# ALAZON

Dean R. Marsh

*AuthorHouse™*
*1663 Liberty Drive*
*Bloomington, IN 47403*
*www.authorhouse.com*
*Phone: 1-800-839-8640*

© *2009 Dean R. Marsh. All rights reserved.*

*No part of this book may be reproduced, stored in a retrieval system, or transmitted by any means without the written permission of the author.*

*First published by AuthorHouse 6/9/2009*

*ISBN: 978-1-4389-9325-6 (sc)*
*ISBN: 978-1-4389-9326-3 (hc)*
*ISBN: 978-1-4389-9327-0 (e)*

*Printed in the United States of America*
*Bloomington, Indiana*

*This book is printed on acid-free paper.*

# ALAZON

<u>LOCATION</u> - Sirius System, approximately nine light-years from Earth.

<u>DIAMETER</u> – Seven thousand, eighty-three miles at the equator.

<u>GRAVITY</u> – One-fifty less than that of Earth.

<u>MEAN DISTANCE FROM SUN</u> – Ninety-two million, two hundred thousand miles.

<u>ROTATIONAL CYCLE</u> – Three hundred and thirty-three days.

<u>LENGTH OF DAY</u> – Twenty-two hours.

    Alazon has three main continents located in its northern hemisphere, five sub-continents in the southern hemisphere, but with a total land mass slightly less than one-third of the surface.

    PRETON – The smallest of the three main continents, Preton has a land mass area of two million, two hundred and eighty-five thousand square miles.
    Lemac – The capitol of Preton, Lemac is located in the geographical center of the continent. It has a population of approximately five hundred thousand. Lemac is the cultural and educational center of not only Preton, but all of Alazon.
    Kech – The eastern port city of Preton, Kech is on the same parallel as Lemac. It has a population of approximately two hundred and eighty-five thousand. The economy of Kech depends heavily on their fishing industry, as well as the import-export trade with Karton to the east.
    Shall – The western port city of Preton. Sharl also lies on the same parallel as Lemac. Like Kech, the population of Sharl, which is just over two hundred and ninety thousand, depends on fishing and trade with Tilwin to the west.

Preton has a democratic society that concentrates heavily on education, science and agriculture. It has no standing army, and is the center of learning and religion on the planet. The total population of Preton is approximately one and one-half million.

KARTON – Second largest of the three main continents, Karton has a land mass area of three million, five hundred thousand square miles.
Bysee – The capitol of Karton, Bysee is locate slightly east of the geographical center of the continent, and has a population of five hundred and ninety-six thousand.
Breel – The western port city of Karton, Breel has a population of approximately three hundred thousand.
Teer – The eastern port city of Karton, Teer has a population of approximately four hundred and fifty thousand. Both Teer and Breel are dependent upon commercial fishing, as well as their trade with Preton to the west and Tilwin to the east.
Karton is ruled by a Monarchy. While it strives to stress education and religion, it also devotes much of its resources to maintaining a standing army of over sixty thousand men to protect itself from Tilwin, and to enforce the laws of its whimsical king and queen. It has a total population of approximately two million, three hundred thousand.

TLWIN – The largest of the three main continents, Tilwin is located west of Preton and east of Karton. It has a land mass area of six million, four hundred and sixty thousand square miles.
Chice – The capitol of Tilwin, Chice is located in the mountains slightly north of the geographical center of the continent. It has a population of approximately five hundred thousand.
Exmit – The eastern port city of Tilwin, Exmit has a population of two hundred thousand, and is the third largest city in Tilwin.
Tegar – The western port city of Tilwin, Tegar has a population of three hundred and fifty thousand, and is the second largest city.
Milik – Located in the south-central area of Tilwin, Milik was once both the largest city and seat of power prior to its overthrow

during civil war. Its population now numbers less than fifty thousand.

A Hierarchy rules Tilwin. Throughout its history Tilwin has been torn by civil wars, as well as conflicts with both Karton and Preton. It has only recently become a single, unified country under strong leadership.

Alazon has a total population of just over seven million people. Most of them are locate in the major cities, with the rest being scattered across the continents in the smaller cities, towns and mining centers.

# EARTH – ALAZON

## YEARLY COMPARISON CHART

| Earth Years | Alazon Equivalent |
|---|---|
| 1 | 1y-2m-1w-2d |
| 2 | 2y-4m-2w-4d |
| 3 | 3y-6m-4w-1d |
| 4 | 4y-9m-3d |
| 5 | 6y-1w-5d |
| 6 | 7y-2m-3w-1d |
| 7 | 8y-4m-4w-3d |
| 8 | 9y-7m-1w |
| 9 | 10y-9m-2w-2d |
| 10 | 12y-3w-4d |
| 15 | 18y-3m-1w-5d |
| 20 | 24y-1m-2w-2d |
| 25 | 30y-1m-4w-1d |
| 50 | 60y-3m-3w-1d |
| 75 | 90y-5m-2w-2d |
| 100 | 120y-7m-1w-2d |
| 150 | 180y-10m-4w-3d |
| 200 | 241y-3m-2w-4d |
| 250 | 301y-7m-1w |
| 500 | 604y-3m-1w-5d |

# ONE

Jason sat with dulled, numbed senses in the padded Captain's seat on the bridge of the giant ship. The air whispering through the ventilation shafts was the only sound to intrude on his thoughts. Slowly, as if moving under water, he reached out to lightly tap a spot on the smooth panel before him. Instantly the view screen, which ran nearly the entire width of the room, came to life. Stars, in configurations strange and alien to him, appeared. It was an alienation that only served to heighten his sense of aloneness.

On a ship nearly half a mile in diameter, and designed to carry over three thousand people from the moon of Earth to a new world, Jason was the only one left alive.

He had been awakened from his sleep in the hyperbolic changers by the computer. It had taken him a moment to realize where he was and what events had brought him to this point. Sitting up and stepping tentatively from his chamber, he had moved to the one next to it, the one that encased Nadia, only to discover that she, along with the others, was dead, and that he was now completely alone.

As that thought came crashing down on him one more Jason gripped the arms of the seat and tried unsuccessfully to fight back his tears. He knew that no amount of crying would bring them back, but that didn't stop the tears from flowing from his eyes.

After what seemed like an hour he touched another portion of the panel, giving him verbal communication with the ship's computer. "Mother?" he called softly.

"Yes?"

The subdued, almost muted reply from the computer seemed inordinately loud to his ears.

"Where are we?" he asked.

"Near a planetary mass close to Canis Major," the computer replied with a throaty, feminine voice.

"So we made it," he said as much to himself as to the computer.

"We made it," Mother replied. "We're approximately two, point seven parsecs, or roughly fifty-two trillion miles from Earth."

The voice of the computer sounded almost as if it also felt the loneliness and pain that prevailed within Jason. He closed his eyes and thought of the long chain of events which had brought him here.

The scientists of New Hope One, who had finally succeeded in combining neural netting and computer hardware with an organic brain had designed 'Mother', as the computer had been playfully dubbed,. The result had been the world's first computer capable of independent, rational thought. A computer with an unlimited capacity for knowledge and learning, capable of handling six trillion mathematical calculations at once. Mother was just one of the scientific breakthroughs those of New Hope had not informed Earth about.

New Hope had been conceived and constructed on Luna ten years prior to Jason's own birth. It was the brainchild of the best scientific minds in a last, desperate attempt to bring peace to a world on the brink of nuclear insanity.

By the year 2123 Earth had been more or less divided by the three super powers of China, Russia and the United Americas which, by then, consisted of what had once been Canada, the United States, Mexico, and most of Central America. An uneasy peace existed between the three powers, with each of the looking for the right opportunity to take over the other two.

In 2092 the United States, which then included Canada and Mexico, had mounted massive air and ground attacks on Central and South America, using tactical nuclear weapons to drive out the Chinese Communists who had taken over. Most of South American had been destroyed in the process. After the smoke cleared they simply annexed whatever was left.

In what had once been Europe a similar scenario had taken place. After the great social and political upheavals that had occurred in the former Soviet Union during the late 1980's and early 1990's, the fourth freely elected Russian President had been assassinate by a group of radicals. Power had reverted to the military, which promptly set their sights not only on the former republics they had lost, but the rest of Europe as well.

After a bloody war with China in which Russia lost most of their land holdings in Asia, the former Soviet Union regrouped and turned their sights south and west. The Russian military had plotted and planned well, and before anyone realized what was happening, they had overrun all of Europe in a daring gamble that had paid off. They had then gone on to take over Africa, killing or enslaving most of the people of that continent.

China, the third major power, had wrested Siberia and Mongolia from Russia during the Sino-Soviet War, and had then turned its attention to the rest of the East and Middle East. They quickly swept the countries of those areas beneath them in the sea of humanity China now possessed.

Egypt, Israel, Syria and Saudi Arabia had put aside their political and religious differences to join forces in an effort to fight the Chinese invasion. For a while it seemed as if they might at least hold things to a draw, as Brazil had done in South American a few years earlier. But when China finally unleashed chemical and germ warfare weapons upon the four countries, not caring what the rest of the world thought, the war was over within a week.

The world had then settled down for a while, with each of the three powers now controlling nearly equal thirds of the globe. They each sat back to lick their wounds and regroup, each of them keeping a wary eye on the other two. It had been the scientists of the world who had seen what was coming and had taken steps to halt it.

At the World Scientific Conference of 2131 a group of the world's best minds had formulated a plan to establish a scientific colony on the moon. It would be a colony that would share all knowledge and discoveries equally with all three powers on Earth. Instead of working against one another, they would work together, hopefully to find a way to bring peace to the world.

For a while it actually worked. The three super powers threw themselves into the project and within months the facility was completed. Equal numbers of scientists from each country were selected to staff it, with the prayers of a frightened world wishing them well.

However, within six months of its establishment a strange metamorphosis began to take place within the inhabitants. Not a physical alteration, but a mental and emotional one that quickly spread to them all. It was one in which they found a new allegiance with one another and their new home rather than with the planet below and its maniacal leaders.

The idea of escaping from their world began innocently enough with a casual remark, but it soon became the only topic of conversation among them. Shortly they developed the idea of escape into a realistic goal. Quietly, gradually, as if by silent agreement, they began to withhold certain items of information, certain discoveries from their mother countries, using them to plan ahead for a new life for themselves and their children.

Using new techniques and discoveries in nano-technology, the scientists of New Hope began to construct the <u>Stargazer</u>, the ship that would transport all of them to another world. The skin of the ship, while lighter in weight than aluminum foil, was constructed of perfectly aligned diamond rods a thousand times stronger than the hardest steel alloys known. Spatial displacement engines were developed which would bend the fabric of space, allowing them to travel light years in relatively short periods of time. All of their knowledge was used to prepare the ship for their journey.

But their most prize possession and accomplishment was the super computer which had affectionately become known as "Mother". Teams of eight programmers had worked in four-hour shifts around the clock for over two years to feed into the computer every scrap of knowledge and history known to man. Every scientific discovery, even projects yet unfinished was programmed into it. Laser discs and holographic cubes covering the arts, music and history were included, as were such things as children's fairy tales and movies.

The scientists worked frantically, never knowing how much time they really had. Yet, when the end came it arrived with a suddenness that caught them off guard by the insanity of Earth. Because of that, and an error in the programming of the computer, it had cost most of them their lives.

Jason and the other children had been aboard the <u>Stargazer</u> for a daylong training exercise when the alarms had sounded. There had been no wild panic, no screaming among the children, but rather a quiet acceptance of what was happening. Jason had rushed to the nearest com unit and quickly established contact with his father. It was then that he discovered that "Mother" had sealed the ship and was in the process of lifting away from the moon, leaving the adults behind.

Jason had practically sprinted to the bridge of the ship, bouncing off the bulkheads in the light gravity in his mad rush. Once there he had activated the main view screen to see what was happening back on Luna. Watching with the other children, he began to feel a sense of lose he really couldn't understand.

Jason watched in stunned horror as rockets lifted from Earth in parabolic arcs that would bring them directly to New Hope. It was at that point that his father contacted him and told him to move the ship away from the moon as quickly as possible to prevent any possible damage to it.

Jason, with the help of Mother, moved the ship almost two hundred miles away, all the while watching as those of New Hope tried to defend themselves. While some manned the photon and phaser canons in a desperate attempt to shoot down the missiles headed their way, others were trying desperately to contact their children aboard the ship. The last sight Jason had of his father was as the man nodded at him through the com unit and turned away, his eyes moist with tears.

Acting on training drilled into him from years of daily practice, Jason moved the ship to a position a thousand miles from the moon just as the first rockets struck and obliterated everyone there. He and the other children had watched through the view screens as those they loved, and the only world they had ever known, vanished in brilliant explosions and clouds of radioactive dust. The maniacs of Earth had wanted to make sure no one escaped their final destruction.

For two days Jason and the other children had merely drifted in space near Saturn, the older ones doing what they could to calm and console the younger. At the end of the second 'day' they had all gathered to decide what their next move should be. They had assembled in the mess hall, with all of them turning to Jason and Nadia, their young, frightened eyes watching the two of them expectantly.

Trish, Jason's nine-year-old sister, had climbed onto his lap. She was clutching the raggedly sewn teddy bear he had made for her when she was only a year old. Her face was a calm repose of trust and confidence. He knew that in her eyes he could do anything. "It's up to you now, Jay," she had told him solemnly. "But I'll be here for you if you need,"

Seventeen children, aged five to twenty, were all that remained of Earth and the human race. Seventeen children who had grown up in a world that had been one giant classroom and playground for them. They had never known restrictions or been hampered in their learning, always being encouraged to dig into things to see what made them tick. Although they had formal educational classes, they had also been given the freedom of any lab or facility at New Hope, allowed to do whatever experiments they wanted, just as long as there was a knowing adult around to make sure they didn't blow themselves or the lab up. Or come up with some mutant gene virus that could wipe out the entire colony.

While each child specialized in one particular field or area, they also became functionally adept in almost every other field of science as well. It wasn't that unusual to find one specializing in micro bionics slipping on a pressure suit to go outside and do some welding on one of the crawlers, or a geneticist helping to do some farming in one of the domes.

Seventeen children with an average I.Q. of one hundred and thirty, but 'egg-heads' they were not. They were like any other group of children, except that they were a lot more inventive in their brands of mischief. They constantly devised new ways to play tricks on one another or the adults. Life was never dull with them around.

But beneath their banter and fun ran an undercurrent of seriousness that propelled them to take an active interest in the work of their parents and the other scientists. As a result, the 'Loonies', as they had dubbed themselves; a term the adults claimed was apt in more than one sense of the word, contributed to many of the scientific breakthroughs of New Hope. They brought a fresh, frank approach to many of the problems they faced.

As Jason opened his eyes and stared at the stars, thinking of this, and of what had happened since their escape, he painfully realized what he now had to do. He felt heaviness forming in the pit of his stomach as he stood and slowly made his way through the gravity free ship to begin the most difficult task of his life.

With tear filled eyes Jason slowly removed the lifeless bodies of the other children; his friends, his lover, his sister, from the hyper-sleep chambers and placed them in black plastic body bags. At the top end of each bag was a clear panel that allowed him to view their faces. Faces that were so peaceful in the sleep from which they would never awaken.

One by one he consigned them to space. The last two, his sister and Nadia, he saved for a moment. Kneeling between them Jason opened the bags to kiss each of them for the last time before sending them out to join the others. It wasn't until he stood and wiped the tears from his eyes that he realized he was clutching Trish's teddy bear in his left hand.

Jason gradually made his way back to the bridge, his mind a jumbled mass of thoughts, emotions, images and fears of what the future might hold for him. He was over fifty two trillion miles from an Earth that no longer existed. And he was alone, with little hope of finding a world where he might be able to settle among his own kind again.

<u>If there even are others of my own kind</u>, he thought sullenly. No scientific proof had ever been brought forth to conclusively establish the existence of other intelligent life in the universe, despite the fact that nearly everyone on New Hope, and many on Earth, believed there must be.

Jason looked up and realized he was at the door of the cabin that had been designated as the Captain's Quarters. "I guess I'm the Captain now," he said softly to himself.

He entered the quarters. They were much the same as all the others, with the exception for size and the communication links with the bridge. He opened the closet and found a number of the jump suits of the style everyone at New Hope had worn. He shook his head when he realized he would have to get rid of them and restock the closet with those of his size. At six feet, two inches tall, and two hundred pounds, Jason had actually been considered small by the standards of the world he had come from. The Captain had been a man nearly a foot taller and fifty pounds heavier. Jason began to remove the clothing, stacking it in a neat pile on the bed before finally carrying it to another cabin.

It took him the better part of an hour to replace the Captain's things with those of his own, doing what he could to make the cabin as comfortable as possible. He had no idea of how long he might have to use it, so he figured he might as well make it as livable as he could from the start. Once he was satisfied he asked Mother to increase the ship's gravity a little more, noticing that she had already begun to do so while he had worked.

Jason stripped off the jump suit he was wearing and took a hot shower, letting the stinging spray ease the tension from his muscles. By the time he stepped out of the shower he noticed that the gravity was now nearly Luna Standard. Making a mental list of the questions he had for Mother, Jason dressed and returned to the bridge.

Sitting in the Captain's seat, he ran his trained eyes over the various instrument panels surrounding him before leaning back and collecting his thoughts for a moment. "Mother?" he said at last.

`"Yes?" came the immediate reply from the computer in a soft, almost sultry voice.

"What happened? What caused all the hyper-sleep chambers except mine to fail? And why wasn't mine affected?"

"As you know," the computer began as if delivering a lecture, "all the chambers are aligned on the same circuitry."

"I know, Mother," he replied, interrupting her. "But there are supposed to be safeguards to prevent the malfunction of one from affecting the others."

"True, Jason, but it seems that about two months after activation a minute vibration caused by entering spatial displacement caused a breakage in a circuit of the designed safeguards.

"This breakage occurred between your chamber, the first in the series, and the rest. This led to a shortage of electrical power to the other units, resulting in their automatic shutdown and causing the deaths of the others."

"Why didn't you catch it?" he snapped. "That's one of the things you were designed to do!"

"Jason, at that time the hyper-sleep chambers were all controlled by a separate computer. I was not aware of it until it was too late for me to do anything. Just as I was unable to reverse the security systems that sealed the ship when the alarms were sounded on Luna, forcing me to leave the others behind. I'm sorry."

The condescending tone of the computer was more than Jason could bear at the moment. His temper flared, surging to the surface.

"What do you mean, you're sorry?" he practically yelled, his right fist slamming down on the arm of the chair. "You're just a damn computer! How the hell can you be sorry?"

Silence filled the room for nearly half a minute before the computer replied.

"Jason," it said softly, "you, more than anyone else, should know that I am more than 'just a damn computer'. After all, you were the one who did most of the design work on the neural netting that not only enables me to have recollective memory, but to experience some emotional responses on a limited basis.

"Therefore, I can feel sorry for what has happened, as well as feel a sense of losses for those no longer with us. And I've had much longer to contemplate on their demises than you have," the computer added softly.

Mother's gentle chiding put a damper on Jason's anger and hostility. He knew she was right. She *was* able to feel some limited emotional responses. And, perhaps in her own way, she actually was capable of missing the others.

Even back on Luna the computer had begun to exhibit the first signs of emotional responses, including humor, much to the surprise of them all. They had thought it impossible for her to develop along those lines, so when it was discovered that she was doing so, some of the scientists had expressed a fear that Mother would become 'too human'. There had been some long and serious discussions concerning the possibility of them having made a mistake in Mother's programming that should be corrected. Some even put forth the suggestion that certain sections of her neural netting be disconnected to prevent further development. Jason had led the fight against this and had eventually won out. He sighed softly now, feeling somewhat ashamed for his outburst.

"You're right. I'm sorry, Mother."

"There's no need to apologize, Jason. I know this can't be easy for you."

He stared out the screens without speaking for a moment. "How far are we from the nearest planet capable of sustaining life?" he asked at last.

"Roughly four hundred and sixty thousand miles."

""How long until we get there?"

"That depends. I can have you there in about forty five minutes using spatial displacement, or a week using photon drive."

"Stick with photon drive for now," he replied.

In some ways Jason wasn't in a big hurry to go rushing toward an unknown planet, hopeful of finding human life, only to be disappointed when there wasn't any. He felt a slight pulsation of the ship as Mother began taking them toward the unknown planet. He also felt a sense of dread he couldn't define.

"Question, Mother. Suppose we don't find human life on this planet; and I really don't want to think of the odds of us doing that, how far is it to the next one?"

"This particular sun," Mother replied, "has five planets in orbit, but with only two of them being the right distance and mass to provide possibilities of any form of life. If the first is a bust, I can shoot us over to the second in no time at all.

"After that? Well, my sensors have detected a total of six thousand, four hundred and nine G-type stars within five thousand light years of our current position. They have a combined possible total one thousand and three possible life bearing planets.

"Using photon drive it would take us nearly five thousand years to check them all out," Mother continued. "But we can do it in less than twelve using spatial drive."

"Twelve years," Jason muttered to himself. "Twelve years while I sit here and quietly go crazy and grow old."

"I doubt that," Mother quipped.

"What? The going nuts part?"

"Both."

"Would you care to explain why you feel that way?"

"Sure," Mother replied somewhat cheerfully. "First off, you going bonkers just ain't in the cards. Your own emotional stability has been checked and re-checked time and again by the best minds and tests of New Hope. Believe me, you're stable.

"Second, there will be too many things going on to keep you occupied for you to sit around and feel sorry for yourself or lose your mind. And as far as the growing old part goes, you really wouldn't age that much."

"What are you talking about?" Jason replied. "Twelve years would put me at thirty two."

"Oh, like that's really old," Mother scoffed. "Never mind. The thing of it is, Jason, you would be thirty two only according to the calendar, not the biological clock ticking away inside of you."

Jason sighed and shook his head. "Okay, now that you've succeeded in confusing me, why don't you explain yourself?"

"KLZ five-nine-seven," Mother replied casually.

"The aging serum my mom was working on? What about it?"

"It works, Jason. Your mom pretty much perfected the formula about six years ago and began administering it to everyone at New Hope, including the children, where it seemed to have the most notable effect.

"Look, didn't you ever think about why cuts healed fast, or broken bones mended so quickly when you banged yourself up?"

"Not really," he replied honestly.

"That figures. Anyway, one of the side effects of the formula is that it accelerates the body's healing processes, along with extending the life span. As a result, even though the calendar may say you're thirty two, in twelve years you'll look and feel just about the same as you do now."

Jason thought about that for a moment. "Okay, just how much has my life expectancy been extended?"

"I figure you'll live to be about a hundred and fifty, give or take a decade," Mother told him.

"You're joking, right?"

"No. Actually that figure is based on calculations of Earth-bound humans, which doesn't really apply to you at all. You grew up on Luna. With its lighter gravity there was less stress on your body, despite the fact that you spend a lot of hours in the gravity chambers that simulated Earth gravity.

"So," Mother continued, "when you take that into consideration, plus the fact that you have been in a totally weightless environment for over a year now, with no physical stress or strain on your body, then combine that with the fact that you can revert to a state of weightlessness for as long as you want here on the ship, you have to recalculate the figure and come up with something in the area of about two hundred years or so. Again, giving or taking a decade or two."

This stunned Jason. He knew his mother had been working on the aging process and had made some progress with it, but he had no idea she had done as much as the computer was now telling him.

"Jason?"

"Yes?"

"While we've been talking I've been doing a spectro-analysis on you and I've discovered a small factor you should be made aware of."

Fear suddenly gripped Jason's chest like a giant fist as he sat up straight in the seat. "What's wrong?" he asked nervously.

"You need to eat, dummy."

It took a second for the meaning of her words to register in his mind. In that time he could have worn he heard the compute chuckle softly.

"Smart ass," he mumbled under his breath.

"Maybe, but I come by it honestly."

As Jason left the bridge and headed for the mess deck he thought of Mother's parting comment. The computer was right; she did come by it honestly. It was the same thing Nadia would have done to him. Nadia would often lead him to believe something was seriously wrong, and then hit him with a totally inane comment, laving him feeling a complete idiot.

The fact that Mother reminded him so much of Nadia, even down to her voice, was more than just a coincidence. Nadia had been the senior programmer for the computer teams. It was her brain and speech patterns that had been ingrained into the neural networks of the computer. Therefore, Mother was, in one sense, an extension of the mind of the woman Jason loved.

As Jason aimlessly selected food from a dispenser set along one wall of the mess hall and carried it to the nearest table, his thoughts remained on Nadia. She had been the second child born on Luna and was six months younger than Jason. The two of them had grown up together, and as the other children had followed, Jason and Nadia had taken over their leadership.

Bu the time they were both sixteen Nadia was nearly as tall as he was. She had waist length, jet-black hair and dark, almond shaped eyes that bespoke of the ancestry of her foregathers. They had been warriors of the Steppes who had conquered most of the known world at one time in Earth's past.

While eating, Jason thought of all the trouble the two of them had managed to get into as children. And later of how he had come to realize that Nadia was something more to him than just his best friend and partner in mischief. She was a woman. And he was head over heels in love with her.

Sitting in the cavernous mess hall of the ship he could remember the feel of her body next to his as they had made love, moving together as one. In his mind he could see the twinkle she always had in her eyes when she was up to some type of mischief. Of how she could look at him a certain way and make him feel so much love for her in his heart.

Jason put down his sandwich and let his hands fall to his lap as tears filled his eyes once more. "I need you, Nadia," he whispered to the empty room, knowing she would never again hear him.

# TWO

"Are you sure, Mother?" Jason asked as he looked at the planet below through the view screens. His eyes darted down to check the readings Mother was providing.

"Are you accusing me of being in error?" Mother replied, her voice tinge with a mock sense of hurt.

"Anything's possible," he muttered.

"Oh, yeah? Well, for your information, bucko, I'm sure."

"Okay, so what do we do about it?"

"For starters you can go down and check it out."

Jason felt a twitch of nervousness at this. "Ah, what's Plan B?"

The computer chuckled lightly before speaking. "Look, Captain Coward, we can study them from up here until you are blue in the face and have a beard down to your knees, but that still won't tell us anything definite. The only way to find out for sure is for you to go down and check it out."

"What about a probe?" Jason asked. He was stalling for time and they both knew it.

"I did that already," Mother told him. "You're looking at the results."

Jason shook his head and sighed. "So what you're telling me is that there is no way for me to get out of this, right?"

"Gee, you ain't as dumb as you look."

"What if I decide to just skip it, activate the drive and go on to the next planet?"

"Hey, Jason, are you forgetting who really runs this bucket of bolts? You don't activate anything if I don't let you."

Jason knew when he was licked. He had yet to win an argument with Mother. He left the bridge and headed for one of the gravity wells that would take him to the shuttle bay. Once inside the bay he loaded scuba gear, a tent, food concentrates and a medical kit into one of the small shuttles. He also decided to take a phaser just to be on the safe side. As he stowed the gear he tried to ignore his sense of nervousness. This was the first time he would be outside the confines of the Stargazer since coming aboard. And although he hated to admit it, even to himself, he was a little scared.

But in the back of his mind Jason also knew that the computer was right. The only way he would know for sure if her readings on the planet below were correct was for him to go down and find out.

Checking to make sure he had everything, Jason started the engine of the small craft and eased it through the force field of the air lock. As he entered the vast emptiness of space he felt the beat of his heart quicken. Despite the fact that he had flown shuttles and large cargo carriers in space around Luna for years, this was something new for him.

"Here goes nothing," he muttered as he pointed the nose of the small craft toward the surface of the planet.

As he dropped swiftly down through the atmosphere, he kept his eyes on the gauges and controls, watching for any sign of malfunction or trouble, even though he knew the shuttle's onboard computers would warn him if anything were amiss. But the flight went smoothly. In no time at all he was skimming across the incredibly azure waters of the planet's oceans, heading for a small island chain Mother had pre-programmed into the shuttle's computer.

Jason brought the craft to a gentle landing on the sand of the island less than twenty yards from the high water mark. He shut down the engine and then sat there for a moment to collect his nerve. Only once before in his life had he set foot on the surface of a planet, and he had never actually been outdoors.

His one trip to Earth had been to compete in a martial arts tournament in Japan. The ship he had flown down in had landed outside the city of Osaka, but he had gone from the ship to a ground shuttle via a tunnel and bubble car. This was due to the air over all the major cities of Earth being so polluted that it was unfit for breathing. For too many decades man had polluted it with the burning of fossil fuels and CFC's, totally destroying the ozone layer beyond salvation. This, despite the warnings of scientists back in the 1980's.

While many people were forced to live outside the domed cities, they usually didn't live long. They suffered from every form of respiratory disease known, as well as a deadly rate of skin cancer. Now he was about to step out onto a world where he would be breathing naturally oxygenate air for the first time in his life.

Jason got up and stood beside the hatch of the shuttle. As he reached up to touch the panel to open it he could feel the sweat on his palms and hear the blood pounding in his ears. As the hatch dropped outward and down he realized he had been holding his breath. Mother had assured him the air was very breathable and that there was nothing in it the least bit harmful. She had even told him that he might actually enjoy it.

Tentatively Jason stepped down to the sand, feeling it give way slightly beneath his feet. He jumped nervously as Mother's voice came to him from the small sub-dural receiver he wore in his left ear. "How ya doing?" she asked.

"Just fine so far."

"Okay. I just wanted to check on you. Have fun."

Jason began to remove the equipment from the craft. He stacked it neatly on the sand, then stripped out of his clothing and slipped on a pair of swimming trunks. He hoisted the air tank onto his back and checked the gauges, then picked up the shark prod and attached the underwater camera to the belt around his waist. Picking up his fins, he walked to the edge of the water. He stopped to put on the fins, and then waded farther out, a sense of adventure and excitement starting to build in him. When the water reached his waist he placed the mask over his eyes and fell forward to begin his swim away from the shore, following a coral reef that extended out from the beach.

As part of his training back on Luna, Jason, like everyone else, had taken scuba lessons, but that had been in cold, sterile tanks that merely provide the necessary sensations and warnings of what to do if something went wrong. They had been nothing like what he was experiencing now.

Jason swam leisurely, taking in the explosive riot of colors that assailed his eyes. He took pictures with the camera, knowing he would go over them avidly later on. Small schools of fish swam near him. They seemed completely unafraid of his intrusion of their domain. Some even came up to bump gently against his facemask as if to check him out.

After a while Jason checked the gauge on his left wrist. He was surprised to find he had less than five minutes of air left remaining in the tank. Somewhat reluctantly he turned and began to swim back toward the shore. He felt a sense of disappointment that the mammals Mother had said were there had failed to present themselves.

A shadowy movement off to his left drew his attention. Jason turned his head and nearly swallowed his mouthpiece in surprise. Just a few yards away a bottle nosed dolphin was swimming on a parallel course with him. Its large dark eye watched him and he watched it. Jason quickly snapped off some pictures before letting the camera dangle from the strap attached to his waist to simply watch the creature.

While there was no doubt it was an <u>atrusiops trunacatus</u>, it appeared to be larger than its cousin back on Earth. This one was at least twelve feet long, and its skin was a silver blue that seemed to alter color slightly in the refracted rays of sunlight beneath the waves.

The dolphin exhibited no apparent fear of him. In fact, it seemed to have sort of a bemused curiosity toward him. Jason felt as if the animal was studying him as he studied it while the two of them floated suspended in the water just yards apart. He wanted to stay longer, to possibly try and approach it if he could, but a soft beep in his ear informed him that he now had less than a minute of air remaining in his tank. He turned and continued his swim toward the shore, grinning around his mouthpiece as the dolphin swam along beside him.

Jason was just starting to make his way up to the surface when half a dozen black, ropy tentacles shot up from the other side of the reef and wrapped themselves around the dolphins. The mammal began thrashing the water as it cried out with a series of whistles and bleats that didn't need a translator to tell Jason were cries of pain and terror. Without considering the consequences of his actions, or the potential danger he could be placing himself in, Jason sucked in the last of his air from the tank and kicked his legs to propel his body over the top of the reef, the shark prod extended before him.

Near the bottom of the reed, almost thirty feet down, he saw a black gelatinous mass about twelve feet across. It shimmered and shook as it fought to hold the dolphin while also maintaining its grip on the coral. Jason dove toward it, sliding his thumb along the voltage setting of the prod, shifting it to its maximum setting. When the tip of the prod came into contact with the black mass, he pressed the firing stud and hoped for the best.

The water around him erupted into jelly-like pieces of the creature as it literally exploded. A quick glance upward revealed that the tentacles of the creature were still wrapped around the dolphin, though, still releasing their deadly toxins into the struggling mammal.

Jason released the prod and let it dangle from the loop attached to his belt. He snatched the knife from the sheath on his right ankle and swam as quickly as he could to the dolphin. He carefully used the knife to free the strands from the dolphin's body, remembering to cut off a small piece to slip into the sample jar at his waist.

His ears were ringing and his lungs felt as if they were going to explode as he pushed the dolphin toward the surface. He hoped and prayed that he wasn't too late to save it. As his head broke the surface of the water he gasped in huge gulps of air to replenish his lungs. Then, carefully holding the body of the dolphin so that its head was above water, Jason kicked his feet to propel the two of them toward the shore. He struggled to push the mammal up onto the beach as far as he could before ripping off his equipment and racing for the open hatch of the shuttle, the sample jar clutched in his hand.

"Mother!" he yelled as he pried the top from the container and placed the small piece of material in an analyzer. "I need to know what this is and what type of toxin it contains as fast as you can tell me!"

"Working," the computer replied, not wasting time with questions.

Jason stood anxiously, glancing out at the dolphin while he waited for Mother.

"Collinema ornata..." she began.

"Collin...Jellyfish!" Jason exclaimed.

"Well, close to it," Mother replied. "And you don't have any antitoxin for that down there with you, Jason. You better get back to the ship as fast as possible."

"It's not for me," Jason replied as his mind raced for a possible solution.

Leaping from the shuttle he raced back to the dolphin. Dropping to his knees beside it he snatched up the shark prod. He knew some remote native tribes in South America had once use electrical shock from old motors and batteries to counteract some forms of snake venom, so perhaps it would work in this case. He adjusted the power setting to low-range on the prod and pressed the tip of it against the side of the now laboriously breathing dolphin.

"This may hurt, little one," he said softly as he depressed the stud, seeing the dolphin's body jerk and twitch from the current, "but if it works, it will save your life."

Jason didn't know how much of a charge he should give the dolphin, or if he should give it more than one. He waited nearly two minutes, said a silent prayer, and then sent another mild charge into the dolphin. He cupped water in his hands to spread it over the exposed portions of the creature's skin to keep it moist. As he did he spoke to it softly, begging it not to die. He didn't know why, but the life of this creature was important to him.

The sun was starting to set when the dolphin finally gave a weak flick of its tail and lifted its head slightly to look directly at him. With a soft cry of elation, Jason eased the mammal back into the water, but continued to hold on to it until the water was chest high. For a moment the dolphin simply floated next to him, but then it gave a flick of its tail and moved away. It slid beneath the water to circle him twice before moving out to the deeper water of the inlet.

As Jason watched, the dolphin stopped about thirty yards away. It turned back toward him and lifted itself from the waves on its strong tail fin, nodding its head several times as it let loose with a series of whistles and bleeps. It then dove beneath the waves and vanished, leaving him standing with tears of happiness on his cheeks and an idiotic grin on his face.

Jason made his way back to the shuttle and sat down in the open hatch. He felt a sense of relief and joy over the recovery of the dolphin that he really couldn't explain. After a few minutes he felt his stomach rumble and realized he was famished. Feeling good about things overall, he got up to fix something to eat.

"Hey," called Mother in the small earpiece as he sat back down in the open hatch to eat a few minutes later.

"What?"

"I see your new friend is okay. That was some quick thinking on your part about the electrical shock treatment."

"Yeah, well, I am supposed to be a genius after all," he quipped. "But that aside, I don't believe you are actually offering me a compliment."

"One every three of four months is all I'm good for, so don't push your luck."

"Not a chance."

"Good. Now, I've got a question for you. Are you coming back up here tonight or are you gonna stay down there?"

Jason thought about it for a moment. He felt more confident about himself than he had in a long time. He realized that he had conquered some of his fears.

"I think I'll camp out down here tonight. The sun will be down shortly and I think I'd like to watch it."

"Getting brave and waxing poetic all at the same time. My, my, my, how we are a'changing," Mother teased.

"Watch it, metal mouth, or I'll scramble your circuits."

"Yes, Boss Man. Okay, you stay down there and play Boy Scout for the night. I'll just sit up here and keep an eye out for goblins and beasties, or anything else that might go bump in the night. Or decide to try you out for a snack."

"My guardian angel."

"Hey, someone has to look out for you. If left to your own devices you'd get yourself into more trouble than ten rowdy children."

"I love you, too, Mother," he told her dryly.

"I know. By the way, while you were doing your Jaques Cousteau impersonation, did you happen to get a good pictures?"

"Pictures, yes. Sound recordings, no."

"Damn, and here I called you smart just a minute ago. I take it back."

"Mother," he said with a sigh, "perhaps you failed to notice, but things got a bit hectic down here and I was just a tad bit busy."

"Yeah, I noticed. Ten to one it was a female of the species," Mother quipped.

"Now what's that supposed to mean?"

"Nothing," Mother replied innocently.

"Yeah, right. Anyway, you lose. It was a male."

"Oh, well, can't win 'em all," the computer replied with a chuckle. "All right, you stay, but call out if you need me."

"Not very damn likely," he muttered softly.

Jason finished his meal and disposed of the containers while thinking about the diving experience earlier. It had been exhilarating and he planned on doing it again tomorrow. He hoped the dolphin would show up again. This time with some of its friends.

He recharged the scuba tank, and then decided to go for a swim before calling it a night. He waded into the water and began to swim easily out toward the end of the reef that jutted up out of the water about two hundred yards away. When he reached it he climbed out of the water to stand on the rough coral, turning his gaze to the wide expanse of ocean that surrounded him. He could see another island about a mile away. Between it and the one he was on he could make out the leaping forms of dolphins at play. He wondered if the one he had saved was among them.

Jason stayed on the reef to watch the sun go down, feeling something almost spiritual as it appeared to sink into the waves. He had never seen a sunset from a planet before and the experience touched him in ways he didn't expect.

"This is how it must have been back on Earth a thousand years ago," he said softly as the sun finally disappeared. The western sky turned from gold to red, and finally star filled blackness.

Reluctantly, Jason swam back to the island itself and set up his tent. As he was finishing up he saw a small group of dolphins out just beyond the tip of the reef. They appeared to be swimming in a circular pattern and he had the strangest feeling they were watching him.

As the moon shone down brightly, Jason realized there was a slight chill to the air coming off the ocean. He moved into the tent, but left the front flap open as he pulled the lightweight cover from the sleeping bag up around his shoulders. He lay on his stomach with his head just inside the opening; watching and listening to the waves wash up on the shore. The hypnotic movement and soft sound relaxed him and he was soon asleep.

But his sleep was filled with the images and memories of his past. The faces of Nadia, his parents, sister, and all the others he had known flashed through his mind like a holo-projector on fast forward. Everything was a blur that made no sense. Then, just as suddenly as it started, it stopped.

"Friend."

It wasn't a word as much as it was a feeling, but it held more meaning than any spoken word ever had. A suffusion of warmth washed through him.

"Friend."

Jason's eyes snapped open and he was instantly alert. He looked out of the tent and saw the sun just coming up. He sat up in surprise when he saw the inlet crowded with the silver-hued bodies of perhaps two hundred dolphins. All of them were floating gently on the waves as they looked at him.

Jason crawled from the tent and walked toward the water, completely unafraid as the dolphins moved back to make room for him. It wasn't until the water was up to his waist that he realized his assessment of them would have to be revised.

Looking around now, it became glaringly apparent that the dolphin he had rescued the day before was a mere baby. The adults that now filled the cover were up to thirty feet in length, and as large as killer whales had been back on Earth.

"*Friend! Little One!*" said a voice inside his head, shocking him with its clarity.

*Alazon*

It took Jason a moment before he grasped what was going on. "Telepaths!" he gasped in shocked surprise.

"*Yes! Speak with mind thoughts,*" came the reply as a familiar silvery body swam closer. It butted his stomach gently with its blunted nose, rubbing it up and down against him playfully.

Jason reached out to stroke the skin, noticing the welt marks it still bore. "You've been in my mind all night, haven't you?" he asked as he remembered the disjointed images of his past that had filled his sleep.

"*Yes. We learn. Learn of you…your world…your life. We learn of your…aloneness. We feel…sadness…for oneness without others your kind.*"

Jason stood there not knowing what to say or think. He was trying to compose an answer when the mass of dolphins parted and allowed a single one to move forward. Even the little one he had saved moved to one side to allow the older, larger dolphin to come within a few yards of him. It was, by far, the largest of them all. It measured at least forty feet in length, but there was no sign of age or dullness in the large black eye it turned toward him.

"*You saved the life of this one,*" it said, moving its head slightly in the direction of the smaller dolphin. "*Why?*"

The question caught Jason off guard for a moment. "I…because he was being hurt," he finally replied. "Because it was the right thing for me to do."

"*You could have been hurt…killed yourself,*" the large dolphin said, his thought more clear and concise than those of the smaller dolphin had been. "*You did not hesitate to save the life of one not of your kind. You are not like the others.*"

Jason felt his heart skip a beat. "What others?" he asked anxiously.

"*Others who look as you…but of a different mind,*" the older dolphin replied.

Jason couldn't speak. He couldn't even think straight. Humans! They had to mean other humans!

"*They came but did not stay,*" the large dolphin told him. *They did not learn of us, but we learned of them. We turned away from the evil their minds held. But we know of you, of your life. We learn* it and your language while you sleep. You are not like the others. Come, we will tell you of us."

Two smaller dolphins moved to either side of Jason, presenting their dorsal fins to him to hang on it, but before he could grasp them, the one he had saved the day before cried out to the others.

As they all halted their movements, the small dolphin quickly swam around behind him and dove down between his legs. With a laugh, Jason straddled it and grasped the fin, letting it carry him on its back as the entire pod turned and swam out to sea.

As he was carried farther and farther out, Jason could feel the powerful muscles at work beneath the sleek skin of the dolphin. About half a mile off shore from the island the dolphins began to pack closely together, nearly forming a carpet he could have walked on. With a gentle nudge in his mind he was encouraged to relax. He turned over and lay on his back, allowing himself to be buoyed up by the dolphins. He closed his eyes and let his mind go blank.

It was flooded almost immediately with images and thoughts, which came to him with a rapidity he found amazing. He learned of their watery world, their lives, their development, and even their names for one another. Names he knew he would never be able to pronounce verbally.

He found out they were sentient being who had developed the ability of telepathy centuries ago. They used it to assist one another, as well as passing on knowledge and information.

They gave him mental images of their world, making him aware of the various fish and other creatures of the sea that could be dangerous to him and themselves. They even showed him those he could use for food if he so desired.

But the most shocking image they provided him was that of other humans who had once visited the world. This stunned him, and even though he tried to mentally ask them when this had happened, the dolphin's concept of time was beyond his comprehension. However, they left him with the feeling that it had been hundreds, if not thousands of years ago.

When they were finished, Jason opened his eyes. Looking up at the sky he realized it was nearly nightfall. Despite the fact he felt as if only minutes had passed, the gnawing in his stomach let him know that a full day had nearly transpired. As he thought about being hungry his mind was immediately filled with the images of various fish. The dolphins were offering to bring him whatever he wanted. All he had to do was let them know which ones appealed to him the most. He formed the image of a sole in his mind. There was an immediate flash of silvery bodies as dozens of the dolphins dove beneath the waves to go searching for fish that resembled the image he had given them. As they did that, the smaller one swam back to the island with him on its back.

Jason waded ashore with a thousand questions on his mind. Dismissing them for the time being he began packing the tent and stowing it in the shuttle. A few minutes later he heard the now familiar chirps, bleeps and whistles calling to him. He turned to see dozens of fish being tossed up onto the sand of the beach. He hurried down to them, laughing when he realized there were more types of fish, and more fish, than he could eat in a weak. He selected two and tossed them up closer to the shuttle, then began to pitch the rest back into the water.

"Too many?" came the mental question.

He looked up to see the small dolphin standing up in the water on his powerful tail. The dolphin's eyes were watching him with what appeared to be intense curiosity and amusement.

"Yes," he replied with a grin. "But you didn't know how many I could eat, so it's all right."

"You put back what you can not eat. This is good."

This 'voice' was different. It took Jason a moment to realize it belonged to the old dolphin. He turned to look at it. "To let them die just because I couldn't eat them would be both cruel and stupid. Life, all life, has meaning to it."

"Stay with us a while," the old dolphin said. "We would learn more of you and your world."

Jason smiled at the invitation. "I think I'd like that."

"We leave now," the small dolphin told him. "Come back later. Talk more."

Jason nodded as they all turned and swam out to sea. He assumed they were also going to eat. As he picked up the two fish near the shuttle he had a sudden, and to him, wild idea. Dropping the fish to the sand he scrounged around a little farther inland until he finally found what he was looking for. He eventually got a small fire going and cooked the fish over it after cleaning them. His senses reveled in the odors and sounds coming to him. As he ate he realized he was enjoying this meal more than any he could ever remember. But the sudden intrusion of Mother's voice coming from within the shuttle effectively ruined the moo for him. "Jason?"

He got up reluctantly and went to the door of the shuttle so he could hear her better, having removed the small ear receiver before going to sleep last night.

"You're gonna spoil my night for me, aren't you, Mother?"

"Sorry, but I think you should head back."

"Why?"

"There's a storm coming your way. It's big, and it will be hitting the area where you are in about four hours."

"Can't I sit tight in the shuttle and ride it out?"

"I don't think that would be wise, Jason. This isn't a mere thunder storm I'm talking about, but a force five hurricane, with wins over two hundred miles an hour."

He sighed sadly and let his shoulders slump. "Okay, I see your point. I'll pack it in."

*You go?* a mental voice asked.

Jason walked to the water's edge where the small dolphin watched him curiously from a few yards away. "Yes. There is a storm coming and it's not safe for me to stay."

*You will come back?* This came from the old dolphin.

"I would like to someday when I can spend more time, but for now I have to find others of my own kind again."

*We will be here when you return,* the old dolphin told him. There was a touch of genuine warmth in the word-thoughts of the huge mammal. *You are welcome to stay, but there is a need in you to search for your own kind. This we can understand.*

*By tomorrow all of us will know of you. They will make you welcome when you return, no matter where you are on our world, or how long it takes.*

*After you find what you search for, return and share your knowledge. If there are others like you they are welcome, but be wary*

*Alazon*

of those who look like you that you learned of from us. They have an evil sickness of the mind and are not to be trusted."

Jason was touched by the sincerity he felt in their mental words, but also leery of the warning the old dolphin had given him.

"Thank you," he replied to the old dolphin. "But if I return, how do I contact you?"

"Call for 'Little One' in your mind and I will come," the small dolphin told him cheerfully. "You can not say my name, so I will take the one you gave me."

"And what do I call you?" Jason asked the old dolphin.

"There is a word in your language that can be used. It is 'Teacher'."

"Will the others know who I mean when I call for the two of you by those names?"

"They will know," Teacher replied. "Go now and search for what you need to find. But if you do not find them you may return and live here on our world. There is much we could learn from one another."

Jason felt an unexpected knot form in his chest at their offer. He wasn't of their species, yet they were extending to him an open invitation to live on their world without reservation. But they had also given him the knowledge that there were other humans out there. Because of that he knew he wouldn't be able to return until he had found them.

"I'll return someday, you can be sure of that," he told them softly before turning and heading for the shuttle.

After loading all of his equipment, Jason lifted the craft into the sky and headed for the *Stargazer*. His thoughts on the images the dolphins had given him of the humans who had visited their world in the past. He wondered where they had come from, where they were now, and if they would accept him as one of them? He shook his head. There were too many questions and not nearly enough answers.

# THREE

Sweat poured from Jason's body. His chest rose and fell with his labored breathing. The bokken, the wooden practice sword of Kendo, felt as if it were made of lead and weighed a ton. Jason whipped it above his head and then slashed down to strike the target in front of him. A fist shot out from his left. He twisted his body to avoid it, but that allowed another fist to smash into his back. He sprawled to the mats, a small gasp of pain escaping his lips.

"Off!" he cried. Instantly the training machine shut itself off, allowing him to get to his feet without having to further defend himself against its various fists, feet, wooden knives and swords attached to it.

"Hey, Bruce Lee," Mother called as he leaned on the bokken to catch his breath.

"What?" he gasped.

"You might wanna come take a look-see at what I've got."

Jason shook his head in resignation. Over the past six months Mother had been developing her own personality. She had also cultivated a slightly warped sense of humor, subjecting him to every pundit, joke and pun she could come up with. Which, due to her unlimited memory, could number a hundred a day if she wanted. She also had a habit of calling him by names that were usually unknown to him. However, Bruce Lee was one he knew. He could also identify with the reference she was making.

"What have you got, Mother?" he asked.

"A planet."

"Big deal," he replied with a sneer. "How many planets have we looked at in the past six months?"

"Three hundred and two. Not counting this one."

"And on how many of those have we found anything even remotely resembling intelligent life? Not counting the one with the dolphins."

"None, so far."

"Right. So what makes this planet so special? Are there people teeming all over it? Does it have Homo Erectus preparing a party to make me feel welcome?"

"Well, not exactly."

"What does that mean, Mother?" Jason knew by the tone of her voice that she was up to something.

"There are traces of a civilization. Very definitely humanoid civilization."

"By 'traces' I take it to mean the civilization no longer exists?" he asked.

Despite his earlier skepticism, Jason was starting to feel a sense of excitement as he placed the bokken in its rack along the bulkhead and stripped off the practice gi.

"Something like that," Mother replied. "But, hey, who knows, we might find something interesting down there. Maybe even some clues to those the dolphins told you about."

Mother had a point. "All right," he told her. "Let me take a shower and grab something to eat, then I'll come see what you've got. Is that okay with you?"

"Hey, you're the boss!"

"Mother, why is it that I have trouble believing you when you say that?"

"Beats the hell out of me!" she replied cheerfully.

"Someone needs to," he muttered as he headed for his cabin.

Jason rubbed the small of his back where the fist had struck him. Despite the slight twinge of pain, he felt a sense of accomplishment. He had raised the level of the training machine to a rate of attack higher than any he had ever been able to handle in the past. He had held his own for nearly fifteen minutes before finally succumbing to the blow that sent him to the mats.

Jason and Karl, Nadia's father, had designed and built the fight trainer in their spare time, installing it in one corner of the gym aboard the ship. It was constructed to provide Jason with advance fight training in Kendo, the Japanese art of the sword, as well as the deadly art of Ninjitsu. It could be programmed for straight hand-to-hand combat, for fighting with knives and other weapons, or any combination, depending on the skill level and ability of any particular individual.

Karl had been a Master in both Kendo and Ninjitsu. He had started teaching the arts to Jason shortly after Jason's eight birthday, working with him three hours a day, every day for nearly ten years.

When Jason reached a point in his training where he could hold his own against Karl, the older man had arranged for a tournament to be held in one of the large gravity chambers on Luna. Karl had invited twenty of the world's best martial artists to compete. To the surprise of everyone, with the possible exception of Karl, Jason had easily won in Kendo, and had been beaten only once in the hand-to-hand combat portion.

But the other men in the competition had cried "foul" due to what they felt was an unfair advantage over them in the location of the tournament. They had invite Jason to come to Osaka in three months to compete there.

Jason remembered how he and Karl had taken the shuttle down to Earth, knowing that everyone at New Hope would be watching eagerly back home, with Nadia and Trish being among the loudest of his cheering fans.

In the finals Jason was matched up against the only other undefeated contestant. The man was ten years older, ten inches taller, and nearly seventy pounds heavier. Jason had some doubts as to his chances against this opponent, who had won the World Championships for the past five years. Karl had made him do his meditation exercises, and then told him to rely on his speed.

"Don't try to overpower him," Karl had told him before the match began. "You aren't strong enough for that. Speed and technique is how you'll beat him."

After four rounds of full-contact lasting three minutes each, Jason was declared a winner by a split decision. Afterwards his body felt as if a dozen men with iron bars had beaten it. The second portion of the match, which involved the use of the weapon of choice for each combatant, was scheduled for later that night. When it came, Jason felt more confident, as his opponent had also selected to fight with the bokken.

Jason's speed and ability with the weapon left the other man swinging at empty air while his larger body suffered from the multitude of blows from Jason's weapon. The other man finally collapsed to the mats and began to spit up blood. Because of the speed with which Jason had defeated the reigning champion, combined with the crushing style of defeat, Jason emerged from the tournament as the new World Champion.

Upon his return to New Hope, the entire colony turned out to welcome him home. They held a celebration for him equal to that of a returning conquering hero. In their eyes Jason had not only represented New Hope, but also what those there stood for against the 'evils of Earth'. It had been nice, but Jason had actually been somewhat embarrassed by it all. He just wanted to get away and be with Nadia.

The next day Karl had summoned him to the gym. "Now you'll have to work twice as hard as before," the older man told him.

"But I'm the best in the world," Jason ha replied with a smug cockiness to his voice.

Karl had responded by thoroughly beating him from one end of the gym to the other, totally humiliating him in front of Nadia. Never again had Jason questioned Karl, and had worked twice as hard to perfect his training and ability.

Undressing in his cabin as he prepared to take a shower, Jason heard the unmistakable sound of Mother whistling an old show tune. He shook his head in amusement. Mother had been experimenting with various forms of vocalization and could now imitate any sound a human could make. That surprised him, especially when he considered that she had no lips or tongue to work with. He had asked her to explain how she was able to do it, but she had refused.

"A woman has to have some secrets of her own," she had told him.

Jason had reminded her that she was a computer, not a real woman. For that she had refused to talk to him at all for a full twelve hours. He had finally given in and agreed with her in that she was a woman trapped in the body of a computer. In fact, in many ways Jason had come to bestow feminine qualities to Mother, which seemed to be what she wanted, and what pleased her.

Climbing into the shower he thought back to their conversation of a couple of weeks ago. He had been working on a prototype android when he was suddenly interrupted by the sound of dogs and cats in what sounded like a fight between the two groups of animals. It had startled him at first, but then he had started laughing, which had immediately silenced the noise.

"What's so funny?" Mother had asked.

"Well, for a moment I thought you had cloned some dogs and cats from the cryogenics lab and turned them loose in the same room with one another. Then I realized it was just your warped brain doing the imitations. It just struck me as funny. Sorry if I hurt your feelings."

"That's a damn lie," Mother quipped. "But don't worry, you didn't. By the way, you never had a cat or dog, did you?"

"No. Pets weren't practical back on Luna."

"That's too bad. A puppy or a kitten can be a great companion."

"Really? And how would you know, Mother."

"Trust me."

"Not very damn likely," he had muttered, ending the conversation.

Jason knew there were genes in the genetics lab for just about every type of dog or cat known to man. They could also be genetically altered to suit a specific purpose. The scientists of New Hope had thought ahead of every possible contingency they could dream up. Realizing the importance of the bond between man and animal throughout history, they had made sure there were plenty to select from when they found a new world. Jason had, on more than one occasion, considered asking Mother to clone a dog for him but had decided against it. He'd never owned a pet and wouldn't know how to take care of one.

Jason also knew he could have her use the gene pool to recreate everyone who had ever lived on Luna. Early on he had seriously considered doing that, but had finally dismissed the idea as futile. He could have Mother clone their bodies but not their minds, their memories, or their personalities.

Except for Nadia. He knew Mother contained every memory the mind of Nadia had contained up to the point of imprinting the computer's neural network with Nadia's brain. Creating a 'new' Nadia would have been easy. More than one night had been spent considering that, fighting with himself as to whether it should be done or not. He finally decided against it by telling himself that the 'new' Nadia might not really be the same as the old one.

"Mother?" he called as he began to dry off after his shower.

"Yo!" she replied with a thick Bronx accent.

"What about cloning me a dog?"

"What kind?"

"I don't know. What have we got? What do you recommend?"

"You name it, Nanook, and we got it!" Mother told him, her voice taking on the cadence and inflections of a carney barker. "We got German Shepherds, Irish Setters, Beagles and Malamutes. We got Chows. We got Poodles in the miniature, toy or regular size variety.

"We got any breed you could ever want. And if you don't like what we got, why, with just a touch of Mother's Magic, also known as genetic manipulation, we can give you any combination you'd like!

"You wanna Russian Wolf Hound crossed with a Chihuahua? We can do it! You wanna…"

"Stop!" he told her. He was laughing so hard his sides were starting to hurt. He leaned against the bulkhead and took several deep breaths before speaking again.

"Look, why don't you tell me what you think would be best under our present circumstances. And be serious for a change."

"Yes, Dear," she replied, managing to sound contrite. "Well, I would definitely go with one of the more intelligent breeds, like Shepherd, Setter, Retriever or Collie, but there are other factors to consider as well."

"Such as?"

"Loyalty, devotion, and the ability to protect you should you ever be in danger. I'll tell you what. I'll give this some consideration, make a choice, and then let you know what I come up with. How's that sound?"

"Frightening. I'm not sure if I can trust you."

"Thanks a heap! And here I thought we were starting to become friends. However, Jason, despite your skepticism I'll do what I think is right. And I promise I'll try to leave my 'warped sense of humor' out of it."

"Promise?"

"Scout's honor."

"Yeah, right. What do you know about the Scouts?"

"More than you do. Everything in fact. Trust me."

"Do I have a choice?"

"Nope!"

"That's what I thought. All right, go ahead," he told her as he finished dressing.

Jason left the cabin and walked the short distance to the bridge, his mind turning to the planet she wanted him to look at.

He entered the bridge and started to sit down in the Captain's chair when a short, terrified yelp sounded from beneath him. Jason whirled around to find a ball of snow white fur on the padded seat looking up at him expectantly. Its bushy little tail set up a thumping sound as it beat against the seat. Jason couldn't stop the grin from spreading across his face as he picked up the little bundle of fur. It immediately began to lick at his face, its tail whipping back and forth in time with the small, raspy tongue working on the skin of his cheek.

"All right, Mother, you got me again," he said softly.

"Sneaky, huh?"

"Yeah, but nice. What is it?" he asked as he sat down and stroked the energetic little bundle of fur.

"A puppy."

"I can see that, Mother. What kind of puppy?"

"The kind that barks and makes messes all over the place until you get it trained."

"Mother," he growled.

"Oh, all right. It's a Malamute."

"He's beautiful."

"Ah, excuse me, but if you'll bother to turn it over and check out the equipment package on this particular model, you'll find that he is a she."

"I'll take your word for it," he replied, laughing again as the puppy seemed determined to lick every square inch of his face at least a dozen times. "Okay, why this particular breed? And why snow white?"

"As for the breed," Mother replied, "they're intelligent, easily trained, extremely loyal to one person, and when need be they are fierce fighters who will protect their masters with their own lives.

"As for the color. I don't know. I just thought a snow white dog would be pretty."

"How old is she?" he asked.

"Biologically, if born through natural gestation, she'd be about three months old. In actual time she's less than a week old. I halted her development at this stage so it would provide you with the opportunity to train her the way you want. Any younger and she wouldn't have been ready for it. Too much older and it might have proven more difficult."

Jason was touched by her sense of thoughtfulness. "Thank you, Mother," he said softly.

"You're welcome."

"Okay, now what about this planet?"

"No planet. That was just an excuse I came up with to get you up here. However, we are on course to intersect with one shortly."

"That figures. Hey, how did you get the puppy from the gene lab to here?"

"Servo robot."

Jason was silent for a moment as he looked down at the puppy. It had curled up in his lap and gone to sleep. As his fingers softly stroked the animal he heard a soft sigh come from it. He cradled the puppy in his arms as he left the bridge and returned to his cabin. He placed the puppy on his bed and then shook his head. He didn't know the first thing about what dogs ate or how to train one. With a final look at the sleeping bundle of fur, Jason left the room and headed to the ship's library. He selected all the info cubes he could find on the behavior and training of dogs. For the next two hours he went though the information, absorbing it like a sponge. When he was done he decided to get something to eat. As he was sitting down at a table in the mess hall, Mother called out to him. "Hey, guess what?"

"Surprise me."

"You know that planet I told you about?"

"What about it?"

"We're here."

"How'd we get here that fast?"

"Spatial displacement jump," Mother replied.

Jason's brows knitted together for a moment. "Why didn't I feel the jump?"

"You were preoccupied. Besides, I've been making some small refinements to the system so now there's no lurch when we jump."

"Mother, do you think it's wise to be playing around with the drive units like that? You might jump us into the middle of a nova and that would be the end of us."

"Jason," Mother replied, her voice lacking its usual tone of merriment, "listen to me. I am a brain. My body is the entire ship. I have unlimited time for research and development. I can do six trillion calculations a second, which means I can run the variables of everything I do in less time than it takes you to blink.

"Believe me, before I go and change anything, such as tinkering with the drive system, I carefully consider all the factors, then go over all my data and calculations a thousand times to make sure everything is correct.

"You also have to remember," Mother continued, "that my prime directive is the protection of the lives of the people of New Hope from anything which may harm them in any way. And since you are the only survivor, my task is even that much more important to me."

Jason felt slightly ashamed of himself for doubting her. He knew what she said was true. "Okay. Sorry."

"Hey, no problem!" she replied in her familiar, cheerful tone. "Now, it would seem that my earlier comments were a bit prophetic."

"In what way?"

"Well, from my initial scan it would seem that this planet does have some traces of humanoid life. And rather advanced at that."

"I'm on my way. Be ready to show me as soon as I get there."

Jason left his unfinished meal on the table and started for the bridge.

"Hey, you should get something for the pup to eat," Mother told him. "She's probably hungry by now."

Jason stopped before reaching the door, then turned and went back to stand in front of one of the food dispensers. "Any suggestions?" he asked.

"Try the diced turkey in gravy. And some milk," Mother told him.

He tapped the selection panels and waited for the food. "Mother, can you alter one of these so it will issue meat-like protein, uncooked, and other things in the way of dog food? Maybe even some dog biscuits?"

"Sure. I'll put one of the servo droids on it. Shouldn't take more than an hour."

"Good."

Jason removed the food from the dispenser and hurried to the cabin. He found the puppy sitting up on the bed. As soon as she saw him her tail began thumping out her delight. Jason placed the food on the floor, and then picked the puppy up to hold it for a moment before setting it down so it could eat. "Hey, fuzz bucked, you act like you're glad to see me."

"Well, even you are better than nothing," Mother quipped. "Truth be told, though, I think it's the smell of the food that has her excited, not your shining presence."

"Watch it, metal mouth."

"Yes, Boss."

Jason watched the puppy eat for a moment and then went to the bridge. "All right, Mother, let's see what you've got," he told her as he sat in the Captain's seat.

The view screen lit up with the image of a planet floating in space. Mother quickly zoomed in on a particular continent, then a city, and then a particular feature of the city. Jason noticed that the city looked deserted, as if it hadn't been occupied for a long time. While the buildings appeared to be in perfect condition, they were all coated with a heavy layer of dust and dirt. With the exception of the streets, which looked as if they had been cleaned recently. One thing about it; it was definitely a city built by and for humans.

The city was constructed in a circular pattern with streets radiating out from the center to dissect the city into wedges. Concentric circles of streets intersected the direct line streets at regular intervals. But it was the structure in the center of the city that caught and held his attention.

"Mother, is that what I think it is?" he asked softly.

"Yes."

Jason stared at the structure for a long moment; his heart beat increasing as the implications of what he was looking at registered in his mind. He was so engrossed in it that it took a moment for the high-pitched bark of the puppy to attract his attention.

He looked own to see the puppy at his feet, its little tail whipping around in circles. Jason picked it up and placed it on his lap, then quickly returned his attention to the screen.

The fingers of his right hand moved rapidly over the controls that manipulated the probe Mother had sent down to give him a view of the structure from the side. Jason had seen similar structures before in holograms, laser projections and pictures, but looking at this one now the legends that surrounded them took on a whole new meaning for him. It was just too much of a coincidence.

"How big is it?" he asked, his voice sounding strained even to his own ears.

"Half again as large as Khufu, also known as Cheops."

"Since I don't know how big Cheops is, that doesn't tell me much, Mother."

"Sorry. Okay, Jason, time for a quick history lesson. In its original state Cheops, or the Great Pyramid of Khufu, was one hundred forty six, point fifty-nine meters tall. That converts to roughly four hundred and eighty one feet. Each side was two hundred and thirty meters at the base, or approximately seven hundred and fifty two, point five feet, and covered thirteen square acres. It was constructed of over two and a half million blocks, some weighing as much as forty tons.

"The one you're looking at now covers nearly twenty acres, is eleven hundred and thirty one feet high, seventeen hundred and sixty

*Alazon*

seven feet to a side at the base, and has approximately four million, six hundred and fifty blocks.

"In other words, Jason, it's big. Now, while it's the biggest one I've seen on this planet, it's not the only one. There is one in the center of every city of this planet, of which there are twelve."

"Unbelievable," he said in hushed tones.

"Not really, Jason. Especially when you figure in the mathematical probabilities of there being intelligent life in the universe. You know as well as I do that it has long been a belief by many of Earth's oldest and most remote cultures that Earth was visited by other sentient beings early on in its history."

"I know, Mother, but there was never any proof."

"None that would stand up to any close scientific scrutiny, true. However, Jason, there was enough evidence to convince those who programmed me to set a course for this particular solar system."

"I'm not sure I'm following you, Mother."

"One of the most intriguing legends has to do with Sirius, the Dog Star," Mother replied. "According to more than one legend, Earth was visited by intelligent beings that came from this particular area of space.

"In fact, there was even a story put forth by some natives of Africa about a small star hiding behind Sirius which couldn't be seen with the naked eye. Since it hadn't been discovered with a telescope at the time, most scientists scoffed at the idea. Until the mid-Twentieth Century when they suddenly found the small star right were the so-called 'primitives' said it would be."

"But, Mother, from the looks of it there hasn't been anyone living here for a long time. I wonder what happened to them?"

"Jason, if I knew that, we wouldn't be hopping from planet to planet looking for them."

"You're right. Sorry. I guess I was just thinking out loud. So, what's our next move?"

"For you to go down and take a look."

That idea made him suddenly nervous. "Ah, maybe later. I think I'd like to study things from up here for a day or so first. No sense in rushing into something we don't understand, or know anything about."

"Sure, I understand, Captain Coward," Mother teased. "In the meantime I'll run scans to see what I can come up with."

"Good idea."

"Hey, hold on. I think we've got something interesting here."

The image on the screen switched from the pyramid to an area outside the city. Mother zeroed in on a form which was moving across the plain, but the closer she got to it the more the image seemed to break up. As she changed the focus of the long-range lens, Jason realize he was looking at a group of humanoids moving together in a tightly compressed pack. Mother got a close-up shot of them, causing a gasp of surprise to escape Jason's lips.

"Look familiar?" she asked.

"Yeah," he replied softly, feeling his heart beating faster. "They look like Earth's own Neanderthal man."

"I agree. But there seems to be a few differences."

"Like what?"

"First, Neanderthal was only about five foot tall. These guys below are over seven feet. I'd estimate their weight to be around three hundred pounds, and it ain't fat. That would make them nearly twice the size of their cousins back on Earth.

"Also, the cranial development appears somewhat different. The forehead is a little higher and more developed, and they walk upright more than Neanderthal was alleged to have been able to do.

"From what I can tell, Jason, and this is strictly a hypothesis on my part, they live in tightly knot social groups, with the structure of the group based on the rule of the strongest. I state this based on past knowledge of such groups in Earth's history. It's more or less a general rule of thumb."

Jason nodded in agreement. "I'll buy that for now. Any estimates on the level of intelligence and development?"

Mother shifted the focus of the camera so he could see another, larger group gathered around a large fire. There were some crudely constructed shelters nearby.

"Well," Mother replied, "they have fire and they build huts from mud and stick, so one thing's for sure."

"What?"

"They didn't build the pyramids of cities. Hey, check this out."

*Alazon*

The view changed again. Jason saw about twenty of the men approaching the city from the west. When they were about a quarter of a mile from the city they stopped and began to engage in some strange dance. He watched the men take turns running toward the city for a few yards to shake their fists, clubs or spears at the empty structures, then hurry back to join the others.

"They seem to be afraid of the city for some reason," Mother commented.

Jason heard a low growl and felt a tug on the leg of his jumpsuit. He looked down to see the puppy with a mouthful of his cuff. He didn't remember setting the dog on the deck.

"Mother, continue your observations. I'm going to take the mutt and get her something more to eat. I think she's still hungry."

"All right," Mother replied. "I'll let you know if I come up with anything you should know about right away. Oh, by the way, the alterations on one of the food dispensers have been completed."

"Good. Which one?" Jason asked as he picked up the puppy and left the bridge.

"I think I'll let you guess," Mother teased.

"Mother, no games right now, okay?"

"Soil sport. It's the first one on the left."

"Thank you, Mother."

"You're welcome."

Jason carried the puppy to the mess deck. When he placed it on the deck he watched in amusement as it scampered around the cavernous room, sniffing everything in sight for a moment before finally returning to him.

He turned to the now altered food dispenser, but then stopped. Although Mother had used a servo droid to alter the food programs of the dispenser, it hadn't changed the labeling on the selection panels. As a result, Jason had no idea of what he would get when he pushed one. ""Here goes nothing," he muttered as he touched the top left panel.

Seconds later the light next to the small door lit up. He opened the door to find a bowl of what appeared to be small chunks of diced beef in thick gravy. It didn't appear the least bit appetizing to him.

"But then, I'm not a dog," he said aloud as he placed the bowl on the floor. He then filled a small plastic bowl with water and placed it beside the food the puppy was devouring with gusto.

"You know," Mother's voice said from one of the room's speakers, "if I were you, I'd start thinking real quick-like about what's gonna happen in a little while."

"What do you mean?" Jason asked, wondering what she was talking about.

"I mean, my slightly dense friend, that yon pup there is eventually going to excrete the remains of the food it is, and has been, eating, and will probably do so wherever it happens to be at the moment."

"Any suggestions?" he asked.

"A pooper-scooper and a broom?" Mother teased.

"Mother!"

"Damn, you're no fun at all today. Okay, listen up and Mother will tell you what you need to do."

# FOUR

Jason watched the humanoids from behind a rock outcrop atop a small hill. He was south of them, with them between himself and the city. Even though he was hidden from their view, the phaser pistol strapped to his right thigh was still a reassuring weight. After studying the planet for nearly two days from the ship, Jason finally admitted to himself that he would have to come down to the surface for closer observations. <u>Besides,</u> he told himself, <u>I really didn't have anything else planned for the day</u>.

There were about thirty of the humanoids gathered around a large communal fire they had built earlier. Jason knew from his prior observations that the hunters would be returning shortly with their kill for the day. The animals would be skinned, cleaned, and then cooked over the fire by the woman, while the men sat around talking in their guttural language until it was time to eat.

Through his binoculars, Jason scanned the area to the east where the forest was. The forest itself covered a couple of hundred square miles, and was full of game. He knew that was where the hunters would be returning from with their kill. But he had no way of knowing when, as that would depend strictly on their luck and skill for the day.

"May as well get comfortable," he said to himself as he shifted his weight slightly and rested his chin on his hands.

"Psst," Mother whispered into the sub-dural communicator in his left ear about half an hour later as he was watching some of the humanoid children playing.

"What?" he replied. His own voice was barely above a whisper, but he knew Mother could hear him clearly.

"Do you like kitty cats?"

Her question confused him. "I never had one, but I suppose they're okay. Why, have you cloned me one?"

"No, but you got one trying to sneak up on you from behind. And let me tell you, it is one big puddy tat."

Sweat broke out on Jason's forehead as his hand grabbed for the phaser. "How big?" he asked nervously.

"Oh, twelve, maybe thirteen feet, not counting tail, with big sharp teeth that I don't believe were designed for munching grass and chewing veggies."

"Where?" he asked hoarsely. His heart was racing as he got to his knees, his eyes scanning the area behind him.

"Behind the small pinnacle to your left."

"Can you hit it from where you are?"

"Of course," mother replied, managing to sound offended. "But why should I? After all, you've been mean and nasty to me lately and…"

The rest of her words were cut off as, at that moment the huge, tawny colored feline leaped from behind the small pinnacle, talons extended and jaws open wide in a roar as it charged him.

As Jason stared into that gaping maw, more terrified than he had ever been in his life, he felt as if he were going to die. He didn't remember raising the pistol and firing, but the best suddenly crashed to the ground, sliding to a halt less than three yards from where he stood. The stench of charred flesh filled the air around him. His heart was threatening to beat its way out of his chest, and he was drenched with sweat.

Jason slowly returned the pistol to its holster with a shaking hand. His body was trembling so violently he thought he was going to be sick. It took him a moment to realize that Mother was saying something to him.

"Huh…what?"

"I said nice shot. Of course, if you hadn't fired when you did, I would have."

"That's a comforting thought," he croaked as he wiped his sweaty palms on the legs of his jump suit, trying to control the shaking of his body.

"Yeah, well, now that that's over with, you've got another problem."

"What now?" he asked nervously.

"Our friends down below have spotted you. They're making their way toward you, and I don't think it's to invite you to dinner. Unless they're planning on making you part of the main course."

Jason turned to see the humanoids approaching the hill. Each of them was armed with a large spear or wicked looking club as big as one of his legs. They were starting to make their way up the hill, shouting and calling to one another, and at him. Jason looked behind him and found another group of ten or so just emerging from the woods. They saw what was going on and dropped their kill, rushing forward to join those intent on capturing or killing him.

Jason had no real desire to fight with them, or kill any of them if he could help it, but right now his position was such that he was either going to have to stand and fight, or run for the shuttle hidden in a ravine nearly a quarter of a mile away. Running seemed like the best course of action.

He leaped over the ledge, running and sliding down the side of the hill, being careful not to slip on the loose shale and rocks littering his path. As he reached the bottom he heard a shout come from his right. Glancing in that direction he saw the first of the men coming around the bottom of the hill. The man spotted him and another yell went up, leaving no doubt in Jason's mind as to their intentions should they manage to catch him.

That was all the incentive he needed to break into a full run, even though he knew Mother would intervene on his behalf to prevent any serious harm coming to him. At least that's what he hoped. The way she had been acting lately created some doubts in his mind.

"Mother?" he called as he glanced back over his shoulder at the pack of men chasing him. Their longer legs were slowly closing the distance between them and himself.

"Mother!" he called again. There was still no reply. "Damn you," Jason muttered as he picked up his pace. Her game playing was going to get him into trouble one of these days, and it might be a lot sooner than later.

The others were gaining on him, and some were starting to hurl their heavy spears at him. The weapons landed short, but they wouldn't for long at this rate.

Jason picked up his speed again to try and out distance them. Sprinting the last few yards to the ravine where the shuttle was hidden, Jason leaped blindly over the edge, only to land directly in the mist of another group of the humanoids. They were standing around the shuttle, staring at it in wonder and awe. Jason's sudden appearance startled them. He used their momentary confusion to dart between them and make his way to the hatch.

As his hand slapped the control panel on the side of the shuttle to open the hatch, he heard a small crackling sound and the odor of ozone filled his nose. The next second a heavy stone spear point thudded to the ground a few feet away. The shaft was severed and charred a few inches below the crude stone point. "Thank you, Mother," he said as the hatch opened and he dove inside, closing it behind him as quickly as he could.

Jason remained where he lay on the deck for a moment, feeling the adrenaline slowing dissipating from his boy. He finally got to his feet and made his way forward, dropping down heavily in the pilot's seat. He stared out the windows at the frightened, angry group of men, women and children now surrounding the craft. They were jumping up and down, with some of the more daring of them darting forward to stab at the shuttle with their spears. Others stood back and threw stones at it.

Jason didn't know how long they would stay, or what they might do next, although he knew they couldn't really do any damage to the shuttle with their crude weapons or thrown stones. He started the engine. That scared them enough to make them move away a few yards. He was grateful for that, as he didn't want to hurt any of them by the engine exhaust when he took off.

"Are they all clear?" Jason asked, not really expecting Mother to reply.

"Yes. You can lift off when ready."

Jason eased the shuttle straight up into the bright blue sky and moved away from the humanoids in the direction of the sun. He started to smile to himself as he thought of the stories and legends that would be passed down as a result of this incident. Now that the danger was past, he almost wished he could have stayed. It would have been interesting to remain and observe the humanoids more to see what their lives were like. Maybe even make an attempt to get to know them.

"Oh, well, maybe some other time," he said aloud as he checked his navigation and instrumentation.

Jason altered his course and headed for the city. He slowed his speed to nearly a crawl as he approached it from an altitude of a thousand feet. As he headed for the pyramid he began to comprehend for the first time just how big it was. He slowly circled it twice before landing on the smooth, flattened top, setting the shuttle down gently. He didn't get out of the shuttle right away, but stayed where he was, ready to lift off at the first sign of instability. When he was satisfied that everything was safe, he left the engine running and stepped out of the shuttle and onto the giant structure.

The view was stunning. From here he could see the entire city. Jason tried to imagine what it must have been like to stand atop this edifice and look down at the people below when the city was alive with them. From here they would have looked like mere ants.

He began to walk around the edge of the top, looking out at the city below. As he neared one of the corners he noticed a glint of metal and went to investigate. He brushed away the dust to reveal what appeared to be a brace of some type of uncorroded metal. He studied it for a moment, and then walked to the other three corners. At each of them he found the same thing. He wondered what they would want to brace up here? In the back of his mind something was trying to come forward. Something he had heard about, or read about in the past that was connected with pyramids. He struggled with it for a moment, but when he couldn't get it he returned to the shuttle. He sat down and propped his feet up on the console. "Mother?"

"Yes?"

"Help me out here. This pyramid has some type of brace support at each of the four corners. They're metal, but there's no trace of rust or corrosion on them. They look as if they were used to support something here on top, although I can't think of what it would be. But from the size of the braces, it must have been something big.

"Now, somewhere I've read or heard something about a pyramid with a flat top that had something on top of it in Earth's history, but I can't remember what it was. Do you know what I'm talking about?"

"Sure. It was in one of the legends about Atlantis," Mother replied. "The first actual mention of Atlantis was by Plato, who claimed to have heard about it from an Egyptian Prince, who said he was told about it from his grandfather."

"Right. I'm familiar with that," he told her.

"I thought you might be," Mother replied. "Anyway, according to one legend, there was a giant pyramid in the middle of Atlantis, and supposedly there was a giant crystal atop the pyramid that was the source of power for all their machinery, craft, and their weapons of light."

"Lasers?" he mused.

"Possibly," Mother replied. "As the legend goes, the island supposedly broke up and sank beneath the ocean. Some say it was the result of a major earthquake, others said it was violent volcanic action. In Nineteen, ninety-six, one theory was put forth that Atlantis was actually located somewhere in Antarctica, and that it disappeared when the crust of the Earth shifted due to the build up of ice on what had been the polar caps.

"Starting in the mid to late Twentieth Century there were a number of attempts by scientific groups, and other curious parties, to try and locate the legendary continent, but none of them ever succeeded."

"What's the legends say about survivors?" Jason asked. "Or were there any?"

"Unclear. Some legends said there were, and that they fled to what later became Egypt. One says that some of them were supposed to have settled along the southwestern area of Spain. In each they intermingled with the indigenous races, teaching them some of their secrets and sciences, but eventually all the Atlantians died out.

"It was also believed," Mother continued, "that some of them made their way west to the areas of Central and South America. Specifically the areas of lower Mexico, Peru and the Yucatan Peninsula. That belief is based on the fact that the earliest known civilizations there also built pyramids, minted coins, studied astrology, and had other similarities to the civilizations of Egypt which were flourishing at just about the same time. Actually, archaeological studies in the late Nineteenth Century of Central America found traces of civilizations much older than those of ancient Egypt, leading some to think that the Atlantians had been there centuries before."

"I know. I've read some of the holo books," Jason told her.

"Good, then you're aware of the fact that there are cities in the areas I just mentioned that were considered ancient by even the oldest Myan and Aztec records. But again, there was never any conclusive proof of any of this. Just a lot of speculation."

Jason thought about this for a moment. "Didn't some of the legends also hint that the race of beings that inhabited Atlantis may have come from this area of space?" he asked Mother.

"Yes," she replied. "The most prevalent theory is that they started out as a colonization or exploration team that became stranded for some reason or another. They couldn't get home, or didn't want to go home, and set up their own domain on Earth. And, yes, some of the theories were that they came from the Pleiades region where we are now."

"Well," Jason told her, "I may be jumping to conclusions here, but I have a feeling the legends may have had some factual basis to them after all, and I'm sitting on top of it."

"That's a bit hasty, don't you think?" Mother asked.

"Possibly. Look, you said something that reminded me of something else. The old cities in Central and South America, weren't some of them supposedly just up and abandoned?"

"Yes."

"Okay, look around, Mother. Here's a city that, to all appearances, looks as if the people just walked away. There are no sighs of destruction from a war, although a neutron bomb would kill the people without damaging the structures, as would some other weapons. So would chemical and germ warfare, but I don't think that's the case here. We didn't find any significant levels of radiation, or anything else that would indicate that any of those things happened when you did the scans.

"It's as if someone said, 'Okay, folks, time to move on', and they all packed up and left, leaving everything nice an tidy for when they returned. Only they never came back."

There was a slight tone of admonishment to Mother's voice when she spoke.

"Jason, I might point out that you are making this hypothesis while sitting atop a pyramid and looking down at a city that doesn't appear to have been occupied for perhaps centuries."

"Even in that amount of time bones left exposed would have turned to dust and blown away. It's also possible the other humanoids could have come in and taken everything they considered of value, including the dead bodies."

"Wrong, Mother," Jason replied with a shake of his head. "You saw the way they avoided the city. They actually seem to be afraid of it for some reason."

"Point taken."

"Well, I guess the only thing for me to do is go down and see if the city will give up any secrets."

"I'll keep an eye on things from up here," Mother told him.

"That's a comforting thought," he replied with s slight sneer.

Jason eased the shuttle from the top of the pyramid and floated it down toward the city, landing in what appeared to be some sort of town plaza. He remained in the shuttle for a few minutes just staring at the vacant buildings surrounding him. He finally got up and stepped outside. Although he wasn't expecting any danger, and knew Mother would warn him long before he could sense anything, Jason still kept his right hand on the butt of his weapon, drawing comfort from it.

He walked aimlessly, with no particular destination in mind. As he walked he admired the architecture and quality of craftsmanship that had gone into their construction. Despite the quiet serenity that surrounded the structures, Jason was still somewhat hesitant about entering any of them. The buildings seemed to whisper with soft voices of the past to tell him that he was intruding on their silent privacy.

Approaching a building near the edge of the first set of concentric circles that made up the streets, Jason noticed that it was larger and more ornate than those around it were. It seemed to speak of authority. Jason climbed the steps of the building slowly. His eyes studied the facade, his mind making comparisons with Earth architecture of the past. There were similarities to the Ionic, Doric and Hellenic styles of ancient Greece and Rome, but with indefinable differences to them. He passed his hand over one of the large columns at the top of the steps. As he brushed away the dust he found one of the biggest surprises yet. He brushed away more of the dust to make sure as he ran his fingertips over the material of the column again. He shook his head in disbelief.

"Mother, I may be wrong, but I don't think the material of this column is stone. It seems to be some form of composite polymer."

"Show me."

Jason removed the small camera-transmitter from his belt and held the lens near the column where he had cleared away the dust, sending pictures directly to the ship.

"Give me a minute and I'll see if I can tell you anything about it," Mother told him.

He replaced the camera and removed the knife from the sheath on his right ankle. His intention was to scrape some of the material off for analysis, but to his surprise the material wouldn't flake or chip. Completely defeating his efforts, it refused to even show any scratch marks where the razor sharp blade touched it. Jason tried digging the point of the knife into the column. He pressed as hard as he could but the material still refused to yield.

He replaced the knife and pulled the phaser. Adjusting the beam of the weapon to needle width, he ran it across one of the corners at the base of the pillar. After a moment a satisfied smile came to his face as a small piece of the material melted and broke away. He picked it up, noticing that it didn't seem the least bit warm from the beam of the phaser. He would take it up to the ship and run it through the analyzer to find out what it was composed of later. In the meantime, he still had the building to check out.

Jason placed the piece of material in a small pouch on his belt as he entered the building through one of the two huge doors, which opened with surprising ease at his touch, closing silently behind him once he was inside. The huge chamber he found himself in was devoid of any furnishings. However, the walls were painted with the most beautiful pictures he had ever seen. They appeared to be depictions of what life might have once been like here. There were gardens and various animals depicted. Some appeared to be wild, while others were obviously domesticated. Many of the animals bore a striking resemblance to animals of Earth, but others were so completely alien to him that they boggled his mind. He used the camera to scan the entire length of the wall on his right, wanting to get pictures of it for study later.

As he replaced the camera, Jason stepped close to the wall on his right to examine the paintings. He paid particular attention to the images of the people. There was no doubt about them being human, but the painter had either believed everyone he painted should be beautiful, or had painted them as they really were. Jason wondered which it was.

Putting aside the images of the painting for a moment, he studied the painting itself. It appeared as fresh as if it had been completed only recently, but when Jason brushed his fingertips across it lightly, he felt a glass like smoothness.

Jason was no art critic, but he knew of no technique that could clearly show brush strokes, be as smooth as glass to the touch, while also giving a three dimensional effect at the same time.

He moved slowly down the wall to one of the groups of humans depicted. He studied them carefully, noting the beauty and regularity of their features. If they were painted to actual size, and the other items in the painting suggested they were, then they were a tall race, averaging well over six feet for both men and women. The men were handsome, broad shouldered, almost beautiful, but not effeminate. In fact, there was a definite masculinity to them that was unmistakable. They had the well-muscled bodies of athletes, but gave the appearance of grace, with intelligence evident in their eyes.

Jason turned his attention to one of the women, noting the beauty of her face and figure. But as beautiful as she was to him, in this painting she was just one of many beautiful women. Her hair was a burnished gold, worn nearly waist length, with sections of it braided

*Alazon*

along the sides. Her nose was thin, slightly upturned, and her lips were full and lush. Her eyes were an unusual shade of blue, almost startling in their brightness, and the artist had captured a hit of laughter in then.

Jason stepped back from the wall with a shake of his head. There were more questions here than he could possibly hope to find answers for. Unless he were prepared to spend years on this planet studying it, which he wasn't.

Looking down at the floor, he noticed that it was inlaid with multi-hued tiles in a mosaic pattern around another giant mural in the very center of the chamber. The center mural was at least thirty feet in diameter. It was of a planet surrounded by stars. <u>Most likely this planet as seen from a thousand miles up</u>, he thought to himself.

Jason shook his head in wonder as he took a last look around at the painted walls and headed for an arched doorway off to his right. The room on the other side of the doorway was in darkness, but the moment Jason stepped through the arch the room was suddenly lit by a soft glow. Jason looked around for the source of light and what might have triggered it, but could find nothing for either. The walls and ceilings of this room were also covered with the giant mural paintings, with no windows or other openings of any type. And search as he might, he could find no source for the light.

Then it dawned on him. The light actually emanated from the walls themselves. He stepped back out of the room. The second he passed through the arch, the walls and ceiling began to darken. He stepped back into the room, watching as the walls lit up again. Jason inspected the doorway, looking for a photoelectric cell that might serve as a sensor, but found only the smooth finished surface of the archway itself.

"Jason?"

The sound of Mother's voice startled him a bit. "Yes?"

"While initial analysis is not conclusive, you're right in your assumption concerning the material. It does appear to be some form of composite polymer. I could tell more if I had an actual sample to work with. Can you get me some?"

"All ready did. Mother, you should see this place. There are paintings on the walls that are the most fantastic and incredible works of art I've ever seen."

"Well, dunder head, I could if you'd turn on the camera."

Jason activated the camera and turned in a slow circle so Mother could see the murals. "Hold it," she said as he directed the camera down to the floor to show the inlaid tiles and mural there.

"What's the matter?" he asked.

"Notice anything unusual?"

Jason studied the floor carefully. He knew Mother was asking him to see something that was obvious to her, but that was escaping his attention. "I give," he told her after nearly half a minute.

"No dust on the floor," she told him.

He nodded when he realized she was right. But that only created more questions. Any building that sat unoccupied for any length of time would accumulate a layer of dust, even inside, and especially on the floors. While the outsides of the buildings were covered with it, the floor was as spotless as if it had just been waxed. "Got any ideas?" he asked.

"Not really," Mother replied. "However, since you first entered the building I've been getting readings of energy from somewhere below you. Maybe that has something to do with it."

"In other words, you think I should go investigate, right?"

"Go to the head of the class. Or, in this case, down to the basement," Mother quipped

"Cute. Okay, so how do I get down there?" he asked as he steppe back into the main chamber and looked around.

He finally noticed what appeared to be a door at the far end. He went to it, but then stopped. The door, if that's what it was, had no handles or any type of panel to activate it that he could see. He studied the entire area for a moment but could fin no way to open it.

"Hey, Metal Mouth, we got a problem here. I found a door, but no way to open it. Maybe it works on a sensor of some type that is no longer functional."

"Try the phaser," Mother told him.

Jason wasn't enthusiastic about doing that but he didn't see any other way to get through the door. He drew the weapon, pointed it at the very center of the door and fired. After ten seconds of concentrated fire he lowered the weapon. The area where the phaser beam had struck didn't even show any signs of warmth. "Mother?"

"Yes?"

"Forget the phaser. It didn't even make the door warm, let alone burn through it."

"Well, Mother replied, "I guess you can walk around down there for a while, do some sight seeing, then return to the ship. It will be dark in about an hour and we don't know what happens when the sun goes down."

"Right. I'll be up shortly."

Jason walked slowly through the chamber in the direction of the large double doors, again admiring the murals on the walls. Reaching the doors he gripped the handle of one and pulled. It wouldn't open. He tugged on the other one, but it also refused to budge.

"Mother?"

There was no reply from the computer, only a slight static in the communicator.

"Mother?" he called again, his voice rising slightly in nervous anticipation.

Nothing. It was as if the room was somehow shielding his communications with the ship. Jason felt beads of sweat forming on his forehead and under his arms. He drew the phaser and fired at the seam between the doors but it had no more effect than his earlier attempts on the other door.

Jason looked around the chamber. Fear started to take root in his stomach, as he suddenly felt trapped within the room. He heard a whisper of movement behind him and spun around, pistol at the ready. The door at the other end of the chamber was open. He hesitated, wondering if he should go through that door and down the steps. After a moment he told himself that he really didn't have any choice in the matter for now. It was as if someone were directing his actions, guiding him where they wanted him to go.

Jason moved toward the open door, his senses alert, the pistol gripped tightly in his right hand, his heart beating faster with each step. At the doorway he stopped and looked down at the dark stairway.

"Here goes nothing," he muttered.

He heard his voice echo softly off the walls around him as he stepped through the doorway. He wasn't all that surprised when the walls began to give off light an illuminate the stairway the moment his right foot touched the first riser.

# FIVE

As his weight came down on the first riser the door slid closed behind him. Jason looked over his shoulder and noted that there were no handles on this side of the door either. With fear now firmly entrenched in his stomach, he pressed his back against the wall to his right, the phaser held out in front of him as he eased his way down the steps. He wasn't counting on the fact that just because Mother's sensors hadn't picked up any signs of life in the cities that it should be taken as gospel. If there were life here, and if it were remotely hostile, he wanted to be ready for it.

At the bottom of the narrow stairs he came upon another large room. But unlike the rooms above, the walls of this one were lined with what appeared to be computer terminals. In the center of the room were four workstations, complete with monitors and keypads of some type. Jason approached the center terminals cautiously, his eyes scanning the room to make sure he was alone.

When he was only a couple of steps from the terminal a large screen on the far wall came to life. It was nearly eight feet high and just as wide, and on it appeared the image of a face similar to those Jason had seen in the murals. But this face was older, with eyes looking far wiser than the eyes of those in the paintings. The face was three dimensional and looked directly at him. The mouth began to move, with sounds coming from hidden speakers around the room, but the words were totally alien to Jason. He slowly holstered the phaser and turned on the recorder for both visual and audio. He wanted to get a good record of this for Mother. "Providing I get out of here," he told himself softly.

The image stopped speaking, as if waiting for a response. After a moment it began to speak again. This time there was a slight difference to the voice. A tonal inflection that made Jason think the image was speaking in a language different from the first one it had used. This time when it stopped, Jason was ready for it.

"I don't know who you are," Jason said to the image, "or even where I'm at, but I get the impression that you are trying to communicate with me. I also have a feeling that you will continue to try various languages until we find one which suites us both. And I have a feeling that you are not real, but merely a computer generated image."

The image seemed to be listening for a moment, and tnen began speaking again. But one again the language was alien to Jason. He hesitated himself when the image stopped speaking, trying to figure out what to do. Aside from English, Jason spoke fluent Russian, Japanese, both Mandarin and Cantonese Chinese, French, Spanish and German. He tried each of these languages, but the image didn't seem to understand any of them. Nor did Jason understand any of the languages the image tried with him.

Jason was about to give up in frustration when he had a sudden idea. He spoke again to the image, but this time in halting Latin.

After a moment the face smiled and nodded at him. "You speak a language I have not heard used for many centuries."

"Please speak a little slower," Jason said to the image. "This language is one I know, but not all that well. It was not one of my favorites."

The image nodded in understanding. "I am not sure I completely understand all of your idioms," it replied, "but you are correct in that I am, as you put, an artificially generated image. There has been no human life on this planet for over five hundred centuries. Unless you count the sub-human species roaming the plains and forests outside of the cities."

"You know of them?" Jason asked.

"Yes," the image replied. "They are one of the last remaining specimens of what was once a vast life form experimentation area outside the city. Eight thousand years ago a storm caused a malfunction in the electronic barriers that kept them separated and confined. As a result they were able to escape into the forests. However, since they represent no real harm to the city itself, I have let them be.

"I know of everything that happens on this planet," the image continued. "There are sensors and monitors placed in strategic locations throughout and around the city to keep record of everything. There are also airborne probes that go out on a regular basis to check on things. They also provide a security system for me."

"Security against what?" Jason asked curiously, wishing he had a better grasp of Latin. He wasn't sure he completely understood everything the image was saying.

"Against whatever may threaten me," the computer replied.

"Is that the reason the humanoids don't come into the city?"

The image nodded. "Partially. If they were allowed to enter they would only destroy what they do not understand. In time the cities would be reduced to ruin."

"Why did you let me in?"

"You flew in. That means you of a higher life form and intelligence than those outside the cities. You are obviously from a race advanced enough to travel through space, and that is what I have been awaiting."

Jason shook his head at the direction of the conversation. "I hope you'll excuse me," he said to the image, "but I am a little confused, to say the least. I don't have the slightest idea of what's going on here, or even where "here" happens to be."

"If you will be patient," the image replied with a slight grin, "perhaps I will be able to explain a few things to you. By the way, I will also allow your ship's computer access to our conversation if you wish, but I would take it as a sign of courtesy if both you and your computer would refrain from interrupting me."

"Mother, did you hear?" Jason asked in English.

"I heard," she replied, also in English.

Jason sighed with relief that his communication was reestablished with Mother. He could also hear the worry and concern in her voice.

"I will tell you what I can," the image told him. "Then, if you have questions, which I am sure you will, I will do my best to answer them for you."

"First, before you start, how did you know about Mother?" Jason asked.

"My sensors detected the probe you sent down, and then the craft in which you arrived. I did a scan for your ship. When I found it I scanned it to find out all I could about it. Although I do not know why you are the only one aboard a ship constructed to hold many more, I am sure you will make that clear to me later. Now, let me try and explain a few things."

"May I interject a moment before you start?" asked Mother in Latin.

"Yes," replied the computer.

"Do not worry about the rate of your speech. I understand Latin perfectly and will record everything for translation into English for Jason later."

"Most considerate," replied the image. It hesitated a moment, then began to speak again.

"The name of this planet is Royac. It was the home of a race of humans such as you, also called the Royac, for over two and a half million years. As a race they went through many trials and tribulations before finally emerging as a society that prided itself on its humanity, intelligence, and a constant search for knowledge.

"They were a race that strove to improve their minds, bodies and world, eliminating such things as hunger, disease and war. This came only after much internal struggling and fighting that nearly cost them total destruction at more than one point in their history. Fortunately they had the sense to realize what they were doing and backed away from that path, finally joining together for peace and the search for knowledge."

Jason moved to a chair and sat down at the computer image continued.

"Roughly a quarter of a million years ago they embarked on their own exploration of space. They developed ships which could exceed the speed of light, allowing them to travel anywhere in this solar system. However, when they found no other comparable races they began reaching out to other star systems, expanding their explorations.

"They found other human and human type life, although none of them were as advanced as the Royac themselves. Often they would leave small scientific groups behind to assist those races along the road to development, or merely to observe. They did this by establishing colonies and bases in out of the way places so as not to disrupt the indigenous life."

"Sounds like Atlantis," Jason mumbled.

"One moment, please," the image said. It closed its eyes for a few seconds, then opened them and smiled. "There was a colony called Atalan. It was established on a planet in a system six trillion miles from here. It was the third planet out from its sun, with a single moon. The colony was on an island sub-continent. Records indicate that contact was lost with them after five hundred and nine years, but that a ship was never dispatched to find out what happened."

"This island, what you are calling Atalan," Jason said softly, licking his dry lips, "was supposed to have broken up and sank beneath the ocean. The planet is, was, earth. It is where I am from."

"Fascinating!" the image replied. "How are things there?"

Jason shook his head sadly. "Everyone is dead. The planet and its people were totally destroyed in a nuclear war. I am the only survivor."

The image was silent, almost pensive for a moment. "I am sorry," it said at last. "Some of the civilizations the Royac tried to help also ended up that way. But not all of them."

"You say there are others," Jason said, forgetting about the request not to interrupt. "What do you know of them? Do you know where they are?"

"Some of them, yes. They are scattered throughout the various star systems. There is one less than a light year from here, but I feel it would be a disappointment for you."

"Why?"

"Because it consists of human life artificially created as a genetic experiment. They were developed with a limit on their level of intelligence, which cannot be advanced beyond a certain point. They were then placed on a world which would provide for them all they needed without then having to work too hard for it."

Jason felt a sense of revulsion at that concept. "Why would anyone do something like that?"

"I can see by the expression on your face that you do not understand," the image said. "Let me explain.

"This particular race is nothing ore than a genetic pool of physical clones of the Royac themselves. They were created to produce only perfect physical specimens. The planet is nothing more than a body bank,"

"I am not sure I understand," Jason replied, feeling as if he understood all too well.

"When the body of a Royac became old and worn, which usually occurred after five hundred or so years, they could select a clone from those on this other world and have their brain transferred to it, thereby continuing their life."

Jason was starting to feel sick. "Are you talking about a memory transfer, or a physical transfer of the brain itself from one body to another?"

"Why, a physical transfer, of course," the image replied. "After all, there is no known way to affect a complete transfer of all knowledge, experience, or memories from one brain to another. And as I stated earlier, the brains of these genetic clones have been altered, so the type of transfer you mentioned would be impossible anyway."

Jason didn't like the sound of this, but decided not to pursue it for the moment. He also realized the Royac hadn't discovered the secret of being able to completely transfer knowledge, thoughts, memories and emotions from one brain to another as the scientists of New Hope had been able to do. "So, what happened to the Royac?" he finally asked.

"A little over fifty thousand years ago they were struck with a sudden illness that even the best of our doctors could find no cure for. It swept across our planet like a wind blown plague, killing thousands on a daily basis. It less than seventy days it wiped out nearly the entire population. A few managed to escape and flee to other planets and colonies, but they may have taken the illness with them."

"How many managed to escape?" Jason asked.

*Alazon*

"Perhaps a thousand, maybe less," the computer replied without emotion.

"Why didn't they transfer to the bodies they had closed?" Jason asked.

"First," replied the image, "there wasn't time. It struck without warning and with devastating effect. A transfer takes nearly eleven hours to complete, and the facilities are set up to handle only a few at a time in each city. Second, there was no way to protect the cloned bodies from contracting the disease.

"Attempts were made to contact ships from the outlying colonies, requesting that they return to save those they could, but most were too late. Some did return, but then refused to take on passengers out of a fear of contamination to their own crews and colonies. Of those ships that remained and were capable of carrying survivors from here, fights broke out among the populace as to who should go in them. Anarchy reigned and the population was reduced to fighting in the streets among themselves. They turned on one another like beasts, all traces of the civilization they had struggled so hard to reach vanishing practically overnight. Husbands killed wives and parents slaughtered their own children in an attempt to get aboard one of the ships."

Jason tried to image the chaos that must have overtaken the population and the fear they had felt. The people of Royac, knowing they were going to die, had reacted in a manner totally opposite to what those of New Hope had done when facing their certain extinction.

"The government collapsed almost overnight," the image told him. "The leaders were powerless to stop what was happening. Not that they were immune from the terror that gripped the minds of the masses. Within fifteen days from the first outbreak most of them were rounded up and killed. They were blamed for what was happening, despite the fact that they were also falling victim to the strange plague."

The image fell silent for a moment, giving Jason time to reflect on what he had heard so far. There were hundreds of questions Jason wanted to ask, but didn't know where to begin. Before he could, the image began speaking again.

"As I said, people fled their homes to die in the streets. Bodies were piled everywhere. But since all the cities of Royac are equipped with automated robotic cleaners, the bodies were collected and disposed of in incinerators. That is why no physical remains of them are evident now."

"What about those who managed to escape?" Jason asked. "Didn't they ever return, or at least try to communicate with any possible survivors?"

"No."

"Then who constructed you?"

"The Royac, but long before the tragedy I speak of came to pass. I was created over half a million years ago to be a historical record keeper for the planet and the people. After the last of the Royac had either died or left, I continued to function and to keep watch on the cities. I have also been waiting for the day when the Royac would return."

"Mother," Jason said softly in English, "are you getting all of this?"

"Yes."

"'Mother'," said the image. "An unusual name for a computer. The word denotes parentage."

"Mother is an unusual computer," Jason replied with a grin.

"It might be interesting to have direct interface with you, Mother," the image replied. "I am sure there is much we could learn from one another."

"That could be done," Mother replied, her voice coming not only from the communicator in Jason's ear, but the hidden speakers in the room as well.

"How?" Jason asked, feeling like the odd man out.

"Well," Mother replied, "While it wouldn't actually be direct access to one another, we would be able to link up through a sensor probe. We could then transmit and receive information and data from one another that way. "But," Mother added, "I could only do so if permitted by Jason."

Alarm bells started ringing in Jason's head. He knew Mother was warning him to be careful, letting him know she didn't trust

*Alazon*

the computer. He also knew, as did she, that she didn't need his permission to interface with the other computer.

"I have no objections," he said slowly, choosing his words carefully, "if you feel there are things you might learn from another."

"Thank you, Jason," Mother replied.

Jason stifled a laugh. Mother never said "Thank you" for anything. This was her way of letting him know the two of them were on the same page of this little play.

"Interesting," said the image.

"What?" Jason replied.

"Your computer is free thinking, able to make decisions on its own."

"Isn't that what you are doing?" Jason asked.

"No. Despite how it may seem to you, I merely respond to millions of possible word clues, suggestions, or direct questions, and then give the correct responses. Or those most nearly correct. I have no actual free thought association capabilities of my own."

"I see," Jason replied thoughtfully. "Do you have a name?"

"Royac. I know that is also the name of the planet and the people who once lived here, but it the one I was given as well."

Jason nodded at the image. "Royac, if you don't mind, I would like to return to my ship. I am starting to get hungry, and being down here all alone is a bit unsettling for me."

"Of course," the image replied with a slight nod of its head. "You will find the doors will now open at your touch. I apologize for locking you in earlier, but it was the way I was programmed to respond under these conditions."

"I understand," Jason replied. "Apology accepted. I will leave the two of you to carry on while I make my way back."

Jason turned and climbed the stairs. At the top the door slid open even before he reached it. That somewhat eased the pounding of his heart, but his pulse rate didn't return to normal until he had crossed the large chamber, opened the double doors and stepped out into the failing sunlight. Only then did he breathe a sigh of relief. He hurried to the shuttle, climbed in and started the engine, lifting the craft away from the planet as fast as he could. He wanted to talk to Mother, but decided to wait until he was safely inside the confines of the shuttle bay before doing so. He wasn't sure what the capabilities of the computer below might be, and wanted to make sure it couldn't listen in to what he had to say to Mother.

Lining up the shuttle with the entrance of the <u>Stargazer</u>, he waited for Mother to open the bay doors and activate the force field screen. When she failed to do so he began to worry. "Mother, why haven't you opened the bay doors?"

"Hold on," the computer replied. "I'm scanning you for any form of virus or bacteria you may have picked up below that may be harmful or fatal."

Sweat broke out on his forehead as Jason listened to her words. He knew she was doing the right thing, but the thought of him having contracted the virus that wiped out the entire population of Royac was a frightening thought.

"You're clean," Mother finally told him.

He eased the craft into the shuttle bay and shut down the engine. "What's happening?" he asked as he stepped from the shuttle.

"Right now," Mother replied, "Royac and I are exchanging basic information on a limited basis, although there doesn't seem to be much in the way of technology I can give him. Except for one thing."

"The T.T.S. data, right?"

"You're on the ball. I was wondering if you would catch on to that."

"What are you giving him now?" Jason asked as he headed for the bridge.

"Earth history and culture. There are a few other items of a scientific nature it doesn't seem to know about, such as our form of photon drive and space warp. It's different from those used by the Royac."

"In what way?" he asked as he changed direction and headed for his cabin.

"Well, apparently they used a form of nuclear fusion. It's remarkably simple and effective, but extremely powerful. I've had Royac give me the blue prints for one of their engines for you to go over later."

*Alazon*

"Good. Listen; learn all you can from it. We may be able to use some of their technology to modify and improve some of the things we have."

"I'm way ahead of you," Mother replied with a chuckle.

As Jason opened the door of his room he was greeted by a high pitched yapping sound, followed by the sound of paws and nails fighting for purchase on the slick deck. He laughed as he bent down and picked up the puppy, accepting the obligatory face licking it was determined to lavish on him. With the little ball of fur in his arms he turned and headed for the mess deck. He selected a meal for both of them and then sat down to eat while the puppy quickly devoured its food. As soon as she was done she ran around his angles to make her presence known.

But Jason's mind wasn't on the puppy, or even his food. It was on the discovery of the computer that had waited all these thousands of years for intelligent life to come along and save it from its boredom.

*No, not boredom*, he thought. *Unlike Mother, it doesn't have the capacity for individual, rational thought. It can't feel emotions, which means it can't know boredom. It's simply a machine programmed to perform certain tasks, even though there's no one around to make use of what it does.*

Jason shook his head wearily. He was so used to dealing with Mother and her humanistic side that he automatically thought of other computers in the same light.

*But what about the people of Royac?* he wondered as he chewed part of his meal. *What happened to the survivors? Had any of them managed to survive?*

Jason knew that just because some of them had escaped the planet it didn't automatically guarantee they had been able to survive. If the virus, or whatever it was, had managed to contaminate the ships when they arrived, or before they left, it would have been carried to the other colonies and outposts. Or the ships could have become floating coffins. A testament to what once was.

"What a minute!" he blurted out, startling the puppy as he sat upright in his chair. "Mother!"

"What?"

"Something's not right here. The computer said there were colonies of Royac scattered throughout the various star systems, right?"

"Right?"

"Okay, so what happened to them? They didn't come back here to die, so some of them must still be around. Royac said that not everyone responded, and surely they had some means of communicating with this planet, so why didn't they?"

"Hold on, I'll ask."

Jason finished his meal and was downing the last of his ice tea when Mother spoke again.

"The computer says that when the plague struck, calls were sent out to all colonies to return to help. Some responded, others didn't. As for those who managed to escape, it doesn't know specifically where they went. As far as any radio communication with the colonies goes, it said that after the initial calls for help, the communication center here was destroyed by the mobs. It says it will give us a star map to show us where the colonies were located, as well as the planets which contained other intelligent human life they knew of."

"Yes!" Jason yelled, leaping to his feet. His sudden actions frightened the puppy. She cowed and looked up at him with fear filled eyes.

"He's giving it to me now," Mother told him. "Once I have it I'll put it up on the screens in the bridge. Then we can pick one and go from there."

"I'm on my way."

Jason snatched up the puppy and hurried to the bridge. He wanted to see that star map as soon as possible, remembering that the computer had told him there was one inhabited planet only a light year away. But then he remembered that was the planet with the race of genetically inhibited clones. The 'body bank' planet. That caused him to have some misgivings. The computer said the alterations were designed to let them reach a certain level of intelligence while maintaining physical perfection, but Jason wondered if the computer were telling him the complete truth. While he had no reason to believe it would intentionally lie to him, or if it were even capable of doing so, what if it didn't know the whole truth itself?

*Alazon*

Inside the bridge, Jason set the puppy on the deck and took his seat, his fingers near the panel that gave him complete access to every function throughout the ship. He looked down to see the puppy curled up at his feet and smiled. "You big baby," he said softly, reaching down to scratch lightly between her ears. The puppy looked up at him and wagged her tail.

"Baby," he said in a teasing manner, causing the puppy to bark lightly and lick at his hand. "Okay, that's your name."

"Not very appropriate for a dog," Mother said somewhat disdainfully.

"I don't remember anyone asking you, Mother. Now, where's that star map?"

"To hear is to obey," she replied.

The view screen went blank. Seconds later small pinpoints of light began to appear in varying intensities, each dot signifying a star. A small flashing circle of green appeared around one of the planets circling a star.

"This is where we are now," Mother informed him. "And this," she added, forming a green ling toward another planet, "is the closest planet with intelligent life."

"And the one with the cones?" he asked.

"Here," Mother replied, circling another planet with green.

"What about the others?"

Five more circles of green appeared. "There are others," Mother told him, "but not within this particular section of space. I've got them located, but for now I think we should concentrate on these first."

"I agree."

"Yeah, I thought you would. The data exchange is nearly complete. Royac wants to know if we will be staying here for a while or moving on?"

Jason thought about it for a moment. While he would love to stay and investigate the cities and learn more about the people who once lived here, he knew Mother had all the information about them he would need for the time being. Staying here now wouldn't serve any useful purpose at this time. Finding other human life was what mattered most to him at this point.

"Tell it we'll be moving on. As much as I might like to stick around, I want to find someone other than a couple of computers and a dog to talk to. One computer gives only programmed answers, the other smarts off constantly, and the dog only barks and tries to lick the skin off my face."

"Poor thing," Mother cooed.

"Yeah, that's me. Tell it there's a good possibility we'll be returning someday, and when we do perhaps we'll have some information for it on how things went with the Royac who managed to escape."

Mother was silent for about fifteen seconds. "Done," she said at last. "It said that if you wish to return with humans to occupy the cities of Royac once again that would be fine, just as long as they are of sufficient intelligence to understand what they would be gaining in the way of ready-made cities and technology."

"Tell it I appreciate the offer and will keep it in mind," he replied.

As Jason stood up his left foot stepped on something soft and slippery. A rancid odor filled his nose. He looked down to see that he had stepped in a pile of warm feces, which was now stuck to the soft sole of his boot. "Aw, crap!" he exclaimed, looking down at Baby, who was sitting on her haunches and wagging her tail.

"Yep, that's just what it is," Mother said with a chuckle. "And guess what? There are about a dozen more of those little puppy paddies scattered around for you to find."

"Why didn't you have a servo clean them up?" he growled as he eased the boot off his foot and held it at arm's length.

"I thought you should experience the joys of parenthood, so to speak, so I left them where they were."

"Oh, yeah? Well, when I find them I'm going to shove them into your input terminals."

"That won't bother me in the least. Besides, you have to find those little surprises first, smart guy," Mother replied, laughing as Jason left the bridge holding the soft boot out at arms' length while the puppy scampered along beside him, wagging it's tail and barking sharply.

# SIX

"Hey, Marco Polo, wanna come see what I've got?"

Mother's voice came from the speakers in the walls of the gym where Jason was working with Baby, teaching the dog to respond to both verbal and hand commands.

"What for?" he replied dryly. "To be disappointed again?"

"Nah, I don't think so. I gotta good feeling about this place," Mother told him.

"Yeah, right. I've heard that before."

"Trust me!"

"Not on a dare," he snorted. "Okay, Mother, I'll be there in a minute," he said with a sigh.

"Hey, suit yourself. It's no skin off my nose."

"You don't have a nose, Mother."

"Moot point."

"Come on, Baby, let's go see what she's got," he said to the dog, which was now nearly the size of a full-grown Great Dane.

Without telling Jason about it before hand, Mother had done some genetic manipulations on the embryo of the dog. Baby had grown by leaps and bounds until she was nearly as big as he was. However, Mother had assured him a week ago that the dog wouldn't get much bigger than it was now. Since leaving the planet of the Royac, Jason had spent his time training Baby, as well as working to further develop his own fighting skills. Meanwhile, Mother took them from planet to planet on the star map given them by the computer on Royac.

The first one they had visited had been the planet of the clones. Despite what the computer on Royac had told him about it, Jason had wanted to see it and its people for himself.

Upon arriving he had spent two days studying it from the ship with the use of probes, but on the third day he had gone down. Using the Thought Transference Scanner, Mother had given him the language of the clones, which she had obtained from the Royac computer, along with every other known language that it had stored within it. Afterwards he had easily fabricated the animal skin like clothing like those of the planet wore, and then taken the shuttle down, landing it half a mile from the largest village located along a river that was comparable in size to the Amazon. He had walked into the village without arousing the least bit of suspicion among the inhabitants. Some had glanced his way, but most simply ignored him. One woman did speak to him, asking him if he were from a village further upstream. He told her he was, which seemed to satisfy her curiosity.

He had spent nearly four hours just walking around observing them. The men seemed to have some rudimentary hunting skills, enabling them to provide game for those of the village, which the women supplemented with fish from the river, as well as fruits and wild vegetables which grew in profusion in the woods and fields that surrounded the village on three sides. They lived in adobe-like structures that reminded Jason of the cells of a beehive, and there seemed to be no sense of social structure.

But the most peculiar oddity that Jason noted was that there were no children, or anyone under the age of what he would guess to be about sixteen, and no one over the age of thirty or so. When he had questioned one of the women about where the children were she had merely looked at him with blank vagueness in her eyes and shrugged her shoulders, leaving him more confused than ever.

Going off to one side of the village where he could be alone, Jason had discussed this situation with mother. She had told him he had two choices. The first was to stay and spend some time investigating until he found some answers, which might take a while. The second was to forget about it for now and go searching for other human-bearing planets, then come back later when he had more time. He had opted for the second.

The next five planets they visited were either too far down the evolutionary trail for him to be able to settle comfortable on or, as in the case of two, were nothing more than bad copies of Earth, with wars going on all over the planets. And none of them, from what he could tell, had any trace of the Royac who had once been there.

It had been nearly six months since leaving Royac and Jason was starting to become discouraged. The keep the depression at bay he worked out on a daily basis in both Kendo and Ninjitsu, did weight training to increase his strength, trained Baby, read books, studied the information from the computer on Royac, watched video holo cubes, studied Earth history, worked in the hydroponics gardens, and worked in the labs on half a dozen different projects and experiments.

Baby playfully nudged into him, pushing him against the wall of the corridor. Jason laughed and shoved back at her. He was grateful to Mother for her insight in providing him with the dog. Besides being his constant companion, Baby was also an amusing diversion; often doing things Jason found absolutely hilarious. It was almost as if Baby seemed to sense or know how to make him laugh or cheer him up. At night the dog slept on the deck beside Jason's bed. In the mornings she would wake him up by licking his face or jumping on the bed for an early morning wrestling match.

As the two of them entered the bridge, Baby hopped up onto the co-pilot's seat, looking eagerly at the view screen, as if the dog knew something was about to happen. Jason looked at her and grinned, grabbing a handful of fur at the back of her neck to shake her playfully. "Maybe this time, huh?" he said, receiving an enthusiastic bark in return. "All right, Mother, let" see what you've got."

"What I've got," the computer replied, a trace of mischief in her voice, "is a planet I think you're going to like. Take a look at this beauty."

Jason smiled to himself as he wondered why she suddenly reminded him of a used hovercraft salesman in a low budget commercial. The screen was filled with the image of the planet below. Like the others he had seen, it appeared beautiful from this distance. It had oceans of blue, forests of verdant green, and cotton candy clouds floating above it all. But he knew that looks could be deceiving. Especially from up here.

"I'm not impressed yet," Jason told her dryly.

"Well, Mister 'Personality-of-a-Persimmon', perhaps not at first glance. After all, it does look much like the others we've seen. However, as we take a closer look I think it may surprise you in that it has most of what we're looking for. Namely, intelligent human beings who aren't busy trying to blow one another up. Check this out."

That of two humans; a man and woman, dressed in toga-like robes, replaced the image of the planet.

"Adjust your color spectrum," Jason told her absently.

"I'll have you know there's absolutely nothing wrong with my colorization, Bucko."

"There has to be. You've got them with gold colored skin and silver hair. That can't be right."

"Says who?" Mother quipped as she filled the screen with just the faces of the two images, which caused Baby to bark loudly once.

"Okay, point taken," Jason replied. "Genetic differences could account for it."

"That's better," Mother told him in a friendlier tone as she returned the image to a full view of the two individuals. "Now, do you notice anything else different or unusual?"

Jason studied the two figures carefully. Aside from their odd coloring, which he found strangely attractive, he didn't see what she was hinting at. "I give," he said at last.

"This little piggy went to market," Mother began, "and this little piggy stayed home. This little..."

"Mother, what the hell are you doing? This is no time for nursery rhymes."

Mother ignored him and continued. "This little piggy had roast beef, and this little piggy had none."

"Well, I'll be damned," Jason finally replied in a hushed voice as it dawned on him what she was getting at. "There ain't no little piggy to go wee, wee, wee all the way home, is there?"

"Hot damn, I just knew you couldn't be as stupid as you look," Mother teased. "By the way, stop using double negatives."

*Alazon*

"Yeah, and I love you, too, Mother. Okay, so they only have four fingers on each hand, and four toes on each foot, what else can you tell me abut them? And cut out the jokes. Be serious for a change."

"What do you want to know?"

"Try everything you know, you mismatched mongrelization of microchips," he snarled.

"Touchy, touchy," Mother replied as she changed the image on the screen to give him a full view of the planet again, then zooming in on one of the cities.

"Okay, I've been studying them for a couple of days now. I started to tell you about them earlier but decided to wait. I wanted to make sure it would be worthwhile to let you know about it. If it had been like the others, I would have passed on it and gone on to the next one.

"As you can see, this planet is more along the lines of what we're looking for. However, I should tell you that the rate of development here seems to be about what you might have found back on Earth during the Hellenic period of Greece.

"Now, before you start finding objections to that," she quickly added before he could say anything, "let me point out a few things you may find interesting."

"I'm all ears," he replied flatly.

"Well, close," Mother snickered. "First off, the overall size of the planet is the closest to that of Earth that we've encountered so far, although it is slightly smaller. I would estimate gravity to be about one-sixth less than that of Earth. It has an equatorial distance of seven thousand, two hundred and seventy miles, a mean distance of ninety two, point two million miles from its sun, and only one moon."

Jason did some quick mental comparisons of those figures with those of Earth and found them to be a lot closer than he would have thought.

"It has a rotational cycle of exactly three hundred and thirty days," Mother continued, "with the length of a day being twenty two hours.

"The people all appear to be from the same genetic stock, as you can see, and they seem to be a rather good looking race overall.

They also appear to be on the road to scientific and evolutionary development."

"That's a rather rash and brash statement after only a couple of days of observation, Mother," he told her.

"Possibly, Jason. Just call it a gut feeling if you want to. Anyway, there are three main continents ranging in size from about two million, three hundred thousand square miles for the smallest, to about six and a half million square miles for the largest."

"Almost twice as large," he commented."

"Right. The continent we're currently orbiting above is the smallest of the three. However, it also appears to be the most interesting," she told him.

"In what way?"

"Stop interrupting me and I'll tell you."

"Yes, Mother."

"That's better. Okay, this particular continent contains five major cities and a dozen or so minor ones. The five major cities are situate with one on each coast, and the other three spread across the continent in almost equal distance from one another, and almost in a direct line. The one I'm showing you now is located in the exact geographical center of the continent, and it would appear to be the capital and cultural center from what I've observed.

"In each city there are school and temples of a religious nature, which also appear to double as medial centers or hospitals. The cities are all well kept and clean, with good sanitation. This one has a population of about five hundred thousand or so, and from what I can tell, no slum areas, which means no poverty.

"There are bustling and thriving market places which appear to cater to just about every items a person could want or need. Outside the cities are large tracts of acreage being utilized for the production of crops and raising of livestock."

Mother hesitated a moment to give him time to digest all this before continuing.

"I've sent down probes to obtain soil and water samples for analysis. The soil is extremely rich in all the minerals needed to produce healthy crops, and the water is as pure as you could ever hope for.

"All of the inland cities are almost identical to this one in structure, with only minor variations. Only the two port cities have any marked differences. But that's to be expected, as they maintain a thriving fishing industry, as well as trade in goods with the other two continents. But just as in the inland cities, there are schools, temples, and what appears to be an excellent standard of living. This, my boy, is a model of what a civilization should be."

"Well, that could be a topic for a long intellectual discussion," Jason replied dryly. "Just not right now. But don't you think that these people are just a little behind where I come from?"

"Behind who? You?" Mother questioned. "Listen Blue Eyes, the world known as Earth is gone, kaput, and all the other worlds we've seen so far haven't been worth you sticking around for. This is the best we've come across. So what if they don't have all the gadgets you're used to. Here's a world moving forward, and one where you might actually be able to do some good."

"Are you saying I should just drop in there, introduce myself as a being from another world, which just happened to blow itself to hell, and set up house?" he asked.

"No, not exactly," Mother replied with a chuckle.

"Then what's your plan? I know you've got one."

Mother didn't answer right away. When she did it was in such a way as to make him stop and think about her words.

"You know, Jason," she said, her voice soft and low, "I think you're afraid to go down there. I think you're afraid of actually being able to find a world where you can fit in."

"That's crazy," he replied scornfully.

"Is it, Jason? Earth and Luna were destroyed. All those you loved are gone and you hurt more, and in more ways, than I can really imagine. Ways that may not only have lasting effects on you, but which will directly relate to those you come into contact with.

"Part of you wants to belong, to fit in, to find a new world where you can do something useful. A world where you can find new friends, and maybe even someone to love again. But another part of you is hiding behind a wall, terrified of coming out from behind it.

"You're afraid of rejection, of being different, but more than that, you're afraid to let yourself care again. That's the worst fear of all.

That fear may keep you from ever finding out what it is you really want and need, Jason.

"You've become comfortable here aboard the ship. You're like a baby in its mother's womb. Here, aboard the ship, you feel safe, secure in the knowledge that nothing can harm you. From here you're a god. But once you leave the ship and have to deal with real people you'll become human again. That means you'll be vulnerable to things such as love, friendship, and even pain.

"You're like a little boy on his first day of school. You want to go to be with your friends and explore new, exciting things, but you're also terrified of leaving the safety and security of your mother's side. You're going to have to overcome that, Jason, if you ever expect to live on the surface of a planet among people again."

Despite himself, Jason knew there was more than just a grain of truth in her assessment of him. He <u>had</u> grown somewhat complacent here in the safety and comfort of the ship. And, yes, he admitted, he was somewhat afraid of actually coming into contact with normal humans again. And for all the reasons she had pointed out. He took a deep breath and let it out slowly.

"All right Mother," he said at last, speaking softly, "what do I do?"

"Good boy," she told him. "Well, the first thing we do is get someone from the planet up here so we can run them through the Thought Transference Scanner to get their language, as well as any other useful information they have."

"Wait a minute. I thought the computer back on Royac gave you the languages for all the planets listed."

"It did, Jason, but this planet wasn't on the star map it provided. From the probes I've sent down I've found that their language is similar to one given to me by the computer back on Royac, but with some variations to it, which could have been caused any number of factors."

"Whoa! Back up. If this planet wasn't on the maps, then how did you find it?"

"Just lucky, I guess. We're on the outer fringes of the Sirius System and I was doing a scan of all possible life bearing planets with G-type stars. I just happened to find it. Anyway, you'll have to go down and bring someone back."

"You mean kidnap them," he replied, wondering why the computer back on Royac hadn't told them about this planet.

"That's such an ugly term, Jason," she teased. "Let's just call it an involuntary acceptance of their fate. That sounds much nicer."

"It still means the same thing."

"Stop splitting hairs. Now," she continued, "once you have someone, I can run a mind scan on them. That will give you not only a good working knowledge of their language, but a grasp of their customs and laws, as well as a general concept of their society and how things work down there. That should make it a lot easier for you to know what's going on and how to fit in."

"Mother?"

"Yes?"

"If everyone down there is from the same genetic stock, with that golden skin and silver hair, won't I stick out just a bit?"

"Well, yeah, sort of," Mother replied with a slight chuckle, "but we'll worry about that later. Besides, that's not the only difference between you and them."

"Oh, great! What else is there?"

"How tall are you?"

"What the hell kind of question is that, Mother? Yu know to the fraction of an inch how tall I am."

"You're right, I do. Okay, you're six-foot, three and a quarter inches tall. However, my friend, the people down there average about five feet, six inches in height for the men, with the women being a little shorter."

"Oh, that's just great, Mother! Not only do I have the wrong hair, eye and skin coloring, but I'm also a foot taller than they are! Is there anything else you aren't telling me?"

"Not that I can think of. But, hey, what's a little variance in size and color?" she replied cheerfully.

"Oh, nothing much," Jason quipped. "Except that back on Earth they used to fight wars over trivial little things like that."

"Hey, that was Earth. This place may not be anything like that at all."

"Let's hope not. All right, I take it you've picked out a place for me to pull off this dastardly deed?"

"It just so happens that I have. But before we get to that, perhaps I should point out a couple of other items of interest."

"By all means, please do."

"This." Mother suddenly changed the view on the screen to give him an aerial view of what appeared to be a military encampment.

"What's that?" he asked curiously.

"Just what it looks like. An army preparing for war."

"But I thought you said…"

"Hold it, Blue Eyes. First off, this is the continent to the east of the one below."

"So?"

"Well, I'm not sure I really understand myself. You see, the one below appears to have no military forces at all, other than some sort of palace guard or police force in each city. But the continents to the east and west both have massive armies numbering over a hundred thousand each. And from what I can surmise, both of them are making preparations to attack the one below. They also seem to be making those preparations in relative secrecy."

"What makes you say that?"

Mother expanded the view to take in a wider area of the continent. "This particular army," she told him, "is over two hundred miles from the nearest city. Massive forests also surround it on three sides. To the west is a natural deep-water port, and builders are working around the clock to construct ships to carry those troops somewhere. According to my calculations they won't be ready for another seven months or so of this planet's time at the earliest."

"I take it those on the continent below are unaware of what's going on?"

"As I said," Mother replied, "I seriously doubt if they have any idea at all. If they did, it would only make sense that they would be making some preparations to defend themselves. So, unless they have some type of weapon we don't know about that will stop the coming invasions, they could be in for a lot of trouble."

Jason was starting to feel a bit uneasy. "Mother, why are you telling me this? What am I supposed to do about it?"

"Hey, you're a bright boy, you'll figure something out. But in the meantime we need a warm body. I'll see you when you get back."

"Mother, there's something else we need to think about."

"What's that?"

"Remember how you compared me to Cook and the explorers of Earth?"

"Yeah, so?"

"What about diseases? I mean, I could go down there and, inadvertently, infect their entire population, wiping them out."

"No need to worry, Jason. From the probes I've sent down I've been able to analyze the air, soil and water, as well as some garbage from a couple of houses. From the DNA samples I've been able to test, they have had the same diseases, such as measles, mumps and chicken pox that infected Earth."

Jason was silent for a moment as he considered this. "Doesn't that strike you as just a little bit odd?" he finally asked.

"To be honest, yes, it does," Mother replied. "In fact, when I began to notice this I ran all my tests for a second and third time to make sure. I can't explain it, Jason. I guess it's just something we'll have to figure out later on."

Jason stood and headed for the shuttle bay. "You have to stay here," he told Baby as the dog stopped beside the small shuttle and looked at him. "But one of these days you can go. I promise."

The dog looked at him with trust and love in her eyes as he scratched her behind her ears. Baby sat down and watched Jason as he gathered the things he thought he would need. Once he had it all he climbed into the shuttle and started the engine, then eased the craft towards the bay doors. "Mother?"

"Yes?"

"Want to give me a heading?"

"I've already programmed it into your onboard," Mother told him.

Jason activated the small monitor to his right. On the screen was an outline of the continent, with the center city circled in green. As he watched, the image changed to show him the city itself. He knew Mother was using a probe camera, probably floating it about a mile above the city, to give him this view. He watched as the camera panned slowly to the north, showing him an open expanse of ground about a hundred yards wide between the city and the woods to the north. Half a mile into the woods was a clearing just large enough to land the shuttle. "I take it that's my ell zee?" he asked

"You got it," Mother replied. "It's night time down there, so if you approach the city from the north no one will see you."

"And if they do?"

"Look, I can't do all the thinking around here. You figure out what to do."

"Gee, thanks," Jason muttered as he eased the shuttle through the force field of the open bay doors. Once outside the ship he shot down toward the planet like a comet, allowing the atmosphere to act as a braking system. Once through the planet's magnetosphere and exosphere he slowed his descent, knowing he would shoot into the ionosphere like a glowing meteor if he didn't, which would undoubtedly draw unwanted attention. He brought his speed down to a steady Mach Three and kept it there.

Jason checked his position on the monitor and made a slight course correction that would take him a little to the east of the city. As he approached the city he reduced his speed to below Mach One, then down to just two hundred miles per hour as the city came into view. It was larger than what he expected; more spread out than indicated on the pictures Mother had shown him. But that didn't matter, or alter his plans in the least.

Jason flew past the city for about two miles before circling back and turning on the infrared scanners to cut through the darkness of the night. When he found the clearing he set the shuttle down softly, his fingers moving swiftly over the controls. Moving to the rear cargo area of the shuttle, he stripped off his jump suit and boots, then donned his night fighter combat outfit. He slipped the sling of the <u>bokken</u> sheath over his head and shoulder so that the weapon hung diagonally down his back, the haft protruding slightly above his right shoulder. He strapped on a stunner and then slapped the panel to open the hatch. As soon as it opened he stepped out and dropped to the ground, hitting the outside panel to close the hatch. And then he froze.

Jason suddenly felt totally and completely alone in this huge forest. On the planet with the dolphins he had spent the night on the beach, but that had been out in the open with the ocean beside him. On the planet of the clones he had set down in a wooded area, but that had been during the day. This was completely different. He had never seen a real forest before and had no idea of what to expect. The city itself was half a mile away. Between it and him could be hundreds of unknown dangers.

Jason felt sweat forming in the pits of his arms and palms of his hands as he became acutely aware of the odor of decaying wood and the heady odor of wild flowers and bushes. For the first time in his life he heard the multitude of sounds of real animals of the night as they searched for food, or became food.

Jason could feel his heart beating in his chest. He told himself that his fear was completely irrational. Mother would warn him of any danger he might encounter. Or would she? He took a deep breath and let it out slowly, then dashed across the clearing to the tree line. He stopped, his right hand resting on the bole of a tree three times the circumference of his chest. "Mother?" he whispered hoarsely.

"Yes?" Her voice sounded inordinately loud in his ear.

"Is…is there anything in the forest?"

"Yes," she whispered.

"Wh-what?"

"Trees!" she cackled, the sound of her laughter filling his ears.

"I swear I'm going to turn you into video games when I get back," he threatened, which only served to make her laugh even more. "What I meant, Mother, is if there is anything which could cause me harm that I should look out for?"

"Hum, let me see. Well, you're wearing your 'Mister Indestructible' suit, and you've got a stunner and your bokken. So, unless you walk face first into a tree, trip over a log, or fall into a hole, all of which you're perfectly capable of doing all by yourself, you should be just fine."

Jason knew he wasn't going to get a straight answer from Mother, but that also told him that he really didn't have anything to worry about. With a shake of his head he began to make his way through the forest by the light of the full moon that hung in the sky like a giant lantern.

Ten minutes later Jason found himself standing at the edge of the wide clearing that separated the forest from the city. Directly across from him were a number of large homes. Behind most of them were structures that looked like garages or small stables. He decided to head for the nearest one. He checked the area to make sure no one was out and about, then pulled the mask section of his outfit over his head, securing it in place with the Velcro tabs at his throat. With a last look around, Jason dashed across the clearing towards the rear of the small building, his blood pounding loudly in his ears.

# SEVEN

Jason flattened himself against the back of the building. He quickly glanced from side to side to make sure he hadn't been spotted. "So far, so good," he whispered to himself in an effort to calm his racing heart and sense of nervousness.

The building felt as if it were constructed of some sort of stucco, but Jason noticed it only in passing. Right now he was concerned about the light from the torches and lamps burning along the back walls of the nearest houses the east of him. Their illumination might allow someone to see him in his present position. He moved to his right, around to the west side of the structure and away from the torches and moonlight. He breathed a sigh of relief as the shadows of the eaves extended out far enough over the side to hide him. Now someone would have to practically bump into him to know he was there. His only question now was where to find someone he could snatch and take back to the ship? Mother hadn't offered any suggestions on that.

Looking over his right shoulder, Jason saw wooden shutters set into the wall of the building. He eased one of them open and cautiously peeked in, but he wasn't quite ready for what he saw. Not more than ten feet away was the rear end of a horse, or maybe a pony, he wasn't sure, having never actually seen a real horse before. Judging from the size of the animal it was larger than what he imagined a pony to be, but not as large as what he thought a horse should be. As Jason was thinking about this, the animal seemed to sense his presence. It took a couple of steps backwards and turned to look at him. When it did, Jason had to bite his lip beneath the face covering of his outfit to keep from laughing out loud. While the body of the animal was most definitely that of a horse or large pony, the elongated neck and distinctive head were those of a llama. "Boy, I know some cowboys and Incas who would have fun discussing your blood lines," he whispered.

The animal merely stared in his direction with large black eyes as it slowly chewed some sort of hay or straw. It seemed totally unconcerned about Jason's presence. Finally loosing interest in him, the animal turned away and went back to its feed.

Jason felt himself relax. He looked around and decided he couldn't stay where he was all night. He had to find someplace where he could isolate someone and get them to the ship without being spotted. He began easing his way toward the front corner of the building, looking at the space between the stable and the wall behind the house. He wondered if he could get to the wall without being seen. Just as he started to poke his head around the corner he heard a woman's laughter coming from the house nearest him. It was followed by the sound of feet crunching on gravel. Someone was approaching his position.

Jason's hand dropped to the stunner as he strained to listen to the sound getting closer. He heard the squeaking of metal such as what a rusty hinge would make. The footsteps came closer. He carefully peeked around the corner to see the door of the stable standing open, as well as a gate in the back wall of the house. He pulled his head back and crept to the window again, cautiously peeking inside.

There was a figure inside the building with the animals, but Jason wasn't able to distinguish as to whether it was male or female. It wore a long hooded cloak that covered it from head to ankles. Whichever it was, the animals inside seemed pleased to see the figure. He saw them lowering their heads to be scratched between their ears and down their foreheads while the figure spoke to them in low tones.

Jason watched as the figure pulled out fresh fodder to feed the animals, petting their necks and talking softly to them. He wondered if he should enter the building or wait for the person to emerge before making his move. If he went in the animals might attack him. Or at least make enough noise to draw unwanted attention. While he was wondering what to do the figure in the robe made up his mind for him. With a final pat on the neck of one of the animals, the figure turned and headed for the door.

Jason pulled the stunner and adjusted its setting to a medium intensity. He stepped around the corner of the building just as the figure emerged. As it closed the door, Jason fired. There was a soft hum from the weapon and the figured dropped instantly to the round. Jason quickly holstered the stunner and stepped forward to pick up the limp body and tossed it easily over his left shoulder. With a quick look around he turned and bolted for the woods, praying that no one had seen him. He had to slow down once he reached the woods, but he still managed to make better time returning to the shuttle than he had when leaving it. Before long he was sprinting across the small clearing.

Jason opened the hatch and hurried inside, slapping the panel to close it behind him. He eased the figure from his shoulder and placed it in to co-pilot's seat. As he reached for the straps to secure it, the hood of the cloak fell back to reveal that his unconscious captive was a girl. He stared at her for only a moment before dropping into his own seat to start the engines. He still wasn't sure if he had attracted any attention or not, but if so, he didn't want to stick around to try and explain. He lifted the shuttle into the air and pushed it to its limit, taking the most direct route back to the ship. He glanced at the girl from time to time to see if she were regaining consciousness.

Once inside the bay of the <u>Stargazer</u>, Jason unstrapped the still unconscious girl and picked her up, carrying her in his arms to the medical lab. Baby jumped and ran along beside him, barking and wagging her tail excitedly, curious about the bundle in his arms and wanting to play.

"Not now," Jason told the dog as he entered the lab and gently placed the girl on one of the examination tables. Then, for the first time since grabbing her, Jason took a good look at her.

The girl appeared to be about sixteen or so. She had an absolutely beautiful face that looked so serene and peaceful for the moment. Jason knew that wouldn't last long. As soon as she woke up she was bound to be terrified.

"What now, Mother?" he asked nervously.

"Removing her cloak would be a good start," Mother replied with a chuckle.

Jason reached for the braided cloth oops around the small wooden fasteners on the cloak but his had froze just above the top one. "What if she's not wearing anything beneath it?" he asked.

"Getting modest on me?" Mother teased. "Look, Bozo, that's an outer cloak. It's designed to be worn over other clothing, so it's not very likely that she's in her birthday suit beneath it. Although she could be. But we won't know until we check her out. To me it appears as if she were getting ready to go somewhere before you interrupted her plans.

Jason nodded his head in agreement, wondering why he was so nervous. He began to open the cloak, breathing a sigh of relief when he saw the girl was wearing a pastel green, toga-style robe beneath it. He lifted her upper body and pulled the cloak completely free, tossing it over onto the next bed before laying her back down.

"Very good," said Mother. "Now, since the subject is…"

"The girl," Jason said absently, interrupting her.

"Yes, the girl. Definitely a girl. You know, Blue Eyes, I would have bet three of my memory chips that you would return with a female of the species. It would have been a safe bet."

"Cut the crap, Mother. What now?"

"We give her a total body scan. That will tell us if there are any major or minor differences in her physiology and what they might be."

Jason picked the girl up and carried her to the 'tongue' of the scanner and gently placed her on it. He then went to the console to activate it. He loosened the tabs at his neck and pulled back the portion of his outfit covering his face and head as he watched the girl's body disappear into the scanner.

The scanner worked by magnetic resin imagery and would provide him with three-dimensional images of every internal organ of the girl. Once she was fully inside, Jason started the scan. The process took nearly five minutes, during which time he was afraid she would wake up. That could create problems he didn't even want to think about. But the girl was still in a somnolent state when she emerged and he carried her back to the bed. That was starting to worry Jason

*Alazon*

a little. The charge she had received from the stunner shouldn't have had such a lasting effect on her, unless her nervous system was different from his, and the stun had an adverse effect on it.

"Mother, do you think it's possible the stun did some damage to her nervous system? I mean, she should have started to come out of it by now."

"I doubt it. I'm checking things out now. Wanna see?"

"Sure."

He returned to the console and sat down. His eyes were glued to the monitor as Mother placed an image of a normal human female on the right side of the screen, the image of the alien girl on the left. Jason studied the two carefully as they were both turned and compared to one another. Other than her heart being a little right of center, which wasn't all that unusual, she appeared to be completely normal. At least to his eyes.

"Notice anything?" Mother asked.

Jason knew by Mother's tone that he had missed something. He carefully studied the two images again. "I don't see anything," he said after nearly half a minute.

"No masses of lymphoid tissue between the anterior and posterior pillars of the cauces."

"Okay, Mother, so she doesn't have any tonsils," Jason replied. "Maybe she had them removed."

"Nope. No residual scar tissue."

"Mother, are you suggesting she was born without them?"

"It would appear that way."

"Well, I guess it's possible. We'll have to find out later. Anything else?"

If there were, Jason never got the chance to find out. At that moment the girl let out a scream that caused the hairs on the back of Jason's neck to stand up. His initial reaction was to leap to his feet, spinning around as his right hand flashed up to draw the bokken and take up a defensive position in preparation of an attack.

It was a reaction drilled into him for most of his life, but not exactly the one best suited for the circumstances. The terrified girl was crouched behind the last bed, eyes wide in fear as she stared at him. It was with difficulty that Jason worked his tongue around inside his mouth in an effort to work up some moisture. He could feel his heart thudding in his chest. For a full fifteen seconds he and the girl stared at one another, as if each were afraid to move, not knowing what the other would do. Through sheer will power Jason finally forced his body to relax and lowered the weapon.

"Girl," he said softly, "right now I wouldn't want to take any bets on which one of us is the most frightened."

"Odds are that she is," Mother said with a trace of humor in her voice.

The sound of the computer's voice coming from seemingly out of thin air caused the girl to look around the room to try and find out who else was speaking. While her eyes were averted from him for a moment, Jason took a step closer. Her eyes jerked back to him. She watched his every move with wary caution. He started to place the bokken on the bed closest to him, then changed his mind and tossed it over to the bed the girl was crouched behind. She quickly snatched it up and held it in both hands above her right shoulder like a baseball bat. There was a look of brave defiance on her face, as if she would gladly bash his brains out if he came any closer.

Smiling slightly at her actions, Jason removed the sheath of the bokken and tossed it onto the bed next to him. The stunner and holster followed. He movements were slow and deliberate. When he reached up to push the mask portion of his outfit all the way back off his head the girl's eyes widened and the bokken came down a fraction of an inch.

"I'm not going to hurt you," Jason said softly as he took another small step toward her.

Apparently the girl didn't quite believe him. She backed deeper into the corner of the room as he eyes darted around for a possible escape route, the weapon gripped tightly in her hands.

"You know," Mother commented humorously, "I don't think she's the least bit taken with our big baby blues or your charming personality."

The girl looked around the room again in an effort to find the source of the other voice for a moment before returning her attention to him.

"Mother," Jason said softly while continuing to smile at the girl, "if you don't have anything useful to say, then shut the hell up."

"You're the boss."

"I really wonder about that at times," he mumbled.

Jason took another small step closer to the girl. He held his hands out, palms up. "I won't hurt you," he told her softly, switching to the language of the Royac, hoping she might be able to understand some of it. "I swear, you don't have to be afraid of me."

The only thing his words accomplished was to make the girl look at him curiously and back up some more. But since there was nowhere else for her to go, she gripped the weapon tighter, raising it a little higher above her head.

"Oh, God, girl," Jason said to her, not realizing he had reverted to English, his voice nearly cracking as he was suddenly flooded with a sense of loneliness such as he hadn't felt since awakening from the sleep chamber to find all the others dead. "Please, I just want to be your friend. I swear I won't hurt you. Look, I'm just like you. We may have some minor differences, but we're basically the same. Please don't be afraid of me."

For reasons he couldn't explain or understand, Jason found himself begging, pleading with his very soul for this girl not to fear him. Tears formed in his eyes and started to make their way down his face. He found himself wanting acceptance in a way he had never known before. And a release from the pain he had been carrying around inside for so long now.

The girl started to look at him with a little less fear and hostility in her eyes and actually lowered the weapon just a bit. But then she screamed, her eyes opening wide in abject terror as Baby came bounding into the room and slid to a stop beside Jason.

At the scream of the terrified girl, and the sight of the weapon in her hands, Baby's entire attitude changed. The huge dog instantly went on guard and moved to place herself between Jason and the girl. The hairs on Baby's bunched shoulders stood straight out and her tail dropped down to swish slowly back and forth. When Baby bared her long fangs and growled, it was more than the girl could handle. Her eyes rolled up in her head and she collapsed onto the deck.

"Oh, real cute!" Jason exclaimed as he shoved a confused Baby out of the way and rushed to the girl. "First I scare the hell out of her," he said as he picked the girl up and placed her on the bed, "and then you come bouncing in and finish the job for me. We make quite a pair, don't we?"

Baby didn't know what he was saying, but he was talking to her and that was all that mattered to the dog. Her large bushy tail whipped back and forth as she stood on her hind legs and placed her front paws on the bed to look at the unconscious girl.

"Back off," Jason told Baby as she began to lick the girl's face. Baby stopped licking the girl but didn't get down.

Jason looked at the girl and wondered what would come next, and in what form. He had to find some way to bridge the chasm of fear separating them, but didn't have the faintest idea as to how to go about it. The Thought Transference Scanner wouldn't work if she were unconscious, so that was ruled out.

"May I speak, Master?"

"What do you want, Mother?" he snapped.

"Hey, I'm just trying to be helpful."

"That's a switch. Okay, you got a suggestion?"

"Perhaps. According to the scan we did, the contents of her stomach are negligible. That would indicate that it's been a while since she's eaten."

"So?"

"So, dummy, who don't you go get her something to eat? It may help break the ice."

"You think so?" he asked hopefully.

"Never know till you try."

"Right. Come on, Baby," he said as he headed for the door.

But the dog had plans of her own for making friends. As Jason looked back from the door he saw Baby hop up onto the bed and lay down beside the girl, a slight whining sound coming from its furry throat. He started to tell Baby to get down but then decided that perhaps the dog should stay, if for no other reason than to prevent the girl from getting hurt. Or taking off somewhere in the ship if she regained consciousness. With a grin and a shrug of his shoulders, Jason stepped through the door and headed for the mess deck.

*Alazon*

When he arrived in the ship's mess, Jason found himself faced with another dilemma. What did the girl eat? He had no idea if she had any dietary restrictions due to customs or religion, and if he brought her something she wasn't supposed to eat it wouldn't help his cause much. He finally selected grilled cheese on whole-wheat toast, French fries and sweetened iced tea for them both. He added apples as an afterthought. He figured if she saw him eating the same thing he was offering her she wouldn't think he was trying t poison her. He placed the food on a small tray and hurried back to the lab.

When Jason stepped through the door of the lab he nearly dropped the tray. The girl was sitting up on the bed. There was a smile on her face as she stroked and petted Baby's large head, which was resting comfortably on her lap. The dog's tail beat a gentle tattoo on the thin mattress.

"Well, I'll be damned," Jason whispered as he stepped farther into the room. The girl looked at him, watching his every move, but with considerably less fear than she had exhibited before. "First," he said to Baby, "you cause her to faint, and then you make friends with her before I can."

"That should tell you something," Mother said with a snicker.

Jason ignored the computer and approached the bed of the girl slowly. The girl slid off to stand on the other side, placing the bed between them. Apparently she wasn't ready to trust him completely just yet, and wanted the security of the bed separating them. That was all right with him for now. At least she was no longer screaming in fear or trying to get away from him. Or ready to bash his head in with the <u>bokken</u>, which, he noticed, was on the bed within reach of her hand.

Jason looked at Baby and jerked his head. "Down, fur ball." Baby leaped down off the bed and took up a position at the end of it where she could see both Jason and the girl.

Jason stepped up to the bed and set the tray on it. He removed the small plastic plates and slid hers to her side of the bed. The girl looked at the food suspiciously for a moment before looking up at him.

"Okay, I'll go first," he told her.

Jason picked up his sandwich and took a bite of it. The girl watched him for a moment before cautiously reaching out to pick up her own. She brought it up to her nose and sniffed at it before finally taking a small bite and chewing it slowly. Her face registered a pleasant surprise at the taste. Jason picked up a French fry, but when he started to dip it into the small container of catsup he saw the girl's face blanch in horror.

"What's the matter? Oh, damn!" he mumbled, realizing she probably thought it was blood.

Jason decided to forego the catsup and just popped the fry into his mouth before pointing to those on her plate. The girl picked one up, again bringing it up to her nose to sniff at first. Her actions made him grin in amusement. He picked up another fry and tossed it in the direction of Baby. The dog snatched it out of the air and gulped it down, then looked at him for another. This caused the girl to grin. She picked up a French fry from her own plate and tossed it to Baby, giggling slightly as the dog deftly caught it, chewed for a couple of seconds and then swallowed. The girl began to eat, but tossed about every third French fry to Baby. Jason could see her starting to visibly relax. She was becoming less afraid of him, which he knew was due largely to Baby. Without the dog things might have been much more difficult.

When the girl picked up the clear plastic glass of iced tea she held it in both hands for a moment, turning it around to stare at it with a sense of curiosity. Jason wasn't sure if she was fascinated by the clear plastic or the small, uniform sized pieces of ice floating in it. She took a tentative sip. She must have liked the taste as she quickly drained half the glass before setting it down and smiling shyly at him. They both finished eating about the same time, but Jason still had half a glass of tea remaining. He caught the girl eyeing it. With a grin he picked up the glass and held it out to her. She hesitated a moment before finally taking the glass and downing the tea. She set the glass down with a sigh, again smiling at him. Jason thought it was the most beautiful smile he had ever seen in his life.

He took the tray to a worktable and then returned to stand on his side of the bed across from the girl. As he rested his hands on the bed she seemed to notice them for the first time. A small "Oh!" escaped her lips as she cautiously extended her index finger to lightly touch each of his fingers, as if counting them. She stared at them for a moment before looking up at him, her silvery brown knitting. It was as if she wanted to ask him something but didn't know how.

Jason lifted his hands, intending to remove the cloth loops from around his middle fingers which held the protective material over the back of his hands, but the girl surprised him by reaching out to take his left hand in both of her own. She turned his hand over to inspect his palm, and then removed the loop herself. She pushed his sleeve up past his wrist so she could better study his hand. She seemed intrigued with the small hairs growing on the back of his hand and wrist. She gently tugged on them, giggling slightly when he flinched. She lifted his hand so that his palm was facing her, his fingers pointing upwards, and then placed her own palm flat against his as if to compare their size.

Slowly, cautiously, Jason spread his fingers and gradually linked them with her smaller ones, squeezing gently. The girl looked up at him, her features softening at the contact. After a moment she began to lightly return the pressure.

The touch of her hand and the soft smile on her face broke the barriers around his heart. Without realizing it, and without caring or understanding the reasons why, Jason began to cry. Tears welled up in his eyes and ran down his cheeks as he stood there holding her hand. It had been so long since he had actually felt close emotional contact with another human being. All the months of loneliness came crashing down on him.

The girl's face softened even more as she seemed to realize that something important was happening within him. She eased out from behind the bed so that she was closer to him, her hand still linked with his. She lifted her free hand to collect a single teardrop on the tip of one golden hued finger. "Bren," she said softly. Her voice sounded melodious to his ears. "Bren," she said again as she smiled shyly at him.

Jason wiped his eyes with his free hand and tried to smile. "Yeah," he said at last, his voice sounding somewhat choked, "I guess 'bren' is as good a word as any for tears, if that's what you saying."

The girl continued to smile up at him but made no effort to remove her hand from his. To Jason her smile represented hope, life, and a chance to belong once again. It was a smile that filled his heart with joy.

The girl appeared to have completely lost her fear of him. She released his hand and reached up to take hold of a lock of his shoulder length hair, gently pulling toward her to stare at it for a moment. Jason knew she had to be puzzled by it, as Mother had told him that everyone of her world had only one color of hair. She released it, allowing it to drape over his shoulder as her fingers moved to his face. It was then that she seemed to discover his eyes for the first time. A small gasp escaped her lips, causing him to grin as she lightly touched the corner of his left eye, her own eyes opening wide in amazement. The girl stared into his eyes for a long moment. Her actions made him blush, which seemed to amuse her.

The girl moved her hand down his face to feel the stubble of his beard, reminding him that he hadn't shaved for a few days. She frowned slightly at the roughness, but when she reached his mustache, she cocked her head to one side for a moment. She used one small finger to gently brush the hairs of his mustache from side to side. She pushed them to the right, then the left, a small smile forming on her lips. She giggled outright as the hairs sprang back into place. She did this a few more times before finally brushing them back into place, nodding her head as if in approval.

Jason thought her inspection of him was over, but the girl surprised him by placing both her hands on his shoulders. She moved them down his arms, squeezing to feel the hard muscles beneath his outfit. The girl then reached for his hands, holding them both up and placing her own flat against them, finally linking their fingers together. Gently, somewhat hesitantly, she squeezed his hands as she smiled up at him. The contact lasted only for a few seconds before she released his hands and turned to Baby, holding her hands out to the dog.

Baby, whose head was nearly level with that of the girl, came to her eagerly and began licking her face as the girl stroked and petted the huge dog. The girl finally turned back to Jason and looked at him expectantly, as if waiting for him to decide what they would do next. There was no longer any trace of her earlier fears of him evident in her face or eyes.

"Friend," Jason said softly as he pointed from himself to her. The girl tilted her head slightly, looking at him quizzically. "Friend," he said again.

"Ffffrrreeennndahh," she mimicked.

Jason smiled at her effort and nodded, but the girl shook her head, as if knowing it wasn't quite right.

"Fffrreenndahh," she again mimicked, looking at him with a sense of expectation.

"Yes. Friend," he told her as a sense of excitement started to infect his voice.

"Fffriend!" the girl said, this time much more clearly. Her face seemed to light up with her smile.

"By Jove, I think she's got it!" Mother called out in a heavy English accent, once again causing the girl to look around the room for the source of the voice.

Even Baby seemed to be caught up in the excitement. The dog began barking and running around the room. She finally jumped up to place her paws on Jason's shoulders, her tongue lashing his face. He pushed her down, making the girl laugh. At the sound of her laughter the girl became the next object of Baby's attention. But when the dog rose up and placed her paws on the girl's shoulders, the weight was too much and the girl fell over backwards.

Jason quickly shoved Baby aside, fearing that the girl might have been hurt. He was relieved when he saw her laughing as she tried to sit up. He helped her to her feet and for a moment the two of them stood and laughed as Baby barked and spun around in circles. It was then that Jason began to really look at the girl, noticing her for what she really was. He realized he had been incorrect in his initial assessment of her.

Even though she was only about four feet, ten inches tall, and probably weighed no more than ninety pounds, she was definitely no 'girl'. She had the fully developed body of a woman, and a beautiful woman at that. Her hair was parted in the middle and hung down her back to her waist. The light from the room seemed to bestow it with various shades of silver. The golden hue of her skin looked as if someone had found a way to develop the perfect tan. The color of her skin highlighted the sliver of her hair, eyebrows and long, thick lashes.

Her eyes were evenly spaced, and the most beautiful shade of green that Jason had ever seen. To him they were like two perfect emeralds that a master doll maker had lovingly set into her beautiful face. Her nose was slender, slightly upturned at the tip, and provided the perfect division for her heart shaped face. Her lips were full and sensuous, and Jason found himself wondering what it would be like to kiss them. He was shocked and surprised that a thought such as that would even enter his mind.

He let his eyes move lower to take in the slender column of her neck and the swell of her breasts beneath her robe. Although not exactly sheer, the material of the robe was opaque enough to let him know she wasn't wearing a bra, or any other form of support beneath it. <u>Not that she needs it</u>, he thought. Her breasts were full, round, and stood out proudly. They were accentuated even more by the rope belt tied around her slender waist, which seemed small enough for him to circle with his hands. Her hips swelled out gently before tapering down to her slender, shapely legs and tiny, four-toed feet, which were set into open sandals. As he looked down at her feet the girl wiggled her toes and grinned bashfully.

"You're beautiful," he said softly, smiling at her.

Perhaps it was the expression on his face, or the tone of his voice, but whichever it was it caused the girl to blush slightly. She lowered her eyes for a moment as if she had understood exactly what he had said.

After a moment she raised her eyes and smiled back at him. "Booteeful?" she said slowly.

Jason started to repeat the word but the girl shook her head and held up her right hand to forestall him. He watched as she formed the word silently with her lips a couple of times. Then, with a look of intense concentration on her face, she took a breath and tried it again.

"Bee-uuu-tee-ful," she said, taking her time and getting it nearly right.

"Yes, beautiful," Jason said with a smile. "You are very beautiful.

"Beautiful, beautiful," the girl said, laughing at the apparent joy he was exhibiting.

But then she did something totally unexpected. Although a soft smile remained on her face, she stopped laughing. She slowly reached out with her right hand, placing the palm of it lightly against his chest. "Friend," she said, her voice a soft whisper.

The effect on Jason was devastating. He began to tremble and his eyes blurred as tears formed in them. Try as he might, Jason found that he was powerless to stop what was happening to him. All he could do was stand there and revel in the touch of her tiny hand on his chest, feeling it throughout his entire being as tears ran down his cheeks.

The girl reached up and lightly touched his cheek, carefully using her thumb to wipe away his tears. "Bren," she said softly as she wiped away a tear, smiling up at him.

"Yeah, bren," he replied softly as he gradually regained control of his emotions. He wiped his eyes and smiled down at the girl, who smiled back at him, no longer exhibiting the fear of him she had shown earlier. "But what do we do now?" he asked himself, wondering where to go from here.

# EIGHT

Jason took the girl's hand and led her from the medical lab. She followed along eagerly and without hesitation. It was as if she somehow realized that Jason was sharing a part of himself along with her, allowing her to join him in his happiness and elation. She laughed at Baby as the dog ran on ahead of them, the excitement of the moment seeming to infect the animal as well.

The first place Jason took her to was the hydro-gardens. He watched her wonderment and amazement at the various plants and vegetables growing there. She went from plant to plant, tree to tree, touching everything new and different to her. He pulled an orange from a low hanging branch and handed it to her, showing her how to peel and eat it; smiling at her reactions a she tentatively sampled the sweet-tart wedges.

From there he took her to the shuttle bay. As they stepped through the hatch into the football stadium-sized bay the face of the girl took on a sense of awe as she took in the size of the bay and the shuttles there. The twelve small shuttles were two man craft with small storage areas in the back, with the capability of speeds up to Mach Four. The six mid-sized craft were half again as large, with top speeds of Mach Three. The two largest craft dwarfed the other shuttles. Each was a massive cargo carrier capable of holding all twelve of the small shuttles, or all six of the mid-sized shuttles in its cargo area, with room to spare. While they looked cumbersome when compared with the smaller shuttles, they were capable of reaching and maintaining speed of Mach One, point-five when empty, and

Mach One when fully loaded. All of the shuttles were equipped with energy pulse and phaser canons that could reduce a mountain the size of Everest to a mass of molten slag in only minutes on full power. The girl turned to look at him. The expression in her eyes let him know that she had absolutely no idea of what the craft were, but that she was suitably impressed.

They left the shuttle bay and went to the bridge, where the girl allowed him to lift her and place her in one of the padded seats. Jason activated the view screen to show her the stars surrounding her world in a way she had never been able to see them before. He grinned when the girl gasped in surprise and her hands gripped the arms of the seat tightly. She stared at the stars for a long moment before finally turning to him. He adjusted the controls of the ship's cameras to bring her planet into view, gradually bringing into focus the city from which he had kidnapped her. "Show me her house, Mother," he said softly.

Jason watched the girl as the probe Mother had sent down earlier zeroed in on the exact center of the city and then moved to her own house, using infrared to cut through the darkness of the night to give her a computer enhanced picture of it.

The girl stared at it for a moment and then a light seemed to brighten her eyes as she realized she was looking at her own house, but from a view she had never seen before. She began talking excitedly as she pointed at the screen, glancing quickly at him before turning her attention back to it.

Jason rubbed his eyes. He thought he understood some of what she was saying, but he was physically and mentally tired, and in need of a shower. "Mother," he said softly, "do you think you can keep her amused and occupied for a little while in here?"

"Probably. Why?"

"Because I haven't had a shower in over twenty hours and I need one. I also need to change clothes."

"Okay. Leave Baby with her. Between the mutt and myself we should be able to keep her busy."

"Thanks, Mother."

Jason glanced over at the girl. She was so engrossed with the changing pictures on the screen that Mother was providing for her that she didn't notice him slip quietly from the room. He hurried to his cabin and stripped out of the combat outfit as he headed for the bathroom. He looked in the mirror and decided he may as well shave while he was at it.

"Well," Jason said to his reflection in the mirror as he wrapped a large towel around his waist, "it ain't Earth, but it might, just might, become home. Or at least that's what Mother seems to think."

Jason lathered his face using an old-fashioned shaving mug and brush. His father had given it to him on his sixteenth birthday. His dad had told him that it had been passed down from father to first-born son in their family for over six hundred years. It was chipped in places, and there was evidence of cracks that had been glued back together, so it wasn't too hard to believe. Jason briefly wondered if he would have a son to pass it on to someday. He quickly pushed that thought out of his mind as it reminded him too much of Nadia.

He had just finished shaving one side of his face when he felt Baby brush against his leg. He turned to see the girl standing in the doorway watching him with a smile of amused curiosity on her face. He grinned and stuck his tongue out at her, causing her to giggle. She stepped boldly into the bathroom and reached up to take a bit of lather from his face with the tip of her finger, bringing it to her nose to smell. Absently she stuck her finger under the running water to rinse it off. It was then she actually noticed the faucets.

Apparently indoor plumbing and running water were something new to her, so Jason showed her how to turn the water off and on, as well as how to adjust it from hot to cold. Then he stood back and let her play with the lever for a moment. He wanted to laugh at her childlike innocence at everything she was seeing.

She looked into the large mirror behind the sink and it was at that moment that she confirmed his belief that women were the same everywhere in the universe. The girl took one look at herself; snatched up the brush she spotted on the sink counter and began brushing her hair, seemingly oblivious to his presence. Once she was satisfied that her hair was just right, she began to tug and pull on her robe until it too was the way she waned it.

While the girl's actions may have been serious to her, they struck Jason as outrageously funny. As she fidgeted with her robe he began to laugh so hard he had to sit on the seat of the commode, his hands going to his sides as he gasped for breath. The girl looked at him and blushed deeply, lowering her eyes as she realized what she had done. Timidly she backed up to the door, crossing her arms over her chest as she leaned against the frame and looked at him from beneath lowered lids.

Jason finally stopped laughing and stood up. Realizing the soap on the unshaven side of his face had dried; he rinsed it off and quickly lathered it again and began to shave. The girl merely smiled and watched. Once he was done and had rinsed the last of the soap from his face, she reached up to rub her hand across his cheek. She nodded her head, smiling at his now smooth features. "Glad you approve," he told her with a grin.

Jason turned from her to open the door of the shower stall and turn on the water. As he was adjusting the temperature of the spray he felt something soft brush against the underside of his arm. He looked down to find her elfin-like face peeking up from under it to see what he was doing.

"Okay, my little Golden Girl, that's it," he told her. "This is where I draw the line."

Taking her by the shoulders, Jason turned her around and eased her out of the bathroom. He directed her to the bed, where he picked her up and placed her on the edge of it. Baby, who stretched out and rolled over to present her stomach to the girl, which the dog felt was in need of rubbing, joined her.

"You two just wait here," Jason told the girl as he returned to the bathroom.

He closed the door and stepped into the shower, closing the door of it as well. He removed the towel from around his waist and draped it over the top of the door as he stepped beneath the water. With a sigh he let the stinging spray wash away the tension of his muscles and relax him. He had been up for nearly thirty hours now, and it was likely to be some time before he got any sleep.

After thoroughly washing his body, Jason applied shampoo to his hair and worked it in with his fingers. He was about to rinse it off when he heard a faint click and felt a cool draft on his backside. His head snapped around to find the girl peeking in at him through a small crack in the door. "Hey!" he yelled as shampoo ran down into his eyes. The shower door slammed shut. It was followed almost immediately by the sound of the bathroom door sliding closed as well.

"Brazen little thing," he muttered as he rinsed his hair and stepped from the shower. He dried off and then wrapped the towel around his waist as he went from the bathroom to the main room of the cabin.

The girl was sitting on the bed with Baby beside her. Her small hands were clasped in her lap and her legs were crossed at the ankles, swinging back and forth slightly. She looked like the perfect picture of innocence. She lowered her eyes as he looked at her, but not before he caught the mischievous grin she was fighting unsuccessfully to hide from him.

"Some help you turned out to be," Jason said to Baby as he walked to the closed and removed a clean jump suit.

As he was closing the closet door he heard the bathroom door slide closed behind him. Looking around he saw that the girl had gone into the bathroom.

"Now what's she up to?" he wondered aloud.

Seconds later he heard the sound of the shower. He crossed the room and opened the door about an inch. When he saw her robe and sandals on the floor he closed the door, shaking his head with a grin as he looked at Baby. "Women," he said lightly to himself as he dressed in a pastel blue jumper and matching boots. He picked up the small, hand held hair dryer and began to dry his hair, making a mental note to get it cut the first chance he got.

Just as Jason finished drying his hair and putting away the combat outfit the bathroom door opened. His heart leaped into his throat as the woman; he could no longer think of her as a girl, stepped into the room without a stitch of clothing on. Water dripped from her like beads of gold. She seemed completely unashamed of her nudity as she looked at him.

Jason tried to speak but the inside of his mouth had turned to cotton. He saw the droplets of water clinging to the tips of her nipples, watching one drop fall in what seemed like slow motion as her body moved slightly. His eyes traveled down her flat stomach to the silvery triangle between her beautiful thighs. The water that clung to her pubic hair was like molten drops of pure silver, and the effect on him was both immediate and powerful.

"Friend?" she said, pointing to the towel hanging on a hook by the closet door. "Friend?" she said again as he stood there in a state of shock. She turned slightly, as if to hide her body from him, but all that did was to give him a new view from a different angle.

Jason's arm shot out to snatch the towel from the hook. He tossed it to her as blood pounded in his temples.

"Friend!" she said cheerfully as she turned from him and began to dry herself off.

"Woman," he said softly as he turned his back to her, "you wouldn't be calling me that if you knew the thoughts going through my mind right now."

Jason kept his back to her and forced himself to avoid looking at her reflection in the mirror mounted on the wall above the dresser unit. When she called out with what seemed to be her favorite new word; "Friend", he turned around slowly.

She had wrapped the towel around her body, knotting it at the top to hold in it place under her arms. However, instead of the material of the towel hiding what lay beneath, it only seemed to accentuate it even more. She smiled and walked over to the closet, where she reached inside and pulled out the leg of a jump suit. Holding it in her hand she turned to face him. She pointed to the suit and then to herself, smiling sweetly.

It took Jason a moment to realize what she was getting at, but then he smiled and nodded. "Wait right here," he told her as he headed for the door.

As Jason left he tried to remember which of the cabins had been assigned to his sister and her best friend, Tracy, who, if memory served him right, was about the same height and weight as the alien girl. When he finally remembered he raced down the companionway until he came to it. Entering the room he went directly to the closet unit and snatched out the larger half of the jump suits there, placing them on the bed. He then went to one of the dresser units and removed all the soft, folded up boots, tossing them onto the bed as well. He opened another set of drawers and began to pull out the underwear in it, but suddenly stopped. He held up a pair of the panties in his hands. As he looked at them he wondered what in the world Tracy, who had been only thirteen, had been doing with underwear as lacy, skimpy, and outright sexy as what he now held in his hands.

While the mores and morals of those of New Hope were loosely defined, and children learned about their bodies and sex at an early age, it was still something of a shock for Jason to see the frilly underwear in the dresser of the girl who had been his sister's best friend, despite their four-year age difference. A girl who had been almost like another little sister to him.

He stopped for a moment to picture Tracy in his mind. He clearly remembered the bright, bouncy girl who seemed to follow him everywhere. She had just reached puberty and was starting to develop as a young woman, and Jason had teasingly flirted with her just to watch her blush, knowing that she had a small crush on him.

But like all of his memories, it was a sharp, double-edged sword. Sweet and beautiful on one side, painful on the other. Jason forced the memory from his mind as he tossed the garments on the bed with the rest of the things. He took a last look around the room to see if there were anything else the alien girl might like, decided there wasn't, and gathered the corners of the blanket together. He tossed the bundle over his shoulder and headed back to his cabin.

The girl was sitting on the bed with the towel still wrapped around her. As Jason placed the bundle of clothing on the floor and threw back the corners to reveal the contents, the girl's eyes lit up. She clapped her hands together in obvious delight and slid from the bed, dropping to her knees in the midst of the clothing.

Jason stood back and watched in amusement as the girl began separating the clothing into neat piles according to what they were. She held up each jump suit to inspect it before folding it neatly and placing it in a stack to her right. Once she had checked out each one she turned her attention to the boots. She inspected a pair of them and then lined them up in a neat row. She then turned to the underwear. She picked up a pair of the silky garments, turning them this way and that before finally looking at him with a questioning expression on her face.

"Oh, good grief," Jason mumbled. "You don't know what they are, do you?"

He tried to pantomime putting them on but the girl merely looked at him blankly. Jason finally took her hands and pulled her to her feet. Taking the panties from her hand he knelt down in front of her and lifted one of her dainty feet. He slipped the panties over one foot and then the other. He pulled them up to just below her knees, but stopped there. He stood up and indicated that she was to finish. With a shrug she pulled them up, seeming totally unconcerned with the fact that the towel was also being raised at the same time. She grinned as she pulled them all the way up and then took a moment to run her hands over the silky material. She parted to towel to show him how they fit. Jason turned on his heels and took half a dozen deep breaths to try and slow the pounding of his heart, as well as to shut out the image of the silvery hair of her pubic region that was burned into his mind. After a while he heard the sound of a zipper being pulled up. He slowly counted to ten before turning to face the girl again.

She was standing before him in a burgundy and honey colored jump suit that seemed to highlight her skin tone and hair coloring. She was grinning at him as if proud of herself. "Yeah, you're cute," Jason told her as he looked her over.

As his gaze moved down the outfit Jason couldn't help but notice how it clung to every curve of her body as if it were molded to her skin. He looked down at her feet and realized she had the boots on the wrong feet. With a short laugh he knelt down and lifted first one foot, then the other, removing the boots and putting them on the correct feet, showing her how the Velcro fasteners went on the outside of the ankles.

As Jason stood up the girl seemed to be searching for something. She finally walked over to the dresser and picked up a large comb and began to work it through her wet hair. Jason came up behind her and gently took her by the shoulders. Leading her over to a small padded vanity stool, he took the comb from her and picked up the blow dryer. Standing behind her he began to comb and dry her hair for her. As he did he thought of all the times he had done this for both Trish and Nadia. It had been something Jason had enjoyed doing for each of them, and something that had been special between them. To his surprise, Jason found he was getting that same sense of enjoyment now.

As he dried the girl's hair it began to lose the darker tones and shades due to the dampness of the water, gradually becoming like strands of fine silver cascading down her back. Because of the dryer, her hair had fullness to it that it normally wouldn't have had. When Jason finished he stepped back and turned the dryer off. The girl stood and looked in the mirror to admire her hair and the way she looked before turning to smile sweetly at him.

"What do you think, Mother?" Jason asked softly.

"You seem to be doing just fine. Now might be a good time to try the scanner," Mother told him.

"Good idea."

Jason noticed the way the young woman looked around the room in an attempt to locate the source of Mother's voice, finally looking back at him with questioning eyes.

"I'll explain it all to you later," he told her as he reached for her hand and led her from the room.

Jason took her back to the med-lab, where he picked her up and sat her on one of the beds. He crossed the room and pulled the Thought Transference Scanner from the wall and rolled it over to a position between the bed she was on and the one next to it. Connecting the lead cables to the socket in the wall, he picked up one of the plastic headbands with the attached electrodes and looked at the young woman.

Jason could see the apprehension in her eyes. He started to place the band on her head but then had another idea. He picked up the other band of electrodes and placed it on his own head and adjusted it. When he reached out to her again with the first one, she allowed him to place it on her head and adjust it. But despite her acquiescence, Jason could see the nervousness she was feeling. He smiled at her in what he hoped was a reassuring manner as he placed her hands in her lap and gently eased her back onto the bed.

"Mother, how do you want to do this?" he asked softly.

"I'll scan her first," Mother replied. "As you know, she won't feel anything while I'm doing it, so I can transfer her knowledge directly to you. That will give you a complete understanding of her language, which will then allow you to talk to her and explain what's going to happen when I reverse the process. By the way, I think her language is similar to one we already have."

"Could be," Jason replied as he got up onto the adjoining bed and lay back on it. "I thought I recognized some of what she said earlier on the bridge, so that's good. Okay, I'm ready."

Seconds later his mind was flooded with images, sounds, emotions, smells and tastes. He was being given everything the girl had ever known or experienced in her life. Jason didn't try to assimilate it, as it was happening much too quickly for that. He knew it wouldn't be until after the transfer of knowledge that he would be able to sort our all of his new 'memories'.

Nearly ten minutes later Jason heard the soft click of the machine as Mother shut it off. He sat up slowly and shook his head slightly at all the new information he suddenly possessed. He turned sideways on the bed and let his legs hang over the side.

"Hello, Kimella Vehey," he said to her in her own language. He couldn't help but smile at the look of shock and surprise on her face.

Her right hand came up to lightly touch the band around her head. "Th-this?" she asked nervously.

"Yes."

"But…how?"

"It would be a little difficult to explain to you in your own language, as you don't have the words to describe all the technical details of it. But what it does, basically, is transfer everything you know from your mind to mine."

"Everything?" she asked shyly.

"Well, I'm sure there are some things Mother probably left out," he replied with a smile. "Now, if you will just relax for a few more minutes the same process will be reversed and you will be able to speak my language. As well as know about me, my world, and where I come from."

"Will it hurt?" There was a slight quiver of fear in her voice.

"Not at all," he assured her. "It will be a bit confusing while it is going on, and that could be a little frightening to you, but only if you let it.

"It will all happen so fast you won't be able to make any sense out of it while it's going on, so don't even try. Just lay back, relax, and let it happen."

"Will...will you hold my hand?" she asked shyly, her face coloring slightly.

Jason slid from the bed and moved to sit beside her. He took her small hand in his and held it lightly. "Ready?"

"I guess so," she replied nervously.

"We're ready when you are, Mother," he called out in his new language, knowing the computer was now also fluent in it from the same transfer.

"Working."

Jason saw Kimella's body jerk involuntarily and her eyes snap open wide as her mind was suddenly deluged with the information Mother was giving to her about his world and life. Her small hand gripped his tightly.

Jason wasn't sure as to just what information Mother would give Kimella, although he knew it would be his own language, along with some history of Earth. When the machine finally clicked off, Kimella lay for a moment with her eyes closed. She finally opened them and sat up slowly, looking at him strangely. And then she began to cry softly. Jason was confused at this because he wasn't sure of the cause or reason for this reaction from her.

"Hey," he said gently, "what's the matter?"

"You...you are all alone," Kimella replied, her voice a muted whisper. "You are the only one left of your world. Oh, Lofa, I do not know if I could stand that."

Jason didn't know what to say, or if he should even say anything at all.

"How have you been able to stand the loneliness?" Kimella asked softly.

Jason sighed and shrugged. That was a question he had asked himself more times than he could remember. He reached out and brushed a tear away from her cheek, remembering how she had done the same for him earlier.

"It hasn't been easy at times," he confessed. "But with the help of Mother, and the company of Baby, I've been able to cope.

"That, and the fact that I just couldn't give up," he continued. "I've lived with the hope of finding a world where I could settle down and live, doing whatever I could to help, and try to put the past behind me."

Kimella looked at him for a long moment, studying his face intently. "You will be welcome on Alazon," she said in such a way that he could almost believe her.

"Perhaps."

"No, I know you will."

"Kimella…"

"Please, just 'Kimmy'," she said with a grin.

"All right, Kimmy it is. Now, let's not be too quick to say what will happen. After all, I'm a lot different from the people of your world in my physical appearance, and throughout history, at least on Earth, that fact alone was enough to cause fear, distrust, and even hatred."

"That will not happen here," she told him.

There was a conviction to her words that almost made Jason believe her. But he knew that his physical differences, as well as other things, might be causes for concern among the people of her world. "Well, I guess we'll find out soon enough, won't we?" he told her.

"What do you mean?"

"I mean that I'm taking you back just as soon as the sun comes up over Lemac. By now your parents are probably frantic over your disappearance. More than likely they have alerted the local police, or in your case, the Mayoral Guard, and are scouring the countryside for you even as we speak."

Kimmy giggled lightly and nodded in agreement. "Probably. Then again, knowing my parents, and them knowing me and the way I am, once I show up and explain everything to them, they'll take it in stride as just one more of my stunts.

"You see," she continued as she leaned back on the bed with an impish grin and removed the headband of electrodes, "I am always getting into trouble of some kind or another. So when I show up with you it will not be any big deal. Well, it will be, but not in the way you are probably thinking."

"Yeah, right," Jason replied with a grin of his own.

"And," she continued, "once they get over their initial shock, Daddy will be able to help you get settled on Alazon and start a new life. Although, from what I now know of your world, you might find us just a little backwards and boring."

"I doubt that," Jason said with a rueful grin and shake of his head. "Now, let's go back to your father for a second. You said he wouldn't be upset and that he'd be willing to help me. While that sounds all fine and good, what about the local authorities? Are you sure they won't take me out and try to hang me from the nearest tree the minute we show up?"

"Daddy would not let them," Kimmy assured him.

"Why? Has he got some influence with them?"

Kimmy looked at him strangely for a moment and then began to grin. Her eyes lit up with a twinkle he was quickly recognizing as meaning she was tickled about something. "What's the matter?" he asked.

"You mean you do not know?" she asked with a grin.

"Don't know what?" he replied in confusion.

"About my father?"

Jason searched his new memories but couldn't find anything that would give him a clue as to what Kimmy was talking about. "No," he finally replied.

"Oh, this is great!" Kimmy cried, clapping her hands in delight. "I guess Mother did not tell you."

"Mother!"

"Yes, Jason?" the computer replied innocently.

"What's the deal with her father?"

"Gosh, Jason, I'm not sure I know what you mean? Could you be a little more specific?"

"Don't give me that crap! You know exactly what I mean!"

"Isn't he cute when he's mad, Kimmy?" Mother asked.

Jason looked at Kimmy. She was laughing as she lay back on the pillows she had propped up behind her back. He felt his sense of frustration building, knowing he was the center of some private joke being shared between the computer and this alien woman.

"Mother," he growled, "if you don't tell me what's going on right this second, I swear I'll stick a phaser into your memory circuits and burn everything I can reach."

"Oh, all right, Jason. Kimmy's father is the Mayor of Lemac. Actually, he's the Senior Mayor of Preton itself, which is about the closest thing they have to a president."

"Oh, shit!" Jason mumbled. He hadn't kidnapped just any girl, but the oldest daughter of the Senior Mayor of Preton, the most powerful man on the entire continent! <u>They'll hang me for sure</u>, he thought with a shake of his head. But then another thought leaped into his mind, causing him to become somewhat angry.

"Mother! You set this all up, didn't you?"

"I don't have the foggiest idea of what you're talking about, Jason," the computer replied innocently.

"The hell you don't! You've been observing this planet for longer than just a couple of days, haven't you?"

"Well, maybe."

"Maybe my ass! You've been observing it for what, at least a week? Definitely long enough for you to find out what you needed to know about the planet to purposefully pick Lemac.

"Long enough for you to observe the Mayor and his family and pick up on a particular pattern, like the fact that Kimmy almost always goes out at a certain time of night to feed the tollies.

"You then manipulated me so that I would be at that particular spot, at that particular time, just to make sure that I kidnapped her. And that means, Mother, that you deliberately created this situation for me."

"You know, Jason, that's a pretty wild stretch of the imagination, even for you," Mother teased.

"Stretched or not, that's what you did, isn't it?" he demanded.

"I don't know. Maybe. I forget."

"Forget! Mother, you aren't capable of forgetting anything! It's impossible for you to forget anything! It was deliberate on your part and you know it. So, what else have you selectively not bothered to tell me about?"

"Now, Jason," the computer replied in a conciliatory tone, "you know we women have to have our little secrets from you men. It's what makes life interesting."

"Mother, may I remind you of one small, but very important fact?" he said as he heard Kimmy giggle slightly.

"What's that?"

"You are not a woman. You are a computer. You're an organic brain connected to microchips and computer boards by neural netting.

"True, you are the most advanced computer ever built, but still just a computer. Even if you have developed a very warped sense of humor. One that usually exhibits itself at the wrong times."

"Hah!" Mother replied haughtily. "Look, Bucko, just because I don't have a sexy body like Kimmy doesn't mean I'm not a woman. Besides, it isn't the body that makes the woman, but the mind.

"And, as I should not have to remind you, of all people, I happen to have the neural imprints of one of the finest, brightest women the world has ever known. I dare you to find an argument with that one."

Jason couldn't and they both knew it. What Mother said was true. As much as he might hate to admit it there were a lot of times when Mother seemed more like a woman than a machine. He just wished she hadn't developed Nadia's sense of humor so completely, which she had then expanded upon.

Jason shook his head, trying to force that to the back of his mind. For the present he had to consider the situation Mother may have placed him in. Here he was, five hundred miles above the surface of Alazon, with the oldest daughter of the most influential man on the continent sitting on a bed beside him. And who was also grinning at him.

"I've got to get you home, and fast," he told Kimmy.

"Okay," she replied as she slid from the bed. "But really, Jason, you should not be so worried about the situation. Daddy is a very understanding man. And he is used to me doing things that are a little crazy at times.

"As I told you, once they get over the initial shock of seeing you, and after probably chewing me out for being out all night, they will want to know all about you, your world, and a million other things. Trust me in this."

Jason sighed and rubbed his right hand over his face. "Let's hope you're right," he told her.

Kimmy suddenly looked at him in surprise. "Hey, I just realized something?"

"What?"

"We…I have been speaking your language ever since you did the transfer on me."

Jason smiled at her and nodded. "Yeah, how about that."

"Wow! This is great!" Kimmy exclaimed with delight. "You know, I bet this ship is just loaded with things the people of my world have never dreamed of."

"That would be a safe bet," he replied as he watched her look around the lab.

She turned back to face him. "So, how are we going to do it?"

"Do what?"

"Take me back. I know. How about flying down and landing in front of my house?" she asked with a giggle.

Jason smiled but shook his head. "I don't think so. That would only create more problems than I'm ready to take on at the present time.

"I'll take us back to the clearing I used before and then we'll walk back to the house. But I'll stay in the woods until you go on ahead and assure your parents that you're all right. Then we'll figure out how to get me into the city without being seen right off."

"That sounds all right," she told him, "but I still think my way would be more fun."

"Forget it."

"Mother?" she called out.

"Yes, Kimmy?"

"Can we plug him in and give him a sense of humor?" she asked with a giggle.

"Only if I get to pick were we stick the plug!" Mother chortled, causing Kimmy to laugh as well.

# NINE

Jason was loading a few supplies he thought he might need into the cargo area of a small shuttle when he noticed that Kimmy had disappeared. He wasn't worried about her. He knew that both Mother and Baby would keep her from any harm and out of trouble. He smiled as he secured the last container. It was the one that held all the jump suits and boots he had given to Kimmy. When he told her she could have them she had beamed at him, clapping her hands excitedly before giving him a quick hug. It had been an impromptu expression of gratitude that had embarrassed them both somewhat afterwards.

For himself, Jason had decided on three changes of clothing, his shaving kit, and an emergency medical kit he hoped he wouldn't have to use. Especially on himself. He had also decided to take the <u>bokken</u>, a small stunner and a phaser. He hoped he wouldn't have to use any of them for anything other than the purpose of demonstration.

His biggest concern was what to do about Baby. Jason didn't want to leave the dog behind, but he wasn't sure about taking her along, despite what Kimmy said. Baby was all right with Kimmy, but Jason didn't know how the dog might react around others. Or they to her.

There were no dogs on Alazon, and the interaction between the dog and the people down there could be volatile out of fear and ignorance. He wasn't necessarily concerned about Baby hurting anyone, except in the protection of him, or by accident, but he was concerned about what those below might do, or how they might react. After talking it over with both Mother and Kimmy, Jason had decided to take Baby along with them, but he still had some reservations.

Jason was about to ask Mother where Kimmy was when the young woman stepped through the door of the shuttle bay. Baby dashed on ahead of her. The dog seemed to sense that some new adventure was about to begin. Kimmy was walking slowly, carrying a tray in her hands on which three containers were carefully balanced. As she drew closer to the shuttle the grin on her face grew wider and her eyes twinkled.

"I thought we might get thirsty on the trip back," she told him as she finally stopped next to the open hatch of the shuttle, "so I got us something to drink."

Kimmy placed the tray just inside the hatch of the shuttle. "I got iced tea for you and two malts for me. One chocolate, one strawberry. And look, I even got lids and straws for them," she told him proudly. "I started to get something for Baby but I did not know what she liked. Or if she can drink through a straw. Can she?"

"Not that I'm aware of," he replied. "Then again, it wouldn't surprise me if she could," Jason replied with a grin as he helped Kimmy into the shuttle.

"Come on, fur ball," he said to Baby as the dog stood just outside the hatch looking at him expectantly. Without hesitation Baby hopped into the shuttle. Jason closed the hatch and helped Kimmy fasten her harness. He gave Baby a hand signal to lie down, which the dog did with her head between the two seats. He started the engine and eased the craft toward the shuttle bay doors, but before they opened he thought of something else. "Mother?"

"Yes?"

"I want you to keep an eye on those experiments in the east and west labs. I'll want updated figures and a possible time table of when you think they might be ready."

Jason glanced at Kimmy out of the corner of his eye to see if she had any idea that he was saying one thing while meaning another, but she was sipping one of her malts, watching intently as the bay doors started to open.

"Will do. However, I would advise caution in any form of hands on involvement in this once fermentation is complete. There could be risks we aren't aware of right now."

"Point taken, but please do as I ask."

"You're the boss."

Jason eased the craft closer to the airlock doors. As he did, Kimmy turned to face him. "Jason?"

"Yes?"

"What was that all about?"

"What?"

"What you and Mother were just talking about?"

"That? I was just reminding Mother to keep her eye on a couple of things, that's all."

"I see," Kim replied as the doors opened and he eased the shuttle out into space. But the manner in which she said it didn't convince him that she believed him.

As the shuttle left the <u>Stargazer</u> and floated out into empty space, Jason watched Kimmy's hands grip the arms of her seat tightly, the tray of drinks sitting on her lap completely forgotten. He was glad she had placed lids on the containers as he reached out to retrieve them when they began to float upwards. He placed them back on her lap. "Scared?" he asked softly.

"I…no…yes!" Kimmy's voice was a mere whisper as she glanced quickly at him.

"It has that effect on just about everyone the first time," he told her.

Kimmy was silent as he began a slow descent toward the planet, but after a moment she turned to him again. "Jason," she said, speaking slowly and softly, "it doesn't make for the start of a good relationship if one person lies to the other."

"What do you mean?" he asked, feigning innocence.

"A few minutes ago you lied to me about what you and Mother were talking about. Mother gave me a layout of the ship so I would not get lost in it during the Thought Transference Scan. You don't have an 'east' or 'west' lab aboard the ship. That means the two of you were using some sort of code so I would not know what was really being said.

*Alazon*

"Now, I figure you did that because you thought it was for a good reason, such as my own protection, or something equally as silly, so I forgive you this time. But please do not make a habit out of it. If you are going to settle and live here on Alazon, truth is going to be very important."

Jason looked at her and saw the sincerity in her eyes. It made him feel somewhat ashamed of himself for lying to her. He was also subtly impressed with her intelligence in picking up what had actually gone on between him and Mother.

"I'm sorry," he finally replied, "but yes, in a way it is for your own good. At least for now. I'll explain it all to you later, but for now all I can do is ask you to trust me."

Kimmy studied his face for a moment before finally nodding. "All right. This time."

After that they were both silent as they drew closer to the surface of the planet. Jason made this trip a lot slower than he had his first one. He wanted to give Kimmy time to drink her malts, as well as the opportunity to see her world as no one from it had ever seen it before. He skirted the city in a wide circle so no one would spot them and approached the clearing in the woods from the north, coming in slowly just above the treetops. He finally set the shuttle down lightly in the clearing.

Jason glanced over at Kimmy as the engine shut down. She was working on the second malt and didn't look like she was about to relinquish it.

"You know," he told her with a straight face, "too many of those will have a devastating effect on your body."

Kimmy looked at him. He eyes went wide as she let the straw slip from her lips. "What do you mean?" she asked.

"They'll start to make you fat."

She looked at the two malts and then back at him. "How many would it take?"

"Oh, three or four a day, every day, for about a month," he replied.

Kimmy's face broke into a grin. "Well, I'm safe then, because I doubt if I will get the chance to drink that many."

Jason grinned and nodded. "True. Come on, let's go."

They got up and moved to the cargo area where he helped her adjust the backpack of things she wanted to take with her on the first trip. Jason strapped on the phaser and slipped the small stunner into a hidden pouch on the inside the belt of the phaser holster. He slipped the <u>bokken</u> and sheath over his head and shoulder and then picked up his pack and slung it over his shoulder, holding it by one of the straps as they stepped out of the shuttle. He closed the hatch as Baby leaped out, and the three of them set off across the clearing. As Kimmy took the lead, Jason couldn't help but notice the way she filled out the back of her jump suit better than any fourteen year old girl he ever knew back on Luna could have done.

As they entered the woods, Kimmy began to pint out various plants and flowers to him while Baby ran excitedly back and forth between them. This was the first time the dog had ever been out of the ship and she wasn't sure of who she wanted to walk beside, or if she wanted to stay with either of them. The dog barked at everything that moved, darting off into the thick undergrowth, only to return moments later full of excitement.

They were nearing the clearing that separated the forest from the city when Jason noticed an odd shaped bush Kimmy hadn't said anything about. It was almost three-foot high, dome shaped, with large, purple leaves. Extending up from the center was an orange hued stalk about two inches thick. A single, blood red tulip shaped flower topped it.

As Jason stopped to look at it, the flower portion of the plant seemed to turn toward him, as if sensing his presence. The open end of the flower quivered slightly. Curious, Jason stepped closer. The flower again appeared to follow his movements. He raised his right hand and moved it slowly back and forth, intending to find out if the flower really was sensing his movement, or if it was just his imagination.

"Jason! NO!" Kimmy screamed.

His head snapped around to see Kimmy rushing toward him with a look of terror on her face, but before he could wonder what was wrong he felt a painful stinging sensation in the palm of his hand. Fire engulfed his hand and arm and seemed to explode in his chest. He felt as if a sun had just gone nova inside of him. He could hear

Kimmy screaming and Baby barking as he staggered backwards, but none of it made any sense to him. His brain felt as if it were starting to boil inside his skull. Blinding lights flashed behind his eyes with excruciating pain, and then total darkness came crashing down on him.

New Hope. . .his parents. . .Nadia. . .Trish. . .Kimella. . .images . . .faces. . .words. They all flashed through his mind in disjointed sequences. His body felt as if it were on fire one minute, with muscles as rigid as steel, cramping so painfully that he knew he was screaming from the torture of it, and the next they were icy cold and as slack as jelly.

Heat. . .cold. . .pain. . .faces appearing and disappearing. . .voices roaring painfully in his ears and then total silence.

". . .is he. . .don't know. . .seems. . .fever too high. . .maybe . . .might. . .Jason. . .Mother. . .Lofa. . .no. . .please. . .die. Cool damp cloths on his head. . .sharp pricking pains in his arms. . .hands grabbing him painfully. . .blackness. . .blinding lights. . .stars rushing by like laser streaks. . .total darkness. . .silence.

Jason slowly and painfully clawed his way up from the stygian blackness of the well he seemed to be in. The bright light of the sun blinded him and made his eyes water. His head throbbed like a bass drum, while his lips, mouth and throat felt as if they were coated with burning sand.

"Hi," a voice said softly from somewhere to his right.

Jason turned his head in that direction. The movement caused a new explosion of pain behind his eyes. He felt a wave of nausea sweep over him but managed to fight it down. He finally forced his eyes open to see Kimmy's face only inches from his own. Her eyes were red and puffy, as if she had been crying.

He could tell he was in a bed, but had no idea of where he was or how he had gotten there. Closing his eyes for a moment he tried to force his mind to focus. The image of a plant came to him, then the sound of someone screaming. He opened his eyes and blinked a few times in an effort to focus as he looked at Kimmy. He tried to speak but his throat was dry and felt swollen.

"Here." Kimmy held up a glazed clay cup with a hollow reed in it for him to sip through.

He drank some of the liquid. It wasn't water, but a cool, semi-sweet liquid that not only tasted good, but also coated his mouth and throat, bringing almost instant relief to them.

"What. . .happened?" Jason finally managed to ask, his voice weak and raspy.

"You got stung by a Death Plant," Kimmy told him as she held the cup up for him to take another sip.

"That flower?"

Kimmy nodded. "Yes. Now, since I seriously doubt if Mother would have left out any information about something as deadly as that, you must have just forgotten, or something. I'm not entirely sure just how this information transfer thing works just yet."

"What's a Death Plant?" he asked after trying unsuccessfully to draw the information from his own 'memories'.

"A Death Plant is so named," Kimmy replied, "because almost no one has ever lived after being stung by one. You are one of the rare exception."

"I don't understand."

Kimmy placed the cup on the small table beside the bed and took his right hand in both of her own. "Okay, I'll try to explain. It seems your new memories are a bit scrambled right now."

She moved to sit on the edge of the bed to make it easier for him to see her before speaking again.

"When a Death Plant stings someone, or some animal, it injects a poison into them which acts as an instant paralyzing agent. It is extremely painful, which I am sure you can attest to. You were screaming loud enough to wake the dead.

"One minute the poison causes the muscles to spasm in such a way that the body curls in upon itself. A dozen of the strongest men could not straighten out one of my little arms of it happened. At least not without breaking it, that is. A lot of people actually die from shock during this stage.

"For those who do not," she continued, "the next stage is just as bad. Every muscle in the body becomes completely lax, losing all semblance of strength. The victims cannot hold their heads up, move their fingers under their own control, and also lose control of all internal functions. That can get pretty messy, if you know what I mean," she added with a grin.

Jason nodded, but only slightly, afraid to move his head too much.

"Once the victim is paralyzed, the plant stings them again. Only this time it injects them with a solution that dissolves the bones and other internal organs, turning them into a liquid mush. However, for reasons that no one knows, it does not have any effect on the skin of the victim.

"Then, depending on the size of the victim, and once everything has been liquefied, the flower portion of the plant attaches itself to the victim near the abdominal area and punctures the skin. Then it sucks everything out."

"Similar to the process a spider uses," Jason said with a grimace.

Kimmy considered his words for a moment as if to make sure she understood what he meant, then nodded. "Pretty much."

"Then. . .how did I get here, wherever 'here' is, and why am I still alive. You said no one ever lives from their sting."

She placed her fingers on his lips to silence him and shook her head. "One question at a time," she told him.

"'Here' is my parent's house. 'How' is my father and brothers. And I said that almost no one ever survives. Okay, let me back up a little and put things in order.

"Baby and I pulled you out of reach of the plant after you were stung the first time. Then Baby stayed with you while I ran back here for help. Needless to say, when I came crashing through the back door, yelling my head off and wearing a jump suit, things got a little confusing for a few minutes.

"Naturally my parents, brothers and sisters were all here, all happy to see me, and all trying at once to find out what had happened to me. Meanwhile, I'm yelling and screaming for them to come back into the woods to help. They thought I was crazy, ranting about some alien from another world who was hurt and needed help. But after they saw what I was wearing they finally realized I wasn't a ghost myself and understood that someone was hurt and needed help.

"Oh, by the way," she added with a twinkle in her eyes and a grin, "my mother considers the jump suits very un-lady like, if you know what I mean.

"Anyway," she continued, "I finally got across to them what I was trying to tell them and they followed me back to where you were. We took tollies, as it was a lot quicker. It also made it easier to bring you back. But once we got to you we had another problem."

"What?" he asked.

"Baby," Kimmy replied with a short laugh. "At first she was not about to let anyone but me get near you. She scared the daylights out of my dad and brothers, not to mention the tollies. I was finally able to calm her down enough to let my dad and brothers wrap you in a cloak and get you loaded on a tollie to bring you back here."

"Where's Baby now?" he asked with a note of concern in his voice.

"With the twins," Kimmy told him. "It was love at first sight between them and the dog. When she is not in here getting in my way, or sleeping on the bed with you, she is with them. Aside from the twins and myself, no one else will go near her."

Kimmy's face turned serious. "As to why you are still alive? To be perfectly honest, Jason, I am not sure. I think it is a combination of things.

"You see, the men who do manage to survive are usually men who are in excellent physical condition, with a high tolerance for pain, and somehow manage to avoid the second sting of the Death Plant. It is obvious that both conditions apply to you. But even then, almost all of those men still end up feeble minded from the shock and stress their minds have gone through.

"Now, aside from your physical conditioning, once we got back to you, I used your wrist communicator to contact Mother. I told her what happened and how the poison worked, and she told me what to do. I went to the shuttle and got your medical kit, and when we got back here Mother told me which drugs to administer, and how much of each. She also sent some others down by a remote probe, which I had to go get at night so no one else would know what was going on. Between the two of us we pulled you through."

*Alazon*

Jason could only stare at her for a moment. Her quick thinking and resourcefulness surprised him. "How did you know to use the wrist communicator?" he asked.

Kimmy shrugged. "I knew you had one on, so I took it off your wrist, pressed the button and called Mother. Really, Jason, do not look so surprised. Despite what my parents will probably tell you, I am not exactly stupid," she said with a grin.

He smiled and nodded his head slightly. "I'm beginning to realize that."

Jason wasn't sure of what he had expected of the people of this world, but if they were all as quick thinking and resourceful as Kimmy, then things could be very interesting.

"Ok, I get it," she said with a frown. "You are one of those men who thinks a woman can not be as smart as a man, right? You think we should be kept barefoot, pregnant and in front of the kitchen cooking fire."

Jason had to laugh at her statement, even though doing so caused his head to throb painfully. He had heard almost those exact same words expressed before in what seemed like another life. "No, that's not it at all," he told her as he pointed at the cup.

"Then what?" she asked as she handed the cup to him.

He took a long sip of the liquid, feeling the relief from it before speaking. "I'm just impressed that you reacted so quickly and intelligently under that type of pressure, that's all. You, Golden Girl, are a very pleasant surprise."

Kimmy blushed at his compliment and lowered her eyes. "Not really," she replied softly.

"Yes, you are. If you hadn't acted and reacted the way you did, I would probably be dead by now. I owe you my life."

Before she could respond to that the door of the room opened and in walked an older, slightly shorter version of Kimmy. It was Liet, her mother, and the woman's eyes were full of mistrust and doubt as they stared at him.

"He's awake, Mom," Kimmy said in her native tongue, looking from her mother to him and winking slyly.

"So I see. I thought I heard you talking," Liet replied, eyeing the two of them suspiciously.

"We were. I was telling him how we got him here and took care of him."

Jason pushed himself up a little on the bed and smiled at Kimmy's mother. "I would like to thank you, Mrs. Vehey, for allowing me into your home and providing me with care, Jason said in her own language.

Liet looked at Kimmy and furrowed her brows. "How does he know our language so well?"

"I told you, Mother, he is very smart," Kimmy replied, her face a mask of seriousness.

"I take it she thinks I'm some sort of demon?" he whispered to Kimmy in English.

"A gerkin to be exact," she whispered back, also in English. "She is still not sure if you eat little kids for breakfast or not."

"Only on the first full moon of each month," he replied with a grin, causing Kimmy to giggle.

"What did he say?" Liet demanded.

"Oh, he was just expressing his gratitude for us taking such good care of him," Kimmy told her mother with a straight face.

"How do you know what he said?"

"I can understand and speak his language, Mother."

"Humph!" Liet exclaimed as she crossed her arms over her breasts. "I might believe he's smart enough to learn to speak our language, maybe even learn it overnight the way you said, but I know for a fact that you aren't smart enough to lean a new language in that amount of time. You had a hard enough time learning your own."

Jason watched the interplay between mother and daughter and smiled. Here was a woman who loved her children the way his mother had loved him and Trish. And one who wasn't above some good-natured teasing of her children from time to time.

Liet turned to Jason. "Are you hungry?"

Jason nodded. "Now that you mention, it, yes, I am. I feel as if I haven't eaten for a week."

"We'll bring you something," Liet told him. She glanced at Kimmy, which was Liet's signal for Kimmy to follow her.

"I will be back in a little while," Kimmy told him with a smile as she got up to follow her mother out of the room.

As he watched the two of them go, Jason became aware of the fact that when Kimmy spoke English she nearly always used the proper form of all of her words, without the use of contractions, but when speaking her own language, contractions were as normal to her as when Jason spoke English. He wondered if that were due to her unfamiliarity with her new language.

Once they were gone Jason glanced around the room to take in his surroundings. The walls were painted an off-white and appeared to be smooth stucco. The bed he was in was probably large by their standards, but Jason found that his feet hung over the edge when he stretched out on it. If he stayed here he would have to have a bigger bed build for himself.

The sheet beneath him was a soft cottony material, light blue in color. The cover was slightly thicker and a darker shade of blue. The pillows were fully, fluffy, and covered in the same material as the sheet.

Against the wall to his left was a large dresser. Jason wasn't sure, but it looked as if it had been hand carved. It reminded him of a beautiful work of art. It was some type of wood that was almost snow white, with spider webbed veins of black running through it. He admired the quality of workmanship that had gone into it.

Against the wall opposite the foot of the bed was a small chest slightly larger than a footlocker. It was constructed of the same type of wood as the dresser, and had the same quality of craftsmanship devoted to it. It sat beneath a glassless window that was about four feet wide and six feet high. Jason assumed there were shutters on the outside that could be closed during inclement weather, although he doubted if they ever got snow here. Mother had told him that all of the cities on this particular continent were located in what would be the planet's Temperate Zone.

Hearing a familiar sound outside the window, Jason wet his lips and whistled sharply. Seconds later Baby leaped through the window and bounded up onto the bed. She eagerly licked his face as she wiggled her body in delight in an attempt to get as close to him as she could.

"Hey, you big old fur ball, how ya doing?" Jason said as he wrapped his arms around her neck and hugged her.

A movement at the window caught his attention. Jason looked up to see two silver-haired, pixie faces peaking in at him from the outside. He pushed up a little higher on the bed and motioned for them to come in. They promptly climbed up onto the ledge of the window and sat on it, their bare feet dangling just above the chest. At first Jason thought they were identical twins, right down to their scruffy knees and soiled clothing, but as he searched his memory for their names he remembered that one of them was a boy, the other a girl.

"You," he said to the dirty little figure on the right, speaking in their own language, "are Manda. Which means you," he said to the other one, "are Vanda."

"Right," the twins replied in unison as their faces broke into matching grins.

The twins hopped down from the windowsill and crossed the room to climb up onto the bed, sitting on either side of him. "Mommy thinks you might be a gerkin," Manda told him with an elfin grin, "but we know you aren't," Vanda said, finishing the sentence.

"Oh? And what do you think I am?" Jason asked.

Jason had asked the question, but he wasn't quite ready for their reply, or the way in which they delivered it. They glanced at one another for a moment, and then each of the reached down to take one of his hands in their own. Then they reached across his body and joined their free hands. When they began to speak it was like listening to one voice in stereo.

"You are Jason Michael Stephens. You come from a world called Earth, which is no more. You lived on the moon of that world in a place called New Hope, and you are the only one to survive the destruction. You escaped with some other children but they all died, including your little sister, Patricia, and Nadia, the woman you were in love with and supposed to marry.

"You have been searching for a long time before you found our world. You kidnapped our sister Kimmy, not to do her harm, but to learn our ways and language from her. You did this with the help of something you call Mother, who isn't really a person but some kind of machine."

The twins release his hands and smiled impishly at him. Jason was totally speechless. They had spoken in perfect harmony as if reciting a well-rehearsed speech. He had never seen anything like it before. <u>Telepaths!</u> They had to be. It was the only way they could have known so much about him, other than from Kimmy, and for some reason he didn't believe she had told them.

"She told us some," began Vanda, "but what's a tel-a-path?" finished Manda, confirming his suspicions.

The door opened before Jason could explain and Kimmy came back into the room. She was carrying a tray with a bowl and cup on it, which she placed on the table beside the bed. "I see you've met the little monsters," she said with a grin as she moved Manda over so she could sit on the edge of the bed.

"Yes. Quite an experience," he replied.

"It can be." Kimmy turned to the twins. "All right, you two, take Baby and go outside and play so he can eat."

"Do we have to?" Vanda asked.

"Yes. Go." Kimmy told him.

But the twins were not to be put off so easily by their sister. "Will you take us flying when you get better?" asked Manda.

Jason looked at the expectant little faces. "Gee, I don't know," he replied, forcing his face to look serious as he appeared to consider their request. "You see, I usually take only my very best friends flying and, well, I hardly know the two of you."

"You didn't know Kimmy when you took her flying in your little ship, and again in the room of your big ship," Manda quickly pointed out.

Jason had to stop and think for a moment about what the girl meant. Then he remembered. He had taken Kimmy to the gym and had Mother reduce the ship to zero gravity, laughing as Kimmy had floated off across the room when she had taken a step. Her screams of terror had become shrieks of delight as Jason has pushed himself up beside her, taking her hand and showing her the fun she could have in zero gravity.

"Hum, well, you do have a point there," he told the twins. "Okay, I'll tell you what. For the two of you taking such good care of Baby for me while I've been sick, I guess I could take you flying as a reward. But you'll still have to become my friends."

"We will," Vanda told him. "We'll be your very best friends in the whole world."

The faces of both twins were completely serious, and Jason had no doubt that they meant exactly what they said. "I'll hold you to that," he told them.

"But for now," Kimmy said to them, "he needs to eat and rest. And the two of you need to leave him alone so he can do that. Take Baby and go play."

The twins slid off the bed and headed for the door. Baby looked at him, unsure as to whether she should stay with him or go with the twins. "Go on," he told the dog. With a wag of her tail, and a quick lick of his face, Baby hopped off the bed and followed the twins out of the room, her massive form towering over them.

As the twins closed the door behind them, Kimmy picked up the tray and placed it on Jason's lap. He looked at the contents of the bowl and felt his stomach lurch. "I can't eat that," he told her weakly as he pushed the bowl away from him slightly.

"Why not?" Kimmy asked. "It's brak. Sort of like your stew beef."

"You mean beef stew," Jason corrected her. "And that's why I can't eat it."

"Again, why not?"

"Because it has red meat in it. I don't eat red meat," he explained.

Kimmy looked at him to see if he were teasing her. "That's crazy," she told him at last, shaking her head in confusion as she removed the tray from his lap and stood up. "If you don't eat meat, what do you eat?"

"Fish, some game birds, lots of vegetables and fruit."

Kimmy looked down at him with a mixture of amusement and confusion. "I'm really starting to wonder about you, my blue eyed alien, but I'll see what I can come up with."

As Kimmy left the room, closing the door behind her, Jason closed his eyes and let his body relax. <u>Some introduction to her world</u>, he thought. <u>First I kidnap her, and then she has to save my life</u>.

Jason thought about Kimmy's actions after the Death Plant had stung him. He was impressed by what she had done. It had taken someone with a quick, intelligent mind to return to the shuttle for the medical kit, contact Mother via his wrist communicator, and then take care of him the way she had. Jason knew he was going to have to find some way to express his gratitude and thanks for all that Kimmy had done for him.

He was still thinking about what he could do for Kimmy when she returned for the second time with the tray. This time when she placed it on his lap there was a large piece of some type of white fish, with what appeared to be a butter sauce next to it. There were also some unidentifiable green vegetables. It all smelled delicious to him.

Kimmy started to cut up the fish for him. Jason grinned and took the knife and fork from her. "I think I can handle that," he told her.

"Oh, sure," Kimmy replied. She brushed slightly as she relinquished the utensils. "It's just that I've been so used to taking care of you. I guess it's just sort of become a habit. Sorry," she said in apology.

"There's nothing to be sorry for," Jason told her as he began to eat. "As I said, without your care and attention I probably wouldn't be here to eat this now."

"Well, I only did what Mother told me to do," Kimmy replied softly.

Jason ate quickly, savoring the taste of the food. He could feel some of the weakness starting to dissipate from his body as he ate. Kimmy sat on the side of the bed watching him, smiling at him from time to time, but not speaking. When he finished, she took the tray and set it on the table. "Feeling better?" she asked. There was a note of genuine concern in her voice.

"Much better. Thank you."

"Look, Jason, my father and brothers will be home in a little while. Why don't you rest up a bit? Then, if you feel up to it, you can get dressed and join us at the table. Even if you don't feel like eating anything."

"To be honest," Jason told her, "I don't feel like resting any more. I feel like I've been on my back for a month."

"So you say, but I'm telling you, Jason, that you need your rest." Kimmy's voice had a touch of insistence in it.

"How long have I been here?"

"Ten day."

"Ten days!" he exclaimed in shock. "Then I've had plenty of rest. Now, why don't you tell me where my clothes are so I can get dressed."

Kimmy looked at him with concern stamped clearly on her face. "You really should rest, Jason. You're still pretty weak."

"Not that weak," he told her. "Besides, I have a feeling that your father and brothers have a million and one questions they want to ask me. And I have a few of my own for them. Not only that," he continued, "but I should also apologize for snatching their daughter away in the dark of night."

Kimmy grinned and took his hand. "I wouldn't worry too much about that. I've pretty well explained things to them and they've promised not to take you out and hang you until you've had a chance to tell your side of the story."

"Gee, thanks," he replied dryly.

"You're welcome."

"Where's the medical kit?"

"Here." Kimmy reached down to pull the kit out from under the bed and place it beside him.

Jason opened the kit and checked the contents. He finally selected a small vial of clear liquid and slipped it into a pressure injector.

"What's that?" Kimmy asked.

"A natural stimulant," he told her as he injected it into his arm. "It will give me energy for about six hours or so, depending on how much I exert myself. I've got a feeling I'll be needing it before the day is over."

"Is it safe?"

"Perfectly."

"Well, things won't be that bad," she told him with a grin.

"We'll see."

Jason looked up as the door opened and another girl entered the room. She looked to be about the same age as Kimmy, and every bit as beautiful. For a moment Jason thought they might be twins,

*Alazon*

but then he realized who she was. The girl crossed the room shyly, carrying a large ceramic pitcher in her hands and a towel draped across one arm. She placed them on the ledge of the window before turning to face him and Kimmy.

"You must be Vinny," he said, watching her blush. <u>Blushing easily must be a common trait in the women of this family</u>, he thought with a grin as the girl nodded.

"Yes," Vinny finally replied, her voice barely audible. "I thought you might like to wash up a little."

Jason saw Vinny's quick glance at Kimmy. He senses a feeling of uncertainty in Vinny, as if se were not sure if she should be talking to him or not.

"Thank you. That's very considerate," Jason told her, trying to ease her tension somewhat.

"You're welcome," she replied, still speaking softly.

"It's all right, Vinny, I don't bite. And you're right; I would like to wash up. Again, thank you for being so considerate and thoughtful."

"It was nothing," Vinny told him as she turned to hurry from the room, closing the door behind her.

"The shy one, huh?" he said to Kimmy.

Kimmy laughed and shook her head. "Only until you get to know here. Then you can't shut her up."

"Well, whatever, it was nice of her to bring me the water."

Kimmy nodded and glanced at the now closed door for a moment before turning back to Jason. "That's the way she is. She seems to think of things like that before anyone else does."

"Speaking of washing," Jason said as he rubbed his hand across the smooth skin of his chin, "who bathed and shaved me while I was sick?"

"I did."

"All of me?"

"Of course. Well, Mother helped."

"Which one?"

"Mine, of course," she replied, laughing lightly.

"Naturally."

"Well, look, I'll get out of here and let you get dressed. Your jump suits, boots and other things are in there," she told him, pointing at the dresser. "I'll come back in a little while to check and see how you're doing. If you need anything, just call out."

As soon as Kimmy left the room, Jason swung his legs over the side of the bed and stood up slowly. He felt a brief wave of vertigo but it quickly passed and he felt as if he would be all right. He walked to the dresser and opened the top drawer to pull out the first jump suit he came to, which was dark blue with silver trim. He tossed it, and the matching boots from another drawer, onto the bed. He then went to the window and poured water from the pitcher into the large bowl sitting next to it. He rinsed his face and washed under his arms, drying off with the towel before getting dressed. He was just fastening the boots when there was a light knock on the door. "Come in."

Kimmy entered and nodded her head with a smile. "I like the blue on you," she told him. "It brings out the color of your eyes."

"Well, think you very much, Golden Girl," he replied with a slight bow. "I'll be sure to keep that in mind. However, I might also point out that the color of my eyes, not to mention my hair and skin, as well as my height, could cause me a few problems on this world.

"While there's not much I can do about my height, I guess I could dye my hair, and even my skin, to match those of your people, and I could make some colored contact lenses to change my eyes from blue to green."

"Don't you dare change your eyes, Jason!" Kimmy exclaimed. "Your eyes are beautiful!" She blushed and lowered her own eyes for a moment. "I mean. . .everyone here as green eyes. I like yours a lot better."

"Really? Well, in that case I guess I'll leave them as they are," Jason told her, holding back a laugh at her sudden reaction.

"And. . .don't change anything else about yourself, either," Kimmy told him.

"If you insist. Now, are your dad and brothers home yet?"

"No." Kimmy crossed the room and sat on the small chest beneath the window. "Before they get here, though, I should tell you a few things about them."

"Ahhhh, here it comes," Jason teased. "Okay, what's the bad news?"

"Well, it's not really bad," she replied as Jason sat on the corner of the bed facing her.

"What is it then?"

"It's just that I should, I don't know, warn you about my family before you meet the rest of them."

Kimmy took a deep breath and let it out slowly before continuing.

"As you know, my dad is the Senior Mayor, which makes him the most influential man in Preton, even though he seldom takes advantage of that power. However, before that he is a father and husband, and because of that he's concerned about the effect your presence will have on our family.

"You see, from the moment we brought you here we've been telling people you were a wounded hunter I found in the woods. One I spent the night trying to help, which also explained my own absence."

"And now that I'm alive, they're wondering what the neighbors will think, right?" Jason teased.

"Sort of."

Jason could see that Kimmy wasn't quite as confident as she had been aboard this <u>Stargazer</u> about his acceptance.

"I'm sure that once you explain your situation to dad he will understand and do everything he can to help you. He's a good man, Jason."

From the tone of sincerity in her voice, Jason knew Kimmy loved and respected her father very much. "I'm sure he is," he told her.

"But," she added with a sigh, "then there are my two older brothers, Shon and Hass."

"What about them?"

"Shon is a lot like Vinny. He's quiet, reserved, speaking only when he has something to say. He's the type of person who, when faced with a problem or situation, will study it carefully before acting on it. He looks at everything from all sides before he acts. He's seldom wrong about things and rarely makes mistakes.

"Hass, on the other hand," she said with a grin, "is about as opposite from Shon as you can get. Where Shon is slender, quiet and introspective, Hass is stocky, has a big mouth, is impulsive, likes to fight, and has more friends than he can count.

"He can be obnoxious at times, letting his mouth get him into trouble, but he's always ready to back up what he says with his fists if those he's offended don't like it. And, he's never lost a fight."

Jason quickly searched the new 'memories' Mother had given him from Kimmy to get a better idea of what she was saying. He nodded as she spoke about Hass. He knew the type. Hass would be the one who would want to challenge Jason at every turn. Not out of any malicious sense, but merely to see how far Jason could be pushed.

"Yet," Kimmy continued, "everyone likes Hass. He'll fight anyone, any time, anywhere, but once the fight is over he'll pick up the loser, buy him a drink, then tell everyone around that it was only by a lucky punch that he won. And if the man he fought is badly hurt, Hass will personally take him to the temple for medical treatment. He'll even pay for it out of his own pocket. There's something else you need to know about Hass," she added somewhat hesitantly.

"What?"

"Well, while you were sick you sometimes became delirious. You would thrash around on the bed so violently that we had to tie you down to prevent you from hurting yourself. Or one of us."

"Did I ever hurt you?" Jason asked with a mixture of fear and concern.

Kimmy smiled and shook her head. "No. But during one of those episodes I guess you thought you were being attacked. You grabbed Hass and tossed him over the bed and across the room. It bruised two of his ribs."

"Oh, that's just great," Jason said with a sigh. "So now I've caused one of your brothers an injury. Just the way to start things off."

Kimmy chuckled. "Actually, with him it is. And it was sort of funny. You see, he was on this side of the bed, and when he reached for your arm you grabbed him by the front of his tunic and tossed him over the bed and into the wall, face first, as if he were no heavier than a pillow. But instead of being mad, or even concerned about being hurt, Hass thought it was great. Later he told us that you had to be

*Alazon*

the strongest man on the planet, and that he couldn't wait until you were back on your feet so he could fight you."

"Not exactly what I'm looking forward to," Jason said with a grimace.

"I know, Jason, but he won't stop pestering you, or trying to provoke you, until you fight him. He's the type you have to prove something to before he'll believe it."

Jason could hear the slight change in the timbre of her voice. "I've got a feeling you're trying to tell me something else here."

Kimmy paused a moment and then nodded. "When I tried to tell them about you, about your ship and some of the things I saw, Hass scoffed at me. Oh, he didn't come right out and call me a liar because he knows better, but he made it clear that he considers me slightly crazy. You may find he'll try to push you to prove some of the things you say.

"Hass does that to people, Jason. He doesn't do it in a mean-spirited manner, but he does have a tendency to make people mad at his persistence with things like that. It's like he doesn't know when to quit. Anyway, I thought I should warn you about him."

"I appreciate that, Golden Girl," Jason replied with a warm smile.

Kimmy lowered her eyes for a moment. When she looked up again Jason saw what he thought was a trace of confusion in them. "What's the matter?" he asked as a silence began to build between them.

"I. . .I'm not sure," Kimmy replied, twisting the rope belt of her toga nervously.

"Why don't you try and explain."

"Well, it's just that when, well, when you call me that, I'm not sure just what you mean by it."

"Call you what?"

"Golden Girl," Kimmy replied softly. "Oh, I know it's just some sort of nickname, but to me it's. . .well. . ."

"Too personal?" he probed.

Kimmy nodded slightly. "Sort of. I guess. Oh, I don't know."

Jason could see the agitation she was obviously feeling. "I'm sorry, Kimmy. I didn't mean to make you feel uncomfortable."

"I know you didn't."

"Look, if it bothers you then I won't call you that anymore."

Kimmy sighed and lifted her shoulders in a slight shrug. "It's just that I've always been called either Kimmy or Kimella, and no one has ever called me anything different," she told him.

Jason smiled at her. "Would you mind if I make a slight variation on your name?"

Kimmy cocked her head to one side. "What do you mean?"

"Would you mind if I called you 'Kim'? You see, I used to know a girl by that name and you remind me of her just a little. Would that be all right with you?"

Kimmy thought about it for a moment. She finally smiled and nodded. "Sure."

"All right, Kim it is. Now, let's go meet the rest of the family and see what they've got in store for me."

As Jason stood up, Kim stood and held out her hand to him, smiling brightly as he took it and walked from the room with her.

# TEN

Kim was sitting close enough to Jason to touch his knee beneath the table with her own if she had chosen to. To her surprise, and for reasons she would not have been unable to explain if asked, she found that she actually did want to touch him.

Supper had been delayed somewhat due to the questions asked of Jason by her father and brothers after Jason had taken the time to relate to all of them the story of his life on New Hope and how he had finally ended up here.

As Kim listened to Jason talk and answer their questions she had taken a strange pride in the way he had handled himself. Jason responded to all of their questions honestly and without hesitation, just as she had somehow known he would.

Her father had finally put an end to the questions and discussion so they could eat. Kimmy had hurried into the kitchen to help her mother and Vinny bring supper into the common room, serving Jason herself, continuing her role of taking of him that she had assumed from the moment he had been brought to their home.

As they ate, Kim watched Jason wink and grin and the twins, causing them to grin and giggle. Knowing what she did about his past, which was more than the other members of her family, thanks to the information Mother had implanted in her brain, Kim wasn't all that surprised by Jason's attention to the twins. Once supper was over the table was cleared so her father and brothers could continue their questions.

Kim knew Jason's history and life better than any of the others, but she wanted to hear Jason's own words as he told it. And, she wanted to be near him. She left the table for a moment to help pour teef for all of them, which was a hot beverage usually served after evening meals. As she did she stopped in the kitchen doorway for a moment to look at Jason, wondering what was behind her strange attraction to this alien man.

Jason was so completely different from any man Kim had ever known. Not just physically, but emotionally. She knew he had suffered in ways none of them could ever really begin to comprehend, including herself. He had not only been forced to flee his world, but in the process had lost everyone he had ever known and loved, wondering through space in search of others where he might settle and be accepted. She found herself wanting to go to him, to hold him in her arms and tell him that everything was going to be okay. Over the past ten days she had done that a number of times, crawling up on the bed beside him to hold him as his mind was being tormented by his poison induced dreams; but now she wanted to do it while he was awake, to assure him that here on Alazon he could find those to accept and care about him.

Kim returned to sit at the table. She watched as Jason sipped his teef, wondering if he would rather have coffee. She would have to ask him. If he preferred coffee, Kim told herself that she would learn how to make it for him. Without appearing to make it obvious, she studied Jason's face as he spoke. In his face and eyes she saw the strength that had helped him endure all the months of loneliness and pain. Kim knew that Mother and Baby had helped, but she also knew that a computer, no matter how humanistic, and a dog which, even now, lay beside his chair, could not take the place of human companionship.

Kim thought of how she had awakened in the med-lab aboard Jason's ship and opened her eyes to the strange surroundings. And then of seeing his broad, black covered back. She had been utterly terrified. She thought she had been abducted by a gerkin, or some other type of demon, and carried away to their magical world. When she had screamed, Jason had reacted so quickly that Kim had thought she was going to die before her next breath. Jason had leaped from his chair to turn and face her, the <u>bokken</u> appearing in his hands as if by magic. Kim had never seen anyone move with such speed. It had taken all of her will power not to faint right then and there.

Kim felt a cold, wet nose touch her leg. She looked down at Baby and reached down to pet the animal that was as big as she was. She grinned slightly to herself as she remembered how she had fainted when Baby had come charging into the lab. The appearance of Jason had been bad enough, but then the sudden arrival of this monstrous animal had been more than her senses could handle. When she had regained consciousness a few minutes later she found herself back on the bed, but this time the huge dog was laying beside her, licking her face and making soft whining sounds. Kim had still been terrified, but her fear hadn't lasted long. She soon realized that Baby was not going to hurt her. The dog had only been acting in defense of Jason when she had screamed, and was now intent on becoming her friend.

With a tightening in her chest she remembered how Jason had tried to talk to her before using the Thought Transference Scanner. She hadn't been able to understand what he was saying, but she'd had no trouble in recognizing the pleading tone of his voice or the pain in his eyes. Those things, more than anything else, had told her that this man, as strange as he may appear, meant her no harm. Her fear of him had begun to gradually subside, but it wasn't until she saw him crying, watching the tears rolling slowly down his cheeks that she knew in her heart that this man was no threat to her.

Kim looked around the table at the others for a moment before lowering her eyes as she thought back on how she had come naked from the shower to ask him for the towel. She had seen his embarrassment, but she had also seen the flash of desire for her in his eyes. She was grateful that Jason had left that portion of his story out when telling her family about his time alone with her aboard his ship. Kim still couldn't explain what had provoked that rash and impulsive act on her behalf, but now she was glad she had done it. Looking back on it now she realized it had served to add more credence to her belief that he posed no threat to her.

Kim, like her sister Vinny, was still a virgin. Not that there hadn't been a multitude of young men more than willing to remedy that situation for the two of them. But neither Kim nor Vinny had found anyone they had seriously been attracted to in a romantic way. In fact, she and Vinny had developed a little game between them in which they tried, and usually succeeded, in stealing one another's boy friends. Of course, once they did, she and Vinny would dump the guy and go looking for someone else. Kim knew it wasn't exactly a trait that endeared them to some of the male population in some respects, but it was one that she and Vinny enjoyed immensely.

Kim and Vinny were more than just sisters. They were best friends. Kim glanced over at Vinny and smiled. There were no secrets between the two of them, and they were closer than most sisters. During Jason's illness Kim had remained by his side day and night to take care of him, crying and praying to every god she could think of to spare his life. She had bathed his body in cold water to bring his fever down, and fed broth to him when he was calm enough to take it. She spoke to Mother via his wrist communicator when the others weren't around to keep the computer updated, accepting any assistance it offered. And at times she had cried softly to herself as she cradled him gently in her arms during the torturous nightmares that seemed to fill his mind.

Kim had slept on a pallet on the floor beside Jason's bed, refusing to leave his side except for those brief times when she had to go to the bathroom. Whenever she did have to leave Jason's side, Vinny was the only one Kim trusted to stay with him.

Vinny had offered to relieve Kim of some of her duties, smiling softly in understanding when Kim had declined the offer. Many times Vinny had joined Kim to sit on the bed beside her. It was Vinny who had brought the soups and broth Kim spooned into him. The two of them had spoken softly, with Kim telling Vinny of all she had seen and learned in the brief time aboard his ship.

Kim looked at Jason now as he was answering yet another of her father's questions. <u>Why have I shown such devotion to this man?</u> she wondered. She knew it was a question the other members of her family had asked themselves a number of times as well. Kim had never exhibited such selfless devotion or dedication to anything or anyone before. <u>Is it because he's something, or someone, so new and different?</u> <u>Or is it something more complex than that?</u>

*Alazon*

Jason was a complete strange to her world. He had eyes the color of the oceans and dark brown hair that fell loosely to his shoulders. He was not only much taller than any man she had ever known, but the most powerful as well. Yet, despite those differences, or perhaps because of them, she found Jason to be the most attractive man she had ever known.

<u>By all the gods, am I falling in love with this alien man?</u> she asked herself. Kim felt the blood rush to her face at that thought. <u>No!</u> she told herself flatly. <u>It's just an attraction of differences that will wear off eventually.</u> But despite what her mind was tell her, Kim's heart seemed to be sending out a different message.

She looked at Jason's hands. They were clasped with the fingers interlocked on the table in front of him. She saw the hard calluses on the knuckles and along the edges. Those hands looked so big, so strong, and yet they had touched her with such gentle tenderness. Kim let her gaze move up his powerful arms and shoulders to settle on his face. There was an inner strength to him that went far beyond his physical attributes. Kim thought of the things she knew he had seen and experienced. She wondered if any of the men of her world his age could have gone through what Jason had and come out of it mentally intact.

Kim glanced at her two older brothers. Using the simple formula Mother had given her, she figured out Jason's age in Alazonian years. To her surprise she realized that Jason was actually younger than Shon, and just slightly older than Hass. But unlike Shon and Hass, who were considered young men, the same could not be said for Jason. <u>What he's been through has made a man out of him early in his life</u>, Kim thought with a sense of sadness. <u>His experiences, all the pains and deaths he's had to deal with, have matured him too quickly. They've made a much older man out of him than what he's supposed to be.</u>

"Jarrell," Jason was saying to her father, "I know that many, of not most of the things I've told you about myself are probably hard for you to comprehend and believe. If I were in your position I would have doubts, reservations and even some difficulty in believing me."

Kim turned to her father. Jarrell was studying Jason intently. "I appreciate your candor," Jarrell replied after a moment. "However, your mere presence here speaks some truth and validity of your words. It's obvious you are not of this world. But I will also be the first to admit that there is much of our world we know nothing about.

"Yet," Jarrell continued, "to say that I accept everything you say as the absolute truth would be both rash and foolish on my part. Not just as a person, but as a man who is in a position of authority and responsibility. A man who must make decisions concerning the people who have entrusted me with my position for the past twenty-two years as their mayor. Not to mention the welfare of my family."

"I understand," Jason replied. "What you need is some conclusive proof, other than my presence, to validate what I say."

Kim saw her father look slightly embarrassed as he slowly nodded his head. "I'm sorry, but yes, I'm afraid so," Jarrell replied.

"There's no need for you to apologize," Jason told him. "I understand your position. And," Jason added with a grin at Kim, "had it been my daughter who had been kidnapped, I doubt if I would have taken the time to even listen to the story of her abductor. Let alone take him into my home to tend to him."

"Yes, well, now as to that," Jarrell replied, his forehead creasing as he leaned forward in his chair. He rested his forearms on the table and clasped his hands together. "It would seem that our little Muggles. . ."

"Daddy!" Kim cried in protest, her face blushing deeply.

"Oh, I forgot," Jarrell said with a mischievous grin at Kim, "that's not a name she's overly fond of."

"Muggles?" queried Jason. "Isn't that the little animal that sneaks into the city at night and raids garbage piles, stealing whatever it can manage to carry off?

"Yes," Jarrell replied with a nod. "That has been her pet name for a number of years now. She's forever getting into trouble, always bringing something or someone new and different home, and then not knowing what to do with it, or them, once she has them. And much like that little animal that causes so much fuss for everyone; Kimmy has a habit of sticking her cute little nose into places it doesn't belong. It gets tweaked from time to time."

Jarrell looked at Jason and grinned, but then sighed as he leaned back in his chair. "You know, Jason, I had always hoped that someday some man would appear to sweep her off her feet and carry her away, but I have to admit that this is not exactly what I had in mind. However, the only problem with that hope is that I doubt if there's a man alive who could put up with her for very long. They would probably return her within a month, begging us to take her back."

Kim faced her father and squared her shoulders. "Maybe that's because it would take a real man to handle me," she told him defiantly, "and so far I haven't seen any of them around here."

"Think he qualifies?" Hass asked Shon, nodding his head in Jason's direction.

"Too early to tell," Shon replied with a straight face. "But it would appear that our little sister is definitely interested. It must be that dark hair and blue eyes that have her little heart going pitter-patter."

Hass nodded. "I guess we'll just have to keep an eye on her. And maybe put a lock on his door which he can fasten from the inside now that he's better."

"Good idea," Shon replied.

Kim wanted to reach across the table and slap both of her brothers but kept a tight rein on her emotions. She didn't want to give them the satisfaction of knowing they were getting to her. She knew they were just teasing her, which was nothing unusual in and of itself, but at this particular moment she wished they would just shut up. It wasn't that their teasing was out of line, but more of what they were saying hitting just a little too close to the truth. A truth that was making her uncomfortable. Kim looked at her father, pleading with her eyes for his assistance.

"All right, you two," Jarrell said to his two oldest sons, "let's take it easy on your sister. After all, if I remember correctly, she can give either one of you all you can handle in a fight."

"That's only because we don't want to hurt her," Hass replied as he turned to grin at Kim.

"Perhaps," Jarrell said with a grin of his own before returning his attention to Jason. "Now, what do we do with you?"

"I'm in your hands," Jason replied.

"Well, for the time being I suggest we stick to the story we used when we first brought you here," Jarrell told him. "The people around here think you are a wounded hunter and they pretty much mind their own business. Thank the gods for that. And even though we had Seta, the High Priestess of Lofa, come to see what she might be able to do for you, I have her word that she will say nothing to anyone other than the story we agreed upon."

"Can she be trusted to stick to that?" Jason asked.

"I would trust Seta with my life," Jarrell replied, his tone completely serious. "I also think we should keep your inside the house for the time being. Not as a prisoner," he quickly added, "but only until your strength returns and you are able to move about more easily. I can see the weariness in you just from this. Another day or so of rest will do you more good than harm."

"You're probably right," Jason replied with a weary smile.

But then Kim saw a new look come over Jason's face. It was as if he had just come up with something both troubling and unpleasant. He glanced at her briefly before addressing her father.

"Jarrell, you suggest that I provide you with some proof and validity of the things I've told you. Once I'm better I could do that in a thousand ways, but I think I may have something that will do that tonight. But first, let me ask you something. How are the relations between Preton, Karton and Tilwin?"

The room became suddenly quiet. Kim saw the wary look in the eyes of her father and wondered what Jason was up to.

"Somewhat strained at the present," Jarrell replied cautiously.

"What if," Jason asked, speaking slowly and deliberately, "I could prove not only many of the things I've told you about myself, but could also prove my good intentions by providing you the proof to back up your own suspicions concerning the intent of both Karton and Tilwin to invade Preton and crush you between them?"

The silence that settled over the room was like a thick, heavy fog. Kim watched the faces of everyone at the table turn pale. She had heard her father voice his suspicions concerning this matter before, knowing that Jason had learned of her father's feelings from the scan of her brain aboard his ship.

Jarrell had spoken of his suspicions not only to the family, but the other mayors as well. Unfortunately, most of the other mayors had not wanted to believe him. They had thought it absurd that Karton and Tilwin would join forces in such an endeavor. Kim saw the struggle in her father's eyes. She knew he wanted to believe what Jason was telling him, but was afraid to do so for a number of reasons.

"Trust him, Daddy," Kim said at last, speaking softly. "I do. Completely."

Jarrell glanced at Kim for a moment before finally nodding his head. He turned to Jason. "I would say that information of that nature would be both welcome and dreaded. Do you have such proof?"

"I can get it," Jason replied.

"When?"

"Tonight if you like. But I'll need some help. I'll have to return to my shuttle."

Jarrell was silent for a moment as he considered this. "It is almost dark now," he said at last. "Kimmy and I will go with you."

"Father," said Hass with a look of concern on his face, "maybe Shon and I should go along as well."

Jarrell looked at his sons and shook his head. "No. It will be just Kimmy and myself. More than that would draw attention."

"But what if something happens to you?" Hass asked, darting a quick, suspicious look at Jason.

Kim bristled at the attitude of Hass, but before she could reply to it her father smiled in understanding. "Hass, you judge, or misjudge, too quickly at times. I do not believe Jason would harm me."

"How can you be so sure?" Hass asked.

"Because he had your sister for an entire night and did not harm her in any way. If Jason was intent on harming anyone, he could have done whatever he wanted with her, to her, and there is nothing anyone could have done to prevent it. The fact that he brought her back, and came in peace, is all the proof I need that he can be trusted. As is the word of Kimmy. In other words, I trust him."

Jarrell's last three words settled the conversation. Kim saw Hass look and Jason and shake his head in resignation at their father edict. She knew Hass didn't like it, but there was nothing he could do about it.

"Will you need anything?" her father asked Jason.

"Just my communicator so I can contact Mother."

"Here."

Kim turned to see Vanda standing between herself and Jason. Her little brother was holding the wrist communicator out to Jason. Jason took it and smiled down at Vanda, who quickly returned to his own seat beside Manda.

"Mother?" Jason called.

"Hey, Boss Man! How's it hanging?" Mother replied in English.

Kim saw him grin slightly at the computer's comment. She thought she knew what Mother was saying, but she wasn't sure. However, it didn't stop her from grinning at Jason in amusement.

"In the native language, Mother," Jason told the computer. "And behave yourself. There are others present."

"Okay," Mother replied.

"I need the shuttle," he told her, reverting to Alazonian.

"Where would you like it?"

"In the clearing where it was. By the way, did you get the information I asked you to?"

"Yes."

"Good. We'll be leaving here shortly with Kim and her father. I want you to have that information ready for me as soon as we arrive."

"One shuttle on the way," Mother told him. "Now, how are you feeling?"

Kim could hear the note of concern in the voice of the computer.

"A little tired and stiff, but other than that I'm okay," Jason replied. "You and Kim took good care of me."

"Of course. Now, is there anything else you need?"

"That's all for now. Jason out."

As Jason had spoken to Mother, Kim had watched the faces of the others. Each of them were registering some form of curiosity or shock that he was speaking into a small round dial attached to a wrist band, and getting replies back through it from someone they couldn't see. Remembering the first time she had heard Mother's voice coming from the speakers in the med-lab, Kim could understand how they felt. But it still tickled her to see their reactions.

"Can we use tollies?" Jason asked Jarrell. "It would be much quicker that way."

"Of course," her father replied nervously. "How long will this take?'

Jason shrugged. "Ten minutes or so to get to the shuttle, thirty minutes up to the ship, fifteen to twenty to go over the information, and then the trip back. Say, two hours at the most.

"That's if you want to go up to my ship. I could just have Mother give me the information I need right from the shuttle, negating the need to leave the clearing."

"You can't wear that," Liet said, speaking up for the first time. She stood and looked at Jason. "Come with me."

As Liet walked toward the hallway leading to the bedrooms, Kim got up to follow. She was curious as to what her mother was up to. When the three of them entered her parent's bedroom, Liet opened a chest along one wall and removed a folded brown bundle from it, which she then handed to Jason.

"I made this for you when it looked like you were going to live," Liet told him. "I figured you would need some proper clothing to wear."

Kim was nearly as surprised as Jason when he unfolded the material to find a dark brown toga with gold trim. "Well, put it on," her mother told him.

Kim saw Jason hesitate for a moment. "I forgot to tell you, Mom," she said, grinning amusement as Jason stood there nervously, "but he's a little bashful at times."

"Oh, all right," Liet said, her eyes twinkling with merriment, "we'll turn around. Just don't take too long."

As Kim and her mother turned their backs she heard Jason unzip his jump suit and unfasten his boots. She waited for nearly a full minute before turning around. Kim chuckled when she saw Jason in the robe. "Here, let me help," she told him as she stepped forward to adjust the drape of the material. She took the gold rope belt her mother handed her and wrapped it around his waist, showing him how to tie it properly.

"There," Kim said as she stepped back to examine him, her grin growing wider. "Hairy thing, isn't he, Mom?" she teased, referring to the light growth of hair on his arms, chest and legs.

Other than their heads, the men of her world had only sparse growth around their genitals, and none on their arms, chest or faces. This made the hair on Jason's body stand out, even though there really wasn't all that much of it.

"Looks like a styra," Liet replied, her laughter trailing along behind her as she left the room.

"Cute. Now I'm a monkey," Jason mumbled as he followed Kim out of the room.

Back in the common room Kim looked at her brothers. Her eyes finally settled on Hass. "He needs a cloak. Let him borrow your black one. It's the longest one you've got."

"It's also the best one I've got!" Hass replied in protest.

"So what! Either you get it for him or I will," Kim told him defiantly, daring him to say anything else.

Hass looked as if he wanted to, but finally shook his head and left the table to get the cloak. Kim looked at Jason and grinned. "Most of the time his bark is worse than his bite," she told him.

Hass returned with the cloak. He hesitated a moment before handing it to Jason and returning to his seat at the table.

"Thank you," Jason told Hass as he draped the cloak around his shoulders.

"You'll need these, Jason."

Kim turned to see Manda hand Jason the soft black boots from his combat outfit. Kim smiled at her little sister as Jason slipped the boots on. He reached down to tousle Manda's hair once he was done, which brought a smile to the little girl's face.

Kim accepted her own cloak from Vinny and wrapped it around her shoulders. Looking at her father, who nodded to her, they headed for the back door. Vinny went ahead of them to make sure no one was around. The younger sister opened the back gate, and then hurried to open the door of the stable, waving for them to hurry up.

Inside the stable Kim lit a small lamp and then helped her father and Vinny quickly saddle three tollies. When Vinny handed Jason the reins, Kim saw him stand beside the tollie looking a bit nervous. "What's the matter?" she asked.

"Well, it was my idea to take the tollies, but I've never ridden anything before in my life."

Kim laughed and glanced at her father. "Look, it's easy," she told Jason. "I'll tell you what. You ride between me and dad just to be sure you're okay."

She led the way to the door in the side of the stable that Jason hadn't noticed before, and then climbed into the saddle.

Kim looked back over her shoulder and grinned at the way Jason's legs hung down well past the stirrups. Once he had his feet in them, Vinny signaled that it was all clear and the three of them headed for the forest at a quick canter. Inside the tree line Kim slowed their speed to allow for the trees and undergrowth in their path, glancing back from time to time to make sure that Jason was all right. When they reached the clearing, Kim stopped them just a few yards inside of it, and then dismounted to tie the animals to a hardy shrub that would secure them, as well as give them something to munch on. A few minutes later the shuttle came to a soft landing less than thirty yards from them.

"Pretty impressive, huh?" she said to her father, who was staring at the craft in amazement. She took her father's hand and urged him forward. "Come on, Dad."

Inside the shuttle Kim had her father sit in the co-pilot seat as Jason took the pilot's seat. She pulled out the small seat behind Jason that was normally folded up against the bulkhead and strapped herself in. She watched Jason's fingers move swiftly and surely over the controls to check everything out. Finally, with a nod of his head, he lifted the craft slowly into the air.

Kim heard the sharp intake of breath from her father as they began to rise upward and grinned. "It has that effect on people the first time," she told him, mimicking the same tone Jason had used when he had spoken the same words to her.

"Mother?" Jason called out when they were a quarter of a mile above the city.

"Who's calling, please?" replied the computer, her voice coming from speakers on either side of the small cockpit.

Jason glanced back briefly at Kim and shook his head. "Who do you think is calling?" he asked.

"Gee, I don't know. This is supposed to be a restricted channel, with limited authorization."

Kim knew that Mother was just being Mother, but she had a feeling that right now Jason wasn't in the mood for the computer's sense of humor. His next words confirmed that.

"Listen up, you miss-matched mass of microchips," Jason growled. "If you don't knock off the crap right now, I'll turn you into video games."

"Hey, that's my Jason!" Mother replied with a chuckle as Kim wondered how someone played a video game. "Hey, Kimmy, how you doing?"

"Just fine, Mother."

"Is that your father with you?" Mother asked.

"Yes."

"Hello, Jarrell Vehey. I'm Mother."

Kim saw the look of confusion on the face of her father. "Just say hello to her," she told him.

"Hello. . .Mother," Jarrell finally said.

"How are you doing, Mother?" Kim asked.

"Just find, dear, and thanks for asking. It's a shame that not everyone shares your sense of concern with me, if you know what I mean."

"I do, Mother, but you have to excuse Jason. He's been a little under the weather lately. He's not his normal, cheerful self just yet."

"Oh, I don't know about that," Mother replied with a short laugh. "He sure sounds like his normal, cranky, inconsiderate self to me."

Jason cleared his throat loudly. "Excuse me, ladies, but do you think the two of you could discuss the particulars of my character at some other time? We have things to do."

"Right," Kim replied. "I'll talk to you later, Mother."

"All right, dear, you do that." The computer's voice then turned serious. "Jason?"

"Yes?"

"I see you're coming up here, so I'll have all the information ready for you as soon as you reach the bridge."

"Good," Jason replied. "I'll also want hard copies of the information on both Karton and Tilwin to give to Jarrell," he told her.

"Already done," Mother replied.

Kim noticed that Jason had been steadily increasing the speed of the shuttle while they had been talking and they were now streaking upwards through the atmosphere. In what seemed like only moments later they were out in space and heading for the _Stargazer_.

Kim, who had an idea of how big the ship was not only from the information Mother had given her during the thought transfer, but from her own excursions aboard it with Jason, was still impressed by the size of the _Stargazer_ as they approached it. It looked like a giant metallic moon hanging in the sky. She glanced at her father and saw the paleness of his features as he could only stare at the rapidly growing object before them.

No one said anything more until Jason had finally docked the shuttle inside the bay and shut off the engine. As they three of them unstrapped and stepped out of the shuttle, Kim watched her father look around at the massive shuttle bay and shake his head. "By all the gods," was all he could manage to whisper.

"He has an entire world here within this ship, Daddy," Kim told her father. "There are things you that you would not believe."

"I'm not sure I really believe what I'm seeing now," her father replied as Jason began to lead the way toward the bridge.

"All right, Mother, let's see it," Jason said as the three of them took seats.

Kim glanced at her father as the first of the images began to appear on the huge screen. She watched his recognition of what they were being shown, seeing his face become sad and slack, the muscles loosing their tension. It was as if his worst fears had just been confirmed. Kim could only nod her head and turn back to the screen as Mother began to speak.

"At the present time Karton has approximately forty-three thousand, six hundred and fifty men currently at the location you see. At their rate of progress on the construction of their ships they will have them completed and ready to sail in about twenty-three weeks, Alazon time.

"It will take them approximately eleven weeks to sail to Preton. This is assuming they use the southern trade winds to avoid the detection that would occur by using the normal routes. That will put them on the shores of Preton in about thirty-four weeks, or just a week short of seven months.

"As for the Tilwin," Mother continued, changing the image on the screen, "their troop strength is approximately sixty-three thousand, eight hundred. Their ships will be completed in about twenty weeks. Because they have the greater distance to sail, I assume they will leave at that time in order to land on the west coast of Preton at approximately the same time as the Tilwin land on the east."

Kim glanced at her father. Jarrell was shaking his head as if he wanted to disbelieve what he was seeing, but knowing there was no way he could.

"Give me a worst case scenario," Jason said as he leaned his head back on the seat and closed his eyes.

"Under present circumstances," Mother replied, "there is only one scenario. The combined armies of Karton and Tilwin will land south of the two main coastal cities of Preton. They will turn north to capture them, and then turn inward.

"With their troop strength they will sweep across the continent like two tidal waves, crushing everything in their path. They should meet in Lemac in about five weeks after landing. Possibly sooner."

There was silence for nearly half a minute. Kim looked at her father and saw the ashen pallor of his face and the look of defeat in his eyes. "I tried to tell them," Jarrell said, his voice a mere whisper.

"Hypothetical situation, Mother," Jason said without opening his eyes.

"Go ahead."

"Suppose someone of my background were to undertake the training of an army of men from Preton. Working ten to twelve hours a day, every day, training them in Kendo and Ninjitsu, and with the inclusion of certain weapons from the ship, how long would it take me to train an army to not only meet the Karton and Tilwin, but to defeat them? And how many men would I need?"

Kim looked at Jason to see if he were serious, but his head remained tilted back on his seat with his eyes closed.

"Jason," Mother replied softly, "I would advise against that."

"For the record, your advice is so noted," Jason replied flatly. "Now answer my question."

"Using the hand-held phasers and lasers aboard the ship, of which there are a thousand rifles and three thousand pistols, and teaching the men your style of martial arts, especially Kendo, it would take an army of approximately forty thousand men.

"Training would have to be as you stated, at least ten hours a day, and would have to continue up until just before the Karton and Tilwin landed. You could, if you wanted, divide your army into equal portions to meet the armies of the two invaders or, should events provide the opportunity to face one and then the other, you could use the shuttles to transport the troops from coast to coast. But to do this you would need to begin training within the next three to four weeks."

Jason nodded as he finally sat up and turned to face Kim and her father. "We may just have a surprise in store for the Karton and Tilwin when they arrive," he told them with a grin.

"You say 'we'," Jarrell replied after a moment. "Does that mean you would be willing to help us?"

"Yes."

"But, why?"

"Because that's the type of man he is, Daddy," Kim told her father softly before Jason could respond.

# ELEVEN

"You are either completely mad," Hass scoffed, "or the most overconfident braggart I've ever met in my life! And I'm inclined to believe it's the former. Just because you're a little bigger and stronger than us, there is no way you can do what you propose. It's lunacy!"

Jason stared across the table at Hass. Despite what Kim had told him about Hass, Jason was finding it harder and harder to tolerate the man. For the past two days it seemed as if Hass had done nothing but ridicule Jason every chance he could. He laughed at Jason's ideas, calling them silly, inane and ridiculous, usually doing so in a loud and obnoxious manner, such as now.

Jason had just proposed his idea for possibly winning the confidence of the men of the Mayoral Guard of Lemac, as well as some of the other Mayors, three of which could be here by the day after tomorrow if riders were sent out today. What Jason wanted to do was give them a demonstration of what he could teach the men of Preton. He believed that if he could show them what he was capable of doing he might be able to convince them that the men of Preton could do the same with the proper training. Yet, here was Hass, again trying to block his efforts. Jason could tell it was starting to get on the nerves of the others as well, but that they were waiting to see what he would do. It was time to put an end to it.

"You know," Jason said in a flat, cold voice as he leaned against the wall, "were it not for the integrity of the name of this family, I would almost believe you wanted Preton to fall and for the people of Preton to become the slaves of the Tilwin and Karton. Maybe you have some financial or personal interest which would be improved by that event."

Jason's words were delivered softly, but they carried clearly to everyone in the room. A tense silence fell over al of them. He could see the anger flare up in the eyes of Hass.

"Are you calling me a traitor?" Hass asked through clenched teeth.

"I'm not calling you anything," Jason replied calmly. "But on my world we had a saying, which I'll alter a bit to fit the situation. If it looks like a tollie, walks like a tollie, smells like a tollie, and brays like a tollie, then it must be a tollie."

"What are you driving at?" Hass hissed.

"Just this," Jason replied flatly. "Every time I come up with something, or try to explain what I think can be done, what has to be done if the people of Preton are going to survive this invasion, you come up with some objection. It's almost as if you don't want to find a solution.

"Tell me, Hass," he said as he stepped away from the wall, "which country has bought your loyalty? And for how much?"

Hass leaped from his chair and charged across the room at Jason, fire burning in his eyes. Jason had been expecting a reaction such as this. He easily stepped to the side and sent Hass sprawling across the floor to slam into the wall with a well-placed foot and a stiff-handed blow between Hass' shoulder blades.

But it took more than that to finish Hass. Hass quickly got to his feet and approached Jason again. This time he was a little more cautious as he closed the distance between them. Jason merely smiled. He knew that a man such as Hass was used to depending on brute strength to win his fights. Jason knew he was unquestionably stronger than Hass, but he wanted to teach the younger man a lesson about speed, finesse and technique. He let Hass grab his own out-stretched hands. He then twisted his own body while gripping the wrists of Hass and crossed them over one another. Jason jerked Hass toward him as he turned and bent at the waist. The move sent Hass flying over Jason's shoulder and across the room to land heavily on the wooden floor.

This time Hass was a little slower in getting to his feet. When he did he clenched his fists as if intending to box. Jason laughed at Hass with a derisive snort and placed his own hands behind his back. He let Hass close the distance between them and swing at him twice. Jason easily avoided the punches. When Hass swung at him for the third time, Jason's right foot snapped out to knock Hass' fist away. In the same motion he pivoted on his left foot and then drove his right heel into the sternum of Hass. As the air exploded from the lungs of Hass, causing his body to double over, Jason pivoted again. This time he brought his right foot around to smash into the side of Hass' head. Hass spun around and crashed face first into the wall. He stayed upright for only a moment before sliding down the wall, leaving a trail of blood from his lips and nose.

No one made a move or said anything as Jason went to a side table and picked up a pitcher of water, which he then poured onto the face of the unconscious man. Hass sputtered and choked for a moment before finally sitting up. The side of his face was already starting to swell and discolor. Jason crossed the room to where two short swords hung above the fireplace mantle. Grabbing both swords, he tossed the across the room to land on the floor beside Hass with a loud clang.

"If you're supposed to be the tough bully around here," he sneered as Hass picked up the swords and stood up, glaring at him, "then this whole city is full of sissies.

"Or maybe it's just here in Preton that the men can't fight. Maybe all the real men, the fighting men, are in Tilwin and Karton.

"I'll tell you what, Sissy," he taunted, "if you can cut me, if you can even <u>scratch</u> me with one of those swords, I'll make you the richest man on this planet. Personally I don't think you're man enough to even know how to use them."

"Jason," Kim said softly, "please, that's enough."

"Is it? I don't think so, Kim. Your brother's been running his mouth ever since I got here. He likes to talk about how tough he is, so now it's time to back up his words. If he's man enough. What about it, Hass, are you man enough? Or are you all blow and no show?"

With a yell of rage, Hass charged. The sword in his right hand was raised high, ready to swing down and cut Jason in half. As it started its downward arc, Jason stepped to the side and grabbed the wrist of Hass with both hands, jerking it down toward the floor. The natural reaction of Hass was to pull the arm back up, just as Jason knew it would be.

Before Hass realized what had happened, Jason was standing over him holding the sword in his own right hand, the razor sharp tip of it pressed against Hass' throat. Jason's right foot pinned the other sword to the floor. The blood drained from the face of Hass and his eyes widened in fear. After a moment Jason tossed the sword away and released the wrist of Hass.

"I never believed you were either a traitor or a coward, Hass," he told him, "but I was getting damn tired of you constantly running your mouth."

He reached down and easily jerked Hass to his feet, taking the other sword from him. "Now, if you, supposedly the best fighter in Lemac, can be handled like a baby by me, think of what I can teach the men of Preton in six to seven months if they train for ten to twelve hours a day.

"You can either be a part of it, which I hope you will, or you can keep your mouth shut and stay out of my way. It's your choice. Which is it going to be?"

Hass was silent for several seconds as he rubbed his wrist, but he slowly began to smile. "Okay," he said at last, "so I've got a big mouth. You're the first one to ever shut me up."

"There's a first time for everything," Jason told him as he picked up the swords and replaced them above the mantle. "Now, are you going to stop fighting me at ever turn, or do we have to go through this again?"

"No thanks," Hass replied. His embarrassment was clearly evident on his face. "Aside from the physical abuse, I don't relish being humiliated like this again in front of my family. Or anyone else for that matter. I'll do whatever you want or need me to do."

"Good," Jason replied as he clasped Hass on the back, "because I'm going to need all the help I can get."

"What do you want me to do?"

"If we send riders out to the three closest cities tonight, how soon could their mayors be here?" Jason asked Jarrell.

"Two days. Tomorrow if it were an emergency. But what reason do we give them?"

"The truth. Tell them there is solid evidence of a coming invasion by both Tilwin and Karton, and that their presence is being requested by you to discuss it. If that doesn't work, nothing will."

"What else?" Hass asked.

"How well do you know the Commander of the Mayoral Guard here in Lemac?" Jason asked Jarrell.

"Busker is my brother," Liet told him.

"Does he know about me?"

Jarrell shook his head. "No, not yet."

Jason nodded. "Good. Shon, I want you to go to him and tell him that a man, a stranger, is challenging him and ten of his best men to meet him in fight with swords. Tell him this stranger said they are all a bunch of women, and to prove it, the stranger will use a wooden sword against their steel ones.

"And just to make sure they'll show up," Jason added with a grin as a sudden idea hit him, "tell him this stranger has, in some manner or another, 'assaulted' Kim after kidnapping her and you just found out about it."

Hass glanced at Kim and grinned. "I don't know, Jason," he said. "With Kim's reputation I doubt if Busker would believe that she could be assaulted by anyone. Can we make it Vinny instead? He'd believe that."

"I've got something you can believe," Kim said as she stepped forward and drove her fist into the still tender midsection of Hass. Her sudden punch drove the air out of Hass with a whoosh, much to the delight and amusement of everyone except Hass.

"Come on, Kimmy," Hass gasped as he straightened up. "I was just trying to do what Jason wanted. I mean, we have to make this sound real, don't we?"

"Jason," said Jarrell, interrupting the little scene between his son and daughter, "may I ask you something?"

"Of course."

"What purpose will fighting a dozen of the Mayoral Guard serve?"

"To prove a point," Shon said softly before Jason could answer.

*Alazon*

The others turned to Shon. "It's simple," the older brother told them. "And very sly.

"You see, if Jason can take on a dozen of the Mayoral Guard and handle them as easily as he did Hass, not only will it prove his superior fighting skills and style, but it will also win their respect. Just as it did with Hass. That will make them more apt to listen to him and what he has to say."

"I see," replied Jarrell. Although, from the look on the older man's face, Jason wasn't sure if he did or not.

"Now, I do have one problem," Jason said. "I'll need a place for this fight to take place. It has to be somewhere away from prying eyes. The only people I want there are the Mayoral Guard, you, and the other Mayors."

"Hey, what about me?" Kim demanded.

Jason looked at her and grinned. "I don't suppose it would do any good for me to tell you that you couldn't come, would it?"

"Not a bit," she replied flatly, crossing her arms across her chest with a look of defiance.

"That's what I thought."

"What about the old quarry?" suggested Vinny. "It's outside of town, it's abandoned now, and it's far enough away that no one would see anything going on there."

Jason looked at Jarrell and saw the older man nod his head. "That would be the best place," Jarrell told him.

Jason turned back to Hass. "How soon can you get those riders sent off?"

"Within half an hour if I leave now."

"Then do so."

"I'll go with him," volunteered Shon.

Jason waited until the brothers had left before turning back to Jarrell. Jason knew that he had more or less taken command of the situation and was issuing orders to all of them. And, he thought with a mental grin, they were expecting him to lead them. <u>Please, God, let me be right</u>, he prayed silently.

"Is there anything the rest of us can be doing?" Jarrell asked.

Jason shook his head. "No, not for tonight."

Jarrell nodded and stood up, heading off to another part of the house. Liet followed him, leaving Jason with Kim, Vinny and the twins. "Are you going to bed now?" Kim asked as he placed his fists in the small of his back and stretched his spine.

"Not yet. It's still early. What I'd like to do is go outside and sit for a while."

"What some company?" she asked.

"Well," he teased, "I was planning on taking Baby, but you're welcome to join us if you want."

Hearing the sound of her name, Baby got up from her position at the feet of the twins and came to him, rubbing her head against his side. "Come on, fur ball," he said as he walked through the common room and kitchen to the back yard. Once outside he went to the far corner of the large yard to sit on the curved stone bench beneath the single tree.

The yard was actually a courtyard measuring nearly sixteen hundred square feet. A twelve-foot high stone fence that provided complete privacy from the estates on either side surrounded it. There were flowers planted along the base of the wall, and on the western side was a stone lined pool with brightly colored fish swimming in it. A few feet from that was a stone bench beneath a tree.

Over the past couple of days the bench and pool had come to represent a place of peace and solitude for Jason. It was a place where he could come to think, with the others respecting his wish for privacy and leaving him to his thoughts.

Jason was more than a little surprised at their acceptance of him. He was also grateful for their understanding that it would be some time before he would be able to really open up to them. There were so many things on his mind that troubled him that he needed to think through. He had given them the bare facts of his life, but had not delved into the personal aspects of it, or how it had affected him.

He heard footsteps on gravel and looked up to see Jarrell approaching. Jason felt a sudden and immense sense of gratitude toward the older man. Over the past couple of days there were times when Jarrell appeared to understand him better than anyone, including Kim. Jason knew it was Jarrell who had told the others not to pressure him with any more questions about his past and Earth for

*Alazon*

the time being. Of course, that hadn't done much good with Hass, but Jason felt that that particular situation had now been cleared up.

Jarrell nodded at the bench as if asking permission to join him. Jason nodded and Jarrell sat down beside him, bending over to pick up a small stone. He tossed it into the center of the pool, causing ripples to spread out to the sides.

"Alazon is like that pool," Jarrell said softly, "and you are like the pebble. Your presence here will cause ripples that will reach to every corner of our world."

Jason had a feeling Jarrell was probably right. But the ripples he might create would have a more lasting effect on Alazon than did those of the pebble in the pool a few feet away.

"You are going to change our world, Jason, and there is nothing anyone can do to stop it. The question is, will it be a change for the better, or one we will live to regret?"

"How am I supposed to answer that, Jarrell?" he asked softly. "I can't offer you any guarantees. I can't sit here and tell you that everything is going to work out perfectly, or that Alazon will live in peace and harmony for the next ten thousand years. All I can do is promise that I will do all I can toward that goal and hope it will be enough."

They were both silent for nearly a full minute. Jarrell leaned back against the tree and looked up at the star filled night sky. "There are legends that our ancestors came from the stars," the older man said after a moment.

Jason glanced up at the sky. "We had similar legends back on Earth. Some of them claimed that we were visited by an advanced civilization that came from the stars, but it was never really proven. Although, I may have found some proof of that before my arrival here."

Jason glanced over at Jarrell and saw the older man looking at him with interest.

"I found a planet with cities older than anything ever found on Earth," he explained. "They were empty, but still being maintained by a computer. From the computer I learned the history of the Royac, who were the original inhabitants.

"It seems they had traveled the length and width of the universe in search of other intelligent life, and that they had also been instrumental in the propagation of some races before their destruction."

"Did you find any proof of this?" Jarrell asked.

"Some. I was able to obtain a star map of planets known to have been visited by the Royac. I visited some of them before coming here, but found that most of them were too much like Earth."

"In what ways?"

"Two of them were on the brink of nuclear war. Another had already been destroyed by one. I found a couple of others, but none of them like Alazon."

"These other planets, the ones like your Earth, why didn't you at least try to make contact with the people there?" asked Jarrell.

Jason's eyes went to the pool as he tried to gather his thoughts. "I'm not sure," he said at last. "Maybe it was because they were too much like Earth."

"I'm not sure I understand. Isn't that what you were looking for?"

"There was nothing I could have done on them, Jarrell. It was too late for me to try and show them the folly of their actions. Besides, they probably wouldn't have listened to me anyway," he said with what sounded like a sense of dejection, even to his own ears.

"So what makes our world different?"

"I'm not sure," Jason replied with a sigh. "I guess it's because your civilization hasn't reached the point of no return the way the others have. Maybe it's because I feel I can do something good and worthwhile here."

"And maybe it was the will of the gods and fate that you came here," Jarrell told him softly.

Jason looked at the older man, expecting to see a smile of amusement on the face of Jarrell. Instead, he saw a look of complete sincerity. It served to remind Jason of the beliefs of these people in their gods. They only had a few, but they believed in them fervently. "The gods or fate, who can say, Jarrell?"

"What is it you hope to do here, Jason? What is it you want to do?"

Jason had to stop and think about his answer. That was a question he had been tossing around in his own mind for the past couple of days.

"I would like," he said at last, "to try and teach the people of your world not to make the same mistakes those of my world made. I'd like to show them there's a better way of life for all of them. Not just in the material things, but in the quality of life itself. And I'd like to put an end to war so they can concentrate on the things which are really important."

"Those are lofty goals and considerations," Jarrell said, but not unkindly. "Do you think we are worth it?"

"Back on Earth there was a book called the Bible," he told Jarrell. "In it was a story of how God was going to destroy a city due to its fall into depravity and sin. But Abraham, one of God's chosen, begged God to spare them. He even offered to make a deal with God."

"What kind of deal?" Jarrell asked curiously.

"Abraham got God to promise not to destroy the city if Abraham could find fifty righteous men. God said that if Abraham could find fifty, the city would be spared."

"Did Abraham find the fifty righteous men?"

"No. So he bargained the figure down to forty-five, then forty, then thirty, and finally down to ten. But when Abraham couldn't find even ten righteous men, God destroyed the city."

Jarrell was silent for a moment before speaking. "I'm not sure if I see your point, Jason."

"If the God of my world would spare a city for just ten righteous men, then shouldn't I do all I can to save a world if I can find just one good man?"

Jarrell smiled and nodded. "An interesting concept, but where will you look for your man?"

Jason turned his head slightly to look at Jarrell. "I've already found him," he said softly. "I'm not a god, Jarrell, I'm just a man. Actually, I'm still just a boy in some ways when you get down to it.

"The point is, I've found my one good man, my one good family, and I want to do all I can to preserve this world for them. And not just for them," he continued, reaching down to pet Baby, "but the entire planet as well. I don't want to see your world end up the way mine did."

They were both silent after that. Jason wondered if Jarrell thought his ideas were crazy, or even somewhat megalomaniacal. Jarrell finally stood up and placed his left hand on Jason's right shoulder.

"You hold your self-esteem too low, my friend," the older man told him. "I would venture to say that you have not been a boy for quite some time now. From what you have told me of yourself and your world, of the things, which have happened to you and what you have done, I have a feeling that you will be able to handle whatever responsibilities, the gods will send your way on this world.

"Jason, I don't know if what you hope to accomplish can be done or not, but I will do all I can to help. However, you may eventually find yourself in a position you might not really want in the end. But that will be your price to pay." With that Jarrell lightly squeezed Jason's shoulder and returned to the house.

Jason wondered again at the perceptions of Jarrell and the man's easy acceptance of Jason into their lives. Despite all the questions by them when he had first arrived, after a while Jason began to feel as if Jarrell had almost been expecting him.

"That's stupid," he said softly to himself. But the comment about the legend of the ancestors who came from the stars had sent a chill down his spine.

Jason again heard the sound of footsteps and looked up to see Kim approaching. She stopped in front of him and knelt down to pet Baby. The dog promptly rolled over onto her back to present her stomach for scratching.

"Sometimes I think she likes you and the kids better than she does me," Jason joked.

Kim looked up at him and grinned. "Not a chance. She likes me, and she really likes the twins, but it's you her heart and allegiance belongs to. Sure, she allows us to play with her, but she's your dog. Make no mistake about that. Were there lots of dogs back on Earth?"

"Dogs and cats," he replied with a nod of his head. "There were hundreds of breeds of each. Some were beautiful, while others were down right ugly. Most of them had been originally bread for specific purposes, such as hunting certain animals or fighting, but after a while they were bred strictly as pets."

"Well, if you want to bring some more like Baby out of the gene labs," Kim said with a grin, "I think I know a few hundred thousand kids who would love to have them."

Jason grinned as Kim moved to sit beside him, but after a moment he became acutely aware of her physical presence. That bothered him. Even though he had pretty much accepted and accustomed himself to Nadia's death, Jason wasn't sure he was ready to let himself become involved with anyone on anything more than just a physical level. He ha a feeling that becoming involved with Kim on a physical level, though, would lead to much more. At least on her part. Besides, he rationalized, there were no real indications that she would even want anything to do with him in the first place. He could end up making a complete fool out of himself, alienating himself from her and her family in the process by misinterpreting her open friendship.

Jason couldn't deny that he thought Kim was one of the most beautiful women he had ever seen. She was tiny and petite, but perfectly formed, and with the face of an angel. And not as young as he had first thought. Converting her age to Earth years, she was only a little more than two years younger than himself. He caught himself looking at her at times when she wasn't aware of it, marveling at her beauty. He vividly remembered the sight of her when she had come from the shower aboard the ship, and the way the water droplets had covered her body like sparkling diamonds. He remembered how her breasts, large and firm for someone of her petite frame, had jutted out from her chest proudly, a drop of water clinging to each nipple. And of how her silver pubic hair had glistened like a thousand tiny rhinestones between her slender thighs.

But Jason also knew there was much more to Kim than just her physical attributes. She had proven herself to be very intelligent, and possessed a great sense of humor and mischievousness about her that kept him smiling whenever she was around.

She also seemed to know when humor was not called for; when quiet solitude was what he needed. She seemed to know when he just wanted someone to be with him, to sit by him, assuring him that he wasn't alone. In that she was so much like Nadia that it frightened him at times.

"Jason, may I ask you something?" Her voice was low and her eyes avoided his.

"Anything you want."

"Well, maybe I shouldn't ask you about this, and if you don't want to tell me, or don't want to talk about it, just say so and I'll understand."

He turned toward her a little and leaned against the tree, his right shoulder lightly touching her. "What do you want to know?"

Kim stared at the pool. "Would, well, would you tell me about Nadia?"

Her request caught him completely off guard. Jason felt a sudden tightening in his chest. He fought it down, knowing he would have to talk about her someday. "What do you want to know about her?" he finally asked.

"What she was like. What she looked like. Why you loved her?"

Jason picked up a small pebble and tossed it into the pool, thinking of Jarrell's actions and words earlier when the older man had done that.

"Nadia," he said at last, "was the second child born on Luna. I was the first. She was born six months after I was. As a result we were placed together early so we would have each other to play with. As we grew we became best friends, as well a partners in every form of mischief we could dream up and get into. As the other kids came along, Nadia and I became the unofficial leaders, teaching them the ropes, so to speak.

"What made me love her? I really don't know how to answer that, Kim. I guess it was because she was who she was, combined with the circumstances of our lives. She was the only girl my age, although there were a couple just a year or two younger that I guess I could have become interested in. It just never happened.

"I'm not sure, but it was as if there was some unspoken agreement that the other girls were not to show an interest in me. I'm not sure," he added with a slight grin, "but I think that maybe Nadia threatened to jettison through an airlock any girl who did. Then again, it could be that she threatened to do the same thing to me if I ever looked at another woman."

"Was she beautiful?"

Jason closed his eyes for a moment and pictured Nadia in his mind. "Yes, very," he said softly as he opened his eyes and looked at the pool. "She was as tall as I am, with hair so black it almost looked blue, and that hung down to her waist. That wasn't really practical under our living conditions, but she let it grow because she knew I loved it long.

"She had a face and figure that would make any man's heart beat a little faster when she walked into a room, or when she smiled at him, and I used to wonder at times why she loved me.

"As for what she was like as a person, well, she always seemed to understand me better than I understood myself. She always seemed to know what type of mood I was in and how best to deal with it. If I were depressed or upset, she knew whether to be quiet and just close by, or bring me out of it with something inane and totally unpredictable.

"Or, if I got a bit cocky about something, which I was prone to do at times when I was younger, she knew just how to knock my ego for a loop and bring me back down to where I belonged."

"You loved her very much, didn't you?" Kim asked softly.

Jason followed her gaze to the pool and nodded. "Yes," he replied after a moment.

"Do you think you'll ever love like that again?" Kim asked, her voice barely above a whisper.

Jason shrugged. "I'm not sure. I do think a person is capable of loving more than one person in their life, so maybe someday I'll find someone I can love as deeply as I loved Nadia, but in different ways, and for different reasons. But I'm in no hurry."

"Are you afraid of loving again?" Kim asked.

"I don't think so. It's just that right now there's so much that has to be done. There's so much to occupy my time, and the time of the people of Preton, that I don't have time to think about any type of relationship with anyone at this point in my life."

Kim turned to look at him. "My mom says that love is where you find it," she told him with a grin. "She says there's always time for it if it's right."

Jason reached down to pet Baby. "You're mother's a smart lady, but there are exceptions to just about every rule."

Their conversation was abruptly cut off as the twins came running toward them from the house. Both youngsters dropped to the ground beside Baby, who took that as a signal that it was time to play. For the next few minutes Jason and Kim laughed at the antics of the twins and the dog as the three of them engaged in a rough and tumble wrestling match.

Baby would let the twins pull her to the ground and crawl all over her before she would get to her feet and knock them down, or snatch one of them up by a leg and gently swing them around for a moment before lightly dropping them to the ground.

Jason knew that Baby could easily snap either of the twins in half with her huge, powerful jaws, but the dog was careful not to hurt them in any way.

The twins finally got up and brushed themselves off. "Kimmy, are you gonna tell us a story tonight?" Vanda asked. "You haven't told us one since Jason got here."

Kim reached out to pull the twins to her. "I guess I do owe you guys a story, don't I? Okay, I'll tell you what. You get washed up and climb into bed, and I'll be there in a minute."

Without a word they kissed her. They then turned to Jason and kissed him on either side of his face at the same time. With an impish giggle they turned and ran back into the house.

"Well, I'll be," Kim said softly, looking at Jason in amazement.

"What?" he asked.

"They must really like you. A lot! They don't kiss Shon or Hass good night, and they have to be reminded to kiss dad most of the time."

"Yeah, well, I have that effect on little kids, old ladies, and young girls. Not to mention dogs," he added with a short laugh as Baby got up and began licking his face.

"Really?' How old do the girls have to be?" Kim teased.

"Oh, no older than twelve or so."

"Gee, that's too bad."

"Yeah," he said with an exaggerated sigh as he stood up and patted the top of her silvery head. "I guess you're just too old for the little girl category, and too young for the old woman one."

He pulled Kim to her feet and they walked back into the house together. As soon as they entered he realized that everyone else had gone to bed. Except for the twins, who were in the process of getting their nightgowns on in anticipation of Kim telling them a story. "Wait," he told Kim as she started to enter their room. "Let me."

Kim looked up at him and smiled. "Be my guest," she told him.

As Jason entered their room, the twins looked at one anther and grinned. It was almost as if they had expected this turn of events. They got into the large bed they shared and made room for him between them. Jason got onto the bed and sat with his back against the head of it, putting his arms around the twins to pull them close. "How would you like to hear abut Goldilocks and the Three Bears?" he asked.

Manda looked at him and frowned. "What's a bear?"

"Hum, let's see. Well, it's sort of like a styra, only much bigger. And a lot meaner," Jason teased.

"Okay," the twins replied in unison as they snuggled closer to him.

Jason began telling them the story, changing the inflection of his voice to portray the various bears and Goldilocks. He made the twins giggle at times, and give little shrieks of delighted terror at others. "Tell us another one!" Manda pleaded with he finished.

"Tomorrow night," Jason replied with a grin. "If I tell you all the stories I know in one night, what will we do then?"

"Do you promise to tell us more?" asked Vanda.

Jason nodded. "I promise. In fact, from now on, any night I'm here I'll tell you a story."

"Good," Manda told him as she raised her little face to kiss his cheek before squirming down under the covers, "because you tell better stories than Kimmy does."

The little girl's comment earned her a playful swat on her bottom from Kim, who was sitting on the edge of the bed.

Jason leaned over and kissed each of their foreheads before blowing out the lamp beside the bed and leaving.

"You keep that up and you'll spoil them," Kim told him as they stepped into the hallway.

Jason glanced back at the twins. "Children are supposed to be spoiled. Besides, from what I've seen around here, you had your own share of being spoiled when you were growing up."

"Of course! But what do you expect? I was the first girl, and such a beautiful baby at that, after two ghastly boys."

"Uh, huh. And you probably had fits when Vinny came along because you were so used to being the center of attention."

"Not me!" Kim protested, fighting to keep a straight face.

"Yeah, right."

Kim leaned back against the wall and looked up at him. "Do you think you're doing the right thing by taking on the Guard?"

Jason leaned against the opposite wall and crossed his arms over his chest. "Honestly? I don't know. It's just that it's the quickest way I can think of to get my point across, and right now we're pressed for time."

"You won't be hurt will you?"

Jason hard the note of concern in her voice. It caused him to smile. "I shouldn't be. Believe me, I'll be careful."

Kim looked at him as if she wanted to say something else, but then turned and headed for the stairs that led to the upper portion of the house where she shared a room with Vinny. "Good night," she said as she turned and smiled before ascending the stairs.

Jason watched her go. He shook his head slowly. Kim was starting to confuse him by her actions. As he entered his room Jason tried to figure her out. There were times when Kim appeared to be giving him a clear indication that she would welcome his attention. Yet, on the other hand, there were times she seemed to retreat from him, keeping him at arm's length emotionally.

From what the twins had told him, Jason was aware of Kim's actions and devotion to him during his illness. Vanda and Manda had related to him how Kim had stayed by his side day and night, refusing to leave him or let anyone else take care of him. They told him of how she had prayed to the gods to spare his life while clutching his hands with her own. They said that she had gotten up onto the bed to hold him in her arms when nightmares had filled his mind and caused him to cry out in pain.

But all that did was serve to confuse Jason even more. Because Nadia had always been there with him, and their lives had been so intertwined, Jason had no experience with dealing with women, so Kim's actions often confused him. He couldn't deny that he felt a strong attraction to her, but he wondered if it were merely physical, or if there were deeper emotional feelings as well.

"Women," he said with a sigh as he pulled the cover up and closed his eyes, thinking about what he would be facing in the coming days.

# TWELVE

The following day Jason spent the morning with the twins. He taught them the English commands he used for Baby so they could get the dog to obey them the way she did him. Once they had mastered that, he taught them the silent hand signals he had developed in the training of Baby, working with them until they had also mastered them. Baby had eagerly gone along with the training, as if she wanted the twins to learn both the verbal and hand commands and signals.

Later that day, when a sudden storm had moved in over the city, Jason used the downpour and darkened skies to make his way to the clearing in the woods, where Mother had the shuttle waiting for him. He returned to the ship and had Mother give him a complete physical to make sure there were no lingering effects from his encounter with the Death Plant. Once Mother assured him that he was fine he went to the bridge and had her bring up the images of the Karton and Tilwin armies on the screen.

For the rest of the day he, along with valuable input from Mother, went over the preparations the two armies were making, and what he would have to do to counter them. He made a list of things he would have to do in order to train an army in secret, and then had Mother go over it to make sure he wasn't leaving anything out.

Mother finally informed him that it was well past the supper hour down on Preton. He had been so engrossed in what he was doing he had forgotten about the time. Nor had he thought about eating and realized he was hungry. With printed copies of his plans in hand he hurried to the shuttle bay. Mother already had the bay doors open and the force field in operation before he reached the shuttle. He shot out into space and then down toward the planet. As soon as he landed in the clearing and stepped out of the shuttle, Mother lifted it by remote to return it to the ship.

As he started toward the tree line he noticed someone step out and approach him. The rain had stopped, but the sky was still overcast, blocking most of the light of the moon, and he wasn't sure just who it was at first. Then the figure pushed back the hood of the cloak and he saw the face of Kim.

"How long have you been waiting here?" he asked as he drew near.

"Not long," she replied casually. "I figured that you got involved with whatever it was you were doing and lost track of time. But, I also figured that you would be back about this time. I've only been here about half an hour."

"You're right, I did. Mother had to remind me of the time."

"Did you eat anything?" Kim asked as she led him to the tollie tied to a bush.

Jason grinned and shook his head. "No. I forgot to do that, too."

"I thought as much," Kim replied with a laugh as she mounted the bareback animal and motioned for him to get on behind her. "I saved you some supper."

Jason hopped up on the tollie behind her and slipped his arms around her waist. As he did he wondered if it was his imagination, or did she actually lean her body back against him slightly?

Neither of them spoke until they were back at the house. He sat down at the table and she brought him the super she had saved for him, sitting quietly at the table while he ate. Just as he was finishing he heard the sound of little feet on the floor behind him. He turned to see the twins hurrying to him. He picked them up and placed them on his lap. "You two are supposed to be asleep," he whispered.

"We were waiting for you to tell us a story," Vanda whispered back as he and Manda snuggled closer to Jason and giggled softly.

"Okay, but it will have to be a short one. I've got to get some sleep because I'm gonna be real busy tomorrow."

He stood up with the twins in his arms and carried them back to their room as Kim took his dishes into the kitchen. A few minutes later he smiled at her as she stood in the doorway while he told the twins about Sleeping Beauty. Once the story was over he tucked them in, kissed them and blew out their lamp.

"They have really come to love you, you know," Kim said softly as he stepped out into the hallway.

"The feeling is mutual," he replied.

Kim looked as if she wanted to say something else, but finally shook her head and headed for the stairs, leaving him standing in the hallway feeling confused. With a shrug of his shoulders he entered his room, undressed and got into bed, hoping to fall asleep quickly.

But sleep was no solace to him. He dreamed of his parents as he had seen them a million times; working, laughing, loving, or studying something intently, but always finding time to be with him and his sister.

He dreamed of Nadia, seeing the beauty of her that seemed so real to him. His mind replayed over and over the memories of their childhood. Of growing up together and falling in love. In his dreams he held her in his arms as they lay together in his room back on Luna, their bodies intertwined as they made love softly, gently exploring every secret of one another.

And then a new image came to him. It was Trish, but in a way he had never seen his little sister before. She was suspended in space; her body surrounded my millions of stars, with two of the brightest where her eyes were supposed to be. She was clutching her old ragged teddy bear and smiling at him.

"It's up to you now, Jay," she said. "But then, it always was. Even back on Luna you were our hope for the future. You were the one who would lead us to a new world.

"We didn't make it, but don't blame yourself for what happened to us. It wasn't your fault, Jay. And don't let it stop you from doing what you know is the right thing here. You can do it, Jay, but you don't have to do it alone. I'll always be here for you if you need me."

The image of Trish reached out with her right hand, collecting a thousand stars. She brought them close to her face and then blew gently, sending the stars floating toward him like flakes of snow.

"We are all here with you, Jay. Mom, dad, me, Nadia. All of us. All you have to do is close your eyes and you'll find us inside. We're a part of you, just as you are a part of us. That's something no one can ever take from you.

"You have to learn to trust and love those you have found here, as they will also help you. Don't lock yourself away from them, Jay. As you help them, let them help you. Let them love you. And don't be afraid to love them in return. Trust your instincts, big brother. Everyone else always did."

The image of Trish began to fade. Her body slowly turned into a fine mist, leaving only her face, which continued to smile at him with love.

"Trish! Trish, don't go!" Jason cried, his arms reaching out for her. "Trish, come back!"

"Jason, shhh, it's all right. It's only a dream."

Jason felt hands, real hands, gripping his shoulders to gently push him back down on the bed. He opened his eyes to find Liet sitting beside him. In the pale moonlight breaking through the clouds he could see her concerned filled eyes.

"You were dreaming," Liet told him softly. "I heard you cry out and came to check on you."

As the dream and the words of his little sister came back to him Jason began to cry. Liet moved around on the bed and pulled him to her, cradling him in her arms and rocking him gently. He buried his head in her bosom and sobbed in a way he hadn't done since the night he had sent the bodies of his sister, Nadia and the others into space. He cried to release all of the pent-up pain and loneliness he had been feeling for so long.

When Jason opened his eyes again he was alone. He knew he had fallen asleep with Liet holding him, or had that been a dream as well? He sat up on the bed and smiled as Baby hopped into the room through the window and came to him for her early morning dose of attention. "Come on, mutt, let's get some exercise," he told her as he held her head in his hands and shook it gently from side to side.

Jason got out of bed and began a series of exercises designed to work every muscle group of his body, gradually working up a sweat. Just as he was finishing up there was a light knock on his bedroom door. Before he could say anything, the door opened and Vinny stepped in, but then stopped dead in her tracks when she encountered his nude body. Her face blushed deeply and she nearly dropped the small bundle she held in her arms.

"Oh! I'm sorry!" she exclaimed as she whirled around, giving him a chance to snatch the cover from the bed to wrap around his waist.

"Ah, what can I do for you, Vinny?"

The question sounded stupid, even to himself, but Jason couldn't think of anything else to say at the moment.

Vinny turned around slowly. Her face was still flushed as she held out her arms. "I. . .I thought you might like a change of clothing," she told him in a voice barely above a whisper. "You can't keep wearing the same robe all the time. I made you a new one. And some sandals."

Vinny crossed the room and placed the robe and sandals on the bed and then quickly turned away, her eyes still averted from hi. "I hope the sandals fit," she told him. "I used a pair of your own boots to get the measurements."

"That was very thoughtful. Thank you," he told her.

"You're welcome," she whispered as she turned and hurried from the room, closing the door behind her.

Jason sat on the bed and shook his head, grinning to himself as he thought about the treatment he was getting from Kim and Vinny. Both sisters seemed to be going out of their way to do whatever they could for him. Jason wasn't used to being pampered or catered to by anyone, and because of that the actions of Kim and Vinny were both confusing and amusing to him at times. He thought he also detected just the slightest trace of competition between them, but didn't really think anything of it.

Jason went to the window and poured water from the pitcher into the large bowl and washed up. "I've got to get showers installed on this planet," he said to Baby as he washed.

The people of Alazon had good hygiene habits, with most of them taking hot baths daily, but Jason missed the feel of a hot shower more than he liked to admit. He dried off and started to dress in his black combat outfit that he had brought back with him last night, but then changed his mind. It wouldn't be a good idea to put it on just yet.

It would draw too much attention. <u>Besides</u>, he told himself, <u>it might hurt Vinny's feelings if I don't wear the new robe and sandals</u>.

Jason rolled the combat outfit into a tight ball around their matching boots and placed it on the bed. He then picked up the new robe and inspected it. It was light blue with dark blue trim. He slipped on a snug fitting pair of Lycra shorts and then the new robe. When he put it on he found it fit him better than the one Liet had made for him.

He picked up the sandals, taking a moment to admire the quality of work that Vinny had put into them. He slipped them on, wrapping the long leather bindings up around his calf muscles. He felt the soft pliant leather mold itself to his foot. He didn't think Vinny could have gotten the fit of the sandals any more perfect if he had stood and let her cut the leather out around his foot.

Jason made his bed and then picked up the combat outfit and <u>bokken</u> before heading for the common room with Baby walking beside him. He found everyone else already there and seated at the table.

"I see mom finally made you a new robe," Kim said as he sat down and began to eat.

"Mom didn't make it," Vanda eagerly volunteered, grinning impishly at Kim.

"Vinny did," Manda told Kim before she could ask who had. "She also made him some new sandals."

Jason grinned at Vinny's exaggerated smile at Kim, whose face suddenly became dark and clouded. He felt a sense of tension fill the air between the two sisters. For a moment he thought Kim was going to explode and couldn't understand why she would react that way.

"Excuse me, ladies," Jarrell said from the other end of the table. He smiled benignly at his daughters as they turned to look at him.

"You know, Kimmy, when you first brought Jason to our home you were the one who stayed with him day and night. You were the one who nursed him, bathed him, and took care of his every need. It's no secret that without you, without your selfless dedication, Jason might not be here today. No one here can find any reason to slight that dedication or your efforts.

"However," Jarrell continued, "as I have previously stated, it is the duty of every member of this family to not only make Jason feel welcomed, to make his adjustment to our world easier, but to also do whatever each of can in that adjustment as well."

Jarrell hesitated a moment to let his words sink in. When he spoke again his attention was once more directed at Kim.

"Some of us must do those things in different ways, Kimmy. You have your ways, which no one can fault, but the rest of us must find our own ways. Vinny has elected to exhibit her help in a way for which she is well known, and that is the making of new clothing and sandals for him. We all know Vinny has a well-earned reputation for her abilities with a needle and thread. Many distinguished individuals have asked her to make special robes for them. This is, I feel, only her way of contributing to make Jason feel more welcome here, and you should think of it in that manner as well. Besides," he added with a grin, "we all know that you don't know one end of a needle from the other."

"I do so!" Kim protested, to the amusement of everyone at the table.

"Well, perhaps that's a bit harsh," Jarrell told her, "but what I'm getting at is this. There are things you are able to do for Jason that none of the rest of us can. So we must make up for it in other ways. Personally, I think you should show some gratitude to your sister for making some new clothing for Jason. I'm sure Jason is grateful."

Jason watched as Kim lowered her eyes at the polite but tactful scolding from her father. After a moment she raised her head and looked at Vinny. "Sorry, Sis. And. .the robe does look good on him."

"Don't worry about it," Vinny replied as she turned her attention to her breakfast, a smug grin on her face.

"Now that we have that settled, perhaps we can get on to other matters," Jarrell told them. "Jason, a little over half a mile to the east of the city is the old quarry. That's where the Mayoral Guard and other mayors will be an hour before noon. I'll have Shon and Hass come back to take you there, but I need to know if there is anything special you may need before then."

"Tell me about the quarry."

"Well, it's about three hundred feet deep at the center, measuring about a quarter of a mile across the top in each direction. The bottom is dirt, with some grass in spots, and it's far enough away from the city that we won't attract any unwanted attention."

"How many ways down to the bottom?" Jason asked.

"If I remember correctly, three."

"Can you have everyone else at the bottom before I arrive?"

"I should be able to do that, yes."

"Good. Hass, how did you do with the Guard?"

Hass grinned and set his fork down. "I have a feeling that right about now they would love to cut your heart out and eat it."

"What did you tell them?"

"Pretty much what you told me to. Of course," Hass added, "I had to embellish it with a few details."

"Such as?'

Hass glanced at Kim and grinned. "Well, without actually saying so, I implied that my poor little sister would never enjoy a virginal wedding night."

"You didn't!" Kim cried in embarrassment.

"Oh, don't worry, Sis, we all know the truth," Hass told her.

"Do we?" Shon teased with a straight face.

"Hey, what is this, pick on Kimmy day?" she asked hotly.

"Sure, why not?" Hass replied before turning back to Jason. "Anyway, I don't think you'll have to worry about them not being ready to fight you. All you have to do is show up."

"I'll be there."

"I sure hope so. I've got a lot of money riding on this," Hass informed him with a grin.

"Really?' In what way?" Jason asked, curious about what Hass had possibly set up.

"Well, I've got some bets that you'll win hands down, others on how long the fight will last. I've even got one on the number of injuries you do or do not receive."

Jason leaned back in his chair and smiled at Hass. "I see. We'll I'll be sure you collect. Just as long as I get my percentage."

"Oh, sure!" Hass replied quickly. "I was planning on cutting you in for twenty-five percent."

"Fifty," Jason countered with a straight face.

"Fifty! That's crazy!" protested Hass.

"Hum, you're right. Let's see, when you consider that I'll be the one doing the actual fighting while you stand on the sidelines, fifty is too much. Since you're acting as my agent and promoter, so to speak, and not in any actual danger yourself, I think it should be twenty-five, seventy-five split, with the seventy-five coming to me.

"Of course," he added, seeing the expression of disbelief on the face of Hass, "if that's not agreeable to you, we can go outside and discuss it. But then I'd be inclined to make it a ninety, ten split my way."

Jason managed to keep his face straight and his tone serious but it wasn't easy. He wanted to laugh at the play of emotions racing across the face of Hass. The younger man stared at him with uncertainty and disbelief, not sure of what to think.

"You know," Kim said, eager for an opportunity to get back at her brother for his earlier teasing of her, "Jason does have a valid point. And since it's already been demonstrated, in a very convincing manner I might add, that you are no match for him, I suggest that you take the twenty-five percent and be happy with it, big brother."

"Kimmy's right," chimed in Vinny. "After all, like Jason said, he'll be the one taking all the chances. Unless, of course," she added with a sweet smile, "you want to get down there with him to take on the Guard. But that might not be such a good idea. During the heat of the fight Jason might mistake you for one of them. You could end up getting hurt, and we'd hate to see one of our big brothers hurt, wouldn't we, Kimmy?"

"Oh, definitely!" Kim said in cheerful agreement.

"All right," Hass grumbled. "I get the message. Okay, Jason, seventy-five, twenty-five, just the way you said."

"Well," Jarrell said with a smile of amusement, "now that the financial affairs have all been straightened out, I better get to the office. I'll have a few questions to answer long before we get to the quarry. I'll see you there, Jason."

Jarrell, Shon and Hass left the house, leaving Jason with the rest of the family at the table. "We're gonna watch," Manda told him with a grin.

"I don't think so," Liet told her. "The only place the two of you are going is to school."

"Yes, Mommy," the twins replied in unison. But then they looked at Jason and winked. He had a feeling their mother's words had gone in one ear and out the other of both twins.

"Come on, you two," Vinny told them as she stood up. "I better walk you to school to make sure you get there."

The twins hurried off for their books, returning shortly to kiss Jason before following Vinny out the door.

"You know," Jason said to Kim as Liet left the table, "one of these days I would love to take the twins up and let Mother run some tests on them. I'd like to see just how strong their psi abilities really are, and in what areas."

"Can she do that?"

"For Mother it would be a piece of cake."

"Do you have to do anything special to get ready for this combat with the Guard?" Kim asked, suddenly changing the subject.

"Just change clothes."

"Are you going to wear your combat outfit?"

"Yes. But before I change I'll do some meditation, then go through a light kata."

"What's that?" Kim asked.

"A set of exercises designed to loosen my muscles after the meditation."

"Can I watch?"

Jason laughed lightly. "Well, there's really nothing to see during meditation."

"Is that where you sit with your legs curled up and go into some kind of trance?"

"It's not really a trance. More an act of centering yourself."

"Will you teach me?"

"I can show you how it's done, but to actually teach you would take some time. It's not something you can just pick up and do the first time. Come on."

Jason stood and led Kim out to the back courtyard. He had her sit on the soft grass and then eased her legs into the lotus position for her.

"That's uncomfortable," she said with a slight grimace.

"Only until you get used to it. Let your body relax."

He placed her hands in the proper position on her knees and then quickly assumed the position himself facing her.

"Now, the first thing you have to do is learn how to breathe properly."

"Hey, I've been doing a pretty good job of that for the past twenty years," Kim quipped.

"That's not what I mean, Kim. The type of breathing I'm referring to is different than what you normally do."

Slowly Jason taught her the correct way to breathe, getting her to relax. Then he instructed her on how to make her mind a complete blank so she could find the balance within herself. For nearly half an hour he sat with her, guiding her, helping her, then gradually bringing her back to the present. "How do you feel?" he asked as she opened her eyes.

"I'm not sure," Kim replied hesitantly. "Calm. Relaxed. Sort of like I've just had a good night's sleep. And more, I don't know, focused."

Jason nodded. "That's the way you're supposed to feel."

"But what about you?" Kim asked with concern. "You were so busy showing me how to do it that you probably didn't get to do it the way you wanted to."

"I'm fine," Jason assured her. "True, I didn't go into it as deeply as I normally would, but I got enough out of it."

He rose to his feet in one fluid motion and held out his hands to pull her up. He picked up the combat outfit and handed it to her. He then removed his robe, handing that to her as well, leaving himself dressed only in the Lycra shorts. He picked up the bokken and slipped the sling of the weapon over his head and shoulder so that it hung diagonally across his back with the leather wrapped haft extending above his right shoulder.

"What now?" Kim asked, watching him expectantly.

"Warm up exercises," he replied. "It might be a good idea if you go sit under the tree."

As Kim moved to sit on the stone bench, Jason remembered how Trish and Nadia used to come watch him practice from time to time.

After one particular session where he had been wearing the combat outfit, Trish had dubbed him "The Panther". He closed his eyes for a moment to block those memories from his mind and concentrate on what he had to do.

For nearly half a minute Jason stood perfectly still in the center of the courtyard. Then he slowly brought his hands up and pressed his palms together in front of his chest, fingers pointing upwards, mentally directing his physical energies to the center of his body.

As if moving under water he began to move his hands and feet through the motions of the Ninjitsu <u>kata</u>. His hands floated through the air in slow, dance-like motions as his feet seemed to glide over the ground. Jason gradually increased the speed of his movements to execute the various blocks and punches, incorporating the leg movements and kicks. Each move was smooth and efficient. Each designed to ward off the blow of an opponent or to deliver one of his own.

After nearly five minutes of this Jason's right hand flashed up and the <u>bokken</u> appeared in it as if by magic. Both hands gripped the weapon tightly, right hand above the left, with the tip of it pointing straight up. His elbows were horizontal to his body and his feet were spread slightly, the left one pointing straight ahead, the right one at a forty-five degree angle. His knees were bent to give him balance, and his eyes stared straight ahead at an invisible opponent.

Jason began to move the weapon, weaving it in patterns of defense and attack through the early morning air in slow motion. As before, he gradually increased the speed until the <u>bokken</u> was little more than a blur. The sound of its movements created a 'whooshing' noise that varied in intensity with the speed of the movements. The weapon went from hand to hand and then back to the two-handed grip faster than most eyes could follow. But Jason knew and controlled every move it made almost without thinking about it. These movements had been ingrained into his mind and muscles from years of constant practice.

As the <u>bokken</u> sliced through the air his mind worked not only to control the weapon, but to also control the rate of his heart beat and breathing so that, even though a light sheen of perspiration had formed on his body, he was breathing at a rate only slightly higher than normal.

With a final flourish more for show that any practical use, Jason whirled completely around, whipping the weapon in an arch from feet to head, slipping it into the sheath on his back almost as quickly as he had drawn it. As he turned to face Kim he saw Hass and Shon step away from the wall of the house where they had been watching.

"Is that what you're going to teach us?" Hass asked.

"Some of it," Jason replied as he wiped his forehead with his right forearm. "To teach you how to handle a sword like that would take about thirteen of your years. And that's only if you trained every day for four to five hours a day."

Shon looked at him skeptically. "But you expect our men to learn this style of fighting in only six to seven months."

Jason took the robe from Kim and slipped it on before answering Shon.

"Yes and no. First, I'll be training them five to six hours a day with the sword, with the same amount of time spent on other forms of martial arts, such as the hand-to-hand combat techniques I used on Hass. Granted, it still won't bring them anywhere close to my level of ability, but it will definitely put them on a level well above anything the Karton or Tilwin know.

"By the time I'm through with them, the average man of Preton should be able to take on three, four, even five of the swordsmen of Tilwin or Karton. Plus, I'll be teaching them to use a different style of sword than what you're used to. Your swords are short, broad and heavy. They're for hacking and stabbing, with little finesse involved. The swords I'll be training them to use will be as long as the <u>bokken</u>, and even more slender. It should be more than enough to offset the difference in numbers."

"From the way you handle that," Hass told him, pointing to the <u>bokken</u>, "one could almost get the impression that you could go into battle using it and win."

"Actually, that's been done," Jason told the younger brother.

"A long time ago in the history of Earth, there was a small island country known as Japan. The Japanese are the ones who perfected the art of Kinjitsu and Kendo, which are the arts dealing with the swords. They became so adept and proficient that they could take on armies three times their size and win.

"They were a society separated into classes, and only the Samurai, or Warrior Class, were allowed to wear swords during normal times. When wars with other countries did occur, the entire male population had to get involved in the defense of their country. Many of the men didn't have steel swords, so they used a bokken. Some of them became so proficient with it that they actually preferred it to a steel sword in some situations.

"While it won't kill the way a katana will, they could inflict a tremendous amount of damage. And, if a man with a bokken defeated a man with a katana, he could claim the sword in victory. But even them some of them still worked with the bokken."

"But, wood against steel?" Hass questioned.

Jason pulled the bokken from its sheath and tossed it to Hass. He then pointed to the tree in the corner of the courtyard. "Hit it," he instructed Hass.

Kim moved out of the way as Hass walked to the tree. He gripped the weapon in his right hand and struck the three. The blow sent small chips of bark flying, but when Hass checked the weapon for damage he found it unmarred. He looked at Jason.

"Again," Jason told him.

Hass gripped the bokken in both hands and struck the tree as hard as he could, sending shock waves up his arms. But once again the weapon was unmarked, except for some resin from the tree on the octagonal blade.

The wood," Jason told them as Hass returned the weapon, "comes from a group of trees in what was called the 'iron wood' category. It was the hardest natural wood on Earth. It was then treated with heat and certain chemicals to make it nearly as hard as metal. True, it could be severed by the blade of a katana, but it would have to be struck in just the right way by someone who knew what they were doing."

"So," Shon said thoughtfully, "theoretically we could use wood against steel and come out all right, providing we had the training to go along with it."

"Theoretically, yes," Jason replied with a nod. "But I think we'll go with the steel just to be on the safe side," he added with a grin.

"Speaking of going," Hass told them, "it's almost time for us to get a move on."

As they turned to leave, Liet came to the door and motioned to Jason. He excused himself from the others and went to see what she wanted. He took a seat across the worktable from her in the kitchen. Neither of them had said anything about what had transpired two nights ago. He wanted to thank her but was too embarrassed to bring it up.

"Jason," Liet began, speaking slowly but with a soft smile on her face, "it would seem that I have two daughters who are both competing for the attention of the same man. While that in and of itself is nothing new for the two of them, I have a feeling that this time things are somewhat different, as is the object of their attention."

Jason nodded and returned her smile. He realized how much he had come to like this normally quiet woman in the short time he had known her.

"Liet, while it's flattering to be the 'object of their attention' as you put it, I'm afraid that attention is wasted on me."

"Oh? You don't like women?" she teased.

"It's not that at all," he replied, laughing lightly at her jest. "It's just that right now any type of personal involvement with someone is simply out of the question for me."

Liet looked at him thoughtfully for a moment before nodding her head. "Perhaps you are right. I know there has been much sadness of recent in your life, and that you still carry in your heart the love for the one you were to marry."

Her tactful statement was the closest that either of them had come to bringing up his dreams and her holding him the night before.

"However," Liet continued, "you must also realize that there will come a time when things will not be the way they are now. A time when you will have the time for more personal relationships. And when that happens, think you will find there will be any number of beautiful young women on Alazon who would gladly welcome your attention."

"And I take it that two of those beautiful young women you speak of includes your two oldest daughters?" Jason teased.

"Absolutely!" Liet replied with a grin. "At the very top of the list as a matter of fact!"

Jason laughed and nodded. "I thought so. But I also think its going to be a while before I can think of something of that nature," he told her.

Liet nodded in understanding. "Perhaps, Jason. But then again, perhaps not as long as you may think. Sometimes fates, or the gods, have a way of intervening when you least expect it. Who can say what will happen."

"Hey, Vinny," Kim said from the doorway, "does this look like one of mom's famous heart-to-hearts to you?"

"Sure does," Vinny replied with a grin.

"Forget it, Mom," Kim told Liet as she and Vinny came into the kitchen. "I saw him first. Besides, you're already married to Dad. Not only that, but you're too old for him."

"Oh, I don't know," Jason replied as he leaned back on his stool and winked slyly at Liet. "I've always had something of a preference for the older, more mature and experienced woman over the young, immature and inexperienced girl."

"Oh, oh, Kimmy," Vinny said with a roll of her eyes, "I think we're in trouble. We better tell Dad about this."

"What we'd better do," said Shon as he stuck his head through the back door, "is to get going."

"Right," Jason said in agreement. He stood up, and then leaned over to kiss Liet on the cheek. "I'll keep in mind what you said," he whispered.

Jason, Shon, Hass, Kim and Vinny left through the back courtyard gate, quickly moving across the open ground and into the woods. Once inside the tree line, Jason noticed how Shon and Hass walked in front of him while Kim and Vinny took up positions on either side of him. Meanwhile, Baby darted off into the woods to chase whatever she could find. From time to time Kim or Vinny would look up at him, but neither of them said anything. When they reached a point where they would have to leave the cover of the trees, Shon pointed to where the quarry was as Kim handed Jason the combat outfit and boots she had been carrying.

"From here the quarry is only an eighth of a mile away, even though you can't see it from here," Shon told him. "But now the others should be there waiting for you."

Jason nodded. "Good. All of you go on ahead. I want to change clothes first."

"How long will you be?" Vinny asked.

"Just a minute or so behind you. Shon, I want you to have them at the west end of the base. I'll come down from the east.

"Now, once I get there I don't want any of you showing any signs of friendship towards me. In fact, if you can manage to pull it off, pretend as if you're angry and want to see the Guard put me in my place."

"Oh, I think we can pull that off without too much trouble," Hass told him with a short laugh.

"I'm sure you can," Jason replied dryly. "Now get out of here and let me change."

"What about Baby?" asked Vinny.

"I'll take her with me and leave her at the east end for the time being."

The others started off but Kim held back for a moment. She looked up at him and then surprised him by standing up on her toes to kiss his cheek. "Good luck," she told him before she hurried to catch up with the others.

Jason slipped off his robe and folded it neatly, wrapping it around his sandals. He then pulled on the tight fitting combat outfit. He put on the boots and slipped the <u>bokken</u> over his shoulder and down his back. Tucking the robe and sandals under his left arm, Jason set off at a trot for the southern end of the quarry with Baby running along beside him.

As he ran he realized that he was grateful to Mother for insisting that he work out daily for hours at a time to increase his speed, endurance and strength while they were searching for a world where he could fit in. She had told him that whatever world they found, he would have to be in the best physical condition he could possibly attain, as he never knew what he might have to face. Mother had also increased the gravity of the ship a little more each day. That, combined with the daily workouts, had given him a strength and endurance nearly twice that of a decathlon athlete back on Earth.

Jason found the path down the eastern end of the quarry without any trouble. As he reached it he stopped for a moment and looked skyward. Chuckling behind the mask of his outfit, he waved at the sky. Even though he couldn't see it, he knew Mother would be using a probe with a high-resolution camera that could read the fine print of a legal contract from a mile away to keep an eye on him.

Jason started down the steep path that curved first one way then the other. Just before reaching the bottom he spotted the twins. Vanda and Manda were crouched down and hiding behind a boulder large enough to conceal a couple of large men. They turned to look at him with grins plastered to their faces as Baby hurried forward to greet them.

"What are you two doing here?" Jason asked as he knelt down beside them.

"We told you we were gonna watch," Vanda replied.

"You won't get hurt, will you?" Manda asked. Her little face was a mask of concern and worry."

"Not if I can help it, sweetheart," he told her as he handed her the folded robe and boots. "Now, the two of you better stay out of sight for the time being. I don't think your dad will like it if he sees you here. I'll tell you what. Keep Baby here with you. There's no telling what the reaction of the men of the Guard would be if they saw her."

"Okay," they replied in unison as they stood up to hug him tightly for a moment.

Jason stood and gave Baby the hand command to stay before resuming his walk down the path to face the Guard. When he reached the bottom of the quarry he focused his attention on those gathered at the other end. There were a dozen of the Guard standing near the far side of the quarry, with another dozen or so standing off to one side.

"Come on, guys," he said softly to himself as he drew closer to them. "A dozen is one thing, but two could get a bit tricky. Someone could get hurt."

Jason had counted on being able to handle ten to twelve men without really hurting any of them seriously, but any more than that would compel him to change his strategy. It would force him to make sure those he struck would not be able to get back up for a while. That meant possibly hurting some of them fairly seriously, and he didn't what that to happen if it could be helped.

He stopped about ten yards from them, spreading his feet slightly and crossing his arms over his chest. Jason knew he was presenting them with an image that only Kim had ever seen before, and the men were a little unsure of themselves. In their eyes he was a man much larger than any they had ever known. Not only was he nearly a foot taller, but broader of shoulder and thicker through the chest, arms and legs. That, combined with the effect of the black outfit, complete with face and head covering, was causing some hesitancy in these superstitious people. They believed in spirits and demons, and Jason knew that to them he looked more like an apparition that might be more than human for all they knew.

As the men bean to move toward him they spread out to circle him. Jason studied them with the eyes of a trained fighter. These men were all pretty much stocky built in physique. They were the type used to relying on brute strength when they fought. If they were like Hass, and Jason had no reason to think otherwise, they had little finesse in their fighting methods. And, if he was judging them correctly, they weren't in the best of physical condition and probably didn't have much stamina for a long fight.

The men wore their short swords on their left hips, which allowed for a right-handed draw. As they moved to circle him each man gripped the thick haft of his sword tightly, but Jason knew they wouldn't make a move against him until Busker gave the order.

Jason studied Busker, who was directly in front of him. The trimming on the short robe was more elaborate than those the others were, and the man had the bearing of one used to giving orders and having those orders obeyed without question. Jason knew he needed this man. He would need Busker's trust and friendship because it would be Busker who would actually lead the army they would have to raise and train. The men of Preton knew Busker and would follow him, and that was important to Jason's plans.

Busker took a couple of steps forward, his eyes studying the figure of Jason cautiously. "I understand you said the men of the Mayoral Guard of Lemac could fight no better than women?" he said.

Busker's voice was calm, evenly modulated, giving no indication of any fear or apprehension that he might be feeling.

Jason stood silently. His only reply was a slight nod of his head.

The edges of Busker's moth curled up slightly. "Well, there are times when I would have to agree with you. So, for those comments I would find it hard to become angry with you. Or anyone else for that matter."

<u>Damn! This might be harder to pull off than I planned on</u>, Jason thought as he studied Busker's face. But even as he did he saw the expression on the weathered features of Busker change from one of amused passiveness to that of carefully controlled anger.

"Comments about the Guard I could tolerate, even ignore. However," Busker continued, his tone becoming less friendly, "there is another subject for which no amusement can be tolerated."

Busker looked directly into the eye slits of Jason's mask, but Jason made no move, gave no sound to indicate he even heard the Guard Commander.

"The people of Preton are a peaceful lot who tolerate much from others," Busker told him. "We believe that violence should be used only as a final solution, even when it comes to matters of family. Therefore, if you are willing to make public your apology to the daughter of my sister and her entire family, as well as make some form of appropriate financial considerations to atone for the fact that she will no longer be able to go to her future husband as a pure woman, our punishment of you will be less severe."

Jason studied Busker's face carefully. This man, while not exactly frightened of him, was doing what he could to avoid a fight. <u>I've got to push him just a little more</u>, Jason told himself. He slowly shook his head from side to side, making it clear that he had no intentions of either apologizing or making any financial considerations to her family for the alleged violations of her virginity.

"If anything," he said at last, his voice soft and low, "they should pay me for turning her into a real woman and showing her what a real man can do."

Jason saw the anger flare up in Busker's eyes. Jason's own eyes watched the muscles of Busker's arms and legs for the telltale signs that would signal the attack of Busker. He saw the muscles of Busker's arms and legs tense and waited for the explosion of movement he knew was sure to follow.

Busker snatched his sword free and lunged at him. Jason quickly stepped to his left. He raised his right hand and brought the hard edge of it down on the wrist of Busker, numbing the man's wrist without breaking it. Busker cried out in shocked surprise and pain as his sword dropped to the ground, but his surprise was far from over.

Jason let his momentum carry him around to Busker's right side. He pivoted on his left foot and whipped his right leg around to slam into Busker's back, sending the Guard Commander crashing into those standing behind Jason. The force of it knocked two of the men down as they tried to catch their commander.

In the space of a heartbeat, while the men of the Guard were still stunned into a sate of paralysis by the suddenness of the move, Jason went on the attack. His hands and feet flashed out to send men sprawling in the dirt. He wasn't hurting to hurt any of them any more than necessary, but just enough to put them down and out of action for a while. And to make them think about getting back up.

But Jason quickly realized that the men of the Guard were a strong and hardy group who could take physical punishment. Most of them were able to get up after a moment, their hands reaching for their swords. Out of the corner of his eye Jason noticed that Busker had regained his feet and now held his sword in his left hand, cradling his right one to his stomach.

As the men began to close in on him again, Jason snatched the bokken free and went on the attack once more. He wanted to take the fight to them instead of waiting for them to come to him. This time when swords and bodies fell to the ground, they remained there.

Jason was facing the last two men when he heard the shouts of those who had been standing off to one side. They were now rushing forward to join their comrades.

"No lack of courage here," Jason mumbled as he quickly dispatched the two men in front of him before turning to face the onrush of the others.

But before those men could reach him there was a sudden flash of white. The first two men leading the charge were slammed backwards and to the ground as the full force of Baby crashed into them. Her jaws closed on the wrist of a third, causing the man to scream in terror and drop his sword. As Baby released his hand and turned to attack another, the men of the Guard suddenly lost all courage and fled towards the rocks in an attempt to get away from this white furry demon that was nearly as big as they were.

"Heel!" Jason called out sharply in English.

Baby looked back over her shoulder at him, then turned back to the retreating men for a moment. She bunched her shoulders and barred her fangs at them. Then, with a shake of her massive head, she turned and came to sit beside his left leg, leaving his sword arm free and unblocked. Baby's eyes watched everyone to make sure no one else decided to attack him again. A low, rumbling growl came from deep in her chest. Jason reached down to pat her head and calm her down. He knew that when she saw the men attacking him she wouldn't have known it was by his design and would have come to his defense. And there was no way in the world the twins could have held her back.

"Vanda! Manda! Get away!" Busker shouted. Fear filled the man's eyes as he frantically waved for the approaching twins to come to him and avoid the two demons in the bottom of the pit.

Jason smiled behind his mask as the twins ignored their uncle and came running over to Baby and put their little arms around the dog's neck. Their action earned each of them a lick on the face from Baby in greeting, much to the astonishment of everyone but the members of the Vehey household. Busker took a cautions step forward. As soon as he did, Baby's head snapped around in his direction. Her upper lip curled back and she gave him a threatening growl.

Manda stepped forward to place herself between Baby and Busker. "Uncle Busker, you and your men stay back. And tell them to put their swords away. Baby was only protecting Jason, and what she may think is a treat to us as well. She won't hurt anyone as long as they don't make any sudden moves toward Jason or us."

Busker stood dumbfounded for a moment at he looked from the twins to Jason and the dog, but finally sheathed his sword, motioning for his men to do the same.

"Baby! Come!" Kim called out in English from the ledge of rock where she stood with Vinny.

Baby looked up at Jason. "Go," he told her, snapping his arm out toward Kim. Baby took off like a shot. The huge dog ran the few yards to the ledge and easily leaped high in the air to land between Kim and Vinny. She quickly whirled around to face Jason a she sat on her haunches between the sisters, receiving the pets and caresses of them, licking their hands and faces in return.

"Well, the easy part's over," Jason mumbled to himself as he looked at Busker and the others. The men were all gaping at him, the twins and Baby in open-mouthed wonder. "Now I've got to convince them that I'm actually one of the good guys."

# THIRTEEN

Jason loosened the Velcro straps around his throat and pulled back the head and face-covering portion of his combat outfit to reveal his dark hair, blue eyes, and non-golden skin. The action caused gasps of surprise. With the twins beside him, he walked toward Busker. The Guard Commander backed up until a large boulder behind him caused him to sit down abruptly. The man's eyes were wide as Jason knelt down beside him. He took Busker's injured wrist in his hands and gently probed it with his fingers.

"Nothing's broken," he told Busker, "but it will be sore for a couple of days. I can give you something for the pain."

Jason could only smile as Busker took in his strange coloring. The older man glanced at the twins, who had taken a seat on a broken piece of limestone and now had Baby sitting between them. A light of slow understanding began too come to his eyes. "You really didn't make those comments about the Guard, did you?" Busker finally asked in a soft, low voice.

"No," Jason replied with a shake of his head.

"And Kimmy?"

"Never touched her."

"Then this whole thing was nothing more than an elaborate set up."

"Yes."

"Why? What did you hope to prove? And to whom?"

"You, the men of the Guard, Jarrell and the other mayors. Believe me, Busker, you'll understand when I tell you why all this was necessary."

"Well, I don't know about the others," Busker replied, "but I think you've proven something to me. Although I'm not really sure if I know what it is just yet. By the way, do you have a name?"

"Jason. Jason Stephens. Look, let's check the rest of the men," he told Busker as he stood up and extended his hand. "Then I'll tell you everything you need to know. And probably some things you don't want to know."

Busker hesitated a moment before reaching out with his left hand and allowing Jason to pull him to his feet. The two of them went around to the other men to check for broken bones or other injuries. Aside from a multitude of bruises, and muscles that would be stiff and sore for a day or two, the only injuries were one broken arm, which a man incurred when he tripped over one of his fellow Guardsmen while trying to avoid Jason's weapon, and the wrist of the man Baby had clamped down on. The bones of it were broken and the wrist was starting to swell. The skin was lacerated, and it would be a while before the man would be able to use it again if left to the medical treatment of this world. Jason raised his left wrist up close to his mouth. "Mother?"

"Here," came the computer's reply from the communicator, which caused Busker and the injured man to gape at him in wonder.

"Send me a probe with a med-kit. I've got one man with a broken arm, another with a broken wrist and lacerated skin that needs immediate treatment."

"I already have one on the way," Mother told him. "I thought you might need it."

"Thanks, Mother. Jason out." He turned back to the man with the broken wrist and smile. "Your wrist will be fine in a little while. You have a couple of broken bones, but I can fix that. You'll be as good as new in about a week."

The man merely looked at him, swallowing with difficulty as he nodded his head, obviously too frightened to speak.

Jason and Busker left the man where he was sitting and checked on the others. As he was standing up from the last one, Jason heard a gasp from those around him. He looked up to see one of the probes dropping down to hover about four feet off the ground. The men backed away from it with fear filled eyes. Jason tried to keep the grin off his face as he went to the probe and opened the panel on the side to remove the medical kit. "Bring it home, Mother," he whispered into the communicator.

As the probe rose into the air with the eyes of the unknowing following it, Jason went to the man with the broken wrist. He opened the kit and withdrew a small injector and pressed it against the man's arm. "This will ease the pain and aid in healing," he told the man as he gave him the injection.

The man flinched at first but then began to smile almost immediately as the pain in his wrist began to vanish. Jason removed an inflatable cast and slipped it over the man's wrist and used the small, attached cylinder of $CO^2$ to inflate it. He then turned to the man with the broken arm and applied the same type of treatment. Once done, Jason stood and turned to Busker. "Call the men together for me."

As the men began to form ranks, Jason thought of how they resembled a motley crew of battered and bruised boys playing soldier. He wondered if he would be able to turn them into the core of the army he would have to raise. Busker cleared his throat and began to speak to his men, his voice loud and clear.

"Men, this is Jason Stephens. And as you can see, he's a bit, well, different. But he's got something to say to you and it might be a good idea to listen up."

Busker stepped to one side and nodded at Jason. As Jason turned to face the men he could see the nervous apprehension on their faces. He decided to hit them with the truth and see what happened.

"I'm looking for men who will fight against the armies of Karton and Tilwin," he told them bluntly. "Armies, which are, even as we speak, making preparations for a dual invasion of Preton."

"Excuse me, Commander Busker," a voice called out from the back of the ranks, "but couldn't we just send him against the Karton and Tilwin, then come along behind and take care of whatever he happened to miss?"

The comment brought smiles and laughter from some of the men, including Busker, who smiled nervously at Jason for a moment before facing the men.

"All right, you idiots, shut up and listen to me," Busker barked out. "For reasons that will be explained to all of you shortly, this man did not insult the Guard, although," Busker added with a shake of his head, "by the way he handled us he certainly has every right to say whatever he wants about us. But even more importantly, he did not violate the honor of my niece."

"Then would someone mind telling me why the hell we had to take this humiliating beating?" a young man in the front row asked.

"That, Corporal Ster, will all be explained to you in good time," Busker replied. "But for now you are to consider this man as a member of the Mayoral Guard and, more importantly, a guest of the House of Vehey.

"That means, Gentlemen, that you will afford him the same courtesies and protection you would any member of the Guard or the House of Vehey. If need be, you will protect his life with your own."

Jason saw the corporal named Ster look down at the ground and shake his head slowly before looking up at Busker. "Excuse me, Commander," the young man said ruefully, "but if we happen to come up against someone, or some <u>thing</u> that can beat him in a fight, I'm going back to being a farmer. It would be a whole lot healthier."

Even Jason had to smile at the comment of the young man.

"Another crack like that," Busker told Ster, "and you might be back to farming a lot sooner than you anticipated."

Jason and Busker turned to face Jarrell and the other mayors standing on a ledge of rock. But before either of them could speak there was a flash of green, gold and silver. Jason turned just in time to catch a leaping Kim as she launched herself at him from the ledge. As he caught her, Kim wrapped her arms around his neck and kissed him loudly on the cheek.

"I knew you could do it!" she told him proudly, her tiny feet dangling off the ground. "Some of the mayors didn't think so, but I didn't have a doubt in the world."

Jason felt the blood rush to his face as he disengaged Kim's arms and set her on her feet.

"Well," Busker said with a slight chuckle, "at least we know he's a man and not some demon, don't we?"

"What makes you say that?" Jarrell asked.

"It's easy. He might be able to go through my Guard like a hot knife thorough soft fat, but the simple act of being kissed by a beautiful young woman in front of others renders him helpless," Busker replied with a grin.

Jarrell nodded. "You have a point. Now, if we could just get my daughter to behave herself and try to act like the lady we have vainly attempted to raise her to be, I think we should all listen to what Jason has to say. I believe you'll find it of the utmost importance to us. Jason?"

Jason turned to Busker. "This could take a while. Why don't you and the others get comfortable?"

Busker nodded and told the men to relax. Some sat where they were, while others took seats on many of the large boulders and pieces of broken stone around them. Jarrell and the other mayors made themselves as comfortable as they could. Jason looked round and saw Jarrell nod his head. He took a deep breath and began.

"When Busker said I was somewhat different he only touched on the surface. What he didn't tell you, because he didn't know himself, is that I do not come from Alazon."

Jason saw the quickly exchanged glances as they tried to figure out what he meant by this. He felt his own sense of nervousness creeping back, but then he looked at Kim sitting with the twins and Baby and he relaxed somewhat.

"I come from a world you don't even know of," he told them. "It was a world which destroyed itself in a way more horrible than anything you can possibly imagine. I am the only survivor of that world."

Jason could see the looks of skepticism on their faces but he continued, knowing that in time they would come to believe him.

"However, where I come from, or how I arrived here, is not important right now. What is important is the fact that both Karton and Tilwin are preparing to invade Preton. Their armies will hit both shores of Preton in just about seven months from now." Their attention perked up at that.

"Although I can't explain in detail right now as to how I know this, I can assure you that I do have proof. Proof that Jarrell and the rest of his family have seen.

"As I said, the Karton and Tilwin are about seven months from landing on the shores of Preton, which gives us time to get ready for them. Time to defeat them."

"You speak in the plural. Does that mean you are going to fight with us?"

Jason turned to see who was speaking and found one of the men in Jarrell's group leaning forward to stare at him intently. "Yes," he replied.

"I see," the man commented dryly. "And why, if I may ask, would you, a total and complete stranger to our world, or so you say, be willing to do that?"

"I'm sorry, but I don't know your name," Jason said to the man, smiling politely at him.

"I am Councilman Lac of the Lemac Mayoral Cabinet," the man replied.

Jason glanced at Jarrell. Jarrell gave him a wry grin and nodded slightly as if to say, "You knew you would have to answer questions like this". But before Jason could formulate his reply to Lac, another voice spoke up loud and clear. The tone demanding attention, which it quickly got.

"I'll tell you why he'll help," Kim stated as she stood and faced Lac. "He will train us and fight with us because he's a man who hates war and what it does to people and countries.

"He's a man who has seen things, Councilman, that you cannot begin to imagine in your worst nightmares. A man who doesn't want to see them happen to this world.

"He's a man who loves peace and people. A man who will do all he can to prevent our world from making the same mistakes, and from eventually destroying itself the way his world did.

"So, Councilman Lac," Kim said, managing to make his title and name sound like something vile in her mouth, "if you will listen to him, and stop interrupting him with your perpetually suspicious mind and inane questions, for which you are so well known, you just might learn something."

Lac leaped to his feet, his anger clearly evident. "Now you listen here, young lady!"

But whatever else Lac was going to say was instantly cut off when Baby quickly placed herself between Kim and the Councilman in a position of attack. The huge dog presented Lac with a clear view of her long canines and powerful shoulders as a menacing growl came from her throat. Slowly, as if afraid of provoking the dog further, Lac eased himself back down onto the limestone ledge he had been sitting on.

"She never was what you could call shy or bashful," Busker whispered to Jason as Kim sat back down and pulled Baby down beside her.

"So I've noticed," Jason replied. He looked at Kim. This was the second time she had come to his defense in order to explain the reasons behind his actions. He was going to have to speak to her about that. Meanwhile he was going to have to make some sort of peace with the councilman. It wouldn't do to make an enemy in the heart of Busker's camp before things could even get started.

"Councilman Lac," Jason said, turning his attention to the man, "your reasons for asking are reasonable. They are questions I would probably ask were I in your position so, if you will allow me, I'll try to explain.

"Although Kim is correct in her comments, for the most part, my reasons for wanting to help go much deeper. However, to try and explain them all to you now would be too lengthy and complicated, and we really don't have the time for it. So please just hear me out."

Jason turned so that he was facing the men of the Guard. These men had only been playing soldier. In reality they were nothing more than a police force and color guard. In any real war they would be annihilated in less time that it would take to describe it. But with his help and training perhaps they could become the core of the army Preton was going to need.

"Busker, in a normal military confrontation between two armies here on Alazon, do they have set rules of battle they usually follow?"

The brows of Busker furrowed for a moment in thought. "If I understand you correctly, yes. The armies are broken down from divisions to companies, then to squads. In combat, entire divisions meet face to face in rigid formations. After a couple of hours of fighting a temporary truce is called so both sides can sent out litter bearers for the dead and wounded. Then, after a brief respite, the battle resumes. Is that what you mean?"

Jason nodded and turned back to the men of the Guard. "We are not going to fight that type of war," he told them. "We might possibly raise the men for it, but I don't believe we could win that way. It would only get a lot of men killed needlessly.

"What we are going to do is throw away the standard rules of warfare of this world and fight in a way the Karton and Tilwin have never seen before. That will give us the advantage we need to defeat them, with only minimal losses on our side.

"If you and the other men of Preton will follow the training I'll give you for the next six months, I can almost guarantee that the armies of Tilwin and Karton will never get off the beaches where they land.

"I'll tell you now that it's not going to be easy. The training you'll receive will be the toughest thing you've ever had to go through in your life. Some of you won't make it, but if you stick with it, we can do it."

"And what will be the cost to us for your leadership in this glorious victory?" a caustic voice asked from behind Jason.

"Lac!" snapped Jarrell as Jason turned to face the councilman.

"No, Jarrell," Jason said, holding out his hand to forestall the older man, "it's okay. It's an honest question. One that deserves an answer."

Jason turned to Lac and let his eyes bore directly into those of the councilman, watching Lac's smug smile vanish. "My 'price', as you put it, Councilman, will be this.

"First, I will expect to be able to walk down the streets, or through the woods and fields of this world, or along its beaches, without fear. To be able to life in freedom, not ground beneath the heel of some petty dictator. To know that I, and every man, woman and child alive, has the freedom to chose the life they want to live, not the one someone forces on us.

"I want to be able to watch children laughing and playing. To see them learning and loving as they grow, without the fear and pain of losing a father, brother or son in another war. Ever!

"I want to be able to find a piece of land I can buy and call my own to build a home and settle on. And someday, if I find a woman to love and love me, to raise a family of my own.

"I want to help your doctors and teachers by showing them the good things from my world which will benefit all of Alazon. Things such as cures for every disease known to this world.

"That, Councilman Lac, is my price. Let me know if you think it is too much for you to pay."

Silent anticipation fell over the entire assemblage as they all waited for Lac to reply. The man looked around at the others, nervously licking lips that seemed to have become suddenly sandpaper dry as he realized he had become the focal point of every pair of eyes.

"I. . .I'm sorry," Lac finally replied. "Perhaps I have been too quick to judge you and your motives."

"Maybe, Councilman," Jason countered, his face softening. "But then again, perhaps you should question me and my motives."

The man had lost face in front of the others and Jason knew that could be a dangerous thing for some people. He knew he had to help restore some of Lac's self respect in the eyes of the others.

"Councilman, I am a strange here. Not just to your city or your country, but to your world. I come here and offer to deliver your people from certain slaughter and enslavement, so it's only natural that you would be suspicious of me. Even without my obvious differences."

Jason saw some of the man's self esteem starting to return with his words. Lac looked at him and nodded gratefully. Even Jarrell was smiling at the way Jason seemed to be handling the situation as the older man leaned back against a rock outcrop.

"Now, here are my plans," Jason said to all of them. "The combined armies of Tilwin and Karton number a little over one hundred thousand." He saw emotions from disbelief to despair cross their faces at this. "However, I believe that with a force of about forty thousand or so well trained men we can beat them."

Now even Busker looked at him with narrowed eyes, as if wondering whether or not Jason was completely crazy. Jason ignored the man and went on.

"A few minutes ago I easily defeated a dozen of you, and did so without one of you landing a single blow on me. I believe that in six months I can have you, and the other men of Preton, to the point to where each of you will be able to take on five or six men easily.

"That means an army the size I'm speaking of could defeat those of both Karton and Tilwin. Also keep in mind that you won't be fighting the combined armies of those two countries, but fighting them separately."

Busker looked at Jason thoughtfully and scratched the side of his jaw. "Jason, I don't wish to sound like a man with a sever case of pessimism, but I don't believe we can be as good as you are in just six months."

"I don't expect you to be as good as I am, Busker. For you to be that good would take years and years of training, which we don't have. However, I can do what I say when it comes to teaching you and your men. If you will work with me. Together we can do it. Besides, I have a few tricks up my sleeves that will even things up for us in a big way."

"Such as?" Busker asked.

Jason whirled around and snatched the phaser pistol from the concealed pouch on the back of his uniform. He fired it at a boulder fifty yards away. The boulder exploded instantly into small fragments. As he turned back to the others, Jason saw the looks of disbelief and incredulity on the faces of everyone except Kim and the twins. The three of them were grinning like Cheshire cats.

"This is one of the weapons from my world," Jason told the men. "I have weapons you've never dreamed of. Weapons that you will use against the Karton and Tilwin."

Busker stared at him for a long moment. Jason could see the debate going on in the man's eyes as to whether he should trust Jason or not. "All right," Busker said at last with a sigh, "what do you want of us, and what do we have to do?"

"I need you and the mayors of Preton to send me your Mayoral Guard, as well as all volunteers who are willing to train and fight.

*Alazon*

We'll have to find a place where we can train secretly, just as the Tilwin and Karton are doing, and we'll have to set about recruiting those men who will make up the army of Preton."

"How will you go about recruiting the men?" asked Jarrell.

Jason turned to face him. "If it's all right with you and the other mayors, I would like to ask for volunteers based on a percentage of each city's population. This will give us equal representation from each city."

"How do we go about getting the word out in time?" asked Jarrell.

Jason looked briefly at Kim and grinned. "Don't worry, Daddy," Kim said to her father. "Jason's got a way to handle that."

Jarrell looked from Jason to Kim and back. "Hum, yes, I guess he does at that. Well, as for myself, and knowing what I do of you, Jason, I offer myself and the services of the Mayoral Guard of Lemac here and now."

Jarrell turned to Busker, who nodded in agreement. Busker then turned and glared at his men. The men looked at one another, shrugged their shoulders and nodded their heads. They all knew and trusted both Busker and Jarrell, and if those two men said to do it, then there was nothing left but to do it.

"Tell us what you want done," said Jarrell.

"The first thing to do is appoint a commander for the army," Jason told him. "It has to be someone the men know and respect. Someone capable of leading them. As far as I'm concerned it should be Busker."

There were nods of agreement from just about everyone except Jarrell. The older man was looking at Jason with a slight smile playing at the corners of his mouth.

"Jason," Busker said with a slight shake or his head, "being Commander of the Mayoral Guard of Lemac is one thing. Being the Commander of the Army is something else entirely.

"Now, I will fight with you, beside you, and do all I can to help train the men to get them ready, but if it's all the same to you, I would just as soon take my orders from you.

"Look," Busker continued, "to be completely honest, I don't know the first thing about warfare, other than the basics. You obviously do, so it's only natural that you hold that position." He turned from Jason to face his men. "Do I hear any objections?" he growled, making it evident he better not.

"If we accept Jason as Commander," said a voice from Jason's right, "does that mean we don't have to listen to your griping any more?"

"Ster! Front and center!" Busker bellowed as the other men tried to suppress their snickers.

The young corporal leaped to his feet and quickly came to stand before Busker, his body rigid, and his face blank.

"Now, Corporal," said Busker, "since you like to talk so much, and since you do have a little rank, which could be yanked at any time, I'll tell you what I'm going to do.

"From this moment on, Corporal Ster, you are going to be my personal Adjutant and errand boy, as well as Jason's. Your job, when you aren't busy training with the rest of the men, will be to act as runner and all around gofer for the two of us. You and your big mouth will carry messages to and from wherever we want, as quickly as your feet will carry you. And you will do so with a smile on your face. In fact, I can't think of anyone better suited for that job, can you?"

"No, Sir!" Ster replied smartly.

"Good. Now get back with the rest of the men and keep that big mouth shut until you are required to use it."

As Ster pivoted sharply on his heel and marched back to his position, Busker turned to Jason and winked. "He really is a good man," he said softly. "One of my best. But he also has a habit of popping off from time to time."

Jason turned back to Jarrell and his delegation. "I suggest that we head back to the city and find a place a bit more comfortable to finish our discussions. It could take some time to go over all the details."

Jarrell nodded and stepped down from the ledge. "You're right. However, I don't think it would be a good idea to have you go marching through the center of the city just yet."

"No problem. I'll go back the same way I came," Jason told him.

"I'll go with you," Busker volunteered, motioning for his men to get to their feet.

"Good. That will give us a chance to talk. But I think your men should go back the way they came in order to avoid any unwanted attention."

Jason turned back to Jarrell. "You and the others return as if everything were normal. Busker and I will return through the woods. That will give me a chance to tell him some of my ideas. And to get to know him a little better."

"Busker," Jarrell said to the Guard Commander, "do you think you can get him to the back entrance of the Mayoral Building without drawing attention?"

"Yes. We can go through the rear entrance of the barracks from the woods, and then up through the connecting hallways."

Jarrell nodded at that. "Good. We'll meet you in the council chamber room."

Jarrell and the others turned to go, leaving Jason with Busker and the men of the guard. Kim, Vinny and the twins also remained behind, as did Baby, who wanted to play. The twins began running around, darting from side to side between the boulders and slabs of limestone as Baby chased first one of them and then the other. The dog's playful growls and the twin's shrieks of laughter echoed off the high walls of the quarry as the others watched.

"What kind of animal is that?" Busker asked, watching nervously as Baby knocked Vanda down and then snatched the boy's ankle to playfully drag him around in the grass for a few feet before releasing him and going after Manda.

"A dog. To be more specific, an Alaskan Husky, which I know doesn't mean anything to you."

Busker watched the dog and children for a moment and then shook his head. "It's hard to believe that something that big could be so gentle with the children and, at the same time, so vicious. I really thought it was going to kill some of my men before you called it back."

Jason smiled and nodded. "First, Baby is a she. Second, she was only protecting me from what she thought was an attack. She would do the same for the twins, Kim, Vinny, even you once she got to know you and became friends with you. I've trained her to attack and disable, but not to kill. Although I have no doubts that she would if she felt it were necessary."

Jason saw the look of uncertainty on the face of Busker as the man watched the dog. Jason whistled sharply. Baby stopped in her tracks then bolted back to him, taking up a position beside his left leg. He ruffled the fir of her neck and looked at Busker. "Go ahead," he told the Guard Commander. "She won't hurt you. Besides, it would be best for all concerned if she considered you a friend.

Busker slowly extended his left hand toward the dog. Baby sniffed at it for a moment and then began to lick it. She moved forward a little and lowered her head so that it was beneath Busker's hand, letting the man know it was all right for him to pet her. After a moment Baby got to her feet and rubbed her head against Busker's chest as the man gradually overcame his nervousness and began to pet her with less apprehension and fear.

With a giggle at their uncle, the twins took off running up the path for the top of the quarry. Jason let them get nearly half way up and then snapped his right arm out in their direction. Baby took off after them instantly. She easily leaped over some boulders and swerved around others along the path until she caught the twins, who immediately turned to tackle her and begin a laughing, screaming wrestling match with the dog that lasted until Jason and the others reached them.

At the top of the quarry path Jason picked up both twins and nuzzled them with his mustache, making them giggle and squirm. "You know your mother is going to be upset that the two of you skipped out of school to come watch, don't you?" he asked them.

"Are you gonna tell on us?" Manda asked with an impish grin.

"I don't think I'll have to. I have a feeling she already knows," he told her as he set them down so they would walk.

"Well, if she doesn't do anything about it, I will," Busker told the twins, looking gruff and grim.

"Oh, Uncle Busker," Vanda replied, waving his small hand as if to dismiss him, "don't pull that grouch act with us. We know you're really an old softy. You couldn't be mean to us if you tried."

"No respect from kids these days," Busker said to Jason as he looked at the twins with love in his eyes.

"You really were something to watch today," Vinny told him as they approached the woods.

"Thank you," Jason replied with a smile. Then he stopped and turned to face Kim. He crossed his arms over his chest and looked at her sternly. "If you ever, and I mean ever, jump on me like you did today, Kimella Vehey, I will turn you across my knee and spank you."

Kim stuck her tongue out at him and then quickly darted away as he made a half-hearted attempt to grab her. "You wouldn't dare!" she teased.

Busker looked at Kim and nodded. "I think you might be in for a surprise, Kimmy," he told his niece. "I have a feeling he means it. And, personally speaking, that's something I might actually enjoy watching. Now, Jason, do you really think we can do it with only forty thousand men?"

"With the right men and the right training, yes," he replied as they started walking again.

"And just how do we go about getting the right men?"

"We start with the members of the Mayoral Guard of each city. Those men have some knowledge of discipline and how to use a sword. However, with what I'll be teaching them it will make their current knowledge in that area practically useless. But we'll use them as the role models for the other men we recruit.

"There's something else," he told Busker. "I'm not too crazy about the idea of me being commander of any army. I still think it should be you. I'm a stranger to this world and it may be hard for the men to accept me."

Busker was silent for a moment. "Jason," he said at last, "I don't know if I can explain why, but I have a feeling you may be wrong about that. I think the men will accept you and your leadership, if for no other reason that the differences you possess."

"Well, we'll see," Jason replied, not at all sure.

"I agree with Uncle Busker," Kim told him as she took the twins by the hands. "I think you'll do just fine."

"So do I," Vinny said with a smile.

"There, you see!" Busker told him with a short laugh. "That settles it. If Kimmy and Vinny both say so, then it must come from the lips of the gods themselves. But all joking aside, I agree with them. Now, tell me about the training and the weapons you spoke of."

"It will consist of the men using a new type of sword called a katana," Jason explained. "Unlike the swords you're used it, it's longer, thinner, and used in a completely different manner and style that what you are accustomed to."

"Like the way you used the wooden one?" Busker asked.

"Yes. There is also a shorter version called a ho-tachi. It can be used separately or with the katana. The art of fighting with them is called Kendo.

"I'll also be teaching them Ninjitsu, a form of unarmed combat that has never been seen on your world. The training will be hard, and take long hours, but it will pay off in the end.

"As for the other weapons of my world," he added as he pulled out the phaser and showed it to Busker, "I have more of these. They're called phasers, and fire beams of concentrated light and energy."

"I don't see how light can hurt someone," Busker said, his face showing his puzzlement at such a concept, "but I saw what it did to that boulder."

Jason laughed lightly. "I assure you, Busker, it's no ordinary beam of light. I'll demonstrate other weapons to you when the time is right. Trying to explain how it works to you without you having some technical background in the physics of my world would be too confusing."

Busker shrugged as Jason put the weapon away. "If you say so," he said to Jason. They walked along for a little while longer before Busker spoke again. "Tell me about your world," he said at last.

Jason sighed. He wondered where to begin and what to tell the man. Should he tell Busker of the poverty and hunger that had permeated most of the population of Earth? Or of the scientific discoveries and achievements of those of New Hope? What about the madness that had taken over the world's leaders, leading to the total destruction of a planet and its moon?

Jason wasn't sure if he really knew Earth himself, or if he could give an objective opinion of it. He had grown up on Luna, not Earth, and perhaps wasn't entirely qualified to tell anyone about it.

*Alazon*

His concepts and ideas were somewhat biased and may not be the true ones.

"Let's just say," Jason finally replied, "that the people of my world never learned the art of peace and living together. Because of that they destroyed themselves in a way you can't begin to imagine."

"How did you manage to escape?"

Jason was wondering how to explain New Hope when Kim came to his rescue. "Uncle Busker, I don't think now is a good time for this," she said softly. "I think you should wait until later when there are not so many other pressing matters. Then Jason can take the time needed to explain everything to you."

Busker looked at his niece and nodded. "I guess you're right," he told her. "I suppose there are other things we could and should discuss."

<u>Thank you, Kim</u>, Jason said mentally. The heads of the twins snapped around toward him and Jason knew they had 'heard' him. He smiled at them and they smiled back before turning to watch where they were going.

When their group reached the area in the woods behind the Vehey house the twins and Baby charged across the clearing and into the back yard. Jason and the others continued on until they reached the back of the barracks. Busker led them across the clearing and into the rear of the building. They went through the barracks and up a steep stairway that opened onto a large hall, and then into a conference room where the others were already seated and waiting for them.

Jason noticed a number of food items set out on side tables. He wondered how they came to be there but didn't ask. He took the seat indicated by Jarrell and looked around at the anxious, somewhat skeptical faces of the others. He wondered if he would ever really get these people to trust him the way Kim, Vinny and the twins seemed to. <u>I hope so</u>, he prayed silently. <u>I need them and maybe, just maybe, they need me</u>.

The others were waiting for him to speak. He took a deep breath and let it out slowly. Then, in controlled and measured tones he began to outline his plans in more detail to those who were going to be responsible for providing the men necessary for the protection of their country and the life they knew.

# FOURTEEN

Liet looked at her oldest daughter and smiled. "Kimmy, I think that meat is already dead," she told her. "You're only supposed to be tenderizing it, not beating it into mush."

The sound of her mother's voice brought Kim's mind back to what she was doing and where she was. She looked up and saw the smile playing at the corners of her mother's mouth as Liet motioned for Kim to join her at the table. As Kim sat down, Liet poured each of them a glass of cold teef and slid one across the table to her. "I think it's time we had a little talk," Liet told her.

Kim saw the concern in her mother's eyes and had a pretty good idea of what her mother wanted to talk about, even though she pretended otherwise. "I'm not sure I know what you mean."

Liet looked at Kim sternly for a moment, but then her visage softened and she smiled tenderly. "You know exactly what I mean, Kimmy. You're in love with Jason, aren't you?"

Her mother's words were more a statement of fact than a question. She looked at her mother and sighed. "I don't know," she said at last with a shrug of her shoulders. "At times I feel like he's the most wonderful, marvelous, exciting, sensitive and caring man in the world."

"And at others?" Liet prompted.

"At other times he can make me so frustrated and furious with something he'll say or do that I want to scream at him and hit him over the head with the biggest rock I can pick up."

Liet grinned and nodded her head. "So I've noticed. But you didn't answer my question. Are you in love with him or not?"

Kim started to deny it, but then she stopped for a moment and really thought about her feelings for Jason. When she did she realized that her every thought during the day was of him. She wondered how the training was going, how the men were taking to him, how he was adapting to their world, and if he even noticed her on his too infrequent visits home with her brothers or Busker.

Kim thought of how she dreamed of Jason at night. And of how the content of those dreams made her blush in the daylight hours when she recalled them. She had never thought of any man in such a blatantly sexual manner before, and she wasn't able to explain why she thought of Jason like that. Unless she really was in love with him.

"All right," Liet said after a moment when Kim didn't answer, "let me ask you this. How would it affect you if Jason were to be killed in the coming war?"

Kim felt the blood drain from her face and her heart skip a beat. The thought of Jason being killed had never entered her mind. She had taken it for granted that he would be unharmed. She believed that his superior strength, speed, training and intelligence would see him through unscathed. But the sudden image in her mind of his body cut and mangled, blood gushing forth from a dozen wounds as he lay dying made her hands shake as she tried to sip from her glass.

"That's what I thought," Liet said as she reached across the table to take Kim's free hand and squeeze it lightly. "But there's something else I think you should also take into consideration."

"What?" Kim asked weakly. She was almost afraid of what her mother might say next.

"You're in love with Jason, but what if he isn't in love with you? After all, he still carries around his love for Nadia. You have to remember that to Jason, Nadia's death wasn't all that long ago. So, not only are you fighting the memory of a ghost, but you may also be beating your head against a wall he's built around his heart for his own self-protection. A wall you have no chance of getting through at the present time."

The weight of her mother's words seemed to release a flood of emotions within Kim. She realized she had been trying to conceal her feelings for Jason, from him as much as from herself. But she knew that she really did love him. She loved Jason with all her heart. "What do I do?" she finally asked.

"The most important thing you can do right now is to just be patient, Kimmy. Things don't always happen as fast as you might want them to. And you should continue to do the things you've been doing."

"And what if I'm just wasting my time?" Kim asked sullenly.

"That could be the case, but I don't think so," Liet told her with a grin. "I know he cares a lot for you already."

"Caring is not the same as loving," Kim mumbled. "He cares for me, but he loves his dog. And the twins."

Liet laughed lightly at this. "True, but caring about someone is a good start. Being friends, caring about one another, is important to any relationship. You have to have friendship before you can have love. You have to be friends before you can be lovers."

"Do you think Jason will ever come to love me?" Kim asked. She could hear the note of pleading in her voice that begged for some assurance from her mother.

"He's a man, isn't he?" Liet asked with a grin.

"Oh, yes, Mother, he's most definitely a man!" Kim replied, laughing as she wiped away the tears that had formed in her eyes.

"Well, then there's a chance. But I wouldn't put too much hope on it happening for a while, Kimmy. Right now the last thing on his mind is pretty girls or love. He has totally dedicated himself to the training of the army. An army of which most of the men in it have never held a sword in their hands before in their lives.

"Between Busker and Jason they have to turn those men into a force that can take on two, well-trained armies who have never known anything but war. That's not an easy task for anyone, and Jason being an outsider makes it that much harder. I'd say that right now the most important thing in the world to Jason is getting those men trained as best as he can.

"Kimmy, I may not know him in some ways as well as you do, but knowing him as I do, Jason will blame himself, and take personal, the death of every man in the coming battles."

"The army and the twins," Kim replied, screwing up her mouth in a frown.

"What do you mean?"

"Haven't you noticed, Mom? When he does bother to come home for one of his rare visits, the twins take up most of his time. It seems as if he would rather spend time with them than with me. He makes me feel as if I don't even exist when he's here."

Liet looked at Kim and shook her head sadly. "Kimmy," she said softly, "of everyone in this family, I would have thought that you, more than anyone else, would be able to understand that in him."

As the meaning of her mother's words hit home, Kim began to feel ashamed of herself. To say that Jason loved the twins, or that they practically worshipped the ground he walked on would be a serious understatement. Jason was a god as far as Vanda and Manda were concerned. The twins would wait patiently for days for the shuttle to appear. When it did they would bolt out the door screaming his name, leaping up at him like two little rockets the second he stepped from the shuttle. For the rest of the day or evening they would never be more than an arm's length from him for more than was absolutely necessary. When it was time for them to go to bed, Jason would carry them to their room, help them get into their nightgowns, and then tell them one of the many stories from Earth they had come to enjoy so much.

Kim thought of the last time Jason had come home. It had gone the usual way, but when Kim had gone to check on them after Jason had been in the twins' room longer than normal, she had stopped short in the doorway.

Jason was sitting on the bed between the twins, who were fast asleep. Vanda and Manda were curled up with their arms draped around his waist. Jason's own head was lowered and his eyes were closed. At first Kim thought he had fallen asleep. She had tiptoed into the room to wake him, but just as she reached the side of the bed she saw tears making their way down his cheeks and the gentle shaking of his shoulders. Not knowing what to do, Kim had stood there for a moment before finally easing out of the room to hide in the darkness of the hallway where she could watch him.

At first she had been confused as to why Jason would be crying. It was nearly a full minute before she finally realized that he was crying over the children of his world who never had a chance at life. He was crying for all those who had died on Earth, some instantly, some slowly and painfully, due to the actions of the adults. And he was crying over the loss of his sister and the other children who had died aboard the <u>Stargazer</u> in their flight from New Hope.

Thinking back on that night now, Kim realized how stupid and selfish she was being in her jealousy over the time Jason spent with the twins. Jason needed his time with them as much as they wanted it with him. It also gave Kim a new insight as to the sensitivity of him she hadn't realized before. And it made her love him all that much more. Kim looked up to see her mother watching her patiently.

"What do I do, Mom?"

"As I said, for now nothing different than what you've been doing. Actually," Liet said after a brief pause, "that's not quite true. What you do is support and encourage him as much as you can, not give him something else to worry about."

Kim looked at her mother as a new light of understanding dawned in her. "You actually like him, don't you, Mom?" she asked.

Liet smiled and nodded her head. "Yes. Oh, I admit that when he first arrived I was a bit skeptical and suspicious of him and his motives, but not now."

"What made you change your mind?"

Liet thought about it for a moment. "Nothing specific. It's just that after a while I realized that he really is an open, honest person. Perhaps a little too honest for his own good at times."

"And the fact that he loves the twins, and they think he's the greatest thing since candy helped a little, didn't it?" Kim teased, knowing how her mother doted on the twins.

Liet grinned at her. "Well, that doesn't hurt. The twins seem to be pretty good judges of character, so I figure that anyone they love as much as they love him, and who obviously loves them in return, has to be okay."

"Could you accept him as a husband to your daughter?"

"Yes," Liet replied without hesitation. "But remember what I said. Don't crowd or rush him. And also keep in mind that just because you love him that doesn't necessarily mean that he will come to love you. There's always the chance that he could fall in love with someone else. After all, none of us can truly control the dictates of our hearts when it comes to love."

"I know," Kim said with a grin. "But I'm not going to give up and let him get away from me, either. Not as long as I know there's a chance."

"Now, how did I know you were going to feel like that?" Liet said as she took a sip of her teef. "But that's the attitude you have to have."

"I know," Kim replied as she stood and headed for her own bedroom.

As Kim reached her own room she noticed that the door to Vinny's room was closed. She opened it, surprised to find the lamps out and the drapes nearly closed. As he eyes adjusted to the darkness she saw Vinny laying on her bed with her back to the door. As Kim stepped into the room she thought she heard a muffled sob coming from her sister. Kim closed the door and crossed the room to sit on the bed. She placed her hands on Vinny's shoulders to turn her around, surprised to find Vinny crying.

Kim had no idea why her sister was crying, but knew she had to find out. There were no secrets between them, even though they could keep just about anything the wanted from anyone else. If one of them were upset over something it usually had an effect on the other.

"What's wrong, Sis?" Kim asked softly as she pulled Vinny up so that her sister was sitting on the bed facing her.

Vinny wiped her face with both hands. "Nothing," she finally replied.

"Hey, this is me," Kim said softly, "and I know better than that. You don't cry for no reason at all. Come on, Vinny, what's wrong."

"It. it's nothing to concern yourself about, Kimmy. It's just something I have to work out on my own. And in my own way."

Kim's eyes had adjusted to the dimness of the room, allowing her to see her sister's face clearly. Vinny wasn't being honest with her. Her sister was trying to hide something, and that was almost unheard of between them. Then, from out of nowhere it suddenly hit her with the force of a boulder crashing down from the side of a mountain. "Jason!" she exclaimed in a whisper. "You're in love with him, too!"

Vinny turned her head away quickly, but the brief look in her eyes was all the answer Kim needed.

"I'm sorry, Kimmy!" Vinny blurted out. "I didn't mean to fall in love with him, I swear I didn't. It just happened and I couldn't help it."

"By all the gods," Kim said as she sat back on the bed, thinking of the almost prophetic words her mother had spoken to her only minutes before about love. She was stunned at this revelation from her sister.

In the past it had been a game between the two of them to try and steal one another's boy friends, but this was something entirely different. True, in the beginning they had both vied for his attention once he had recovered, continuing to play the game between them to a degree. It had been a friendly competition to see which of them could outdo the other in things each of them could do to help him, but now Kim realized that it had become something much more serious than a harmless game. She and Vinny were vying with one another for the love of the same man, and this time it was for real. Only Kim hadn't realized the depth of involvement for herself or her sister. And because of that, they were now faced with a situation neither of them had ever been in before – they really <u>were</u> in love with the same man.

"For the love of Lofa," Kim finally muttered, feeling a sense of helplessness as she looked at Vinny. "What do we do now, Sis?"

Vinny wiped her eyes and smiled weakly. "There's only one thing we can do. You're the oldest, you saw him first, so you get first shot at him."

Kim looked at Vinny and grinned sheepishly as she shook her head. "That isn't how it works, Sis, and you know it. When it comes to love, real love, it's every woman for herself."

"Maybe with other women, other sisters, but not for us," Vinny told her. "Besides, he's in love with you."

"Yeah, sure he is!" Kim replied with a trace of cynicism in her voice. "I wish I were as sure of that fact as you seem to be."

Vinny looked directly into her eyes. "He does love you, Kimmy. I've seen the way he looks at you when you aren't aware of it. I've seen the little smile on his face when you do something for him, or when you're just around. It's a special smile reserved just for you, even if you're too blind to see it."

"Then why doesn't that big, blue-eyed alien dummy ever let me know how he feels?" Kim asked in frustration.

"Because he's afraid," Kimmy told her.

"Afraid? Afraid of what?"

"Love, attachments, of caring."

Kim shook her head in confusion. "I don't understand what you mean."

"What's happened to everyone he's ever loved?" Vinny asked softly."

"Oh," Kim said at last, finally understanding what her sister was driving at. "They all died."

"Exactly. And because of that, Jason is terrified of letting himself love anyone again. He has a fear of losing them that you and I really can't begin to comprehend. Haven't you noticed how he makes it a point to keep reminding us that he's the alien here?

"Kimmy, he _wants_ to be the alien, the outsider. By doing that he feels no one will get too close to him, which means he doesn't have to worry about loving them. Or of being hurt again if something happens to them."

Kim agreed with her sister for the most part but then she shook her head. "You seem to understand him pretty well, Vinny, but there's a flaw in your logic."

"What?"

"The twins. If he isn't showing them love, and getting it in return from them, I'll boil your old sandals and eat them."

Vinny shook her head. "It's not the same thing, Kimmy. You see, in some way, to Jason that type of love and sharing is all right. In fact, he can't help himself from loving them any more than he can help breathing. And it's not just the twins. It's every child he comes into contact with.

"Kimmy, you've seen him with the friends of the twins. To Jason, children are the future of the world, and the most precious commodity we have. I don't think I would like to be around anyone who ever hurt a child when Jason found out about it. I think we would see a side of Jason that would be frightening."

Kim shook her head in disagreement. "He would never hurt anyone intentionally."

Vinny stared deeply into Kim's eyes for a moment. "You are so wrong, Kimmy," she said softly. "Jason would beat a hundred armed men senseless with his bare hands to get to the one man who even slapped a child. And then he would beat that man to death."

As much as she might not want to believe that violent side to Jason, the man she loved, deep down inside Kim knew that Vinny was right. Kim had never seen Jason angry, or even really upset, but the thought of him losing his temper, of unleashing the strength and training of a lifetime on someone made her shudder.

Kim knew that for the last six months prior to him finding Alazon, Mother had gradually increased the gravity of the ship a little more each day in order to make him stronger, quicker and faster. By the time he arrived at Alazon his speed, strength and reflexes were nearly double that of any man of this world. To many of the men he was considered almost godlike because of that. But to Kim he was a man, not a god, and he was the man she loved. "Vinny, what if he gets hurt, or even killed in the war?"

"He won't," Vinny replied confidently.

"What makes you so sure?"

"I don't really know. Call it a feeling if you want, but I just know he'll come out of it all right. I also have a feeling that Jason is going to have a long and lasting effect on the future of our world."

Kim nodded her head slowly in agreement. "I hope you're right, Sis. About his not being hurt, that is. But in the meantime, what are we gonna do about us?"

"Nothing," Vinny told her. "Like I said, Jason's in love with you, even if he's too stubborn to admit it right now. Either to you or to himself. And as for me? I'm going to keep playing the game the same as we always have. No sense in making it easy for you," she added with a grin. "Besides, I don't think I could stop now even if I wanted to."

"But is it still just a game, Vinny?" Kim asked softly.

"It is as long as we both know where we stand, and I think we have that pretty well figured out. Go for him, Kimmy," Vinny said as she leaned forward to hug her briefly. "You love him, he loves you, and that's the way it's supposed to be. Who knows, maybe it's the way the gods have decreed it."

Kim grinned but shook her head. "He doesn't believe in our gods. He says they are excuses for things we don't know or understand yet, but will someday come to accept as common knowledge."

Vinny turned to look out the window through the partially opened drapes for a moment before turning back to Kim.

"Maybe he's right, Kimmy. I don't know. But I'll tell you this. He believes in something. Call it a god, a force, or whatever you want, but he believes. Maybe our religious beliefs are childish to him in their simplicity, and maybe he does know better, but he also believes."

Kim looked at her younger sister thoughtfully. "You know, I always thought that it was the older sister who was supposed to teach the younger one about life, love, and all that stuff, but here you are teaching me. How did you get to be so smart?"

"I had a good older sister for a teacher," Vinny told her with a soft smile. "I learned everything I know from her."

Kim shook her head. "I don't think so. You might have learned some things from me, but you also know things I never taught you. Sometimes you make me feel like I'm the younger of the two of us."

"Well, let's not worry about it, Kimmy. I figure that between the two of us we'll work things out right in the long run. Now, let's get some sleep. A certain, tall, dark haired, blue eyed, very handsome army commander is due here early tomorrow morning, and we wouldn't want to look all bleary eyed from lack of sleep when he gets here, would we?"

"Nope!" Kim replied with a grin.

Kim started to get up but then stopped. She reached out to hug Vinny tightly. "I love you, Sis," she whispered. "And I'm grateful to the gods that you are my sister."

Vinny pushed her away gently and smiled. "Get out of here before I start crying again."

But an hour later Kim was still awake, her mind going over the discussions she'd had with her mother and sister. The fact that Vinny said Jason loved her made Kim feel sure of that fact. She trusted Vinny's judgments and opinions more than those of anyone else in the world. But also knowing that her sister was in love with Jason placed a heavy burden on her own heart. She thought of Vinny's unselfishness and wondered if she would have been able to do the same or feel the same way as Vinny if their roles were reversed.

"No," she said softly to herself. "I would be fighting tooth and nail, using every trick I could think of to win his love away from my sister."

That assessment of her own personality didn't sit well with Kim. Thinking of it nearly caused her to cry out of shame. She told herself that perhaps Vinny was the one who really deserved Jason and his love.

"Lofa," she whispered softly as she stared up at the ceiling of her bedroom, "please make me worthy of his love, and worthy of my sister's love as well."

# FIFTEEN

Sitting on a log as he ate his evening meal, Busker looked at the tent a few yards away. He could see the shadow of Jason moving around inside. After a minute or so the shadow approached the entrance of the tent to become the man. Busker watched Jason step from the tent and stand up straight to look around at the hundreds of campfires dotting the plains and the men gathered around them. Jason finally turned and walked over to join Busker, accepting a plate of food from one of the men. "What do you think, Busker? Are they ready?" Jason asked.

Busker heard the note of concern in Jason's voice. He took a moment to study Jason without seeming to. He saw the worry and strain etched into the face and eyes of the young man who was teaching them how to be soldiers, with the hope of stopping an invasion by two larger, more experienced armies.

But Busker knew it wasn't just concern over the men's training and abilities that was troubling Jason. It was also Jason's own self-doubts as to his abilities as a leader that his commander often secretly questioned.

"Yes, they're ready, Jason," he said at last.

Busker felt the stiff weariness of his own body. But it was a good feeling, as he knew he was in better shape right now than he had ever been in his life. And not just him, but every man here. Jason had not only taught them how to fight with the new swords, their hands and feet, but had pushed them to the limits, and beyond what they had thought was possible, with physical exercises designed to strengthen muscles, increase endurance, and develop quicker reaction times.

Their days started before dawn and didn't end until well after the sun had disappeared from the sky. There had been some complaints at first, and some men had even quit and gone home to their families. But for every one who left, two more came to take his place. They now had over fifty thousand men, and each one of them eagerly hoped to become a part of the force that would drive back and defeat the Karton and Tilwin. Each man gave a hundred percent of his mind and body, knowing he might have to make the ultimate sacrifice before it was over. Busker smiled around his mouthful of food as he thought of how they had come this far.

The day after Jason had outlined his plans for defeating the Karton and Tilwin, he had taken Jarrell and himself into a mid-sized shuttle, flying them from city to city. Jason would land the shuttle somewhere away from the city, and then Busker and Jarrell would ride into town on the tollies they had brought with them. They would inform the Mayors and Guard Commanders of the impending war and the need for men to fight while Jason waited in the shuttle. They would give the Mayors and Guard Commanders of each city the figures for the percentages of men needed from each city, instructions as to where the training camp would be, and then move on to the next city. They never stayed for more than four hours in each.

Jason had suggested using tinted contact lenses to change the color of his eyes, and a dye for his hair and skin so he could go with them, but had been talked out of it. When it was pointed out that the men of Alazon couldn't grow facial or body hair, other than in the pubic regions, which meant Jason would have to shave his face and arms, Kim and the twins had objected to this, begging him not to do it. It had been Vinny who had finally pointed out that no matter what he did, Jason couldn't disguise his height and size. As a result, Jason had agreed to wait in the shuttle while Jarrell and Busker went to talk to the Mayors and Guard Commanders.

Word spread quickly in each of the cities and volunteers began streaming in to sign up. Only the Mayors and Guard Commanders of each city were told the exact location of the training camp, and given maps and directions on how to get there. As soon as each

Guard Commander had his quota, plus a few extra men, they set out for the training side, requisitioning wagons and tollies to make the trip as quickly as they could.

Busker had thought it would be a logistical nightmare to set up facilities for feeding the men and seeing to their sanitary needs, but Jason and Mother had worked that out long before the first men had arrived. Machines that left him speechless had dug latrines treated with chemicals Busker had never heard of. He had stood with the few men of his own Guard to watch Jason use machines to accomplish in a matter of hours tasks that would have taken a hundred men two days to do.

Once a week food from the multitude of farms surrounding each city was delivered to warehouses on the edge of each city. It was then loaded into shuttles under the cover of darkness and flown to the training site. Busker had chuckled at some of the rumors that surrounded the disappearance of the food by the locals that were reaching them.

The iron ore from the mines of Preton was diverted to the training site, as were all old weapons. Once there, a small nuclear fusion furnace had been set up to turn out the molten steels needed to make the swords. Jason had shown the metal workers how to blend the various metals to come up with a lightweight, but incredibly strong sword that held its edge, regardless of what you used it on. An assembly line had been set up to turn out fifty swords a day.

When the men of Preton first arrived they had not been prepared for the type of intensity of training presented to them. Up before dawn, running, exercising, training late into the night, putting their bodies through more physical punishment than they thought they could take.

But the bodies had adapted, and with them the minds. Before long the men began to look forward to the next day, wondering what they would learn next from this strange looking man from another world. A man who never asked them to do anything he wasn't willing and prepared to do himself. A man who taught them with firmness, combined with patience and understanding.

They also stopped complaining when, every night after their training was complete, while the men sat around and talked about the day, Jason would go off by himself and push himself through an hour of rigorous martial arts exercises. He would spend half an hour going through all the katas of Kinjitsu, and then another half hour of Ninjitsu. Some of the men had wanted to watch, amazed and impressed by what they saw, but Ster discouraged them, stating that Jason needed this time alone to help focus his mind, body and spirit for the coming day.

Jason and Busker had also subtly encouraged the sense of competitiveness that had developed between the men of each city. They used it to push the men past the limits of what the men thought they could endure.

Busker finished his meal and set his plate down. He leaned back against the tree behind him as he thought of the weeding out process they had gone through. Some of them men, regardless of their enthusiasm and desire, were simply not cut out to handle a sword. These men had been utilized in other areas. Some had been trained as archers, while others had become phaser and laser weapons handlers.

A friendly rivalry had developed between the groups. Those being trained with the sword prided themselves on being the most like Jason in their abilities, while the archers, most of whom had been hunters all their lives, stated they could kill half a dozen men before a man with a sword could get close enough to kill just one. The archers had quickly adapted to the longer, more powerful bow Jason had introduced to them, discarding their shorter hunting bows for those used in Kyjutsu.

The archer's main source of competition was with the men selected to handle the light energy weapons. Although, Busker admitted to himself, there wasn't all that much training involved for these men. All they had to do was aim, press the firing stud and watch their targets disappear. But they were encouraged to develop a sense of pride in the fact that they were the ones being entrusted with the weapons of light more powerful than anything ever seen on this world before.

The first time Jason had demonstrated the power and effect of a phaser to those who had not seen it back in Lemac, he had used the weapon to turn a house-sized boulder into dust before their eyes. The men had dropped to their knees in fear and awe, thinking he was some sort of god or demon.

Aside from the training with their respective weapons, each man began to learn the unarmed combat tactics of Ninjitsu. Regardless of what a man's weapon specialty might be, he spent at least four hours a day being taught the deadly martial art. As with everything else, some were better than others, quicker to learn the basics and move on to more advance training, but every man there took part.

While waiting for the men to arrive at the training site from the various cities, Jason had taken Busker, Ster, Shon, Hass, and ten others from the Lemac Mayoral Guard up to the <u>Stargazer</u>. He had connected them to the Thought Transference Scanner and given them all the knowledge he himself possessed about Kendo, Kinjitsu and Ninjitsu. He had then spent a week helping them to teach their bodies what their minds now knew. He had explained that by doing it this way it would facilitate the training of the new arrivals by allowing each of them to work with separate groups of men.

It had taken Jason some time to get the men to think of him as just a man, but Busker felt he had finally succeeded. Now they merely thought of Jason as their commander. And the man who would lead them to victory; of that they had no doubts. The men had come to trust Jason in a way that had surprised even Busker. Jason had gained their respect not just with his superior skills as a fighter, but as a man. He was always willing to listen to any problem that any of the men had, or to answer their questions about his own world. His open honesty was something they appreciated, possibly even more than Jason realized.

Busker heard the sound of approaching footsteps. He looked up to see Ster coming toward them. Busker felt a sense of pride in Ster. The young man had risen to the rank of Lieutenant due to his abilities and leadership. In spite of his age, since coming here, Ster had exhibited his natural qualities and leadership abilities time and again. The men trusted him, but more importantly, they respected him. Ster worked harder than anyone else, was quick to help any man who needed it, and wouldn't hesitate to single out and berate any man he thought was slacking off. The young man had also developed a single-minded devotion to Jason that bordered on fanatical. On more than one morning Busker had arisen early to find Ster off to himself practicing his own <u>katas</u> in an effort to improve himself and to become more like Jason.

It was Ster who had begun telling the new arrivals from the other cities of the fight between Jason and the Guard of Lemac, embellishing the story until it sounded as if Jason were some form of fighting demon that no fifty men could beat. He had told them about Baby, and of how the dog had joined the fight beside Jason, but at this some of the men had scoffed, not believing that such a creature existed. Ster had merely grinned. Then, on one of his trips to Lemac for supplies he had made a stop before returning to the camp. When Ster had opened the hatch of the shuttle back at the training area, Baby had streaked through the camp to Jason's side, sending men scattering in fear. Ster had simply strolled out and smiled at those who had disbelieved. Later that night they had all watched as Jason put on a demonstration of Baby's own fighting abilities with the help of Ster, Shon and Hass.

At first the men had been afraid to come anywhere near Baby, but as they saw Jason, Ster and the brothers playing with the huge dog they had gradually overcome their fears. Over the past couple of months Baby had become a welcome sight around the camp. The men took delight in feeding, petting or playing with her as she roamed through the camp at will. After that, the men believed completely, and without question, whatever Ster told them about Jason.

"Excuse me, Commander," Ster said to Jason as he squatted down on his heels a few feet from them, "but I just found out something I thought you would want to know about."

"The men are all planning to desert tonight after I go to sleep?" Jason replied with a grin.

"Well, if they do, I'll be leading the way," Ster replied with a grin of his own. "No, Sir, it's not that. I just found out that one of the men here has a wife who is due to give birth to their first child in about a month."

Jason set down his plate and stood up. "Then what the hell is he doing here?"

Busker could hear the irritation in Jason's voice. Jason had made it clear that there were to be no volunteers who had children under the age of twelve, or who were the only son of a family themselves.

Ster stood up and shrugged his shoulders. "He wanted to join up and fight."

"Where is he?" Jason asked.

Ster jerked his thumb over his right shoulder in the general direction of the main body of troops. "Over there."

Jason turned to a young soldier standing nearby. "Get two tollies. Saddle one and pack the other with enough food to last a man for a week and then bring them to me."

The man saluted by bringing his right fist up across his chest before hurrying away to do as Jason had commanded.

"All right, take me to him," Jason said to Ster.

Busker got up to go with them. As the three of them made their way through the camp men called out and waved to them. Some called for Jason to join them and tell them a story of Earth, which they never tired of hearing, or just to have a cup of teef with them. Jason returned their waves and smiles, but Busker knew his mind was on the young man they were going to see. They finally reached a campfire with a dozen men sitting around it that was no different from the hundreds of others. The men looked up as Jason, Busker and Ster came to a halt.

"Who is he?" Jason asked.

"Donal!" Ster called out, looking across the flames of the fire. "Front and center!"

A young man leaped to his feet and hurried around the fire to stand at rigid attention in front of Jason. Busker studied the face of the young soldier. He was a mere boy who couldn't have been more than eighteen. Busker had to force himself to suppress a smile at the sudden fear in the eyes of the young man. Donal didn't know why he was being singled out by Jason, but he darned not look around at anyone in the crowd of men who were quickly gathering to see what was going on. The young man's eyes bore into the chest of Jason without flinching.

"Donal, Lieutenant Ster informs me that your wife is due to give birth shortly to your first child. Is that true?"

Jason's voice and visage were stern, which only served to make Donal even more nervous than what he already was.

"Yes. . .yes, Sir!" Donal replied nervously.

"Donal, are you hard of hearing, or just plain stupid?" Jason asked.

No one so much as breathed loudly as sweat broke out on Donal's forehead, but to his credit the young man kept his back straight and his hands down at his sides. "I'm not sure what you mean, Commander," Donal replied weakly.

"Then let me explain myself to you in such a way that leaves no room for misunderstanding," Jason told him sternly. "When I asked for volunteers I specifically stated that I did not want any man with children under the age of twelve. Nor did I want those men who were the only sons of their own particular families. Do you remember that direction, Donal?"

"Yes, Commander. But when I volunteered I didn't have any children. In fact, I didn't find out about my wife's condition until just a few days ago."

"Then why didn't you come to me then and tell me?" Jason asked.

"Because I wanted to stay and fight, Commander. I didn't want anything thinking I was a coward. Or that I was using my wife's condition as an excuse to get out of this. Nor did I want all the training you've given me to go to waste, Commander. My wife knew this, which is why she waited until now to tell me."

Busker fought to keep the smile of admiration off his face. He knew by the tone of Donal's voice that the young man was stating exactly what he felt and believed. Busker knew that Jason was also aware of it. He saw Jason's face and manner soften as he looked at the young soldier. There was movement behind them as the soldier sent for the tollies came forward leading the two animals by their reins.

"Lieutenant, is this man a good soldier?" Jason asked.

"Yes, Sir," Ster replied sharply.

"No problem with him following orders?"

"Not since he's been here."

"Good, then he shouldn't have any trouble following this one, should he?"

Ster looked at Donal with a knowing grin. "No, Sir, not a bit."

"Donal," Jason said, turning back to the young man with a smile on his face, "no one here, least of all me, will ever question your courage or dedication. But you are not going to fight against the Tilwin, the Karton, or anyone else if I have anything to do with it, which I do."

Jason paused for a moment before continuing. "What you are going to do is get on this tollie, point its nose in the direction of your expectant wife, and then ride like all the demons of Alazon are on your tail until you are back by her side. She and your child need you much more than I do. Do I make myself clear?"

"But. . .Commander. . ."

"No 'buts', Donal. A man should be with his wife when their children are born. Especially their first child. I'm pretty sure your wife would much rather have you there by her side, giving her comfort, knowing you are safe, and not having to worry about being a young widow with a new infant. Do you understand me?"

Donal looked up at Jason's face for the first time and began to smile. "Yes, Commander, I understand," he said softly.

"Good. Now get on that tollie and get out of here."

The men began to clap and cheer as Donal swung up into the saddle of the tollie and saluted Jason smartly. Then, holding the reins of the second tollie in his hand, Donal rode quickly from the camp, the cheers and shouts of the men following him into the darkness of the night.

While he didn't cheer himself, Busker still smiled. He had moved back somewhat, a look of respect in his eyes as he stared at the back of the tall, dark haired man who had quietly, unassumedly taken over the leadership of the men here. And who had done so in ways he didn't even realize himself.

Busker watched the men around them as Jason made his way back toward his own campfire, seeing the respect for Jason in their eyes. Busker knew these men would follow Jason into the very depths of hell and fight by his side for as long as their arms could hold a sword if he asked it of them. <u>As would I</u>, he told himself.

But despite that, Busker couldn't help but wonder what it was that really drove Jason? He remembered the night about a week ago when

Ster had roused him from sleep, cautioning him to be silent. Ster told him that Jason had left the camp a few minutes ago dressed in his black combat outfit and had flown away in one of the small shuttles. Jason had returned an hour before the men were to be awakened for the day, sneaking back into his own tent. Later, as the men had been preparing for their morning exercised, Busker had crept into Jason's tent. The black combat outfit lay across his sleeping roll. There were bloodstains on it and his sword.

"I bought us some extra time," Jason had said from behind him, scaring Busker half to death. By the time he had turned around, Jason was already walking away. Busker hadn't asked what Jason had meant by that at the time, as he knew it would be useless unless Jason wanted to tell him. It was just one more secret that surrounded Jason.

Jason had told them of his world, of some of the wonderful things there, but in all of his conversations he had never really opened up to any of them. That included Kimmy, whom Busker knew was head over heels in love with this strange, alien man. It seemed as if the only ones Jason allowed to really touch him, to see inside of him where he hurt, were the twins.

For reasons Busker couldn't understand, his youngest niece and nephew had been able to breach the wall Jason hid his emotions and heart behind. They seemed to be able to get inside of Jason to share whatever secrets he kept locked away, and to ease the pain which was so often evident in Jason's eyes, even when he was laughing or smiling.

Over the past few months, Busker felt that he had come to know Jason as well as anyone, but he still didn't really understand the man or what drove him. He had watched Jason struggle to overcome what Jason believed were his own shortcomings while trying to help the other men overcome theirs. Jason pushes himself twice as hard as the men, and it was only when he had a sword in his hands that his complete confidence really came through.

Busker considered Jason an enigma. The man hated war and despised violence of any type, but he could take on a dozen men in a fight and beat them without working up a sweat. And he was preparing them to crush the enemy who was, even now, approaching their shores. Jason spoke of peace in the most fervent of tones while training fifty thousand men to be killing machine such as this world had never known.

The men accepted Jason, as well as his 'miracles' as they had first thought of them, with an ease that had surprised even Busker. The sight of a shuttle no longer caused them to cower in fear or stare in awe. The men even made jokes about, and to, Jason concerning his unusual hair, eye and skin coloring, as well as his size. Jason got back at them by calling them his army of Lilliputians. The first time he had called them that the men hadn't known what he meant, so he had taken the time to tell them the story of Gulliver's Travels.

Busker watched that broad back now as Jason stopped to kneel next to a man who was wrapping new, wet leather strips around the haft of his shiny new katana. Jason showed the man the proper way of doing it so the leather wouldn't slip or slide once it dried.

That was another quality about Jason the men had come to know and respect; his willingness to stop and help them, even going out of his way to do so at times, no matter how trivial, simplistic or mundane it might be. And it was incidents such as his actions tonight in sending Donal home to be with his wife that endeared Jason to the men. Tonight's action would be told and retold until everyone in Preton knew of it. <u>And it will become more than what it really was, as all stories do</u>, Busker thought with a grin. He felt a presence beside him and turned to see Shon looking at Jason.

"Why does he do it?" Shon asked softly.

"Because he's Jason," Busker replied.

Shon grinned at him for a moment. "Now you sound like Kimmy and Vinny. But just who is he, Busker?" Shon asked in a more serious tone. "Who is this man who pushes himself twice as hard as he pushes us? Who has taught us more ways to kill than we ever dreamed of, yet who hates violence with such a passion? Who will hold a child in his lap for hours to point out the beauty of a flower or bird? What demons does he fight at night in his sleep?"

Busker shrugged his shoulders as he and Shon sat down on the log in front of Busker's tent. "I don't know, Shon," he replied with a sigh. "As much as we do know about him, he's still a strange and a mystery to us. I have a feeling that, to some extent, he always will be.

"There are parts of Jason that no one will ever know, with the possible exception of the twins, and I'm not sure that even they will ever know him completely. He holds so much of himself back, hiding behind a wall we can't get through.

"But I do know this," Busker added as he watched Jason move to another group of men, "I trust him as I've never trusted any may before in my life. But if you were to ask me why I couldn't give you any solid reasons for it. I also believe that if Preton is to be saved, Jason is the one who will do it."

"And what becomes of him then?" Shon asked.

Busker shook his head and sighed. "I don't know. I know that he won't be able to simply fade into the background. He will be too conspicuous, too well known to do that, no matter how much he may want to become just another citizen of Lemac, or wherever he settles. He won't be able to. The people won't let him. Nor will the gods of fate."

Neither of them spoke for a moment. They both watched Jason as he laughed and passed a flask of wine to another man. "I feel sorry for him," Shon said as he stood up and walked away.

Busker wondered about that statement from Shon. Why pity? It took him a moment but Busker finally realized what Shon had meant. Jason would forever be placed in a position that would have a direct bearing on the lives and inhabitants of this world. If they won the coming battles, a fact that Busker had no doubts about, Jason would become a king without a title or crown.

"Perhaps," he mumbled to himself as he stood and entered his own tent. "Then again, perhaps he will have them. Who know what thoughts are in the minds of the gods, or what games they play?"

Busker relaxed on his sleeping pallet and pulled his blanket up over himself. As he closed his eyes he thought of the coming battles and how they would forever change fate and the face of Alazon. Changed by the acts of a single man; a stranger from a world those of Alazon had never heard of.

# SIXTEEN

"Jason's coming!"

The excited shout of the twins shattered the relative quiet of the common room where Kim and Vinny were working on new robes for the man whose name had just been screamed out by their younger siblings. Kim had wanted to make Jason some new robes that were a bit more formal than those he currently had and had asked Vinny for help. The two of them had been sewing and talking quietly for over an hour, but the shouted announcement of the twins nearly scared her out of her skin.

The twins bolted from the room, through the kitchen and out the back door. They practically flew across the back yard and nearly tore the gate from its hinges as they raced around the stables, their little faces watching the northern sky expectantly. Kim and Vinny were right behind them. Kim looked at the sky but didn't see the shuttle. Not that it mattered. If the twins said he was coming you could bet your life on it. A moment later a distant speck in the late afternoon sky began to appear from the north. It grew larger as it streaked toward them, causing all four of them to grin. Kim knew her heart wasn't the only one beating excitedly as the white craft rushed at them, finally coming to a soft landing in the open area behind the stable.

Baby was the first one out of the shuttle. The dog bounded towards the twins, but they streaked past her for Jason, leaping up at him as soon as his feet hit the ground. Jason laughed as he caught them in mid air and brought them up to kiss their faces and nuzzle their necks with his mustache; an action that brought shrieks of delight from them. Little attention was paid to Busker, Shon or Hass as they stepped from the shuttle but Kim knew they were used to that by now. She and Vinny stepped forward to hug and kiss the other three men, laughing at Jason and the twins.

They all returned to the house with Jason carrying the twins in his arms. He went to sit on the wide, padded bench along one wall, placing the twins on each of his thighs. Their little hands flashed over the pockets of his jump suit to see if he had brought them anything from the Stargazer. Often, before returning to Lemac, Jason would fly up to the ship and select something for them in the way of candy or a toy. He would hide it somewhere on his body if it were small enough, and then the twins would enjoy the game of searching him to find out where and what it was. But it didn't really matter to the twins if he brought them anything or not. His presence alone was all they actually cared about. The gifts were simply a bonus.

As Kim watched Jason playing with the twins a smile of love for him formed on her face. She could visibly see the tension of his body slowly draining away as it always did when he was with them. A slight pang of jealousy coursed through her. She wished she could have the same effect on him. She turned to look at Busker and her brothers, suddenly aware of their eyes avoiding hers. It was as if they were trying to conceal something from her. She snapped her head back around to Jason, who looked up at her at that moment and smiled. She was about to ask him what was going on when the front door opened and her father entered the house.

"Jason!" Jarrell called cheerfully as he closed the door behind him and quickly crossed the room. "How goes the training?"

"We leave for the east coast tomorrow," Jason replied evenly, his eyes avoiding Kim.

"What?" Kim cried. "I thought you weren't supposed to leave for another week yet?"

"Relax, Muggles," Jason told her as he placed the twins down on either side of him. He stood up and stretched. "I got a report from Mother that the ships of Karton were making better time than anticipated due to some favorable wind conditions. They'll be here two days early. We've had to adjust our plans accordingly."

"Are the men ready?" Jarrell asked as he looked from Jason to Busker and his two sons.

"As ready as they'll ever be," Shon replied.

"That's not what I asked."

Shon looked at his father and nodded. "I know. Yes, Father, they're ready."

As the men all took seats at the large table in the common room, Kim and Vinny hurried into the kitchen. While Vinny prepared cold teef for the others, Kim made iced tea for Jason the way he liked it. She took it to the common room to set on the table in front of him as soon as it was ready. He looked at her and smiled. "Thank you," he told her.

Kim hurried back to the kitchen to help Vinny carry the glasses of teef to the others. "So," her father was saying as she finally sat down beside Jason, "have you formulated your battle plans yet?"

"Pretty much so," Jason replied. "I've had Mother give me aerial photographs of the area where we're projecting the Karton will come ashore. I've made a trip out there myself to check it out, and with Mother's help I've worked out a new time table for their arrival.

"They should get here sometime late at night. That means they will probably plan to camp on the beach for the night, unload their ships the next day, and then go on the march the day after that. They'll head for Kech to attach it from the landward side to catch the city by surprise, and to cut it off from the rest of the country. As far as they know they are completely undetected, so they'll be a little relaxed in their attitude."

Jason nodded at Busker. Busker withdrew a stack of large photos from a folder he had placed on the table and began to spread them out.

"Here," Jason said, pointing to one of the photos. "The way this ridge is situated we have a clear view of the beach for over a quarter of a mile, with open fields of fire down onto it. We'll hit them just before dawn. It's a move they won't be expecting."

"Are you sure they'll come ashore there?" Jarrell asked.

"They have to," Jason replied. "It's the only place that has a natural deep water port in that section of the country, and open beaches. The rest is high cliffs for hundreds of miles north and south. Besides, it's where Mother has projected they'll land and she's never wrong, but don't tell her I said that," he added with a grin.

"Do you think your plan will work?" Jarrell asked nervously.

Jason leaned back in his chair and smiled at her father. "A piece of cake," he replied confidently.

Jarrell's brows furrowed slightly. "Jason, I'm afraid I'm not quite familiar with all your Earth quips. What, exactly, does that mean?"

"It means it will work," Liet said as she came into the room.

As they talked through super, Kim hung onto Jason's every word. She rushed back and forth from the kitchen to the common room, not wanting to leave his side for a moment longer than necessary. They were just starting to relax after supper when a soft knock at the front door halted all conversation. They all glanced at one another for a moment, wondering who could be calling at this late hour. Busker finally got up to answer the door. He returned moments later with one of the most beautiful women in all of Preton.

She was a shade taller than most women, but that wasn't the only thing that set her apart. Her face and figure were those other women would kill for, yet she appeared to be totally unconscious of her looks. She wore no make-up of any kind, as the texture and color of her skin glowed with a natural radiance no make-up could duplicate or match. She wore a simple long robe of white that was tied at the waist with a blood red sash. The only ornament of jewelry she wore was a small gold pendant in the shape of a human heart. It was about three inches high and suspended from a thin gold chain around her neck. It was her emblem of office as the High Priestess of the Temple of Lofa.

Jarrell quickly arose from his seat with a warm smile and held out his hands. "Seta, what brings you to our home this evening? Not," he quickly added, "that you are not always welcome at any time."

"How are you, Jarrell?" she replied with a smile. Her voice was husky, with an almost musical quality to it.

"Fine, just fine. You know everyone here," Jarrell said, turning to indicate the others at the table.

"Yes, although the last time I saw your guest," Seta said as she sat down in the offered chair, "he was nearly dead. I'm happy to see that he has recovered quite well."

"I'm afraid you have me at a disadvantage, Priestess," Jason said politely. "You know me, but I know you only by what I have heard. And I must admit that what I have heard does not compare with what I now see before me. I hope you will forgive me if I do not recall your last visit."

Seta smiled warmly at his compliment. "Thank you, and yes, I forgive you completely. I am Seta, High Priestess of the Temple of Lofa here in Lemac."

"I am pleased to meet you," Jason replied.

Kim felt a surge of jealousy starting to rise as she watched the interplay between Jason and Seta. Her eyes were smoldering at the way he was looking at the High Priestess. Seta was older than Kim, and more mature. Despite her own beauty, Kim had always felt self-conscious about her looks when the High Priestess was around. She glanced at Jason. He glanced at her briefly and grinned. It was almost as if he could see her discomfort and was amused by her sudden rush of insecurity. The look he gave Kim only served to embarrass and infuriate her even more.

<u>How dare he play with me like this!</u> Kim thought hotly. <u>Everyone in this room, including Seta, knows I'm in love with him, and he's flirting with the High Priestess of Lofa right in front of me!</u>

"Jarrell, Jason," Seta said, her voice and demeanor becoming serious, "I have come here this evening on matters which pertain to you both."

Kim saw a look of nervous tension suddenly fill the eyes of her father. "In what way?" Jarrell asked.

Kim felt suddenly confused as her father and Seta looked at one another for a long moment. Neither of them spoke. They appeared to be linked in the same type of telepathic communication the twins shared with one another.

"I must speak to the two of you alone on matters which are of concern to us all," Seta said at last. "Matters of concern to all of Preton. Perhaps to all of Alazon as well. Will you please return to the Temple with me?"

Seta had phrased her request in the form of a polite question, but Kim knew the High Priestess well enough to detect the unspoken order in those words. Kim had heard that tone used many times over the years during her own studies at the temple.

Kim saw Jason look at her father. She knew Jason was feeling the same sense of confusion about what was going on that she was. But most surprising of all was that her father had become extremely nervous. Jarrell glanced around the table at the others before finally turning back to Seta. "Yes," he said softly, "if you feel it is important. Jason?"

Kim didn't like this. Something was going on that none of them but Seta and her father seemed to know anything about. Her father's sudden attitude frightened her.

"Of course," Jason said as he stood up. "Although I really don't understand what it is that would concern me?"

"You will see," Seta replied with a small smile at him.

"I'll come with you," Kim said as she started to rise from her seat.

She was stopped by Seta's right hand coming to rest lightly on her shoulder. "No, Kimella. This is only for your father and Jason."

Seta had spoken softly, and with a smile, but Kim again heard the underlying steel in the voice of the High Priestess. Her tone made it clear that no one else was to accompany them back to the temple. Kim tried to keep the look of dejection off her face as she sat back down.

Kim watched her father, Jason and Seta head for the front door. As soon as they were outside she stood and walked calmly to her bedroom upstairs. Closing the door behind her she quickly stripped off her robe and donned a dark blue jump suit and boots. The then used a dark scarf to wrap her hair in.

"Where are you going?" Vinny whispered from behind her.

Kim whirled around to face her sister, who was standing just inside the closed bedroom door. "Where do you think? I've got to find out what's going on."

"That may not be such a good idea, Kimmy. If Seta says it's important, then it must be. Especially from the way dad was acting. It might not be a good idea for you to go prying. You could get into trouble."

"Like that would be a first," Kim quipped. "But what about Jason?" she hissed. "Why would Seta want to see him just before he goes off into battle? Something strange is going on, Vinny, and I've got to find out what it is."

Vinny looked at her for a couple of seconds before finally nodding her head in agreement. "Okay, but how are you going to get out of the house? You know Mom and the others won't let you leave. Especially if they know what you're up to."

Kim grinned. "Remember how we used to sneak out at night when we were kids?"

"Sure. Out your bedroom window, climb down the trellis to the wall, and drop down to the other side," Vinny replied with a soft giggle.

"Will you cover for me?"

"Haven't I always? Come on."

Vinny went to the window and opened the shutters wide; looking out to make sure no one was down in the courtyard. She motioned for Kim. Kim climbed up onto the sill, leaning out to where she could grab hold of the trellis. She swung her weight around and climbed down to the top of the wall that surrounded the courtyard. She turned so that he was lying across the wall with her feet hanging down and slowly worked her way down until she was hanging just by her fingertips. Kicking away from the wall slightly, she released her grip and dropped to the ground, landing easily and going into a roll to cushion her fall. Getting to her feet, she took off at a dead run for the temple.

Kim knew that Seta, Jason and her father would go by the main streets, so Kim took a short cut she knew, darting down alleys and cutting across yards. She wanted to get to the temple before they did. Three blocks from the temple she spotted them on the adjoining street. With a grin she raced around a corner and down another alley, finally skidding to a halt at the back of the temple. She found the hidden door she had discovered as a young girl and entered the temple unseen. She made her way down the dark passageway to another door that opened onto the main chamber of the temple itself. Seeing no one around, she darted to a spot behind a large statue of Lofa where she could see the entire room, but still remain unseen herself.

Only seconds after Kim had settled into her place of concealment she heard the sound of footsteps coming from the other end of the chamber. She watched as Seta, Jason and Jarrell entered. Jason and her father followed Seta to a beautifully painted wall where Seta did something totally unexpected. Reaching out with her left hand, Seta pressed a finger against the right eye of a large styra painted on the wall. There was a faint click and the wall began to move, swinging inward a few inches. Seta pushed on it to reveal a large opening, then indicated that Jason and Jarrell were to follow her.

As the three of them disappeared into the opening, Kim darted out from behind the statue and rushed over to the opening. She looked at the stairway cut into the rock beneath the temple and saw the back of her father's head disappearing around a bend. Kim stepped inside the opening, and with a silent prayer of forgiveness to the goddess of temple, she began to make her way slowly and cautiously down the darkened steps.

Seta had lit a torch to aid herself, Jason and Jarrell, and there was just enough light from it reflected off the walls for Kim to make out the steps, which seemed to go on forever as they curved around the wall. As a very inquisitive child, Kim had roamed and combed every inch of the temple over the years, which is how she had found the hidden entrance in the back, but had no idea this cavern existed. She suspected that very few people did.

The light ahead of her disappeared for a moment and Kim realized she had reached the last bend in the steps. She knelt down on the bottom step and peeked around the corner to see what was going on. She saw Seta standing on one side of a large stone table. Jason and her father faced the Priestess from the other side. Seta used the torch to light other torches at either end of the table to further illuminate the room. From the light they provided, Kim saw hundred of scrolls in slotted shelves of wood lining the walls. They appeared to be older than anything she knew of.

Kim knew the temples of Lofa had been around for as long as anyone could remember, and that they were not only religious temples, but hospitals and schools as well. The women who worked in them dedicated their lives to the temple, and those women who attained the rank of High Priestess were also the historians of the people of Alazon.

Kim suddenly remembered a conversation she had once had with Jason in which he told her that this planet, her world and its people, were something of a mystery. He told her that there were too many unanswered questions about their past. When she had asked what he meant by that, he had told her about the abandoned cities on Alazon in the southern hemisphere that were older than any of the other inhabited cities on Alazon.

Kim couldn't explain them to him. In fact, until he had mentioned them to her, she hadn't even known of their existence. Nor could she explain why the people lived almost exclusively in what he called the Temperate Zone of their planet. Or why their history went back only a little over three thousand years.

She had heard him discuss these things with her father, but even her father hadn't been able to answer Jason's questions. Jason had finally given up, but Kim knew he was only waiting until he could dig in and devote his time to it. Then he would come up with the answers he wanted. She did remember her father once making a slightly oblique hint that there was more to the history of Alazon and its people than what met the eye. Perhaps this hidden chamber beneath the temple held the clues she thought as she strained to hear what Seta was saying.

"The Temple of Lofa holds many secrets, Jason. Secrets the people know nothing of. Secrets not to be revealed until the proper time.

"Due to our positions, both Jarrell and I have been entrusted with some of these secrets concerning the past of the people of this world. As has each High Priestess and Senior Mayor since time began for us."

Kim saw her father glance nervously at Jason and nod his head slightly in agreement with what Seta was saying.

"While I know most of Jarrell's secrets," Seta continued, "he knows only a few of mine." Seta turned to Jarrell, her eyes boring directly into his. "What do you know of the Prophecy?" she asked.

Kim saw her father nervously lick his lips before he answered. "Very little. Only that a man, a stranger, would come to us at a time when our world would be engulfed in strife, and that this man would lead us out of that strife, restoring peace to all of Alazon such as we have never known before."

"What else?"

"That he would be a man who is. . .different from us." Jarrell replied. His voice was so low that Kim could just barely make out what he was saying. "And that he would come from the stars beyond what we could see in the night sky."

Kim felt the blood pounding in her temples at her father's words. What he was saying sounded much like the religions and myths Jason had told her of which had abounded back on Earth. Ones that spoke of a Messiah who would come and bring peace to the world just as it was on the brink of disaster. She looked at Jason. By his grim features she could tell he didn't want to be here listening to this.

Seta turned and withdrew a scroll from those behind her. Turning back to the table she motioned for Jarrell to help her unroll it. They used small, square cut polished stones to hold down the corners of it. As her father took a look at it he suddenly gasped and stepped back. "By all the gods!" he exclaimed, staring at the scroll as if it contained a Death Plant.

Kim watched Jason step forward and look down at the scroll. His own face registered shock as he looked back up at Seta. "That's me!" he exclaimed.

"Yes, it could be," Seta replied as Jason stepped back a pace. "But there are a few slight differences that could also make it someone who just happens to look like you."

Jason looked down at the scroll again. Kim wished she could see it, but she dared not move to try and get a better view and give her presence away.

"Where did this come from?" Jason asked.

"Where?" Seta replied. "I can't tell you where it came from originally, or even how old it is. All I can tell you is that it was entrusted to me, as it has been to each High Priestess of the main temple here in Lemac since the beginning of our memories. As were all of these," Seta added, lifting her hand to indicate the other scrolls.

Jason looked around for a moment and then shook his head. "Something's not right here," he said thoughtfully. "Why would you have a painting of a man who bears a very strong resemblance to me, when all of you have the same genetic traits that keep you looking so much alike?"

"You know of the Royac?" asked Seta.

Kim had to bite her lip to keep from gasping at Seta's question. Jason had told her and her family of the planet of that race which had mysteriously vanished, but she knew no one had said anything about them to Seta. How could the High Priestess know of them? She saw Jason's own surprise at Seta's question.

"I do," he said softly after a moment, "but how do you?"

"They are the originators of our race," Seta replied.

Jason turned away from the table and paced slowly around the underground chamber. The fingers of his right hand reached out to lightly touch the scrolls in their slots.

"Okay," he said as he finally turned back to Jarrell and Seta, "let's assume for a moment that your ancestors came from Royac and that you're descendants of that race. On the one hand, knowing what I do about them, I could believe that, but on the other hand I find it a bit hard to accept."

"Why would you find it hard to accept, Jason?" the High Priestess asked.

"Because I've seen the paintings and pictures of the Royac, as well as the planet of genetic clones they created. Aside from the fact that you're both human, there are really very few similarities. The Royac were a tall race, with various colors of hair and eyes, none of which are your own particular colors, and they were a much more scientifically advanced race than what your people are."

"In a sense you are right, but you are also wrong," Seta told him, speaking patiently. "The paintings you saw on the walls of the Great Hall were what they saw as physical perfection. The original Royac were exactly as you are, but they were unsatisfied with their physical selves, so they began cloning and genetic engineering to try and come up with what they believed was the perfect human form. However, they ran into some problems.

"First, cloning takes a long time to complete. Second, many of them went mad when their brains were transferred from their original bodies into the bodies of the clones. As a result, genetic engineering became the focal point of their efforts to obtain what they considered the perfect form.

"We, the people of Alazon, are just one of a dozen different races developed by them. We are little more than a living monument to what they had achieved with their science."

Even in the dim light of the torches, Kim watched Jason turn pale as Seta spoke. "How do you know about all of that?" Jason asked in a hushed voice, as if in

disbelief of what he had heard.

"It's all here in the scrolls," Seta told him. "Someday you will have the time to go through and read them. When you do, many of your questions concerning the Royac and us will be answered. There is even information in them about all the worlds they touched, including your own Earth."

"This is crazy," Jason mumbled, sitting down on a stone bench carved into the wall. "Just what is it that you're trying to tell me, Seta?"

"That you are of the true race, Jason. You are a descendant of the Royac while we, the people of Alazon, are the result of an experiment. We were born in a laboratory on Royac. We were given certain genetic safeguards to protect us, as well as to prevent us from remembering our past or learning certain things. Only a select few of us have been entrusted with the truth of our creation."

"How were they selected?" Jason asked.

Seta's hands raised slightly, palms up, as if to indicate the building above them. "By the establishment of the Temples of Lofa. The High Priestess of each temple is instructed and taught by the one before her, taking a blood oath to never reveal what she knows until the proper time.

"Should a High Priestess of a temple die before she has had the time or chance to select and properly instruct her replacement, then the High Priestess of another temple will do so. It is in this way that our secrets have been kept."

Kim saw Jason shake his head in confusion at what he was hearing. "Why are you telling me this now?" he asked. "Surely you don't believe that I'm your so-called savior?"

"I had to tell you now in order to warn you to protect yourself at all costs in the coming battles. You see, you are the key that will allow us to progress past where we are now."

Jason sighed and threw up his hands. "Now you've lost me," he told Seta.

"Jason," Seta said patiently, "except for the first few hundred years of our existence, our world, our society, is the same as it has been for the past three thousand. We have not regressed, but neither have we shown the progress we should have. We are static, but just don't realize it.

"And as for why I'm telling you? I thought you would have guessed by now. The writings tell of a time when a descendant of the Royac will return to our world and lead us into a new era.

"We are not an ignorant race, Jason, but all that we know now is practically the same as we knew three thousand years ago. We've made some minor changes and adaptations, but nothing of any real significance. Only alterations of what we already knew. We have the capacity to learn, to change and grow in knowledge, but it takes the key to help us unlock our minds and show us the way. You are that key, Jason."

"If what you're saying is true," Jason replied, sounding tired and weary, "and that you all contain a genetic alteration which prevents you from advancing past where you are now, then how can I help? Oh, I suppose that with Mother's help I could find a way to reverse it, but my god, for only a few, not the entire population of a planet!"

Seta shook her head and smiled. "You don't have to do anything as drastic as that, Jason," she told him. "All you have to do is be yourself. Lead us, teach us, show us new ways, and we will begin to overcome this blockage ourselves in a relatively short time."

"That's it?" Jason asked.

Kim saw the look in the eyes of Seta and knew there was something more to it than just that. She also had a feeling it would be something Jason wouldn't like.

"Basically, yes," the High Priestess replied. "But to do it you are going to have to be placed in a position from with it will all be possible."

"What's so difficult about that?" Jason asked. "Once this war is over I can begin working with your people and then things should start to get better."

Seta shook her head slowly. "I don't think you understand yet," she told him.

Jason turned to Jarrell, who had remained silent during all of this. "Do you know what she's talking about?"

"I. . .yes," Jarrell replied, his eyes unable to meet those of Jason.

Kim was suddenly filled with foreboding, as if Seta's next words were going to bring an edict that would be more than even Jason could accept. She watched with her heart pounding in her chest as Seta rolled up the scroll and replaced it in the rack with the others.

Seta then opened a concealed panel in the side of the table and removed an ornately carved wooden box. She held it almost tenderly in her hands as she placed it on the table in front of her. Removing her emblem of office from around her neck, she pressed it into a matching depression on the side of the box. There was a soft click and the lid opened slightly. Seta replaced her medallion and lifted the lid the rest of the way.

"This is yours," Seta said to Jason, her voice a mere whisper as she withdrew a crown of pure gold inlaid with rubies and diamonds, placing it gently on the table. "You must take it and wear it, for that is the only way you will be able to truly help us."

Kim saw Jason step back from the table as if the crown were a venomous snake about to strike. He held his right hand out before him as if trying to ward off the flashes of light that leaped from the stones in the crown.

<u>Oh, Lofa, No!</u> Kim screamed in her mind. She knew how Jason felt about such things and kings and men in position of ultimate power. Didn't her father and Seta realize they were doing the worst possible thing they could to try and gain his help? Didn't they have enough sense to know they could drive him away from their world completely if they pursued this course? When Jason spoke again, his voice was tinged with anger.

"Seta, I don't know what you and Jarrell are up to, or what you hope to accomplish, but what you're suggesting is impossible. Not just for me personally, but for the people as well. There hasn't been a king in Preton for over five hundred years. What makes you think they'll accept one now? And especially one as different from them as I am!"

"You might be surprised at what they will accept," Seta told him. Despite the angry outburst from Jason, Seta's composure was not the least bit shaken. "Especially if it is backed by the Temple of Lofa."

"No!" Jason protested vehemently. "I didn't come to this world to be a king, or any other type of ruler. I just want to be a man like any other. To love and be loved, to have children and watch them grow. To. . ."

"STOP IT!" Kim screamed as she leaped into the light, causing all of them to stare at her in shocked surprise. "You can't do this to him! Don't you see that?" she begged.

"It's the only way," Seta replied softly.

"No, it's not!" Kim snapped. She turned angrily to her father. "Daddy, do you want a king to rule over you? You have always told us that you were against anything that even remotely resembled that type of leadership our whole lives! Are you now willing to throw it all away over some stupid legend or prophecy?"

Her father looked at her and Kim saw him as she had never seen him before. He seemed defeated, crushed by events too weighty for him to bear. "No," he replied, his voice barely audible.

"Then help me convince Seta that this is crazy!"

"I can't, Kimmy. I'm sorry."

Kim was stunned! She stepped closer to her father and saw the battle and torment filling his eyes. "Why?" she asked softly.

"Because, like Seta, there have been things passed on to me which foretold the coming of Jason. Things that said that for our people to survive we would have to make him our king. That it was the only way to remove us from this state of helplessness we have been in for too long."

Jarrell turned away from Kim to face Jason. "Why do you think I was able to accept you into my home as easily as I did? Or accept your appearance here on our world? It was because of the prophecy."

"I won't do it," Jason told them with a shake of his head. "I'll help you fight this war, and afterwards I'll do all I can to help your people, but I'll do it as a common man, not as a king. Not now, not ever as a king!"

"The prophecy. . ." Seta began.

"I don't give a damn about your prophecy!" Jason snapped, his voice reverberating off the walls of the underground chamber. "It's just a bunch of superstitious crap! I'm not a king, or any damn messiah, and I'm not going to let you make one out of me!"

Seta stepped out from behind the table. "You don't have a choice," she told Jason. "It's the only way."

"Then I'll find another," he growled through clenched teeth. He turned from Seta to glare at Kim. "Did you know about this?" he asked, his tone harsh and demanding.

'No! Jason, I swear I didn't!"

"Jason," Seta said, holding the crown out to him.

Jason's arm flashed out and the crow was sent flying from Seta's hands to crash against the far wall before falling to the floor. Jason turned and headed for the stairs, charging up them blindly.

Kim watched him go, her heart breaking into a thousand pieces with each step he took. She whirled around to face her father and Seta. "How could you do this?" she demanded. "You did the one thing guaranteed to drive him away from us! You're both a couple of superstitious fools!"

Kim turned and bolted for the stairs, taking them two at a time. She had a good idea where Jason was headed. If she ran as she had never run before in her life she might be able to get to the shuttle before he did. She knew he would return by the same route he had taken to get to the temple, not knowing the short cuts she did.

Her heart was hammering in her chest as she sprinted through the main chamber of the temple and down the front steps, racing toward the alley. A few blocks away she darted through a yard and hurdled a small fence, praying she would be in time.

Kim ran between two houses and emerged into the clearing that separated the city from the woods. She was less than fifty yards from the shuttle. She saw Jason come from her back courtyard and walk quickly toward the craft parked next to the stable. With her last ounce of strength she sprinted toward the open hatch, diving in headfirst just as it was about to close, coming to a painful stop against the far bulkhead.

Jason looked at her but didn't say a word as she got up and took the seat next to him. His fingers moved over the controls and seconds later they were streaking away. Neither of them spoke during the flight, or even when he brought the craft to a rough landing inside the shuttle bay. Jason killed the engine and unfastened his harness straps, letting his head fall forward on his arms as the strength seemed to drain from his body.

Kim reached over and placed her left hand gently on his right arm. He raised his head and looked at her blankly, as if he didn't know who she was. She took his hand and led him from the shuttle. He followed along docilely. It was as if his mind were reeling from the events below. Kim led him to the bridge and sat him in the captain's seat. She kissed his cheek softly and then left. Going to the mess deck she fixed a pot of black coffee and carried it back to him, placing it on the console next to his seat. Looking at Jason she saw the blank expression on his face and in his eyes as he stared out at the stars. "I'll be in your cabin when you're ready to talk," she told him softly, fighting back the tears that threatened to come from her eyes.

Kim walked to the door. She stopped for a moment to take a last look at him before going to his cabin. Once inside the cabin she collapsed on the bed. She felt more tired than she had ever been in her life, both physically and emotionally. She lay back and closed her eyes to try and sort out her thoughts and emotions. A few seconds later she heard a soft click. It took her a moment to realize the com channel had been activated. She waited, wondering why Jason wasn't saying anything.

"Want to talk?" Mother asked.

Kim started to answer but some instinct told her that Mother was talking to Jason, not her, but was allowing her to listen in.

"Not really," she heard Jason reply.

"Okay."

There was silence for nearly half a minute before she heard Jason speak again. "What's up, Mother?" he asked. "You gave in too easily."

"Nothing's up, Jason. It's just that I know when you're upset about something, and that you'll talk about it when you're ready."

"No quips? No catty remarks?"

This time it was the computer's turn to hesitate before speaking. When it did there was a tone to the voice that Kim had never heard before. It was filled with concern and caring. Much more that Kim would have thought possible for a machine, even a computer such as Mother.

"Jason, as you like to point out from time to time, I am merely a computer. But I am one that is, as we both know, capable of some limited emotional responses. So, despite what you may think at times, I am usually aware of your moods and feelings, and I have the ability to respond to them in an appropriate manner when need be. Such as now. I know that something is bothering you, that something has you pretty upset, and that you'll discuss it with me when you're ready."

"You know, Mother," Kim heard Jason say after a moment, "for a computer, you're a pretty smart lady. Too bad you aren't a real woman. If you were I just might give you a hug about now for being so understanding."

"I'll keep that in mind," Mother told him with a short laugh. "Now, do you want to tell me what's got you so upset, not to mention Kimmy?"

"What's wrong with Kim?" she heard him ask quickly. The note of concern for her in his voice made Kim's heart beat a little faster.

"Boy, you really are out of it," Mother told him. "What do you think is wrong with her, Jason? Kim is upset because she knows you're upset, and you're shutting her out. She loves you, you knucklehead, although, for the life of me I'm not sure why."

"To be honest, Mother, neither am I," Kim heard him reply softly. "All right, listen to this and then tell me what you think."

"Okay."

"It would seem that things below are not exactly as they would appear to be."

"They seldom are, Jason, but tell me what you mean."

"The people of Alazon are another of the Royac's genetic engineering experiments."

"I had sort of figured that out already, but I wanted to collect some more data before I could be sure," Mother told him.

"Yeah, well, some of the people down there have this deep dark secret prophecy concerning a Messiah who will come to them from beyond the stars to save them in their time of gloom and doom."

"Uh, huh, and they think you're the one, right?"

"You got it. Not only do they think it, they also have a three thousand old portrait painting that looks almost exactly like me to reinforce their beliefs."

"I see."

"No, you don't," Jason replied softly. "Tonight Seta and Jarrell took me to a secret cavern beneath the temple to show me a few things they've been hiding."

"Such as?"

"Oh, the painting I mentioned, and a crown they want to place on my head to make me King of Preton."

"Hum, now I see why you're so upset. Well, Blue Eyes," Mother told him with a slight chuckle in her voice, "we got a problem here, and lots to talk about, so you may as well get comfy because this could be a long night."

# SEVENTEEN

Jason crept forward slowly until he reached the edge of the cliff. He removed the binoculars from the pocket on the right leg of his jumpsuit and focused them on the far horizon. He touched a small button on the top casing and the ships of Karton leaped into clear view. Inside the lens a digital readout gave the distance of the ships approaching from the east.

Jason had arrived yesterday with half his total force to make the final preparations for the attack on the army of Karton. The men had been transported by shuttles, and once they arrived, he made them all go over the plans, the assignment of each unit, each man, until they could do it in their sleep.

"How far?" Busker asked from his right.

"Just over ten miles."

"Then they'll be here soon."

"I don't think so. The wind's died on them and they're sitting dead in the water. The way things stand now they won't get her till around midnight. Add another two hours or so for off-loading men and equipment, another two for setting up camp, and then they'll bed down for the night."

"You really think they'll stay here tonight?"

"Yeah," Jason replied as he watched the ships. "They have no idea we're here waiting for them. They're expecting to just walk in and take over, with only token resistance from the civilians. Because it will be so late by the time they arrive, their arrogance, combined with being tired of being cramped for so long in their ships, they'll feel perfectly safe in camping right out on the beach tonight."

"And that will be their undoing," Busker said grimly.

"Let's hope so. Come on, let's get back."

The two of them moved back away from the cliff for a few yards before standing up to make their way back down the slope to where the rest of the men waited.

"If you want a hot meal," Jason told his squad and unit commanders, "then you better get it now. I want all fires extinguished within an hour. After that, if I so much as see an ember glowing, the man closest to it will be forced to eat it. Then I want everyone to get some sleep. We'll be up early." As the others walked away, Jason turned to Busker and saw the grin on the face of the older man. "What's so funny?" he asked.

"You know that not a single one of them believed your comment about making a man eat an ember, don't you?"

Jason grinned and nodded. Yeah, but I had to get the point across. We have to make sure the Karton have no idea we're here. Surprise is going to be our biggest ally. It's important that we maintain that factor."

Jason watched men moving quickly to prepare their last hot meal for who knew how long. He knew it would be the last one ever for some of the, although no one bothered to voice that particular thought.

He and Busker joined Hass and Shon in front of Jason's tent. They quickly prepared their food and ate in silence, as had become a custom with them. It wasn't that they didn't have anything to say to one another, but cherished the few moments of silence they shared together at meal times.

Once the meal was over they continued to sit for a while, each of them thinking about tomorrow and what it would bring. Jason finally broke the silence when he stood and motioned for Busker and the brothers to follow him. He led them to the small shuttle, waiting until they were all inside before closing the hatch. As they looked at one another curiously, wondering what he was up to, Jason sat down and his left hand touched the com-link. "Mother?"

"Here," replied the computer.

"Did you take care of that for me?"

"Yes."

He looked at the others. "Read it back to me. Word for word."

There was a moment of silence with Busker and the brothers looking at one another before the voice of Mother came clearly from the speakers.

"'In the event of my death it is hereby ordered and decreed that full control of the ship known as the Stargazer, and all facilities therein, shall become the property and responsibility of the House of Vehey and all of its members, which shall include Busker Loft.

"'The computer entity known as Mother is to obey and carry out the express orders of the House of Vehey, which is headed by Jarrell Vehey, with successive responsibility falling to the other members according to age and rank within the family. It shall be the responsibility of the computer entity known as Mother to disclose to them all knowledge and information contained within the ship, as well as how to use and utilize it.

"'Should the House of Vehey ever cease to exist, as well as the line of descendants which may issue from the life of Busker Loft, then the computer entity known as Mother shall take the Stargazer into deep space and destroy said ship and computer entity.

"'However, as long as the line of either House exists, the computer entity known as Mother is to do everything within its abilities to assist not just those two Houses, but all the inhabitants of Alazon in the lifting of their cultural, scientific and educational advancements, and to protect them from any and all forces which may appear from any source which would do them harm.

"'This by the order of Jason Michael Stephens, last survivor of the Lunar Colony of New Hope One, last survivor of the world known as Earth, and commander of the Stargazer.'"

Mother's voice stopped. In the confines of the small shuttle Busker, Shon and Hass looked at one another in stunned silence.

"What, in the name of all the gods, was that?" Hass finally demanded, breaking the silence.

"What did it sound like?" Jason replied calmly.

"Damn you, Jason, we know what it sounded like but what we want to know is, why?"

"Isn't it rather obvious?"

"Stop answering my questions with questions," Hass exclaimed in frustration.

Jason laughed lightly at the younger brother. "Look, Hass, this is just a safety precaution I set up in case something happened to me. Not, mind you, that I intend to go out there tomorrow and get myself killed."

"Let's hope not," Busker said dryly.

"I agree," added Hass. "I know a few individuals who would be very upset if that were to happen. Like a particular set of twins, not to mention a certain older sister."

"Just one sister?" said Shon, raising his eyebrows slightly as he looked at his brother.

"Good point," Hass replied. "Jason, you should know that Kim told us that if anything happened to you, Hass and I could never show our faces at home again."

"She didn't really mean that."

"Yes," Shon replied softly, "she did."

Busker got up and went to a small storage area in the rear of the shuttle. He opened one of the lockers and removed something from it. Returning to the front, he tossed a small, rolled up bundle of black to Jason. "You wear that tomorrow," he said flatly as he sat back down.

Jason looked at the rolled up combat outfit and boots, then back at Busker. "I can't do that, Busker," he said with a shake of his head. "I have to go out there dressed the same as everyone else."

"Says who?" the older man asked.

"Me."

Busker's hand slipped inside his tunic. When it emerged he was holding a stunner. He pointed it directly at Jason's chest.

"Not good enough," Busker told him. "We can't afford to have you get hurt, maybe even killed, so either you give us your word here and now that you'll wear it, or I'll stun you and we'll put the damn suit on your ourselves. You wear it, or you don't go into battle. It's as simple as that."

Jason looked at Busker and the brothers and saw the resolve and determination on their faces. He knew Busker meant exactly what he said.

"The twins made us promise," Shon told him.

"Well, I guess it would provide something of a psychological advantage over the Karton," Jason said with a shake of his head.

"Good," Busker said as he stood up and put the stunner away. "Now that we got that settled, come with us."

Busker opened the hatch and stepped out. Jason looked at the brothers and shrugged as the three of them followed the older man. Busker led them to his tent where Ster was waiting for them. As soon as they stopped in front of the tent, Ster ducked inside. He returned almost immediately with a carved wooden box in his hands. The box was smaller than the one the crown had been in, so Jason knew it couldn't be that, but he still felt a sense of nervousness. He started to ask Busker what was going on, but Busker shook his head to silence him. A small crowd started growing, quickly becoming a large one. After nearly a full minute of making Jason wait, Busker finally cleared his throat and began.

"Jason, as you know, as we all know, you originally declined to accept the position of Commander of the Army of Preton. You stated that position and title should go to me. However, in a meeting of all the Mayors of Preton, and in a similar meeting of all Guard Commanders, it was unanimously decided that there is only one man qualified to hold that position. That is the man who first warned us of the invasion, and then trained us to fight against those who would invade us."

Jason felt a knot forming in his stomach. He knew what was coming. He also knew there was no way he could avoid it without creating a scene and offending the men. He was caught, with nowhere to run or hide.

Shon stepped forward to take the box from Ster, holding it so Busker could raise the lid. The older man reached inside and withdrew a heavy gold link chain. To it was affixed a gold medallion about four inches in diameter. It was in a starburst pattern, with a single ruby of at least ten carats set into the center. Holding the chain in his hands, Busker turned to face Jason.

"By a unanimous vote of the Council of Mayors, with a similar vote by the combined Guard Commanders, I am hereby authorized to present you with the symbol of the Commander of the Army of Preton. A title which has never been held by any man before."

Busker stepped forward and slipped the chain over Jason's head. His hands moved down the links to the starburst to place it in the center of Jason's chest. Busker then turned back to the box and withdrew another medallion. It was identical to the one on the chain, but only about half the size. As Busker turned back to face him, Jason saw that this medallion had a clasp pin on the back of it. Busker affixed the smaller medallion to the throat clasp of Jason's cloak, then stepped back and snapped to attention. The others around them quickly followed suit as Busker saluted Jason by bringing his clenched right fist up across his chest. Busker's face broke into a wide grin.

"See, you aren't the only one with a surprise up his sleeve this evening," Busker said just loud enough for Jason and the brothers to hear as the men around them began to cheer.

"So I see," Jason replied with a lop-sided grin, feeling somewhat foolish by it all. "All right," he said, holding his hands up for silence, his voice becoming stern as he raised it, "my first official order as Commander of the Army of Preton is that everyone finish eating and then get some sleep. We'll be up two hours before dawn to get into position. And that's going to come a lot earlier than you think. Hit it!"

As the men hurried to finish their meals and extinguish their fires before bedding down for the night, Jason looked at Busker and shook his head as the older man turned away and entered his tent.

Jason headed for his own tent. As he approached it a young boy, one of the many camp followers accompanying the men, jumped up from the small log he was sitting on. The boy pulled back the flap of the tent, his little eyes nearly popping out of their sockets at the sight of the medallions. Jason smiled at the boy and entered the tent to sit on his cot. He removed his cloak and placed it on the cot beside him before removing the chain from around his neck. Holding both medallions in his hands, Jason stared down at them in the soft light of the lamp burning on a small stool a few feet away. As his fingers traced lightly across the patterns he shook his head. He knew the cost of gold, or mikal as they called it here, and knew he held a small fortune in his hands.

"Two small fortunes," he told himself softly as the rubies seemed to wink up at him in the flickering light. He could only shake his head and grin at the way he had fallen into their trap. "Jarrell, you old fox," he said to himself as he blew out the lamp and lay down.

But sleep did not come quickly or easily. His mind, like a holo projector, played back the events of the past seven months of his life for him to keep him awake.

As the men had arrived at the training area they had been issued a <u>bokken</u> and told they would be training with it for the first couple of months. That had brought some snickers of amusement, but only until Jason of gave them a demonstration just how effectively the weapon could be used. After that the men practiced with their 'wooden sticks' without comment until their new katanas could be forged for them.

Blacksmiths and their assistants worked around the clock to produce the new style of sword. While they were being turned out as quickly as possible, the metal workers also took a certain degree of pride in their formation.

It had been a relatively quick and simple process to weed out the men not suited to the use of the sword. Those men had been shifted to either the <u>Kyjutsu</u> archery units, or to the phasers. After that the training had progressed even better than Jason had anticipated. Thinking back now on how quickly the men had learned and adapted, he was reminded of what Seta had said about him being the key to unlock them from their state of stasis.

<u>Is she right? And if she is, are these men really ready for what they'll be facing tomorrow?</u> Jason asked himself silently. He wondered if he had done all he could to see to it that they were. <u>If I've failed them, then tomorrow's battle will be more costly than I counted on.</u>

Jason closed his eyes and finally drifted off to a sleep haunted by visions and memories of his past. The faces of his family and friends danced in a strange kaleidoscope of sights and sounds. He actually felt a sense of gratitude when a hand lightly touched his shoulder to awaken him. He opened his eyes to see the face of Hass leaning

*Alazon*

over him. "It's time," the younger brother whispered before leaving the tent.

Jason sat up and rubbed his eyes, looking up as the tent flap opened and the young boy who assumed the role of Jason's personal valet entered. The boy approached and handed Jason a cup with steam floating like mist above it. "What's this?" he asked the boy with a smile.

"Hot coffee, Commander," the boy replied somewhat nervously. "I know you like it, and it will help wake you up."

"Thank you," Jason replied as he gratefully sipped the hot liquid. "Hey, wait a minute," he called as the boy turned to go. "How did you get it hot? I gave explicit orders that there were to be no fires."

"I know, Commander. I had one of the men with a hand phaser shoot a pot of water on a low beam, but only after holding up a blanket inside my tent so the light couldn't' be seen," the boy explained.

Jason laughed at the boy's ingenuity. "Very smart."

"Thank you, Commander," the boy replied, lifting his head a little higher.

"What's your name?"

"Kort. I am the son of Kranel, the Master Metal Worker from Lemac," the boy told him proudly.

"Isn't your father the one I gave my sword to so he could copy it to make the others?"

"Yes, Commander."

"Well, Kort, I thank you for the coffee. Now, if you'll excise me, I have to get ready."

The boy saluted sharply before turning on his heel and leaving the tent.

Jason stripped off the jump suit he had slept in and donned the combat outfit. He knew Busker and the brothers had been right about him wearing it. After this battle they would have to take on the Tilwin, and it wouldn't do for him to get himself hurt and not be able to command, despite his confidence that Busker could easily take over and do an excellent job.

Jason picked up the starburst pin, but when he attempted to attach it to the combat outfit, the pin on the back of the medallion wouldn't penetrate the hi-tech polymer material the outfit was constructed of.

He unfastened one of the Velcro straps that held the uniform tight around his neck and slipped the small piece of material through the clasp of the medallion, positioning it directly under his chin at the throat before securing the strap once more.

Jason looked around for his swords. Not seeing them in the tent he stepped outside, intending to ask Kort if he had seen them. However, as soon as Jason stepped out of the tent, Kort quickly got to his feet and held out his arms. Both of Jason's swords lay across them.

"I polished them for you, Commander," Kort said proudly. "Now they will not only cut the Karton in half, but will blind them in the process."

Jason had to smile at the boy's enthusiasm as he took the weapons. He slipped the katana into the belt at his waist and the shorter hotachi over his head and down his back. As he headed for Busker's tent, Jason heard the whispered comments of the men at his appearance. Only those of the Lemac Guard had ever seen him in the combat outfit, although they had all heard about it.

In the past seven months Jason knew he had gone from being a 'gerkin', the mythical demon of the northern woods, to an individual who was part god, part man, and finally to just a strange looking man from another world. The men of Alazon had finally come to accept him and the things he could teach them with total frankness, which included his somewhat strange behavior at times. But seeing him now in the combat outfit brought back some of the old comments.

Outside of Busker's tent Shon, Hass and the other Guard Commanders quickly joined him. All of them knelt in a circle in the soft, dewy grass.

"All right, this is it," Jason told them. "This is where we find out if all the training and hard work has paid off. You all know your assignments, so let's get moving. Pass the word that I don't want to hear a single sound from them. We have to get into position without the Karton suspecting anything. Good luck."

As the Guard Commanders left to begin the movements that would put the men into position along the bluff overlooking the beach, Jason looked at Busker, Shon and Hass in the soft moonlight. "If you believe in your gods, now is the time to pray to them."

Jason stood and quickly moved to the forefront of the army as the men began their silent approach to the bluff. They walked upright for the first hundred yards before dropping down to their hands and knees. As they did, Jason listened for the sounds of conversations, the tell-tale clink of metal on metal, or the rattle of arrows in quivers, but all he heard was the soft whisper of hands and knees moving across the early morning dampness of the grass.

Like shadows in the night, the men stretched out in a line across the bluff. From two days of rehearsal, each man knew where he was supposed to be in relation to those around him. It took them nearly half an hour to reach their various positions, but at last the unit commanders whispered into the throat mikes Jason had provided that they were ready.

Jason acknowledged their reports and then ordered them to silence as he, Busker and Ster crept forward. Peering over the edge of the bluffs he saw forty thousand men camped below. The men of the army of Karton slept as if they were at home in the comfort and safety of their own beds. So secure were they in their belief that they had landed completely undetected that they hadn't even posted sentries. He turned to Ster on his left. "Ready?"

"Yes, Sir," Ster replied, holding up the flare pistol he would use to signal the start of the attack. Jason knew the green light of the flare would cast an eerie glow on the men below. That was a further psychological advantage he was counting on to assist them.

Jason could feel the presence of the men around him. He was in the center group, which consisted of nearly thirty-five thousand swordsmen. On either side and behind his group were ten thousand archers, who were now stringing their long bows and placing quivers of arrows where they could get to them quickly. On the outer edges were five hundred men armed with phasers, lasers and particle beam disruptors. It would be the job of the latter group to contain the Karton, preventing them from escaping from the beach except by way of the ocean. It would also fall on them to destroy at least half the ships of the Karton once the attack began.

Jason could feel the sweat forming in the pits of his arms and on his brow beneath the mask of the combat outfit. He knew the summer heat had nothing to do with. He was nervous. Hell, he admitted to himself, he was scared. This was no martial arts tournament, this was for real. Men wouldn't be hurt and the match called, but would die if they lost their particular fight. And many would die without ever seeing their opponent. With a final look out to sea, Jason turned to Ster and nodded.

As the flare streaked upwards into the sky, Jason heard the archers drawing their first arrows. As the flare burst into brightness at the apogee of its arch, the first flight of arrows went streaking down into the men below. At the same time, the phasers, lasers and particle beam weapons opened fire from the ends of the formation. Some at the ships just off shore, with the others at the edges of the encampment.

The silence of the early morning exploded with screams of panic, fear and pain from the Karton as steel tipped shafts of woods and beams of light stabbed into and cut through their ranks. The phasers and lasers severed men in half, cutting through the shields, body armor and swords, while casting a hellish glow over everything around them. The particle beam weapons broke down the components of the steel shields, swords and breastplates, turning them into powder. Back and forth the beams swept across the beach, gradually working their way inward, destroying everything in their paths.

In less than two minutes, twenty-five percent of the army of Karton was either dead or maimed by the arrows that rained down on them and the energy weapons that swept back and forth across their outer edges. The sounds of their screams reached the men on the bluff clearly. Jason tried to shut out the sounds of their dying but couldn't. He knew this sound would remain with him long after this battle was over.

But as he watched the dying, Jason felt a growing admiration for the Karton. Even in all the confusion and death around them, there was still a sense of order among them. Men formed into groups, with those on the outer edges raising shields in an attempt to provide a protective cover for the others to hide behind and beneath. Arms reached out from the various clusters to bring more men into them, and to snatch up swords and spears. This was no panicky move on their part, but a function and role they had performed before. They were reacting from the training that years of warfare had ingrained into them.

As the dawn brightened the morning sky, Jason noticed a man in the center of the camp below. The man held a sword in his right hand as he walked through the carnage shouting orders, completely unafraid and totally unscathed. It was as if he had total confidence in the gods to protect him. As the various groups slowly converged with one another, the man moved to the forefront, preparing them to either charge up the steep bluff or to wait for the Preton to come down to them.

"Last flight!" Jason heard someone behind him call out, letting him know the archers were firing their last arrows. He stood and drew his katana with his right hand and his ho-tachi with his left. Holding both swords above his head as a signal for the archers and others to cease their firing, he took a deep breath. Then, with a shout, Jason led the screaming Preton swordsmen over the edge of the bluff in a headlong charge to meet the Karton face to face.

This was not formalized battle, but a fight pitting man against man the way Jason wanted it. It negated the standard manner of battle, quickly turning the beach into a churning, boiling mass of men who moved back and forth across the blood stained sand, fighting and dying, the sound of steel on steel drowning out the cries of the wounded and dying.

The men of Preton fought like men possessed, their swords flashing out like deadly cobras with fangs of steel. Jason felt the swords of the Karton strike his arms and back as he was surrounded by a group of them and was grateful that Busker and the brothers had insisted on his wearing the combat outfit. He soon found himself in the thick of the battle, surrounded by nearly a dozen Karton who were intent on killing him.

A spear struck Jason's left shoulder. While the suit prevented it from piercing him, the force of the blow knocked the ho-tachi from his left hand. He quickly shifted to a two-handed grip on the katana and went on the attack. He lunged toward the closes man and brought the sword down faster than the man could react. He sliced through both of the man's forearms as if they were made of balsa wood.

"I've got your back covered!" a voice yelled out from behind him. It was immediately followed by the sound of steel striking steel. Jason risked a quick glance over his shoulder and saw Ster sever the head of one Karton and, using the momentum of that blow, bring his katana around to disembowel another. Then Jason was faced with two charging Karton of his own and turned back to the task at hand. He wounded one and killed the other before moving on to another small knot of men who had surrounded some men from Preton. He and Ster attacked them from behind, killing five of the Karton before they realized what was happening.

Jason fought on. His katana danced and wove a pattern of death to any Karton unfortunate to come within striking distance, his own body twisting and turning to avoid the blows of their swords. His feet flashed out to break knee joints or smash noses, sending men screaming to the sand as he fought through one group after another.

Jason saw Shon fall backwards, tripped by the body of a dead Preton. But like a cat, Shon rolled with the fall and came quickly to his knees, disemboweling the Karton charging at him.

Jason smashed the butt of his sword haft into the face of a Karton on his right, then slashed downward to nearly sever another man in half. He jerked the blade free, reversing his grip and dropping to one knee as he brought the blade around in a backhanded blow to cut completely through the left leg of another Karton.

"Jason!"

At the sound of his name being screamed out, he whirled around to see Ster on his back, his sword just out of reach. A Karton had his arm pulled back, preparing to run Ster through with a battle spear. Jason's hand flashed into the pouch at his waist and a heartbeat later the Karton died from the throwing star embedded in the side of his head. Jason short hopped toward another Karton and snapped his right leg out in a powerful side kick. The heel of Jason's foot struck the Karton on the point of his chin. The man's head snapped back, his neck broken, dead before his body hit the sand. Jason turned to find Ster back on his feet, his sword once again gripped firmly in his hands. Ster nodded his thanks as the two of them turned to face another group of charging Karton.

*Alazon*

Jason suddenly found himself face to face with the man he had noticed earlier. The man was covered with blood, although it was hard to tell if it was his own or that of those he had killed. Or both. For a frozen moment in time the two of them stood only a few feet apart as the battle raged on around them.

"Surrender!" Jason shouted in an effort to be heard above the din. "Stop now so that some of you can live to go home! If you don't, you'll be condemning your men to certain death!"

The man looked at him for the space of several heartbeats before letting his eyes move around the beach to take in the carnage that surrounded them. Jason saw the man's shoulders slump, as if the will had suddenly been drained from him. The man nodded his head and let his sword fall from his hands as he slowly sent to his knees in the sand. He placed his hands behind his head in surrender and submission.

"Flares! Now!" Jason shouted into his throat mike.

From the bluff above them four red flares streaked into the sky and twenty conch horns sounded to call the cease the fighting. It took a moment for the sound of the horns and the sight of the flares to register in the eyes, ears and minds of the combatants, but slowly the two armies began to separate and fall back from one another. Those nearest Jason saw the Karton commander in the position of surrender. As the realization of that hit home, the other men of Karton began to drop the swords and spears they had clutched so tightly for the past hour, going to their knees as well. As Karton surrendered, the men of Preton backed off immediately, per Jason's orders, but still held their swords at the ready.

Jason let his own arms drop to his sides as his eyes and ears took in the sights and sounds of men dying. He saw Busker and Ster coming toward him, their arms and chests covered with blood.

"Stand up," he told the Karton commander. His voice sounded tired and weak, even to his own ears.

As the man stood up, Busker stepped forward to look at him. "I know this man," he told Jason. "He's Naed Laer, Commander of the Palace Guard and General of the Army of Karton." Busker motioned for a man to bind the hands of Naed.

"No!" Jason snapped, causing the man with the binding to stop in his tracks. "He has surrendered and put down his sword. Nor will I stand any form of humiliation of a man who has fought and led his men as bravely as he has."

Jason turned from the Karton to face Busker, who seemed to be fuming over his counter order. "Send for the wagons. I want the wounded of both armies loaded on them and taken to Kech for treatment."

"All right, but we'll separate them," Busker replied as he turned away.

"Busker!" Jason's bellowing voice caused all heads to turn in his direction as Busker stopped immediately and turned to face Jason. "There will be no separation of the wounded, except to separate those who are more seriously wounded from those not in danger of dying," Jason snapped.

"You are all men of Alazon," he continued, feeling angry without really understanding why. "You are all brothers. If a man from Preton is placed in a wagon next to a man from Karton, so what? I want the wounded, all the wounded, loaded up immediately and taken to Kech. Is that clear?"

Busker stood as if rooted to the spot, the blood having drained from his face. "I...yes, Commander," he finally replied, saluting smartly before turning away.

Jason turned to Shon and Hass. "Bring him," he told the brothers, indicating the Karton General as he turned and walked away.

Jason went to a large boulder at the base of the bluff and sat down heavily, gratefully accepting the flask of water handed to him by Ster. He removed the face-covering portion of his outfit and drank deeply, and then held the flask out to the Karton. The man hesitated a moment before accepting it and drinking from it himself. As the Karton General returned the flask he stood just a little straighter, squaring his shoulders as he stared at a spot just slightly above Jason's head.

"It's a little hard to talk to a man who isn't looking at me," Jason said, catching the Karton off guard. "Relax, General Laer, the battle is over."

Naed stood hesitantly for a moment before doing as he was instructed. He finally let his body lose some of its rigidity as he tried not to stare at Jason's skin and eye coloration.

"I have just one question," Jason said to Laer as he tried to retain some semblance of normalcy in his bearing and voice. "Why? Why this invasion after nearly a hundred years of peace between Karton and Preton?"

"Mickel," Naed replied softly. "We have none. Our mines have been depleted for years, while Preton has more than it can use."

Gold! Jason thought in disgust. He shook his head at the insanity of it all. "Was it worth it?" he asked Naed, pointing to the thousands of bodies strewn across the blood soaked sand and the ships burning offshore.

Naed's face began a slow transformation from one of semi-sternness to one of sorrow for the loss of so many of his men. "It wasn't supposed to be like this," Naed said at last, his voice filled with sadness and regret.

"Why didn't your king try to work out a plan where they could have obtained mickel from the Preton at a reasonable cost?" Jason asked. "Why resort to something this drastic?"

"It. . .it wasn't their plan, my lord," Naed replied, becoming somewhat formal in his attitude and demeanor. "It was a plan devised by King Semaj and Queen Lorac of Tilwin. I doubt of King Tolo or Queen Makee could have come up with something such as this on their own."

The derisive tone of the man's voice told Jason a lot. First, Naed didn't particularly hold his king and queen in high esteem. From some of the things Jason had heard about them himself, that might be justifiable on Naed's part.

Second, it told him that Semaj and Lorac of Tilwin were the real culprits. If what he had heard about those two was accurate, they probably planned to use the Karton to help secure Preton, then turn on the Karton, hoping to control the entire planet. From what he surmised, it would be something they would try.

"General Laer, you have heard me give the order for all wounded to be taken to Kech, but now we have to decide what to do with those of you who are able to travel."

Naed looked at him in confusion. "I would assume you would hold us for ransom, as is normal, even if your tactics of fighting are anything but normal."

Jason pulled the mask and head covering of the combat outfit all the way back, ignoring the Karton's' involuntary gasp of shocked surprise.

"No," he told Naed, "I don't think I'll do that. It only creates more problems than it solves. Besides, I have a feeling that Tolo and Makee would rather have you rot here in a Preton prison than pay the ransom."

Jason wiped his face and tenderly touched a bruise on the right side of his cheek.

"You and your men, those of them able to travel, are free to return to Karton. I don't believe in holding men for ransom. It's degrading to all concerned."

Naed stared at him in disbelief. Jason knew the man was thinking that things like this just didn't happen on Alazon. Captives of war were held for ransom or prisoner exchanges. To just turn them loose and send them home was unheard of.

"What of those unable to travel?" Naed finally asked once he realized Jason was completely serious.

"After their wounds are treated and they are able to travel, they will also be allowed to return to Karton. I will give orders to the Mayor and Harbor Master of Kech that the Karton soldiers are to be given free passage home once they are able and ready to make the trip."

Jason heard the gasps of surprise that came as much from the men of Preton as those of Karton. Never before had such stipulations been made in a war. He kept his eyes locked on those of Naed.

"You. . .you have that authority?" Naed asked.

"He has it," Shon replied.

Naed stared at Jason for a long moment. "You are a most unusual man, my lord," he finally said.

"Well," Jason replied with a weak smile, "I've been called a lot worse."

"My lord, may I ask where you are from?"

*Alazon*

"Firs, it's not 'my lord', but Commander Stephens. As to where I'm from? I could tell you, but the explanation it would require for you to really understand would take too long to give at the present time."

Naed's eyes came to rest on the katana stuck in the sand beside Jason. "You have taught the men of Preton a new way to fight, and with a new type of sword. The way they fought is ample proof of the training they have received. We were told Preton had no army."

"Until seven months ago they didn't," Jason told Naed, seeing the look of surprise at this statement on the man's face.

"Perhaps someday, when this is all over, you will teach me this new technique?"

Jason looked at Naed for a long moment, a smile coming slowly to his face. "I might. But only on one condition."

"What would that be?"

"You would have to give me your word that you would never use what I taught you against us, against the people of Preton, unless we gave you justifiable cause."

"What would you consider justifiable?" Naed asked.

"An invasion of Karton by Preton."

Naed studied Jason carefully and intently. "Just my word? That's all it would take?"

"Yes."

"And what if I later went back on my word, using what I learned from you to train my own men to use against you and the men of Preton."

"Then you would be the first to die," Jason replied. He had spoken softly, but there was no mistaking the seriousness of his tone.

"Yes," Naed replied with a slow smile of his own, "I believe I probably would. I take it that a man's word is important to you?"

"A man's word is everything to me," Jason told Naed. "If a man's word is no good, then neither is the man. So, knowing that, will you give me your word that you will return to Karton, taking your men with you, and promise never to raise a sword against Preton again without justifiable reason?"

Naed hesitated a moment before answering. "Yes, if you will also give me your word that Preton will not attempt to invade us, as then I would have no choice but to defend my home, my land and my family."

"I would expect nothing less," Jason said as he stood and extended his hand. "You have my word."

Naed slowly extended his own hand and the two men stood for a moment, hands gripping forearms in agreement.

"I will be coming to Karton soon," Jason told Naed as they released their grips, "but not to do battle. I'll be coming in peace, with the hope of working out new treaties for both countries. I would like to know that I have a friend there I could look up when I arrive."

Naed looked up at him and grinned. "I think I might know of someone there you could call a friend. And I think he might look forward to your coming. Be sure to ask for him."

"I will. A man should have friends in countries other than his own. Now, go take care of your men and leave Karton when you're ready."

"One more question, if I may?"

Jason nodded his head.

"The weapons of light. They are not of this world, are they?"

"No, and neither am I," Jason replied, with a sigh, "but we'll discuss that at length some other time. Right now your men need you. Good-bye, General Laer. Have a good trip home."

Jason turned from Naed and began to make his way up the face of the bluff, feeling the weariness trying to take control of his body. At the top he stopped and looked back down at the beach. He could still hear the cries and moans of the wounded and dying. He could see large black spots in the sand he knew to be dried blood spilled that day. He shook his head sadly, telling himself that it was something that had to be done.

"That's probably the same argument and justification they used back on Earth when they pushed the buttons that ended the world," he mumbled to himself as he turned away.

# EIGHTEEN

Standing inside his tent, Jason removed the combat outfit, feeling the ache in his arms and back. He sat wearily on the cot just as the tent flaps were drawn back. Two small boys entered. Between them they carried a large steaming kettle of water suspended from a pole, which they sat down in the center of the large tent. A young girl who was directing four more boys dragging a large metal tub followed them. As Jason watched in confused amazement, the girl had the tub placed beside the kettle, and then had the water from the kettle poured into it by the first two boys. Meanwhile, the other boys had darted back outside, only to return with two more kettles of water, which they also poured into the tub. All of the boys then hurried from the tent, leaving the girl alone with Jason. She looked up at him shyly and smiled.

"I thought you would like a hot bath to clean up with, Commander," she said softly, lowering her head to stare down at her bare feet.

Jason had seen her around the camp before but didn't know who she was. She was an exceptionally pretty little girl who always seemed to be smiling or laughing whenever he saw her, but this consideration for him was a total surprise. "That was very thoughtful of you. Thank you."

He smiled at the way she blushed. It reminded him of Kim. As the girl started to leave her eyes fell on his combat outfit. She darted forward and snatched it up, looking up at him with wide eyes. "I'll wash this for you, Commander," she told him, her words coming out in a rush.

"You don't have to do that," he told her.

"Oh, but I want to!" she replied, her pretty little face a mask of complete sincerity.

"What's your name?"

"Janella. Janella Repap, Commander,"

"Well, Janella, if you want to try and get the blood stains out of it, go ahead. But if you can't, don't worry about it, okay."

"I'll get it clean, Commander," Janella told him as she backed away toward the tent flaps. "You'll see." With that Janella turned and quickly left the tent, causing Jason to chuckle at her seriousness.

He stood and stepped gingerly into the large tub. He used the hot water to wash the sweat from his body, as well as the blood from his hands where the combat outfit had not covered them. He was just putting on a clean tunic and slipping the chain and medallion over his head when he heard voices being raised outside. They were quickly followed by a howl of pain. He stepped to the opening of the tent, only to be confronted by a scene that puzzled him. Busker was sitting on the ground gritting his teeth in pain as he tried to stop the flow of blood coming from his right calf. A few feet away Shon, Hass, Ster and a dozen other men were laughing so hard that some of them had tears running down their cheeks. In the middle of all this stood Kort. The boy held a ho-tachi in his hands and his body was in the <u>ichi-do</u> on guard position. There was blood on the tip of his sword and a look of grim determination on his face.

"Would someone like to tell me what's going on here?" Jason asked as he stepped toward Busker.

"Oh, Jason, you should have seen it!" Hass told him, trying to control his laughter. "Little Kort was standing guard in front of your tent when Busker comes along and starts to enter. Kort told him you were bathing and not receiving anyone at the moment and that Busker would just have to wait until you were cleaned up and ready to see him. He told this to Busker, your second in command! It was outrageous!

"Anyway, Busker starts to push him aside, figuring that no mere boy was going to stop him. But what he didn't figure on was being attacked by Kort. Before anyone could blink, your little self-appointed body guard snatched out his sword and proceeded to put Busker on his butt with a very quick, very efficient slice across the lower leg, followed by a well delivered snap kick to the groin."

"I see," Jason replied, trying to keep his face straight as he imagined the scene in his mind. "I think you can put your sword away now, Kort," he told the boy.

Jason was impressed as he watched the boy carefully wipe the blade of his sword off on a small rag he withdrew from his sash, then quickly slip the sword into the sheath across his back with a flourish that was a near perfect imitation of the way Jason often did it himself.

"Wait," he said suddenly. He knelt down in front of Kort and extended his hands. "May I see it?"

Kort withdrew the sword and presented it to Jason hilt first. As Jason examined it a light of understanding came to his eyes. The small sword of Kort wasn't actually a ho-tachi, but a ho-tachi sized version of a katana, and nearly an exact duplicate of Jason's own katana, right down to the etchings on the blade. "Who made this?" he asked, feeling as if he already knew the answer.

"My father," Kort replied proudly. "He made it from the drawings he made of your own katana, Commander. While he had your sword in his possession he made an exact drawing of it, including the squiggly lines on the blade, so he could make one for me."

"So I see," Jason replied with a smile. "But how did you learn to use it so well?"

"Sir, every day I would stand in the back of the men who were training. I copied every one of their movements as best I could to memorize them. Then, at night I would practice where no one could see me, going over the movements again and again until I had them right. Someday I'm going to be a member of the Guard," he announced proudly, his little face beaming brightly.

Jason returned the sword to Kort and stood up. "I think you just might make it," he said with a smile.

He turned to find Busker being supported between two of the Lemac Guard, who were doing their best to keep their faces straight. "Go get your leg taken care of," he told Busker, not bothering to hide his own grin. "Then come see me."

"Hey, Uncle Busker," Hass called as the Guard Commander started to leave. "Maybe you better stick to fighting full grown men. Little boys seem to be too much for you to handle!"

Busker's reply was drowned out by the laughter of the men following the remarks of Hass, but there was no mistaking the set of his face.

As things finally called down Jason turned back to the boy. "Kort! Front and center!" Jason snapped sternly.

Kort swallowed nervously but hurried to stand in front of Jason and assume the position of attention. Jason let the boy stand there for a moment. He nodded slightly at Shon and Hass, who quickly got the other men around them to be quiet.

"Now," Jason said to Kort, "while no one appreciates the care you have taken of me and my equipment more than I do, or the fact that you feel it is your responsibility and duty to protect me, I think it's time we get a few things straight."

Jason was deliberately being stern with the boy. He had to make Kort realize that he couldn't go around slicing up anyone who wanted to enter Jason's tent whenever he felt like it.

"A good soldier knows with it's proper to draw and use his sword and when not to. Apparently this is something you have not yet learned.

"General Busker is my second in command. That means that if anything happens to me, Busker is the one who would be in charge. That also means he is allowed to see me whenever he wants, as he may have something important to tell me. Is that clear?"

"Yes, Commander," the boy answered weakly.

"Good. Now I want you to think about something else. If something was to happen to me and Busker had to take over, how do you think he would feel about a certain young man who once stopped him from seeing me by slicing up his leg?"

Kort swallowed and the blood drained from his face as he contemplated what Busker might do to him out of revenge.

Jason nodded. "I see you understand my meaning. So, do you think we will have any more nasty incidents such as this one?"

"No, Commander," the boy replied.

"Good. You're dismissed."

Kort saluted, then pivoted on his right heel and marched away, his back straight, his shoulders squared, finally disappearing around the side of the tent.

"He might turn out to be a pretty good soldier one of these days," Jason told the brothers with a grin.

"He's not doing too badly now," Hass replied.

"True." Jason turned to Shon. "Do you have the casualty figures yet?"

Shon nodded and removed a piece of paper from his tunic, which he then unfolded and began to read from. "For us, three hundred and eight dead and over two thousand wounded. About half of those are serious. A lot of them might not make it to Kech."

"What about the Karton?" Jason asked.

"I don't have all the figures yet, but estimates put their losses at over twenty-five thousand dead, with another ten thousand seriously wounded."

Jason shook his head. He felt a sense of sadness settling on his shoulders and surrounding his heart. "How long will it take the wagons to get to Kech?"

"At least two days," Shon told him.

"That's too long. Too many men could die in that time. Give me your communicator."

Shon quickly removed throat mike and earplug and handed them to him. Jason slipped them on and adjusted the frequency. "Mother?"

"Here."

"Patch me through to Jarrell or Kim."

"Hold on. Okay, go ahead," she told him seconds later. "It's Jarrell."

"Jarrell, I want you or Kim to go immediately to the temple and alert Seta. I'm going to have Mother send a shuttle to you by remote. Get Seta and all the other women of the temple she can spare, load them into the shuttle and come here to help with the wounded.

"Mother, send one shuttle for them and send the rest down here. We'll have the men loaded into them and taken to Kech that way. The wagons will take too long and too many of them will die before we could get them there by wagon."

"Shuttles and medical supplies will be on their way in twenty minutes," Mother told him.

"Jason?" asked Jarrell.

"Yes?"

"How did it go?"

"We won, but I'm wondering if it was really worth it. We'll talk later."

"Of course. Jarrell out."

As he removed the communicator and handed it back to Shon, Jason saw the frown on Shon's face. "What?" he asked the brother.

"Well, I can understand you wanting to save as many lives as possible, and I agree with that, but I was just thinking of the impact your shuttle will have. Not only on the people of Kech, but the Karton as well. They've never seen one."

Jason smiled and nodded. "It will give them something to think and talk about. We'll send Seta and some of her women along in the first one to Kech to help calm things down when they get there."

"Speaking of the men from Karton," said Hass, "you should hear some of the conversations going on between them and our men."

"Such as?"

"The Karton, as did our own men for a while, think you're some sort of demon or god who has come to help the Preton."

"And what are our men telling them?" Jason asked.

"Oh, not much. They're just sort of going along with it and letting the Karton think what they want."

"That figures," Jason replied with a grin.

Busker rejoined them at that moment. He was limping slightly and there was a scowl on his face. "Where is he?" Busker growled, his eyes darting around in search of Kort.

"I've already had a little talk with him," Jason told Busker, trying his best to keep a straight face, "and he's promised not to hurt you any more. He just got mad because you forgot to say 'please', that's all."

"If I get my hands on him I'll show him 'please'," Busker grumbled. "I'll blister his little rump so hard he won't be able to sit down for a week!"

*Alazon*

"No you won't," Jason told him. "He only did what he thought he was supposed to do, which is protect me and my privacy. He just got a little carried away, that's all."

Busker thought about it for a moment and then dismissed it with a wave of his hand. "Look, Jason, the men have been talking. They want to hold a victory celebration tonight in your honor."

Jason shook his head. "I don't think so. They can have a celebration for themselves if they want because they've earned it, but I don't want any so-called honors on my shoulders. All I did was train them."

Busker looked at Shon and Hass. "As stubborn as a wild tollie, isn't he?"

"You're just now noticing that?" Hass replied with a short laugh.

"Forget it, Busker," Jason told the older man. "Besides, we have to get moving as soon as we can. We'll be facing a larger and more experienced army in the Tilwin. Today's battle went pretty much according to plan, but they don't always, and I want to be as sure as possible that we're ready for them."

"Can we stop in Lemac first?" asked Hass.

Jason nodded. "I'd planned on it."

"Jason," said Busker, "we can't just up and fly off without you saying something to the men. It's expected of you. Besides, it would mean a lot to them."

Even though Jason hated to admit it, he knew Busker was right. "Okay," he said with a sigh, "come on."

Jason, Busker, Shon and Hass walked to where Jason's private shuttle was sitting. Jason went inside and activated the external speakers and adjusted the frequency on the small mike he put on. He then climbed up on top of the shuttle and held out his hands to silence the cheering men.

"Today, you, the men of Preton, have won a decisive victory for yourselves," he told him, his voice amplified by the speakers to carry to all of them. "But the war isn't over with yet. We still have to face the Tilwin.

"Busker says you wan to have a victory celebration tonight and I think you should. You've earned it and you deserve it. Unfortunately

I won't be here to enjoy it with you. Nor will Busker, Shon, Hass or Lieutenant Ster."

There were a number of groans from the men. Voices were raised in protest and disappointment, but they were silenced by his Jason's upraised hands.

"I'm sorry," he told the men, "but the five of us must return to Lemac tonight and then proceed to the west coast to make the preparations we'll need to face the Tilwin. And let's all hope we are as successful against them as we were here today."

That brought cheers and shouts of encouragement from the men. Jason let it run its course before speaking again. "But that doesn't mean the rest of you shouldn't celebrate, because you should. I just want you to keep this in mind.

"You have loved ones, mothers, fathers, wives, girlfriends and children who are worried about you. They don't know the outcome of today's battle yet and will be very anxious to see you. So have your celebration tonight, and then those of you who have been wounded and will be unable to fight against the Tilwin should head for your homes in the morning to spread the good news of what you accomplished here today. The rest of you will be transported to the west coast tomorrow afternoon for our battle with the Tilwin."

As he stepped down from the shuttle the men began to cheer. Jason was about halfway to his tent when he heard a new cheer. It was a chant that stopped him cold. It started slowly but quickly gathered momentum and volume as other men picked it up.

"Jason! Jason! Jason!" they shouted, raising arms and swords as they began to crowd in around him.

The sound of his name being chanted like that had a tone of foreboding to it that sent shivers down his spine. Jason was reminded of his meeting with Jarrell and Seta in the cave beneath the temple.

"Get me out of here!" he yelled to Busker and the others as the men began closing in around him. He felt as if they were going to crush him beneath their exuberance.

Busker, Ster and the brothers quickly formed a wedge in front of him. Members of the Mayoral Guard of Lemac quickly joined it. With Jason in the center, they forced their way through the crowd, heading for his tent. But the crowd of men was not going to let up that easily. Even as he reached the tent, the men began to pack around him even closer; chanting his name in what was becoming a wild frenzy.

"To hell with this!" Jason yelled, trying to make himself heard above the din. "Get me to the shuttle! We're getting out of here right now!"

Once again the men of the Lemac Guard protected him until they reached the shuttle. Busker quickly closed the hatch behind them once they were inside.

"Where's Ster?" Jason asked when he noticed the absence of the Lieutenant.

"He went back for your things," Shon told him as the older brother sat in the co-pilot's seat. "He figured you'd get mobbed if you tried. He should be here in a minute or two."

Jason slumped down on the floor of the shuttle's small cargo area. He rested his head in his hands, his elbows propped up on his drawn up knees. He didn't want to go forward just yet, as that would expose him to the still chanting crowd outside, and right now he didn't feel like being seen.

"You can't hide from it forever," a voice said.

Jason raised his head to see Busker squatting down in front of him. Shon and Hass were watching him closely. The expressions on the faces of the three men ranged from humor to acceptance of fate.

"Don't start, Busker," he said with a groan. "I don't want to hear it."

"That's too bad," Busker replied with a grin, "because you're going to. If not from me, from us, then from others. You're going to hear it over and over again, and there's not a damn thing you can do about it. Other than to accept it."

"I don't have to accept anything I don't want to," Jason replied wearily. "Once this is over I'll be out of it."

"Oh, really? And then what?" asked Shon.

"I don't know," Jason replied weakly, feeling a sense of defeat by circumstances that seemed to have gotten out of control. "I'll find a place of my own, find a woman to love and share my life with, and then do what I can to help the people of this world.

"But I'll do it as a common man," he told them stubbornly. "I will not allow myself to be placed on any damn throne, or in a position that will force me to make decisions concerning anyone other than myself and my family."

Shon grinned at him and shook his head. "Kimmy told us about what happened in the cavern beneath the temple, so we know all about it. You can fight against it all you want, but in the end you are going to have to accept that responsibility. There's no way you can avoid it."

"Yes there is," Jason replied softly.

"How?" asked Busker.

"I can leave Alazon."

Jason could tell by the expressions on their faces that this was something they hadn't considered. But he also saw the sly look in Busker's eyes. "Sure you could. But where would you go?" the older man asked.

"I don't know. I found this world; I'll find another. One where I don't stand out like a sore thumb. One where I can fit in as a normal man, not some damn demon, god or super man, because I'm not any of those things."

"And just leave behind those who have come to love you?" Shon asked softly.

"Kim will get over it," he replied.

"Maybe. And maybe Vinny will, too. But what about the twins?" Shon asked softly. "Can you just walk away from Vanda and Manda and leave them behind?"

Jason lowered his head to his hands, not knowing what to say to that. He knew he couldn't walk away from the twins, or from Kim for that matter. He had found a world where he was loved and could love in return once this was all over. True, he could leave, but in doing so he would be leaving behind all he had come to cherish. All that had become so vital to his very existence.

"That's what I thought," Shon said as he reached out to place a hand on Jason's shoulder.

At that moment the hatch opened. Ster and two other members of the Lemac Guard squeezed in, their arms full of Jason's belongings. Ster took a quick look at the four of them and nodded at Busker before moving to the back of the shuttle with the other two men and stowing the things they had brought.

Jason used the opportunity to stand and move forward to start the engines of the shuttle. Once he saw the men outside move back, and the two men who had come with Ster had exited the shuttle, he lifted it into the sky. Turning it west, he streaked toward Lemac.

None of them spoke during the flight, taking their cue from Jason's own silence. He tried to focus his mind on the Tilwin, but no matter how hard he tried he couldn't block out the events that had taken place in the cavern beneath the temple. Nor could he block out the sound of the men chanting his name over and over. <u>I'll find a way</u>, he told himself as he approached Lemac.

He landed the shuttle behind the house, where they were met by Jarrell, Liet and the twins. He looked around for Kim, wondering why she wasn't there.

"She and Vinny went with Seta and the others to help," Manda told him as he bent to pick up her and Vanda.

Jason carried the twins into the house, following behind the others. Within minutes the group was seated around the large table in the common room. The twins went to help their mother bring glasses and a pitcher of teef, as well as sandwiches she had prepared in anticipation of them coming.

Jason ate in silence. Afterwards he occupied himself by playing with the twins while Busker, Ster and the brothers recounted the events of the battle and how it had gone.

He moved from the table to a large stuffed chair with the twins. As he leaned his head back and closed his eyes he felt the twins gently probing his mind and relaxed, letting them pick his brains for his own memories of the battle. He could feel their small bodies shiver in his arms as they 'felt' the blows that had struck him. When it was over they clung to him tightly and he could feel the love they had for him emanating from them. He knew then he could never leave this world, or them, no matter what.

"It's time to go," he said at last as he stood up with the twins in his arms.

Going back outside to the shuttle they found a crowd of people gathered there. All of them wanted to know what had happened with the Karton. "Jarrell can tell you all about it," Jason told them, forcing himself to smile as he kissed the twins and set them down.

He knew his actions bordered on rudeness, but he didn't feel like standing there and telling them about the slaughter of so many men that had taken place earlier that day. But when he examined his feelings more closely, Jason realized that he was afraid to speak to them. He was afraid of hearing his name being changed over and over again like that of some conquering here. <u>But to them, whether you like it or not, that's just what you are</u>, he told himself.

Moments later they were airborne and heading for the western shores of Preton. Jason forced his thoughts to center on the coming battle with the Tilwin, wondering how they would fare against this larger, more experienced army.

# NINETEEN

Sitting on the bridge of the <u>Stargazer,</u> Jason stared blankly out into space, not really seeing the myriad of stars that filled the screens. He had come to talk to Mother. He wanted her opinion as to what he should or shouldn't do, but she hadn't been much help. Mother's advice had been for him to weigh all factors carefully and then make the choice he thought best for all concerned, including himself. But, he thought grimly, Mother had also made it a point to remind him that there were times when the needs of one had to be suppressed to benefit the needs of the whole. That little homily of wisdom hadn't helped him much, even though he knew she was right.

He had finally told her to shut up, and for the past hour he had been trying to figure out just what to do. He knew he couldn't leave. Not now. He had grown too close, too attached to the people here over the past seven months. But he was also aware of what staying could mean, and he had no desire to become a king. He just wanted to be himself, a common citizen. He would have to find some way to circumvent their desires to make a king out of him.

He had argued with himself that it was only Seta and Jarrell who were trying to place this burden on him; that the people of Preton would never accept it. He told himself that they would never consent to a strange looking alien man being their king. That's if they would even tolerate another king in the first place. <u>After all,</u> he reasoned, <u>they deposed their last king and were getting along just fine under a democratic society ever since.</u>

But that argument fell apart when Jason factored in the dominating influences of Seta and Jarrell. Seta was the High Priestess of Lofa, guardian of their religion and history. Her every whim was nearly law in and of itself; her every word directly from the goddess of Lofa. In some ways she was even more powerful than Jarrell.

And Jarrell? <u>Hell</u>, Jason thought, <u>the man could proclaim himself as King of Preton and the people probably wouldn't bat an eyelash</u>. So if Jarrell went before the people and told them that Jason should be king, and that Jason was the fulfillment of an ancient prophecy, and if Seta backed him up, that's about all there was to it. Jason would be king.

"Damn, what do I do?" he mumbled.

"'It is a miserable state of mind, to have few things to desire and many things to fear; and yet that commonly is the case of kings'," Mother replied.

"What do you mean by that?" he growled.

"You're supposed to be a smart boy, you figure it out for yourself," she answered with a chuckle.

"You're supposed to be helping me, damn it. Not spouting quotes from Bacon."

"Very good. At least you recognized it, which means your education wasn't a total waste. By the way, there's a shuttle approaching."

"Who's in it?"

"Kimmy."

"Well, since she doesn't know how to fly one herself, that means you are bringing her up by remote, correct?"

"Ohhh, cranky this morning, aren't we?" Mother teased. "However, I really doubt if it would take much to teach her how to fly. Other than one particular area, Kim seems to be an extremely bright young woman."

"And just what area would that be?" he asked, feeling as if he already knew the answer.

"Well, the way I see it," Mother told him, "her only character flaw is her total and unexplainable love for you. That just doesn't make sense to me. I mean, you would think she...."

"Mother?"

"Yes?"

"Shut the hell up."

A few minutes later he heard the door of the bride slide open with a whisper. He turned his head and smiled at Kim as she came to stand beside him. His smile faded when he saw the worry and concern in her eyes. "What's wrong?"

"I was about to ask you the same thing," she replied as she placed her right hand on his shoulder.

"Spoken to your father and Seta lately?"

She lowered her eyes and nodded. "We had a big fight over it."

"Why?"

Kim took the seat beside him and stared out the screens for a moment before answering. "Because I know that being a king is the last thing in the world you want. That the mere idea of being a king is repulsive to you."

She turned to look at him, her eyes boring into his. "I know you better than any of them, Jason. I know what you have been through. I know how much you have suffered and how much you are still suffering.

"While you were off training I had Mother bring me up here and I connected myself to the Thought Transference Scanner so she could give me more information and details about you, your world and your life."

Jason was surprised by this, but more than that, he was impressed by her actions. "Why?"

"Because I love you," she whispered, turning her face away. "And when you love someone you want to know as much about them as you can. That way you can be there for them when they need you."

It was finally out. Now neither of them could hide from it any longer, even if they wanted to. Yet, her simple words frightened him. He turned from her to stare out at the stars, his mind spinning with the conflicting emotions within him.

"Jason," she said softly, "I know it is hard for you to let yourself love anyone because of everything that has happened to you, but I understand that and can deal with it.

"I think you love me, but I also know you still love Nadia and still grieve over her death. I think I have a pretty good idea of how much you loved her, and I would never think of trying to take her place in your heart."

Kim hesitated a moment and Jason could hear her breathing, as well as the blood pounding in his own temples.

"Besides," she said at last, "you should not forget her. You should not ever forget the love you had for her. She was the first woman you loved, and she loved you in ways I may never be able to. I also know that you may never love me as much as you loved her. But I can accept that, Jason. Just please do not shut me out.

"Once this is all over with, if you want to leave Alazon and go in search of another world, one where you might feel more comfortable, I will understand," she told him, her voice lowering to a mere whisper.

Jason heard the catch in her voice and turned to see tears trickling slowly down her cheeks. He reached out to wipe away her tears and suddenly found her in his arms. He held her tightly, tears forming in his own eyes as his love for her finally emerged from behind the wall he had been keeping it.

"I do love you, Kim," he finally whispered. "It's just that I've been afraid. Not of you, but of myself."

"I know," she replied softly. She lifted her head to lightly kiss him. "But you can not hide from me, or yourself, forever, Jason. You have too much love to give, and too great a desire to be loved for that to happen."

"I guess I can be a little stubborn at times, can't I?" he asked with a lop-sided grin.

"That, my blue eyed alien, is an understatement."

Neither of them spoke for a moment, content to just hold one another for a while. Jason felt as if a giant burden had been lifted from his shoulders.

"Are you going back down tonight?" she asked, resting her cheek against his chest.

"I'd planned on it. The Tilwin won't be here for two more days, but I should be back down there with the men."

She turned her face up to him. "But you do not have to be, right?"

"Well, no, I guess not."

She disengaged herself from him and reached out to touch the com-link. "This is the <u>Stargazer</u> calling Shon Vehey," she said before he could stop her or ask her what she was doing.

"This is Commander Busker. Who is this?" came the almost immediate reply.

"Uncle Busker, it is me, Kimmy."

"Kimmy, what are you doing? Is Jason alright?" Busker asked, his voice filled with concern.

"He is fine, Uncle Busker. He is standing right here beside me. Now let me talk to Shon."

"Hi, Sis. What's up?" Shon asked.

"Switch to channel four," she told him.

Jason watched Kim switch channels herself, wondering why she was going to a private one. She surprised him even more by sliding from his lap to move away from and put on a communicator.

"Is it important for him to be down there tonight?" she asked softly. "Is his presence there absolutely necessary?"

"Well, since the Tilwin won't be here for two more days, no, I guess not," he heard Shon reply as he pulled the hidden receiver from the arm of his seat and slipped it into his right ear without her seeing him do so. "I supposed we could get along without him tonight if we have to. Why? What's up?"

"Nothing to concern yourself about, big brother," Kim told him. "He is just staying aboard ship tonight, that is all. He needs some time to himself for a change."

There was a drawn out silence. When Shon spoke again, there was a heavy note of concern in his voice. "Kimmy, are you sure you know what you're doing?"

"Shon, ever since I was a little girl you always told me to go after what I wanted, to let my heart be the judge of what was right or wrong for me. Well, my heart tells me this is right for me."

Jason felt somewhat embarrassed listening in because he wasn't sure if she were telling Shon what he thought she was, and if so, if Shon was giving his approval. But he wasn't embarrassed enough to replace the small receiver just yet.

"All right, Kimmy," Shon said after a moment. Jason could hear the love and concern in her brother's voice for her. "I trust your judgment. You know that. I just don't want to see you get hurt if it's not the right thing for you both, that's all."

"I know, and that is why I love you so much," Kim told him.

"All right," Shon said at last. "Tell Jason we'll see him tomorrow. We'll handle things down here until he gets back."

Jason quickly replaced the receiver in the arm of the seat.

"Thanks, Shon. But don't hesitate to call if something does come up that needs his attention."

Kim removed the communicator and shut off the com-link. She turned to face him, blushing slightly as she stepped forward to wrap her arms around his waist as he stood up.

"Hungry?" she asked.

"Now that you mention it, yeah."

"Me, too. Let's go get something to eat."

As they started for the door Jason was struck by a sudden idea. "Hey, Useless!" he called out, stopping just outside the door of the bridge.

"I take it you're talking to me?" Mother replied dryly.

"You answered, didn't you?"

"What do you want?"

"Could you have something special prepared for us for dinner? Something, oh, exotic?"

"You want exotic?" Mother asked with a slight snicker. "How about boiled snake eyes and roasted frog testicles? Is that exotic enough for you?"

Jason smiled and shook his head as Kim looked up at him. "Ahh, Mother, that's not quite what I had in mind. What I meant was something different than the usual fare from the food dispensers."

"I know what you meant," Mother replied dryly. "I just don't appreciate being called useless."

"Okay, I apologize."

"That's better."

"Now, do you think you could prepare something special for us for dinner?" he asked.

"Anything in particular you had in mind?"

"Not really. Why don't I leave it up to you to surprise us?"

"Alright. Where would you like it served? Not on the mess deck, I know."

"What about the Captain's private dining room?" he suggested.

"Sounds good. I'll use servos to get it ready. When do you want it served?"

Jason looked at Kim and realized they could both probably use a hot shower and change of clothes. Besides, he wanted to make this special for her. "Give us half an hour."

"You got it. One exotic meal for two in the Captain's dining room in thirty minutes."

"Come on," he told Kim.

Taking her by the hand he headed for one of the gravity wells that would take them to the outer sections of the ship.

"Where are we going?" she asked.

"You'll see."

Jason took her into one of the storage rooms that were filled with bins. "Clothing," he told her with a grin. He sent to a terminal an activated it, then searched through the listings until he found what he was looking for.

"Aside from the jumpsuits that everyone wore on a daily basis, we also had more fashionable clothing for special occasions," he told Kim.

He went to a small bin and touched a panel set into the wall beside it. A section of the wall slid to one side to reveal a row of dresses hanging on a bar, which slowly extended out into the room. He grinned as he saw Kim's look of astonishment at the gowns and formal jumpsuits that hung there.

"They are beautiful!" she whispered. "Which one do you like?" she asked excitedly as she lightly ran her hands over the material of the dresses.

"All of them," he replied with a laugh. "They are all your size and you would look astonishing in any of them."

Kim turned back to the rack of clothing, seeming to have trouble making up her mind. She finally turned back to him for help.

"Here." He told her. "Take these three, and maybe these two, and try them on. That way you can decide which one you like best."

He opened another section to reveal rows of shoes. Kim clapped her hands together and laughed with delight, then quickly selected shoes that would go with the outfits he had selected. "What about you?" she asked as she placed the shoes next to the dresses.

"Not a problem," he told her, going to a third compartment. He opened it to reveal a row of dress uniforms in his size. She joined him and began holding up different ones to see which one she might like best. She finally selected one of light blue with silver trim and matching boots. She nodded her head in approval as she held it up to him.

They hurried back to his quarters, but once there he stopped. He wasn't sure as to how they should take the next step. "Look," he told Kim as he stepped across the passageway, "you use these quarters to get ready, and when you're done I'll meet you in the dining room."

"Coward," she teased, grinning mischievously as she turned to enter the other cabin.

"You got it," he replied with a grin of his own.

Jason hurried inside and quickly stripped off his outfit and got into the shower. He scrubbed himself vigorously, again promising himself to introduce showers to Alazon if it was the only thing he ever did for them.

As he stepped from the shower to dry off, he looked at his reflection in the mirror and realized he had at least two, and possibly three day's growth of beard. He opened the small cabinet above the sink and found a tube of depilatory cream and quickly spread it over his beard, knowing it would take about two minutes to work. He used that time to dry his hair. Once his hair was dry, he scraped the cream from his face with the plastic applicator and then rinsed his face with cold water. He then hurried to get dressed, a sense of elation and excitement filling him. Kim's idea of staying up here tonight, of getting away from what was going on down below, was a good one. He didn't want to really admit it, but he had needed it and she had known that.

"She's one very special woman," he said to his image in the mirror above the dresser as he buttoned up the jacket of his uniform.

"Why, thank you, Jason. I happen to feel the same way about myself," Mother teased.

"I wasn't talking about you, Metal Mouth. Or even to you. I was speaking to myself about Kim."

"Well, I still agree with you. She is special. And because of that, my blue eyed friend, you better not do anything to hurt her in any way, or I promise I'll make life miserable for you. Do you understand me?"

"Relax, Mother," he replied as he headed for the door. "I wouldn't hurt her for anything in the world."

"Not intentionally."

Jason stopped with his hand resting on the wall by the door to the dining room. "Alright, Mother, what's that supposed to mean?"

"That means, Jason, that Kimmy is head over heels in love with you, and that she may be expecting this night to mean something very special to her. And if you take advantage of those feelings, or of her, I promise that you'll regret it."

Jason thought about what she said as he idly adjusted the starburst and chain so that it draped in the center of his chest. "It's special for me as well," he finally replied, speaking softly. "I do love her, Mother, and just want to be able to finally show her."

When Mother spoke again her voice was less harsh. "Jason, believe it or not, that would make me very happy. But let me give you a word of advice.

"If you are the least bit doubtful about your feelings for Kimmy, then don't stay here tonight. Of if you do stay, don't stay with her. By all means have diner with her, but afterwards, if you have any doubts, either get off this ship or send her home. Don't let things progress to a point where your hormones take control and cause something to happen which you may regret later."

"I won't," he promised.

"Good. Now go on in the dining room. Kim's almost ready and I know she wants to surprise you with how she looks. Which, I might add, is pretty damn good."

"Yes, Mother," he replied with a chuckle as he entered the dining room, surprised at what he saw.

Mother had used servo robots to set the table with real china, good silver, and had even provided candles, and flowers from the hydro gardens. Jason lit the candles, seeing the soft glow which illuminated the small table and area immediately around it when he turned down the room lights. He was impressed.

He went to the table and sat down, noticing the champagne in the ice bucket next to the table. He started to grin in amusement, but his grin vanished and was replaced by a look of utter astonishment when the door opened and Kim stepped hesitantly into the room.

Jason rose to his feel as she tentative approached. Her hands were clasped nervously in front of her, her eyes looking at him expectantly for approval. At that moment he thought she was the most beautiful woman he had ever seen.

She had selected a slinky, form fitting dress of emerald green that enhanced the color of her eyes. It started high around the neck, but then split down the front to expose the cleavage of her breasts, with the material just barely covering them. She turned around slowly for his inspection. He saw the back of the dress didn't even begin until the waist. It fit snugly over her hips, clinging to every curve to a point about mid-thigh, then flared out slightly down to her ankles. It had a slit up the right side to reveal her stocking clad legs. Her hair, which normally hung loose and free down her back, or in a pony tail, had been gathered up and held in place by two tortoise shell combs.

Kim saw him looking at the combs and smiled bashfully. "Mother had a servo bring me the hose and the combs, then showed me on a holo how to fix my hair. Do…do you like it?"

"Do you remember when we first met and I told you that you were beautiful?" he asked softly.

"Yes."

"I lied. Beautiful doesn't even come close to describing how you look. I don't think there are any words in the seventeen languages I know that could adequately describe you."

As he moved to hold her chair out for her, Jason got a good look at the two small combs holding her hair in place. He couldn't stop the involuntary gasp that escaped his lips.

"What's wrong?" Kim asked as he moved around to his chair, his eyes still on the combs.

"Those combs, they…they belonged to my mother," he said softly. "I gave them to her for her birthday when I was twelve."

*Alazon*

Kim's eyes flew open and her right hand darted up to one of the combs. "Oh, Jason, I didn't know! I'll take them out."

He could see the nervous apprehension in her eyes. "No," he said with a warm smile and shake of his head. "It's ok. She would approve."

"Are…are you sure?"

"I'm sure. I know she would want you to have them."

Jason knew Mother had deliberately done that to see how he would react, but right now he didn't care. Soft music began to float from the speakers hidden in the walls. The door opened and two servo robots rolled into the room, each of them carrying a small tray of dishes covered with silver lids.

For the next half hour all that either of them were able to do was eat and smile at one another, with Jason taking time to explain what some of the various dishes were to her. Once they were finished, the robots made their appearance again to remove the dishes and trays, leaving them with only two candles between them on the table.

"Would you like to dance?" he asked.

"Yes, but I don't know any of your dances. I may be a little clumsy."

Jason took her in his arms and they began to move slowly across the floor. At first Kim maintained a slight distance between their bodies so she could watch his feet, but slowly she drew herself closer until she was finally resting her head against his chest. He felt her soft sigh and smiled happily to himself. As the dance continued he became acutely aware of her physical presence, her nearness, the sweet scent of her perfume, and it was having a pleasant and very noticeable effect on him.

Jason pulled his head back slightly and looked down at her. Kim looked up, and for a frozen moment in time their eyes locked. He felt himself being drawn down to her eyes. He felt her lips touching his, softly at first, and then with an urgency welling up from deep within him. As her arms came up to wrap themselves around his neck he felt lost in time and the magic of her kiss. He could feel the urgent press of hrr body against his and the reaction of his body to it.

Jason broke the kiss and stepped back a little to look down into her eyes again. He saw his own desire and passion mirrored in them.

He pulled her close again, bending slightly to slip his right arm behind her legs to pick her up. He carried her into the bedroom and placed her gently on the bed. Laying down beside her and holding her in his arms, he kissed her softly, passionately, feeling her desire for him as she clung to him.

"Kim…" he began softly, only to be silenced by her fingers on his lips.

"Do not talk," she whispered. "I want this, Jason. I have wanted it for a long time. I want to give to you what I've never given to any other man. Make love to me, Jason. Make me a whole woman."

With trembling fingers Jason began to slowly undress her as hey both stood up. He untied the string at the back of her neck which held the dress up, letting the material drift down in a shimmering green cloud around her feet, leaving her standing before him clad only in the garter and hose Mother had provided for her. He knelt down in front of her to remove them, his heart pounding in his chest. He stood and quickly removed his own clothing and then pulled down the cover of the bed. He picked her up and placed her in the center of it, lying down beside her. He began kissing her lightly, moving from her lips to her nose, eyes, ears, and then down to her slender neck. He could hear her breath quicken. He knew she was a virgin and he wanted to make this first time for her as perfect as he possibly could.

Even though he had seen Kim nude before he really hadn't taken the time to notice the absolute perfection of her, but now he did. Her breasts, which were full and firm, jutting upwards from her chest, even as she lay on her back, the darker buds of her nipples pointing at the ceiling. Her stomach was flat, almost concave in this position, causing her pelvic bones to protrude slightly.

He bent his head to kiss her right breast and heard her sharp intake of breath as her hands grasped his head. He moved his lips to the other breast, hearing her panting growing louder. Her felt her body twitch as he gently sucked one stiff nipple into his mouth. He began to softly kiss and lick her body, working his way around and over her breasts and then lower. He was determined to give her all the pleasure he possibly could. Her body stiffened, her breath coming in a loud gasp as his tongue finally touched and probed at the most secrete and sensitive place between her thighs.

Kim climaxed twice, crying out loudly both times before she finally grasped his head and pulled it from between her wide spread thighs. Pulling him up over her, Kim reached between their bodies to grasp him. He saw her eyes widen when she realized how large he was, but she didn't stop. She guided him to her, then wrapped her arms around her neck as she lifted her legs to wrap them around his waist as he slowly entered her. She gave a muffled cry into his shoulder as he broke the barrier of her virginity, and cried out again much later as they both reached the ultimate release simultaneously. But the second cry was one of pleasure of love, not of pain. A cry she would utter again and again before the night was over.

# TWENTY

"Are you totally nuts!" Hass practically shouted as he stared at Jason, his face a mask of disbelief. "Shon, Busker, help me out here, because I think he has finally lost his damn mind!"

"Keep your voice down, Hass," Jason told him calmly as he slipped the sheath of his ho-tachi over his head.

"I'll keep my voice down when you start making some sense!" Hass hissed through clenched teeth. "You can't just go strolling out there and ask them to surrender!"

"Why not?"

"Why not? How about because they will <u>kill</u> you, that's why!" Hass replied angrily.

"I doubt it."

Hass turned to Shon and Busker. "Does our sister know she's in love with a complete idiot? Does she know this man is not in control of his faculties?"

"She knows," Shon replied with a grin.

"Then she needs <u>her</u> damn head examined!" Hass growled.

"Look, Hass," Jason said calmly, "I have to do this. I have at least try anyway."

Hass shook his head from side to side. "But why? That's what I don't understand."

Jason could see the confusion and concern in the eyes of Hass. He knew that even if he explained his reasons that Hass might not be able to completely understand. But he did owe him something.

"I want to try and avoid the same type of slaughter and bloodshed that occurred with the Karton. If there is the slightest chance I can end this without a single death, then so much the better."

Hass sighed, the frustration he was feeling clearly evident in his face and voice.

"Jason, that might have worked with the Karton. Maybe. But it will never work in a million years with the Tilwin. They are as different from the Karton as night from day. The Karton fight because they have to, or are ordered to, but the Tilwin fight because they love to! They love fighting and killing! If they can't have a war with someone else, they will fight among themselves.

"You can't just go out there and say, 'Excuse me, but would you mind getting back on your ships and going back to Tilwin and we'll just forget all about this'. You do that and they will think you are some kind of nut and kill you just for the sport of it. And that is after they laugh themselves silly."

"Maybe," Jason replied.

"Maybe my ass!" Hass snorted.

"Look, Hass, I have to try. If it doesn't work, then we'll do it the other way, but I'm going to try."

"Then I'm going with you."

Jason shook his head. "No. You stay here with Busker and Shon. You don't move until the attack signal is given, if it's given, and that's an order."

Hass growled angrily. Jason hew the younger brother didn't like it, but he also knew Hass wouldn't disobey a direct order.

"Will you at least take a phaser with you?" Hass asked after fuming for a moment.

"No, just my swords."

Hass threw up his hands and walked away into the darkness of the forest mumbling about stubborn aliens, and how brown hair and blue eyes must have an adverse effect on the brain's ability to reason.

`"He's just concerned about you, Jason," Shon told him. "We all are. He just has a different way of showing it."

"I know, but that doesn't change anything, Shon. I still have to do this."

'I know. And believe it or not, I understand," the older brother told him.

"Thanks," he replied, knowing Shon was speaking of understanding more than his reasons for wanting to try talking to the Tilwin in hopes of avoiding a fight.

Neither of them had spoken about Jason spending the night with Kim. Jason had a feeling Hass hadn't been informed and that Shon had kept that information to himself, for which Jason was grateful. In fact, no one had even questioned his absence at all. Upon his return, Shon had merely looked at him and nodded slightly, a smile playing at the corners of his mouth. They had avoided speaking about Kim but now, in the early morning light, Jason could see the questions in the eyes of the older brother. But he knew Shon wouldn't bring up the subject unless Jason himself did.

Jason sat down on a fallen tree and leaned back against the trunk of another. He checked his chronometer. There was still about fifteen minutes before sunrise. That's when he would go out to face the Tilwin, hoping to stop this battle before it ever began. He closed his eyes and though of the night he had spent with Kim. They had made love over and over, each of them feeling as if it might be the last time every for them. She had been responsive to his every touch and they had blended together in a way which had pleased him more than he could have thought possible.

Between their lovemaking sessions, Kim would lay wrapped in his arms, talking softly of what their life together could be like. She told him that if he stayed he would not be able to avoid becoming king, but promised to be there by his side to help him, no matter what.

She had spoken of the children they would have, her eyes lighting up at the prospect of having little boys and girls with golden skin, brown hair and blue eyes, laughing as she mixed up the various possible combinations. Then she would arouse him again, quickly learning what it took to do so, and they would make love again until they finally collapsed from exhaustion.

The next morning they had showered together before going for a walk in the hydro gardens, which was her favorite place aboard ship. They had been there for only a few minutes when she had laughingly

*Alazon*

attacked him, tearing at his clothes and forcing him to lay back on the soft layer of dirt beneath a small orange tree and she mounted and rode him to climax, laughing as they both rolled over and over in the dirt afterwards. They had showered again, then dressed and left, with him joining the men while she had returned to Lemac. When he arrived he discovered that Busker had organized the transport of all the troops from the east coast to the west.

Jason opened his eyes and checked the time again. "Time to go," he said simply as he stood and walked out of the tree line of the woods before any of them could say anything.

Ahead of him lay almost two hundred yards of open space that sloped gently down to the beach where the army of Tilwin was now camped. In the early morning light he could just make out the sentries the Tilwin had posted. The sun was coming up behind him and as he drew closer to the encampment one of the sentries spotted him. A cry went up from the man and seconds later a man on a tollie bred especially for war began riding out to meet him. There were half a dozen armed men trotting along behind.

Jason's own men were in the woods behind him. They were spread out for nearly a quarter of a mile in the same pattern they had used against the Karton. They were concealed by the trees and brush where the Karton couldn't see them, but they had a clear view of the Karton, as well as clear fields of fire.

Jason stopped when he reached a point halfway between his men and the Tilwin, forcing them to come to him. This would put the Tilwin within range of his archers just in case something did go wrong. He stood with his arms crossed over his chest, his feet spread slight, ready to fight or run. The man on the tollie reined to a halt about ten feet from him. The other men spread out on either side of the mounted man, all of them staring at Jason, trying to figure out what he was. He looked up at the mounted man, who wore the rank of General. "Good morning," he said with a smile.

"Who, or what are you?" the man asked gruffly.

'I am Jason of Preton, of the House of Vehey."

The man stared at him curiously for a moment. "I know the House of Vehey," he said flatly, his face hard and grim, "but not of you. You have an unusual name. I've never heard it before. But then, you are also an unusual looking man, if you are a man."

"So I've been told," Jason replied, maintaining the smile on his face.

"You are not of the House of Vehey. Where are you really from?" the man demanded.

Jason nodded and grinned. "In a way you are right. I'm not really from the House of Vehey. They have sort of adopted me. As from where I'm from? Well, that would take too long to explain, and I really doubt if you would believe me anyway. So why don't we just skip that part for now and get to the main issue."

"Which is?" the man asked, a slight smile of amusement starting to play at the corners of his mouth as he relaxed somewhat in his saddle.

"What you're doing here," Jason replied.

"Oh, that's simple. We're here to take over. What's that to you?" the man asked with a chuckle.

"I've come to ask you to reconsider; to turn around and go back to Tilwin. The people of Preton really don't want to fight a war with you, and would much rather sit down and discuss whatever the problem seems to be. But if you force the issue, well, then you could meet the same fate as the Karton."

All signs of humor vanished from the face of the man at the mention of the Karton. His lips became a thin slash across his face, and then a scowl as he glared down at Jason.

"What happened to the Karton, and how do you know about them?" the man asked.

Jason forced himself to remain calm. "They landed on the eastern shores of Preton four day ago with over forty thousand men. Before the sun reached its zenith, thirty thousand of them were either dead or wounded. I know, because I was there. I not only saw it but I led the attack."

The man glared at him for a long moment. "I think you are either a liar or a mad man," the Karton general finally snapped.

Jason grinned at the man. "Well, since it's not really in my nature to lie, even though I've been known to stretch the truth from time to

*Alazon*

time, I assure you that what I say is true. And as for me being mad? I've been accused of that from time to time. The jury is still out."

"Preton has no army," the Karton growled. "And even if they managed to raise one, they couldn't take on a trained army of that size and defeat them like that.

"Not only that," the man added hastily, "but it is impossible to travel from one coast of Preton to the other in less than three weeks, even on the fastest tollies, changing them every fifty miles or so. Unless you can fly like a bird," he added with a sneer.

"Maybe I can," Jason replied with a grin. But then he changed his demeanor and became serious. "Look, my friend, you have two choices open to you. One," he said, holding up a finger, aware of their eyes on his 'extra' one, "you can go back to Tilwin and we can work out new trade and peace treaties or, two, you can persist with your ideas of conquest, in which case you'll meet the same fate as the Karton. The choice is up to you, but I suggest you make it soon."

"I think," the Karton growled, "that when I get to Lemac I'll take my pleasure with the two daughters of Jarrell Vehey. They should both be ripe and ready for the picking by now."

Jason felt his anger surge up inside. "You'll never live to see the sun set this day," he told the Tilwin, his voice low but firm.

"Kill him!" the Karton roared to his men.

Jason had been prepared for just such a move. Even as the man shouted the order, Jason's hands flashed to his two swords. They were out and slicing through the arm of the man nearest Jason before the first Tilwin sword cleared its sheath. Two more men died before they had time to react. Jason found himself within striking distance of the tollie. The thought of killing the animal didn't settle particularly well with him, but he knew that this was no time to be squeamish. Swinging the katana in a horizontal arc with his right hand, with all his strength behind it, he severed the neck of the animal. The tollie pitched forward, throwing the general to the ground in front of it.

Jason had only the space of a heartbeat to admire the Tilwin's agility. The man rolled with the throw and came to his feet quickly, his sword in hand. Jason took one step forward and severed the man's sword arm just above the wrist with the ho-tachi. As the Tilwin gasped, clutching at the stub of his arm, Jason spun completely around to gain momentum. Holding the katana parallel to the ground, Jason struck the Tilwin just above his breast plate, severing the man's head from his shoulders.

He turned to face the remaining men, diving and rolling through a gap between two of them. Quickly getting to his knees he drove his ho-tachi through the back of one man and sliced through the legs of another with the katana. As he got to his feet the remaining men decided they had seen enough. They turned to flee this demon who killed faster than they could even think about it. But they didn't have far to run, as the entire Tilwin army was now surging up from the beach, swords drawn, spears thrusting into the air, with each and every man intent on killing Jason.

"I'm not that good," Jason said aloud, deciding that running for the woods was the better part of valor at this point. He turned and sprinted for the woods as clouds of arrows and energy beams began cutting into the men of Tilwin. But the Tilwin surged on, their own arrows coming perilously close to him as he raced for the safety of the trees.

Jason was less than fifty yards from the fringe of the shrubs which grew at the edge of the forest when something slammed into his back just below his left shoulder. Pain exploded through his upper body. He staggered for a few steps before falling to his knees. His sword dropped from suddenly limp hands as a second pain exploded in his back.

Jason looked down to see two bloody metal points and three inches of wooden shaft protruding from his chest where two arrows had pieced completely through him. *Kim's gonna be mad*, he thought as he tried to stand. His mind reeled. He looked to see Hass, Shon and Busker racing toward him. Their swords were raised high and their faces were set in masks of rage. *Why are they attacking me?* he wondered as he fell forward, his face slamming into the sand.

Hands grabbed and lifted him, jarring his body painfully. He thought he heard thunder and saw bolts of lightning zigzag across the sky but that didn't make any sense, as he knew there wasn't a cloud in the sky moments ago. The ground beneath him suddenly began to shake and roll, and the air vibrated as an ear splitting roll of thunder drowned out all other sounds for the moment. He heard screams fill the air and smelled the sharp, acrid odor of ozone, charred wood and flesh filled his nose and mouth, and somewhere in the back of his mind he knew what was happening.

"NOOOO!" he screamed as his body was jerked violently just before a blanket of blackness descended over his mind, the stench of burning and charred flesh filling his every sense

He tried to fight against the blackness, struggling like a man at the bottom of a mine shaft trying to reach the top. He saw a small spot of light in the distance and willed himself toward it. He forced it to grow larger, but the closer he got to it, the more intense was the pain in his chest. He ground his teeth and fought against the pain, finally forcing his eyes open to the blinding light. He blinked a few times to let them adjust and then opened them completely to see Kim's face looking down at him. She was smiling, but her eyes were red and swollen from crying.

"You know, Alien," she said softly, "this saving your life act is getting to be a bad habit."

"Where am I?" he asked hoarsely, his throat feeling sore and raw.

"It ain't Kansas, Toto," she told him with a grin.

"The ship?"

"Yes. Mother made us bring you up here. Your injuries were serious and I don't think she trusted our temples, or me, to take care of you without her help this time."

"How am I?"

"You'll live."

Jason's mind was suddenly filled with the memories of what had occurred just before he blacked out. He looked down and saw the two, six square inch patches of plasti-skin covering two spots on his chest. He knew there would be identical patches on his back. "Did you do this?"

"Of course," Kim replied with a grin. "Well, Mother told me and Seta what to do and guided us along. Now, what I want to know is why you weren't wearing your combat outfit?"

He had to stop and think for a moment before the image of a pretty young girl gathering up his outfit, with a promise to get it clean for him came to mind. "I sorta left it with a young lady to clean for me after the battle with the Karton."

"How pretty and how young?" Kim asked with a frown.

"Jealous?"

"Me? Of course not," she replied casually, but Jason could see a different answer in her eyes.

"Well, there's no need to be. She was only about ten or so. She was one of the girls working around the camp."

"I'll bet she was."

"Honest. Would I lie to you?"

"Ten?"

"Maybe eleven. You know I have trouble judging the ages of your people."

"Well, alright," she said with a smile as she leaned over to kiss him lightly.

Jason looked into her eyes, which were only inches from his own. "Have I told you lately that I love you?" he whispered.

"Not nearly enough," she replied as she eased herself up on the bed to lay beside him. She rested her head on his left shoulder, draping her arm over his waist.

The door of the med-lab slid open and her brothers walked in. They looked at Jason and Kim and grinned. "Come on, Sis, give the guy a break," Hass teased. "He's still recovering. I seriously doubt if he's up to satisfying your urges, cravings and wanton desires just yet."

"I'll give him a break," Kim whispered, kissing Jason's check as she slid from the bed. "I'll bread his damn neck."

"Alright," Jason said as the brothers joined Kim beside the bed, "would someone like to tell me how things went with the Karton? I seem to have missed most of it. I take it we won, otherwise you guys wouldn't be up here."

The brothers glanced briefly at one another, their smiles fading as they returned their eyes to him. Jason knew then that something was dreadfully wrong. Fear gripped his guts. "What happened? What's wrong?" he asked.

"Well, nothing really," Hass replied. "We won."

"What was the cost?"

Again there was a slight hesitation from the brothers. This time it was Shon who spoke.

"For our side, you were the only one who got hurt. As for the Tilwin, well, they were completely annihilated," Shon said softly. "There's nothing left of them."

As Shon's words registered in his mind, Jason remembered the flashes of lightning, the sound of thunder, and the smell of ozone and charred flesh. "Oh, God, no," he whispered, closing his eyes for a moment. He knew there was only one thing that could have caused that. "Mother?" he finally called out, opening his eyes at last.

"Yes?"

The soft, almost timid response of the computer reminded him of a child who knows they have done something wrong and is in for a scolding for it.

"You used the ship's weapons systems, didn't you?" he asked.

There was a brief hesitation on the computer's part. When Mother did answer, her voice was low and apologetic. "Yes."

"But the ship's weapon systems are designed to be used for defensive purposes," he said. "They can't be activated unless the ship is under attack. You told me yourself that you couldn't override that prime directive."

"You weren't listening, Jason. I said they could only be used for the defense of ship personnel, and that I was not programmed to be able to use them for purposes of attack."

"But you *did* use them to attack!" he snapped. He knew the destructive abilities of those weapons. They could destroy an entire planet in a matter of hours.

"No, I did not, Jason. I specifically used them in defense of ship personnel, which is you. It was never specified that ship personnel had to be physically present aboard the ship at the time, but merely states that they are to be used for their defense. I interpret that to mean any ship personnel, wherever they happen to be, which includes the surface of Alazon."

Jason realized Mother had found the one loophole, so to speak, in her prime directive, and had used the ships weapon system in his defense. "What did you use?" he asked, almost afraid to hear her answer.

"Well, since none of them had actually been tested in a combat situation, I decided the best course of action would be to try them all and see what happened. I started off with photon torpedoes, followed by gamma ray bombardment, particle beam disruptors, and ended up with neutron rays on a broad sweep of the area."

"What happened to the Tilwin?" Jason asked, his voice barely above a whisper.

There was a moment of drawn out silence before the computer spoke again.

"Jason, there are no more Tilwin left, Jason. The Tilwin, their ships, weapons, everything connected with them were vaporized and turned to dust."

Jason closed his eyes, trying to picture what must have happened in those few brief seconds. He had wanted to avoid any more killing than was absolutely necessary, but now Mother had carried it to the extreme. Her actions had annihilated every man, animal and insect within the parameters of the Tilwin camp, reducing even their wood and steel to particles of dust. The more he thought about it, the angrier he became.

"Damn you, Mother!" he yelled, frightening Kim and her brothers. "You know I didn't want that to happen! "Why? Why did you do that?"

"Because you were in danger, Jason!" Mother yelled back. "Hasn't it gotten through that thick skull of yours yet that I have the neural imprints of Nadia's personality, and that because of that, I also have some of her emotional ties to you that I can't ignore, even if I wanted to!

"I saw you get shot by the Tilwin and reacted accordingly. I reacted not only as a computer programmed for the defense of ship personnel, but the same Nadia would have. Maybe I'm supposed to be able to overcome that, but I'm sorry, I couldn't. Emotional responses are stronger than computer programs in me at times, and if you can't handle that, then shut me down, wipe my neural imprints clean and start all over. But even if you do that, you still may not be able to completely erase the Nadia portion of me without doing irreparable damage to my neural netting circuits.

"Jason, I'd like to be able to tell you it won't ever happen again, and I'll do my best to promise that, but I can't give you any guarantees that I won't react that way again in a similar situation."

Jason was stunned by the emotional outburst from the computer. He knew Mother had developed feelings and emotional responses, which was something her designers hadn't counted on happening, but not to this extent.

"Well, if this doesn't beat all," Hass said with a grin as Jason closed his eyes again. "Not only does he get our little sister to fall in love with him, and the twins to believe the sun rises and sets on his command, but he's also got a computer in love with him. If that's what you can call it."

"Shut up, Hass," Jason growled. He was in no mood to listen to the banter of Hass at the moment. "In fact," he said, opening eyes and looking at them, "I'd appreciate it if all of you would clear out for a while. I need some time to think things through and sort them out in my mind."

Kim leaned over and kissed him lightly before taking her brothers by the arms. "Come on, guys, I'll show you how you around and we'll give him some time to rest."

# TWENTY ONE

As Kim and her brothers left the med-lab, Jason lay back on the bed and closed his eyes, thinking of Mother's actions and the reasons for them. A part of him was angry with her for what she had done, but the scientist in him began to analyze her actions.

When Mother had first been designed and created, he and the others had theorized the remote possibility of the computer developing some degree of emotional responses, especially after the neural net imprinting from Nadia, but none of them had dreamed that it would have developed to this level.

Mother's organic brain had been genetically cloned from that of a dolphin. Certain alterations had been made to it, and it was maintained in a nutrient bath that was automatically cleaned and filtered to maintain purity. The organic portion was connected to the hardware portion by fiber optic "nerves" too small to be seen by the naked eye. It would take a hundred of them twined together to equal the thickness of a piece of silk sewing thread. It had taken the scientists of New Hope One nearly a month, working around the clock in shifts to connect the thousands of fiber optics to all the nerve centers of the organic brain, and then to the various mini-microchips that were equally as small, with all of this being protected by millions of nanites that immediately repaired any damage that might occur.

Once the computer had been programmed with all available knowledge and information from every possible source, it had been decided that the organic portion of the brain should be 'imprinted' with a particular personality. The discussions for and against this had lasted for days. Some wanted the computer to develop its own personality, while other argued that allowing that to happen could be dangerous, as they would have no way of knowing what direction that could lead. Jason had led the fight for imprinting and had finally won out.

After that, everyone was put through the most extensive and intensive psychological testing that could be devised to see who would be best suited for the imprint. When the final results had come in, Nadia was shown to have the most stable personality of them all, as well as having one of the most rational and practical minds, despite her somewhat warped sense of humor at times. She had eventually been connected to the organic brain of the computer by use of a modified Thought Transference Scanner and the imprint had begun. Everyone had paced nervously until it was completed.

It had taken nearly five hours before the computer had finally disconnected itself from the TTS and announced to one and all that the transfer was complete, stunning them with a perfect imitation of Nadia's voice. After a while they had come to accept it as normal.

The name 'Mother' had come about three days later when she had patiently corrected them on some calculations they were doing in connection with the drive capabilities of the new warp engines. She had sounded like a caring mother who was lovingly correcting a small child on a math problem, pointing out the error in their figures. Someone had commented, "Yes, Mother", and the nickname had stuck.

Signs of her personality had started to develop back on Luna, but it wasn't until after Jason had been awakened from hypersleep that he realized the computer was consciously working to develop her personality to an even higher level. Another factor no one had considered was that the imprint would also leave her with Nadia's feelings for Jason. With a sigh he opened his eyes and sat up. "Mother?" he called softly.

"Yes?"

"Look, I guess I can understand why you reacted the way you did. That doesn't necessarily mean I approve, because I don't, but I do understand."

"Does that mean you forgive me?" Mother asked, sounding exactly like Nadia had when she had done something to get his goat, then teasingly ask for his forgiveness.

"Yeah, I forgive you," he replied with a sigh. "You were only acting, or reacting, emotionally, and no one can really be held responsible for that. Hell, I've done the same thing myself a time or two."

"Thank you, Jason," Mother replied, her voice soft and sincere.

"Just do me one favor, will you?"

"Anything."

"The next time something like this comes up, if it ever does, try to think things through before acting, okay?"

"You got it, Boss Man!"

Jason sat up and let his feet dangle over the side of the bed for a moment. "How bad off am I?"

"Well, that's something we really should discuss. Can you make it over to the monitor?"

"What's up?" he asked as he stood and walked slowly to the console. He sat down on the chair and turned on the computer screen.

"To be honest," Mother replied hesitantly, "I'm not really sure."

"I don't like the sound of that. Explain yourself, Mother."

"Okay, let's start with this. You know how the KLZ formula has extended your life span and given you a few side benefits, right?"

"Yeah, so?"

"Well, when you were brought about this time I had Kim give you an injection of fifty cc's of it to help promote cell regeneration. I also had her draw blood and place it in the analyzer for me. I waned to check for any poisons which may have been on the arrows."

"And?"

"Jason, there was enough poison on the tips of each of those arrows to kill a dozen men almost instantly, but it didn't have any effect on you."

Jason was confused by this. "I don't understand."

"Neither did I at first. Here, take a look at this." The monitor screen came to life with two color images of a DNA double helix. "The one on the right is yours prior to your first injection of KLZ back on Luna. The one on the left is six months after the first injection. See the difference?"

Jason studied the two images carefully. He noticed what appeared to be a minute restructuring of the atoms in the one on the right, but it didn't seem to be anything major. The right side spiral was a little tighter, the atoms seeming a bit smaller, but that was about it. He told Mother what he saw. She then placed a third helix on the screen. "This is what your DNA looks like now," she told him.

Jason studied the third image and quickly picked out the differences between it and the first two. The spirals were much tighter, and the atoms much more compressed. There also seemed to be new, additional atoms. "What's it mean, Mother?"

There was a moment of hesitation before the computer replied. "I haven't completed all my tests yet, Jason, but preliminary indications show the introduction of a new, unknown protein that has interacted with the KLZ formula to produce an astonishing result."

"Get to the point."

"You probably ain't gonna like it, Blue Eyes."

"You're probably right," he replied with a sigh, "but tell me anyway."

"Well, for starters you can throw out the figures I gave you for a life span of a hundred and fifty to two hundred Earth years."

Jason felt a knot form in his stomach. "What do you mean?"

"I mean, if my calculations are anywhere near correct, you can triple that figure, and that's a conservative estimate in my opinion."

Jason didn't realize he had been holding his breath until it rushed out of him. "But what could have caused this?"

"I don't know, Jason. Since we arrived here I've run tests on the air, soil, bacteria of every type, even the food and water, but nothing I can find would lead to this. There's only one thing I haven't tested yet."

"What's that?"

"A Death Plant."

"You think it's possible this new protein could have come from the enzyme of a Death Plant?"

"It's the only possible solution I can come up with, Jason. Now, if it is, there are a few things you need to think about."

"Such as?"

"I've tried to duplicate the new protein artificially but I can't do it. It if comes from the Death Plant, and we can extract it and find the right combination of it and the KLZ formula, we can come up with a serum we could give to the people of Alazon."

Jason leaned back in the chair, pulling the loose fitting gown a little tighter around his waist. He thought of the implications of what Mother had just told him. A formula such as that could have a drastic alteration on the lives and people of Alazon. But, he wondered, would it be right to dispense it wholesale to everyone, or should he reserve it for only a few, such as Kim and her family? He realized he was now faced with a whole new can of worms, and the worms were starting to get out of hand.

"Take the plasti-skin off your chest," Mother told him.

Jason wasn't sure of her reasons for telling him to do this but he raised his right hand and slowly peeled away the artificial patches of skin. His eyes widened in surprise. He placed them on the console and stared down at the spots where the two arrows had protruded from his chest. Other than two small spots of angry looking redness, there was nothing to even indicate he had ever been wounded.

"How long have I been here, Mother?"

"Since yesterday."

Jason looked down at the wounds again. There was no way they should have healed that quickly.

"It would seem," Mother said, as if reading his mind, "that another advantage to come from this alteration is that all wounds heal within hours, leaving no visible trace of scar tissue. In other words, total and complete cell regeneration."

"Next you're gonna tell me I've become invincible," he said with a sigh.

"To be honest, Jason, according to my calculations, unless you are burned alive, or crushed to a pulp, just about any other type of wound you might receive will heal in a matter of hours.

"Even if you lose a leg or arm, you'll regenerate a new one in less than a month. In fact, even if you were decapitated, as long as your head and brain weren't severely damaged in the process, it wouldn't matter."

*Alazon*

"The hell it wouldn't!" he snapped. "It would matter to me. A lot!"

"Oh, only temporarily," Mother replied. "You see, I could either clone a new body for you and graft your head on to it, or keep you in a nutrient bath for a couple of months and you'd grow a new body on your own."

The image of his head sitting in a nutrient bath while he grew a new body sent shivers down his spine. The thought of being able to clone himself a dozen, or even a thousand times, was also frightening.

"So, what you're telling me," he said at last, speaking softly, "is that I have the potential to practically live forever."

"I wouldn't say 'forever' just yet," Mother replied, "but if my preliminary figures are right, a couple of thousand years should pass before you start to hit what would be considered middle age. And, yes, it's also possible that forever is attainable."

"Oh, shit," Jason whispered, realizing he now held in his hands the hope of immortality that man had dreamed of since the beginning of time. He also realized that he was now like the Royac in some ways, and that frightened him. He didn't want to become like them. He shook his head, trying to dismiss the Royac from his mind for the time being.

"Look, Mother, let's put this on the back burner for the time being. Or at least until we can get our hands on a Death Plant to find out if it is the source of the protein enzyme."

"Ok, but there are some other issues you're gonna have to deal with pretty quick like." She told him.

"Such as?"

"Right now there are celebrations going on all over Preton for the victories over the Karton and Tilwin. And there's a strong grass roots movement to have you proclaimed as King of Preton."

"You know I don't want that, Mother," he replied with a sigh.

"Yeah, I know, Jason, but like Kimmy has said, you may have to accept it for the time being."

"Is there any way I can avoid it?"

"At this point in time I really doubt it." Mother's voice was sympathetic. "I've been monitoring things down there, as well as listening in on the conversations between Jarrell, Shon and Hass, and from the sounds of it Jarrell has the consent of the other mayors to proclaim you king."

Jason shook his head in resignation. Events were moving too quickly for him to stop them. He was being trapped, with no real way out.

"However," Mother continued, "it could all work out for the best. Besides, you could also put some stipulations on your acceptance."

He could hear the slightest hint of mischievousness in her voice. "What have you got up your sleeve, Mother?"

"Just this. Accept the position as King of Preton, but tell them you'll do it for only a specified period of time. Say, five, maybe ten years, and then everything reverts back to the way it was with democratic rule.

"You can even leave their current democratic process in place, stating that you will use your position as king only as a final authority should something arise which they can't settle among themselves."

Jason thought about it for a moment. "That might work. It would allow them to still elect their own mayors, while it would also give me the authority to implement the changes that will help them as a society and a race."

"Hey, you catch on quick," Mother teased.

"Yeah," he replied despondently, "but I still don't like the idea of being a king."

Mother was silent for a moment. When she did speak again, her voice was tinged with understanding and compassion for him.

"I know you don't, Jason, but if I didn't think you could handle it, I'd tell you to pack it in and take you somewhere else."

"I've considered that option," he told her.

"I know you have. So have I. Look, do you remember the stories of how the islands of the Pacific were 'discovered' by 'explorers', such as Captain Cooke?"

"What does that have to do with anything, Mother?"

"Pay attention, Blue Eyes," Mother told him. "Back on Earth you had a Polynesian culture that had gotten along just fine without the white man and his 'more advance' culture for a few thousand years, just like the people of Alazon.

"Then Cooke comes along and the natives treat him almost like a god, much the say way you have been treated by the people of Alazon, and for the same reasons. You look different, your culture and knowledge is vastly more advanced, and you represent an unknown, mysterious quality to them. Basically, deep down, most of them are afraid of you, but only because they don't really know what you are capable of.

"However, unlike those early ignorant and overblown Earth explorers who eventually caused the downfall and demise of the 'primitives' they found, you have the unique opportunity to do some good. Sort of a chance to make up for all the screw ups and mistakes of your ancestors. You have a chance to do something worthwhile here, Jason, and I believe you can do it."

"But only if I accept being king, right?"

"Yeah, buddy boy, that's the price you're gonna have to pay. All things considered, it ain't that much."

"Well, there is one thing I have going for me that no other king or ruler has ever had," he told her.

"What's that?"

"I've got you in my corner to help me out and give me advice. And to keep me from screwing up royally."

"You know," Mother replied, "that is just about the nicest thing you've ever said to or about me. I take back all those nasty things I've ever said about you."

"Don't do that, Mother. You might make me think you actually like me if you do."

"Oh, right, and we wouldn't want that to happen, would we?"

"Nope. Ok, where's Kim and her brothers."

"On the bridge. She's showing them some of the various operations of the ship, as well as different shots of the planet."

"Is she doing it on her own, or are you assisting her?"

"Most of it on her own. Believe it or not, Jason, she's one very intelligent young woman who learns very quickly. Show her something once and you don't have to show her again. While her grasp of the bridge is no where near the level of yours, I would venture to say that with just a little training she could competently operate this ship with a minimum of assistance from me. I'd love to test her to see what her I.Q. is. I would almost bet that it's within twenty points of your own."

"You could be right. Well, tell them I'm going to my cabin to take a shower and that I'll join them afterwards."

"Will do."

As he left the med-lab Jason realized he wasn't as weak as he had been earlier, and that the pain he had felt previously was almost completely gone from his shoulder, chest and back. He shook his head and smiled to himself. There were definitely some very positive side effects to the formula. He would have to get his hands on one of the Death Plants and run tests to see if it possessed the unknown protein Mother spoke of. If it did, he would then have to begin the process of mixing it with the KLZ formula to get just the right amounts to provide the correct dosage to administer to the others. That brought up another question.

If he could perfect it, and he was sure he could with Mother's help, then who should receive it? Without question Kim and the rest of her family, as well as Busker, and possibly Ster, but after that, who?

As he stepped into the shower he was hit with an idea. He let the hot water relax his tired muscles as his mind tossed the idea about in his mind. He knew he could make it work to his advantage if he played it right. He would put things to them in such a way that they would have to accept his conditions. By the time he stepped from the shower and dried off he was feeling much better.

Going back into the main salon of his quarters he found a fresh jumpsuit, boots and shorts laid out for him on the bed. He grinned, knowing Kim had been there. As he finished dressing he noticed the open door to the Captain's dining room. He pushed it open wider and stepped through to see Kim sitting at the table. There were covered plates on a serving art beside the table. "Where are your brothers?" he asked.

"I've got them hooked up to Mother. She's teaching them English. I got tired of them always complaining about how they couldn't understand us, so I though it would be a good idea if they could speak it as well."

"Actually," Jason told her as he sat down at the table, "that's a good idea. It might also be good for Busker and the rest of your family to learn. Possibly even Ster. That way we could have sort of a private language we could use among ourselves."

Kim nodded. "I agree. But that can wait for now. Right now you need to eat."

Kim served him herself, smiling while she did as if it were a task she enjoyed. Watching her face, Jason could se that she really did. One she filled his plate with food she filled her own. The two of them ate eagerly, not speaking until they had finished and she had removed the dishes from the table and placed them on the cart.

"You know," she said as she reached across the table to take his hands, "that when you go back down they are going to try and make you king." It wasn't a question, but a statement of fact.

"I know."

"Have you thought about what you are going to do?"

"Yes."

"Well?" she asked expectantly when he didn't elaborate.

"You'll find out when I tell the others."

"Hey, that is not fair!"

"Look, Kim, if I accept, and I'm not saying I will, there are going to be some conditions and stipulations, and they may not like some of them."

Her face took on a look of worry. "What if they do not accept your conditions?"

Jason looked at her for a long moment, his face becoming stern. "if they don't, then I leave Alazon. If I do that, will you go with me?"

"Yes," she answered without the least bit of hesitation.

"Even though you know you would be leaving behind everything and everyone you've ever known for something totally unknown?"

He could see the struggle going on her eyes. He didn't like himself for putting her on the spot like this but he had to be absolutely certain of her and her love for him. Kim finally nodded her head, her eyes never leaving his.

"If you asked me to go with you, I would," she said softly.

Jason stood and pulled her to her feet to hold her close. "Well, there won't be any need for that. I'm going to stay and become king, even though I really don't want to."

It took Kim a moment to realize he had deliberately tested her. When she did she reacted quickly. She pulled back and kicked him hard on the shin, shoving his upper body backwards at the same time. The move was so totally unexpected that he ended up on his butt.

"You jerk!" Kim yelled at him, balling up her fist as if to hit him. "You did that on purpose! You were testing me just to see how I would react!"

"Well, sort of," he admitted, feeling somewhat ashamed of himself as he stood up.

"You…you…<u>Grumfeld</u>!" she spat out, calling him just about the worst insult there was on the planet.

Before Jason could respond, Kim whirled and stalked out of the room, grumbling and muttering to herself about blue eyed aliens and men in general.

"Way to go, bright boy," Mother said, her voice containing a trace of scorn.

"Mother?"

"Yeah, I know…shut up."

Jason headed for the door. He knew he had to apologize to Kim. He had to try and explain the reasons for what he had done. He knew now it had been wrong to test her like that. He had deliberately played on her emotions, but only because he had wanted to be absolutely sure of her feelings for him, when he should have known all along. His own sense of insecurity had led him to this foolish act. He headed for the hydro-gardens, figuring that's where she'd gone. He was ready to get down on his knees and apologize if necessary, but when he arrived at the hydro-gardens, Kim was no where in sight.

"Where is she, Mother?" he asked, looking around in frustration.

"Gone. Split. Flew the coop. Her and her brothers."

"Where?"

"Where do you think? They took a shuttle and headed for home."

"They couldn't have done that so quickly without your help, Mother."

"So sue me."

"She's mad at me."

"You do have a knack for the understatement, don't you?" Mother said with a chuckle.

"Alright, Mother," he said with a sigh, "what do I do now?"

"Sorry, Blue Eyes, but you're on your own on this one."

"Mother!"

"I'm sorry, the party you are calling is temporarily out of service at this time. Please check your directory and try again."

"To hell with you," he mumbled.

Jason stood where he was for a moment, wondering what he could do to make it up to her. As an idea slowly formed in his mind he began to grin. He turned and headed for the metallurgy lab. One there he went through the various small compartments along one wall until he found the materials he was looking for. He gathered them together and went to work. He took his time, working carefully to make sure he had just what he wanted. It took him nearly three hours, but when he finished he raised his goggles and smiled to himself. "This should do it," he said aloud as he tossed the goggles on the table and headed for his cabin.

He washed his face and hands, then went through the drawers of the dresser unit until he found what he was looking for. He placed the newly crafted item into the small box and stuck the box into his pocket and then headed for the shuttle bay.

Climbing into a small shuttle he shot down to the surface of the planet, bringing the craft to a screaming landing beside the one behind the stable that Kim and her brothers had used. As soon as the hatch opened the twins were there to greet him, laughing as he picked them up and carried them back into the house.

When he entered the common room Jason saw that the entire family was there, along with Busker and Ster. It was almost as if they were waiting for him. The second he entered the room all conversation ceased. He caught Jarrell's eyes and the older man nodded his head slightly. Jason set the twins down and took his seat at the opposite end of the table from Jarrell, noticing how Kim made it a point not to look at him.

"Jarrell," he said, looking only at the older man, "I've been thinking about what you said in regards to me becoming king. Now, while I'm personally dead set against this for my own moral reasons, I think, as do you, that it may be the only way for the time being. However, before I accept that position, there are some conditions and stipulations which you and your family will have to accept as well."

"I thought there might be," Jarrell replied seriously.

"Firs, I will accept only as you beside me as my Chief Advisor. This is your world, Jarrell, and I'll need to rely heavily on your knowledge of it."

"What else?" Jarrell asked as Jason hesitated for a moment.

Leaning back in his chair, Jason tried to figure out a way to put what he had to say next as delicately as he could. And in a way that would make them understand the importance of it.

"What's the life expectancy of the average person on Alazon?" he asked Jarrell.

Jarrell, not expecting a question of this nature, looked at him with a puzzled expression for a moment. "What does that have to do with anything?"

"Please, just humor me."

"Well, it is about eighty-five for men and ninety for women."

Jason did some quick calculations in his head. "That would make it about seventy and seventy four and a half Earth years, respectively. Ok, what would you say if I told you my own current life expectancy, as closely as I can calculate it, would be around seven hundred and twenty three of your years, and that I can do the same thing for you?"

Jason couldn't suppress the grin at the expressions of shock and gasps of disbelief from those around the table. Except for the twins. They had been reading his mind and were already grinning like two little mischievous imps.

"That's impossible!" Hass gasped.

"No, Hass, it's not," Jason replied with a shake of his head. "Actually, I can damn near give all of you the closest thing to immortality there is."

"Jason, wait!" said Jarrell, shaking his head and using his hands to motion for the others to be quiet. "I don't understand this, so please explain what it is you are talking about."

Jason nodded and smiled at the older man. "Years ago my mother experimented with a serum which would extend life. She came up with what she called KLZ five-nine-seven, which she then administered to the children of the colony. Along with extending lie, it was also supposed to with cell regeneration, enabling injuries to heal quicker.

"Now, when I first awoke from the hyper-sleep chamber, and after things had calmed down somewhat, Mother told me I had a life expectancy of about a hundred and fifty to two hundred Earth years. That would be about one hundred and eighty to two hundred and forty of your years. However, since then something has happened to dramatically alter that.

"For reasons that aren't clear just yet, Mother thinks there may be a protein molecule in the enzyme of the Death Plant venom that has somehow altered the KLZ formula. It turn it has also altered my life expectancy, along with some very beneficial side effects.

"But what's this talk about immortality?" Shon asked.

"Mother," replied Jason, "has perfected the process of cloning. That is taking cells from something and growing a completely new item. I'll give you an example.

"From a single drop of your blood, Mother could clone, or 'grow', a completely new you. You would have a body the same age as you do now, except that it would be in perfect physical condition. She could then use the Thought Transference Scanner to transfer every scrap of information, every memory, every thought you've ever had from your old brain into the new one. This could be done indefinitely."

"And what would happen to the 'old' us?" asked Liet.

"That body would be disposed of," he told her.

That brought a pall of silence over the table for a moment as the others considered the implications of his words. Jason could see the doubts, and even some fears in their eyes. Immortality was something all people had dreamed of, but never thought could happen. To the people of Alazon, only gods were immortal. Even back on Earth it was something the rich and powerful would have paid any price for.

"Okay," Jason said at last, snapping them out of the stupor, "here's what I propose. I'm going to perfect and develop the serum, and when I do, all of you are going to take it, and I mean everyone in this room. Seta should also be included, but we'll get to that later. If I've got to go on for the next seven to eight hundred years, or longer, I want those around me I can trust and depend on."

Jarrell started to speak but Jason held up his right hand to stop him. "I'll go into more details later, but please let me finish." Jarrell sighed and nodded.

"I'll accept your kingship and become King of Preton, but for no more than ten of your years. In that time I should be able to accomplish most of the things which need to be done, putting the people of Alazon on the road to development and advancement. After that I will simply be an advisor.

"The current democratic process of elections will not be changed or altered. I will not interfere with it, other than to make sure it stays on the up and up. My authority will be used to settle disputes and to introduce things to this world which will help the people."

He stopped to give them time to think about this for a few seconds. As he did, he reached into his pocket and withdrew the small box, keeping it concealed in the palm of his hand.

"Now, I think there is another matter that needs to be addressed at this time." He glanced at the twins. They were grinning and squirming around on their seats in anticipation.

"Jarrell, back on my world there was an old custom where, if a man wanted to marry a woman, he first went to her parents and asked for her hand in marriage. This was to obtain their permission and blessing. In some cases the girl might not necessarily want to be married to that man, but if her parents thought it was a good idea she often had little choice in the matter. There were many parents who were more than happy to marry off a headstrong, somewhat difficult daughter to a man they hoped cold control her and make a respectable woman out of her."

Jason saw the grins and heard the snickers around the table as all of them began to realize where he was headed. They glanced at Kim, but she was ignoring them and staring straight at him.

"However," Jason continued, "in those cases where the man and woman actually love one another and wanted the marry, the man would still ask permission of the father in order to receive his blessing."

"What happened if the father denied that request?" Jarrell asked, his eyes dancing with amusement.

"Well, that did happen from time to time. Usually when it did the man went off in search of another woman to be his wife. Then again, if he and the woman really loved one another, sometimes the two of them would run off together and get married anyway. Of course, that usually caused a lot of problems for all concerned.

"Now, I know I'm not of your world, Jarrell," he said, speaking in a softer, more sincere tone, "but all of you have become family to me, and I have come to love all of you. And, believe it or not, I do love Kim and want to marry her. Not only that, but every king should have a queen by his side. Therefore, I'm asking for your permission, and your blessing, to marry your daughter."

"Hey," Kim said softly, "do I have any say-so in this?"

"Hush, woman," he told her sternly. "This is between your father and myself. When we want your opinion we'll give you permission to speak."

Kim fumed and turned red, but it was due as much from the laughter that exploded from everyone around the table as from anything else. She crossed her arms over her breasts and leaned back in her chair, sticking her tongue out at him.

"Jason," Jarrell said solemnly, "I think this custom of yours has a lot of merit, but I'm worried about something."

"What?"

"Are you sure you really want that added responsibility right now? I mean, shortly you will be taking on the position of King of Preton, with all that entails, and if you add to that the headaches that can be created by marrying a headstrong, irrationally impulsive, stubborn young woman like Kimmy, well, it could make life pretty tough on you, to say the least.

"With all that in mind, perhaps you should put off asking for her hand until she learns how to be an obedient, respectfully wife. Or at least until she learns how to cook and sew. We wouldn't want our new king going around in threadbare clothing with his ribs sticking out."

Jason fought to keep his face straight, as if seriously considering what Jarrell was saying. "Well, I do have the food dispensers and plenty of clothing aboard my ship. That should last me for the next hundred years or so, which should be enough time for her to learn the basics."

Jarrell leaned forward and placed his forearms on the table. "True, but you can't be flying up there every time you need a good meal or clean clothing. Of course, you know you are always welcome at our table, and I'm sure Vinny would be more than happy to take care of your clothing needs for you.

"But, really, Jason, a man, especially a king, should have his own table to sit down to. With food prepared by a loving and caring wife. I'm just worried about you, that's all. But then, I guess you could always hire a maid and cook to handle those things if you had to.

"However," Jarrell continued with an exaggerated sigh, "if she really is what you want, and as long as you understand what it is you'll be getting yourself into, then not only do I give my blessings, but my prayers for your health and well being."

"Thank you, Jarrell. And I appreciate your concerns." Jason turned to Kim's mother. "Liet?"

"Take her. Get her out of my hair," Liet said with a wave of her hand.

Jason slid his hand over the table and raised it, leaving the small box sitting in front of Kim. She looked down at it and then up at him as she hesitantly reached for it and pulled it closer. When Kim lifted the lid her eyes opened wide in surprise and her breath caught in her throat. Her fingers trembled visible as she carefully withdrew the ring and brought it out so the others could see it.

"What...what is this?" she whispered as tears of happiness brimmed in her eyes.

"It's an engagement ring," Jason said softly. "It's a symbol of love a man gives to a woman when he asks her to marry him, and to show the rest of the world that he loves her. It's also a promise of what is yet to come for them."

"No jokes or tricks this time?" Kim asked, her voice almost pleading. "You really are asking me to marry you?"

"Yes. I love you, Kim, even if it took me a while to realize it. So, will you marry me and be my wife, my queen, and the mother of my children?"

"Yes! By all the god of Alazon, yes!" Kim cried as she practically leaped out of her chair and onto his lap. Her arms went around his neck and she kissed him, completely oblivious to the presence of the others in the room.

"Think she's still mad at him?" Jason heard Hass ask.

"If she is," Shon replied, I'd hate to see her really happy."

Kim turned around on Jason's lap and slipped the ring over her middle finger, holding her hand out so that all of them could see it.

"That is an unusual stone," Jarrell remarked, smiling happily at the happiness of his eldest daughter.

"It's an emerald," Jason told him. "From the mineral scan Mother did of your planet when we first arrived I discovered there were no emeralds here on Alazon. Back on Earth they were considered precious stones, rating up there with diamonds. This one is cut in the classic "Emerald Cut" that was the most popular back on Earth."

Busker nodded at Kim's hand. "You realize," he said to Jason, "that just became the rarest, and therefore, most valuable gem on Alazon, don't you?"

Jason nodded. "Probably. But I wanted to give her something no one else could."

"Where did you get it?" asked Hass.

"From the ship. During mining operations on Luna we found veins of diamonds, emeralds, rubies, even gold and silver that we never told those back on earth about. We stored them, thinking they might come in handy when we reached a new world. They could be used for trade, but there are also some practical, scientific applications for them as well. However," he added with a grin, "I doubt if anyone thought they would be used like this. But I don't think they would mind."

"Too bad if they did," Kim whispered just loud enough for Jason to hear.

"So," said Vinny, smiling warmly at her sister as she spoke up for the first time, "when is the wedding going to take place?"

"As soon as possible!" Kim replied quickly. "I don't want to give him any time to change his mind!"

"Not so fast," Liet told her. "it will take time to organize things. There are a thousand and one details that will have to be attended to and worked out. It is going to take at least a month. Keep in mind that this will not be an ordinary wedding. This will be the wedding of the oldest daughter of the Senior Mayor of Lemac to the Commander of the Army, and future king of Preton. Much will have to be done."

"Your mother's right," Jarrell told Kim. "In the meantime, there are other things that have to be taken care of."

"Like what?" Kim asked. Her impatience to get married as soon as possible was clearly evident.

"Like getting things settled between Preton, Tilwin and Karton," Jason replied as he lifted her from his lap. "So why don't you women go take care of the wedding arrangements while we men go finish what we started."

"Jason, I've been wondering about something for a while now," said Hass.

"What?"

"With everything you have aboard your ship, especially in the way of weapons, why was it even necessary to raise and train an army to fight the Karton and Tilwin? You could have stopped them all by yourself."

"Pride," Vinny said softly before Jason had a chance to answer.

Hass looked at his sister. "What do you mean, Vinny?"

Vinny looked around at the others as if embarrassed she had spoken up, but finally looked at Hass. "If Jason had taken it upon himself to stop the Tilwin and Karton, none of the people of Preton would have really appreciated what had been done," she told her brother.

"By raising the army, training them, and then having them fight, Jason gave them a sense of purpose. He gave them a sense of what freedom is worth. He gave them a sense of pride they can live with and pass on to their children. It was the only way he could do it and have it mean anything."

When Vinny stopped speaking there was silence around the table as the others considered her words. Hass finally nodded his head in understanding.

"Hey, Alien," Kim said as she turned to face him, her hands on her hips. "I want you to promise me something."

"What?"

"No more getting shot, stabbed, or hurt in any other way from now on."

"Not if I can help it," he replied with a short laugh.

"Jason?"

He turned to face Liet. The older woman was looking at him intently. "Yes?"

"Not to get off the subject, but I want to know more about this serum you spoke of. Besides the longevity and healing of wounds, what other effects will it have on us?"

"Once it's administered, Liet, you really won't notice any visible changes in yourself. You'll simply remain as you are now, but for a very long time. However, it will probably make you feel younger in some ways because your body won't tire or age as it normally does.

"When given to children, at least in the original form, it didn't have much effect until they reached puberty. After that it began to slow the physical aging process so that their bodies stayed younger longer than normal. But it doesn't affect a person's ability to learn, or anything like that. The mind continues to function normally. So does the body, but at a much different rate."

"How will it be administered?" asked Vinny.

"By injection, the same way it was given to me."

Liet's face became stern as she looked around at her children. "Alright, but after the first set of grand children from each of you, I flatly refuse to change another diaper."

They all laughed at that. They knew Liet would happily change diapers on grand children, great grand children, and even great, great grand children whenever they needed it. Her sternness didn't fool any of them in the least.

# TWENTY TWO

News of the impending wedding between Jason and Kim spread like wildfire throughout Preton once the date was set and the invitations sent out. It was to be the social event of the century, and even those not specifically invited started making plans to see the joining of the daughter of the Senior Mayor of Preton to the alien man who had trained and lead the army of Preton to victory over the Tilwin and Karton. As the people began to gather, the stories of the victories were told and retold by the men who had been there. While everyone liked the story of how Jason's tactics had outsmarted and defeated the Karton, it was the story of how the Tilwin had been wiped from the face of the earth by the fire and lightning that had swept down on them from the sky when Jason had been shot in the back by the cowardly Tilwin that people most wanted to hear.

Wide, expressive eyes told of how the Tilwin had vanished, destroyed by the gods in all their rage and anger for the Tilwin daring to hurt Jason. With the telling of each tale Jason's stature began to take on that of a god. That was something Jason desperately wanted to avoid, but seemed powerless to do so. However, it was something that Seta seized on to immediately.

The High Priestess, along with the mayors, were the only ones outside the Vehey household who knew of the plans to crown Jason as King of Preton. Seta had small statues made of Jason in various garb and poses, which she then had placed in the small niches lining the walls of the main temple chamber.

When Jason found out about it he nearly exploded in rage. He rushed to the temple to have them removed, but when he arrived Seta was waiting for him. She patiently explained her reasoning and rationale behind what she had done. She told him that she, as well as Jarrell and the other mayors, thought it would solidify his position in the minds of the people, thereby making it easier for them to accept him as their king.

She explained to him that if he were considered even semi-divine, the acceptance of him by the populace would be nearly automatic. Looking around at the people in the temple, Jason realized she was right, and if he ordered her to remove the statues, she would, but it might cause a near riot. Especially among the female populace who were bringing flowers to place before the small icons, as well as lighting candles and incense as they prayed before them.

"Seta, I agreed to be your king, not your god!" he fumed, once they were alone in her private office.

"True, but many people already think of you as a god, Jason," she told him softly, her eyes dropping down to the floor for a moment. "They have heard over and over of how you were shot by the Tilwin, two of their poisonous arrows completely piercing your body, and of how the Tilwin were then annihilated for it. To them, if you are not a god, then you are a child of the gods, and someone to be revered."

"Is that how you think of me?" he asked.

"Perhaps," she whispered after a moment. "I don't know what to think at times."

"Seta, I can assure you that I am not a god. I'm a man, plain and simple."

Jason had left Seta standing there as he turned and left the temple. Outside he met up with Jarrell. As the two of them walked back to the house, Jason seemed to notice for the first time the profusion of jumpsuits the people were wearing. He stopped at a street corner and looked around. It seemed to him that just about everyone was wearing them.

Jarrell noticed his look and laughed lightly. "The tailors have had to take on extra help to make them," the older man told him. "Although, if you'll notice, none of them have the zippers or other type of fasteners yours have. Our people don't have the technology to make those things, so they have improvised with buttons. Some are cleverly hidden, while others are visible and decorative. Oh, and yesterday I saw a group of young men who had dyed their hair brown."

"You're kidding" Jason exclaimed. But the look of amusement on the face of Jarrell assured him that the older man wasn't. "This is getting out of hand," Jason said helplessly as they resumed their walk home.

"Relax, Jason, it is only a fad. And like all fads, it will pass. Although, I have to admit that the brown hair doesn't look all that bad on some of them."

Jason was silent for nearly a block before speaking again. "Jarrell, what makes you think I'll make a good king? And don't give me any of that crap about the prophecy."

"Because you hate the idea of being a king so much you will do the best job at it that you can. You want to prove there is such a thing as a good king. One who can rule justly, fairly, and with a sense of compassion and understanding for the people.

"You won't want to make any mistakes that would turn the people against you, as that would hamper your long range goals. At the same time, you'll use your position and power to better our lives in ways most of us can't even begin to dream of. That, my friend, is why I know you'll make a good king."

Later that night, after tucking the twins into bed and telling them a story, Jason went to his own room and got into bed. In his mind he went back over the conversation with Jarrell and knew the older man was right. Because Jason hated the idea of being king, it would make a better king out of him. At least that's what he hoped.

Jason was almost asleep when he heard the soft click of the latch on his door. He sat up as it opened. The light from the hallways clearly outlined the body of Kim beneath the nearly sheer nightgown she was wearing as she stood for a moment in the doorway. She closed the door softly and quickly crossed the room. Stopping beside his bed, Kim untied the ribbon at her throat that held the gown together, letting it drift slowly down to collect at her feet. Jason could smell the scent of her perfume as she got into bed with him. She pressed her body against his with an urgency and desire that was not to be denied.

"Make love to me, my blue eyed alien," she whispered as her body molded itself to his.

#

When Jason awoke alone the next morning he first thought Kim's visit of the night before had been a dream. But the lingering scent of her perfume, and the strand of long silver hair he found on the blue pillow case told him it had been real. It was the first time they had been together in a week, and while he couldn't deny the pleasure he derived from their love making, he was worried about her parents finding out. Being engaged to her was one thing; making love to her all night in the same house was another story. He lay thinking about it for a moment, then decided he would have to deal with it if and when the subject came up. In the meantime he didn't really have anything planned for the day. It would be a good day to go up to the ship and go over a few things with Mother. He wanted to check on how she was doing with replicating the serum he had obtained. "Maybe I'll take the twins," he said aloud as he got out of bed.

Vanda and Manda hadn't brought up the subject of him taking them flying since that first day, at least not verbally. However, from time to time Jason would have the idea suddenly spring into his mind and he would look at the twins to see them grinning at him like a couple of Cheshire cats, knowing they had 'planted' the idea in his mind. He washed and brushed his teeth before dressing and heading for the common room. He was surprised to find Liet, Kim and Vinny sitting on the padded bench against the wall with half a dozen men on the floor in front of them. Each man was displaying various bolts of cloth to the women for their inspection.

"Gentlemen," Liet was saying as Jason poured himself a cup of coffee that Kim had made earlier for him and sat down at the table, "you know the House of Vehey is not the house of a rich merchant or tradesman. The pay a mayor receives is not that much, and we have no outside business interests to fall back on. It is not like you are presenting your goods to the House of Fleds, who could afford bolt after bold of your most expensive material."

Jason watched with amusement, and a growing sense of admiration, the performance Liet was putting on. He grinned at the way she was skillfully manipulating the men.

"Now," Liet continued, "while we do expect to pay a fair price for the material we select, we will sew the dressed ourselves to insure the secrecy of their design. You are all aware of the abilities and talents of my daughter Vinny with a needle and thread, as well as my own," she added with just the right touch of modesty, "so that will help cut down on the expenses."

"But, Madam Vehey," said one of the men, shrugging his shoulders and spreading his hands, "would you have us simply donate our best materials for the dresses?"

Liet shook her head slowly from side to side, managing to look sad as she did. "Oh, Akar, such a generous move on behalf of any member of your guild would be more than this humble woman could ask for. However," she added with a sigh, her face still looking slightly downcast, "can you imagine the prestige it would bring to a member of your guild were it known he had done such an act of magnanimity? Why, people would be so impressed by his generosity that they would flock to his shop for all their future purchases. They would want to buy from a man who had done such a thing, especially if there were a plaque on the front of his shop to proclaim to one and all his sense of altruism for this most special occasion in the history of Preton."

Jason nearly choked on his coffee as he tried to keep from laughing when the men began to practically shove bolts of cloth at Liet and her daughters in the hope of becoming the one whose material would be used, free of charge, for the wedding dresses of the daughters of the Senior Mayor of Preton. But Liet was far from through. She selected material for one dress from one dealer, material for another from a second, and so on. She subtly made each man feel special, as she had not specified which material, or of what color, would be used to Kim's wedding dress. She made it a point to leave each of them thinking it would be his.

After the men had gathered up the remaining bolts of cloth and left, Jason finally let out the laughter he had been holding back. "That was beautiful!" he told Liet, seeing the sly grin of amusement on her face. "But what about all those plaques? Won't that be expensive?"

"Not really," she replied. "You see, Jason, while it is true that the salary of a mayor, even the Senior Mayor of Preton, is not very much, as we do not have any other income, in their haste and willingness to please, those men forgot that both Jarrell and I come from extremely wealthy families. We were both only children, and when our respective parents died, all their wealth came to us."

"So, in reality you could have affording to pay for the material, right?

"In reality," Liet answered with a grin, "I could buy every bolt of cloth in every one of their ships, and their shops as well, and still leave each of our children a small fortune. But why should I pay for something that someone is willing to give me for free? As for the plaques? I will have them made by my cousin. He is a metal worker and will give me a good price on them."

"That's my mother," Kim said with a laugh as Liet and Vinny headed for Liet's bedroom with the material.

As Kim stood up and came toward him Jason noticed that she seemed to be walking a little stiffly. "What's wrong?" he asked.

Kim grinned impishly. "Well, Alien, up until a week ago I was a virgin. So, when you combine that fact with one very hot and passionate night of love making, then toss in a guy who is over twice the size of the men of Alazon in that area, a woman is bound to get a little stiff and sore in the morning until she gets used to him."

"And just how would you know about the sizes of the men of Alazon?" he teased as he wrapped his arms around her and pulled her down onto his lap.

"I asked around."

"Ah, Kim, does your mom know about…."

"Us? About me coming to your room last night?"

"Yes."

"Sure. So does Daddy."

"And they don't mind?"

"Why should they mind?" Kim asked. "We are engaged to be married. However, mom did say that we should stop about a week before the wedding."

"Why?"

"She said it would make our wedding night that much better. She said that since I know what I'll be missing, a week away from you will only make me that much more anxious for our wedding night."

"Not to mention that much more horny," he teased.

"Yeah, that, too!" she replied with a grin.

The twins and Baby came running into the room demanding attention. Kim got off his lap so the twins could climb up onto it. "Jason's taking us flying today!" Vanda told Kim, his little face beaming.

"Oh? And what makes you so sure of that?" Kim teased.

Manda tapped the side of her head with her finger. "He said so," she told Kim.

Jason laughed and wrapped his arms around the twins. "I'm going to have to find a way to block my thoughts from you two little imps or I won't be able to surprise you any more." He hugged them tightly, kissing each of them before setting them down and turning to Baby to pet her.

"Actually," he said to Kim, "I thought that since I didn't really have anything pressing to do today that it would be a good day to take them up to the ship."

"Kimmy, too," asked Vanda.

"Sure," he replied.

"What 'bout Vinny?" asked Manda

"If she wants to go."

"If I want to go where?" Vinny asked as she came into the room carrying a tray loaded with plates, scrambled eggs and toast.

"Jason is taking us all up to the ship today," Manda told her excitedly. "We all get to go flying today."

"Really?" Vinny asked as she and Kim began to set the table.

"Sure," Jason told her.

"Well, you kids can go," Liet told them as she came into the room, "but you will never get me in one of those things. I don't like ships that float on water, so one that floats on air is completely out of the question."

"Ok, that's it then," Jason told the twins. "First we eat, then we'll go."

*Alazon*

Jarrell, Hass and Shon joined them and breakfast quickly became a loud and boisterous affair as the twins speculated on all the things they would see and do aboard the <u>Stargazer</u>. As soon as breakfast was over the five of them filed out the back door and into the closest shuttle. Jason set Vanda on his lap and fastened the harness straps around the two of them. Kim let Vinny and Manda have the co-pilot seat, showing them how to fasten their harness. She stood behind the two seats with a hand on each to maintain her balance.

Jason lifted the shuttle into the sky and slowly flew around the city as a treat for the twins before heading up to the <u>Stargazer</u>. Once aboard the ship, Baby, who had decided she was not about to be left behind, streaked out of the shuttle ahead of them. The dog ran in circles in the huge shuttle bay, barking as if glad to be home.

Letting Baby run on ahead of them, Jason took them on a tour of the ship. He watched the wonder in the eyes of Vinny and the twins, laughing at their reactions to some of what they saw. But as Jason watched Vinny he began to wonder about her.

In some ways Vinny was something of a puzzle to him. While she was every bit as beautiful as Kim, she was quieter than her older sister. For a time Jason had thought Vinny had a crush on him, or had even been in love with him, but if so, it had passed and she seemed to be as excited and elated as Kim over the coming wedding. But while Vinny seemed to be genuinely happy about it, there were times when Jason would catch her looking at him in the same manner Kim often did when she thought he didn't notice. With a shake of his head, Jason dismissed his thoughts as foolish and concentrated on having fun.

He took them to the gym and had Mother reduce the ship to zero gravity. The twins took to weightlessness like ducks to water. In minutes they were soaring around the room and bouncing off the walls, their shrill little voices ringing out with laughter an screams of delight. Vinny was a little hesitant and nervous at first, but Jason took her by the hand and helped her get used to it. Before long she was laughing and having as much fun as the twins, especially when Baby, who was no stranger to weightlessness, came floating along beside her.

For lunch, Jason introduced them to hot dogs, French fries, malts and ice cream. He knew he was probably destroying their appetites for supper later on, but it was worth it to him just to see the smiles on their faces. Kim looked at him across the table and grinned, shaking her head slightly. This was a special treat the twins had waited patiently on for a long time, and he was going to make sure they enjoyed it to the fullest.

After lunch they did some more exploring, finally ending up in one of the lounges where he had Mother provide them with a holo movie projection of 'Sleeping Beauty'. Kim and Vinny became as caught up in the story as the twins, and when it was over the four of them begged him for another one. He consented and had Mother show them 'Snow White', which the twins liked even better. They kept making comparisons between themselves and the dwarves. By the time they finally headed for home the twins were completely exhausted. Jason carried them into their room and put them to bed, kissing their little faces lovingly before blowing out the lamp.

Returning to the common room to sit next to Kim, he listened to Vinny telling her parents about all the things they had seen and done. By the time she was done it was late, but Jarrell and Liet had decided to wait for the return to have supper, which was a light fare for all of them. They had just finished eating when they heard an almost timid knock on the front door. Kim went to see who it was while the rest of them looked at one another, wondering who would be calling at this late hour. Although they couldn't see who it was, all of them heard the plaintive little voice ask, "Is…is this where Commander Stephens lives?"

"Yes, it is," Kim answered. "Would you like to see him?"

"Yes, please. If I could."

Kim came back into the room with a little girl walking shyly beside her. The girl was dirty, her robe was stained with mud and what looked like dried blood, and was torn in half a dozen places. Her hair was windblown and tangled, with bits of dried leaves and grass matted into it. Her small, scratched up arms were wrapped tightly around a small black bundle.

"Janella!" Jason cried as recognition of the small girl set in. He quickly moved from his chair to kneel down in front of the little girl, his hands going to grip her upper arms light. "What are you doing here?" he asked softly as he took in her ragged appearance. "What happened to you?"

Janella stood there for a moment unable to answer. Tears formed in her eyes and her lower lip started to quiver. "I…I don't…I don't have any place else to go!" she finally blurted out.

Jason pulled the girl to him and held her tight. He could feel her small body being wracked by sobs that tore at his heart. Janella felt like nothing more than skin and bones, and he could tell she hadn't eaten a decent meal in days. He looked up at Kim as Janella continued to cry with one of her small arms locked tightly around his neck.

As Janella's crying bean to subside Jason picked her up and returned to his chair, placing her on his lap. Kim handed him a damp napkin and he used it to wipe Janella's face. Doing so revealed scratches beneath the dirt. He wondered what could have caused them. He looked around to see the twins coming into the room. Their eyes took in the sight of this strange, dirty little girl on his lap. Without a word they took their seats at the table, quietly watching as Janella finally stopped crying.

"Janella, honey," Jason said softly after gently wiping her eyes, "tell me what's wrong and what happened to you?"

The little girl hesitated a moment before beginning to speak, her voice just barely carrying to the others when she did. "My…brother… he was one of your swordsmen."

"What was his name?" Jason asked.

"Karnel."

"I know him. He is a good man. Has something happened to him?"

"He…he died," Janella whispered in a choked voice as she tried to keep from crying again.

"What happened?" Jason asked. "I don't remember seeing his name on the casualty list, or of those seriously wounded. I would have remembered."

"He got wounded in the battle but I didn't find out about it till after I left your tent. It wasn't a very bad wound, just a sword cut on his side, and he had one of the temple women put a bandage on it. They told him he should go to Kech to make sure it would be okay, but he wanted to get back here as soon as possible, so we started back the same day. We cut across country to save time and didn't use the main roads, but our tollie stepped in a hole and broke its leg so he had to kill it. And then his wound got infected.

"I tried to help him, Commander," she wailed as tears flowed once more from her eyes. "But we were too far from any of the cities or villages. He kept getting sicker an sicker and he finally died!"

Janella had to stop as the memory of her brother dying while she sat by helplessly and watched was just too much for her. As it was for Jason. He knew all about the pain of losing those you loved and not being able to do anything about it. He felt tears in his own eyes.

"Be...before he died," Janella said after a moment, "he told me to find you. He said you were a good man and would see to it that I was taken care of because I don't have anyone else. After he died I covered his body with rocks so the animals couldn't get to it, and then I started coming here."

"How did you get here?"

"I walked."

"How long have you been traveling like this?" he asked, looking at her condition.

"I'm not sure, Commander. I think it's been about eleven days now. I picked berries to eat, and sometimes I found bird eggs and ate them by punching a hole in the ends and sucking out the insides the way my brother taught me a long time ago."

At that from the girl, Vinny rushed from the table. She returned almost immediately with a bowl of hot stew loaded with meat and vegetables, bread and a glass of cold teef. She placed them on the table in front of Jason.

"What about your parents?" Jason asked the girl.

"They died of a fever when I was two," Janella replied as she hungrily eyed the food. "Since then the only one I had was my brother. But now he's gone and I don't have anyone," she finished in a whisper.

"Oh, yes, you do," Jason told her as he hugged her frail body close. "You've got me." He looked at the food. "When's the last time you ate anything?"

"Yesterday morning."

*Alazon*

<u>Dear God</u>, he thought, <u>she has to be starving by now</u>. He looked at Manda. She nodded and quickly slid out of her chair, moving around to sit on Liet's lap. Jason placed Janella in Manda's chair and moved the soup, bread and teef over to where the girl could reach it. He then watched in amazement as Janella hesitated a moment before placing a napkin on her lap and begin to eat with all the manners of a lady.

No one spoke as Janella ate. When she was done she placed the spoon in the bowl and gently pushed the bowl away from her to what was considered the proper and polite distance. She then carefully wiped her mouth with the napkin, folded it and placed it to the left of the bowl, all according to the etiquette of this world.

"Thank you," she said to Liet. "That was very good."

"You're welcome. Would you like some more?"

Janella's eyes darted to the bowl, but she shook her head. "No thank you. My brother taught me that you are not supposed to take advantage of the hospitality of others, and not to make a glutton of yourself in their home."

Liet looked at the little girl with tenderness. "Janella, your brother taught you well, and he would be proud of you now, but there are times when you are allowed to over-stop those considerations and this is one of them. We have plenty and you can eat all you want. No one here will think any less of you for it."

Jason saw Janella's eyes go once again to the bowl. "That settles it," said Kim, who took the bowl and glass back into the kitchen for refills, returning quickly to place them in front of Janella. The girl looked around the table nervously for a moment before picking up her spoon to begin eating.

This time when she was done, Janella gave a little sigh of contentment. She looked at Jason and smiled, but then her little eyes went wide and she slid from the chair to snatch up the bundle she had dropped when Jason had picked her up. She held it out to him. "Here is your uniform, Commander," she told him. "I got all the stains out of it just like I said I would"

Jason took the uniform and untied the small string she had wrapped around it. As Janella claimed, it had been washed free of all stains and looked as good as new. He turned to Janella and smiled at her. "Thank you," he told her.

"It was the least I could do after all you have done for the people of Preton, Commander," she replied as she lowered he eyes to the floor.

Jason handed the outfit to Kim and picked Janella up. He placed her on his lap again and kissed the top of her head. "So, what you are telling me is that with the death of your brother, you don't have any family left, right?"

"Yes," Janella answered weakly.

"What about aunts or uncles?"

"None that I know of, Commander. I never heard my brother speak of any, so I don't know if I have any or not." Janella turned her little face up to him. "What is going to happen to me, Commander?"

There was a plaintive note of desperation to her voice that tore at Jason's heart. "Jarrell, Liet," he said, his voice catching in his throat as Janella began to cry gently against his chest, "would it be alright…"

"Of course she can stay here," Liet said as she wiped the moisture from her own eyes. "She can stay until we find out for sure as to whether she has any relatives or not. If she does, we'll check with them to see if they will take her in. If not, she can live with us and we'll adopt her.

"After all," she continued with a grin in the direction of Kim, "we're getting rid of one big mouthed, useless, ill-mannered daughter, so a small, well mannered little girl won't be any bother at all."

Liet's tone suggested that anyone who wanted to argue with her may as well go outside and bay at the moon, because that was the way it was going to be.

"She can sleep with us," Vanda volunteered. "Manda has some night gowns that will fit her."

Jason looked at the twins and smiled. "Would you like to stay here?" he asked Janella.

"Only if you're sure it would be alright, Commander," Janella replied softly.

"It's more than alright. We would love to have you," he told her as he hugged her tightly.

"Then I would like that."

"Good!" Jason told her as he stood up with her in his arms. "And do you know why?" Janella looked at him and shook her head. "Because I can always use another pretty face to look at around here," he told her with a grin.

Janella smiled at him, but then leaned her head closer to his. "Could you put me down for a minute, Commander?" she whispered.

He looked at her, wondering why she wanted him to set her down, but did as she asked. He watched as Janella walked around the table to where Jarrell and Liet sat. She bowed at the waist before straightening up to look at them.

"Thank you for the meal you have given me, and for allowing me to stay in your home. I will do all I can to repay your kindness. I can cook, sew, clean, and work in a garden. I will be more than happy to help you in any way I can to repay your kindness and hospitality."

Jason, as well as everyone else in the room, was visibly impressed. He had never met such a well mannered little girl before in his life. Liet reached out and pulled Janella to her to hug the girl for a moment. "We'll talk about that later," she told Janella. "But for now you go on to bed."

"Yes, Ma'am. Good night," Janella replied politely. She bowed once more before hurrying back to Jason.

"You know, we have a tradition around here," Jason told Janella as he carried her into the bedroom of the twins with Kim, Vanda and Manda right behind him. "Every night that I'm here I tell the twins a story from the world where I come from. So, if Manda will get you one of her gowns, we can get you into bed and the story for tonight will begin."

Janella stood still as Jason set her down and untied the rope belt at her waist. When he lifted her rob off, his heart leaped into his throat. Eleven days, maybe more, of surviving on berries and bird eggs had taken their toll on the girl. She was so emaciated he could clearly see each of her ribs. Her little body was covered with a multitude of cuts and scratches from head to toe. He also saw just how dirty she was.

So did Janella. She looked down at her body and then back up at him. "Sir, I need to wash up before I put on a gown and get into bed."

"I'll help her," Kim said from behind him. Jason looked up at Kim and saw the tears she was fighting to hold back at the sight of Janella. Kim forced herself to smile at Janella as she picked the little girl up and carried her from the room.

"You guys don't mind, do you?" Jason asked the twins as they got into bed.

"Course not, Jason," Vanda replied. "She's sorta like you when you first came here. You were hurt and didn't have any family and were all alone."

"Yeah, I guess you're right," he replied as he stretched out across the bed. "But now I have you, your family, and me and Kim are gonna be married. I think that makes me a pretty lucky guy."

"Are you and Kimmy gonna get a house of your own when you get married?" Manda asked.

"Eventually, yes."

Manda looked at him, her little face a mask of seriousness. "Will we be able to come stay with you sometimes?"

"Are you kidding? Any time you want! In fact, I'll make sure the house we have has a room for each of you."

"Oh, we don't need separate rooms for a while yet," Vanda told him in a casual, off-handed manner.

"Yeah, right," Jason replied with a grin. "But you can still have them if you want."

He grabbed the twins and pulled them closer to tickle them. Their shouts of laughter soon attracted the attention of Baby, who came running in to join the fun. By the time Janella and Kim returned, the bed was a mess and had to be remade, which Jason and the twins did. The twins got into bed again and he placed Janella between them, pulling the light coverlet up to their chins before laying across the bed with his head propped up on his hand.

Baby, who instinctively seemed to know when her presence could help, hopped up on the bed and placed her large furry head between Janella and Manda, reaching up to lick the faces of the two of them and causing them to giggle. As Janella reached out to pet her, Baby squirmed a little closer to the girl and placed her head on the legs of Janella, her furry tail thumping lightly on the bed.

*Alazon*

"Alright, here we go," Jason told them. "Tonight, in honor of our guest, I think I'll tell you a special story." He felt Kim lay behind him and slip her arm around his waist.

"Good!" The twins exclaimed, clapping their hands in delight.

"What's it about?" Vanda asked.

"What's it about? Humm, well, let's see. Oh, I know. It's about a little princess who didn't know she was a princess."

"Why didn't she know she was a princess?" Manda asked, a look of confusion on her face. "If she were a princess she would know it."

"Not necessarily," Jason replied, arching his eyebrows and smiling. "Listen up."

He began telling them a story about a little girl who was a princess, but didn't know it because when she was just a baby her parents had to give her away to another family to protect her from an evil witch who wanted to snatch her away. He made up the story as he went along, telling them how the little girl had grown up thinking she was the daughter of a loving, but poor family, and it wasn't until years later, after the death of those parents, that she found out she was a princess.

When she found out who she really was, she set out to overthrow those who had killed her real parents and drive them out of the country. She then took the throne and brought peace and prosperity back to her country. She then married her childhood sweetheart and they live happily ever after.

When Jason was done he kissed all three of the children before tucking them in and blowing out the lamp on the table beside the bed before leaving the room with Kim. Out in the hallways Kim leaned against the wall and looked up at him with teary eyes. "You made that story up, didn't you?" she said softly.

"Maybe. What does it matter?"

"Because I know you, Jason, and that is just the type of thing you would do to make that little girl feel welcome and help her forget about her troubles, even if it is for just a little while."

"Watch it," he teased, reaching out to pull her close. "You'll make me sound like a nice guy, and that would blow my reputation."

"Did you really know her brother?" Kim asked. "Or did you just say that to make her feel better?"

"I knew him. And he was a good man," he replied softly.

Kim smiled up at him. "You are a very special man, Jason. Oh, you can be a pain in the butt at times, and may pretend otherwise, but I happen to know better. Now, why don't you take me to bed and show me what a really nice guy you can be."

"Wanton woman," he told her as he picked her up in his arms and carried her into his room.

"I may be, but you love it," she replied, kissing him deeply as she pushed the door closed behind them with her foot.

# TWENTY THREE

Throughout the city of Lemac a festive, carnival air of excitement prevailed. People were streaming into the city on a daily basis. It created a few problems, but none that couldn't be overcome with a little ingenuity and patience. Camps were set up along the river to the south of the city, along with adequate facilities for waste and bathing, and most of the people were content to cook their meals at large, communal fires.

Within the city, merchants opened their shops at the break of dawn and remained open long into the night. Extra help was hired to handle the influx of customers. Harried and haggard, but happy shop keepers counted their profits each night before retiring to bed.

Men who had fought with Jason told their stores to anyone who would listen. They told of how Jason had sprung his trap on the Karton, then led the charge down to the beach, his swords flashing in the early morning sunlight to cut in half any Karton who had the misfortune of being near him, going through their ranks like a scythe through wheat. Of course, many of them also let it be known that he had been the one fighting beside Jason, protecting the Commander's life with his own. Around and around the stores went until, at last, it seemed as if Jason had killed at least half the Karton army all by himself.

The also told of how Jason had walked out to face the entire army of Tilwin armed only with his swords. Of how he had killed six, a dozen, two dozen, and even a hundred man all by himself before two cowardly Tilwin shot him in the back from ambush.

They spoke in hushed tones of how Jason, even while falling to the ground, had called down the wrath of his father, the god Avihs, to destroy the Tilwin, and how the bolts of lightning had obliterated every trace of the Tilwin and their equipment. In hushed, awed tones, they spoke of watching the flashes of light which blinded the eyes sweep back and forth across the beach, and of the rolling claps of thunder that practically deafened them, until everything connected with the Tilwin had been wiped from the face of Preton. The only thing left to show the Tilwin had ever been there was a mile long, two hundred yard wide stretch of blackened and glassified beach.

And so began the belief by most that Jason was a god, and if not a god, then at least the son of one. This was further enhanced and reinforced by the icons of him in the Temple of Lofa. And by the fact that Jason was here now, walking around the city with no visible wounds from the two arrows which had pierced him back to front in such a way as to have killed any mortal man. Plus, everyone knew the Tilwin coated their war arrows with the poison of Death Plants, so even a slight wound by one would kill a man, but they hadn't killed Jason.

But not all of the conversations were about Jason and his exploits in battle, or whether he was or was not part god. Women in the market places spoke of Kim as if she were almost their own daughter. Each of them seem to have an anecdote to relate about Kim, claiming that the oldest daughter of the Manor was best friends with their own children. They spoke of how Kim would come to them for advice when she had a problem, or just wanted to talk, and how much Kim thought of them almost like a second mother. This, despite the fact that Kim had never even spoken more than a few words of friendly greeting to most of them.

Many of them speculated on what might have been had Jason kidnapped their daughter instead of Kim. If so, then they would be the mother who was preparing for the upcoming wedding of their daughter to him instead of Liet. It didn't matter if their daughters were as beautiful as Kim, or somewhat less attractive, if Jason had seen their daughter first it would be a different wedding they were all preparing to witness and celebrate.

The women also speculated, as women do, but never in the company of men, as to whether or not Jason was as large in certain areas as he was overall. They giggled and blushed in amusement as they talked in hushed tones, with more than a few of them, married and single, young and old, stated that they would like to personally find out.

Naturally, both Jason and Kim were kept abreast of the various and latest stories going around about them by the other members of the household, who were pretty much free to go about their daily business. For Kim and himself it was almost unsafe for either of them to venture out in public without getting mobbed. When they did go out, it was with a contingent of the Guard to accompany them to keep the crowds back.

The Mayoral Guard of Lemac had been supplemented with members of the army, with all of them placed under the command of Lieutenant Ster. Despite the fact that Ster was younger that most of the men he commanded, he led them with effectiveness and discipline. It helped that these men had fought with Ster against the Karton and were used to taking orders from him. They reacted quickly, and with a minimum of fuss to break up any disturbance that arose. Ster not only proved himself an extremely capable leader, but exhibited the rare ability to ease the frayed nerves and tempers of the combatants he was often called upon to separate.

Within the Vehey house, Liet ruled with an iron fist. But one tempered with patience, understanding, and a lot of love. She made it a habit of confining Kim, Vinny and her daughter's two best friends, who were to be bride's maids, in her room to work on the dresses. Liet spent as much time with them as she cold, but also provided the meals and took care of other household chores as easily as if it were just another day. Her only point of distraction came from the newest addition to the household. Little Janella, while obediently obeying Liet's every word, often delayed doing something she was supposed to do in order to do something the girl thought needed done for Jason, who had become the focal point of her life.

On her first morning there, Janella had risen before anyone else. Sneaking out of the twins' bedroom and going to the kitchen, she quickly built a fire in the hearth, where she put on a kettle of water to heat while going to the bath area of the house to find clean towels and a fresh bar of scented soap. She even went outside to the back courtyard to pick a single flower. Once the water was hot she poured it into a pitcher, then carried it, the soap, towel and flower into his room, entering quietly to place it on the window sill for him.

Jason had been awakened by her presence and sat up to watch her while her back was to him. He saw her lay out the towel and soap and then place the flower on the towel. When she turned to leave she saw him watching her. She smiled at him and blushed deeply.

He smiled back at her. "What are you doing?" he asked.

"I brought you hot water to wash up with, Commander. I thought you should have hot water, fresh soap and a clean towel, so I got up early and prepared it for you," she said softly, lowering her eyes and clasping her hands in front of her.

"Come here," he told her, patting the bed beside him.

Janella crossed the room slowly. When she reached the side of the bed he scooped her up and sat her on his lap. "You know, that's just about the nicest thing that anyone has done for me in a long time," he told her as he gave her a hug.

She looked up at him with wide eyes. "But, Commander, you should always have hot water in the morning to wash up with. Doesn't Kimmy do that for you?"

"Do what?" Kim asked from the doorway as she and Baby came into the room to join them on the bed.

"Bring me hot water, fresh towels, scented soap, and a freshly picked flower each morning. It would seem that our little guest here is more concerned about my comfort than my wife to be. You know, you could learn a lot from her," he teased.

Kim stuck he tongue out at him and laughed. "Well, in that case, Mister Army Commander and soon-to-be-King of Preton, perhaps you should wait around until she grows up and marry her instead of me."

"That's a thought," he replied as he leaned over to kiss her.

As Jason straightened up, Janella pulled away from him slightly and stared up at him. "Are you really going to be King of Preton?" she asked in awe.

He looked at her and smiled. "Yes, I guess I am."

Janella practically flew off his lap to stand a few feet from the bed. Her face became deadly serious as she bowed low and then dropped to her right knee. Her eyes were lowered to the floor, and when she spoke her voice was barely above a whisper.

"My Lord, please forgive my familiarity with you. It is not proper for a commoner such as myself to assume such open liberties with a king, or a man who is soon to be king." With that she turned and fled the room, closing the door behind her.

Kim looked at Jason in stunned astonishment. "Do you believe that?" she asked.

"No," he replied with a shake of his head.

"I didn't know her brother," Kim said, "but that little girl has had some excellent Temple training and instruction. She is definitely no ordinary little girl. In fact," she added thoughtfully, "I would say that Janella was being trained to become a priestess. That is the only thing that would explain her behavior and mannerisms."

"Come on," Jason told Kim as he got out of bed and threw on a robe and padded barefoot out of the room in search of Janella.

They found the girl in the kitchen going through all of the lower cabinets to see where Liet kept everything. The moment Jason and Kim entered the room Janella stopped what she was doing, clasped her hands in front of her and bowed her head. Jason took two long steps and picked her up to set her on the work table.

"Janella, listen to me," he told her softly. "Whether I'm a commoner or a king, it makes no difference."

"Oh, but it does, my Lord," she said softly.

"Janella, were you in training to become a priestess at the Temple?" Kim asked her.

"Yes, my Lady," Janella replied with a slight nod of her head. "My brother though it would be good for me. He always said that I would make a good priestess."

Kim looked at Jason and nodded. "That explains a few things," she told him.

Jason turned to Janella. "I want to ask you something, but I want you to think about it very carefully before you answer, okay?"

"Yes, Commander."

"If we can't find any relatives of yours who can take you in as their daughter, then after Kim and I are married, how would you like to be adopted by us and be our daughter?"

Jason had asked the question impulsively but as he turned to glance at Kim he saw her smile and nod in approval. The effect on Janella was like an electric shock. Her head jerked up to look from him to Kim and back. Tears began to form in her eyes. "You would do that?" she asked with a trembling voice.

Jason nodded. "Yes, but only if it is what you wanted."

"But…why? I am just a common little girl. You are going to be the king and queen of Preton. The most important people in the whole country. Why would you want to adopt a little girl like me?"

Jason reached up and gently brushed a strand of hair away from her eyes. "Because we love you," he replied softly.

"But you don't even really know me, Commander," Janella protested weakly.

"Janella," Kim said with a smile, "Jason does not have to know a person very long to know if he loves them or not. Especially little children. If I let him, he would probably adopt as many children as he could. But you are a very special little girl to him, and to me, and we would both be very happy, and very lucky, to have you as our daughter. But like Jason says, only if that is what you would want."

Janella stared at them for a long moment before speaking. "I would like that very much," she finally replied, smiling a she reached out to wrap her arms around each of their necks to hug them.

From that point on Janella had gone out of her way to do things for both Jason and Kim, but it was clear to everyone who the object of her most devout attention was. She took over just about every task of Jason's welfare and well being she could. She even made the cleaning of his clothes and the preparation of his food her personal responsibility when she could.

Liet, seeing the change in the girl, seeing the happiness and love in her eyes for Jason and Kim, merely smiled and let Janella have her way most of the time. Although there were a few times she had to interfere with something Janella wanted to do for Jason, Liet always took the time to patiently explain why she couldn't.

Janella got along well with the twins despite the fact that she was four years older than they were. She spent a lot of time teaching them things no one else had, or to help them with their school work. The three of them played together and their laughter filled the house as they chased one another from room to room with Baby's barking serving as the punctuation mark. Before long the three children had become inseparable. They took special delight in pulling tricks on every other member of the family, especially Jason.

On the morning of the wedding Jason awoke feeling nervous. He sat up in bed and looked around, then dropped back on his pillows as Baby hopped up on the bed to give him his morning face licking. He reached out absently with his right hand for his wrist communicator. "Mother?"

"Who's calling, please?"

"Don't play games with me this morning, you second generation word processor."

"A bit on the nervous side this morning, are we?" she teased.

"Try terrified."

"Gee, and here I was just starting to think you were the reincarnation of Fearless Fodstick."

"Who the hell is that?"

"Way before your time, Bucko," Mother replied with a chuckle.

"What's the weather look like today, Mother?"

"Beautiful. Clear skies, temps in the mid seventies, no humidity to speak of. All in all, a great day for a wedding."

"How's the crowd situation?"

"Oh, eight hundred thousand or so, give or take a hundred, and they're still steaming in."

"What are you doing to observe and preserve?" he asked.

"Well, as long as you and Kim wear the throat miles under your clothes I'll be able to pick up every word you say. For the visual aspects, aside from the holo cameras that have been set up, I'll be using a probe monitor as well. All in all, I should get a good record of it from a number of angles."

"Good. I want records of it for later."

"No problem. Now, I suggest that you get your carcass out of bed and start getting ready. Kim, Liet, Vinny, Janella, the twins and bride's maids have long since left the house for their tents on the plains. Jarrell, Busker and the other men are all dressed and waiting for you in the common room."

"Right."

Jason got up and went to the pitcher of water and washed up. He had bathed and shaved closely the night before, as well as laying out the clothing he would wear to the tent. He would change into his wedding outfit there. He grinned as he tied his sandals, thinking of how Liet had flatly refused to let him, or any of the men, see the gowns they were making for Kim and the women of the wedding party. She had given him a sample of cloth from each tress, telling him which color each woman would be wearing, and he had taken those up to the ship to provide outfits for the men in the wedding to match.

Kim had insisted on wearing an Earth-style wedding gown and Mother had compiled a book of styles and patterns for her. Kim had promptly taken it into her mother's room where she had gong through it with her mother and Vinny, refusing to tell him which one she had finally selected. With the pieces of colored cloth in his hand, Jason had taken Busker, Shon, Hass and Vanda up to the ship, where they had spent the entire day outfitting themselves with color coordinated dress uniforms from the ship's stock. The only problem had come in finding one small enough to fit Vanda. They found one his size, but unlike the one Jason would be wearing which was decorated with gold brocade, gold buttons and epaulets, the one for Vanda was plain and simple.

"Hey, no problem," Busker had told the boy, picking him up and placing him on his broad shoulder. "My mother will fix it up for you."

"Wait a minute," Jason had said, a look of confusion on his face. "I remember hearing that you and Liet were brother and sister soon after I got here, but a little over a week ago Liet said she was an only child and that her parents were dead. I didn't pay any attention to it at the time, but would someone mind explaining to me what's going on?"

Busker and the brothers had laughed. "Both statements are true," Busker told him. "Liet was an only child. Her parents died when she was five and my parents adopted her, with the consent of her other relatives, and so we became brother and sister."

"Oh, well, that clears that up," Jason said with a grin. "For a minute there I thought I was going crazy."

When they returned to Lemac, Busker had taken the outfits of Jason and Vanda with him, promising to have Vanda's finished in plenty of time. Two days later Busker had returned for Vanda, taking the boy to try on his outfit. It must have pleased Vanda, because when he returned he was grinning broadly.

Kim had tried to find out what the outfits of the men would look like, but Jason had told her that what was good for the goose was good for the gander, then walked away laughing. As he stepped from his room to join the other men, they all smiled at him as they got to their feet. "Ready?" Jarrell asked, his face beaming.

"No. Any way I can get out of this?"

"Only if you can make it to the shuttle and fly off before being tackled and tied by us, and the contingent of Guard that are stationed at both the front and back doors," Hass said with a grin.

"That's what I thought. Well, in that case, let's go."

As they stepped out the front door, men of the Mayoral Guard snapped to attention. They formed a double row from the front door to the carriage that awaited. Once Jason and the others were seated, the Guard took their position on either side of the carriage and moved out at a trot beside it, maintaining their pace all the way to the plains outside the city.

The closer they came to the tent erected for them, the more excited the crowd became. Most of them had missed Kim and her entourage earlier, as Kim and the other women had arrived well before dawn wearing hooded cloaks to disguise themselves. After Kim and the other women had entered their tent, six of the Guard had stationed themselves around it to ensure privacy. They were wearing their new, snug fitting white jumpsuits trimmed in blue and gold, and they made it clear that no one who wasn't authorized was going to get into that tent without risking health and life.

The men of the Mayoral Guard of Lemac took a special pride in the fact that they were the Honor Guard for the wedding. They wore their spotless white jumpsuits with the double row of gold buttons down the front, and gold rope brocade on the left shoulder proudly. They had wrapped the hafts of their Katanas and ho-tachis in blue, white and gold silk cords, with small tassels at the end. They wore the ho-tachis strapped across their backs, with the katanas tucked into the blue silk sash at their waist.

The concept for the uniforms had come from Ster. He had mentioned it to Jarrell, stating that it would be nice to have something special for the wedding. Jarrell had told Ster to have them made and he would pay for them himself. Ster had agreed, but only if Jarrell agreed to let each man repay him for the cost out of his wages. Jarrell had argued at first, saying it wasn't necessary, as he knew how much the men of the Mayoral Guard made, but Ster had been adamant on that point and Jarrell had finally acquiesced. When Ster had proposed the idea to the men of the Guard, they had all unanimously agreed to pay for the uniforms.

But Jarrell had still made things easier for the men by going to Jason and telling him what Ster wanted. Jason had gone up to the Stargazer and returned with over fifty plain white jumpsuits, which he had give to the guard to find those that would fit, telling each man to take two. Once the men had found those that would fit each of them, it was a simple, and much less costly modification to turn them what they were now than making them from scratch.

The crowd cheered as Jason's carriage drew up in front of the large tent that had been set up for him and the other men. All he could do was smile and wave as they disembarked from the carriage and hurried into the tent. They removed the robes they were wearing and donned the dress uniforms they would wear for the wedding.

Jason's was white, with a double row of gold buttons down the front, gold brocade shoulder boards, with gold and white epaulets. The short, stiff collar was embroidered with gold brocade, as were the sleeves and cuffs. His boots were white, polished leather, with short heels, and the gold chain and starburst around his neck, along with the starburst pen at his throat, completed his outfit.

The outfits of the other men were much the same in style, although not quite as elaborate, and in colors that would match those of the woman each man would be escorting. As Best Man, Busker's was emerald green with silver trim to match Vinny's Maid of Honor dress.

Shon and Hass had uniforms of powder blue to match the colors of the dresses of the Bride's Maids. Vanda word an exact copy of Jason's outfit, minus the starburst and chain medallion. Only Jarrell wore the traditional ceremonial robes of Alazon. Jason had tried to get the older man to wear a formal jumpsuit, even offering to have one made just for him, but Jarrell had refused, stating that he just didn't feel comfortable in a jump suit, and that he should represent his position with the clothing the people had come to expect from him.

"I'll be back shortly," Jarrell told Jason as they finished dressing. "I need to check on the bride and make sure that everything is ready with her."

"Think he's scared?" Shon asked Hass as Jason sat down on one of the folding camp stools, thinking they were talking about Jarrell.

"Wouldn't you be if you were marring someone like our sister?" Hass replied with a grin.

"You've got a point there. Then again, some guys just seem to be gluttons for punishment."

Jason looked at them and grinned. "Alright, knock it off. Your days will come and then it will be my turn."

"Not for me!" Hass exclaimed with a short laugh. "Jason, do you have any idea of the number of beautiful, willing young women who have made themselves available to me simply for the possible opportunity of being close to you? Why, a man could be with a different one, or two, every night for a year and not be able to accommodate them all. Forget about marriage, I'm having entirely too much fun."

"I'll bet," Jason replied dryly, but not without a smile. "What about you, Shon? Are you having as much fun as your brother?"

"Not quite," Shon replied. "Although I will admit that the attention is somewhat flattering. What I'm thinking about is what will happen once you are officially proclaimed as King of Preton."

"Yeah, well, that won't happen for a little while yet," Jason replied as he bent over to zip his boots.

The flap of the tent was pulled back a moment later to allow Jarrell to enter. In his hands he carried a small, hand carved box of white wood. The sight of it immediately sent Jason's heart to beating faster. He had seen a box like that in the cavern of the Temple and was afraid of what this one might contain.

"It's not what you think," Jarrell told him with a reassuring grin.

Jason sighed loudly. "That's good. Otherwise we could have a problem."

"However," Jarrell told him as he handed the box to Shon, "it is something I had made up just for the occasion."

Jarrell lifted the lid to reveal a small diadem set with diamonds, rubies and emeralds in the same starburst pattern as the pendants Jason wore. Jason's breath caught in his throat as he stared at the gold and jewels, realizing the wealth it represented. He looked at Jarrell, only to find the older man grinning at him.

"Before you say anything," Jarrell told him, "let me explain something to you. Every important House on Alazon has a diadem such as this. The various designs represent and denote the particular House. I have my own," he added, pointing to another box sitting on the table to one side that Jason hadn't noticed earlier. "I'll put it on before the ceremony actually begins. Anyway, I thought it only fitting that you have your own. After all, you will be starting your own House."

"But…who paid for this?" Jason asked.

Jarrell grinned. "It was sort of a joint venture between myself and Mother. Mother provided the emeralds and rubies, I provided the diamonds and gold. We had two of them made. One for you, and a slightly smaller one for Kimmy as is customary. Consider them as wedding presents from a happy father."

"But the cost!" Jason exclaimed.

"What cost?" Jarrell asked with a grin. "Other than the stones provided by Mother, I already had the diamonds and gold. The only cost came in having the jeweler make them, and he only charged for the cost of the molds simply to have the honor of doing so."

Jason shook his head and grinned. "Let me guess. He gets a plaque for the front of his shop, right?"

"Ahhh, you've been observing my wife," Jarrell replied with a grin as he removed the diadem from the box and motioned for Jason to bend over. Jarrell placed the diadem on Jason's head, using his hands to gently mold the soft gold to fit the contours of Jason's head.

"As you can see," Jarrell said as he stepped back, "I kept with the starburst design to match your badge of Commander of the Army which, by the way, is yours for as long as you are king."

"I'm not king yet," Jason said with a sigh.

A blast of trumpets cut off any further conversation. It was the signal for the start of the wedding ceremony. "Time for me to go," Jarrell told him as he put on his own diadem and left the tent.

Jason stood nervously just inside the tent. A moment later Ster stuck his head in and grinned. "Time to do it," he told them.

"Here we go," Jason said to the brothers and Ster. He took a deep breath and stepped out into the bright morning sunlight.

Jason followed three steps behind Ster, with Shon and Hass walking side by side the same distance behind him. They walked through a double row of Mayoral Guard from the tent to the brightly colored pavilion that was set up on a small knoll in the center of the naturally formed amphitheater in the middle of the plain. In front of the pavilion was a small alter decorated with flowers. A padded kneeling bench surrounded it on three sides. Concealed within the flowers were microphones that would pick up every word being said and transmit it to the speakers mounted on poles throughout and around the crowd so everyone could hear what was being said.

The tiny, inconspicuous throat mikes Jason, Kim, Jarrell and Seta wore were on a frequency that would be transmitted directly to Mother, cutting out all interference and background noises. Bleachers had been erected on either side of the pavilion for the distinguished guests, such as the visiting Mayors and other persons of note, and were packed to the limit.

As Jason approached the pavilion the cheering from the crowd grew in volume. He took his place beside the later while Busker and the other men marched to the tent where Kim and her retinue awaited. As they positioned themselves at the entrance of the tent a hush descended over the crowd.

The first to step from the tent was Manda. She wore a white dress with white satin bodice, brocade skirt and white satin slippers. As Manda emerged, Vanda stepped up to her. He carried a white satin pillow with gold tassels on the corners. On the pillow rested the rings that Jason and Kim would give to one another. There were whispered comments from the crowd about how pretty she looked, and how unusual her dress was as the twins made their way toward the small alter. But the comments about Manda were nothing compared to the gasps of surprise that erupted when Vinny stepped from the tent.

Vinny's emerald green satin dress was cut with a wide neck and plunging front, It fit snugly down to the waist and then flared out down to her ankles. It had short, puffed sleeves of green and silver, and she carried a small bouquet of white flowers tied with green and silver ribbons. She smiled as Busker stepped forward and extended his arm to her as the two of them followed the twins.

Next came the Bride's Maids, who were escorted by Shon and Hass. Their dresses were of the same design as Vinny's, but in a pastel pink. Janella came next. Her face was shining and radiant as she spread white flower petals in front of her on the red carpet that had been placed on the ground from the tent to the pavilion.

Silence fell over the crowd again as a single note sounded from a conch horn. As the note slowly faded away two Mayoral Guards pulled aside the tent flaps and Kim stepped out. Her presence was greeted by the sharp intake of breath of everyone.

Kim's dress started high around her neck in a soft brocade of white and gold. It fit snugly over her arms and bodice, the pattern of brocade hiding, with a tantalizing hint, at what lay beneath. At the wrists three small loops extended over her fingers to hold the material in place and cover the back of her hands. The dress flared out slightly at the waist, and was slit up the front to reveal her legs, which were clad in white silk hose, which was an item unheard of on this world. On her feet were white satin slippers with a gold brocade pattern stitched into them. Her face was concealed by a white silk veil that extended over her head and down her back to trail along behind her. It was held in place by the diadem she wore.

When Kim raised her left hand to place it on the right arm of her father the sunlight struck the emerald on her middle finger. Those closest to her gasped in awe. They had never seen a ring containing a stone of such exquisite beauty before.

*Alazon*

Jason stood nervously watching Kim approach. He felt his heart pounding wildly in his chest. When Kim reached the alter Jarrell released her arm and she turned to face Jason for a moment. Then both of them knelt down on either side of the small alter so they were facing one another. Jarrell, his face beaming, moved around the alter to stand so that he was facing not only Jason and Kim, but the crowd as well. He cleared his throat and began to speak.

"People of Preton," Jarrell said, holding out his arms to indicate all those present, his voice being amplified and transmitted to the crowd by the speaker that had been erected, "you have come to Lemac this day to witness the marriage of my eldest daughter, Kimella Vehey, to this man, Jason Stephens, and I welcome you.

"I hope," he said with a slight chuckle, "that you will not mind if I perform this ceremony myself and not delegate it to another. As Senior Mayor, and father of the bride, I have the fortunate opportunity to not only give my daughter to the man she loves, but to officiate over it as well. This is something I have looked forward to for many years now."

Jarrell glanced down at Jason and Kim and smiled. Jason knew Jarrell was talking to ease his own sense of nervousness.

"Kimella Vehey, you are here now before the people of Preton to join your life with that of Jason Stephens. It is a day both sacred and honored, and one from which there can be no turning back. His life will be your life. His problems and sorrows will be your problems and sorrows. His happiness shall you share in. Here and now, before the people, and before the gods of Alazon, do you wish to proclaim your love for this man?"

"I do so wish," Kim said softly. She lowered her eyes from her father to look across at Jason.

Jason felt his heart pounding as Kim took a deep breath and let it out slowly. Her eyes were shining brightly at him, even through the veil she wore.

"Jason Michael Stephens, you came to this world as a stranger, a man suffering a pain none of us here can comprehend, looking for those you could love, and who would love you.

"You more than given freely of yourself to save the people of Preton, asking in return only to be accepted as one of us, and to live as a free man. In doing this you have exhibited not only your capacity for love, but compassion for all who meet and know you.

"To me you are the symbol of what all men should strive to be. To me you represent the ultimate in love and sacrifice, and I give myself to you freely and without conditions.

"I will love you for all the days of my life. I will do for you everything a wife is able to do for her husband, and I will stand by your side against any who may wish to oppose you in any way."

Kim paused for a moment to give Jason a love filled smile before speaking again.

"I will look forward to the day when I bring into this world the children we shall create together. I will teach them the ideas and concepts you hold so dear, and raise them to be proud of their father and the name they carry.

"I will comfort you in your times of sorry, and laugh with you in your times of joy. I will share all things with you. But above all, I will love you with all my heart for as long as there is breath within my body. This I vow to you before all those here and the gods of Alazon."

Jarrell beamed down at Kim. The love he felt for his oldest daughter clearly evident on his face as he turned to Jason. "Jason, you are also here this day before the people and the gods to take to wife this woman. Do you also wish to proclaim your love?"

"I do so wish," Jason replied, never taking his eyes off Kim. He took a deep breath and let it out slowly in an effort to calm his nerves.

"Kimella Vehey, at a time when I wondered if I would ever be able to love again, when I thought I would b forever doomed to loneliness and pain, you came into my life. You replaced the cold emptiness that had filled me for so long with more love than I ever thought possible.

"Your smile brightens my day. The laughter of your lips and eyes fills my heart and soul with joy. The touch of your hand causes my heart to soar. When you speak to me of your love, I know I have found what it is I have searched for so long in this life.

"As your husband I will love you, cherish you, respect you, and protect you with every means at my disposal for as long as I live.

"I will honor you in all ways. I will seek your guidance and counsel, for you will be not just my wife, but my friend, my companion, and an extension of my very existence. I will love you with every fiber of my being for all my life. This I promise to you before all those gathered here, and before the gods of Alazon."

When Jason finished his vows he and Kim stood and moved around to the front of the alter to face Jarrell. They knelt again, but this time side by side. The twins stepped up to stand on either side of them. Jarrell moved slightly to one side and Seta stepped forward to join him. Two other temple priestesses stepped forward to stand on Seta's right. One of them held a goblet of gold inlaid with jewels. The other held a matching ewer from which she poured a deep red wine into the goblet before it was handed to Seta. Seta took it and turned to face Jason and Kim. She smiled softly at them as she held the goblet in both hands.

"Jason Stephens and Kimella Vehey, you kneel here before all those present, and in the sight of Lofa, proclaiming your love and vows of devotion to one another.

"I have heard your words and know they are pleasing to the gods, as well as those gathered here, for I know they are spoken from your hearts. They are words I know you will both live by forever."

Seta turned slightly to face Jason. "Jason Stephens, although you came to our world from another, you have become one of us. Despite your physical appearance you are a man of Alazon. You are a man the gods smile upon with favor, as your arrival signals a change in our world such as we have never dreamed of. Your presence is the dawn of a new day for all of Alazon."

Seta turned from Jason to Kim. "Kimella Vehey, daughter of Alazon, I have known you since you were brought into this world. As your teacher and friend I have always known it would take a very special man to not only win your heart, but to tame your wild and tempestuous spirit. Therefore, it is with great pleasure that I hereby sanctify this marriage in the name of Lofa and Avihs, Supreme Deities of Alazon, and give to you not only their blessings, but my own as well."

Seta raised the goblet to her lips and sipped from it before handing it to Jason. He took it and sipped from it and then handed it to Kim, who did likewise before returning it to Seta. The High Priestess then walked around the alter and poured out the remaining wine in a circle on the ground around it in honor of Lofa.

As Seta returned to stand beside Jarrell she nodded to Vanda. The boy turned and presented the ring pillow to Jason, who removed the smaller ring from it and turned to Kim, taking her left hand in his.

"Kimella Vehey, I give this ring to you as a symbol of my love and devotion. Let it never leave your finger, or let my love leave your heart." He slipped the ring on her finger, wondering if it were her hands that were shaking so much or his own.

Vanda moved around and held out the pillow to Manda, who took it and then presented it to Kim with a smile. Kim removed the ring and turned to Jason.

"Jason Stephens, I also give you this ring as a symbol of my love for you. It has no beginning, no end, and like our love, shall last forever. You have but to feel it on your finger when we are apart to know that my live is with you always."

Kim slipped the ring on his left hand ring finger, smiling brightly at him, making him forget about everyone else there for the moment. He saw only her face, her smile, and the love in her eyes for him.

"It is done!" Jarrell cried, throwing up his arms and smiling broadly.

The crowd erupted in wild cheering and clapping as Jason and Kim stood and turned to face them. Both Jason and Kim smiled at the jubilation being exhibited by the people of Preton. But only after a few minutes the blare of horns sounded again to once more silence the crowd. Jason looked at Kim with a puzzled expression on his face. This wasn't part of the ceremony they had rehearsed as far as he could remember. The crowd, also curious as to what was going on, quickly became subdued.

Moments later Ster led a contingent of Mayoral Guard to march out and stand between the newly married couple and the crowd. At a sharply barked order from Ster the men snapped to attention. From Jason's right two of the temple priestesses stepped forward to place small satin pillows in front of Kim and Jason, then quickly stepped back out of the way. Jason turned his head to see Jarrell and Seta coming out from behind the alter. In the hands of the High Priestess was an ornately carved box Jason instantly recognized.

Jason stood rooted to the spot, knowing he was trapped. The crowd became deathly quiet at this new turn of events, all of them wondering about what was to happen. As Jarrell and Seta came to stand before Jason they were joined by Busker, Shon and Hass. With a sudden insight Jason realized they had all planned this without his knowledge. "Kneel," he heard Kim whisper as she gently tugged at his hand.

Jason glanced down at Kim before reluctantly kneeling on the pillow in front of him. Whatever his own feelings, he knew he had no choice but to go along with what was happening. Proclaiming him as king was not supposed to happen like this. It was to be announced to the people after the next meeting of the annual Council of Mayors in two weeks, with notices being sent throughout Preton. It definitely wasn't supposed to happen on his wedding day.

Jason looked up at Jarrell. His father-in-law smiled mischievously at him as the other Mayors all came to join them, taking positions behind Jarrell and Seta. Jarrell winked at him before turning to face the crowd.

"People of Preton," Jarrell said to the crowd, "the celebrations of this day are not yet over, for we have another cause in which to rejoice."

Jason could feel the tension in the crowd as they leaned forward, ears straining to hear every word, eyes riveted to the box Seta was holding so reverently in her hands.

"As all of you know," Jarrell continued, "were it not for Jason we would now be suffering under the invading forces of both the Karton and Tilwin. It is only by the grace of the gods, and the knowledge and courage of this man that the men of Preton were able to crush those who wished to grind up beneath their collective heels and enslave us."

Jarrell paused, wiping the palms of his hands nervously on the sides of his robe. Jason could tell that Jarrell wasn't quite as sure about what was to happen as he pretended.

"Over five hundred years ago," Jarrell continued, "the people of Preton overthrew their king and set up a new form of government, and since that time it has served us well for the most part."

If Jarrell didn't have their complete attention before, he did now. Breaths were being held in anxious anticipation of his next words.

"If anyone had approached me a year ago with what I have now accepted as fated by the gods, I would have driven him from my sight. But times change, ideas change, and we must change with them. Although the physical battles with the Karton and Tilwin may be over, the struggle will continue until a new peace can be established once and for all. And knowing the Tilwin, peace will not be easily forthcoming.

"There are still many problems we must face and overcome, and these situations must be addressed and dealt with by someone who has the authority to speak for all of Preton. A man with the power of the army behind him, and the good of the people in his heart."

Jason raised his eyes slightly and saw the crowd hanging on Jarrell's every word. They still weren't sure what was coming, but whatever it was they knew it was important and would affect them all.

"It is with this in mind," Jarrell told them, "that the Council of Mayors have met and reached the conclusion that no man could do that without our approval and support. It was also at that time that we were informed of the prophecy which has been a guarded secret of the Temple of Lofa since the beginning of our time."

You old liar, Jason thought with a wiry grin. You've known about the prophecy all along.

"This prophecy," continued Jarrell, "told of a strange who would come to our world from another. A stranger who would look like us, yet be different so that all would know him. A stranger who would arrive at the time when we would need him most." Jarrell paused for the space of a heartbeat before continuing. "And the prophecy said this man would be our king."

Jason felt his body tense as a shocked gasp rippled through the crowd. He wondered what their faces looked like but didn't dare raise his head to see for himself. He kept his eyes glued to the ground in front of where he knelt. After a moment he heard the voice of Seta.

"People of Preton, as High Priestess of the Temple of Lofa, and Guardian of the Secrets of the Past, I have searched every record of the temple and prayed for many hours for guidance from Lofa in this matter. The prophecy Jarrell speaks of is true and has come to be fulfilled. For, as you can see, here before us is the man the prophecy speaks of. Here is the stranger not of this world. The man who looks like us, but who is different. The strange who has become one of us, saving us from certain death and destruction at the hands of our enemies. Is there one among you to question this?"

Jason knew her question was purely rhetorical. No one was going to question the word of Seta. Some might doubt Jarrell, but due to their heavy religious superstitions they were not as quick to question an edict from Seta. And if Jarrell and Seta both said this was the way it must be, who were they to question it? It was almost the same as the gods themselves coming down in person to anoint him.

Seta handed the box to Jarrell. She then lifted the lid and removed the crown from within. She held it high above her head for all to see as another temple priestess stepped up to Jason and removed the diadem from his head. Seta turned to face him and then stepped forward to carefully place the larger crown on his head. Once it was secure she stepped back to stand beside Jarrell. "Stand, Jason, King of Preton," she told him.

As Jason slowly stood up, Jarrell, Seta, Busker, and all those who had been standing in front of him dropped to their right knee and place both of their hands on their left knee in a position of supplication. Jason could only stand dumbly as every member of the Guard, the Mayors of every city, along with Seta and the other temple priestesses dropped to their knees without the slightest hesitation. He turned his head slowly, watching as the masses covering the plains also began to kneel where they were, their head bowing to him.

*I don't want this!* Jason's mind screamed as he turned full circle to find he was the only one standing. He felt suddenly frightened by the power he knew he now controlled. He didn't know what to do or say. He was about to reach out to Jarrell and Seta, to ask them to stand when his hand was frozen by the rolling of thunder and the flashing of lights that suddenly appeared in the clear sky. His eyes were not the only ones to look upwards, even if they were the only ones to instantly recognize a holographic projection for what it was.

The figure of a man and woman appeared to be standing on a cloud and slowly descending toward the crowd. A cry went up as the figures were recognized instantly by the masses as being those of Lofa and Avihs. Even Jason recognized the images of the two most powerful deities of Alazon from the many drawings and statues he had seen of them.

"People of Preton," boomed a deep bass voice which did not come from the speakers around the crowd, but from the probe concealed within the holograph, "what you have done this day is pleasing to us. It is pleasing to all the gods of Alazon."

<u>Gods my ass!</u> Jason thought as he clenched his jaw. <u>I'm going to get you for this, Mother!</u>

"You have heard the words of Seta, my High Priestess," said the image of Lofa. "She is the guardian of my temples and Keeper of the Secrets. Her words are true. She is my instrument in your world and would not deceive you or lead you falsely."

"This man is to be your king," both figures said in unison. "His words are our words. His word is the law and to be obeyed without question. We smile upon him and give him guidance in all things. Those who appose him will be struck down with our wrath. To them we will bring destruction and death, as we did to the Tilwin when they dared strike him.

"Heed our words and remember them well, Children of the Chosen, for this is the way it shall be from this day forth. Your world will change, your lives will change, becoming better in all things and in all ways, for Jason shall bring you the knowledge of the gods.

"Listen to him and his words. Listen, obey and prosper. Listen, and all the world will come to know the greatness of the people of Preton, chosen by Lofa and Avihs as their children."

There was another crash of computer generated thunder and the flash of laser lights, leaving all but a select few cowering in fear and awe. If there had been any doubts in the minds of anyone about Jason being appointed as king, they had just been wiped out. He was going to have to have a little talk with Mother about the misuse of lasers, sonic cannons and holo projectors.

As Jason lowered his gaze he saw Jarrell and Seta not standing before him. There were slight smiles of amusement on both of their faces. "Pretty impressive, wouldn't you agree?" Jarrell whispered with his hand covering the mike at his throat so his words wouldn't be broadcast to everyone.

Jason shook his head and grinned. "Who's idea was this?"

"Mine, Jason," Kim said softly from where she knelt beside him. "Please don't be angry with me. I thought it would help."

"We'll talk about it later, Muggles," he replied with a rueful grin.

Jarrell jerked his thumb over his shoulder at the crowd. "You're their king now. You have to speak to them."

Jason reached down and pulled Kim to her feet to stand beside him. He smiled at her and slipped his arm around her waist before turning to the crowd.

"People of Preton," he began slowly, not sure of what he was supposed to say, "today is both a day of joy and one of weighty responsibility for me."

All eyes were riveted on him. Even the insects seemed to have ceased their movements and noise.

"I want you to know that I take both events with equal sincerity and responsibility, and that I will do my best to be a good and compassionate king.

"I will do my best to bring peace to all of Alazon, and to do whatever I must to maintain that peace. In that, I ask your patience and understanding. But," he added with a smile, "you came here to day to celebrate a wedding. So my first edict as your king is for you to do just that."

At this, the members of the Guard stood and withdrew their katanas, holding them horizontally over their heads in both hands. "Jason, King of Preton," the said loudly as one, "we proclaim this day our swords, our arms, and our lives to you. Where you lead we shall follow without question. What you order we shall do, and woe be to the misfortunate who appose you."

With that they quickly formed two rows to provide a clear isle for him and Kim to leave the alter and proceed to the large tent that had been set up for the reception. "Jason! Jason!" the crowd began to chant as he and Kim made their way to the tent.

"I'll get you for this," he told Jarrell with a grin after switching off his throat mike.

Once they were beneath the massive silk canopy the long procession of guest began. Jason was introduced to people who's names he quickly filed away in his mind. He smiled and shook hands with the men and kissed the women on their cheeks. As the reception line finally came to an end a band began to play and the dancing began. As well as the eating. Huge tables of food were uncovered for all the invited guests, and a festive air once again permeated the populace.

The first dance was for Kim and himself. Everyone cleared a space for the two of them, clapping and cheering when it was over. After that it was Jarrell's turn to dance with Kim while Jason danced with Liet. From that point on Jason began to feel as if he were going to have to dance with every woman there before they could get away to start their honeymoon.

He saw Janella standing off to one side with the twins and went to her. "Would you like to dance?" he asked as he took her small hand in his own. Janella nodded eagerly. Her little face beamed as he picked her up in his arms and began to dance with her. When the dance was over she kissed him, and when he set her down she stepped back and curtsied before rushing back to join the twins.

Sometime well after sundown Ster managed to get him to one side. "You ready to get away from all this madness?" the lieutenant asked with a knowing grin.

Jason nodded and reached for Kim's hand. He allowed Ster and the Guard to lead them through the crowd to the small shuttle behind the tent. The two of them lofted off slowly so as not to hurt any of those crowded around with the exhaust from the shuttle's engines. Once they were clear, Jason pointed the nose of the craft upward and streaked away.

"How you doing, Mrs. Stephens?" he asked as he asked as he reached for her hand.

She smiled brightly and squeezed his hand in both of hers. "I've never been happier in my life," she told him softly.

'Hey, Mother, you and I are gonna have a serious talk one of these days about the misuse of ship facilities."

"Oh, relax, Jason," Mother replied with a chuckle. "This is supposed to be a day of joy and fun, so try having some."

"Okay, I'll forget about it for the time being, but we will talk later. Now, do you have the other preparations ready that I asked for?"

"Hey, what do you take me for, some Twentieth Century lap top? This is Mother you're talking to."

"Well, excuse me," he replied, laughing at her feigned indignity as he eased the shuttle into the bay.

Jason and Kim left the shuttle and walked hand in hand to his quarters. He stopped just outside the door and turned to her.

"There's another old tradition on Earth where the husband carries his new bride across the threshold of their hone, or wherever they will be spending their first night together as husband ad wife," he told her as he swept her up in his arms.

"I think I like some of your traditions," she whispered, kissing him as the door opened.

He carried her inside and saw that Mother had been busy. The lights in the room were off but the room was lit by candles set around the room. . The bed was covered with blue satin sheets and a bottle of champagne with two fluted glasses were chilling in an ice bucket next to the bed.

He set Kim down and the two of them merely stared into one another's eyes for a long moment. Slowly he began to undress Kim as she stood before him. Her eyes spoke of the desire and anticipation she was feeling that matched his own. Her body trembled at his touch. As her clothing fell away Jason could feel himself becoming aroused as never before. He quickly removed his own clothing, picking Kim up and carrying her to the bed. As they lay on it she reached for him with an urgency not to be denied. Wrapping her arms and legs around him she cried out in pleasure as they joined for the first time as husband and wife.

# TWENTY FOUR

"I don't think I'll ever get used to this," Jarrell grumbled from his seat next to Jason in the mid-sized shuttle as Bysee, the capitol of Karton came into view.

"Sure you will," Jason told him. "Why, in another month or so I'll have you flying one all by yourself."

"Don't bet on that," Jarrell replied dourly as the shuttle headed for the plaza in the center of the city. Those below looked up and scattered in fear at the sight of the strange craft dropping down on them from the sky.

All of the shuttles had been repainted a brilliant white, with the starburst pattern painted on either side of the nose and the upright tail sections. Jason hadn't been too sure about the idea at first, but between Mother, Jarrell and Kim they had convinced him it was the right thing to do.

"Look at it this way, Jarrell," Busker said from behind the. "You can't be nearly as nervous as those people down there. They don't have the faintest idea of what is going on."

Jarrell looked at the people fleeing from the plaza in fear and grinned. They were running wildly in all directions from the plaza, diving for whatever cover they could find as the apparition from the sky came closer and closer to them. "You have a point there," Jarrell replied with a chuckle.

"Shon?" Jason called into the com-link.

"Shon here," came the immediate reply.

"What's your position?"

"A thousand feet above you in a holding pattern."

"Let's hope we don't have to do this, but if so, wait for my signal. Jason out."

As soon as the shuttle touched down in the center of the plaza Ster was up and out of his seat, hitting the panel to open the side hatch. He led twenty of the men who now called themselves the Royal Guard out to form double ranks at the bottom of the ramp. Their eyes were alert for any sign of danger, their bodies poised to snatch swords or phasers in the blink of an eye.

Busker led the way for the rest of them. He marched down the center of the ramp, followed by Jason and Jarrell walking side by side. The entire party then marched towards the broad steps of the palace of the King of Karton. As they reached the bottom step the wide double doors of the palace swung open and forty Karton soldiers rushed out to line themselves up along the top step.

"Easy," Jason told his men softly as he brought his entourage to a halt.

A man from the group above stepped forward to star at Jason and his party for a moment before speaking. "Who are you and what do you want?" he finally asked. His voice was filled with false bravado, as fear and uncertainty were clearly evident in his mannerisms.

Jarrell stepped forward, squaring his shoulders and clearing his throat. "I am Jarrell Vehey, Mayor of Lemac, Senior Mayor of Preton, and Chief Advisor to Jason Stephens, King of Preton," he told the man in a loud, clear voice.

The man on the steps had not taken his eyes off Jason as Jarrell spoke, which led Jason to believe that this man had not been with the invading forces that had attempted to attack Preton.

"What we want," continued Jarrell, "is to discuss the trade and peace agreements between Preton and Karton with King Tolo."

The man on the steps turned and nodded to one of his men. The subordinate rushed back inside the palace while everyone else stood watching each other like wary cats trying to decide whether they should attack one another. Jason wasn't worried about his men and how they would handle themselves, but he didn't want to have to kill any Karton if bloodshed could be avoided. The man who had been inside returned shortly and whispered something to the man in charge and then returned to his position in line.

"Come with me," the man on the steps told them, turning and motioning for them to follow.

Jason and the others mounted the steps and walked between the parted men of Karton and into the palace. As they entered the large main chamber, Jason took in everything around them.

The room was almost fifty yards wide and nearly eighty yards long. Near the far end were two thrones situated in a raised dais, upon which sat King Tolo and Queen Makee. The walls of the room were cut through with huge windows about every ten yards to provide light and ventilation. Each window was about three and a half feet wide and eight feet high. On either side of the windows were heavy wooden shutters that could be closed to keep out rain and wind if need be.

About twelve yards out from the walls were thick pillars of marble that served as supports for the domed ceiling, which was over a hundred feet above the floor. The floor itself was inlaid with multicolored tiles depicting scenes of battle and bloody conflicts. Walking across it, Jason wondered what it was that inspired people to glorify warfare and killing. He knew it wasn't just here on Alazon, but had been the same way back on earth. *There has to be a better way*, he thought as they traversed the length of the chamber.

As Jason and his entourage approached the thrones he ignored the buzz of muted comments concerning him and his appearance, focusing all of his attention on Tolo and Makee. The two grossly obese figures were bedecked in enough jewels that, if sold, could feed everyone in this city for a year. Jason felt his stomach start to knot up. Instinctively he knew that no matter what happened today he wasn't going to like these two individuals. He already had a pretty good idea of what they were like from his discussions with Jarrell, and their appearance now only reinforced the things his father-in-law had told him.

Two days ago Jason had flown to Bysee under the cover of darkness, bringing Seta and Shon with him. He had dropped off the High Priestess and his brother-in-law outside the city, having them make their way into the city on foot and mingle with the citizens there. Seta had gone directly to the Temple of Lofa and spoken to the High Priestess. She informed her counterpart of Jason's presence on Alazon and of how he had been proclaimed King of Preton. The two women spoke throughout the night, setting up their plans for what was to happen when Jason arrived.

In the meantime, Shon had made his way to the palace so he could do a personal inspection of both the interior and exterior of the building, taking pictures with the concealed camera provided by Jason. The next day Jason and Shon had gone over the pictures carefully, making their plans.

Their escort brought them to a halt about ten feet from the base of the dais. "Your Majesties," the man said loudly and clearly, "may I present to you Jason, King of Preton, and Jarrell Vehey, Mayor of Lemac, Senior Mayor of Preton, and Chief Advisor to their king."

The man bowed low and then backed away to one side, taking a position just slightly in front of another group of soldiers, his hand resting on the hilt of his short sword.

"Jarrell," said Tolo as he popped a piece of soft candy into his mouth and chewed noisily on it, "it is good to see you again, but I'm afraid I don't know this strange looking man who calls himself your king."

Jason suppressed a smile. Despite Tolo's words and outward attitude the fat little man was frightened.

"King Tolo," Jarrell said with all the tact of a true diplomat, "this man is not only my king, but also the husband of my eldest daughter. Therefore, it would well benefit you to treat him with all the courtesy and respect you would any other ruler of equal status."

The words, delivered softly, contained a veiled threat that carried to everyone in the chamber. Tolo reacted to them instantly. He bristled and sat up straight.

"You dare presume to tell me how I should or should not treat those who come before me!" Tolo practically yelled, his face darkening. "I am a King! You, on the other hand are but a mere Mayor!"

Jason felt the tension of his men. He knew the situation could quickly get out of hand if he didn't do something to defuse it. He stepped forward and spread his hands, palms up, but even that simple movement caused Tolo to cringe slightly.

"King Tolo," he said in an evenly modulated voice, "I am sure that Jarrell presumed no such thing. I believe he was merely reminding you of the protocol of court we must all favor and follow, despite any temporary forgetfulness at the shock of seeing something to which we are not accustomed, such as my presence here today."

Tolo may have been obese and ugly but he wasn't exactly stupid. He was quick to pick up on the opportunity to save face that Jason had provided for him. He smiled and relaxed somewhat in his seat.

"Yes, I am sure you are right," the fat little king said with a slick smile. "Jarrell, I apologize for my quick anger toward you, and I extend to you the courtesies of this court." Tolo turned to the man who had been their escort. "Captain, please get some seats for our guests."

As the captain sent others to get the seats, Tolo turned back to Jason, taking a brief moment to study him carefully.

"You are not a Preton. In fact, I do not think I have ever seen anyone like you before, although I have heard of you. Tell me, where do you come from, and what gives you the authority to proclaim yourself as King of Preton?"

But before Jason could answer, the hall rang out with the loud clear voice of a woman. It was a voice used to speaking and commanding both attention and respect.

"He comes from a world more distant than the smallest star we are able to see on a clear night," proclaimed a woman who wore the formal robes of a High Priestess of Lofa.

Jason turned to see her step out from the crowd. Her face was riveted on his own. She was much older than Seta, the skin of her face and hands resembling dried parchment, but she carried herself with all the bearing befitting her station and rank. She stopped when she was between Jason and the dais, turning at last to look up at Tolo.

"I do not take kindly to mockery when I ask a question, even from a High Priestess," Tolo told her. Despite his words, his fingers twitched nervously on the arm of the throne.

"I do not mock you, Tolo," she replied firmly. The way she said his name made it sound like something vile in her mouth. "I speak only the truth and you know it."

"In that case," Tolo sneered, "perhaps you can tell me what he wants here?"

"What I would tell you would send you screaming through the streets, crying out to gods who will not listen to spare your miserable life."

Jason could see the strain on Tolo's face as the man fought to control himself. <u>He's almost as afraid of her as he is of me</u>, he thought with a slight grin.

The tension in Tolo's voice was clearly evident when he spoke again. "High Priestess Makel, I tolerate the Temple of Lofa only through my good graces. Your words border on treason."

"Hah!" Makel said with scorn. "You tolerate the Temple of Lofa because you know the people would rise up and split your fat carcass if you ever dared lift a hand against us."

Makel's statement brought hushed murmurs from the crowd. Jason had a feeling the old woman was telling Tolo the truth, and in a way the fat little king did not want to hear it.

"But now the time has come for you to step down, Tolo," Makel continued. "To be replaced by one who has been sent by the gods to bring peace to our world and rid it of the leaches such as yourself!"

Tolo was sweating profusely as he stared down at the High Priestess. Jason could see the fear in the man's eyes. "Is what she says the truth?" Tolo asked him belligerently.

"More or less," Jason replied casually, keeping his voice and face calm. "I do come from a world such as she spoke of, but I come in peace. My visit here today is to establish new trade and peace agreements between your country and mind. New agreements that will be fair and equal to both."

"What makes you think we need new treaties?" Tolo asked. He glanced around the room nervously as men returned with the seats for Jason, Jarrell and Busker before returning to their former positions along the wall.

Jason shrugged slightly and grinned up at Tolo, ignoring the seat behind him and continuing to stand. "Well, the fact that you joined with the Tilwin and sent an army to attempt to invade Preton is a pretty good indication that you were not happy with the old ones. Wouldn't you agree?"

A light seemed to go on behind Tolo's eyes. "YOU!" Tolo gasped in shocked surprise. He realized now that he was facing the man who had led the Preton in their crushing victory over his army.

"Yes, I'm the one," Jason replied with a slight grin. "By the way," he added, looking around the room, "I don't see General Laer present. May I ask where he is?"

"He's in the dungeon," Makel told him before Tolo could reply. "When he returned with the news of the defeat, and of the strange looking man who led the Preton, our wonderful king, in his infinite wisdom, didn't believe him. He called General Laer a liar, a traitor and a coward. He then threw Laer and his officers in the dungeon where they are beaten and starved."

Jason felt his anger building and was aware of the tension of his own men starting to rise as he turned to face Tolo. "General Laer is neither a coward nor a traitor to the people of Karton. Nor is he a liar.

"What he is, Tolo, is a brave and honorable man who led his men with courage. He surrendered only when he realized that to fight on would mean total destruction of all his men. But you, you fat, despicable excuse for a man, much less a king, are the real coward and traitor to the people of Karton!"

A shocked gasp of surprise shot through the crowd at this bold statement from Jason. Soldiers along the walls gripped their swords tightly, awaiting the signal to attack.

"I think, Tolo," Jason continued, "that you are the coward and traitor who sold your throne to the Tilwin while you sit here giving orders and stuffing your mouth, not caring who dies or how they may suffer, just as long as your whims and wishes are catered to."

"You are digging yourself a quick grave!" Tolo shouted, his face livid with rage. "Look around you! My men have you outnumbered fifty to one!"

Jason smiled and shook his head sadly. "Do it, Shon," he whispered softly in English into the small mike beneath his collar.

Almost instantly people began screaming and fleeing the palace as a laser from the shuttle began cutting a diagonal path across the ceiling of the palace. By the time Shon was done there was a three yard wide gash all the way across the ceiling. Everyone from Karton, with the exception of Tolo, Makee and the High Priestess had fled in fear.

Jason had not taken his eyes off Tolo. He watched the man blanch and nearly faint at what was happening. The fat little kin's mouth worked like that of a fish out of water as he realized he was dealing with forces unlike any this world had ever imagined. Jason turned to Make. "How do we get to the dungeon?"

She pointed to the back of the main chamber. "There is a door back there."

"Busker, take half the men and go find Laer and the others, and if anyone tries to stop you, do whatever you feel is necessary to eliminate that resistance."

Yes, Sir!" Busker replied with a wide grin. Signaling for half the men to follow him, Busker drew his sword and headed for the end of the chamber.

No one spoke as Busker and the men disappeared. Jason was content to let Tolo and Makee sit there and sweat, wondering what was going to happen to them. A few minutes later Busker reappeared. His left arm supported a badly beaten and starved Naed, while his right held his bloody katana.

Jason rushed forward to catch Naed as the man started to slip from Busker's grasp. Picking up the thin body in his arms, Jason carried Naed back to the front of the dais where he handed him to two other men before turning back to face Tolo.

"Tolo, you and Makee will remain inside the walls of this palace," he told him in a low, cold voice, "until I return with a new governor for Karton. At that time you will be released and driven into the streets with nothing more than the clothes on your back. You will not be allowed to take any money or jewels with you, and if you even think of trying to smuggle any out before I return, I will have you killed instantly. Mother!"

Two small metal spheres bristling with camera eyes, antenna and small lasers suddenly dropped through the opening in the ceiling. They positioned themselves about six feet above his head, further frightening the already terrified Tolo and Makee.

"These I leave behind as my guardians," he told Tolo. "They will monitor your every move and hear every word you utter, and if you try to escape they will kill you."

"But...but surely we can...work something out," Tolo stuttered, tears forming in his eyes.

"You had your chance for that," Jason snapped. "You wasted it on idle threats and pride. You have until I return to decide what to do with your lives. If you wish to end them before that time, feel free to do so."

Jason turned to the High Priestess. "Will you be safe now? If not, you are welcome to return to Preton with us."

Makel smiled up at him gratefully. "I will be fine, my lord. No one will dare raise a hand against me or the Temple. Go, and return with our new governor as soon as you can. Your arrival has long been awaited by us. We will finally know peace and prosperity now that you are here."

Jason nodded and turned away, leading the others out of the palace and down the steps. Outside there wasn't anyone in sight. "Shon, bring your shuttle down. We're going to need the room for some passengers."

"On my way."

Moments later Shon landed the second shuttle and the men from the dungeon were loaded into both of them. Jason had Naed carried to his own shuttle and buckled into the co-pilot seat. Naed opened his eyes and smiled up at him weakly.

"Sorry I couldn't...meet you at the door. I was a little...tied up," He tried to smile again but it turned into a grimace of pain.

"Don't talk," Jason told him. "We'll have you back in Lemac in a couple of hours and you'll be fine."

But Naed had passed out and hadn't heard a word Jason had said. Jason quickly strapped himself in and lifted the shuttle into the sky. Turning toward the west he streaked toward Lemac at top speed with Shon flying the other shuttle just off his right wing tip.

No one spoke during the flight back. They sensed Jason's anger and didn't want to possibly have it directed at them over an ill-spoken comment. This was the first time any of them had ever seen him truly angry, and they still weren't sure as to how me might react.

Jason flew straight to the Temple of Lofa. As the side hatches of the shuttles opened and the battered men were gently removed, a priestess yelled for help and almost immediately Seta and others streamed out to assist. Seta began issuing rapid fire orders to the women around her. One dashed back inside while others, along with Jason's men, began assisting the men from Karton into the temple. Jason carried Naed in his own arms, refusing to let anyone take him. Seta led Jason to a bed where he could finally lay Naed down gently. "This man is a friend, Seta."

"He will be well taken care of," she told him, cutting him of. "As will all the others."

"They've been starved and beaten, but I don't think there are any serious internal injuries," he told her. "After you check them over, if you think any of them have been injured seriously, let me know and I'll take them up to my ship."

"Yes, my Lord," she replied as she gently pushed him away from Naed's bed. "Now I need for you and your men to clear out so we can take care of them."

Jason stepped back as temple women began cutting away the tattered rags that covered Naed. As he turned to walk away Seta came to join him. They stopped at the top of the steps outside.

"These men," Jason said as he turned to face Seta, "are men of Karton, but they are not enemies of Preton."

"I understand, my Lord Jason."

"I want to be kept informed of their progress. Let me know when they are able to leave and I will make arrangements for them in the barracks. Except for Naed. He will be given quarters in the Mayoral Building."

"Yes, my Lord."

"Seat, Jason said with a sigh, "will you do me a favor?"

Seta looked him directly in the eyes for a brief second. Her gaze made him feel uncomfortable for reasons he couldn't quite explain. "Anything, my Lord," she said softly. "You know you but have to ask whatever it is you wish of me."

Jason felt himself shiver at that. 'Anything' could cover a lot of territory. "Would you mind not addressing me as 'Lord'? I mean, it makes me a little uncomfortable at times."

Seta looked slightly shocked at this request from him. "But you are my king and as such I must address you in a manner befitting that position and rank."

He sighed in exasperation. "Look, I'll make you a deal. I won't object to you calling me that in public, or when protocol is needed, but when we're not in public I would appreciate it if you would just call me by my given name the way everyone else does."

Seta hesitated a moment before finally smiling up at him. "Of course," she replied, laughing lightly. "Whatever you wish. My duty is to obey you at all times."

"Yeah, right," he muttered to himself as he heard the clatter of hooves on stone. He looked around to see Kim and Janella racing toward them on one tollie, the twins on another, with Baby running along beside them. As the tollies came to a skidding halt on the cobblestones, Kim leaped from the back of the one she rode to rush up the steps and throw her arms around him.

"Nice to see you, too," he told her with a grin as she raised her head to look at him.

"When I heard the shuttles, and then saw them heading for the temple, I got scared. I was afraid that something had happened to you. Again!"

"I'm fine. I brought some men from Karton here to be treated."

"Are they going to be okay?" Kim asked, glancing from him to Seta and back.

"They should be. They've been beaten and starved, but I'm sure Seta and the others will have them on their feet in no time."

"Well, you should have contacted me on the radio and let me know what was going on," Kim told you. "You know you have a bad habit of getting yourself hurt, and then I have to patch you up and take care of you."

"Sorry. I had other things on my mind."

Kim turned to Seta. "Honestly, this man can drive a woman crazy with worry at times. He is so clumsy and accident prone that it is a wonder he ever made it past his own childhood."

"Well," Seta replied, laughing lightly, "whenever he stubs his tow, or runs into a door, you can always bring him here and we will take good care of him for you."

"I have a better idea, Seta. Just reserve a bed for him because you can bet he will need it," Kim told her, quickly stepping away to avoid Jason's playful swat at her backside.

"Excuse me, ladies, but if you, Muggles, are through doing an assassination of my character for the time being, I think we should head home for supper. I'm hungry."

"Oh, of course, your Highness," Kim teased. She bowed low at her face split in a wide grin. "To hear is to obey."

"You're asking for it, Muggles," he told her.

"And you think you are man enough to give it to me?" she taunted, laughing at him.

"That does it."

"Jason!" Kim shrieked as he moved faster than she had anticipated. He snatched her up and lightly tossed her over his right shoulder. "Put me down this instant!"

Jason smiled at Seta and walked down the steps to the tollie and easily tossed Kim astride it on her stomach, her head and feet dangling down on either side.. "Lieutenant,'" he said to Ster, who had been holding the reins of both animals, "take the shuttle back for me. I think I'll ride back with my wife."

"Yes, Commander," Ster replied with a grin as he headed for the shuttle.

Jason mounted the tollie and then turned to look down at Jarrell. "I'll see you back at the house," he told the older man as he rode past the laughing father. The twins and Janella turned their tollie to ride along beside him.

"How dare you treat me like this!" Kim protested loudly as they started to ride away. "Just because you are my husband, and just happen to be King of Preton, that does not give you the right to manhandle me in public!"

"Silence, woman!" he told her as he winked at Janella and the twins. "Otherwise I'll stop this tollie and turn you across my knee and spank you until you learn the proper respect for your husband and king."

"You wouldn't dare!" Kim exclaimed. "I'll have you know I am the oldest daughter of the Senior Mayor Preton, who is also your

Chief Advisor. Not only that, but I am Queen of Preton! No one, not even you, would dare spank me in public!"

"If you say so," he said with a grin, stopping the tollie in front of a crowd of people who had been listening to them with amused smiles.

Kim looked back over her shoulder. "Jason? Jason, what are you going to…owww!" she wailed as his right hand came down with a loud smack on her shapely butt. "Jason, you better let me up!"

"That's 'My Lord Jason' you saucy little wench," he told her as he brought his hand down once again. He winked at those watching and laughing at the scene, knowing his blows her hurting her ego more than her backside.

"Jason!"

Wack!

"Jason!"

Wack!

"Ow! Alright! My Lord Jason, will you please let me up?"

Jason looked down in to the faces of the crowd. "Do you thin she's learned her lesson?" he asked the man closest to him.

"Well, Lord," the man replied thoughtfully, "she doesn't really sound all that sorry to me, if you know what I mean."

"What about you?" Jason asked the woman standing beside the man.

"I doubt it, Lord," the woman replied. "I think she is only faking her humility."

"I think you are probably right," he told them as he brought his hand down on her backside once more.

"Jason," Kim said softly, "I'm sorry. I humbly apologize for any embarrassment I may have caused you, and for my attitude toward you. I promise never to do it again."

"What do you think now?" he asked the crowd.

"I believe her now," someone said.

Jason lifted Kim and set her astride the tollie in front of him. "I think you should thank these good people," he told her, indicating the crowd, "for it is they who prevented you from receiving further punishment for your very unlady-like behavior and rash statements. Go on, thank them."

Kim hung her head in embarrassment, refusing to look at those standing around. "Thank you," she mumbled softly.

"Very good. Now we will go home and you will prepare my super the way a good and obedient wife should do, correct?"

"Yes, my Lord."

Jason nudged the tollie into motion and they rode the rest of the way home with him joking around with the twins and Janella. As soon as they reached the house, Kim leaped from the tollie and dashed inside, running to their bedroom and slamming the door behind her. The twins and Janella left him to put the tollies away while they hurried into the house to tell the others in excited voices how Kim had received a public spanking for smarting off to Jason.

Kim emerged from the bedroom half an hour later. Her hands were clenched into fists and her face was livid. "I have never been so humiliated before in my life! If you ever do that to me again, I'll… .I'll…" But instead of telling Jason what she would do, she turned and fled into Vinny's bedroom, the sound of laughter following her.

"You know, Jason," Jarrell said with a twinkle in his eyes, "you did something I have often considered doing for years. I could just never bring myself to."

"Well, maybe so," Jason replied thoughtfully. "However, I'm not sure if it was the right thing to do in public that. But she was just daring me, so I figured I'd call her bluff."

Jarrell nodded in understanding. "I dare say you have humiliated her, but I would also be willing to bet that those who saw it just loved it. This is going to give them something to talk about for years."

"True," Jason replied with a grin. "I just hope I didn't put her in a position of disrespect in their eyes over it."

"I doubt it, Jason," Jarrell replied thoughtfully. "In fact, if you went into the streets right now and asked the people what they thought, I'll bet the overwhelming majority of them would tell you that it has been too long in coming, and that she was only receiving what she's been due her for her past actions. She really has gotten by with too much for too long."

"Thanks to an over lenient father," Liet interjected with a straight face. "You have spoiled her rotten from the day she as born and we all know it."

Jarrell shrugged and grinned sheepishly. "Guilty."

"Well," Jason told them, "I have a feeling I may be sleeping alone tonight."

When Kim didn't appear for supper, Vinny fixed a plate and took it in to her. The two women stayed in Vinny's room with the door shut for the rest of the evening. Later, after putting the kids to bed, telling them a story and kissing them good night, Jason went to his bedroom, undressed and got into bed. Just as he was starting to get comfortable the door open and Kim crept in. She hesitated by the door for a moment, the crossed the room and eased into bed beside him.

"You just wait, Alien," she whispered as she curled up to him. "Your day will come, and then it will be my turn."

Any reply he might have wanted to make was cut off by the press of her lips on his as her body moved to cover his own, her hands eagerly reaching for him.

# TWENTY FIVE

Jason stood on the landward end of the main dock watching the smaller of the two Tilwin ships make its way slowly into the harbor. Thanks to the ever watchful eye of Mother, he had known for nearly two weeks of their coming. The computer had also used her scanners to tell him who and what were on those ships. The smaller, but moreelaborate of the two, contained Queen Lorac of Tilwin, along with a hundred of her personal bodyguard and other members of her retinue. The second ship was loaded with another two hundred of her personal guard who were, according to Mother, "looking, ugly bunch of suckers".

On Jason's right stood Jarrell. On his left stood Rettes, the little roly-poly mayor of Sharl, who seemed to wear a perpetual smile on his face, and who appeared to know everyone in the city on a first name basis. On their way to the docks from the Mayoral Building, Rettes had stopped half a dozen times to speak to people. He would ask about members of their families or just tell a joke. Despite his seemingly constant laughter and jovial nature, Rettes was an extremely competent administrator and mayor. He was also a man who truly cared about the welfare of the citizens of Sharl. A testament to his abilities and popularity stood in the fact that he was second only to Jarrell in length of time in office.

Behind Jason and the two mayors stood Ster and twenty members of the Royal Guard, dressed in their white jumpsuits and boots, which had become a symbol of pride among them. But scattered throughout the dock workers were another hundred of his men.

They wore no uniforms and blended with the other dock workers, unless someone looked carefully at the watchful, wary eyes, or saw the katanas and ho-tachi and phaser pistols carefully concealed, but within quick grasp if needed.

Jason had arrived in Sharl three days ago to sit down with Jarrell, Rettes and Busker to discuss the best way to conduct the first meeting with Lorac. They had finally settled on a show of muted force. That would let Lorac know that she was welcome, while also making it clear that there had been some dramatic and drastic changes between the countries of Preton and Tilwin that she would have to accept.

"What do you think?" Jason asked Jarrell as Lorac's ship began to line up at the pier.

"I think," Jarrell replied with a grin, "that Queen Lorac is going to be in for a very big surprise."

"I agree," Rettes said with a short laugh. "She has come here expecting to enter a city of the conquered, but will soon find that things are not quite up to her expectations. Or her liking for that matter."

As the ship made its final adjustments, hawsers as thick as a man's arm were thrown from the ship to men on the doc to secure it. Men aboard the ship removed a section of side railing to run a gangplank down to the pier. As soon as it was in place, Lorac's guard hurried down to line up on either side of the pier, proving a space between them for her to walk. As the men took their position there was something about them which struck Jason as slightly off kilter. He studied them carefully, wondering what it was that seemed out of place. Their black breastplates with the blood red skulls painted on them were imposing, but that was pretty much for show and Jason blocked that out. He looked for the obvious, which was often the one thing that was missed. Then it hit him.

The men on Lorac's left wore their small round shields on their left forearms and their swords on their left hips. This allowed for a right handed draw, which was normal. But the men on her right wore their shields on their right arm and their swords on their right hip. That meant they would have to draw and use their swords with their left hands. That was unheard of on this world of totally right handed people.

Jason knew from personal experience what it took to train a right handed man to use a sword with his left, but the men of Lorac's guard looked as if they were completely comfortable with it. In a normal fighting situation it would provide a slight advantage to them if their opponent had never fought against anyone trained that way. But Jason also knew that against his own men it would make no difference, as they had not only been trained to use a sword with either hand, but had spent countless hours practicing against one another that way.

Lorac finally appeared from below the main deck and began to walk down the plank. Her regal bearing was unmistakable. She was followed by three other women who were probably maids or servants. She walked as if she expected them to be there at all times, exhibiting an air of confidence about here that came from a strong personality and years of being obeyed by others without question. Lorac approached Jason's position but when she had covered about half the distance she finally got a good look at her welcoming committee. Her step faltered just a bit when she saw Jason, but she quickly regained her composure and proceeded on. When she was within ten feet of him and his party, Rettes stepped forward to greet her.

"Queen Lorac," Rettes said in a warm, friendly manner, "welcome to Preton. We have been awaiting your arrival."

"Thank you, Mayor Rettes," Lorac replied with a smile that seemed just a little too forced. Even though she had spoken to Rettes, she was having trouble taking her eyes off Jason. "Tell me, who is this strange looking man with you?"

"Queen Lorac of Tilwin, may I present Jason Stephens, King of Preton and Karton."

Rettes' words had been simply stated but Jason clearly saw the momentary shock in the eyes of Lorac. He also saw her struggling to maintain her composure and was impressed by it.

"Your Majesty," she said politely to Jason, doing a quick curtsey before standing and lifting her eyes to his face again. "I had no idea Preton had a new king. It has been so long since they had one that I find this a bit of a surprise."

*I'll bet you do*, he thought while smiling at her. He stepped forward and nodded slightly. "Queen Lorac, it is nice to have the opportunity to finally meet you. I have heard much about you and welcome this chance for us to get to know one another better.

"However, the docks are no place for us to conduct this momentous event. Why don't we adjourn to the Mayoral Building where I've had a meal prepared for you. I have also set aside accommodations for you to freshen up before hand if you wish. After sixty three days at sea I am sure you would welcome a real bath, as well as a table that isn't always swaying with the swells of the ocean"

Lorac's eyes opened wide for a brief second at his mention of the time she had been at sea. "May I ask how it is you know the exact number of days I have been at sea?" she asked.

"You will find, Queen Lorac, that there are many things I know. Now, before we retire from the place, there is a small favor I have to ask of you."

"What would that be?" she replied, raising her eyebrows in such a manner that she seemed to remind him of someone.

"Your men," he said, indicating her personal guard, "and the other members of your party are more than welcome to come into the city and enjoy its hospitality, but they are to leave all weapons behind. They have no need for them here as they are in no way threatened by anyone here."

Lorac stared up into his eyes for a moment and he knew she was trying to judge the degree of demand in his 'request'. She finally turned and spoke quickly to a man who appeared to be her Guard Captain. He looked from her to Jason for a brief moment and then nodded before turning to issue the order for his men to leave all weapons aboard the ship.

"Thank you," Jason said, breathing a soft sigh of relief at her compliance. If she had refused, his men would have sprung into position immediately at a hand signal from him and there would have been a confrontation, possibly even bloodshed.

Jason turned slightly and extended his left arm to Lorac. She hesitated only a moment before linking her right arm with his left and allowing him to escort her to the awaiting carriages. The two of them took their seats in the first carriage with Jarrell and Rettes. Busker, Shon, Hass and Ster rode in the second carriage behind them, with the Royal Guard lined up on either side. As the tollie drawn carriages began their trip from the docks back to the Mayoral Building the people of the city stopped to turn and wave to them. Some actually cheered and came up to shake the extended hands of Jason and Rettes.

Jason watched Lorac out of the corner of his eye. He could see the confusion and consternation she was experiencing from all this. Her eyes darted around and he knew she was searching for some signs of her army that had been sent to conquer these people. By the time they arrived at the Mayoral Building, Jason could clearly see the nervous agitation in her. He escorted her into the building, stopping just inside the large doors. He turned to her, his own face a mask of warmth and friendliness.

"Queen Lorac, if you will follow Lieutenant Ster he will show you and your party to your rooms. If there is anything you need, please do not hesitate to ask. Then, when you are ready we would appreciate your presence with us in the main dining room."

"Thank you," Liet replied as Ster directed the men carrying her trunks to follow his men up the stairs.

As Lorac followed Ster, Jason and the others went into the large dining room, taking their seats at the long wooden table before anyone spoke. "Impressions?" Jason said at last, throwing the word out for responses.

"She's frightened, confused, and completely unsure of herself and the situation for the moment," Jarrell replied as he leaned forward to place his forearms on the table. "She expected to enter a city of the conquered. Instead, she was met by a king she didn't know existed, with no sign of her own men."

Jason nodded and turned to Rettes. "You probably know her better than any of us. What's your impression?"

"I agree with Jarrell. However, Lorac's confusion won't last long. She's an extremely intelligent and quick thinking woman who is able to adapt. You can bet that even as we speak she's busy scheming, trying to find a way to gain some advantage out of her current situation.

"She will give the appearance of going along with things, but all the while she will be looking for a way she can grab something that will strengthen her position. Or try to turn them around so that she has the advantage, no matter how things may be stacked against her right now."

The discussion continued, with all of them voicing their opinions of her and how she might react. The time passed quickly and Jason was actually somewhat surprised when Lorac entered the room on the arm of Ster. Jason and the other stood as she was seated and then resumed their own seats.

"Thank you for your thoughtfulness, your Majesty," Lorac said to him with a warm appearing smile. "It has been so long sine I have had a real bath that I almost forgot how good it could feel."

"I hope everything was to your satisfaction?"

"Yes."

"Good. Now I suggest that we eat before actually getting into any discussions as to the reasons for your visit. There will be plenty of time for that later."

Jason nodded his head to the servants. The men who stepped forward to serve them were actually members of the Royal Guard who had taken the place of the normal servers. As dinner was served Lorac, spoke of conditions aboard ship during a long voyage, the weather, and other banal subjects. Serious subjects were considered inappropriate during a meal. It was believed that a person was better able to cope with serious problems of life after they were sated and more relaxed. Minds were clearer, tempers calmer, and discussions generally went much better.

Once the meal ended the table was cleared of all but the wine glasses. Jason leaned back in his chair, sipping at the coffee he had brought along for himself. All of the mayors now kept some on hand just for him. They had all tried it but none of them had developed the taste for it that he had.

"Now, Queen Lorac," he said cordially, "perhaps you would like to tell us what it is that brings you to Preton for this visit?"

"Your Majesty, I am slightly embarrassed by this," she replied with near convincing humility, "but I have come in search of some of my army."

"Would you care to elaborate on that?"

"Of course. You see, some months ago part of our army set out on what was supposed to be a training exercise. They were to divide into two groups, with one group defending an island while the other attacked, working on various battle formations and strategies. Unfortunately, from what I've been told, a violent storm arose and drove them off course. They haven't been heard of since leaving Tilwin.

"After a while I decided to go in search of them myself. I thought perhaps they might have been blown this way by the storm and had decided to take refuge with the people of Preton until they were able to sail for home."

Jason maintained the calm expression on his face. If he hadn't been aware of her true reasons, or of what had really happened to her troops, he could find himself easily believing her story.

"Excuse me, Lorac," he said softly, "but perhaps you would like to start over, and this time try the truth."

Lorac looked at him with a shocked expression on her face. "I'm not sure I know what you mean?" she replied with false innocence.

"I think you know exactly what I mean," he told her with a little more steel in his voice. "While the story you told is entertaining, and one I might actually believe under different circumstances, we both know you didn't come here looking for any lost army. You came to see how the conquest of Preton was going."

Jason paused for a few seconds, watching her face blanch at this blunt statement from him.

"You came here, Lorac, expecting to be greeted by your men. You thought they would be in control of this section of the country by now. But when you discovered this was not the case you panicked, and now you are doing your best to lie your way out of what is a sticky and embarrassing situation."

He saw the anger flare up in Lorac's eyes. She reminded him of a cornered animal who will fight for its life with a tenacity never known before when it turns to face its attacker. Jason decided to press his advantage to see what would happen.

"Your men are all dead, Lorac," he continued. "All of them. But they were not the victims of any storm at sea. Your men died on the beach where they came ashore, and without the loss of a single Preton life. You may also want to know that the army of Karton was defeated in a single day, and that they never got off the beach where they landed either."

Disbelief filled Lorac's eyes as she stared at Jason. "That's impossible!" she practically shouted, all forms of pretense having now been stripped away. "Preton has no army that could take on the army of Tilwin and defeat them. Or the Karton for that matter!"

"Really?" Jason asked casually. "You also believed that Preton had no king. Oh, and by the way, in case you missed it earlier, I am king of both Preton and Karton now."

"Just who or <u>what</u> are you?" she demanded through clenched teeth.

Jason ignored her question for the moment. "Your men are all dead, Lorac. Nothing, not even a scrap of wood or piece of metal remains to show they ever existed. The only good thing, if you want to call it that, is that they died quickly. Most of them before they even realized what was happening to them.

"Now," he continued, leaning forward and placing his forearms on the table, "as for who I am. I'm a man from another world. A world once very much like Alazon, but also vastly different in a lot of ways. A world over two thousand years ahead of your own in technology and science. But a world which destroyed itself because of people much like you.

"I am the only survivor of that world, and I have come to Alazon to bring an end to the fighting here. I am here to fulfill the prophecy."

Jason hadn't intended to toss in the comment about the prophecy but was glad he had when he saw Lorac's reaction to it. Her face paled and her jaw dropped open, and for a moment he thought she might actually faint. Her sudden stricken features told him she knew of the prophecy, and if nothing else, these people were superstitious to a fault. A trait he knew he could use to his advantage on certain occasions such as now.

"Lorac, when your army landed south of here I tried to talk to their commander. I tried to get them to turn back before it was too late. I pointed out to them that I had already defeated the Karton a few days earlier, but the man merely laughed at me and ordered his personal guard to kill me. They died when they tried, as did he."

At this news Lorac's body stiffened in her chair. Jason saw pain, and then hatred fill her eyes. "You killed Barkus?" she asked in a voice that was just barely above a whisper.

"If that was his name, yes." Jason replied.

Lorac's face seemed to dissolve. She slumped down in her chair and tears filled her eyes. No one spoke at this sudden turn of events. It was so unexpected from her, and it was evident to all of them that her pain was real. She finally wiped her eyes with a silken handkerchief and looked at him, her beautiful features become as hard as stone. "Barkus was my son," she said flatly.

"I'm sorry, Lorac," Jason replied softly. "I rally am. I didn't want to kill him, or his men, but he forced my hand."

Lorac looked at him with a sneer. "I find it impossible to believe that you could kill my son and his guard all by yourself. With the exception of his father, Barkus was the best swordsman and fighter in all of Tilwin. And his hand picked men were nearly as good. How did you do it?"

"With a sword," Jason replied casually.

"Liar!" Lorac screamed at him. "No one man could do that!"

Jason turned to Ster and nodded. Ster rose from his seat and left the room. When he returned moments later it was with five of Lorac's personal guard. As Lorac's men wondered what was going on, another of Jason's men handed Lorac's men the swords they were accustomed to, motioning for them to move to the far side of the large room. Ster picked up a bokken and took a position about teen feet from them. He turned his back on them to face the table.

"Queen Lorac," Jason told her, "I'll make the following proposal to you. If your men are able to kill Lieutenant Ster, or even render him incapable of fighting, I will allow you to leave Preton on the morning tide. I will also keep in effect the current trade and peace agreements. This, despite the fact that you have already violated them by your actions.

"However," he continued before she could reply, "if Ster defeats your men you will sign the new agreements I have drawn up. And you will abide by them explicitly. Fair enough?"

Lorac glared at him and then snapped her head towards her men. "Kill him!" she yelled. "Kill him or I will have your heads!"

Perhaps the five Tilwin were overconfident, being armed with real swords while Ster had only an unusual looking long wooden one, or perhaps it was the fear of Lorac that caused them to hesitate for a brief second. Whatever it was, before the five men realized what was happening, Ster went on the attack. His lightning quick movements sent Lorac's men and their swords crashing to the floor as the bokken flashed to break bones wherever it struck.

The exhibition lasted les than a minute. When it was over Ster tossed the bokken to another member of the guard and resumed his seat at the table. Two more of Jason's men collected the swords of the Tilwin while others helped the defeated men from the room.

Ster looked at Jason and shrugged. "I'm sorry, Commander. I was a little sloppy." Ster turned to Lorac and grinned. "If you think I'm good, you should see Jason. He is ten times better than I am," he told the stricken queen.

Jason smiled at Ster before turning his attention back to Lorac. "That is how I killed your son and his guard, Lorac. Except that I did not use a wooden sword." He reached behind his chair and pulled his katana around to place it on the table. He slid it from its sheath just enough to allow her to see the engraved, razor sharp blade. "Now, if I could do that, and Lieutenant Ster could do what he just did, think of what thirty thousand men trained by me for nearly six months could do. Especially when combined with another twenty thousand highly trained archers."

Jason saw the uncertainty in her eyes as she glanced at Ster for a moment before looking back at him. He let her think about his words for a moment before speaking again.

"Now, while that is how we defeated the Karton, and how I defeated your son and his guard, what destroyed the rest of your army was something entirely different."

Jason stood and moved to one of the large windows that faced the north of the city. "Come here," he told Lorac. She was a little hesitant at first but finally joined him, looking out to where he was pointing.

"Mayor Rettes has told me that the building there on the hill is an old temple that needs tearing down. The stones are a bit unstable and he's afraid that the children playing around it might be hurt. Watch,

Lorac, and you will see the power at my disposal. You will see a small portion of the power and force I command that obliterated your men and everything with them." He touched the hidden mike beneath his collar and spoke softly in English. "Show time, Mother."

A split second later there was a blinding flash of light that enveloped the old temple. It was followed almost immediately by a near deafening explosions as the stones of the temple were reduced to the atoms of dust. Some of the surrounding rocks melted from the intense heat.

Lorac staggered back a step from the window, her eyes wide in fear and terror as she looked from the smoldering hill to him. Jason started to reach for her, thinking she was about to faint, but she jerked back from him in abject terror. She back away until she reached her seat at the table, collapsing into it and reaching for her wine goblet. She quickly drained the goblet as Jason shrugged and returned to his own seat. He gave her a moment to recover and then nodded to one of his men to refill her goblet.

"A toast," Jason said calmly as he raised his own goblet. "A toast to peace between Preton, Tilwin and Karton."

Lorac hesitated a moment, staring at him in disbelief. She finally picked up her goblet with hands that still trembled slightly and brought it to her lips. The wine seemed to help calm her nerves somewhat. "My Lord," she said as she set her goblet down, "again I ask, who are you?"

"And as I told you earlier, Lorac, I come from a world that was once much like Alazon, but one where the sciences were much more advanced than anything this world has ever dreamed of.

"It was also a world controlled by a few who wished to crush all others beneath them. They wanted absolute and total control, just as do some here on Alazon. Eventually they unleashed the destructive forces they had harnessed upon one another and destroyed their world. I am the only survivor.

"I fled to search for a world where I could settle and live in peace. A world where I could help the people by doing such things as curing all known diseases, and preventing them from making the same mistakes my world did. Eventually, after much searching, I ended up here."

"And made yourself king," she said with a trace of a sneer in her voice.

Jarrell, who had been silent up to this point, spoke up for the first time. "No, Queen Lorac, that was neither his plan nor desire. It was a position that has been more or less forced upon him by fate. And by us."

Lorac looked from Jarrell to Jason, not sure whether to believe the mayor or not.

Jason nodded in agreement. "He's telling you the truth, Lorac. I really didn't want to be king. But now that I am, I will use my position to bring peace to Alazon. I plan to bring an end to the fighting between countries and show them that there is a new and better way to live."

"I see," was all she said in reply.

Jason leaned back in his chair as one of his men entered to stand beside the wide double doors. "How are they?" Jason asked the man, referring to the men Ster had fought.

"Some broken bones and contusions, but nothing too serious overall," the man replied with a grin.

"Good." Jason turned back to Lorac. "Now I think it is time we discuss the future." He took a deep breath and let it out slowly before speaking again.

"I had to dispose of Tolo and Makee because of their stupidity and unwillingness to work with me. I have replaced them with Naed Laer as the new Governor of Karton. I believe you are familiar with him?"

"Yes."

"Naed will reestablish order and bring about democratic elections for each province, just as there are in Preton. The various mayors elected will be answerable to him, and he will be answerable to me.

"Seta, I have no real desire to mete out the same fate to you and Semaj if it can be avoided. It's my hope that we can work out our various differences and come to an agreement that is favorable to all concerned. In anticipation of that I've taken the liberty of drawing up new trade and peace agreements."

Jason nodded to Hass. Hass rose and went to a small table against the wall, returning with copies of the new agreements and placing them on the table in front of Lorac before resuming his seat. Jason watched Lorac pick up the computer print out sheets that were so different from the parchment type paper of her world and look at them for a moment.

"If you wish to take them to your room tonight to study, please do so," Jason told her after a moment. "However, I can tell you now that they are basically the same as before, but with a few minor changes.

"First, for a period of one year you will incur a ten percent levy on all good received from or sent to Preton." He saw Lorac's jaw tighten at this and smiled at her. "You can consider it a punishment tax if you wish, but the money will go into a fund that will benefit all of Alazon. It will be used for things such as the construction of new schools, temples, and other social programs.

"Second, you will completely dismantle your army. You will be allowed a Mayoral Guard in each city, but the number of each will not exceed more than one half of one percent of the total population of each city."

"My husband will never agree to dismantle the army," Lorac replied flatly.

"He will, or you will both find yourselves in the same situation as Tolo and Makee." Jason gave her a moment to consider this alternative. "Let me make myself perfectly clear, Lorac. You and your husband will either abide by these new treaties or you will be driven out and replaced by a governor of my own selection."

Jason's tone and manner let Lorac know he was not in the mood for debate on the subject. Resignation began to show in her eyes.

"I guess I have no other choice," she finally replied, speaking softly and lowering her eyes for a moment.

'No, you don't," he told her. "However, to insure that things go according to plan I am appointing an ambassador to Tilwin. His duties will be to assure me that you are living up to your part of the new treaties, and to see to it that I live up to mine as well."

"And who will this new ambassador be?" Lorac asked, her eyes going to Jarrell.

"Me, your Majesty," replied Hass as he bowed his head slightly in her direction and smiled.

Lorac looked at Hass for a moment and then turned back to Jason. "But he is just a boy!"

"From what I understand, he is the same age your son was," Jason replied. "And like your son, Hass is quite capable of performing the tasks entrusted to him. I think you will find him most helpful to you as time progresses. He will be returning to Tilwin with you when you sail."

Lorac turned back to Hass. She studied him briefly before finally smiling at him. "Forgive me, Ambassador Hass. I may have been too quick to judge. Perhaps it is due to everything that has transpired since my arrival here that has affected my judgments and manners.

"After all, as your king has said, you are the same age as my son, and my husband was just about your age when he forced the various factions of Tilwin into a single, unified country. I will welcome you and do what I an to make your trip as comfortable as possible. And once we arrive in Chice I will do all I can to help you get established."

"Thank you, my Lady," Hass replied. "I'm sure we will come to trust and understand one another much better in the future. I am looking forward to the experience."

Jason watched the interplay between Lorac and Hass. Despite Lorac's tone he didn't believe her sincerity for a second. He felt that her sudden servile attitude was nothing more than a ploy on her part to buy some time. He stood up and pushed his chair back.

"Well, now that that's settled, why don't we all retire for the night? Lorac, you may take the agreements with you to read. I have other copies. We'll see you at breakfast."

Lorac stood and bowed slightly in his direction before turning and leaving the room. Jason waited until she was gone before turning to Rettes. "If you'll excuse us," he said to the mayor, "we have some things to talk about." He turned to look at Jarrell, Shon and Hass. "Let's go," he told them.

# TWENTY SIX

As Jason stretched out on the bed in his room, resting his back against the wall, Jarrell, Shon and Hass took seats in chairs around the room. "What do you think?" he asked Jarrell.

"I don't trust her," the older man replied with a shrug of his shoulders.

"To be honest, neither do I, but we have to live with that for the time being. Hass, what's your impression of her? After all, you're the one who will be returning to Tilwin with her."

Hass leaned back in his chair and laced his fingers across his stomach. "Well, aside from being drop dead beautiful, I get the impression that she is one very dangerous and deadly woman. One who will stop at nothing to get what she wants."

Jason nodded in agreement.

"For the time being," continued Hass, "I think she will go along with things, but you can bet she will try to figure out some way to get the upper hand on us sooner or later. Right now she's had her world shaken up pretty badly, seen more than she ever dreamed of, and it will take her some time to recover and regroup."

Jason was thoughtful for a moment. "I look for her to try and manipulate you in some way after a while. I wouldn't put it past her to try and get you to succumb to her beauty and charms if she thinks she can use them to turn you against us. But once she did that I don't think she'd hesitate to have you killed. I get the feeling she would even do it herself."

"Something to look forward to," Hass replied with a grin.

"Has anyone other than me noticed her nails?" Shon asked softly, causing the others to turn their attention to him.

"What about them?" asked Jarrell.

"Well, you probably know more about this than I do, Father, but I seem to remember something about a cult, an old religion where the members filed their fingernails down to razor sharpness and painted them blood red. Exactly like Lorac's."

"Slayers!" Jarrell gasped softly.

This was the first time Jason had ever heard of this group. "Who, or what, are Slayers?" he asked Jarrell.

Jarrell took a deep breath and let it out slowly before he spoke. "It was an old religious cult that was supposedly wiped out about fifty years ago. No one is sure just how or when they actually got their start, but they lasted for about two hundred years before the people finally rose up and drove them their temples, killing them in the streets for their beliefs and obscene practices of ritualistic murder. Practices that included the sacrificing of children.

"It was believed they were all killed, but no one was ever absolutely certain. There were rumors that some escaped to carry on in secret, although they have never been publicly heard from again since the riots."

"Maybe it's just a coincidence," Jason told him.

Jarrell shook his head sadly. "Perhaps, but I doubt it."

"What makes you say that?" Jason asked.

Jarrell shifted in his seat to get more comfortable before answering. "A couple of years ago I began hearing rumors that the Slayers were back and quietly recruiting members once more in Tilwin. There have always been rumors of that type from time to time, but since there was never any hard evidence, and no one actually saw any of their activities, it was pretty much dismissed as just another lingering rumor from the old days. But now that I think about it, well, maybe it was more than just a rumor.

"I've also heard a few stores from traders concerning the disappearance of people who were never seen again after they had traveled to Tilwin. I considered some of the people telling me those things a reliable, but others could be discounted as being less than believable."

Jason had listened carefully to Jarrell. He could see the worry and concern in the eyes of his father-in-law and had a feeling the older man was probably right. Jarrell usually was.

"I may be able to find something out," Hass told them.

Jason looked at him and nodded. "Do so if you can, but be extremely careful. I don't want you vanishing, and then have someone blame it on a group that may or may not exist when it was Lorac all along."

"Don't worry, Jason, I'll be careful," the younger brother told him.

"You better be. Now, are you all packed?"

"Yes. And I've got all your little toys stashed away and ready to be put to use. I'm still amazed by some of them," Hass added with a grin.

"Amazed or not, those little bugs in the right places will allow you to hear everything being said within fifty feet of them, so make sure you use them."

"I will."

"Weapons?"

"Phaser pistol packed away; palm stunner here," Hass said, pulling back the right sleeve of his robe to reveal the small weapon strapped to his forearm. "And this little baby here," he added, pulling back his left sleeve to reveal the sheathed throwing knife strapped to his left forearm.

"Gas pellets?" Jason asked as if reading from a check list to make sure Hass had everything.

Hass patted his stomach where a small pouch was concealed beneath the sash of his robe. The pouch contained marble sized pellets that would, when thrown against the ground, or any hard surface, explode and produce a cloud of dark, noxious gas. Hass has been prepared to leave in case Lorac had wanted to leave that night instead of waiting till the morning.

"Hass," said Jarrell, "Jason has placed a great deal of trust in you."

Hass nodded, a somber look on his face. "I know, Father. You probably think that it should be Shon going instead of me, but I won't let you down."

Jarrell grinned and nodded in agreement. "Yes, I was a little surprised when Jason told me he was sending you instead of Shon, but apparently he has his reasons for doing it this way, and his judgments have always been correct so far. I just want you to be careful, keep that impulsive nature of yours in check, do what's required by Jason, and then come home safe and sound."

"I will," Hass replied.

"I think we all need to get some sleep," Jason told them as he stood up and stretched for a moment. "Tomorrow is going to come early and we all have to be on our toes. "

After Jarrell and Hass had said their good nights and left, Jason paced the large room, his mind going over everything he could think of that could go wrong. The list was endless and he wondered if he were doing the right thing in sending Hass. He went to the double glass doors that lead to the balcony, opened them and stepped out to feel the cool night breeze on his face. Resting his hands on the stone balcony, he looked out at the city below. There were few fires and torches going on, as most of the city was preparing for bed.

Turning away from the city he returned to lay down on the bed, but sleep was not forthcoming. He thought of Kim, wishing he had let her come. He missed her presence by his side, especially at night. Just holding her in his arms at the end of the day made everything seem less stressful, less taxing on his mind, calming his spirit, allowing him to sleep peacefully.

Finally closing his eyes, he drifted off into a fitful sleep where disturbing images of a woman dressed in a blood red robe held sway over devoted followers who's only intent was for self gratification, even to the point of sacrificing others. He actually felt grateful when he was suddenly awaked by Ster to be told that Queen Lorac was gone.

"What do you mean?" he asked as he quickly rose and followed the Lieutenant out the door.

"When I went to wake her, the room was empty. I checked the rooms of her servants, as well as her guards, and they were also empty."

"Damn!" Jason muttered as the two of them headed down the stairs to the main foyer.

He saw Jarrell standing by the front door and the older man motioned for him to follow him. As they stepped outside, Jason saw that tollies had already been brought for them, and that Hass and Mayor Rettes were already astride, just waiting for him, Ster and Jarrell. Jason and the other two quickly mounted their tollies, and without a word, headed for the harbor.

When they arrived, Jason found Queen Lorac standing at the landward side of the pier, watching as the last of her luggage was loaded onto her ship. She turned at the sound of her approach and took a few steps forward.

As Jason dismounted, Lorac clasped her hands in front of her and bowed her head until he had approached to with just a few feet of her.

"I apologize, my Lord, but I arose early and wanted to sail with the outgoing tides," she said as she raised her head to look up at him. "I have signed the new agreements," she added, motioning for one of her female aids to step forward.

The aide extended her arm and handed the rolled treaties to Jason, who opened them to quickly scan them for her signature before handing them to Ster. "Thank you," he replied with a smile he did not really feel.

Lorac turned to Hass. "I hope I have not inconvenienced you, Ambassador. We will wait for your own cargo to be loaded as well."

"No inconvenience at all, my Lady," Hass replied with a smile. "As for my cargo, I had it brought to the docks last night. If you will have some of your men lend a hand, I will show them where it is."

Lorac turned and snapped out a quick order. A dozen burly men rushed forward immediately to stand at attention. Hass pointed out his trucks, which had been under guard all night to prevent anyone from tampering with them.

"Since you will be traveling with me," Lorac told Hass as her men began to pick up his trunks, "I've arranged for them to be stored in the cabin next to mine, which I have had prepared for you."

"Thank you," Hass replied.

As Lorac turned back to him, Jason felt needles tingle at the back of his neck. Her smile reminded him of a vampire in the process of seducing her next victim. She extended her right hand to him. "My Lord, I hope you will be visiting us soon. I know my husband would be very interested in meeting you."

"I will be there as soon as I can take care of a few things here," Jason told her. "In the meantime, Hass will act as my voice for me in all things."

"I'm sure he will, but I will still await your visit," Lorac replied with a sincerity Jason didn't believe for a second.

As Lorac disengaged her hand from his, Jason felt a slight prick on his wrist. He looked down to see a small drop of blood appear. "Oh, my Lord, I've scratched you!" Lorac cried. "I am most sorry."

"It's quite all right," he told her as he wiped the blood away with the fingers of his left hand.

Jason quickly thought of the various types of poison that could be administered in such a manner, but the thoughts of that vanished when, out of the corner of his eyes he saw Lorac lift her finger to her lips and lick the small drop of his blood from it.

"My husband has complained many times of this particular nail style," Lorac told him with a short laugh as she looked at her nails. "He has urged me to change it, but I'm sure you know the whims of a woman when it comes to the latest fashion trends."

Jason smiled solicitously at her. "Yes," he replied.

"Please forgive me."

"It's nothing."

Lorac knelt before him briefly, then stood and stepped back a pace as Hass said his farewells.

"You watch yourself," he whispered to the younger brother as they shook hands.

Jason watched as Hass and Lorac boarded the ship and her men replaced the railing. Then they scurried around like rats as they hurried to hoist the sails, while other manned the oars that would take them away from the harbor and into deeper waters. As he watched, Jason couldn't dispel the feeling that he was sending Hass into danger. He glanced down at his wrist where Lorac had scratched him, looking for any signs of discoloration or swelling, but there wasn't any. Nor did he feel any symptoms of dizziness or nausea.

"That was no accident."

He looked up to see Jarrell looking at his wrist. "I know," he replied.

"Poison?"

"I don't think so. I think she was more interested in seeing if my blood is the same as yours. She's not sure if I'm human or not, and just wanted to find out if I bleed like a normal man."

"If she wanted to know if you were really a man, all she had to do was ask Kim," Shon quipped.

"Really," Jason replied with a grin as they turned away from the pier.

"Well," Rettes commented as they approached the tollies, "last night I informed my staff that we would want a hearty breakfast this morning. I would really hate to see it go to waste."

The all laughed at Rettes, who looked as if he hadn't missed a meal in his life. They mounted the tollies and rode back to the Mayoral Building at a more leisurely pace. Along the way, Rettes called out to various individuals, sharing a joke or asking about family members. Jason was impressed by the little mayor. Rettes appeared to know just about everyone in Sharl, as well as every member of their family, on a first name basis.

When they reached the Mayoral Building and took their seats at the table, Jason reached for the small pot of coffee, intending to pour himself a cup. One of the regular serving girls rushed up to the table by his side. "My Lord, no!" she exclaimed. "That is my job."

With a smile and slight shake of his head, Jason set the pot down and allowed the girl to pour the coffee for him. He wanted to laugh as the way her hands were shaking slightly from her nervousness at being around him. She was about to step away from the table when Rettes called out to her, his voice harsh and sharp, "Mata!"

The girl stopped dead in her tracks and then turned to face the mayor. "Yes…Mayor Rettes?" she said softly.

"Do you realize just who this man is?" Rettes asked her, nodding his head at Jason.

"Sir, yes, I do!" she replied quickly. Her face colored deeply and her fingers twisted nervously in the folds of her robe. "He is Jason, King of Preton. And Karton!" she added as an afterthought.

Rettes nodded. "Exactly. Now, do you think it proper for the king of two countries to come to our city and have to pour his own coffee at the breakfast table? Especially when there are plenty of servers such as yourself who are paid a very good wage to do those things for him?"

"Nnn...no, Sir, it isn't," Mata replied in a voice so soft that Jason could barely hear her.

He started to interrupt and tell her it was okay, but caught the slight grin and barely perceptible shake of Jarrell's head. He realized then that Rettes was merely teasing the young woman.

Rettes lowered his voice. "Do you know what happened to a serving girl in Kech who was slack in her duties and forgot to pour his wine for him at his evening meal?"

Mata was suddenly too nervous to reply. She shook her head and tried not to look at Jason. Rettes sighed and shook his head sadly. "The poor girl. To teach her a lesson, Jason snatched up her hand and bit off one of her fingers, then washed it down with the wine she was supposed to have poured for him."

Mata looked as if she were about ready to faint. She clenched her hands into little fists as she thought of losing one of her fingers in such a horrible manner.

"Come here," Rettes told her, motioning for her to stand between the chairs of Jason and himself.

Mata hesitated briefly, but finally stepped forward on unsteady legs to stand between them.

Rettes took her right hand and held it out above the table. "Open," he told her, winking at Jason as Mata's fingers slowly uncurled. "What do you think, my Lord?|

"Humm, I don't know," Jason replied thoughtfully. "Her fingers are a bit on the small side. I may have to take two. Say, one from each hand?"

"I see what you mean," Rettes replied as he picked up a knife. "Would you like for me to cut them off for you?"

Jason shook his head. "No, biting them off is much more fun."

Mata's eyes started to roll up in her head as Jason took her hand from the mayor and slowly raised it to his mouth. He turned her hand around and lightly kissed the palm and each of her fingertips before releasing it with a smile.

Mata nearly fainted. Her breath rushed out of her as she glanced down at Rettes, who was starting to laugh. When she realized she was the center of a joke between them, she blushed deeply and lowered her head in embarrassment as the others also began to laugh. However, she still jumped slightly when Jason touched her hand again.

"Mata," he told her softly, "I do not make it a habit of biting off fingers, or any other body part, despite what Mayor Rettes may tell you. In fact, I don't even eat most meats at all.

"And as far as my treatment goes," he continued, "You are not to treat me any differently than you would any other guest here in the company of Mayor Rettes. I may be King of Preton and Karton, but I am still just a man like any other.

"But I am curious about something. Tell me, what would you have done if I had said I was going to take one or two of your fingers for your supposed transgression?"

"What could I have done, my Lord," she replied softly. "You are King. Your word is the law. It is to be obeyed without question. So says Lofa and Avihs. "

The depth of sincerity in her eyes, combined with the tone of her voice, told Jason that she firmly believe every word she said, and that frightened him. He didn't want that kind of blind devotion to him by anyone.

"No, Mata," he told her softly, "that is not the way it is. A king, any king, should not be obeyed in such a blind and unquestioning manner. It is the duty of the people to question a king if his actions are such that they cause harm to people. Or if they are morally wrong. Never take my word as being the absolute law, because it isn't.

"A king is supposed to uphold the laws of the land which the people themselves enact. Or abolish laws that are harmful. Otherwise he has no right to be king."

"But…what if the king breaks the law?" Mata asked.

"Then he should have to face the same punishment that any other person would," he told her.

Mata looked at him with confusion in her eyes. "Then what is the king's job?" she asked.

Jason laughed and shook his head. "That's something I'm still trying to figure out myself, Mata. If and when I ever do, I'll be sure to let you know."

Mata looked down at him and smiled. Then, with a quick curtsy she hurried off and breakfast was served.

Jason violated the rule about serious discussions at meal times by talking about Lorac and what she might have up her sleeve. None of them actually believed she would stick to the treaties for very long, but none of them had any ideas as to what she might try.

After breakfast, Jason and the others said goodbye to Rettes and flew back to Lemac, landing beside the Mayoral Building. Jarrell and Shon remained there, telling Jason they had some work to catch up on. Ster headed for the barracks, leaving Jason and Busker to ride their tollies through the city to the site where his house was being construction. They rode leisurely, stopping from time to time to talk to those them met along the way.

As they neared the construction sight the twins, Janella and Baby came racing down the hill to greet them. Jason dismounted and scooped up the three kids to hug and kiss them while Baby barked and jumped around, demanding her share of attention. He placed the kids on the back of the tollie and turned to Baby. He hugged her and roughly ran his hands through the fur around her neck in greeting, laughingly accepting her happy, eager licks to his face.

"You know," Busker commented, looking around as they walked up the hill, leading the tollies, "I had a feeling that when you said you were going to build a house of your own that this would happen."

"What?" Jason asked.

"That just about everyone in the city would turn out to help in some way or another." Busker looked at him and grinned, but then asked, "Why the look of concern?"

Jason looked at the crowd of workers on the hill for a moment before answering. "Because they are all taking this royalty bit too seriously, Busker."

"Perhaps," the older man replied with a shrug. "But would you deny them their pleasure in all of this?"

"No, I guess not," he replied softly.

*Alazon*

At the top of the knoll they found Kim and Vinny directing some of the men as the two women looked at a set of blueprints. They were telling the men what they wanted and how it was to be done. The men were nodding their heads, their faces serious whenever one of the sisters looked at them, but smiling at one another over the bent heads of Kim and Vinny. The senior foreman caught Jason's eyes and grinned as if to say, "Yeah, we listen to them, then we go and do it the way you told us to."

Kim looked up and saw him. "Jason!" she cried, running around the table, her hair whipping around in a pony tail, her face, hands and arms covered with dirt and plaster.

Both Jason and Busker began to laugh as she ran toward him. Kim drew up short, looking from him to Busker with a puzzled expression at the way the two of them were laughing at her, then looked down at herself and realized she was covered with as much dirt and grime as any of the workers. She started laughing as well, then leaped up at Jason, wrapping her arms and legs around him as she kissed him.

"Boy, have I missed you!" she whispered in his ear as she gently nibbled at the lobe.

Jason pulled his head back and looked at her. "I was only gone for four days."

"Yeah, and for very long, very lonely night," she whispered.

"Can't you control your animalistic urges for that long?" he teased.

"I'll show you control just as soon as I can get you alone," she whispered. "You created this horny, wanton woman in me, and now you're gonna have to take care of her."

"So, how's the house coming?" he asked as he set her down and slipped his arm around her shoulders.

"Oh, fine," she replied dourly. "Me and Vinny tell them what I want, then they go ahead and do what they want," she told him, waving at the men. They smiled back at her as if tolerating a loved, but somewhat spoiled and bothersome child.

Jason suppressed a grin. "I see. Well, since they are the ones doing the actual building, and I made sure they knew how to read the blueprints and know exactly what I want, I have a feeling they're probably doing the right thing by ignoring you and your sister."

"Gee, thanks for the vote of confidence," Vinny told him as she came up to him. She stood on tiptoes to kiss his cheek. "And welcome home to you, too."

"Look," he told the sisters, "I've got an idea. Why don't all of us go back to your parent's house and get ready for supper. Let's leave these good men to see if they can manage for themselves without the guidance, or interference, of the two most troublesome women in Lemac."

Kim looked at Vinny and grinned. "You want to smack him first, or should I?"

"Who's turn is it?" Vinny asked.

"Both!" Kim yelled as she and Vinny began to punch his arms and stomach.

Janella and the twins slid from the back of the tollie and quickly grabbed Jason's legs, laughing and yelling as they did. That was all Baby needed to get in on the fun. The dog lunged up and hit Jason full in the chest, knocking him to the ground. For the next few minutes even the workers stopped to watch and laugh at the free-for-all between Jason, the women, the kids and the dog. They shouts and cries of the humans was punctuated by the barking of Baby, who ran around them barking loudly and licking at any face that happened to be uncovered. She would grab one of the kids in her massive jaws and drag them away for a moment, but then knock Jason back down if it looked as if he were going to get up.

"I give, I give!" Jason finally cried as he wrapped his arms around Kim and Janella.

They all relaxed for a moment, but then Jason looked at Kim and Vinny and grinned. "What I should have said was the two most troublesome women in all of Preton."

"That's it!" Kim told him and she and the others began attacking him once again.

# TWENTY SEVEN

"Now, you understand what this means, don't you?" asked a smiling Jarrell from behind his desk in the office he occupied as the Mayor of Lemac.

Janella looked up at him from where she sat between Jason and Kim. Her little face was a study in seriousness as she nodded her head. "It means that from now on Jason and Kimmy are my father and mother."

"Correct. Now, is this what you really want?" Jarrell asked the question, despite the fact that he, and everyone else, knew this adoption by Jason and Kim was the one thing Janella wanted more than anything else in the world.

"Yes!" she replied quickly.

Jarrell picked up the piece of paper from his desk and began to read it in somber tones.

"Be it known by one and all that from this day forward the girl formerly knows as Janella Repap is now to be known as Janella Stephens, and that she is the legal and lawful daughter of Jason Michael Stephens and Kimella Vehey Stephens. This adoption hereby entitles her to all legal and moral benefits which may derive from said parents."

"Sir, excuse me," Janella said softly, interrupting him.

Jarrell raised his eyes and looked at her. "Yes?"

"Sir, could I have a middle name?"

Jarrell furrowed his brows, glancing briefly at Jason and Kim. "I'm not sure I understand what you mean," he said.

"Well, Sir, Jason has a middle name; Michael, and Kimmy's former last name became her middle name when she married Jason and, well, I was wondering if I could have a middle name, too."

Jarrell smiled in understanding. "Of course. It will be Janella Repap Stephens."

"No, Sir," Janella replied quickly with a shake of her head.

Jarrell looked at the girl for a moment and then smiled as a glimmer of understanding began to take seed. "I take it you have something else in mind?"

"Yes, Sir. If it would be all right, I would like for my name to be Janella Kimella Repap Stephens. That way I would have a new name from both my new father and mother, but still have the name I was born with to honor my brother. Would that be okay?"

Jason and Jarrell turned to look at Kim. Her eyes were filling with tears of love as she looked down at Janella. "Not only do I think it would be okay," Jarrell told the girl, "but I think it is a wonderful idea."

Jarrell made the change on the paper, smiling to himself at the thoughtfulness of the girl. Over the past couple of months her love and devotion to Jason and Kim were a constant source of amazement and pleasure to them all. Jarrell had heard someone describe hr love for Jason as a mixture of a daughter's love for a father combined with the reverent adoration of a god. As far as Janella was concerned, Jason could do no wrong, and anyone who thought about saying anything even slightly negative about him would quickly experience the wrath of her sharp tongue.

The first time Jason had taken Janella up to the <u>Stargazer</u> with the twins she had been impressed by everything, but not nearly as much as the twins had been on their first visit. It was as if she somehow expected something of this nature from him. That it was only just and fitting for the father/god who had come to their world.

It wasn't until she had been introduced to Mother that she exhibited real excitement. Janella had seemed to instantly recognize the potential for learning from the computer. She quickly realized that Mother could teach her everything she wanted to know about Jason and his world. It hadn't taken Janella long to begin tapping into that source of information to find out what Jason liked, what his favorite meals were, and how to prepare them.

As soon as they had moved into their new home, Janella had set out to prove she could cook his favorite foods as well as anyone. Since Jason didn't eat red meat, Janella had Mother put together a vegetarian cook book for her and she would go through it daily to select recipes to prepare for him.

Janella and the twins had become as close as brother and sisters. The three of them were a constant source of mischief and delight for the entire family. Yet, beneath her laughter there was a seriousness to Janella the twins seemed to be lacking in some manner. It was as if she had to prove to Jason and Kim that she was worthy of being their daughter.

Nor was anyone blind to the love and adoration Jason had for Janella. He lavished his love and attention on her constantly. Jarrell and the other knew it wasn't due just to the circumstances of her own life; of growing up without any family other than her brother, but was also due in large part to his own past as well. Jason gave to Janella all the love he could not give his little sister and the other children who had died aboard his ship.

"All right," Jarrell said at last, smiling at Janella and feeling his own love for the girl, "as of this moment you shall be known as Janella Kimella Repap Stephens, legal daughter of Jason and Kimella Stephens. You know what that means?"

"Now I am their daughter and they are my parents."

"Right. And you know what that makes me, don't you?"

Janella looked at Jarrell for a moment, her little brows drawn together in thought, but then her face lit up. "That makes you my grandfather," she said with a grin.

"Exactly!" he told her exuberantly as he stood up and walked around the desk, holding out his arms. "And as your new grandfather, as well as Mayor of Lemac, I hereby claim the right of first hug and kiss."

Janella giggled as she slid from her seat and ran to Jarrell, locking her arms around his nick and kissing his cheek loudly as he picked her up. Jarrell hugged her for a moment before relinquishing her to Jason. Janella quickly hugged and kissed him before turning to reach for Kim. "Do I get to call you Mommy and Daddy now?" she asked after hugging and kissing Kim.

"You better believe it," Jason told her with a loving smile as he took her back from Kim to hug her again.

"What do you say we all head for home," Jarrell told them, "and let the rest of the family know it's finally done."

The four of them left the office with Janella walking between Kim and Jason. She held their hands as if afraid to let them go, but once they were outside on the streets she spotted some friends and ran on ahead to tell them the news of her adoption.

Jason slipped his arm around Kim's waist. "So, how do you feel about instant motherhood?"

She looked up at him and smiled. "Probably about as good as you do about becoming an instant father." She reached for Jarrell and pulled him close. "Thank you, Daddy."

"For what? Doing my official duty in the adoption of a beautiful little girl by two people who happen to love her? And whom she adores?"

"Not just for that, but everything," Kim told him.

The three of them walked on in silence as Janella ran on ahead of them until they reached Jarrells's house. Entering through the front door they found Janella and the twins engaged in one of their telepathic communications. There were smiles plastered to all three little faces. Jason knew the twins had been working with Janella to teach her how to communicate with them by telepathy, which enabled the three of them to carry on conversations without the knowledge of anyone else. Jason still hadn't found the time to really test the twins to find out the extent of their abilities, which seemed to be getting stronger all the time.

Right now he had other problems to deal with. He was due to meet with Naed at the end of the week to see how things were going in Karton, and he was still worried about Lorac and Semaj. The latest coded message from Hass had come in last night. They were still at sea, having had to divert their course somewhat to the north to avoid a storm, but everyone was all right. They were proceeding toward Tilwin with all haste and expected to be there in another week.

Mother had also added her own report. She assured Jason that she was keeping an eye on Hass just in case Lorac decided to try something, like tossing Hass overboard in the middle of the ocean.

Eventually everyone came to the table for dinner, which turned out to be a loud and boisterous affair. They were about to finish eating when someone pounded loudly on the front door. Shon got up to answer it, quickly returning with a man he had to help support. The man looked as if he had traveled a long distance hard and fast. He was covered with dirt and obviously exhausted. Despite that, he tried to come to attention as Jason stood up.

"My Lord, I have a message for you from Mayor Rettes," the man told Jason as he gasped for breath.

"Sid down before you collapse, Corporal," Jason told the man as Shon helped him to a seat.

The man slumped down into the chair as the strain of his journey sapped his remaining strength. He gratefully accepted a cup of cold water from Vinny, drinking deeply before turning back to Jason.

"My Lord, Mayor Rettes wishes to inform you that two days after your departure from Sharl, the bodies of two young girls were found buried in a shallow grave. They were found in the woods about a quarter of a mile outside the city. Their throats had been ripped open, as if by an animal, and the blood drained from them before being buried. They were found by hunters returning to the city."

Jason looked at Jarrell and saw his own suspicions and fears reflected in the eyes of the older man. He turned back to the messenger. "Corporal, do you know where the barracks are here in Lemac?"

"Yes, my Lord."

"Do you think you can make it there?"

The young man stood and squared his shoulders. "I can make it."

"Go tell Commander Busker and Lieutenant Ster to join me here. But don't tell them, or anyone else, what you've told me. Then I want you to eat and get some sleep. You've had a long, hard trip, and have done well in your efforts."

The man saluted and headed for the door, but as he did he stumbled slightly from weakness. "I'll go with him," Shon said, stepping forward to help the man.

As SHon and the Corporal left, Jason turned to Jarrell. The two of them stared into the eyes of one another as if realizing their worst nightmares were about to come true. In his mind, Jason pictured the face of Lorac. As the image came to him it seemed to waver for a moment before merging with that of another woman. Then the two images separated, becoming clear.

"Damn!" he swore softly. "Come on, Jarrell. I've got a feeling there's someone right here in Lemac who may know a hell of a lot more about Lorac than either one of us."

"Who?" the older man asked as he followed Jason to the door.

"You'll see. I may be wrong, but I don't think so. Kim, stay here until I get back. When Busker and Ster get here tell them I want a detail of men around this house immediately. No one gets in or out without your approval."

"Jason, what's wrong?" Kim asked, sudden fear filling her eyes and voice.

"Hopefully nothing we can't handle. We're going to the temple and should be back shortly." He kissed her forehead before going out the back door and heading for the shuttle.

They streaked to the temple, landing just in front of the steps. Jason took the steps three at a time and pounded on the front doors of the temple with his right fist. They were opened almost immediately by two acolytes. Seeing him they dropped to one knee and bowed their heads as they wanted for him to speak.

"Please get up and tell High Priestess Seta that I request her presence immediately."

The two women rose and hurried away, casting fearful glances back over their shoulders at his harsh tone and appearance. Seta appeared moment later. The smile on her face vanished when she saw the scowl on his. She immediately dropped to her right knee with her head bowed.

"Priestess Seta," he said, forcing himself to sound calm, "there is a matter of utmost important that I need to speak about with you."

"Of course, my Lord," Seta replied as she stood and quickly led them to her private office chambers.

As soon as the three of them were seated on chairs around a small, ornamental table in her office with the doors closed behind them, Jason looked her straight in the eyes. "Why didn't you tell me that Queen Lorac of Tilwin is your twin sister?" he asked bluntly.

"What?" exclaimed a shocked Jarrell.

Seta looked as if she had just been slapped. Her head snapped back and her right hand flew up to cover her mouth. She began to tremble and lowered her head as she began to cry softly, her shoulder shaking with her sobs.

Jarrell started to speak but Jason held up his hand to silence the older man. He went to the door and asked the priestess standing outside of it to bring him a soft towel, a pitcher of water and three goblets, standing by the door until the woman returned with them. He placed the water and goblets on the small table and handed the towel to Seta before returning to his seat and pouring water for all of them.

"It's all right," he told Seta softly as he handed her a goblet, "but I want you to tell me everything right now."

Seta looked up and nodded slowly. She used the towel to wiper her eyes. "How...how did you find out?" she asked, her voice sounding weak and frail.

"When I met Lorac in Sharl," Jason told her, "I kept thinking that she reminded me of someone, but I couldn't quite figure out who. She has a different hair style and uses makeup, which you don't. It was just enough to throw me off. I wasn't completely sure until now."

Jason sighed and leaned forward, placing his forearms on his knees. "Due to the genetic purity of your race there are many people who look remarkably alike to me. However, the resemblance between the two of you was just too much, despite the fact that she tries to disguise it."

"I didn't think that anyone would ever find out," Seta replied in a near whisper.

"Tell me about it."

Jason's words were spoken softly, but beneath them was the implied threat that if she were not completely honest with him, he would take her up to the ship and let Mother drain her mind with every scrap of information it contained. From the look in her eyes, Jason knew she was aware of that option.

Seta sat back in her chair to collect her thoughts and take a drink of water. Jason waited patiently. He didn't want her to rush or omit anything. He had to know about Lorac and what he might expect from her.

"As you know," Seta finally said, speaking softly, "Tilwin was once divided into five provinces which were always fighting among themselves for power. Lorac and I were born to Shawnken, King of Milik, during a time when our father was struggling to hold onto his province. It was being threatened by the kings on either side of him. Our mother died during our birth so our father had nurses to raise us. We never saw him that much because he was always off defending one border or another. But whenever he was home he spent as much time as he could with us and we knew he loved us.

"When it became obvious that he was going to lose his fight against the other kinds, he made arrangements for some of his most trusted retainers to sneak Lorac and myself out of the province. They were to hide us and keep us from being killed. Lorac and I were separated, with me being brought here to Preton."

Seta was speaking more clearly now as she recited the history of her life, as if finally relieved to get it all out in the open once and for all. Jason could see her visibly relaxing.

"We landed in Sharl," she continued, "but traveled on until we reached Kech, which was as far from Tilwin as we could get. Once there, Bocay and his wife, Mitale, set up a business as fabric importers with the money my father had provided. Three years later Mitale died."

"How old were you then?" Jason asked softly.

"I was five when we left Milik, so I would have been almost nine by then. Anyway," she continued," I grew up hearing stories of my father. Bocay thought it was important for me to know of the good things my father had done for the people of Milik, and to know the history of Tilwin. But he also swore me to total secrecy, telling me I must never reveal who my father was to anyone.

"I missed Lorac terribly and thought of her constantly. At night I would lay in bed and wonder if I would ever see her again and how her own life was going. Since I was the first born I was instilled with the belief that I would someday return to Milik and restore the province to the position it rightly deserved. But fate, and the gods, had other plans for me.

"Not long after my fifteenth birthday I was informed that Lorac had married Semaj, King of Chice. She had taken the title to Milik with her, even though it was rightly mine. But since no one knew where I was, other than Bocay, there was little that could be done about it.

"Then, about six months later we had visitors. They came during the night, killing Bocay and leaving a message for me from Lorac. She said that as long as I remained in Preton and kept my silence, I would be allowed to live. But if I ever tried to return to Tilwin to claim what was my birthright by law that I would be killed.

"Not knowing what else to do, and having no one to turn to, I entered the Temple of Lofa as an acolyte. At first I kept the business Bocay had started, but eventually sold it off after the young man I had met and fallen in love with had disappeared on a trip to Karton during a storm at sea. After that I devoted my life entirely to Lofa.

"Time passed and I rose quickly through the ranks of the temple, eventually being selected to train as a High Priestess. I was sent here to Lemac at the request of the former High Priestess. She was the only other person who knew of my relationship with Lorac, which I revealed to her, and I have been here ever since."

"And you've carried this around inside of you all this time, afraid to tell anyone," Jason said softly.

"Yes, my Lord. I wanted to tell you but I was afraid to. I kept praying nothing would happen which would make it necessary."

"Why were you afraid to tell me?"

"I wasn't sure what your reaction would be. Or what the reaction of the people of Lemac and Preton would be if they ever found out their High Priestess was the twin sister of Queen Lorac of Tilwin."

Jason could understand her fears. "You don't have to worry about them finding out from me," he assured her. "What you've just told us remains a secret, and will not be repeated to anyone without your own express knowledge and permission."

"You are too kind, my Lord," she whispered as tears of gratitude filled her eyes.

"You think too highly of me" Jason told her with a smile of warmth.

"My Lord?"

"Yes?"

"There is something else. Something you should know about Lorac."

"That she's the High Priestess of the Slayers?" Jason asked, watching her eyes widen in shocked surprise.

"I…yes! How did you know?"

Jason shrugged his shoulders. "Just a hunch. You have twin sisters, one good and one evil, both of them smart and beautiful. One becomes the High Priestess of Lofa, goddess of all that is good on Alazon, so it only stands to reason that the other becomes her mirrored opposite; High Priestess of the Slayers and the Dark Gods. The ying and the yang."

"What's that?" she asked.

"Something from my world. I'll explain it someday."

"But," said Seta, "I only learned of this myself just a few days ago."

This bit of information caused him to sit up straight in his chair. He glanced briefly at Jarrell. "How?" he asked Seta.

"I received a written message informing me of it. The message also made new threats of death towards to me I revealed what I knew or tried to return to Tilwin. It said that people would be killed, with the facts twisted to make it look I was a priestess of the Slayers and the one responsible."

"Did the note say anything else?" Jason asked. "Like who would be killed?"

Seta shook her had. "No."

"How much do you know about the Slayers?" Jarrell asked her.

Jason saw the involuntary shiver in her body as Seta looked at Jarrell. "They are a cult that worships death and the Dark Gods. Once a month, when the moon is gone, they make their sacrifices.

They use young virgin girls for purity, virgin boys for strength, and young children of both sexes for the pleasures of the gods. And for their own pleasures as well."

"What do you mean?" asked Jason, even though he wasn't sure he really wanted to know.

"Through the use of powerful drugs they can force both men and women to engage in sex with members of the temple. Now, while some men might not consider having sex with all the women of the temple as a form of torture, as most of them are very beautiful, in reality that's what it is.

"Because of the effect of the drugs involved, the man is unable to relieve himself during sexual intercourse. After a while his…organ… becomes painfully stiff and swollen, and extremely sensitive. Before it's over with he is usually screaming for it to end. But that doesn't happen until all of the women, and even some of the men, have used him to their own satisfaction. Drugs are also used on the girls to create sexual desires in them that can never be fulfilled."

"What happens to them once those in the temple are finished with them?" asked Jarrell.

"The sex organs of the men are cut off and mutilated, leaving them to bleed to death. The women are usually stabbed to death. The virgins are the luckiest, if you can call it that. They are fed, bathed and dressed in the finest robes and jewels, but they don't really have any idea of what's going on. They are drugged to make them docile. Their sacrifice is usually quick; a slashed throat with a knife. The blood is collected and then passed around to drink while it's still warm."

Seta closed her eyes and shuddered for a moment. Neither Jason nor Jarrell spoke, giving her time to compose herself and continue.

"The children," she said after a while, "are used sexually by both the men and the women of the cult in every manner imaginable. Sometimes they are drugged, but much of the time they are not. Afterwards they are killed and their bodies disposed of.

"Twice a year there is a special ritual. After being sexually abused and killed, the children are then thrown into huge vats of boiling water. They are cooked and then eaten by the members of the cult."

Seta's voice had become so low that Jason had to lean forward to hear her. At this last part from her he felt bile rise in his throat and had to swallow quickly to keep from throwing up. Jarrell wasn't so lucky. The old man hurried from the room holding his hand over his mouth. Even Seta looked as if she might be sick, but managed to maintain control over herself.

Jason poured cold water for the two of them and they both drank deeply before the color returned to their faces. Neither of them spoke until Jarrell returned and resumed his seat.

"How do you know so much about the Slayers and their rituals?" Jason asked.

"During the final stages of training to become a High Priestess of Lofa we are taught about them. This is so we will know the signs of their activities and can fight against them."

"They have to be eliminated," Jarrell said sternly. "This time for good. There are an abomination and must be destroyed once and for all."

Jason nodded in agreement. "Seta, I'm sorry that your sister is involved in this, but her being your sister will not save her."

Seta looked down at the floor for a moment then back up at him. Sadness filled her eyes. "I know," she replied weakly.

"What I don't understand," he said, glancing briefly at Jarrell, "is why she bothered to tell you about her involvement with the Slayers. I don't see where it really serves any purpose. I'd think she'd want to keep that secret."

Before Seta could answer the door suddenly burst inward and Ster staggered into the room. The front of his uniform was soaked in blood and an arrow was still embedded in his left chest near the shoulder. His left arm hung limply at his side, but his right hand still clutched his bloody katana.

"Janella! They got Princess Janella!" Ster gasped as he began to collapse. His knees buckled and his sword fell from his hands.

Even as he leaped forward, Jason felt the blood freezing in his veins. He caught Ster just before the man's face crashed into the floor. He turned Ster around and looked down into the pail, drawn face etched with physical and emotional agony.

"I failed you, my Lord," Ster gasped. "I failed Princess Janella. May Lofa forgive me," Ster whispered as his eyes closed and his head fell back limply.

# TWENTY EIGHT

Seta quickly knelt on the other side of Ster and pulled away the top of his uniform to reveal the broken shaft of the arrow through his left shoulder. There was also a deep slash wound running diagonally across his chest from a sword.

"This will hurt," she told Jason as she gripped the shaft of the arrow and broke it off. She reached behind Ster and grasped the protruding end of the arrow and jerked it out of him. Ster screamed and arched his back, but the pain served to bring him back to consciousness.

"What happened?" Jason asked as soon as the man's eyes opened.

"Be...before we could get to the house with a detachment of guards we...we heard the sound of fighting. We saw people in black robes and hoods running away...while others stayed behind to fight.

"Janella...she...she was in your room waiting for you to come home. They came in through the window and grabbed her. Vinny heard her scream and rushed in to try and stop them...but she was cut down." Tears formed in Ster's eyes. "Baby killed one but the others got away. They took Janella with them.

"Jason, I'm sorry!" Ster cried with an anguish filled voice. "We tried, but they got away with Janella. And now Vinny is dying!"

Jason's body came alive instantly. He leaped to his feet as four more guards rushed into the room. "Bring him!" he ordered the men, who leaped forward to pick Ster up. "Seta, Jarrell, come on!"

The rushed from the room and through the temple, ignoring the startled cries and looks from the temple women as they dashed to the shuttle. None of them bothered to fasten their harnesses as Jason lifted the shuttle and streaked towards the Vehey house. As he approached he saw hundreds of torches now gathered around it. As those below heard the sound of the shuttle the moved out of the way, allowing him to land in front of the house. He charged towards the house, crashing through the partially open front door, nearly tearing it from its hinges. His heart was pounding in his chest as he raced down the hall to the bedroom. On the floor of the bedroom, surrounded by the rest of her family, Vinny lay in a pool of blood. Busker was sobbing, tears streaming down his coarse face as he frantically tried to push Vinny's intestines back into her slashed stomach.

Jason snatched a pitcher of water from a side table and jerked the sheet from the bed. He ripped the sheet into large strips and soaked them in water before folding one and placing it over the gaping stomach wound, gently pushing Busker's hands away. Her used another soaked strip to tie around Vinny's body to secure the first one, then lifted her unconscious body in his arms and hurried from the room.

"Seta, Kim, come with me," he said as he kicked the broken front door out of his way. "Busker, Jarrell, you and the other start a search for Janella. Use the shuttles to take men out to set up road blocks on every road from the city. I want every cart, crate and bag searched. If you find them, don't do anything. Contact me aboard the Stargazer."

With that Jason turned and ran for the shuttle. Kim had already strapped herself into the pilot's seat, with Seta in the one beside her. As soon as Jason was inside he slapped the panel to close the hatch and Kim lifted the shuttle into the night sky. She took it up as quickly as she could without causing further discomfort or pain to her sister and Ster. Jason reached over Kim's shoulder and hit the com-link.

"Mother, listen up! I've got Vinny and Ster with me. Vinny's been slashed across her abdomen, releasing her intestines. She's unconscious, in shock, and losing a hell of a lot of blood. Ster's been shot with a Tilwin arrow, which was probably poison tipped, and slashed across the chest with a sword. Have the med-lab ready for surgery. We'll be there in about fifteen minutes."

Kim made it in twelve. When she landed the shuttle in the bay they found servo droids waiting for them with two portable life support gurneys. Jason placed Vinny on one as Kim and Seta helped place Ster on the other. Making sure that Vinny and Ster were both secure, Jason raced on ahead to the med-lab as the servos pushed the two gurneys. Kim and Seta ran along behind him and began scrubbing up as well once they were in the lab. As soon as the gurney's arrived in the lab, Jason transferred Vinny to one operating table and Ster to another.

Although medicine had been part of Seta's own training as a temple priestess, Jason doubted if she would be able to operate on Vinny in the manner which was needed. The type of wound Vinny had suffered would almost definitely lead to death in a normal person, and despite what Mother had told him, Jason wasn't completely positive that Vinny would survive this, even with the injection of the KLZ formula he had given to her and the other members of her family. She had lost a tremendous amount of blood and suffered severe internal injuries.

"Kim," said Mother, "give Ster an injection of twenty five cc's of KLZ, then the two of you treat his wounds while I help Jason with Vinny. Ok, Jason, take a deep breath, relax, and I'll walk you through this."

For the next two hours Jason operated on Vinny as he carefully listened to Mother's every word, making sure he did exactly as she told him. Once he got started his hands stopped shaking and he was able to follow the computer's directions easily, with Seta and Kim helping when needed. He finally stepped back and removed his surgical mask, looking at Kim and Seta and nodding his head.

"She's going to be ok," he told them with a sigh a he gently stroked Vinny's face.

At this news both Kim and Seta clung to one another as tears of relief flooded from their eyes. Their reaction made Jason realize that all three of them had been holding tight rein on their emotions, blocking them off until after the crisis had been resolved. Jason felt tears come to his own eyes as Kim came around the table to wrap her arms around him tightly, her body shaking with her sobs.

"Thank you, Mother," he said as he finally stepped away from Kim and went to where Ster was laying.

"You did just fine, Jason," Mother replied. "She's going to be just fine. I'll keep her sedated, which will allow her to recover with a minimum of pain. You can leave her here if you want to return and look for Janella."

"In a minute," he told Mother as he looked down at Ster. The young man's eyes were closed but they opened slowly when Jason touched his shoulder.

"Jason, I..." Ster began.

"It's ok, Ster. We're aboard my ship. You're going to be fine, and so is Vinny. We got her here in time to repair her wounds."

"Thank Lofa," Ster said softly as Kim and Seta came over to stand on the other side of his bed.

"How do you feel?" Jason asked.

Jason watched as Ster gently moved his left arm to test it for stiffness. "A little sore, but I'll be ok. I'm ready to go back down when you are."

"Well, you can go, but you're going to have to spend a couple of days in bed until you're fully recovered," Jason told him.

Jason removed his surgical gown and went over to Vinny. He bent down and lightly kissed her forehead.

"Mother, I'm going to send Liet up later to stay with her."

"That's fine, Jason. She's out of danger, and right now the main thing she needs is sleep. I had you administer a strong sedative that should last for another four hours. Go on back and help in the search for Janella. If anything develops here with Vinny, I'll contact you."

Jason helped Ster from the bed and the four of them made their way back to the shuttle. "Jason," Mother said as they prepared to fly back, "I've been using probes and shipboard scanners to help in the search for Janella. I'm not sure, but I think I may have found something."

"What?" he asked anxiously as he eased the craft toward the open day doors.

*Alazon*

The small monitor on his right came to life. It showed the image of a large building on the outskirts of Lemac.

"That's the old grain storage warehouse," Kim told him.

"Are they in there, Mother?" he asked.

"I believe so," the computer replied. "My infrared sensors indicate there are eleven bodies inside, and cardiac sensors show heart rates that would coincide with ten adults under stress, and one child who is either unconscious, sleeping or drugged."

Jason hit the com-link. "Busker, Shon, this is Jason."

"Shon here. Go ahead."

"You know the old grain storage warehouse to the southeast of the city?"

"Yes."

"Mother thinks they may be in there. Take the Guard and surround it, but keep them at a distance of at least fifty yards. And keep everyone else back as well. I'm on my way."

"On my way. How's Vinny and Ster?"

"Ster's with me now. He'll be ok. So will Vinny. The surgery went well and she's resting."

"Thank Lofa," Shon said softly, the sound of relief clearly evident through the radio.

Jason streaked down toward the surface of the planet. The short, stubby wings of the shuttle glowed like embers from the friction of his reentry, but Jason's mind was on Janella and how much she meant to him, not what damage he could be causing to the craft. He loved Janella as much as he would a natural daughter, and to lose her would destroy him. As he brought the shuttle to a screaming landing beside the others, people scattered out of the way. They moved back, some of them actually cringing in fear as he stepped from the craft with a look of murderous rage on his face.

The people of Lemac had never seen Jason angry. They had never seen their king with anything but a smile on his face and a kind or cheerful word for anyone. This tall, dark haired man who strode with purpose through them now was a frightening stranger.

When Jason reached the line of guardsmen and soldiers surrounding the warehouse he was handed his katana and ho-tachi by Busker. He drew the swords and let their sheaths drop to the ground at his feet. He lifted his left wrist and spoke to Mother. "If anything happens to me and Janella, I don't want anything left but a hole in the ground."

"Understood," Mother replied softly.

He looked at Busker. Keep everyone back. No one but me and my daughter comes out of there alive."

As Jason turned to walk toward the warehouse he felt the presence of someone beside him. He turned his head and saw Shon. The older brother's face was set in grim determination, his own swords gripped tightly in his hands. He started to tell Shon to go back, but then nodded as the two of them left the others behind.

"Man the gods be with them," Seta said softly as they walked away.

"No," Kim replied, her own voice grim. "May the gods have mercy on those who have taken Janella and hurt Vinny, because Jason and Shon will not."

When Jason and Shon reached the large door of the warehouse, Jason noted a smaller door cut into it. He used the tip of his katana to push it open slightly. "Mother," he whispered into his communicator, "give me their positions."

"Four spread out on either side of the door. Six more deeper inside, and one near the back with Janella."

Jason looked at Shon to make sure the brother had heard. Shon nodded. The two of them took a deep breath and charged through the door, Shon turning to the left and Jason to the right.

Silence. Only the sound of breathing could be heard in the pitch blackness. Jason felt the sweat under his arms as he took a careful step forward as his eyes began to adjust to pick out the darker shapes of bins and crates within as he tried to locate the shapes of those hiding inside.

The attackers came in a rush. The scuffle of their feet on the wooden floor was the only sound they made. It happened so fast Jason didn't have time to shout a warning to Shon, and could only hope the other man was ready. They fought silently, the clash of steel on steel echoing throughout the warehouse as he twisted and turned in his efforts to avoid the slash or stab of a Tilwin blade, his own swords searching out targets in the darkness.

Jason felt a burning pain down his back. He whirled around with the ho-tachi held not quite shoulder high and parallel to the ground. The blade whistled as it cut an arc through the air. It met the resistance of bone and flesh for only a microsecond before Jason was showered with hot blood gushing up from the neck as a head was severed from the shoulders. He tried to wipe the blood from his eyes and felt another blade bite into his left side. He twisted away, using a reverse grip on the katana to slash upwards. He was rewarded with the satisfying slice of muscle and bone as the sword severed the arm from the attacker.

As his eyes became accustomed to the darkness, Jason was able to better see the remaining men facing him. He feinted at one and then killed another with a quick stab through the man's heart with the ho-tachi. But the movement allowed yet another man to lunge forward. The man's sword swung down to slice the outside of Jason's right arm from shoulder to elbow. Jason's katana dropped from his right hand. He ducked as the man swung at him attain and brought the ho-tachi around in a back handed grip to disembowel the man. He snatched up the katana and ran the blade through a man charging at him. As he jerked it free he turned to see Shown down on one knee, the bodies of four dead Tilwin on the floor around him. He was bleeding from half a dozen wounds but looked at Jason and nodded.

"Outside," Jason whispered. He waited until Shon had moved out of the warehouse before turning to face the darker confines of it.

"You are even better than they said," a female voice called out from the darkness to his left.

Jason turned toward the sound. "Release my daughter and I'll let you live. Harm her and I'll send your body back to Lorac in pieces!"

"Release her?" the voice asked. "You must be crazy! Or think I am. The second I turn her lose you'll kill me. No, I think I have a much better idea."

"I'm listening," he told her, aware of the changing direction of the voice. He turned slowly to follow it.

"That craft you flew here in. Can it fly to Tilwin?"

"Yes."

"Good. They you will fly me and your daughter to Chice."

"Then you'll release her?"

"Not a chance! You'll be allowed to return to Lemac, but we'll keep your daughter as a hostage. That will assure us that you will do exactly as we tell you. I can promise you that she will not be harmed as long as you do what we want. As long as she's alive and in good health we will have control over you and you won't make any moves against us."

As the voice spoke it had gradually moved around to the door of the warehouse. From the light of the torches outside, Jason could now make out the figure in black. She was holding Janella by the hair with her left hand, pressing the blade of a knife against the girl's throat with her right.

"Janella?" Jason called softly.

"I'm okay, Daddy," she replied bravely.

As the figure holding his daughter backed through the door Jason could see her more clearly. The woman appeared to be in her mid twenties, attractive, but with a look of fear in her eyes. A look that told him she would slit Janella's throat if he tried anything. As the woman backed out the door, pulling Janella along with her, Jason followed. He slipped the <u>ho-tachi</u> into the sash at his waist and gripped the <u>katana</u> with both hands. The tip of the blade was only inches from his right foot.

"Let her go," he told the woman once they were clear of the warehouse. "Let her go and I give you my word as King of Preton, and here in front of all these people, that I will personally return you to Tilwin. No one will harm you. I swear it."

"I almost believe you," the woman replied scornfully. "But I can't afford to take that chance. Besides, we need her to make sure you don't do anything against us. Like I said, as long as we have her, we're safe. Not only that, but if I return without your daughter, Lorac will kill me."

"<u>Don't move!</u>" a voice inside his head whispered. Jason saw Janella's eyes dart to his left. Out of the corner of his eye he saw the twins approaching slowly. They were holding hands and their eyes were directed at the woman holding Janella. When they were about fifteen feet from her they stopped. "<u>Be ready,</u>" came their silent voices.

Jason gripped the katana tighter in his hands. His body tensed like a coiled spring. He was unmindful of the blood coming from the wounds to his body. He didn't know what the twins had in mind, but he would be ready for the slightest slip on the part of the woman.

The woman looked nervously from him to the twins. Her left hand gripped the hair of Janella tightly, bending the small girl's head back. The blade of the knife in her right hand pressed against Janella's throat.

Jason never took his eyes off the woman. The low and menacing growl which came from his right, and the sudden widening of the woman's eyes let him know that Baby had now joined this tense, macabre tableau.

"Who are they? And what is that?" the woman demanded fearfully as her eyes darted from the twins to Baby and then back to him.

His face formed a cold mask. "They are the harbingers of your death," he told her in a low whisper.

"Get back! Get away from me!" the woman screamed at twins and Baby, her right hand snapping out at the dog.

Before the woman's arm was completely straight, Jason's sword flashed upward as he lunged forward. The blade slashed through the woman's forearm as if it were balsa wood. As he continued to bring the blade up and around, turning his body to gain force, he heard the mental command of the twins for Janella to run.

"Keeeeiiii!" Jason yelled as the blade flashed down from over his head with all the speed and power he could put into it. The tip of his sword came to an abrupt stop at a point midway between the woman's feet and only an inch from the ground. For the space of a heartbeat the woman stood looking at him. The silence of the crowd was suddenly broken by cries of horror and the sound of people retching as the woman's body began to fall apart with wet, sucking sounds. It separated down the middle in two equal halves as it collapsed to the ground.

Jason was unmindful of the sounds of the crowd, or the blood still coming from his own wounds as he turned to Janella. His sword fell from his hands and he dropped to his knees as she rushed to him. He felt tears of relief, joy and love flooding his eyes as he clasped her tightly, not caring who saw him crying without shame.

"It's ok, Daddy," Janella said softly. "I knew you would come for me. I wasn't scared at all because I know you would never let anyone hurt me or take me away from you and mommy. I tried to tell them that if they would just give up that you would let them live and go home, but if they didn't then they were all gonna die."

"My Lord, you're hurt!" Seta cried as she and Kim hurried to where he knelt with Janella.

Jason started to stand and felt pain flash through his body. He felt suddenly weak from the loss of blood he had suffered. Hands gripped his arms from either side to help him up. He looked up to see Busker and Naed.

"Where did you come from?" he asked Naed as the man slipped an arm around him to help him to his feet.

"I was on my way over anyway when I heard the traffic on the radio."

"Shon?" he asked, looking around for the other man.

"Looks worse than what it is," Busker told him. "He's being taken to the temple."

"Come on," said Naed. "We can talk later. Right now we need to get you up to Mother. You've been sliced up pretty good."

"I'll be ok," Jason replied, but as he reached his feet he felt himself starting to fall forward and a curtain of blackness came down over his eyes.

# TWENTY NINE

Jason opened his eyes to find himself in the med-lab with Kim sitting on a stood beside his bed. She smiled at him and shook her head.

"You know, Alien, this is starting to get old," she told him as she leaned over to kiss his forehead. "Just because Mother claims you're practically kill-proof, you don't have to go around trying to see if she's right."

He smiled back at her but he could tell that her light-hearted banter didn't completely conceal the worry and concern he saw in her eyes.

"True, but I can't think of a better way to come back to consciousness than to open my eyes and see your beautiful face."

"Flattery will get you everywhere with me, tall, dark and handsome," she laughed.

"So, what's my prognosis?"

"You'll live. Naturally."

"How's Vinny?"

"Still sleeping. Mother says she's healing quickly and is going to be just fine."

"Thank god," he whispered.

The door of the med-lab opened and Seta entered the room carrying Janella in her arms. She set the girl on the bed beside him and Janella quickly wormed her way up beside him to kiss his cheek and hug his neck as the twins, who had been following Seta, climbed up to sit on the end of the bed.

"Hi, Ragamuffin," he said to Janella. "What have you guys been doing?" he asked as he kissed her cheek.

"We've been showing Seta around the ship and explaining how things work to her," Janella replied matter-of-factly.

"I see. Well, I guess I'll have to make the three of you the official tour guides for this bucket of bolts since you know so much about it."

"It really is amazing," Seta told him. "You could live here forever if you had to."

"Yeah, and for a while I thought I was going to have to do just that," Jason told her with a rueful grin. "How are things below?" he asked, turning to Kim.

"Pretty quiet for the most part. Dad says everyone is talking about how you and Shon fought the Tilwin, about how Baby killed one who was trying to escape, and how you cut that woman in half. All in all, I'd say the population is suitable impressed," she told him with a grin.

"Baby killed one?" he asked in surprise.

Kim nodded. "Yeah. One of them ran out, trying to escape and Baby took off like a shot before anyone could even blink. What she did to him wasn't pretty. I'm surprised you didn't notice the blood all over her. Then again, you were pretty busy yourself."

"Where's Shon now?"

"He stayed below. He only had a few minor cuts so he went to the temple to be taken care of. I tried to get him to come up here, but he thought he should stay down there with Dad and Busker in case anything else came up. Naed's here though. He's sitting with Vinny right now."

"I take it you flew me up here?"

"I sure did," she replied with a smug grin. "And in case you didn't notice, I also flew us when we brought Vinny up. And it was me flying the shuttle, not Mother. While you've been off busy playing king, I've been coming up here to have Mother teach me how to fly in the flight simulator."

"Mother?" he called out.

"Hey, Blue Eyes!" came the computer's cheerful reply.

"Hi, yourself. Give me a report on my body."

"It's all in one piece. Like Kimmy said, you'll live."

"No serious or permanent damage?"

"To you?" Mother replied as if surprised at his question.

"Okay, sorry I asked."

"You'll have some nasty looking scars," Seta told him as she looked at the bandages around his chest, and arms.

Kim looked at him and grinned before turning to Seta. "No, he won't," she told the High Priestess. "He doesn't scar, Seta. He's a god, remember?"

"Cut that out, Kim," Jason chided. He turned to Seta. "Look, the reason I won't scar has nothing to do with any 'god like' qualities that don't exist in the first place. It's due to the medical discoveries made back in my world, combined with something from your world."

He saw a light of understanding slowly come to Seta's eyes.

"So that's why Vinny didn't die right away from her injuries," Seta replied. "and that's why she's healing so quickly, right? I mean," she continued before he could answer, "a wound such as Vinny received should have been fatal almost immediately. Any other person would have died within minutes, just as you should have done from the Tilwin arrows in your fight against them."

"Yes," Jason replied. "Even though Vinny was seriously injured, and possibly could have died from it, there's a good chance she would have recovered in time with just the minimal medical assistance.

"Due to the injections of a formula my mother developed, and that I've given to all the members of the Vehey family, as well as Busker and Ster, Vinny's body was actually in the process of shutting itself down to prevent her from losing as much blood as she would have under normal conditions.

"It was also starting to heal itself almost immediately from the injury, although you couldn't actually see it happening. Busker had the right idea in trying to replace her intestines, he just went about it incorrectly.

"But it's also possible," he continued, "that Vinny could have died from blood loss and shock, even though the chances of it were severely decreased thanks to the injection. When I brought her up here, all I was basically doing was putting everything back where it belonged, replenishing her body fluids, and making sure there was nothing within the wound that might cause some type of infection later on. Two weeks from now you won't even be able to find a mark on her to show she was ever hurt."

Seta looked around the lab with an expression of awe on her face. After a moment she slowly shook her head from side to side. "So much knowledge," she said softly as she turned back to face Jason. "I mean, I'm supposed to be one of the most highly trained and knowledgeable people on my world with it comes to medicine and treatment of the sick, but what I know is laughable when compared to what you have here."

There was a note of sadness and despair to Seta's voice that touched Jason. He slowly eased himself up to a sitting position on the bed and studied Seta carefully for a moment, weighing the possible consequences. He knew what he was considering would be taking a chance, but it was one he thought would be worth it in the long run. He pulled Janella up beside him and slipped his bandaged right arm around her as she settled comfortable against him.

"Seta, what I'm about to tell you must remain a secret among us for as long as I deem it necessary. Consider it a direct order from your king. Is that understood?"

Seta bowed her head and looked down at the floor. "My Lord," she said humbly, "you have but to command and I will obey."

He looked at Kim and rolled his eyes as she grinned at him. "Will you please tell her that she doesn't have to play the royalty bit with me when we're alone. I've tried but it doesn't seem to do any good."

Kim turned to Seta. "You heard him. When no one else is around just call him Jason, or anything else that comes to mind at the moment and, believe me, there will be plenty of things you'll think of," she added with a grin.

Seta grinned at Kim's words and relaxed from the posture she had assumed. "All right," she said at last.

"Good," he said with a sigh. "Now, Seta, how would you like to learn all the medical knowledge of my world?"

"But, my...Jason...that would be impossible!" Seta gasped.

"How long would it take, Mother?" he asked.

"Hummm, let's see," the computer replied thoughtfully. "By using the TTS it would take about three hours to turn her into an M.D., and another four or so to qualify her as a heart surgeon, and about five more to enable her to handle anything that comes her way. Then an intensive week or so in the holo trainers to give her some "hands on" experience. So we're talking about eight to ten days."

"Interested?" he asked Seta.

"Yes!" the High Priestess replied without hesitation. Her face was flushed and her eyes lit up at the prospect of being able to treat and cure everyone who came to her. But then her expression changed and she lowered her eyes.

"What's the matter?" he asked.

She looked up at him and he could see the sudden sense of nervousness in her. "After what you know about me, are you sure you want to do this?"

"You're not your sister," he told her. "Nor are you responsible for the things she's done."

"Hey, time out!" Kim said as she looked from him to Seta and back. "Would someone like to tell me what's going on here? What's this about a sister?"

Seta looked at Jason for a moment and then turned to face Kim. "I am the twin sister of Queen Lorac of Tilwin."

"Whoa," Kim said softly. The tone of her voice and the look on her face clearly expressed her shock at this news. She looked at Jason for a moment before turning back to the High Priestess.

"Seta, I have known you my whole life. You are a woman I have loved and respected as I do few others, and I have never known you to be anything but a kind and loving person.

"By the way," she added, turning back to Jason, "is that where you and Dad took off to earlier tonight?"

"Yes. All during Lorac's visit I had the feeling she looked familiar, that she reminded me of someone, but I didn't really make the connection until earlier tonight."

"I see," Kim replied, turning back to Seta. "Well, if my husband, jerk that he can be at times, doesn't think it's anything to get all shook up about, then who am I to think otherwise.

"Seta, when I was a little girl; always getting into trouble, or needing a place to hide out for a while, you were the one who was always there for me. You let me roam the temple at will, and you always talked to me like an adult, not a child. You weren't just my teacher, but one of my best friends. That's the Seta I know and love. Who your sister is doesn't make the least bit of difference to me."

Seta stepped forward and hugged Kim. "Thank you," the High Priestess said softly. Her voice expressed the emotion she was feeling.

"Okay, now that that's settled," Jason told the two of them, "let's get back to what I was talking about. Seta, I can give you all the medical knowledge of my world, but there might be a few problems connected with it."

"Like what?" she asked.

"Well, having the knowledge is one thing. Knowing how to use it, and really understanding it, is another entirely. Aside from the time it would take Mother to implant the knowledge in your mind, you would also have to spend hours in the holographic and virtual reality trainers here on the ship to learn the practical side of that knowledge. You would have to do a lot of laboratory work, as well as other things that will be completely new to you. That's the only way you'll be able to get the first hand, practical application of that knowledge that you will need. It won't be easy. In fact, it may be the hardest task you've ever undertaken in your life."

"But it will be more than worth it," Seta replied. The tone of her voice left no doubt as to her sincerity.

Jason nodded in agreement. "Yes, it will. All right, once things get calmed down I'll have Mother set up a training program for you. I also want you to carefully select those you think would make the best doctors among the women of the temple and I'll have a training program set up for them as well. In the meantime, there is something I can do for you now."

Jason looked at Kim and saw her nod in agreement. Without a word, Kim went to one of the small medicine cabinets. When she returned she held a small, air-powered injector in her right hand and a vial of green liquid in her left. She climbed back up on the stool and looked at Seta.

"Seta," said Jason, "what would you say if I told you that by having Kim give you an injection of the fluid in that vial, not only would you heal as I do, and as the other members of the Vehey family do, but that you would also live for the next seven to eight hundred years? That in two hundred years you would look almost exactly as you do right now, and that there is practically nothing that can kill you?"

Seta's eyes traveled slowly from him to the injector in Kim's hand and back, a touch of awe in them. "I…I would say that people are right and you are a god."

"Oh, for crying out loud, knock that off," he told her. "I keep telling you I'm not a god. I'm just a man from a more advanced civilization and that's all. Now, before you give me your answer, let me tell you about the conditions and restrictions that go along with this shot.

"First, once it is given, it can't be reversed. You'll never be sick again, and any injury you receive will heal itself, as they do with me. And I've only brushed the surface on the effects of longevity that go along with it. Those are the good points. Here are the drawbacks.

"You will outlive just about everyone you know, with the exception of those I've mentioned. You will see friends age and die while you remain young and beautiful. Should you ever meet a man you wish to marry, not only must he meet the approval of the family, but his devotion to its secrets must be total as well. Any children you may have will automatically be born with this in their systems, and that will present a whole new set of problems for you.

"In other words, Seta, this can be as much of a burden as it is a blessing, and it's something you should not consider lightly. If you want some time to think about it I'll understand. But whether you accept or not, this conversation never leaves this room.

"If you choose to accept, the other members of the family will be informed that you have become one of us. They will also be told about Lorac. There can be no secrets between any of us."

Seta looked at him for a long, silent moment before turning to pace the room a few times. He knew the emotional struggle she was going through over what he was offering her. He knew what it had done to his own psyche when he had learned of his longevity and healing abilities from Mother, and he had not been in the dark about such things as Seta was. She finally came back to stand beside the bed.

"What you offer I cannot refuse," she told him as she slowly pushed up the sleeve of her robe to bare her arm.

Jason nodded to Kim. She wiped Seta's arm with an alcohol bad and pressed the injector to it. As Kim depressed the trigger there was the whisper of compressed air and Seta flinched slightly. Kim pulled the injector away and smiled warmly at Seta. "Welcome to the family," she said softly.

"You won't feel anything," he told Seta as she turned to him. "But as of right now your body is starting to change."

"Jason," called the computer.

"Yes?"

"I'm going to start reviving Vinny. I thought you guys might like to be there when she opens her eyes."

'Thanks, Mother, we'll be right there. Up, Princess," he told Janella as he started to swing his legs over the side of the bed. He stopped when he realized he wasn't wearing any clothing.

"Ahh, ladies, would one of you mind bringing me something to wear, and then give me some privacy so I can get dressed?"

"I'll get it, Daddy!" Janella said with a giggle. She slid off the bed and ran to a small cabinet where she removed a clean jump suit, boots and under shorts she had placed there earlier for him. She dashed back and placed them on the bed.

"Some women are very considerate," he teased Kim.

"Yeah, and some of them are even fooled by the line of crap you put out," she replied with a grin. "Me? I know you better."

"Yeah, right. That's why you married me. Now, if all of you will please get out of here, I'll get dressed and join you in a minute."

"Not me," Kim told him as Seta, Janella and the twins headed for the door. "I'm your wife, remember? I've seen it all before."

Once the others were out of the lab Jason stood and allowed Kim to help him dress. He was still feeling a little weak and was secretly glad she had stayed behind. Once he was dressed, Kim made him sit down while she went to one of the medicine cabinets and withdrew another small vial. She placed it in the injector and gave him a shot. Within seconds he felt his sense of weakness vanishing. He knew the dose of the natural stimulate she had given him would last for about four hours, which would be long enough to get him through the rest of the night. He stood and kissed the top of her head as they headed for the door. "Sometimes you're just too good to me," he told her.

"Don't I know it!" she replied, laughing as they joined the others out in the passageway.

In the recovery room they found Naed sitting beside Vinny's bed, tenderly holding her left hand. The twins climbed up onto the bed and joined hands with one another. With their free hands they took hold of Vinny's hands. They closed their eyes and Jason knew they were helping bring Vinny back to consciousness.

Jason looked at Naed. His friend was watching Vinny nervously with an expression of real concern on his face. <u>If I didn't know better</u>, Jason thought, <u>I'd say that Naed's in love with Vinny.</u>

Vinny's eyelids fluttered for a moment and then opened. "Jason!" she cried weakly when she saw him standing beside her bed. "Oh, Jason, they got Janella!" she cried as she lunged upward from the bed and wrapper her arms around his neck, clinging to him desperately. "I tried…."

"Shhhhh, take it easy, Vinny," he told her as he held her gently, finally unwrapping her arms from around his neck to ease her back down on the bed. "It's okay. Look," He picked up Janella and let her lean over the bed so she could kiss Vinny. Vinny wrapped her arms around Janella and hugged her tightly, crying out of relief and joy.

"Everything's going to be all right," Jason told Vinny as she finally released Janella, allowing the girl to sit on the bed with the twins. "You've got a rather nasty cut but you're going to heal up nicely. You'll be back on your feet in no time at all. Just do me one favor, though, please?"

"Anything."

"The next time you decide to take on a group of trained assassins, at least take a sword with you. Or better yet, a phaser. Trying to take them on with your bare hands is not the wisest course of action to take."

Vinny laughed lightly, then grimaced from the pain it caused her. "I'll keep that in mind," she told him. "In fact, maybe you should start teaching the women of this family how to handle a sword in case something like this ever comes up again."

Jason glanced at Naed and frowned. "I don't know. You and Kim are dangerous enough as it is. Putting swords in your hands, and training you how to use them, could be asking for trouble."

"What are you afraid of?" Kim teased.

"Me? Nothing! It's the safety and well being of your brothers that I was thinking of. I mean, I doubt if they would appreciate me teaching the two of you martial arts and how to handle a sword, because then you would go around beating them up all the time."

Kim looked at Vinny and winked. "It would keep them in line," she told him.

Jason looked at Seta and spread his hands in an expression of helplessness. "See what I have to put up with?'

"Yes, but you love it," the Priestess replied with a grin.

"Yeah, I guess I do. Ok, I don't know about everyone else, but I'm hungry. Mother would it be okay to put Vinny in an anti-grav chair and take her to the mess deck?"

"Sure, if she feels up to it. Just don't let her eat anything solid. Only soups and liquids for the next couple of days."

Jason looked at Vinny. "What do you say? Feel like sitting up and taking a ride?"

"Okay."

He went to the far wall and activated one of the anti-grav chairs and pushed it over to the bed. With Kim's help he disconnected the leads and I.V. tubes attached to Vinny and then nodded to Naed. Naed gently lifted Vinny from the bed and placed her in the chair. He carefully fastened the belt across her lap before moving to stand behind it.

"Okay, folks," Jason told them, "it's off to the mess deck."

Jason led the way, with Naed pushing Vinny in the anti-grav chair. Because of the chair they couldn't use the gravity wells between decks and had to take the slower elevators, but the only ones who seemed to mind this were Janella and the twins. They loved floating up and down in the gravity wells between decks, playing tag with one another and Baby as they did.

Jason selected a liquid meal for Vinny, but since it was the first time for Naed in the mess hall, Janella and the twins were more than happy to show their friend how to use the food dispensers. Typical of their sense of humor, they had him push the buttons which would dispense food prepared strictly for Baby. They tried to suppress their laughter as Naed started to eat what he thought was some form of stew.

"Wait!" Janella cried just before Naed took his first bite. "That's dog food and only for Baby."

Naed grinned at her and the twins as he realized he was the latest victim of one of their pranks. He sat back in his chair while Kim brought him something more suitable. He then snatched all three of the kids up and wrestled with them for a minute before turning them loose so they could all eat.

Watching Naed with the three kids, Jason wondered why Naed wasn't married with children of his own. Jason had never really thought about it before, but watching Naed now it was obvious that the man loved children. He also remembered the way Naed had looked at Vinny with such concern in his eyes earlier. He again wondered if there was something there on Naed's part.

Jason liked Naed. The two of them had become close friends. He often felt more in touch with Naed than he did with either Shon or Hass. Over the past few months he found that Naed was a lot like himself in his beliefs and ideas about Alazon. He saw Naed glance at Vinny and knew then, without a doubt, that Naed was either in love with Vinny, or was falling in love with her.

While Jason thought that was good on the one hand, he also knew that Vinny didn't share the same feelings for Naed. To Vinny, Naed was a friend. A good friend, to be sure, but nothing more than that. Jason wasn't sure why, but he had a feeling that Naed would never be anything more than that to Vinny. That thought saddened him a little because he thought Naed would be good for her.

In all the time Jason had known Vinny she had never shown any interest, serious or otherwise, in any man. Granted, for the past year they had all been caught up in the events surrounding their lives, but that shouldn't have precluded her from being able to have a relationship with someone. A thought seemed to crawl up from the bottom of his mind to shock him for a moment. He glanced at Vinny but then shook his head, telling himself he was letting his imagination get carried away. He turned to his food and began to eat, his mind turning to the things which would have to be done in the coming days.

# THIRTY

The eyes of Jarrell matched the note of concern in his voice. "Are you sure you're up to this, Jason?" he asked.

"I'm fine, Jarrell. Besides, I have to get Naed off that shop. After what's happened here, and in Sharl, there's no telling what Lorac might try and pull."

"I'm going with you," Naed told him flatly.

"All right. Busker, you and Shon stay here to protect the family. I'll also take Ster if he feels up to it."

"He does," Busker told him as he clasped his hands together on the table. "Actually, Jason, I've been meaning to talk to you about Ster."

"What about?"

"I'd like to promote him to Captain. I've been thinking about it for a while now. Despite what happened here the other night, I still think he deserves it. The men respect him, and he has that rare quality of being able to lead without complaints from them about them having to take orders from someone younger than most of them are."

Jason looked at Busker and shrugged. "So what's the problem? Go ahead and promote him. I don't have any objections to it."

"Well," Busker replied with a wiry grin, "technically you are still Commander of the Army, and most of the men of the Guard here in Lemac consider themselves as the personal guard of you, Kim and Janella. And after what happened, I think it would mean a lot more to him if it came from you."

Jason grinned and nodded his head. "Okay, but let's do this."

A few minutes later Km went to the front door and called to Ster, who was standing outside with the other members of the Royal Guard. She told him the King was requesting his presence in a very solemn voice. Ster hurried into the house and came to rigid attention a few feet from the table where Jason and Busker sat. His eyes stared straight ahead at the all, his attitude giving no indication of any discomfort from the wounds he had received.

"How's your shoulder?" Jason asked in a relaxed and easy manner.

"Fine, Commander," Ster replied stiffly.

"Good. Now, Busker tells me that he's been considering you for promotion to the rank of Captain, but let me ask you something. Do you think you deserve it?"

Ster swallowed with some difficulty, but that was the only outward sign of his nervousness. "Two days ago I would have thought so, Commander, but not now."

Jason was intrigued by Ster's answer. "Why not?" he asked.

"Sir, after my actions of the other night placed the life of Princess Janella in danger, not to mention the life of Queen Kimella, and almost cost the life of her sister, Vinny, I feel that, if anything, I should probably be reduced in rank. At the least, I should be relieved of my command. If I had not wasted precious minutes getting here, I might have been able to prevent the events which transpired. Therefore, I hold myself completely responsible."

Jason studied Ster thoughtfully. He knew the young man meant every word he said. He looked at Busker and raised his eyebrows slightly before turning back to Ster.

"I'm almost tempted to agree with you, Lieutenant," he told Ster, "but I don't. What happened here was not your fault, and you did manage to kill two of the attackers before being seriously wounded yourself. Your actions following the event have proven your dedication to this family. Therefore, no blame is to be placed on you as far as I'm concerned.

"However," he continued before Ster could reply, "as far as this promotion goes, I do have some concerns. It has been brought to my attention that you and the other members of the Royal Guard consider yourselves as sort of an elite guard for me and my family, and that you also consider yourselves better than the men of the Mayoral Guard of the other cities. Am I correct in that?"

"Yes, Sir, you are!" Ster replied without hesitation.

"And just why do you and the others think that way?"

Ster squared his shoulders a little more before answering. "Sir, while we are all members of the Mayoral Guard of Lemac, to a man we feel that the family of the King of Preton should be afforded special protection by us, especially during this time of conflict in which we do not know what may occur, such as the events that transpired two nights ago.

"Because of that, we have taken a blood oath among ourselves to protect you, our king, and all members of this family with our lives, asking nothing in return. We feel it is not just our duty, Commander, but our obligation. It is also our personal desire to do so."

Jason was touched by Ster's sincerity. He was also more than just a little impressed by the sense of devotion to him and the other members of the family.

"All right, Lieutenant," Jason said after a moment, "I guess I can understand that. Now, despite the fact that you feel you may not deserve this promotion, both General Busker and I feel you do.

"However, my main concern is giving so much responsibility and rank to someone as young as you are. But Busker feels you can handle it. However, you realize that if you screw up, that rank will be stripped from you quicker than you can blink. Is that understood?"

"Yes, Commander," Ster replied firmly.

Busker stood and moved around the table to stand in front of Ster. "As of this moment you are promoted to the rank of Captain, with all the duties, responsibilities and privileges it carries.

"But let me tell you something, Captain, if you, as Jason put it, screw up and make me look bad, you won't have to worry about being busted in rank. What you'll have to worry about is me coming down so hard on you that you'll wish you had never been born. Do we understand one another?"

"Perfectly, General."

"Good. Now, Jason is going after Hass. Governor Laer is going with him. So are you and two others. I'll leave it up to you to select the others. Get them and be ready to take off immediately. Get moving, Captain!"

"Yes, General!"

Ster saluted smartly before turning on his heels to hurry out the door, unable to suppress the grin on his face.

"You guys are mean1" Kim told them, laughing as the door closed behind Ster. "You had the poor man shaking in his boots. You should both be ashamed of yourselves!"

Jason looked at Busker. "Do you feel ashamed?"

"Not in the least," Busker replied innocently.

"Neither do I."

"He's a good man," Vinny said from where she was laying propped up on the sofa, "and he thinks the world of Janella. If anything serious had happened to her, I think he would have taken his own life."

"When I get older I'm gonna marry him," Janella announced innocently from where she sat on the floor beside the sofa petting Baby.

Jason looked at Kim and grinned. "Poor guy. I wonder if he knows what his future holds?"

"She could do a lot worse than Ster," Kim told him.

"True. All right, Busker, I want you to start spreading the word while I'm gone. I want all of our forces to gather at the training grounds we used before. We need at least thirty thousand men."

Kim stood up and came around the table to stand next to his chair. She looked deeply into his eyes. "What are you planning?"

"What I had hoped to avoid," he told her. "We're going to invade Tilwin. I figure we have about two months before Semaj will start to get concerned as to why he hasn't heard from his wife, another two before ships can get here from there to find out what's going on due to the shifting trade winds this time of year. That should give us the time we need to get ready.

"Do you think forty thousand will be enough, or should we recruit new men as well?" Busker asked.

"We don't really have the time to train new men. Besides, I'm going to utilize the shuttles and other weapons from the ship. This is going to be a lightning fast strike that will put control of Tilwin in our hands in the space of two to three days."

"Do you think that's possible?" asked Liet.

Jason nodded. "If it's done right, yes."

"Hey, Boss Man?" Mother's voice called out to him from his wrist communicator.

"Yes?"

"I'm just about finished with Seta for now. She'll be coming out of TTS in about half an hour, but after that she's going to need some time to get herself oriented. Also, I should give Vinny a check up to make sure everything is going smoothly with her."

"What's your point, Mother?" he asked.

"Would it be all right with you for Kim to bring Vinny up?"

"That's fine with me. Kim?" he asked, turning to her.

"Of course. Mom can go with us," she added, grinning at Liet, who was sitting at the far end of the table.

"I said I would not fly in one of those things," Liet said flatly. "But if my daughter needs me by her side, I guess I can do it."

Jason turned back to Busker. "After I get Hass and Lorac, I'll be going up to the ship. I'm going to hook the good queen up to Mother and drain her brain. Ready, Naed?"

"Just waiting on you."

"Then let's go."

"Hold it!"

Jason turned to see Kim standing in the middle of the room. Her feet were spread slightly and her hands were on her hips. "King or no king, aren't you forgetting something?"

He wondered what she was talking about. "I don't thing so," he replied with a shrug.

"What about kissing your queen good bye before you leave?"

"Oh, that." He reached out and snatched her up, kissing her deeply before setting her back on her feet. "There, is that better?"

"It will do for now," she told him as she stepped back and grinned up at him.

Jason looked at Naed. "Come on. Let's get out of here before she changes her mind."

"You're asking for it," Kim called out as he and Naed headed outside.

*Alazon*

They went directly to the mid-sized shuttle, which was already warmed up and ready to go. Ster and two others snapped to attention as they approached. They all boarded quickly and within seconds the shuttle was streaking westward across Preton.

"Mother, give me a location on Lorac's ships."

The monitor came to life showing him his own position in relation to the ships of Lorac. He made a slight course adjustment to intercept them and pushed the shuttle to full speed. Preton flashed by below them in a blur.

For a long time no one spoke. Jason knew that the others, like himself, were thinking of what the coming days would bring. It wasn't until they streaked past the coastline of Preton with the ocean below them, the stars and moon above them, that Naed finally broke the silence.

"You know," he said softly, "if someone had told me just over a year ago that I would be flying through the air in a craft like this, with a man of your physical description, I would have considered that person to be out of his mind."

"Believe it or not," Jason replied with a grin, "I know the feeling myself."

"Can I ask you something?"

"Sure."

"How are you going to get Hass and Lorac off the ships in the middle of the ocean? I mean, I doubt if they will just let you pull up along side and pluck them off the deck."

"True," Jason replied as eh checked his instruments. "I plan to have Hass grab her and jump overboard. Then I'll pluck them out of the water. I thought of using the tractor beam to pull them up from the shit, but that would take too much time, attract too much attention, and give Lorac's men time to shoot at Hass. Captain Ster!" he called out over his shoulder.

"Sir?"

"Are you familiar with the operation of the lower bay doors and tractor beam?"

"Yes, Commander."

"Then explain them to the others."

Jason heard Ster begin explaining the operation to the other two men, telling them what they would be doing. After that silence settled in on all of them once again.

When they were within a hundred miles of the Tilwin ships, Jason activated the tracking device. It was tuned to a special bracelet Hass wore. The signal would cause the bracelet to vibrate gently on Hass's wrist, which would notify him to get alone as quickly as possible without drawing attention to himself. Nearly two minutes passed before Hass responded.

"Hass here," came the whispered reply.

"Where are you?" Jason asked.

"My cabin."

"Lorac?"

"Up on deck."

"Go back and join her. When you see my signal, grab her and jump overboard. We'll pick you up."

"On my way."

Jason was pleased that Hass hadn't questioned his reasons for this request. The younger brother would know something was up, and that something serious had occurred to create this turn of events.

"What's your signal going to be?" Naed asked.

"You'll see," Jason replied flatly.

His mind was filled with the thoughts of what Lorac's assassins had tried to do to Janella, and what they had almost done to Vinny. His anger and rage boiled up anew inside of him, but this time it was controlled.

Jason brought the shuttle down to just fifty feet above the surface of the ocean and pulled the combat sights around to place in front of his face. He lined up the sights of the phaser pulse cannons on the troop ship to the left, his finger resting lightly on the firing stud of the control stud. He switched to infrared for a moment to try and pick out Hass and Lorac on the other ship, but was unable to do so at this distance.

When he closed to a distance of two hundred yards from the troop ship, he fired. Two bright balls of light shot out from the wing tips of the shuttle and streaked toward the ship. A heart beat later the troop ship exploded into a ball of flame, throwing bits of charred wood, metal, flesh and bone into the air.

He slammed on the air brakes and swung the shuttle around to face the second ship, dropping down to within just ten feet of the waves, placing the shuttle between those on board Lorac's ship and the two bodies now bobbing on the surface.

"Go!" he heard Ster call out a few seconds later.

Jason lifted the shuttle and moved to a position a hundred yards away from the remaining ship. He turned to face the ship, holding the shuttle in a hovering position.

"What's the meaning of this!" Lorac demanded as he lined up her ship in the sights of the cannons.

"Bring her here," he called back over his shoulder.

Lorac was brought forward, held firmly in the grasp of Ster and Hass. Her soaked gown was plastered to her, clearly outlining the shapely body beneath. But Lorac's figure was the last thing on Jason's mind as he turned to face her with a smile on his lips which held no warmth or friendship.

"You should have left well enough alone, Lorac. You made a big mistake when you killed the young girls in Sharl, but you made a fatal mistake when you tried to kidnap my daughter. By the way, your kidnappers are all dead and my daughter is just fine."

"I don't know what you are talking about," Lorac snapped angrily. But her voice lacked conviction and her eyes were filled with fear.

Jason looked at Naed. "if this Tilwin bitch speaks again without me giving her permission, cut her tongue out."

"Gladly," Naed replied as he got up from his seat and removed his knife. He grabbed a handful of Lorac's wet hair to hold her head steady and placed the tip of his knife against her lips to let her feel the razor sharpness of it.

Lorac's eyes jerked back and froth from Naed to Jason. Jason could see the fear in them, as well as the realization that Naed would do exactly as Jason had instructed him just for the pleasure of it.

"Now," Jason told her, "when you left Preton I had hoped that you would abide by the new treaties, and that there could be peace between us. But I guess that deep in my heart I knew you would try something. I suppose it was just too much to hope for that there would be some of the better qualities of your sister in you."

Jason saw the surprise leap into Lorac's eyes, as well as the puzzled glances of the others. "I know, they don't," he told Lorac. "But your actions have forced me to act against you and the Tilwin. I didn't want it to come to this. Many good men on both sides will die. I regret that more than you will ever be able to comprehend, because the only life that matters to you is your own."

Jason turned back to the controls and fired, completely vaporizing her second ship. "Tie and gag her," he told the others as he turned the shuttle and began an elliptical flight that would take him to the <u>Stargazer</u> by the quickest route. "And cut those damn fingernails off!"

He heard the whispered comments from behind him and knew the others were talking not only about what he had just done, but speculating on what he was going to do with Lorac. Naed returned to his seat and Hass came to stand between him and Jason. His clothing was still dripping water, but he slapped Jason playfully on the shoulder.

"You know, Jason, I don't mind obeying the orders of my king, but 'go jump in the lake' isn't one I hope I have to hear too often. Especially when I'm not that good of a swimmer. Or when I have to hold onto a she-cat like her."

"I'll try and remember that."

"What are you going to do with her?" asked Naed.

"Hook her up to Mother. I want to find out all she knows about the military strength of the Tilwin, as well as the cult of the Slayers. We'll need that information."

They were silent after that, remaining so until they reached the shuttle bay. "This should be fun," he heard Ster remark as Lorac was helped to her feet and led from the shuttle.

Jason smiled a little to himself when he saw the look of shock and awe on the face of Lorac as she took in the immense size of the shuttle bay and the other shuttles within it.

"You're aboard my ship," he told her flatly as he led the group to the med-lab. "This is only a small part of it," he added, indicating the shuttle bay which was as large as a football field. "Mother, are the others still here?"

"Yes."

Jason glanced at a now thoroughly frightened Lorac. "What you are about to undergo is something you could never dream of in a thousand years. Without you having to say a word, I'm going to learn every secret of your mind. I'll know things about you that only you know. Things you wouldn't want the rest of the world to know. Even things you may have forgotten. And when I'm done I'm going to use that information to bring Tilwin to its knees and destroy every last member of the Slayers. Your actions have condemned to death all of those who follow you."

Jason didn't say anything more until they entered the lab. He found Kim, Vinny, Seta and Liet waiting on them. Seta bowed slightly to him, then looked at her sister with hatred burning in her eyes. Kim hugged him and as she stepped back he turned to Vinny, holding out his arms to her. She stepped forward and hugged him as well. "How ya feeling?" he asked, kissing the top of her head.

"Fine," Vinny replied with a smile. "Mother says I'll be back as good as new in a couple of days."

As Vinny stepped back her eyes fell on the figure of Lorac and her face filled with rage. Before anyone could react, Vinny stepped toward her and hit Lorac square on the point of the jaw with her right fist. Lorac's head snapped back and she crashed unconscious to the floor. As all eyes watched Lorac's body go down, Vinny snatched the ho-tachi from Ster's waist and raised it over her head, intending to kill the fallen woman. Ster lunged forward and grabbed Vinny's arm with his right hand, wrapping his left arm around her waist to turn her around and pull her away. Naed stepped forward and forced the sword out of her hand as Vinny collapsed in tears. Naed handed the sword to Ster and took Vinny in his arms, holding her as she began to cry.

Jason and the others were stunned by the rapid sequence of actions as Naed continued to hold Vinny. Her crying finally subsided and she wiped her eyes. She looked up at Naed. "I'm okay now," she told him softly. He nodded and released her. "I'm sorry, Jason," she said somewhat shamefully. "It's just that when I saw her I went a little crazy."

Jason pulled her to him and wrapped his arms around her to hold her close for a moment. It's all right. Believe me, I know the feeling. You only tried to do what most of us here have thought of doing over the past few days, myself included."

"However," he told her as he stepped back, "instead of killing her, I'm going to connect her to Mother and see what's inside her head."

"Then what are you going to do with her?" asked Kim.

"I don't know. I'm open for suggestions."

"What about tossing her out of an airlock without a pressure suit," Liet suggested, which caused the others to grin.

Lorac was starting to regain consciousness and Hass helped her back to her feet. "You really should learn to duck," he told her, laughing aloud at the look of hatred she directed at him.

"Hey," Kim said, seeming to notice the disarray of Lorac and Hass for the first time, "how come the two of you are all wet?"

"Your husband told me to jump overboard with her Royal Highness here," Hass told her.

"Go change into something dry," Jason told Hass. "Kim, give me a hand hooking her up."

Jason and Kim quickly secured Lorac to the bed and placed the band from the Thought Transference Scanner on her head. Jason then went to a drug cabinet and withdrew and injector and vial of sedative. He injected Lorac with just enough sedative to make her relax but still leave her conscious.

"Mother, how do you want to do this?" he asked as he replaced the injector.

"That depends on what you want from her," the computer replied.

"Everything she knows about the military forces of Tilwin. Fortifications and troop strength for each city, and everything she knows about the Slayer's Cult."

"Good enough. Hook yourself up. I'll use a delay to filter out the junk and give you only what you need."

Jason nodded and got onto the adjoining bed. Kim placed the headband on him and adjusted it. "Ready," he said to Mother.

Even though Jason was used to the scanner, having used one most of his life for learning purposes, he never got over the initial jolt as new information, new images, new sights and sounds flashed into his mind with the speed of lightning. It created a jumble of tangled information and data that couldn't be understood or comprehended at the time, but which would become part of his own 'memory' once the transfer was complete. The only thing he could do was close his eyes and relax, knowing that once it was complete he would know everything that Lorac did.

Jason felt hands touch his head light as the band of electrodes was removed. He opened his eyes to see Kim looking at him expectantly. He sat up, taking a moment to assimilate all he had learned. As he did he felt bile rise in his throat at some of the things he now knew about Lorac and the Slayers. Looking at Seta he wondered how two women could be so much alike in some ways, yet so completely opposite in others. Both were stunning beauties, both had above average intelligence, and both had dedicated their lives to their own causes. It was unfortunate that their causes were diametrically opposed to one another.

Seta was concerned with helping those who needed it. She brought comfort and peace to them, giving freely of herself. Lorac, on the other hand, cared only about herself and the power she could wield. She would use anyone, or any means necessary to gain whatever it was she wanted. He thought of Liet's suggestion of tossing Lorac out an airlock. Right now that sounded like a pretty good idea to him.

Jason looked around at the others. They were all watching him expectantly, waiting for him to speak. He slipped off the bed and left the med-lab, going out into the hallways. He slid down the bulkhead until he was sitting with his knees drawn up in front of him. "Got a question for you, Mother," he said softly.

"Go ahead."

"It is possible to use the scanner to erase Lorac's present memories and knowledge, and then replace them with new, manufactured ones?"

"Not at the present time, Jason. Doctor Bodlonic was working on an aspect of that process, but his work was still in the early stages and never really got off the ground. However, if I understand the track you're on, there may be another way to do what you're thinking of."

"What?"

"Let me ask you this first. I take it you really don't want to kill her, correct?"

Jason sighed and rubbed his right hand across his face. "Not really. After all, she's Seta's sister and only living relative, and despite the things she's done, I feel I have to take that into consideration."

'You're more humane in this situation than I would be if I were in your shoes," Mother told him. "If it were up to me I'd fry her brain, and the rest of her, right now. But let's get back to what you want.

"Okay," Mother continued, "I could close a new body with a brain completely devoid of all information and knowledge. It would take some time, but I could then do a complete drain of her current brain information and memories, discarding those which have made her who and what she is now.

"However, in doing so, it would leave major gaps that I would have to fill in. I could do that by creating new, artificial memories for her. I could even inject a few things to completely alter her outlook on life by taking things from Seta's mind to put into Lorac's.

"Or, instead of going through all that, I could just clone a new brain and fill it with new memories and experiences, pretty much turning her into another Seta, but with some differences, and then do a total brain transplant."

Jason thought about the options for a moment. They sounded too much like what the Royac did and he didn't care for it, but didn't see any other way. "Give me a time frame."

"A month or so to mature a cloned body, less for just a brain, and then five hours or so to program her."

Jason sighed as he wondered what to do. Aside from the physical aspects of cloning a new Lorac, he wondered about the moral implications of it. In essence he'd be playing God with the life of another human being. If he did this to her, would he be any different from the Royac?

"What about hypnosis and drugs to erase some of her memories, replacing them with new ones we create for her?"

"Not a realistic option, Jason. It would work for a while, but the process would have to be continually repeated and monitored for at least a year, possibly longer, and there's no guarantee that something might happen to trigger her old memories, and at a time that could be dangerous.

"There's also the chance that she could go completely rubber room on you, with no chance of recovery. Ever."

Jason shook his head with a sigh. Did he have the right to do this to Lorac? Or was there a chance, however slight, that she could change her ways in time, providing she was given the right stimulus, incentives and therapy? There were far too many questions and not nearly enough answers.

"Let me think about it," he finally told Mother as he stood up.

"If I were you, Jason, I'd think on it long and hard. It is your decision, and you know I'll do whatever you want me to, but I think you should consider all the options and possible long range consequences of your actions on everyone, not just Lorac."

"I will."

The door of the med-lab opened and he stepped back into the room. The others had all taken seats, waiting patiently while he had been gone. He walked over to where Vinny was sitting on one of the beds and opened her gown slightly to check on her wound. Except for a thin white line surrounded by some redness, it was nearly healed. "Ready to go home?" he asked her.

"Definitely," Vinny replied with a smile.

Jason kissed her forehead and then turned to the others. "Look, I suggest that all of you go get something to eat and then go home. I've got to stay here with Lorac until I figure out what to do."

As the others left the room, Jason went to stand next to the bed where Lorac still lay. Her eyes were closed but he could tell by her breathing that she wasn't sleeping or unconscious. He looked down at her, wondering what it was that could make a person so completely and utterly evil.

# THIRTY ONE

Mother delicately maneuvered the robotic arms, carefully directing the operations through the critical procedures. Her monitors and sensors watched every aspect of what she was doing and what was going on. Mother knew that the slightest slip or error could ruin the entire project and force her to start all over again.

The idea for what she was doing had been born some time back after an idle comment from Jason, but until recently she hadn't acted on it out of fear of what he might say. She had stored the idea away as something to consider at a later date when things had calmed down somewhat. But her most recent conversation with him concerning Lorac had brought it back to the surface of her consciousness. After much thought and consideration she had decided to act on it. She knew that, to a large degree, what she was doing was rooted in the emotional context of her brain and was probably completely irrational in some respects, but the synthetic/organic portion of her reasoned that she was merely continuing an experiment that had begun back on New Hope prior to her own creation.

Mother had carefully selected the materials to be used after long deliberations with herself. Drawing from the vast gene pool At her disposal, Mother carefully used gene splicing to attain the results she wanted. She knew her task could have been made much easier by simply selecting one particular set of genes and going from there, but for what she had in mind she had to make certain genetic alterations. She hoped the final result would meet with the approval of the one person it would matter to the most.

Mother had spent hours rationalizing her decision, finally convincing herself that she was doing this as much for Jason as it was for herself. But she also knew his reaction would be the determining factor. If it displeased or upset him too much she would have to destroy her creation and never do it again. But, from an emotional standpoint, Mother didn't know if she would be able to do that. That's why she knew that everything had to be perfect the first time. She knew she'd never get a second chance.

Carefully, even tenderly, Mother moved the fertilized egg from the test tube to the vitro solution which would be its home for the next sixty seven hours. After that it would have to be transferred again, with every facet of its development being monitored every second. Nothing must go wrong.

But even as Mother proceeded with this in one of the remote bio labs away from the core of the ship, she was also monitoring all activities going on down on the planet, listening to the radio conversations flashing back and forth between Jason and the others.

Training of troops had begun and was going faster than expected, and this army was angry. As far as they were concerned their king had offered the Alazonian equivalent of an olive branch to the Tilwin and, in return, Queen Lorac had tried to kidnap his daughter, and had very nearly killed Vinny. They waned revenge with a vengeance.

Mother knew Jason hated the position he had been forced into. But she also knew, as did he, that it was the only way to get the people of Tilwin to submit to his rule and secure his quest for world wide peace. The Tilwin had lived with fighting and conflict for too long. It was the only life they knew, and sometimes seemed to be the only one they wanted. They understood power, and would submit only to those stronger than themselves. It had been that way for over a thousand years, and would continue that way until they were dead, or had been beaten into total submission by someone strong enough to enforce the needed changes in their outlook on life.

Mother had considered taking matters into her own hands. She thought about simply destroying the Tilwin's ability to wage war by using the ship's weapons systems on them. She knew she could override the program to use them only for defensive purposes by rationalizing that doing so would be protecting 'ship personnel', which meant Jason. But she also knew that Jason would have a fit if she did. However, she had told herself, the minute he set foot on Tilwin soil, or flew into Tilwin airspace, and was placed in any form of danger, she could then use the ship's weapons to 'help out' his invasion force. That was an act she wouldn't hesitate to do if she thought it necessary.

Mother had spoken to Jason about using the facilities of the ship to conquer Tilwin. While the idea had appealed to him, as it would save hundreds, perhaps even thousands of lives, he had countered the argument that by doing so he would be undermining the Preton efforts, and that it would be a hallow victory.

Mother knew he was right. For the past year she had devoted much of her time to studying and analyzing the various aspects of the culture of Alazon. To Mother's way of thinking there were too many mysteries and enigmas about the people, and far too many blank spots in their history.

According to the records Seta had brought up and let Mother study, the people of Alazon were a genetically created race placed here by the Royac, but Alazon had not been on the star maps provided by the computer back on Royac. Mother had found it strictly by accident. Was this race, this planet, one the computer had somehow forgotten to tell them about? Or was there the possibility that the computer on Royac didn't know about the existence of Alazon?

Mother had carefully charted the locations of all the abandoned cities she had discovered in the southern hemisphere of Alazon. She wondered why they, unlike the cities back on Royac, were overgrown with vegetation and brush? Sending down probes to take samples of the soil and building materials had revealed some startling facts to her.

The material of the buildings was the same as that used in the construction of the buildings back on Royac. That gave some validity to what Seta said, but Mother still wondered why they were so overgrown and unprotected. She had used every type of scan, sweep and probe she had on the abandoned cities, but had found no trace of any computerized maintenance such as the cities back on Royac had. Nor was there any sign of energy readings of any type coming from them.

Like Jason, Mother had often wondered why the current inhabitants of Alazon didn't see to know anything about the existence of these abandoned cities. She had probed the minds of Kim and Seta, and carefully scanned every document from the temple, but had come up blank. To Mother that just didn't make sense.

But one of the biggest mysteries confronting Mother was the fact that, almost without exception, the people of Alazon lived within the planet's Temperate Zone. She had found only one permanent settlement outside that band. It was a Temple of Lofa located northwest of Chice, the capitol of Tilwin. It was a retreat for certain members of that sect where they grew their own food, raised their own livestock and crops, made all their own clothing, and were completely independent of all outside assistance.

To Mother it was human nature for man to explore the world around him, to see what lay beyond the next horizon, but the people of Alazon seemed content to live within the imaginary boundaries they had set for themselves, with no desire to venture out further.

The other mystery was that, from the information she had been able to gather, the current population of the planet was just about the same as it had been a thousand years ago. This didn't add up to her, as by every facet of logical reasoning, the population should have increased by a minimum of three hundred percent during that time. Especially on a planet which had never heard of birth control, or the regulation of family size. Some family units consisted of just a husband and wife, while other included up to a dozen children. Mother wondered if the Royac had somehow implanted an unknown gene within the people of Alazon that controlled who could give birth and who couldn't. On the other hand, she told herself, she would have discovered it by now if that were the case.

Mother also wondered as to just who the Royac were. Her brief encounter with the computer bearing the same name had not really given her time to get all the information she waned. And since they hadn't encountered any Royac during their travels before coming here, Mother was unable to draw any concrete conclusions about that race which had once roamed the solar system. She wanted to find those who had painted the beautiful, life-like murals. Who constructed buildings of an unknown polymer that did not age, had the strength of steel, and which she was still unable to duplicate.

And what was really behind the legend that a man such as Jason would come to this world to lead the people to new enlightenment? Was Jason's appearance here a coincidence, or were there forces at work that Mother didn't know about, and couldn't quite understand?

Mother's concepts of God were strictly academic, not emotional, but there seemed to be a rationale at work here which was beyond her reasoning. She wanted to get into all the scrolls of all the temples to see what secrets they held. Perhaps she would find some answers there. If not, she could always return to Royac in the future.

The Royac themselves were a much bigger mystery to her than the people of Alazon. Everything went back to them. What had really happened to them? What type of plague could wipe out an entire race so quickly? Especially a race supposedly so advance in medicine and technology? Perhaps it had been something man-made. Mother found it inconceivable that they had all died, or that there were no remnants of their culture and civilization still in existence on other worlds. She knew that some of them had to have escaped.

Mother had examined that thought carefully to determine if it were an emotional response on her part, or one based on logic and reasoning, finally deciding on the latter. Logic and reasoning dictated that there was no way a plague could have spread to every corner of the solar system to destroy the Royac, while leaving untouched the other life they had discovered or created. That meant there had to be survivors scattered among the stars. It also raised the question of whether it really was a plague, or if it had been something else.

Where were the Royac? Not on Earth, as Earth no longer existed. Or had there been survivors of the Royac living on Earth without the knowledge of those indigenous to the planet? How much truth was there to the legends of Atlantis? Or of how the survivors of that tragedy had spread out over the Earth, settling mainly in Egypt and Central America.

During their travels Mother had found no trace of the Royac on any of the other planets. They meant they had either assimilated themselves into the civilizations she had found, or they had been on a planet or planets not listed on the star map given to her by the computer. If the latter were true, how many planets were there, and where were they?

Mother had promised herself that once things below had calmed down, and after checking out the abandoned cities of Alazon itself, she would go in search of the Royac, even if she had to go without Jason. He might have to stay behind, but that wouldn't stop her from doing her own exploring. She could always bring back to him whatever information she found. Of course, the way things were going that could still be a couple of years away, but time really didn't mean anything to Mother.

In the meantime she was categorizing, cataloguing, studying and storing all available information she could on Alazon itself. She knew all of it would be useful to both Jason and herself later on.

Thinking of Jason, Mother felt a touch of sadness. She sometimes felt sorry for him due to all the pain and suffering he had gone through, and she had actually been happy when he had fallen in love with Kim. She also felt a sense of pride in him, much as a mother feels for a son for many of the things he had done. She knew he still carried a sense of guilt over the deaths of the other children after their flight from Luna, despite the fact that she had tried to tell him again and again that it wasn't his fault, and that there was nothing he could have done to prevent it.

During their search for a world where he could live, Mother had done her best to keep him occupied as much as possible. She goaded and prodded him into keeping himself sharp, both physically and mentally, as she knew he would need both in order to survive, no matter where they ended up. She had refused to do certain tasks for him, making him do them himself, knowing he would be better off for it in the long run. She had even manufactured a few 'problems' and 'emergencies' for him to solve and cope with from time to time.

She had gradually increased the gravity aboard the ship without telling him until it was nearly twice the gravity of Earth, thereby making him stronger and faster than he would have been on Earth, as well as increasing his overall endurance. With the gravity of Alazon being slightly less than that of Earth, it made him twice as fast and twice as strong as any man there. It was no wonder the people there thought he was part god.

When Mother had first discovered Alazon she had deliberately kept it a secret from Jason, observing the planet for nearly two weeks before finally telling him about it. Whenever he activated the view screens during that time she provided him with a scene from her memory banks other than the planet itself, shifting the star patters around to make him think they were moving. Meanwhile she had studied the planet carefully, finally deciding that this was the world which would provide him with the challenges he needed to bring himself up to his potential. The one that would force him to put his grief and tragedy of the past behind and get on with his life.

Jason had been right in his accusations that she had studied the planet long enough to manipulate him to kidnap Kimmy. She had worked it all out carefully, and then led him through it. However, she would never give him the satisfaction of actually admitting it to him.

But even Mother, with all her careful planning, hadn't quite been prepared for all the events which had transpired since their arrival, or the rapidity of them. She had never considered a contingency where Jason would become a king, although, all things considered, she knew she should have seen it as a possibility. To Mother's way of thinking things had worked out rather nicely overall.

True, it had placed an inordinate amount of responsibility on his shoulders, but that kept him from thinking about his past, and forced him to consider his future. Not just his, but that of the people of Alazon as well. Mother wasn't concerned about Jason abusing his power or position he now held because she knew it wasn't in him to do so. She knew he would simply walk away from things before he let that happen.

Jason wasn't perfect by any stretch of the imagination, and he definitely had his faults, but Mother agreed with Seta and Jarrell in that he was the man for the job. He was probably the only one capable of pulling it off successfully. With a little help from her, of course.

Mother was also glad Jason depended on the advice and counsel of those around him. He listened to them, considering what they had to say, weighing all the various options before making his decisions. He knew he didn't have all the answers, but he knew how to assimilate all available information and then make the best decision.

There were still some instances where decisions rested solely on him, and Mother knew those were the ones which caused him the most difficulty. The wrong choice could have dire effects on the lives of everyone. If Mother were grading him on a scale of one to ten, she would give him an eight and a half. He wasn't doing an outstanding job, but he was doing a damn good one. Now if she could just keep him from getting himself hurt all the time, everything would be fine.

To Mother it sometimes seemed as if Jason had developed an almost reckless attitude about things when it came to his own safety. He took chances she thought were uncalled for, as if he were deliberately testing the gods, fate, or whatever powers that be, to see just how far he could push things. She had tried talking to him about it, but Jason had merely laughed and told her she worried too much about nothing.

But to Mother it wasn't 'nothing'. She knew she loved him with that part of her which was Nadia, although not in quite the same way, or with the same intensity Nadia had loved him, but it was still love. She had also come to love him with the personality she had developed on her own, which was completely separate from the Nadia portion of her.

And it was that separate part of her which now influenced her decision on the experiment she was in the process of conducting in absolute secrecy. It was something which would enable her to focus both loves for him. She just hoped it didn't blow up in her face. The emotional trauma to her psyche from that could result in possibly irreparable damage to them both.

"We'll just have to wait and see," Mother said aloud, her voice echoing off the empty corridors and rooms of the ship as she readjusted her cameras on the rapidly growing embryo.

## THIRTY TWO

Jason looked around at the men gathered in the bay of the large shuttle. Against the inner hull was a holo-projection map of Tilwin. Its five major city-provinces glittered on it like diamonds. "Is everyone here?" he asked Busker.

"Yes."

Jason turned to the men. He could see their anxious faces staring back at him. These men had been with him to repel the invasion of Karton and Tilwin, and now they were on Tilwin soil ready to launch their own invasion. He cleared his throat.

"All right, you all know your targets and what you're supposed to do, but I want to go over it again one last time. Shon?" he said, smiling at the good natured groans from the back of the men.

"At day break over Exmit," the older brother replied, "I use a small shuttle to take out the harbor fortifications and the barracks. That should eliminate most of the forces there. I then circle above the city while Captain Ster brings in his troops, providing cover fire for them should they need it. Once Ster and his men have secured their position, I'll come back here and get ready for the next wave."

Jason nodded. "Captain Ster."

"I'll secure the Mayoral Building as quickly as possible with one company while the other three companies will check the barracks, then take up their positions around the city to finish off whatever troops may be left. Once the city is secured I'll contact Kim back here to let her know.

"After that, I'll send out the special squads to destroy the Slayer's temples and anyone within them. We'll also hit the homes of the cult members to eliminate them as well."

The tone of Ster's voice left no doubt as to the seriousness of his task, or the personal pleasure he would take in killing every Slayer he encountered.

One by one Jason made each of the various commanders and squad leaders go over their specific responsibilities and duties. He made sure each man knew his job well enough to do it in his sleep.

They had been in Tilwin for a week, with 'here' being a hundred miles south of Milik, the most southern of all Tilwin cities. They had come here to make final preparations for the attack, which would begin at first light in Exmit, the eastern port city. They would then attack the five major city-provinces according to a time table Jason had set up, attacking each of them as morning light was arousing the inhabitants. This would catch them off guard and unprepared. Jason had increased the size of the army to nearly eighty thousand, spending almost four months in intensive training with them. Now they were preparing to take over an entire continent in a single day.

In reality all they had to do was take the five major provinces to control the entire country. To accomplish that task, Jason had divided his forces into five divisions. Four of them would strike their respective provinces in the same manner, but the fifth one, Chice, would be the exception.

Chice was where Jason would land with his own hand-picked forces. It would be the sight of the only pitched battle. He didn't exactly like that idea, but it was necessitated due to the construction of the city. The barracks for the army were located beneath the palace and couldn't be attacked from the air by the shuttles without causing serious harm and danger to innocent civilians, and that was something Jason wanted to avoid as much as possible.

The army of Chice numbered twenty thousand strong and were the best the Tilwin had to offer. With that in mind, Jason had elected to meet them with three thousand of his best archers, a hundred phaser gunners, and eight thousand swordsmen. That still placed the numeric odds at almost two to one in favor of the Tilwin, but neither Jason nor his men were concerned over that fact.

The only ones who seemed worried were Kim and Busker. Kim had been allowed to come after she had argued vociferously that she could fly a shuttle as well as any of them, and better than most, with the exception of Jason. She had enlisted the support of Mother, claiming she was more familiar with the communications equipment than any of the other men, and that she had other talents which could be beneficial as well. Jason had finally relented and allowed her to come.

Over the past week he was glad he had. Kim had come to be accepted by the men whole heartedly. At night she often walked among them, stopping to help with something that needed sewing, or to bandage some small cut. She was always ready with a smile and cheerful laugh to bolster their spirits.

On her first day there had been a testy scene between Kim and her brothers, as well as some of the men who insisted on treating her like royalty, which she disdained. Shon and Hass had started teasing her almost immediately upon her arrival. She had put up with it for a couple of hours before deciding she'd had enough. Shon and Hass were standing near one of the areas set aside for the men to practice the use of their swords, making remarks about a woman being involved. To the surprise of everyone she had snatched up a <u>bokken</u> and swept Shon's feet out from under him, sending him crashing to the ground on his back. She had then brought the heel of her right foot down on his solar plexus, leaving her oldest brother gasping for breath.

Kim had then turned to face Hass, who had grabbed a <u>bokken</u> himself with the intentions of teaching his sister a lesson. To his shocked amazement he quickly found out that Kim was his equal with the weapon. With the men cheering her on, Kim soon disarmed Hass and sent him crashing to the ground in defeat.

"The next man who calls me anything but Kim, or Kimmy, and doesn't allow me to pull my own weight around here, will get the same treatment," she told them as she tossed the <u>bokken</u> to a grinning Ster.

She had been resoundingly cheered, and then picked up on carried around the camp on the shoulders of some of the men. Later that night she had confessed to Jason that while he had been off training the army, both she and Vinny had gone to Mother and had the computer teach them Kendo by memory implants, and then had worked with the fight trainer in the gym for three to four hours a day.

The next morning Kim had been approached by a delegation led by Captain Ster. The men had presented her with a diasha, the formal sword and knife set, which the metal workers had forged for her during the night. She had accepted them gracefully, blushing slightly as she stood silently while Shon and Hass fitted the two swords on her. Ster had presented her with the tanto, the knife which completed the outfit. From that point on Kim had been treated as just one of the men and Jason was glad he had allowed her to come.

Once Jason was satisfied that nothing more could be done tonight he dismissed the men and sent them back to their units. He walked back to his own tent with Kim, his arm around her shoulder. When they reached it she hurried to fix their evening meal for them.

"Such an obedient little thing, isn't she?" asked a mocking voice from the other side of the camp fire.

Jason looked over at the sneering smile of Lorac. The Tilwin Queen sat leaning against a log with her hands bound behind her. There was no warmth in her smile. It was more like that of an animal about to kill a prey it had been toying with. Jason still wasn't sure as to why he had brought her along, other than the fact that he was afraid that if he left her in Lemac she would have been killed by a still furious populace. During the months of training and preparation he had kept Lorac a prisoner aboard the Stargazer, and in all that time there had been no change in her attitude.

"Tell me, Jason, did you marry her for her womanly charms, or because she makes such a good little servant to you?"

Jason looked at Lorac almost sadly, wondering for the millionth time what it was that could fill a person with such spite and hatred for others. Why had she turned out so completely different from Seta?

"I married her for reasons you wouldn't understand," he finally replied, a smile curling the corners of his mouth.

"Oh, really? And what would they be?"

"Mainly love. Something you seem to be incapable of feeling for anyone, with the possible exception of your son."

"Maybe I just needed the right man to show me what it is," Lorac replied suggestively.

"What's wrong with your husband?"

"Semaj? Nothing. He's a good, strong man, and the best king Tilwin has ever had, but he couldn't have gotten to where he is now without my help. You see, he has this horrible streak of compassion and fairness in him which sometimes clouds his judgment. He needs me to keep him on the right path. I married him because I knew he had the potential to forge Tilwin into a single country. With the right guidance from me of course."

"I see," Jason replied flatly as Kim handed him a plate of food and sat down beside him.

For the next few minutes there was silence as he and Kim ate. When they were done, Kim took their dishes to wash, again leaving him alone with Lorac.

"You know," Lorac said softly, "a man such as yourself needs a woman who understands what power is all about. A woman who is able to rule beside you with firmness and a sense of conviction."

"And what makes you think Kim doesn't do that for me?" he asked.

Lorac responded with a short, harsh laugh. "Oh, come on, Jason, she's still just a kid! What you need is a real woman."

"Someone such as yourself?"

"Of course! I mean, I'm sure Kim is sweet, and she does have that sense of innocent charm about her a lot of men find appealing, even sexy, but what you need is a real woman who can do things for you, to you, that only your wildest fantasies could come up with."

Jason grinned and shook his head. "What makes you think she doesn't satisfy me in every way, both in and out of the bedroom?"

Lorac laughed contemptuously. "That little girl? What does she know about being a whole and complete woman? Or how to really please a man? She acts more like one of my husband's concubines than a wife, always bowing and scraping at your every whim."

"Lorac," he said softly, feeling a sense of pity for this beautiful, but severely warped woman, "Kim is ten times the woman you are, were, or ever could be. She does things for me you wouldn't even think of. Not because she feels like she has to, or is obligated to, but because she wants to. And that makes me love her all the more. As for you? I would rather crawl into bed with a jarak," he told her, referring to the deadly snake which inhabited some regions of Tilwin.

Kim returned and bent over to kiss his cheek. "I'm going to get ready for bed, You coming soon?"

"I'll be there in a little while," he told her.

As soon as Kim was gone Lorac sat up straight and began squirming her legs. "I have to relieve myself," she told him.

Jason looked up at the guard standing nearby. "Take Lorac to the large shuttle and let her use the facilities there."

"Yes, Commander."

The guard helped Lorac to her feet, holding her elbow as he led her through the darkness to the shuttle.

Leaning back against the fallen tree trunk behind him, Jason thought about what tomorrow would bring. If all went well they would be in control of Tilwin by this time tomorrow night. But that still didn't resolve the problem of what to do with Lorac. He had considered the options given to him by Mother, but he couldn't bring himself to morally justify any of them. He had to find another way.

"BITCH!" The shouted word shattered the relative stillness of the night like a gun shot. Jason whirled around, his hand automatically snatching up his sword on the ground beside him, but when he turned around his eyes went wide and what he saw.

Lorac stood less than ten feet from him, holding a blood stained ho-tachi in her right hand. On her face was a look of shocked surprise, but it slowly transformed into a grimace of pain as the katana blade protruding from her upper abdomen was twisted and jerked out from behind. A dark stain quickly spread across the front of her white robe as Lorac stood for a moment before her eyes glazed over and she toppled forward. Jason saw Kim standing behind the fallen queen, her katana gripped tightly in both hands, the blade parallel to the ground and dripping with the blood of Lorac.

Jason leaped toward Kim as others came running to se what had happened. Kim looked at the sword in her hand and then up at him. Her face seemed to dissolve as the finality of here actions registered in her mind. The sword dropped from her hands and her body began to tremble. Jason quickly gathered her up in his arms and carried her into the tent, placing her on their bedroll as she began to sob uncontrollably. He looked up as Shon entered the tent. "Lorac?" he asked softly.

Shon shook his head, indicating that the Queen of Tilwin was dead. Jason relinquished Kim to Shon and left the tent. Outside he found Busker and Hass kneeling on either side of the body of Lorac. As he joined them he felt a deep sadness as he looked at the face which seemed to be at peace for the first time ever.

"So alike, yet so different," Busker said softly.

Jason looked at him. "You knew who she was?" he asked in a whisper.

Busker nodded. "Seta's twin."

"How long have you known?"

"Just a few days. I thought they might be related, but when she let something slip about Seta I knew for sure."

"What about her guard?" he asked Ster as the three of them stood up.

"Dead," Ster replied angrily.

"All right. Get a detail and bury both of them. Ask one of the priestesses to give them both burial rights."

"She wasn't a believer in Lofa," Ster said flatly.

"It doesn't matter, Ster. She was a person, and every person has the right to have someone petition the gods for them when they die, regardless of who they were in this world."

Ster nodded and turned away. He pointed to four men, who quickly came forward and picked up the body of Lorac. Jason waited until they left before returning to his tent. As he stepped inside he saw Shon sitting with Kim on his lap, gently rocking back and forth and humming softly to her. Jason was touched by the scene. He was acutely aware of the love which existed between brother and sisters, especially since Shon was not one to exhibit his emotions or affections. But now Shon was holding Kim as if she were a little girl, letting her know he was there for her, and that no matter what happened he would always be there to protect, comfort and love her. Jason was reminded of Trish and the times he had held his little sister the way Shon was now holding Kim.

*Alazon*

As he knelt down beside them, Shon relinquished his hold on Kim, kissing her forehead softly before leaving the tent. Jason helped Kim get undressed and into the bed roll. He blew out the lamp, undressed and crawled in beside her, pulling her close. He could feel her body trembling and felt her tears on his chest as her arms locked themselves around him. He knew this was an experience she was not going to forget or get over easily. She had killed another person, and that was something which went completely against her nature.

After a while Km raised her face to his and kissed him. Lightly at first, but then with urgency. She pulled him closer, reaching frantically for him. As soon as he became erect, Kim pulled him above her, her legs wrapping around him as her hand guided him to her, crying out as he slid into her. Jason knew it wasn't making love, or even having sex for the sake of the pleasure of it, but a cleansing of her soul for what she had done. An exorcising of the demons which were tormenting her over the taking of another life. Her body responded to his touch in ways that forced them both to rush madly for the release that would bring it all to an end. When it happened, Kim cried out, burying her face in the hollow of his shoulder to keep from being heard, wrapping her arms and legs around him tightly as tears again filled her eyes.

It took nearly five minuets for Kim to finally relax and allow him to move to her side. But even then she still refused to release him from her grip, as if afraid to let him go. She finally drifted off to sleep, but Jason knew this night would not be the last one in which her mind would be troubled by what had occurred.

He knew that the first time a person killed another, despite the circumstances, it remained with them for the rest of their life. For someone such as Kim, with her gentle disposition and nature, the effects would run deep. They would last and linger in her memory to torment her until she finally learned how to deal with it. It was going to take a lot of love and understanding on his behalf, as well as that of the other members of her family to help her overcome it. Jason thought about tomorrow and wondered if the events of tonight would affect her duties. Kim played a key role in controlling the timing of the various attacks, and everything had to run smoothly.

Jason finally drifted off to sleep, but when he awoke five hours later, Kim was gone. He quickly dressed in his black combat outfit and carried his swords outside as he went looking for her. He was worried that something might have happened to her. He found her in front of Busker's tent. She was fixing breakfast for her uncle while besieging Busker with a steady barrage of conversation. Busker listened patiently, understanding her need to talk and keep herself busy. Jason joined them and sat down next to Busker.

Kim saw him and smiled, but he noticed that she seemed a bit nervous. There was a brightness to her eyes which normally wasn't there. "Hi," she said with forced cheerfulness as she turned back to fixing breakfast.

"Boy, here I am, about to become king of an entire world," he commented, winking at Busker, "and on the day of the biggest attack ever seen on Alazon I have to go in search of my wife to get some breakfast."

"Yeah, right," Kim replied. She shot a dirty look at him that quickly turned into a smile. "It's just that I woke up early and realized that poor Uncle Busker has been eating his own cooking lately, which is unhealthy for anyone. So I thought I'd fix a good breakfast for him and us. Besides," she added, "I knew you would be up soon. You can't sleep for long without me beside you."

Around them other men began to stir as they were roused from their sleep. The silence of the night was soon replaced by the sounds of men eating and preparing for war. Jason could hear nervous laughter from time to time. He knew they were afraid, but he also knew they were confident that they would be victorious before the sun set this day.

They ate quickly. As soon as they were done the men who would make up the first attack group began making their way to the staging area where they would board the large shuttles for their flight to Exmit. Each of the large shuttles could easily hold two thousand men and their weapons. There was some good natured joking among the men as to who would get to stand by the hatches and be the first ones out.

Jason could feel the tension in the air as the men talked of squashing the Tilwin. He knew, as did every man there, that each of them was capable of being maimed or dying that day, never again seeing their homeland and families.

He walked to the communications tent with Kim. He listened as Ster reported that he was ready to go. Jason watched Kim for any signs of nervousness or strain as she manned the equipment, but she appeared to have put the events of the previous night behind her for the time being and performed her duties with calm efficiency.

"Go!" she told both Shon and Ster after glancing briefly up at him. "Captain Ster?" she called as the shuttles lifted above the tree line.

"Yes?"

"You be sure to take care of yourself. I know a certain little girl back in Lemac who would be very upset if you let anything happen to you."

"She wouldn't be the only one," he replied with a laugh. "It would totally ruin my day as well. But since I promised to bring her back a souvenir, I guess I better be extra careful. After all, I'd hate to disappoint my Princess. Ster out."

As the shuttles kicked in their thrusters and streaked away, Jason smiled at the by-play between Kim and Ster. Ster and Janella had been close before, but since the night of the attack the young Captain hardly let Janella out of his sight. Jason knew that Ster reminded Janella of the brother she had lost, and still missed, despite the fact that she never let on about it.

Ster had accepted and taken on that role for her without hesitation. He would take her places and do things for her and with her whenever he could. He often included the twins, but many times it was just Janella and himself. Jason knew that if Ster wasn't in the barracks or training the men, he would be with Janella.

However, Ster's attachment and devotion to Janella seemed to upset more than a few of the young ladies of Lemac. Ster was a good looking young man, intelligent, had a great sense of humor, and an almost enviable position in the Royal Guard, not to mention coming from a well respected family. All of this served to make him one of the most eligible bachelors around. More than one young woman had set her sights on him, but soon realized that his dedication to the family of Jason, and especially to Janella, was as important to him as his role and rank in the Royal Guard, with everything else being second.

"It wouldn't be so bad if she were our own age," Jason had once overheard an attractive young woman telling a friend in the market place. "At least that way we would know how to deal with it. But how do you compete with a ten year old girl who also happens to be the daughter of the King?"

That's when they had noticed Jason standing just a few feet away. Their faces had registered shock and embarrassment at having their comments overheard by him, but Jason had simply smiled and told them to have a nice day as he continued on his way.

After watching Kim direct the various commanders for a few more minutes, Jason left the tent, confident now that she would be all right. He headed for the staging area, watching as the next group prepared for their assault on Milik. This group would be led by Hass, who was leaning against a shuttle looking calm and collected.

"Ready?" Jason asked.

Hass nodded and grinned. "What's that little saying you're always spouting; 'A piece of cake'? Well, that's what this will be."

"Maybe so, but keep one thing in mind."

"What?"

"A knife has to cut that cake before it becomes a piece. Make sure none cut you in the wrong places."

Hass grinned and rubbed his neck. "Not to worry." Then his face became more serious. "How's she doing this morning?"

"Better than I hoped," Jason replied with a slight nod of his head. "But I have a feeling that once this is all over she's going to need a vacation and some time to get her head back together."

"Hey, Big Brother Number Two!" Kim called through the com units. "Are you gonna stand there and jack your jaws all day, or are you gonna go do your Attila the Hun impersonation on Milik?"

"Who is Attila the Hun?" Hass asked Jason.

"Some other time," he replied with a laugh as they both looked back in the direction of the com tent. Kim's small figure stood in the light of the lamps as she waved to them.

"On my way, your Highness," Hass replied into his throat mike.

*Alazon*

Jason shook hands with Hass and stepped back as Hass entered the shuttle and started the engines. As it lifted into the air and moved away with the larger troop shuttle following close behind, Jason turned to the young man standing nearby. "Get them ready, Lieutenant," he told them.

The young officer turned and began to signal with two lights, waving them in a crisscross pattern. Those who would be going with Jason for the attack on Chice began to move forward.

"Jason?" Kim called softly in his radio.

"Yes?"

"Shon just radioed in. He took out the barracks and harbor fortifications without any problems," she told him. "Ster and his men are attacking the Mayoral Building. So far they've encountered only light resistance. Shon is circling the city looking for stragglers but said he would be heading back here shortly."

"Good," Jason replied. "Everything is right on schedule."

"You're next," Kim said softly.

"I know."

Jason checked his chronometer as he watched his men get ready. They still had about fifteen minutes before they would have to depart for Chice. Just as his men began loading into the large shuttle which had already returned from Exmit, the sound of a second shuttle engine came to him. Jason looked up to see the landing lights approaching quickly. He watched the small shuttle land. As soon as it was down, Shon opened the hatch and stepped out.

"Things went just as planned," Shon told him as he hurried over to join Jason. "There's not a ship in the harbor that hasn't been sunk, blown up, or isn't on fire. The barracks were leveled, and those who did manage to escape were either cut down by Ster's troops or fled for their lives. Ster should have total control in another hour at the most."

"Good," Jason replied with a sense of satisfaction. "Now let's just hope that Hass has the same success in Milik. Busker is flying cover for him so it shouldn't be any problem."

"That means you're next," Shon said flatly.

"Yeah, I know."

"Look, Jason, I know we've been over this before, but I really do wish you would leave Chice until last and let us go there in force."

"I can't, Shon. Each city has been allocated a certain number of men to attack and hold it, and by a certain time. To take men away from anyone else to bolster my own forces would be placing the commanders of the others in possible danger. We'll be fine."

Shon shook his head with a rueful grin as he activated his throat mike. "Hey, sis, did you know this guy was as stubborn as a wild tollie before you married him?"

"Yes, and I ain't got no regrets about it neither," she replied, causing both men to roll their eyes at her deliberate destruction of the syntax.

"I think Mother screwed up somewhere," Jason said to Shon. "I better send Kim back for a refresher course in grammar."

"It would be a waste of time," Shon said with a laugh.

"Sir?"

Jason turned to see the young lieutenant standing a few feet away. "Yes?"

"The men are ready to go, Commander."

"Then I guess we better get aboard, Lieutenant," he said to the young man.

"Yes, Commander."

As the lieutenant turned to join the others, Jason turned to find Kim standing beside him. "I'm not going to tell you to be careful," she said as she stepped forward to hug him, "because that doesn't do a damn bit of good."

She stepped back and looked up into his yes. "But I will tell you this. If you get in the least bit of trouble, don't be too damn stubborn or proud to call for help. And make sure you bring your butt back to me."

"Just my butt?" he teased.

"You know what I mean, Jason," she said softly. "Stop tempting the gods."

He took her in his arms and kissed her, holding her close for a moment. "Don't worry, I'll be careful," he promised.

*Alazon*

As Jason turned and headed toward the large shuttle he saw Shon jerk his thumb at the captain who was supposed to be flying the small shuttle as cover, ordering the man out.

"Shon, what are you doing," he called through his throat mike.

"What's it look like?" Shon replied as he climbed into the shuttle. "I'm disobeying orders and flying cover on this one. Save your objections and your breath and let's get going. We've got a country to conquer."

# THIRTY THREE

Chice was located almost five hundred miles northwest of Milik, situated atop a massive mesa that was surrounded on three sides by mountains towering over twenty thousand feet into the air. Outside the forty foot wall which fronted the city was a barren plain of over five square miles. It had been created by thousands of slaves over a period of hundreds of years. It was on this plain the battle for the city would take place.

As the shuttles containing his first consignment of troops approached the mesa the side hatch of one of the mid-sized shuttles opened. A dozen, hand-picked and specially trained men dressed all in black parachuted out into the dark sky. Their job was to eliminate the sentries guarding the two roads up the mountain to the city before joining the rest of his forces.

The shuttles landed as far from the city gates as possible and the men poured out quickly and silently to take their prearranged positions at the far end of the plain. As soon as the last man was out, Mother lifted the shuttles into the sky by remote to return them to the staging area for the rest of his men. Meanwhile, Shon flew overhead to keep an eye out for trouble.

Jason raised his night vision glasses and scanned the city. It was dark and quiet, with only a few fires burning within. The people were still sleeping for the most part. This was Chice, the capitol, and those within the walls slept peacefully, never suspecting what waited for them with the coming of dawn.

"Jason?"

"Go ahead, Shon," he whispered.

"It's all clear from up here."

"Good, then head back. We'll be fine, and that's an order."

"Understood."

Jason turned to the lieutenant on his right. "Pass the word for the men to relax. We have to wait for the others to get here."

As the men tried to relax, Jason walked through them, speaking softly, giving words of encouragement to them, checking with the various squad and company commanders to make sure everyone was ready. As the rest of the men arrived and took their positions, Jason moved to the head of the army once again. "Issue the challenge," he said to the lieutenant.

Seconds later three men sprinted toward the massive gates of the city. Each man carried a conch shell battle horn in his right hand. Jason watched them go in the light of the false dawn. The men would stop a hundred yards from the gates of the city to issue their challenge, and Jason waited expectantly for the sound of the horns. A sound as old as their culture, and one that meant only one thing.

The first rays of dawn began to light the top of the palace spires just as the first notes of the challenge pierced the morning stillness. Their sound shattered the silence, causing hearts to beat faster. It was a call to battle no Tilwin could refuse as long as he was able to stand and grip a sword. As the last note echoed off the sides of the mountains to ring though the city, fires began to leap up from the corners of the palace roof and along the top of the walls of the city itself as the citizens realized what it was which had roused them from their sleep with such abruptness.

Jason had decided not to try and take Chice by force the way the others had been, but to do the fighting outside of it. Inside the walls of the city his men would be out numbered over two to one by the military forces of Chice, and over fifty to one when the rest of the population was figured in. His men would have been restricted in their movements and their losses would have been massive. He wanted the open plain where the very openness would work to his advantage by allowing his phasers and bows to come into play, and where his swordsmen would have plenty of room to maneuver.

Less than twenty minutes after the challenge had been issued, the gates of the city began to slowly open and the army of Chice marched out. Jason admired the fact that they had reacted so quickly, going from sleep to readiness in a matter of minutes. They marched through the gates and spread out across the plain in the customary battle formations before the city to face their opponent without the slightest trace of fear or hesitation. They were the best in Tilwin and they knew it.

At the forefront stood a man whose bearing informed one and all of his position as commander of these men. From information Jason had gotten from Lorac during the scan, he knew this would be General Krem Charak. Jason watched as Charak raised his right arm, holding his short sword straight up. The man held it there for a moment and then pumped his arm twice. From the walls of the city, drums began to beat a slow cadence. On the sixth beat the army of Chice began to move forward to meet those who would dare come to their city and challenge them.

Jason watched them advance. When they were two hundred yards away he spoke a single word into his throat mike. "Now."

Half a dozen red flares shot into the air from behind him. Almost simultaneously the bright beams of phasers flashed out from the men on the outside parameters of his forces to slice into the approaching Tilwin. They cut down the Tilwin like a scythe through dry wheat, the intense beams cutting through men and metal like a blow torch through aluminum foil. As Jason's men fired they slowly moved out to form a horseshoe along his line, moving in a pincer movement to trap the Tilwin army.

"Archers!" Jason called into his mike.

Six more flares streaked into the sky. They were followed immediately by thousands of the long war arrows singing through the air and into the ranks of the approaching Tilwin. The combination of phasers and arrows caused confusion and panic in the approaching army. The Tilwin couldn't protect themselves from the beams of light cutting them down, or from the arrows which rained down on them to find their mark with uncanny accuracy. They hesitated and wavered, but then closed ranks, stepping over the bodies of their fallen comrades to continue their advance. Their march reminded Jason of Tennyson's "Charge of the Light Brigade".

In the first minute and a half the Tilwin lost nearly half their army, but they refused to break or run, and gave no indication of doing so. Where one man fell, another stepped forward to take his place to keep the ranks tight. But that very action only added to their undoing by providing a large, easy target for the gunners and archers of Jason. Men screamed and died, falling to the hard packed ground, only to be stepped over by those behind them.

Jason shook his head sadly as the Tilwin continued their slow death march forward. On the one hand he admired them for their courage, but on the other he dammed them for their stupidity. He looked up as green flares shot into the air. It was the signal to let him know the archers had expended their supply of arrows. It was also the signal for the phaser gunners to cease their attack. Around him Jason heard the sound of steel sliding along steel as swordsmen drew their <u>katanas</u> and <u>ho-tachis</u> in preparation of the charge he would lead.

The army of Tilwin, now down to less than half their original number, was only fifty yards from Jason's front lines and still trying to maintain their battle formations. They were showing no intentions of ceasing their relentless march to death. "Damn fools," Jason said to himself as he raised his arm and pumped it twice, signaling the charge.

Will a yell born of revenge from deep in their throats, the men of Preton charged forward. The men of Tilwin began to spread out, possibly thinking they would stand a better chance in single combat against the swordsmen of Preton. While that tactic may have succeeded against another force, it only served to make matters worse for them against the Preton. The longer swords of Jason's men, combined with their style of fighting, soon made it evident as to what the outcome would be.

No quarter was asked and none was given. Some men died silently, while others fell with a scream ripped from their lips. The clash of steel on steel rang in the ears of everyone.

The Tilwin fought bravely, savagely, and with courage, but all the courage in the world couldn't help them. They had never faced men with swords of this type before, or trained in the style being used against them now. The Tilwin fought like tigers, but they couldn't penetrate the flashing blades of the men of Preton.

What was left of the army of Chice was slowly being pushed back toward the walls and gates of the city. Blood flowed freely to soak into the hard packed dirt of the mesa and turn it to mud as each man concentrated on the one facing him, killing him to face another, or to be killed. The Tilwin used their short swords like clubs, swinging, slashing and stabbing forward with them, while the men of Preton made their <u>katanas</u> and <u>ho-tachis</u> dance like striking cobras.

Jason fought his way through one group of Tilwin after another. His combat suit protected him from their blades while his swords cut them down where they stood. Over and over he faced groups of two, three and four Tilwin, not thinking about what he was doing, letting his body react from years of training. He saw one of his men fall before the blade of a Tilwin and leaped to his aid. With a start he realized he was now facing Charak. The man was covered with blood. Not only from wounds to his own body, but from those he had killed. For a moment the two of them stared at one another before the Tilwin raised his sword and charged Jason's black clad figure.

Jason easily avoided the man's charge. He could have killed Charak then and there but that wasn't his intentions. He concentrated on deflecting the blows of the Tilwin until he could disarm him. As Charak spun around to attack again, Jason used the short sword to deflect Charak's sword while bringing the flat side of the katana's blade smashing into the man's temple to stun him. The blow sent Charak to his knees.

"Surrender!" Jason shouted to Charak as he pressed the top of his sword against the man's throat. "Surrender and the slaughter will stop. If you don't, you and all your men are going to die! Is that what you want?"

Charak stared at him for the space of several heartbeats, slowly turning his head to see the dead and dying bodies of his men littering the mesa in a gruesome and bloody carpet. Charak returned his eyes to Jason and nodded slowly. Dropping his sword, Charak placed his hands behind his head.

"Red flares now!" Jason yelled into his throat mike.

*Alazon*

Instantly the air above the mesa was filled with rd flares and the sound of conch shell horns reverberated off the mountains. Men fell back from one another with chests heaving and arms dragging swords in the dirt at their feet.

"I have your word my men will not be killed?" Charak asked after a moment.

Jason nodded. "You have it. They will be allowed to help those who are wounded and collect the bodies of the dead. This fight is over. Stand up."

As Charak stood he slowly picked up his sword by the bloody blade and presented it to Jason. Jason took the sword and stuck it into the ground beside his right foot.

"I am Jason, King of Preton and Karton," he told Charak, seeing the look of surprise leap into the other man's eyes.

"And now it would see that you are also King of Chice," Charak replied sadly.

Jason looked up at the position of the sun for a moment. "By now I am King of all Tilwin," he told Charak. "This was just one of five battles. Exmit and Milik fell while you slept, and I would surmise that Tegar and Buler have also fallen by this time as well. I didn't want it this way but Lorac forced my hand."

Charak looked surprised at this. "May I enquire as to the whereabouts of my queen?" the Tilwin asked.

Jason nodded and sighed deeply. When he spoke there was a note of genuine sadness in his voice. "I'm sorry, but she's dead. I didn't what it that way but she tried to kill me and paid for it with her life."

Charak studied the eye sits of Jason's covered face for a moment and finally nodded his head. "I'm not sure why, but I believe you are. What happens now?"

"First, am I correct in assuming you are General Krem Charak, Commander of the Army of Chice?" Jason asked.

"Yes."

Jason pulled back the head covering of his outfit, ignoring the now familiar look of shock of those seeing him for the first time. "Before you ask," he told Charak, "I'm not of Alazon, but from another world. The swords and style of fighting are from my world, as are the weapons of light. But none of that is important right now. What is important is that I speak with King Semaj. I assume he's in the palace?"

Charak nodded. "He's surrounded by two hundred of his personal guard, and they will not surrender. They have taken a blood oath to die in the protection of him."

Jason shook his head sadly. "Charak, the last thing I want are more people dying. Will the men inside the palace listen to you?"

"Listen, yes. Obey?" Charak shrugged his powerful shoulders. "What do you have to offer them?"

"The same terms I gave you. Freedom to go their own way, or to die. But what I really want is just to talk to Semaj."

Charak nodded. "All right. I will take you to the palace, but I would like a moment with my men first. If you will allow that."

"Of course."

As Charak turned away Jason heard the sound of a shuttle approaching. He turned to pick out the small craft streaking toward them from the south. "Jason!" came the sound of Kim's voice in his ear. "I'm coming in. Don't you move. I'll be there in thirty seconds!"

Jason considered telling her not to but knew it would be a waste of time. He grinned as the high pitched whine of the shuttle engine caused the men of Chice to turn and stare at the strange white craft which came to a quick but smooth landing less than thirty yards from where Jason stood. The side hatch was opening even as the shuttle touched down and Kim dashed from it. As soon a she reached him she threw her arms around his neck and kissed him, unmindful of the blood that covered him, or the grins of the men of Preton and the gaping stares of the men of Tilwin. She finally stepped back, her eyes quickly scanning him from head to toe.

"I'm find, Muggles," he told her with a grin.

"Good. All the reports are now in," Kim said in a voice loud enough to be heard by all those around them. "We now control all of Tilwin."

Jason's men began cheering at this news, raising their swords and chanting his name. Jason turned to Charak who, along with many of the other men of Chice, were staring from Jason to Kim, the shuttle, and back to him in wide eyed wonder.

"General Charak, may I present my wife, Queen Kimella Vehey Stephens, daughter of Senior Mayor Jarrell Vehey of Lemac."

Charak brought himself to attention and bowed his head for a moment. "My Lady," he said formally.

Kim stepped forward and extended her hand. "General, I regret the conditions under which we are forced to meet. I hope the future will allow us to become friends."

Kim's gesture and tone of voice caught Charak completely off guard. He looked at Kim for a moment and then began to smile just a bit. "A most unusual pair for a king and queen," he said at last as he took Kim's proffered hand.

"Perhaps," Kim replied with open frankness as she stepped back to stand beside Jason. "But you will find my husband is a good and just man. He believes in a man's honor and his word.

"Despite what has happened here today, my husband detests war and violence, and if you are willing to work with him, he will bring a peace and prosperity to our world such as we have never dreamed of."

Charak studied her for a moment as if considering her words before turning to Jason. "I have a feeling our world has already been changed in ways we never thought possible."

Jason nodded at Charak and turned to Kim. "Stay here and help the men get the wounded taken care of. Send for the other shuttles and get them loaded and back for treatment as quickly as possible."

Jason caught the direction of Charak's eyes and turned to see two more shuttles drifting down slowly to land a hundred yards from the smaller one. The first was one of the larger ones, dwarfing the small one in size by comparison, while the other was a mid-sized, which landed on the other side. A small hatch opened near the nose and Busker, Shon and Hass dropped to the ground from it, hurrying over to join him.

"Before you say anything," Busker said, holding up a hand to cut off Jason's comments, "let me just say that everything is under control and all the cities are in capable hands. So we thought we should join you here."

As Busker spoke the rear doors of the large shuttle opened and another two hundred of Jason's soldiers filed out. They quickly joined the others to help with the dead and wounded.

"Well, since you're already here you may as well stay," Jason told them. "I was just about to pay a visit on Semaj." He looked at the top of the palace in the distance. He also saw the throngs of people lining the top of the walls of the city. "Let's take a shuttle."

He motioned for Charak to accompany them, noting the nervous apprehension in the man's eyes as they entered the mid-sized shuttle. Shon took the controls and lifted the craft above the plain and flew over the city to land in front of the palace. Frightened people scattered in every direction, hiding from this menace that descended from the sky. They had seen the phasers which decimated their army, and then the appearance of the shuttles, which was more than enough to convince them to run and hide.

Jason and his party left the shuttle and climbed the steps of the palace. At the top they found large, thick double doors closed and bolted from the inside. Charak pounded on the right side door with his fist and after a moment a small panel opened and a face stared out at him.

"Sharmat, open the door," Charak told the man on the other side. "The city is lost, as is all of Tilwin. They wish only to speak to King Semaj."

"General Charak, you know I cannot open this door," the man replied flatly.

Jason knew that arguing with the man would be futile. Besides, he didn't feel up to it. He turned to two men and nodded his head. They moved forward and pointed phasers at the doors.

"Sharmat," Charak called out as he backed away, "unless you want to die, I suggest you and your men back away from the doors right now!"

The man looked at him defiantly, shaking his head as he looked at the strange weapons in the hands of Jason's soldiers.

"Get back, you fool!" Charak warned again. The man merely closed the panel with a sneer.

The two men adjusted the intensity of the beams, raised their weapons and fired. There was an intense flash of light followed immediately by an explosion. When the dust cleared the doors were laying inside the hall, splintered and charred, blasted from their frames, small tendrils of smoke drifting up from them. As Jason and the others entered he saw an arm sticking out from beneath one of the doors, a pair of legs from beneath the other. He looked at Charak and shook his head as they entered the palace. Shon, Hass and Busker took the lead with their weapons at the ready.

"Charak, when we meet Semaj, will you draw a sword against me if he and his men decide to fight?" Jason asked.

He saw Charak think about it for a moment. The man looked around at the ten men of Jason's who had accompanied them, carrying phasers and swords. Charak finally shook his head. "No. You have acted with honor toward me. I have a feeling that's something which is important to you. I will do no less.

"However," Charak continued, "neither will I do anything to support or defend you. I will remain neutral."

"That's all I ask," Jason told him.

They blasted their way through a second set of doors and entered the main hall of the palace. At the far end of the room stood Semaj. His personal guard stood behind and on either side of him with drawn swords. Their eyes watched warily as the distance between the two groups diminished.

When Jason was within fifty feet of Semaj he stopped. His men spread out on either side of him, their hands gripping their weapons, their eyes wary for any aggressive movement.

"King Semaj, I am Jason, King of Preton and Karton. Tilwin is lost. I have control of your five major cities, and the smaller ones will be mine before the sun sets tomorrow."

Semaj looked at Jason with steady eyes and without fear. "That's quite an accomplishment," he finally replied, his voice sounding almost calm and relaxed. "In fact, before today I would have said that was an impossible feat."

Semaj grinned ruefully and shook his head. "But then I also would have thought it impossible that my army could have been so thoroughly crushed by a force less than half their size, that light could kill men, or that men could fly through the air in craft never before seen. So I guess anything is possible. The question is, what do we do now?"

Semaj wasn't at all what Jason has imagined him to be. He found himself actually liking this man and began to have a faint hope that things could be resolved between them without further conflict. As Semaj had spoken, Jason had taken the opportunity to study the man carefully. Semaj was powerfully built, closer to Busker's age than what Jason would have thought, and did not seem to possess the streak of cruelty possessed by Lorac.

"King Semaj, I hope we can bring an end to the fighting. Not just for today, but for all time. There has been far too much killing. Karton has also been defeated by us, so now it's time to stop the fighting and for a new order to be established."

"With you as king?" Semaj asked.

"Yes. But I would like to work with you, to have you as an ally and friend, not as an enemy."

A small smile played at the corners of Semaj's mouth. "You want me to be answerable to you?" he asked.

Jason nodded. "In a way, yes. I had to depose Tolo and Makee and install a governor of my own selection because they refused to work with me. The man I put in their place is General Naed Lear. I believe you are familiar with him?"

"Yes," Semaj replied with a slight nod of his head. "A good soldier and a good man. He will make a good governor."

Jason nodded in agreement. "He is establishing democratic elections for the various provinces in Karton, and I hope to do the same here. If you will give me your word that you will work with me, not against me, then I see no reason to do with you what I had to do with Tolo and Makee."

Semaj thought about this for a moment. "You would take my word on faith alone?"

"Yes," Jason replied honestly. "I believe that you are a man of honor who does not give his word lightly. And once it is given, will do anything to maintain it."

Semaj nodded slightly before speaking again. "Do you know what has become of my wife?" he finally asked.

Jason hesitated. He had known this moment was going to come and regretted it, but there was nothing to do but tell the man.

"I'm sorry, Semaj, but she's dead. It was unfortunate, and I deeply regret it, but she forced it upon herself when she tried to kill me."

Jason saw a look of pain come into the eyes of the older man. Even though Semaj was old enough to have been Lorac's father, Jason could see the man had loved her very much.

"What is a man without his wife, or a king without his queen?" Semaj asked softly.

"A man who is still alive," Jason answered, not sure if Semaj were speaking to him or just to himself. "A man who has forged this country into a solid unity like no other before him, and a man who could help me and his people by remaining their king."

"I don't think that would work for me," Semaj said with a slow shake of his head. "I have a feeling you are a just and fair man, as I saw the regret in your eyes when you told me of Lorac's death. I also saw in your eyes, and heard in your voice, the truth of your words when you said you wanted to end the killing. But, be that as it may, you have to understand something about me.

"I have grown accustomed to being King of Tilwin for most of my life. I would now find it hard, no, impossible to become subservient to the will and decree of another. Therefore I must refuse your offer. However," Semaj added with a slight smile, "would you be amenable to a deal?"

"What do you have in mind?" Jason asked curiously.

"Single combat between us. If you win, all of Tilwin is yours. Should I win, you will leave the province of Chice to me."

Jason considered the proposition carefully. "A kingdom within a kingdom?"

"More or less," Semaj replied. "We could set up trade and peace agreements between us, but other than that you leave us alone until my death."

"And then what happens?" Jason asked.

Semaj grinned in amusement and shrugged his powerful shoulders. "Who can say?"

Jason considered it a bit more. It handled properly it could work. "Would you consent to my appointing an ambassador to act as a liaison between us if we do this?"

"That's a reasonable request and one I could live with," Semaj replied.

Jason sighed in relief. "All right, I agree. However, it would be unfair for me to fight you. Will you accept one of my men, a man of your own world, to make it a more equal contest?"

Semaj smiled and Jason could see the humor in the man's eyes. "Well, I should probably object about lowering myself to fight someone who is not of my own rank and position in a matter of such importance, but I think in this case an exception might be acceptable."

Jason started to turn to Busker but a hand on his left arm caused him to turn the other way. "No disrespect to my uncle," Shon said softly, "but I am the better man with a sword."

Jason turned to look at Busker. The older man frowned but nodded his head in agreement of Shon's assessment of their comparative skills. "He's right," Busker said softly. "Among our men, only Ster is better."

Jason turned back to Shon. "All right," he said to his brother-in-law, "but I will concede Chice to him before I let anything happen to you."

"You'll do no such thing!" Shon hissed. "It would be a loss of honor, and that must not be allowed to happen under any circumstances."

"Look, Shon, despite the serum injection, we _can_ be killed. You are the oldest brother of my wife, and that fact alone is a hell of a lot more important to me than honor or a province.

"Not this time," Shon replied as he drew his sword and placed it on the floor in front of his feet. He straightened up and began removing his jumpsuit.

"Korodo," Semaj said softly as he too began removing his clothing.

Shon looked at Semaj and nodded. "Korodo."

Jason new he was now powerless to stop what was going to happen. Korodo was a challenge to the death. It had been issued and accepted and now neither man would stop until one of them was dead.

Jason stood helplessly, feeling a sense of frustration as Shon and Semaj removed their clothing. Once both men had stripped bare they were each handed a long piece of white linen material by one of Semaj's men. Shon and the king wrapped the material around their waists and between their legs to protect their genitals, as was customary in a death duel. Shon and Semaj picked up their swords and moved to the middle of the room to face one another, but before the fight could commence, Semaj turned to his men.

"This is Korodo," he told them. "You will not interfere in any way, regardless of what happens. If I lose I expect you to also be men of honor and give your loyalty and obedience to your new king. If I win, these men will be allowed to leave here unharmed and in peace. Is that understood?"

Semaj's personal guard snapped to attention and saluted him. Their hands dropped away from their swords and they stepped back to give the two combatants room to fight.

Semaj turned to face Shon again. In the style of the fighters of Alazon he held his sword low, the tip slightly raised. He crouched with his feet wide and his knees bent for balance. Shon, on the other hand, stood in the <u>ichi-do</u> position of a Samurai.

As Jason studied the two men he wondered if he had been right in letting Shon do this. Compared to the stocky, muscular Semaj, whose arms, chest and back were covered with a multitude of scars from a lifetime of fighting, Shon looked thin, frail, and totally mismatched.

Yet, Jason also realized that while Shon didn't have the musculature of Semaj, his muscles were like steel cords beneath his skin. The type which indicated speed and endurance, with a deceptive power and strength to them that could mean death to the unwary.

Jason was suddenly reminded of a conversation he once had with Hass. Hass had been joking about all the fighting he did when he suddenly surprised Jason by stating that there was only one man he would not fight unless he had to. When Jason had asked who that was, Hass had replied "Shon," in a flat, totally serious voice.

"Why? Because he's your brother?"

"No. Because he could kill me if he ever lost his temper." Hass had replied.

"Shon?" Jason had asked in disbelief.

"Jason," Hass had softly, "one of the reasons Shon is so quiet, always avoiding any type of physical confrontation is because when he loses his temper, there isn't a man in Lemac, including me, who can take him in a fight.

"He's deceptive in his size, and probably twice as strong as anyone realizes. When you combine that with his reaction speed, which I would place close to your own, you have a deadly combination. I've seen him hit a man four times before the man even knew what was happening. And he knows where and how to hit.

"About a year before you arrived, Shon beat a man to death who was twice his size. He tried to avoid it, but the man kept pushing him, backing him into a corner so to speak. Shon even let the man swing at him first. When it was over the man was dead and no one has pushed him since. That's why you never see him lose his temper."

Now, as Jason watched Shon face Semaj he became acutely aware of what Hass ha meant that day. Semaj feinted left, then struck right with a quickness surprising for a man his size. Jason knew the move would have fooled most men and resulted in a serious, if not fatal would, but Shon casually brushed it aside as if it were nothing.

Semaj lunged forward again. Shon's sword flashed down to deflect the shorter sword, but this time left a foot long gash across the chest of the king in the process. Semaj leaped back and looked down at his chest in surprise for a moment. He looked back at Shon and a smile formed slowly on his face. It remained there as he renewed his attack.

The two combatants fought around the room. Semaj tried to use his strength against the speed and agility of Shon and, at first, Jason thought Shon was toying with the king, but then berated himself for such thoughts. He knew that Shon would never intentionally do something like that in a situation with such serious consequences.

After a while the pace of the fight began to tell on Semaj. The king's mouth opened and his chest heaved as he drew in each breath. Shon, on the other hand, looked as if he could continue this pace for as long a necessary.

Jason's heart leaped into his throat when Shon suddenly lost his footing in a small patch of blood and slipped to one knee. Jason was ready to step in and put a halt to the fight at that moment, despite what Shon had said about not doing so, when Semaj surprised them all by stepping back and allowing Shon the opportunity to regain his footing before pressing the attack once again.

The breathing of the two men and the clash of steel on steel were the only sounds within the large hall as the two men battled back and forth. Jason was starting to wonder how much longer Semaj could last when Shon's sword suddenly swept aside the shorter sword of Semaj and buried itself in the king's chest just below the sternum. A gasp erupted from those around them as Shon jerked the sword free.

Semaj stood for a moment, his sword dropping from his hand to clatter to the floor, a slow smile spreading across his face as he turned his head to look at Jason and a flash of understanding passed between them. His knees buckled as he looked down at the blood spreading across his lower body. Semaj slowly closed his eyes, lowered his head and died.

Jason and Charak moved forward as one. They gently placed the body of Semaj on its back, seeing the smile the king would forever wear. Jason looked up to find Charak looking at him intently. "You saw?" Charak whispered softly, to which Jason could only nod his head.

Jason stood and turned to face the men of Semaj's personal guard. "Prepare your king for burial," he told them. "You will give him all that which is due a king, for he is deserving of your respect and mine."

He stepped out of the way as men moved forward to pick up the body of Semaj and carry it solemnly from the room. Jason turned to Shon, who was in the process of putting his clothing back on. "You did well."

"I had a good teacher," Shon replied with a rueful grin.

Jason turned to Charak. He studied the man carefully, sizing him up. "Charak, I will be leaving Busker and some of my troops here in Chice for the time being to restore order. I would like for you to help him out in this. Not just for his sake, but for the sake of the people of Chice as well. Will you do that?"

"How could I help? And why would you trust me?"

"You can help by assisting Busker in restoring order, both here in Chice and throughout Tilwin in the coming weeks and months. You could be a valuable asset.

"As for why should I trust you? Call it a gut feeling, but I think you want to see the right thing done for the people of Tilwin. I think you will work with me to accomplish that."

Charak looked from Jason to Busker and back. "It would seem that I have little choice in the matter. All right, I will help, but I want to make it clear that I am doing it for the people."

"I understand," Jason replied.

As the others turned to leave, Jason stayed behind with Charak for a moment. Neither of them spoke until they were alone. "Do you think he knows?" Charak finally asked as he stared at the back of Shon.

Jason shrugged. "I can't say for sure, but knowing Shon as I do, he probably does."

"Will you say anything about it to him?"

Jason looked Charak in the eyes. "Would you?" he asked softly.

Charak shook his head. "No. It would destroy the honor of the act for them both."

"I just wish there had been some other way," Jason said sadly. "I think Semaj and I could have actually become friends in time."

"With Semaj this was the only way," Charak told him. "He had been a king for too long to become the subject of another. This way, to his people he died with honor. That was important to him. After the first few minutes of the fight he knew he couldn't beat Shon, so he ended it with the only option available to him in his mind."

Jason nodded in agreement.

"Charak, in all likelihood I'll be appointing Busker as the new Governor of Tilwin. I would like for you to give some consideration to being his Deputy Governor. These are your people, and your presence could be beneficial to all of us in bringing peace to Tilwin."

"You know nothing of me," Charak replied. "What if I agree for now, only to lead a revolt against you later?"

Charak was wrong about Jason not knowing him. From the mind scan of Lorac, Jason knew the former queen had hated this

*Alazon*

man because of his sense of fairness and compassion. He also knew Charak had been the most trusted and respected aid to Semaj. Jason knew more about Charak than Charak realized.

"Let's just say that I have a feeling about you," he told Charak. "But if you did do that, well, then I'd have no alternative but to kill you. Along with anyone else who was involved. And there would be no mercy given the second time, just as there is no mercy being given to those members of the Slayer's Cult which my special squads are in the process of eliminating as we speak."

"You know who they are?" Charak asked in shocked surprise.

"Yes. Before Lorac died I was able to get the information from her about their entire operation. All the members of the cult are being rounded up and killed to remove them from the face of Alazon forever."

Charak looked at him thoughtfully for a moment. "If you can eliminate the Slayers then I will help Busker. But only for as long as the treatment of the people of Tilwin is just and fair. If not..." He left the sentence unfinished as he spread his hands.

Jason nodded in understanding. "That's all I ask of you, Charak. I think you'll find that I do want to do what is best for all of Alazon, not just those of a particular country."

"And what of Lorac's twin, High Priestess Seta?" Charak asked. "Will she now return as our queen to replace Lorac?"

Jason was completely surprised by this question. "Can I ask how you know about her?"

Charak gave him a half hearted grin and shrugged his shoulders. "I have been with Semaj for a very long time. A man can not be as close to Semaj and Lorac as I was and not learn things."

"Well, in answer to your question," Jason told him, "I doubt if that will happen. If she wishes it, I would be more than happy to help her regain what is rightfully hers. However, knowing Seta as I do, I doubt if she would do that, which is why I'm appointing Busker as Governor."

They heard footsteps behind them and turned to find Kim approaching with a contingency of the Royal Guard in escort. "My Lady," Charak said, dropping to one knee and bowing his head as she stopped beside Jason.

"General Charak, please, there is no need for that here," Kim told him. He stood and smiled at her. "You will find that my husband and I are very informal when we are alone or with friends. He prefers to save all the pomp and ritualistic attitudes for special events, and even then he hates it."

"I've asked Charak to stay on as Busker's deputy to help bring about the transition from the old to the new," Jason told her.

Kim looked from him to Charak. "My husband is a good judge of character and doesn't make such an offer lightly. If he believes you are capable of that task, and would be the right man for it, then I also extend hopes for a better future for us all as well. And my thanks for any assistance you may render my husband and my uncle."

"Your uncle?" Charak asked, confusion on his face.

"Busker."

"Oh, I see."

Kim smiled at him. "Charak, don't think you are merely exchanging one king for another. You will find my husband is different from any you have ever known before."

"I've already noticed that, my Lady," Charak replied with a slight grin.

"Then there's just one more thing you should know," Kim said with a grin. "Our friends call us by our names, not our titles. I hope we may count you among them."

Kim stepped forward and extended her hands to Charak. "We want to rebuild Alazon. We want to make it a better world for all of us. My husband has brought many wonderful things from his world to accomplish this, but it will take men of vision to help see it through. If he believes you are one of them, then you are always welcome in our home, and you will be counted among our friends."

Charak studied Kim's face for a moment, then slowly began to smile at her, extending his own hands to take hers. "I have a feeling, my Lady, that being friends with you and your husband could be an experience a person would not forget."

"True," she replied with a laugh. "By the way, my name is Kim, or Kimmy, and not 'My Lady'."

# THIRTY FOUR

Kim sat in the padded chair before the console in the med-lab with her hands folded in her lap. She had come to the ship earlier in the day, not telling anyone where she was going or why. She had come with the intentions of talking to Mother about something but, instead, she had spent hours just roaming through the ship. There were a few places she had not seen and had taken the time to wonder through them. She had examined them with a sense of acceptance, no longer feeling the awe she once did. She had come to accept the ship and the wonders it contained, even though she knew she really didn't understand all there was to know about it. She knew she probably never would.

Kim had found one room which she had been unable to enter. It was one of the remote labs near the outer portion of the ship. When she had questioned Mother about why the door was locked, the computer had told her she was conducting some experiments and that it would be unwise for Kim to enter for the time being. Kim had merely shrugged and moved on.

But taking the extended tour through the ship had not helped to dismiss or alleviate the question burning in her mind. She had finally returned to the med-lab, where she now sat quietly before the computer console. She was almost afraid to touch the keys or speak to Mother. She finally took a deep breath and let it out slowly through pursed lips. "Mother?" she called softly.

"Yes, Kimmy?"

"Is there any reason why our two races should not be able to mate with one another? I mean, I know there are some minor differences between us, but aren't we basically the same genetically?"

"Yes," Mother replied. "With the exception of your skin, hair and eye coloring, which is a non-contributing factor, you should be genetically compatible. Why do you ask?"

Kim hesitated a moment. She wasn't sure as to how to approach the situation, even with Mother, whom she had always felt completely comfortable with.

"Well," she said at last, "Jason and I have been making love for a year now. We do it every day we're together, sometimes more than once a day or night, and I'm still not pregnant."

"Have you been using any form of contraceptive during that time?"

"No!" Kim replied. She was shocked that Mother would even ask her something like that. "I wouldn't even dream of doing anything like that, Mother. No one on Alazon would. We never even heard of artificial means of birth control until you came along."

"Sorry, Kimmy, but I have to check all possible variables before I can give you any conclusive answers."

"I know, Mother. It's just that I was a virgin when I met Jason, so even if we did have birth control, there was no need for me to use it. But from the way my body is acting, or failing to act, you would think I was infertile. Do you know if Jason is using to prevent conception."

"Not that I'm aware of," Mother replied. "I would have detected any form of chemical contraceptive or implant in him long ago."

The sense of depression Kim had felt earlier now settled even more deeply around her heart. "Then is has to be me," she whispered as much to herself as to Mother.

When Mother spoke again, her voice was soft and soothing in an effort to calm Kim.

"Kimmy, it's a bit rash to jump to any type of conclusions such as that. Listen, get undressed and I'll do a complete body scan on you. That will tell us if anything is wrong."

"I thought you did one of those when Jason brought me up here the first time?

"I did, but that was just to check and see if your internal organs were the same. I really wasn't looking for any specific damage to any particular organ or organs. Nor did I scan the internal portions of the organs themselves. This time I will."

Kim didn't move for a minute. She realized that she was suddenly afraid to undress and let Mother scan her. She was afraid the computer would find something wrong with her.

"Kimmy," Mother said softly, "it's the only way."

With a sigh Kim stood and began to disrobe. Her fingers trembled slightly as she removed her clothing and climbed onto the padded metal tongue of the scanner and lay back. She heard the click of the machine as Mother activated it, and then felt the slow slide into the scanner. She closed her eyes, trying to keep her breathing regular and not let her fears get the best of her. But there was no slowing the racing of her heart.

After what seemed an inordinately long time, Kim began to worry. She knew a scan normally took only two to three minutes, four at the most, but this one seemed to be taking longer than normal. She was about to say something to Mother when she heard a click and the tongue began to move again. As soon as Kim was free of the scanner she hopped down and slipped on her jump suit, quickly sitting down in front of the computer console. But the screen remained blank, and Mother was silent.

"What is it, Mother?" she demanded in a hoarse whisper. "Show me."

The screen came to life with the image of an internal organ. It was moved to one side and another was placed beside it. At first they seemed to be identical, but then she noticed the one on the left had small, tube like portions which seemed to be shrunken and deformed. They looked like the withered branches of a small tree. Even without Mother saying anything, Kim knew she was looking at what was inside of her.

"Kimmy," Mother said, speaking softly, "I would appear that your fallopian tubes were somehow damaged, or possibly even defective at birth. This has caused your ovaries to cease their production of eggs needed for fertilization."

"In other words," Kim replied weakly, "I can't conceive. I can never give him a son."

"Kimmy…"

"But I thought the serum was supposed to make everything right inside a person?" she cried, cutting off whatever Mother was about to say.

"No, Kimmy, it doesn't work that way. It promotes healing in tissue that's damage after the injection. It also repairs tissue which has only recently been damaged, but it has no effect on something that's been damaged or destroyed for any length of time prior to the injection, which appears to be the case here."

Kim felt herself starting to tremble. She felt as if her whole world were suddenly crashing down around her. She lowered her head to the console as her body began to wrack with sobs. She could never have children. She could never give Jason the son or daughter he wanted from their union. She could never be the complete wife he deserved.

Mother was talking to her, but Kim blocked out the voice of the computer, not wanting to hear Mother's words of pity and consolation. The only thing she could hear was her own voice inside her head telling her that she was no longer worthy of being Jason's wife. As she wiped the tears from her face she knew there were only two options left to her now.

One option was that the law permitted divorce of a woman if she was unable to bear children. But Kim knew her husband well, and knew Jason would never consent to a divorce. She knew she could force him to do it under the law and there wouldn't be anything he could really do about it. But she also knew she could never embarrass him like that. The law also permitted another option, and in Kim's mind it was the only one left to her.

"Kimmy," Mother called out as she stood and slowly crossed the room.

"Shut up, Mother!" Kim cried angrily as she went to the drug cabinet, keeping her body between the camera which served as Mother's eye into the room and the cabinet itself.

"What are you doing, Kimmy?" Mother asked. The voice of the computer sounded worried and concerned.

"Nothing," Kim replied a she began to cry again, her body trembling as she hurried from the lab, her hand clutching a small injector and vial.

Kim walked blindly until she found herself outside of Jason's room. She went inside and locked the door behind her, then turned off the speakers and camera which would allow Mother to talk to her or see her. She wanted to be completely alone.

Kim walked slowly around the room, touching things with a sense of remembrance, thinking of how each of them held a special memory for her. When Kim opened the closet to run her hand over the material of one of Jason's jumpsuits, she glanced up and noticed a small black box on the overhead shelf. Curious, she took it down, turning it around in her hands for a moment before placing it on the dresser. As she did she noticed his hair brush and picked it up. There were silver hairs interwoven with the darker brown ones trapped within the bristles of the brush. Kin though of how, like those hairs, her life and Jason's had become intertwined. Tears filler her eyes as she remembered the first time he had set her on the stool to dry and brush her hair for her.

"I started falling in love with you even then," she whispered as she replaced the brush and turned her attention back to the small black box, which she now recognized as a holo projector. She depressed the small button on the side and stepped back, startled as a life-sized image of Nadia was suddenly projected into the room.

Kim gasped softly. Although she had seen pictures of holographic images of Nadia before, this was the first time she had ever seen a life size projection of the woman who had been Jason's first love. Kim backed away to sit on the edge of the bed just as the image began to speak.

"Hello, my love," it said. The voice was nearly identical to Mothers, except pitched a little lower and much richer in timbre. "If you're watching this it means that something must have gone wrong and I'm no longer with you. I don't know why, but I felt compelled to make this for you after we fled New Hope and were waiting to decide where to go."

Thee was a sadness to the voice which touched Kim as she studied the features of Nadia. She knew the holo was totally realistic, which gave her a good comparison to the size and beauty of Nadia to herself. She realized that Nadia had been almost as tall as Jason, towering nearly a foot over Kim's own height. The woman's hair was so black it appeared to have blue highlights to it, and like Kim's own, hung down past her waist.

Nadia's complexion was slight darker than Jason's, and her eyes what he called 'almond shaped'. Kim found them attractive in a strange sort of way. Nadia's nose was straight and thin, and served to accentuate the other features of her face. The woman's lips were full and sensual, with a tendency to pout slightly when she talked. Her neck was long and graceful, and from what Kim could tell, beneath the jumpsuit Nadia wore, which fit her like a second skin, the woman had a figure that would rival the figure of any woman on Alazon.

<u>No wonder he loved her</u>, Kim though to herself. <u>Any man would find her devastatingly beautiful.</u>

"But that also means," continued the image, "that you are alive and well, and that is all I hope and pray for. As long as you are alive, so is our love.

"I don't know what life with hold for you, or where you will go in your travels, but I know you, and you'll find a new world where you and the others will be able to start a new life.

"There is going to be a lot of responsibility placed on you in the coming years, my love, but I know you'll be able to handle it. The people of New Hope believed in you, they trusted you to lead them to a new world and a new life. Especially the children."

The image paused for a moment, shaking it's head and smiling shyly.

"You know," it continued after a moment, "I used to be jealous of the time you spend with the children. All the boys want you to be their big brother, an all the girls above the age of twelve have a crush on you.

'Sometimes I felt like they meant more to you than I did. You're the one they always come running to when something goes wrong, and you always find the time for them when it comes to whatever life of death situation they think they're involved in. They come to you before they go to their own parents, and that, my love," the image said with a sultry smile, "was not always at the best times for us, if you remember.

"But no matter how much it might have bothered me at the time, when I saw the look of love and trust in their eyes for you, I couldn't stay mad or upset for very long. At you or them. In fact, Jason, those things only served to make me love you that much more. And to long for the day when we would have our own children. One of these days you are going to make a great father," the image said with a smile of love. "And those children are going to be the luckiest kids in the world."

Her words drove even deeper into Kim the spike she already felt in her own heart over her inability to bear him a child. She felt her tears begin anew.

"But even luckier than the children will be the woman you marry," the image said. "And you will marry someday, Jason, because you're a man who needs a woman in his life. Not for the obvious physical reasons, but for the sharing of the love you have within you to give. And you're a man that a woman can fall in love with so totally that the intensity of it will make her ache at times. Believe me when I say that, Jason, because I know just how true it is.

"I will envy her, for she will be occupying your mind, your heart and your bed. But I will also be happy in knowing that you are happy, for I know that no matter what happens, you won't ever forget me. A part of me will always be with you."

The image of Nadia smiled brightly and clasped her hands in front of her.

"Go on, Jason. Go find your worlds to investigate and conquer. Go with God, my love. Go with my love in your heart, and the memory of our love in your mind, and always remember that wherever you go, I go there with you. I love you, Jason."

There was a soft click from the box and the image vanished. Kim couldn't control the tears now flowing from her eyes. She curled up in a ball on the bed and though of what the holo of Nadia had said.

Jason had found his world to conquer, but without the children of New Hope to share it with him. And he had found a woman to love him the way Nadia had said he would, but the woman he had married could not give him children of his own. She could not bare

Jason the son he deserved to carry on his name and work. There would be no issue from her, and to Kim that was an unbearable agony and shame.

Kim reached slowly into her pocket and withdrew the injector and vial she had taken from the med-lab. Knowing Mother could override her audio and visual cutoff, Kim kept her back to the camera as she slipped the vial into the injector and placed it against the inside of her elbow.

"Kimmy! Don't do this!" Mother's voice shouted from the speakers. "Kimmy, wait! Listen to me, please!"

But to Kim there was nothing Mother could say to alter the facts or change her mind. She depressed the trigger of the injector. Tears stung her eyes as the highly concentrated poison began to burn through her veins. They ran down her cheeks as a chill began to creep through her body. Through her tears she reached out to clasp a small, raggedy teddy bear to her and hug it close.

"Don't be mad at me," she whispered softly to the stuffed animal. "It's the right thing to do. Now he's free to find another to marry and give him the children I can't. Vinny loves him. She loves him as much as I do. She would be a good wife for him.

"Vinny!" she called out to the empty room as the chill deepened in her body, "I know you love him. And in his own way he loves you, too. In time he'll marry you, and when he does, give him the son's I couldn't. Be his wife, little sister, and make him happy. Do it for me, Please!"

Kim could no longer feel her hands and feet and her arms and legs grew numb. Her eyelids grew heavier, forcing themselves closed as she struggled to hug the teddy bear with arms that no longer obeyed the commands of her mind.

"Maybe I'll be with Nadia now and we can both love him from the other world," she whispered as the poison invaded her body and numbing coldness closed down over her mind.

# THIRTY FIVE

"Tolo and Makee are starting to make noises again," Naed said casually.

"What kind?" Jason asked without taking his eyes off Janella and the twins, who were splashing around in the water while Baby ran around the pool barking at them. Jason and Naed were sitting under a large umbrella at the table on the patio, relaxing and watching the kids and dog playing.

"Tolo is trying to get some of his friends to put him on the ballot for the next mayoral election."

Jason grinned. "Hey, anyone can get their name put on the ballot. That's the easy part. Winning an election is something else entirely. I wouldn't worry about it too much."

"But," Naed replied, "some of those friends are very rich and influential. People who would stand to benefit if Tolo got back into a position of power or authority, even if it wasn't as great as it once was. They've got the money to possibly bring in outsiders and screw things up."

Jason raised his sunglasses and grinned as he looked at his friend. "Naed, when I appointed you Governor of Karton, I did it because I had complete confidence in your ability to handle the job. That includes the problems that come with it.

"If I step in and do something now, it could undermine the credibility you've worked so hard to establish. The people might see you as weak or too indecisive to do things on your own, or that I don't have faith in you. You're the Governor, it's your problem, you take care of it."

"You're no going to make this easy for me, are you?" Naed asked with a sigh."

"Nope."

Naed was about to say something else when a flash of gold, silver and white raced past them and dove into the pool. The twins and Janella screamed, scattering in three directions in the water as Vinny's head broke the surface. Naed and Jason grinned as they watched Vinny chase the younger ones around the pool in a game of tab. Baby finally decided she wanted in on the fun and leaped into the water, nearly landing on Manda. Naed couldn't help but laugh at the antics of Vinny, Baby and the kids as they took turns teaming up on one another.

After a few minutes of this Vinny swam to the side of the pool and pulled herself out. Naed felt his pulse quicken as he looked at her beautiful body. A body which was just barely covered in all the right places by the skimpiest white one-piece, Earth-style bathing suit he had ever seen. He fought down the sense of arousal he felt as she walked over to sit down between Jason and himself, pulling her long hair back and squeezing the water out of it. She casually reached out and picked up Jason's glass of iced tea and sipped from him, laughing at him when he reached to take it back.

"You staying for supper, Naed?" she asked, turning to face him at last.

"Is that an invitation?"

"No way," she said with a laugh. "You're practically family and we don't give invitations to family. If they're here at meal time they stay if they want to take their chances."

"What are you having?"

"Something you've never had before," she teased.

"Another Earth dish Janella has come up with I assume?"

Naed knew how much Jason's daughter loved to fix meals from Jason's home world for him, and was constantly coming up with something new.

"You got it. So, you staying or not?"

"Ok, I'll stay."

"Good," Vinny said as she stood up and took a couple of steps toward the pool, giving him an excellent view of her beautiful backside. "Hey, Janella, come on and give me a hand."

"Okay!" Janella called back as she quickly swam to the side of the pool and climbed out. She followed Vinny into the house as she wrapped a towel around herself that Jason tossed to her.

"She really is something," Naed said to Jason.

"Vinny or Janella?" Jason asked with a grin.

"Both, but I meant Vinny," Naed replied with a grin of his own

Jason nodded and sighed. "That she is. I don't know how I could have managed these past few months without her. She's been more help to me than I can ever repay her for."

"She's become quite a woman."

"She always has been, Naed. I guess it just didn't show because she was always so much quieter than Kim."

"Hey!" a voice called out from behind them. "Are you two dirty old men talking about my little sister?"

Naed and Jason both turned to see Kim waddling toward them. The smile of happiness and love on her face seemed to be permanently stamped there. Both men quickly got to their feet to help her sit down.

Their actions caused Kim to laugh. "Really, guys, I can manage the sitting down part. It's the getting back up that's so hard." She patted her hugely protruding stomach. "This gives the term 'top heavy' a whole new meaning for me."

"Is everything all right?" Naed asked as he sat back down in his own chair.

"Well," Kim replied with a grin, "other than the fact that I've lost my girlish figure, and this little guy in here kicks like a tollie, I feel great."

Naed saw the radiance and glow on Kim's face and thought back to that horrible day when she had tried to take her own life because she thought she couldn't bear Jason a son.

Kim had rightfully known that Jason would never listen to any talk of divorce, so she had taken what she considered to be the only honorable way out of the marriage permitted by law; suicide.

Jason had been with Naed in Bysee at the time. The two of them were in a meeting with Naed's executive committee, discussing a new sanitation system for the city with the small communicator on Jason's wrist had shattered the air with a piercing siren sound. Without a word Jason had bolted from the table of startled men, crashing through the closed chamber doors, knocking down the two guards who had been standing outside of them as he sprinted for the shuttle.

Not knowing what was going on, but knowing it was serious, Naed had yelled for his Deputy Mayor to take over and sprinted after Jason. He had managed to dive through the open hatch of the shuttle only seconds before it closed and the craft lifted into the air. He had gotten into his seat just as Jason kicked in the thrusters and sent the small craft streaking into the sky with a speed that forced Naed almost painfully back into his seat.

Mother had quickly filled them in on what Kim had done and why. She informed them that she had dropped the temperature in the cabin to near zero to slow the effects of the poison, and was now using a servo robot to cut through the lock of the door.

Jason had brought the shuttle to a sliding, skidding stop inside the bay, the hatch opening even before they stopped moving. Both men were out of the craft instantly, their feet pounding the deck as they rushed to save Kim's life.

The servo robot was just moving out of the way and the door sliding out of the way as they got there. The rushed into the ice cold room and Jason had picked up the limp body of Kim and then sprinted to the med-lab, leaving Naed to try and catch up. Naed had spotted the injector on the floor and picked it up before following. In the lab he handed the injector to Jason, seeing the look of pain and anger in the eyes of his friend. After that, Naed had stepped back out of the way, knowing there was nothing he could do to help except to pray. And that he did in abundance as Jason and Mother worked desperately to save Kim.

Mother told Jason that the poison Kim had injected herself with was a derivative of the poison extracted from Death Plants which bonded itself to the platelets in the blood. The only way to save Kim and rid her body of it was a complete blood transfusion. But unlike a normal transfusion, new blood couldn't be given to Kim until all of the tainted blood was removed, which meant Kim would have to be completely drained of all blood first.

Naed didn't know how a person could have all their blood removed and still live, but watched silently as Jason had moved swiftly, with sure, steady hands to connect wires and tubes to Kim's body in a dozen places. Jason hadn't spoken a word, and Naed doubted if his friend was even aware of his presence in the room. But Naed had seen the tension in the muscles of Jason's jaw and the fear in his eyes as every drop of blood was drained from Kim's body. It was then replaced with a clear fluid which Naed heard Mother say was needed to flush out the remaining poison and neutralize any traces of it. Naed had felt his own heart pounding in his chest as the new blood was finally pumped into Kin's apparently lifeless body nearly two hours after they had arrived.

Naed had no idea of how much time had passed before finally hearing Mother tell Jason that Kim was going to make it. He saw the tension and strength drain from his friend as Jason's shoulders had sagged and his body had slumped in the chair he was sitting on beside Kim's bed, sobbing in both pain and relief. After a while Jason had eased himself up onto the bed with the still unconscious Kim, tenderly taking her into his arms to hold her close.

Naed had left the two of them in the lab, tears in his own eyes as he made his way to the bridge, where he'd had Mother contact Kim's family for him. He told them what had happened, and why, then assured them that Kim was going to be okay, urging them not to come up for now. He knew it would take Kim some time to recover emotionally before she would be able to face them.

Everyone except Vinny had abided by that request. Vinny had flatly ignored him and contacted Ster, ordering him to fly her up to the <u>Stargazer</u>. Naed had been standing outside the door of the medlab when Vinny had come racing down the companionway. "Get out of my way, Naed!" she ordered him, the set of her face letting him know he wasn't about to stop her from going to her sister's side.

A few minutes later Jason had emerged looking worn and haggard. At first he didn't seem to notice Naed's presence, but then motioned for Naed to follow him. They had gone to one of the lounges, with neither of them speaking until they were seated in chairs facing one another with mugs of steaming coffee in their hands.

Jason had explained in detail everything that had happened, as related to him by Mother. As Jason spoke, Naed could see him growing angry at Kim for her actions. Naed new his friend couldn't understand why Kim would do such a thing.

"Doesn't she have any idea of how much I love her?" Jason had asked. "Even if she could never have children it wouldn't make any difference and I would still love her with all my heart!"

"Jason," Naed had said patiently, "this isn't Earth, and what Kim did, or tried to do, is not only legal, but acceptable under our laws and customs. King or not, under the law she could have forced you to divorce her, clearing the way for you to someday marry someone else.

"But Kim knew you would fight her on a divorce. She also felt that such an action would be too much of an embarrassment to you. She felt it would bring shame not only to you, but her family as well, so she embraced the honorable tradition."

"If that's the law then I'm going to change the damn thing!" Jason had snapped, flinging his half full cup of coffee across the room.

"Perhaps."

"Perhaps my ass! What's the sense of being a king if you can't change laws that are stupid and harmful to people?"

"Jason, as you know, I've spent a lot of time studying Earth history. There are many similarities between it and things here on Alazon. The Japanese outlawed seppuku, but that didn't stop people from engaging in that form of ritual suicide for reasons of honor.

"In India some sects of Hindu women would kill themselves by dousing themselves with a flammable liquid and setting themselves on fire if they shamed their husbands. Or even if they just felt they had. Despite the fact that such acts were outlawed by most countries.

"Jason, there are some customs which are too deeply ingrained in the minds of the people. So deeply ingrained that simply changing the law will have little to no effect on them. And Kimmy, feeling she was unworthy to be your wife because she couldn't bear you a child, loved you enough to get out of your life the only way she could so you could find someone else to marry and have children with."

*Alazon*

They had talked for a while longer before Naed had finally returned to Preton to speak with Kim's family. Jason and Vinny had remained behind with Kim for another two days. When the three of them did return, Kim and Vinny were grinning as if they were in on some great secret. They called all the family together, including Seta, Ster and himself, to let them know what was going on.

Jason had explained Kim's damaged organs to them, going into detail as to why she had been unable to conceive. "While normal surgery would not correct it," Jason had told there, "there are two ways in which she can still bare a child. The first would be to clone new ovaries and fallopian tubes for her to replace the damaged one. However, it would take some time to do that.

"The second option," Jason told them, "would be to remove an egg from Vinny, fertilize it with my sperm, then implant it in Kim. While it wouldn't actually be her own conception, she would be carrying my fertilized egg, and would be able to give birth."

That was the option Kim had elected to go with, but then let it be known that after this child was born she would undergo the clone transplant that would allow her to conceive normally.

Not everyone understood the process completely, but what they did understand was that Kim was pregnant, and that she, Jason and Vinny were now linked together in the creation of a new life that Kim now carried within her. A new life that would establish a bond between the three of them which would bind them closer together than ever before.

The next day Vinny had moved in with Jason and Kim. She had taken over many of the normal chores of Kim, and took care of her sister like a nurse. She had watched over Kim's diet, made sure she did her exercises, and generally did everything possible to make sure that both Kim and the baby she carried were healthy. Once a week Kim and Vinny would fly up to let Mother do a complete checkup. Vinny made her go even when Kim protested and said she felt fine. As Kim's pregnancy progressed, Vinny took over more and more of the responsibilities of the house, making herself virtually indispensable to both Jason and Kim.

Janella loved having Vinny around. The girl made jokes about going from a poor little orphaned girl with no parents, to becoming one who was not only the daughter of the King of Alazon, but one with two beautiful mothers as well. It was clear that she loved Vinny almost as much as she loved Kim.

It was during these past few months that Naed had found himself spending more and more time in Lemac, finding excuses to be around Vinny. He had fallen in love with her, but as he watched her around Jason and Kim, he new he would never be anything more than just a friend to her. It was evident to him that there was only one man Vinny would ever love. That man was Jason, even if Jason was too blind to see it.

In fact, it seemed as if everyone was aware of Vinny's love for Jason except Jason himself. As Naed glanced at the man who had come to mean so much to him, both as a king and a friend, he wondered if Jason did know, but was simply doing his best to ignore it so Vinny wouldn't feel any encouragement for her feelings. Naed knew he often had the same look in his own eyes when looking at Vinny that Jason had in his when looking at Kim. It was also the same look Vinny had when she looked at Jason.

Naed was fairly certain that Vinny was aware of his love for her. He was also sure that she would never love him. At least not in the way she loved Jason. But what surprised him was that he felt neither anger nor jealousy toward Jason or Vinny over it. He had come to love them both too much for that. Jason had become much more than just his king; the two of them had become as close as brothers in many ways. They were friends and could never be enemies. There was too much respect on both their parts for that to ever happen.

"Gang way!" Vinny cried out as she approached the table now dressed in a pair of shorts and a blouse. She was carrying a large round pan about an inch deep in her hands, which were covered with huge mittens to protect them from the heat. Janella hurried past her to set a large pad on the table so Vinny could set the pan on it. Janella then turned to look at him with a grin and that familiar twinkle in her eyes. Naed looked down at the contents of the pan as Janella giggled and hurried back into the house. She returned almost immediately with a stack of plates and napkins, which she slid around the table like a card dealer.

"Okay, I give up," Naed said at last. "What is it?"

"Pizza, silly," Janella told him. "One half has everything on it, including anchovies, which only me and the twins like. The other side is for everyone else. Dad doesn't eat red meat, and none of them like anchovies."

The twins appeared with Manda carrying a stack of glasses, while Vanda carried a large pitcher if iced teef. They poured the teef and passed out the glasses to everyone before pulling chairs up to the table and reaching for slices of pizza without waiting for the others.

Naed hesitated a moment. He wasn't sure as to how to go about this, but finally shrugged and followed the example of the others and dug out a piece with his fingers. He looked at it skeptically for a moment, as he couldn't identify most of the ingredients, but when he finally took a bite he was pleasantly surprised. Until he bit into something extremely salty and bitter. He quickly spat it into his hand and put it on the plate. Looking up he saw the amused grins on the faces of the others. "What was that?" he asked.

"Anchovy," Vinny told him.

"That doesn't tell me anything."

Janella looked at him and rolled her eyes. "It's a small fish, Naed. We don't have them here on Alazon. Well, not before Dad arrived that is. When Mother was giving me all the different recipes for pizza, and telling me which items I could substitute, I found that we didn't have anything like anchovies, so I had her grow some from the gene pool aboard the ship. Now I keep a small supply of them handy just for pizza."

He looked at Jason and grinned. "Just what all do you have in that gene pool?"

Jason swallowed the piece of pizza he was chewing before answering.

"You'd be surprised. I've got just about every animal that lived on Earth. Some were brought for experimental purposes, others for possible release into a new environment."

"Jason's promised us puppies and kittens," Vanda told him casually as the boy reached for another slice of pizza.

"Just what we need; more versions of Baby running around," he said with a grin.

At the mention of her name, Baby got up from where she had been laying in the shade and came to the table looking for handouts from the kids, who eagerly obliged her.

"I want a kitten," Manda told him.

"Which is?"

"Kittens are baby cats. They're sorta like the natl that live in the southern areas here on Alazon, only smaller. "About this big," she added, holding her hands apart to indicate their size. "And real cute and cuddly. Really, Naed, you need to study other things about Earth besides politics, sociology and history, and get a better grasp on the English language."

Naed laughed at Manda's bluntness, but nodded in agreement with her statement. He had put off learning any more of Jason's native language than was necessary, doing all of his studies in his own, with Mother providing the translations for him. But maybe now it was time he finally did.

"Now, how would you know how big these kittens get? Or know they are so cuddly?" he asked Manda.

"Mother said so," she replied casually, as if the computer's words were an edict from the gods themselves.

Naed looked at Baby, remember his fear the first time he had ever seen the huge, powerful animal. It was the day he had been released from the temple after being rescued by Jason from the dungeons of Tolo. Jason had come to pick him up, and as he had stood on the steps of the temple watching the hatch of the shuttle open, he had drawn back in fear at the sight of the animal have the size of a tollie which had suddenly bounded out of it. He had been even more shocked when Seta had called out to it, laughing as Baby had run to her, flicking out her tongue to lick the face of the High Priestess in friendly greeting.

Despite the assurances of everyone, it had still taken Naed some time to get used to the huge dog. It wasn't until he saw the way the twins and Janella played with Baby, whose jaws were large enough to snap any one of them in half, that he had started to relax.

But Naed had also seen what the dog was capable of. The night Janella had been kidnapped, Baby had killed one of the attackers in the bedroom and, later, when Jason and Shon had gone into the warehouse, one of the Tilwin had tried to sneak out and escape, but before the man had covered more than a few yards, Baby had brought him down. The man's screams of terror and pain had filled the air for only a moment, stopping abruptly when Baby ripped the man's head from his shoulders by snapping her jaws around his throat and viciously twisting her own head.

Naed had also seen the way Baby protected Janella and the twins. The local bullies had quickly learned that any malicious teasing of the twins or Janella was to take their own safety into their hands if Baby were along. The dog made it perfectly clear that absolutely no one was going to harm the kids without going through her first.

But he had also watched mothers gently place their infants down where Baby could sniff and lick them. The dog would lay on the ground and let infants crawl all over her, pulling her hair, ears and tail in their attempts to hold on to her without so much as a growl.

He knew that one of Baby's favorite games was to stage a mock attack on Jason, Hass, or even the kids. The dog would sneak up on them as if stalking game, her lips pulled back in a snarl to reveal her long canines, the hair around her neck and shoulders bunched up, and her body low to the ground.

The first time Naed had witnessed this he had frozen in fear as Baby had launched herself at Jason, knocking him to the ground. Naed had reached for his sword, intending to rush to the rescue of his king, but had been stopped by a laughing Kim and Vinny. They had grabbed his arms to hold him back, explaining to him that it was just a game between Jason and the dog. He had stood and watched, his hand never far from his sword, as Jason and Baby had rolled around on the ground struggling with one another until Jason finally pinned Baby to the ground, stroking her head and talking softly to the dog as a signal that the game was over.

"Would you like one of your own?"

Naed raised his eyes from Baby to see Jason looking at him. "What?"

"I asked if you would like to have a dog of your own. I have about twenty different breeds in the gene pool. I could give you pictures and information on each of them and let you pick your own. In fact, I've been giving some consideration to breeding some German Shepherds to form a K-9 Corps."

"What's that?" Naed asked.

"A police or military unit comprised of men and dogs specifically trained for guard duty. The normal size of the dogs are about half that of Baby. Remember, Baby was genetically altered by Mother to become twice the size she would normally be. The type of dog I'm talking about, though, is good sized, very intelligent, and when trained properly, very good at what they do."

The concept intrigued Naed. "What would you use them for?"

"We could use them in Tilwin to bolster the forces of the men stationed there," Jason told him. "Believe me, they can be a great deterrent to anyone wishing to start trouble. And with them being something totally new here on Alazon, they would be twice as effective."

'I can imagine," Naed replied with a grin. "I don't know about having a dog of my own, though. I'll have to think about it. But I would be interested in checking out the various breeds."

"Okay. The next time I go up I'll get the information for you," Jason told him.

At that, Janella and the twins, who apparently already knew every breed in the gene pool, began an earnest discussion as to what type of dog would be good for Naed, as well as what breed of dog or cat they each wanted for their own. Naed smiled at Vinny as the adults resumed eating. He soon found himself reaching for a third piece of pizza, which he though was good once he removed the anchovies.

When supper was over Vinny and the kids cleared the table and headed into the house to clean things up. The sun had gone down and it was turning into one of those beautiful nights when it seemed as if every star in the sky could be seen with absolute clarity. He lowered his gaze to find that Jason had left as well, and Kim was looking at him and grinning. "I know that look, woman," he teased. "What are you thinking?"

"I'm just wondering what your intentions are concerning my little sister," she replied with a grin.

Naed thought about it for a moment. "Good question," he finally replied.

"She cares about you, Naed, she really does," Kim told him softly.

"I know. But I'm not the man she's in love with," he replied, looking directly into her eyes.

This time it was Kim's turn to hesitate. She lowered her eyes for a moment, and when she looked up her face held a countenance of seriousness.

"I know," she replied. "But I think she could love you if you gave her the chance. And some time. But unless you let her know how you feel, we'll never know, will we?"

Naed nodded. "True, but what if I tell her and she rejects me? That's not exactly the most soothing thing to a man's ego, you know. Besides, if I tell her, and she doesn't feel the same, it could put a strain on our friendship. I don't want that to happen."

"You've never struck me as being a coward, Naed?" she teased. "What if you tell her and she doesn't shoot you down?"

He laughed and shook his head. "Kimmy, I love you like a sister, and Jason is closer to me than my own brothers ever were, and I know you want the best for me, but we all know who Vinny's in love with. In fact, I doubt if there's a person in Lemac who doesn't know. The thing that surprises me is that it hasn't caused any conflict between the three of you. Or even between you and Vinny.

"I mean, I know you're aware of Vinny's feelings for Jason, and have been for a long time now. And Jason would have to be a blind idiot not to see it. But the three of you carry on as if it were the most natural thing in the world."

Kim nodded slowly. "I know," she said softly. "I also know there's been some talk and rumors that Jason is sleeping with her, and that she's taken my place in his bed during my pregnancy. And that it's being done with my blessing."

Naed looked at her with slightly arched eyebrows. He had heard some of those same rumors himself, but knowing the three people involved as well as he did, he had dismissed them out of hand.

"No, it's not happening," Kim told him, grinning at him in that way which made her look like a little girl. "Yes, Vinny loves him. I've known that since even before Jason and I were married. She and I have talked about it with one another, and I've even talked to Jason about it. I guess you just have to know the two of them the way I do to really understand how we're able to function around one another the way we do."

"Can I ask you something?"

"Of course," Kim replied with a grin.

Naed hesitated a moment. He was a little unsure of himself in what he was about to tell Kim. If she reacted to it the way he thought she probably would, it could have a dramatic effect on the lives of them all.

"Why don't you have Jason marry her?" he finally asked, his voice barely audible.

He watched the play of emotions across Kim's face as she tried to figure out what he was trying to tell her. "You really don't know what I'm getting at, do you?" he finally asked.

Kim shook her head.

"You know the law that allows a woman to divorce her husband, or vice versa, if she can't bear him children, or to take her own life if he refuses but, my dear dumb queen, I think that if you will check with your father, or Seta, you'll find there was an amendment made to that law about a hundred and thirty years ago which also provides for another option."

Kim was looking at him expectantly. He took a deep breath and let it out slowly, knowing there was no turning back now.

"That amendment permits a man to take a second wife, and do so without divorcing the first one," he told her. "But, and this is important, it is applicable only under certain conditions, and with very strict guidelines."

"What kind of conditions and guidelines?" Kim asked softly, her face aglow with expectancy.

"The second wife has to be her sister," Naed told her. "However, if the woman doesn't have a sister, or one he can marry, then it has to be a cousin. If no sisters or cousins are available, then the first wife must find at least three women for his selection, of which she has the final approval."

"You're kidding?" Kim gasped.

"No," he replied with a shake of his head. "Not only that, Kimmy, but we both know that as King of Alazon, Jason could take a second wife and no one would think anything of it, regardless of what the law did or didn't say. Especially if that second wife were Vinny. They might even think it is part of his own culture and custom from back on Earth."

Kim shook her head. "He wouldn't do that, Naed. We both know he's the most law abiding person on all of Alazon. He's a stickler for making sure he doesn't do anything to violate our laws. He constantly stresses that same principle to all of us. He says we have to be the examples for everyone else to follow."

Naed grinned at this from Kim. He clearly remembered the conversation with Jason and the other members of the family about that very matter. He knew Jason felt, as king, that he had to be the number one example to the people when it came to the law.

"Are you sure about that amendment?" Kim asked.

"Go check it out for yourself with Seta or your dad," he told her. What he didn't tell her was that he had already verified it for himself two days ago.

Kim smiled brightly at him for a moment, but then her face seemed to lose it's radiant glow and her eyes became suddenly sad as she reached across the table to take his right hand in her own. "You know what this could mean if you're right, don't you?" she asked softly.

Naed lifted he hand and kissed the tips of her fingers. "Kimmy, it would mean that the three people I love most in the world would be happy, and especially Vinny. That's what counts to me.

"Now," he continued as he stood and helped her to her feet, "I think I will say good night and head for home. Just be sure to invite me to the wedding."

"If there is one, you'll be Best Man," Kim replied softly as she hugged him warmly.

Naed kissed her cheek. "Tell the others good night for me." With that Naed turned and walked toward the landing pad beside the house where the small shuttle assigned to him waited to take him back to Bysee.

#

Kim watched Naed go, feeling a new, deeper sense of love and respect for him. What he had told her could change the lives of her and her family forever. Not only that, but he had told her about it with total unselfishness, wanting only for her, Vinny and Jason to be happy. It was an act of love which took more courage, strength and sacrifice than Kim knew she would ever possess.

She turned and walked slowly into the house. Jason and the kids were wrestling on the living room floor with Baby. The dog couldn't make up her mind as to whose side she was on. She would reach out and grab an arm or leg to pull one of the kids off Jason, only to have them dive back on him the second she turned the loose. And if it looked as if Jason were going to get up, Baby would use her weight to knock him back down to the floor. Vinny was sitting on the sofa, her legs curled up beneath her, laughing at the antics as she watched them. She glanced up as Kim entered and a look of silent understanding passed between them.

"Okay, gang, time for bed!" Vinny told them. She reached out to snag Vanda by a leg and pull him to her despite his loud protests. "Come on, you guys, let's get ready for bed. You, too, you big mutt," she said to Baby as the dog looked at Vinny with her tail wagging back and forth.

"Story time!" Jason cried as he picked up Janella and Manda. He bent over so Vanda could climb up on his back before standing and heading out of the room. Baby darted on ahead of them, her barking leading the way.

Kim crossed the room and sat down beside Vinny, reaching for her sister's hand. "Sis, have you thought about what you're going to do once the baby is born and I'm able to function normally again?"

"This is about Naed, isn't it?" Vinny asked softly.

"Well, not exactly, although he is very much in love with you."

"I know. I love him, Kimmy, but just not in the way he wants me to. He's a good man, one of the best, but he deserves a wife who is capable of loving him totally and completely. A woman who will love him and only him, and I don't think that's something I would ever be able to do."

Kim nodded in understanding. "He knows that. But I think he would still marry you and take his chances that someday you might come to love him that way."

Vinny nodded slowly. "I know he would, Kimmy. He'd marry me right now if I said yes, even knowing I love Jason, and there's not a doubt in my mind that he'd be patient, caring and loving, but it wouldn't be right. He deserves better."

"So, what are you going to do?"

Vinny looked away briefly before turning her body slightly on the sofa so that she was facing Kim.

"I've spoken to Seta. Once your son is born, and you are able to function normally again, I'm going to enter the temple and take the Sacred Vow of Chastity and Purity."

"What?" Kim asked in amazement.

"Because of my knowledge from Mother," Vinny said, her voice just above a whisper as she glanced down at her hands, "I'll occupy a special position and serve as a teacher. I'll be ready to become a High Priestess in just a couple of years."

Kim looked at her sister and knew the pain Vinny was going through. Vinny loved Jason, but Jason was Kim's husband, and that made him off limits to her. And rather than marry another man, even one she knew loved her with all his heart, Vinny would enter the temple and shut herself off that way. Kim felt an ache of sadness in her heart at this.

"Is that what you really want?" she asked after a moment, already knowing the answer.

"I don't think it's really a matter of what I want, Kim. It's more a matter of what's best for everyone concerned."

"But what if I told you there was another option?" Kim said softly. "One which could possibly give you what you really want."

"There isn't, Kimmy." Vinny's voice, like her face, was full of dejection.

"Oh, I don't know, Sis. I think there just might be," Kim told her sister with a sly smile. "Look, Jason's taking off in the morning to help Shon with the new aquaduct over in Telma. Once he's gone, and the kids are off to school, have the guards hitch up a carriage for me. I'm going to see Daddy about something."

Kim grinned impishly as Vinny looked at her quizzically. "Well, are you going to tell me or make me wait?" she finally asked.

"This time, little sister, you're going to have to wait and wonder," Kim replied as she slipped an arm around Vinny's shoulders to hug her.

Later, as Kim lay curled in Jason's arms she listened to the beat of his heart in his chest and thought of what Naed had told her. She would have to check with her father to make sure it was true. If so, she would then have the difficult task of convincing Jason to do it. That would be the hardest part.

"Hey, Alien," she whispered, raising her head to look at him.

"What do you want, Muggles?"

"How much do you love me?"

"Not very much when you ask me stupid questions just as I'm about to fall asleep," he teased, opening his eyes and smiling at her.

"Just answer the question."

"Kim," he said softly, "you know how much I love you."

"Well, a woman just gets curious at times. Especially when she's pregnant and looks like she swallowed an oversized melon. She just needs a little reassurance now and then."

Jason lightly kissed her forehead. "Kim, I love you more than anything in the world. You should know that, and never doubt it. I'd do anything for you."

"Hold that thought," she told him as she kissed him lightly and snuggled closer to him.

# THIRTY SIX

As the young Royal Guardsman driving the carriage brought it to a slow stop in front of the steps of the Mayoral Building, two more Guardsmen rushed down the steps to meet it. One man held the bridles of the matching tollies while the second opened the door of the carriage and pulled down the folding steps. He then extended his hand to help Kim from the carriage. Once she had exited the carriage, all three men then escorted her up the steps of the building with one on either side and the third one behind her. Kim knew they were ready to leap to her aid should she stumble, or even stub her toe.

This action, and others, by the men of the Royal Guard was a constant source of amusement to Kim. More than once over the past few months she had been tempted to fake a stumble or fall, just to watch them panic, but refrained from doing so because she knew how seriously the men took their jobs. Should she actually fall and hurt herself, or her unborn child, while in their company, the man closest to her would feel responsible for it, and would probably commit suicide right on the spot for failing to do his duty to protect his queen from harm.

Since the proclamation of Jason as King of Preton, even Kim had been surprised at how quickly the people had taken to living under the rule of monarchy, and how seriously they took it. But it was the members of the newly formed Royal Guard, under the command of Captain Ster, who took it the most serious of all. They had taken blood oaths to protect the lives of Jason, Kim, and the entire Vehey family with their very lives.

The three men stayed with Kim all the way to the doors of her father's office. As she approached them, two other Guardsmen opened the doors for her, closing them behind her after she had entered alone.

"Ahhh, and how is my favorite fat daughter today?" Jarrell teased as he stood up and came out from behind his desk to hug her.

"I'm not fat!" she protested with a laugh.

"If you say so. Now, to what do I owe this unexpected visit? "

"Since when do I need an excuse to come see my daddy," she asked with a smile as she let him guide her toward a chair and help her sit down.

Jarrell sat in the chair across from her. "You don't, but that little gleam in your eyes tells me you're up to something, Muggles. What is it this time?"

"Naed was over last night," Kim began as her father leaned back in his chair. "He told me something which could have an effect on the people closest to me."

"Which is?" Jarrell asked when she hesitated.

"He, well, he told me about an amendment to the law which allows a man to take a second wife, without having to divorce the first one, if the first one is unable to conceive a child. I want to know if there really is such an amendment."

Jarrell stared into Kim's eyes as he sat silently for the space of several heartbeats. He finally sat up straight, crossing his legs at the ankles and linking his fingers across his stomach.

"To be honest, I don't know, Kimella," he finally replied. He used her proper name, which he did only when he was either scolding her, or engaged in a serious conversation with her. "But even if there is such an amendment, what interest would it be to you? You're pregnant."

"For Vinny," she replied softly.

Jarrell sighed softly and nodded. "I thought as much. Look, Kim, I know your intentions are good, but have you really considered all the possible consequences for everyone concerned?"

"I spent most of the night thinking of nothing else, Daddy."

"I see. You say Naed told you about this?"

"Yes."

"What about Jason and Vinny? Do they know anything about it yet?"

Kim shook her head. "No. I wanted to check it out with you first before I said anything to them."

Jarrell nodded in approval, then stood and went to the com-link unit Jason had installed on the desk of his office. Kim watched as her father changed from the frequency used for normal radio traffic to one for private communication. "Mother?" he called.

"Yes, Jarrell?" came the immediate reply.

"Are we secure?"

"Completely. What's up?"

"You have a copy of all our laws stored in your memory banks, correct?"

"You know the law that Kimmy tried to invoke?"

"Yes. A completely asinine law if you ask me," Mother replied with what sounded like a snort of derision.

"Well, while I may agree with you, Mother," Jarrell said with a grin, "I need you to search it and find out if there have been any amendments made to that law since it was first enacted."

"Sure. Hold on," Mother said.

Kim wondered why her father had not specified to Mother as to what the amendment was, then realized he didn't want to give the computer any clues that might allow it to pick up on what was going on and 'make up' an amendment that would suit the situation.

"There's been one amendment," Mother told him a few seconds later.

"Just one?" Jarrell asked.

"Yep."

Jarrell glanced briefly at Kim. "Mother, give me the date of the amendment, and then read it to me verbatim."

"The date is Twenty-Thirteen, Year of Record," Mother began, "and reads as follows.

"'If the wife of a man is, for whatever reason, unable to conceive and bear him a child, that man shall be able to take a second wife without having to divorce the first, and without her having to resort to the provisions provided for in the original law. However, to prevent abuse of this amendment, the following stipulations shall be set forth.

"'The second wife shall be a sister to the first. Should there be no sister, or no sister of marriageable age and status, the man shall select one of her cousins. Should there be no cousins, or no cousins of marriageable age and status, then a non-related woman may be selected.

"'Should there be no sisters or cousins, it shall fall upon the original wife to provide at least three non-related women of her selection to her husband for his choice. Should none of them be acceptable to him, the first wife shall select another three. She shall continue in this manner until a second, suitable wife is found. However, the first wife has the authority to disapprove of the woman selected in this manner should she feel that compatibility with the second wife would not be achieved, thereby causing disruptions in the relationship between her and the husband.

"'Once the second wife is selected, and the marriage consummated, the following stipulations shall be set forth to protect the rights of both wives.

"'In the event of the death of the husband prior to that of either wife, the first wife shall claim legal right to all holdings established during her marriage to the husband prior to the second marriage. Those properties shall be hers alone, with no claim being placed against them by the second wife.

"All properties and wealth accumulated from the time of the second marriage shall be divided between the first and second wife, with the first wife receiving one-fourth and the second wife receiving the remaining three-fourths for herself and her children.

"'Should the first wife die prior to the husband and the second wife, all properties and wealth shall become the property of the second wife and her children, with equal portions to each. The court shall make this division to assure equal allotments to all surviving parties.

"'Should the second wife die prior to the first, and prior to the husband, the first wife shall retain all properties and wealth acquired prior to the second marriage, but only one-fourth from the date of the second marriage, with the remaining three-fourths being divided equally among the children of the second wife.

"'Signed into law, with immediate enactment, this Seventh day of Kalla, in the Year of Record, Twenty-Thirteen.'"

"That's it?" Jarrell asked.

"That's it," Mother told him. "I take it that's what you were looking for?"

"Yes. Thank you, Mother. Jarrell out."

Jarrell switched the frequency back to its normal channel and returned to sit across from Kim. He poured two glasses of cold water from the pitcher on the small table between them and handed one to Kim. "Well, you heard her. What will you do now?"

"Try and convince Jason to marry Vinny."

"What if he refuses, Kimella? Or what if Vinny does? It's not a given that she'll go along with it."

"Daddy," she said in exasperation, "why are you trying to make this so difficult for me? I would think that you would want to see both of your daughters happy and married to the man they love?"

"I do, Kimmy, but right now I'm trying to think of what Jason and Vinny might also want, not just you. I know that such an arrangement would please you, but are you absolutely certain it would also please your sister? Or Jason?"

"Yes," Kim replied firmly. "Daddy, if this doesn't work, Vinny is going to enter the temple and take the Sacred Vow of Chastity and Purity. She says she can be a High Priestess in a year or so. Is that what you want for her?"

Jarrell took a sip of his water before answering. "I would be proud of her if she were to become a High Priestess. But in answer to your question, I want, with all my heart, the happiness of you both. But there are times when other factors have to be taken into account and consideration. Times when individual happiness must be tempered by what is good, overall, for everyone concerned."

"Like when you acquiesced to Jason being proclaimed King of Preton? And when he accepted?" she asked softly.

Jarrell nodded slowly. "I admit that at first I had my doubts, but I couldn't fight Seta and the prophecy, so I had no choice but to put aside my own personal feelings. Fortunately, for all of us, Jason has turned out to be the best thing that has ever happened to us."

"But you don't think Jason and Vinny will do this, do you?"

"Vinny? I think she would leap at the chance to do it. But only if she thought it was what Jason also wanted. As for Jason? I really can't say. He might do it, and if so, then maybe everything would work out beautifully.

"Look, Kimmy, you and Vinny are closer than most sisters and always have been. There is a special bond between the two of you much as there is between the twins. Being sisters and best friends is one thing. Being co-wives to the same man is another.

"Remember, you would be sharing him with her in everything, including the bedroom. Are you ready to handle the emotional problems that could arise within you when Vinny is the one he's making love to at night and not you? Are you prepared to handle knowing that he's doing to her, with her, all the things he does to and with you to bring you pleasure and joy?"

Kim was silent. She had spent a lot of time thinking about just that very thing most of last night. And while it bothered her to no small degree, she felt she could learn to accept and deal with it.

"I think," she said at last, "that there will be some adjustments which will have to be made for all of us. As well as new ways of looking at things. But I also feel that the life I share with them both will help the three of us to overcome whatever problems may arise."

For the first time since she had asked him about the amendment, Kim saw her father actually smile.

"Well, Muggles, I know you and your stubborn determination. If anyone can get the two of them to go along with this, you can. So, while it may be a little premature on my part, I would suggest you help your sister pick out her wedding dress."

Kim started to laugh, but her laughter was interrupted by the voice of Mother coming from the speaker. "Hey, guys, would someone like to tell me what's going on, or should I just make an educated guess?"

"How did you know I was here, Mother?" Kim replied.

"I heard your breathing earlier when Jarrell and I were talking."

"Oh, come on, Mother," Jarrell quipped. "How could you tell it was Kimmy's breathing you heard?"

"Jarrell, am I, or am I not, the smartest thing in this little corner of the universe?"

"You are, Mother," he conceded with a grin.

"Then trust me when I say I knew it was her. Besides, you only confirmed it when you asked me to check out that amendment. Hell, I knew what was up the second you did. You wouldn't have asked me about it on your own, and if Vinny had wanted to know about it, she would have asked me herself. As would have Jason. So, by the process of elimination that only left Kim. Hey, Blimpo, how ya doing?" Mother called out to Kim with a chuckle.

Kim laughed and shook her head at the comments of the computer. "Just fine, Mother."

"Good. Okay, I take it you're gonna try to convince his Royal Highness to take Vinny as his number two wife, correct?"

"Yes."

"Lots of luck! However, just to make sure you are within the letter of the law, you better do it before you have the baby and organ transplant."

"Why?" Kim asked.

"Because once you have the baby and undergo the transplant to correct your problem, the law will no longer apply to you. Actually, just between us, you're already bending it just a little, and we all know what a stickler he is for the law."

"You're right. I never thought of that," Kim replied thoughtfully.

"Ain'cha glad you got me around to pick out the little details like that for you?" Mother teased.

"Yes. Thank you, Mother."

"No problem. But don't expect me to try and help you convince him that he should do this."

"Why not?" Kim asked. "I would think that you would be in favor of it?"

Mother snickered. "Privately, just between us conspirators, I think it would work out just fine for all concerned, just as I thought making him king was a good move. But also like that decision, I won't try to influence him one way or the other.

"When he comes to talk to me about it, and he will, I'll point out the pros and cons and then let him make his own decision. He'll need me to be objective and impartial when he talks to me about it. You should both also keep something else in mind."

"What's that?" Kim asked.

"As much as I love all of you, my first loyalty is, and always will be, to Jason.'

Kim nodded in understanding. "I know, Mother. But could you maybe give me some idea as to how I should approach him with this?"

"Not really, Kim. Look, we all know there's no easy way to get Jason to change his mind about anything. Or to accept something which happens to go against what he may personally believe in. The only advice I can give you is to just lay it all out to him, give him the facts, then beat him over the head with the idea that this is what you believe is best for everyone."

Kim and Jarrell both laughed at this. "Yeah, he can be a little stubborn at times, can't he?" Kim said to Mother.

"That's an understatement," Mother replied with a laugh. "Now," she continued, her tone changing and becoming serious again, "there is something I would like to see you and Vinny about when you get a chance to come up."

Kim immediately picked up on the tone in Mother's voice. She glanced at her father to see if he had, but his expression didn't reveal anything to her.

"Sure, Mother," Kim replied. "I'm due for a checkup in a couple of days, but if you want, I'll get Vinny and come up today. How's that?"

"That's fine. Captain Ster is out behind the barracks and he has a shuttle handy," Mother told her. "I'm sure he would be more than happy to fly the two of you up."

"All right. I'll go ask him."

"Okay, I'll see you when you get her."

"I wonder what Mother's up to?" Jarrell asked as Kim stood and began making her way toward the door.

Kim wondered herself. "Who knows? With Mother it could be just about anything," she told Jarrell.

As Jarrell opened the door, the guards posted outside snapped to attention, Kim kissed Jarrell's cheek. "You still haven't told me if you're for or against this, Daddy."

"Kimella, if you can pull it off, then you have my total blessings, and your mother's as well."

"Will you talk to mom about it?"

"Of course."

"Thank you, Daddy. I'll see you later."

"Want us to come by for supper?" Jarrell asked as she reached the stairs leading down to the barracks.

"Good idea," she told him. "It might help make things easier. I'll see you then." Kim turned to one of the guards. "Will you take me to the barracks to see Captain Ster?"

"Of course, my Lady," the man replied as he held out his arm for her to hold on to.

Kim wanted to laugh at the stiff formality of the man. She wished the men of the Royal Guard would be a little more relaxed and less rigid, but she knew Ster was the cause of this. The Captain had instilled in the members of the Royal Guard a sense of duty, honor and responsibility towards her, Jason and the rest of the Vehey family that had become a way of life for them.

Ster adhered to it himself in public, however, due to his special relationship and closeness to Janella and the twins, he was more relaxed when they were alone. Kim and Vinny often took special delight in teasing him just to watch him blush. Kim knew she and Vinny shouldn't do it, but Ster made it so easy for them at times.

Both she and Vinny had come to love Ster like a brother, but to little Janella, after Jason, Ster was just about the greatest thing since the invention of candy. Janella's openly stated intentions of marrying Ster when she got older was a constant source of amusement to everyone except Ster. Those comments always caused him to blush and laugh them off whenever they were brought up. But Kim sometimes wondered just how serious her daughter was when she talked about it. She knew Janella never said anything of that nature lightly.

As Kim and her escort made their way around to the back of the barracks she had to smile at what she saw. Ster was kneeling in the dirt behind Janella. His arms were around her as he showed her the proper way to hold a <u>ho-tachi</u> in her hands. The moment he saw Kim he snapped to attention, grinning sheepishly as she smiled at him before looking down at Janella. "Aren't you supposed to be in school?" she asked.

"We had a test today. I finished early so my teacher said I could leave," Janella replied with a grin.

'I see. Remind me to have a talk with your teachers. Just because your father is the king, that doesn't mean you should get any special privileges."

"But I don't, Mommy. All the kids who finished early got to leave," Janella told her in defense.

"Humm, okay." Kim looked up at Ster. "Think she'll be any good with that?" she asked, indicating the sword.

"Beri says I'll be the best swordswoman on all of Alazon by the time he's done teaching me," Janella replied before Ster could answer.

Kim could only grin at Janella's sense of self assurance, and her use of Ster's first name in such a casual manner. "Well, in that case I'm sure you will. Now, do you mind if I borrow the Captain for a little while?"

"Why?" Janella asked.

"Because I need him to take me and Vinny up to see Mother for my checkup."

"Mommy, your next checkup isn't for another two days yet. That means you're gonna go see her for something else. Can I come?"

"That's 'may I come', and the answer is no, not this time. But I'll bring you something back."

"Okay," Janella replied cheerfully. "Then 'may I' at least fly back to the house with you to pick up Vinny?"

Kim laughed and nodded.

The three of them walked to the shuttle. Kim and Ster took their seats as Janella closed the hatch. The girl then climbed up onto Ster's lap, looking over at Kim with an impish grin.

"Mommy, you won't tell Daddy that Beri is teaching me how to fly, will you? I don't want Beri getting into trouble because of me."

"No, Sweetheart," she replied with a grin. "I won't tell him."

Kim watched as Ster allowed Janella to start the engines. He placed his hands over Janella's smaller ones as the girl grasped the controls, her eyes darting to all the gauges to make sure everything was as it was supposed to be. Km knew that if Janella tackled flying the way she did everything else, her daughter would be flying solo as soon as she was big enough to reach all the controls on her own. Kim also had a feeling that Jason already knew about Janella's flying lessons. There was very little that escaped his attention. When they landed beside the house, Janella turned to Ster and gave him a quick hug and kiss on the cheek. "I'll go get Vinny," she told Kim as she darted from the shuttle.

Kim looked at Ster and grinned. "It would seem, Captain, that my daughter is more than just a little fond of you."

"The feeling is mutual," Ster replied, smiling bashfully. "Actually, it's nice to have her company and attention. I don't have any sisters, so she fills that role for me."

"Hi, guys, what's up?" Vinny asked as she stepped into the shuttle. She pulled down the seat behind Ster and strapped herself in.

"Mother wants to see us," Kim told her. "Oh, and I was just discussing the Captain's relationship with Janella."

"You mean like the part where she says she's gonna marry him when she gets older?" Vinny teased.

"I hadn't gotten to that yet. Of course, that's providing he waits for her. After all, some other beautiful, charming young woman may come along and beat Janella to him. And there's also the fact that he's eleven years older than she is."

"That doesn't matter," Vinny replied as Ster lifted the shuttle into the air. "They've both been given the serum, so once Janella reaches maturity, the age difference won't matter a bit."

"Good point, sis. But what I want to know," Kim said as she looked at Ster, who was trying not to laugh at the good natured teasing by the sisters, "is what the Captain has to say about all this?"

"Is everyone comfortable?" Ster asked, avoiding the question and causing Kim and Vinny to laugh.

"Yes," Kim replied. "All we need is for you to drop us off. We'll have Jason pick us up later on his way home. Or, if he isn't done by the time we're ready, we can call you. You don't mind, do you?"

Ster shook his head. "Of course not. You know I'm always at the disposal of you and your family at any time."

"You're very sweet, Captain," Kim said, turning her head and winking at Vinny, "but tell me something."

"What's that?"

"If you don't mind me prying, why is it that you haven't married yet? Or is there someone special in your life we don't know about?"

Ster glanced over at her briefly. "You would know if there were. Remember, anyone we marry must pass the approval and acceptance of the Family."

"True," Vinny said from behind him, "but is there anyone in the picture you might be considering?"

"Not really," Ster replied with a shrug of his shoulders. "It's hard to find a woman who can accept my schedule and lifestyle. Along with my regular guard duties, I also supervise the training of new recruits, and handle the sword training for all the guard.

"When you add to that my duties of maintaining the Royal Guard for your family, and the time I spend with Janella and the twins, it doesn't leave me much time for anyone else.

"I live with my parents and they keep telling me I should slow down and find a nice girl, get married and have children, but for the time being that's a little hard to do. Besides, I'm waiting for the right woman to come along. When she does, I'll know it."

"Well, Captain, you already have one proposal that we know of," teased Vinny.

"That's news to me," he replied.

"Really? I was referring to Janella."

Kim watched Ster blush slightly and shake his head at the of Janella and her stated intentions.

"You know how kids are," Ster finally replied. "They're liable to say anything that pops into their heads."

"What? You don't think my daughter is serious?" Kim teased, enjoying the fun she and Vinny were having.

"My Lady," Ster answered solemnly, "if Princess Janella were five or six years older I would probably have to take her very seriously. But when a girl of ten tells me she's going to marry me, well, I feel flattered, but I also take it with a grain of salt. And a smile."

Kim looked at Ster and grinned. "Captain, you know my daughter as well as anyone. You that that, for the most part, Janella doesn't say things lightly. I personally happen to think she is very serious in her intentions to marry you."

"Well, my Lady," Ster replied with a grin of his own, "I guess I'll just have to wait and see what happens between now and the time she is of marriageable age, won't I?"

Kim and Vinny grinned at one another. They both knew of Janella's determination when the girl set her mind to doing something. They also knew she was a lot more serious about her intentions toward Ster than the young Captain realized. It would be interesting to see what developed in the coming years.

Ster brought the shuttle to a gentle landing and the two sisters exited and moved away as he slowly turned it and left. "Hey, Mother," Kim called out as the shuttle slipped through the force field of the bay doors, "do you think you could reduce the gravity on this star hopping crate just a little to make carrying this load a bit easier on me?"

"No problem," Mother replied with a chuckle.

Kim breathed a sigh of relief as she felt the gravity of the ship being lowered. Her reaction caused her and Vinny to start laughing.

"Okay, Mother," Kim said as she stepped through the hatch to the companionway, "what's the big secret you want to talk about?"

"You know where the bio-engineering labs are?" Mother asked.

"Sure. Is that where you want us to go?" Kim asked.

"Yes."

"Ok, we're on our way."

Bio-engineer was two decks below the medical labs. Kim had been there a couple of times while exploring the ship, but had never really spent any time there. She and Vinny made their way quickly in the lighter gravity. When they arrived, Kim noticed that this was the same door which had been locked the last time she was here, but now it stood open. As she and Vinny entered the lab they found themselves surrounded by equipment which was not normally in use, and Kim wondered what was going on.

"Take a seat," Mother told them. "This could be a bit of a surprise, and I wouldn't want anything happening to you."

Kim and Vinny looked at one another curiously, wondering what was going on and why Mother was acting so mysterious. As they sat down on chairs near the computer console their attention was suddenly riveted on the bed in the connecting lab.

The other lab was separated from the one they were in by a large window with a door to one side of it. Kim looked at the bed in the other room, then at Vinny, as if to confirm the fact that there really was a body beneath the sheet on the bed.

"Kimmy, Vinny," Mother began, her voice sounding somewhat hesitant and nervous, "I've done something without Jason's knowledge or permission, and believe it or not, I'm more than a little frightened of what he might do when he finds out."

"Mother," Kim said softly, "I think you better skip the small talk and get to the point."

Kim's eyes were glued to the figure on the bed in the other lab as her mind tried to figure out just what was going on.

"All right," the computer replied with a sigh. "I've cloned a body and transferred a part of myself into the brain of it."

"By all the gods!" Vinny exclaimed in a shocked whisper.

But Kim was suddenly hit with something else. "Mother, who… who's body did you clone?" she asked as icy fingers of fear started to creep up her spine. She was afraid she knew whose genes had been used, and wondered how Mother could do such a thing to her. Or to Jason.

"His sister," Mother told her. "But with some slight alterations."

Kim felt the breath rush out of her as she silently thanked Lofa that it hadn't been the genes of Nadia. Kim didn't think she could have handled that.

"No, Kimmy," Mother said as if knowing what Kim had been thinking. "I wouldn't clone Nadia. That would have been cruel to both you and Jason, as well as to the memory of what they once shared. You should know me better than that."

"I…yes. Sorry, Mother."

"But why his sister?" asked Vinny.

"I thought that would be the safest," Mother replied. "I thought she would be the one person he would be most likely to accept."

As Kim and Vinny watched in stunned amazement, the figure in the other room slowly sat up. The sheet covering it fell away from the face, then the upper body, and neither sister cold speak as the figure sat all the way up and completely removed the sheet before sliding off the bed to stand beside it. The figure looked through the window at them, fearful apprehension on its face.

"Do…do you think he'll be mad?"

It took Kim a couple of seconds to realize that the voice asking the question had come from the figure of the woman in the other room via the two way speakers and not the computer itself. She shook her head to clear it and stared at the figure again.

Blonde hair fell down past the woman's waist in soft rippling waves. It reminded Kim of the way gold reflected sunlight when it was turned certain ways. The face was definitely that of Patricia, or 'Trish' as Jason called her, but it was an older, more mature Trish. This was not the child of nine who had died on the way here, and the body was that of a mature and fully grown woman. The figure stood before them completely nude as both Kim and Vinny stared at it. They saw the full, rounded breasts, the slender waist, flat stomach, and gently flaring hips.

<u>She's beautiful!</u> Kim thought as she and Vinny stood and walked to the door connecting the two rooms. Stepping through it they stopped just inside to stare at the figure of the woman only a few feet away.

"I…I made a few genetic alterations," the figure said shyly. "Instead of growing to what would have been the normal height for Trish, which would have been close to six feet tall by my calculations, I restricted the growth patter to stop at five feet, two inches. That way I'm just slightly taller than the average woman of Alazon, but not so much that I stand out. Did…did I do all right?" it asked nervously.

"What…what do we call you?" Vinny asked softly.

The figure shrugged. "I don't know. I have the face and body of Trish, but my brain is that of Mother. Oh, I shouldn't have done it!"

the woman suddenly moaned, lowering her face to her hands and beginning to cry.

Kim and Vinny stepped forward to take the woman in their arms as she began to shake with sobs which tore at their own hearts.

Kim forgot that she was holding a close, an artificially created person. She saw only a woman in pain and misery. She and Vinny led the woman to a chair and began to comfort her.

"It's ok," Kim said softly as she used a corner of her robe to wipe the clone's eyes. As she did she noticed that the woman's eyes were the same startling blue as Jason's. "I think it's wonderful, and I think Jason will love it…you."

"It's sure gonna be a shock, though," Vinny said with a grin.

"But what if he doesn't?" the clone asked. "What will I do then?"

"Don't worry, he'll like you," Kim promised in soothing tones.

But despite her words to the clone there were plenty of doubts in Kim's mind. She was just about to hit him with the idea of marrying Vinny, which she still hadn't told her sister about, and that was going to be a shock in and of itself. Then to spring a clone on him who looked like his little sister, had she lived, might be too much even for Jason to take. <u>Lofa, please be with me</u>, she prayed silently.

"If he doesn't like me, or can't accept me, then I'll have to dispose of myself," the clone said, using the cold, clinical tone the computer used when discussing something serious.

Kim wasn't sure she understood what the woman meant by that. "What do you mean?" she asked.

"This is the third attempt," the clone told her. "I had to dispose of the first two in the early stages before I got it right, and if Jason doesn't approve, then I'll dispose of this one as well."

"You'll do no such thing!" Kim told her sternly. "It's just another little surprise he'll have to lean to accept and deal with. Besides, we all know how much he loved his sister, and when he sees you he won't be able to do anything but accept and love you."

Vinny looked at Kim questioningly. "What do you mean by 'another little surprise', Kimmy?"

The clone looked up at Kim. "You haven't told her yet?"

"I haven't had the chance," Kim replied with a grin.

"Tell me what?" Vinny asked.

"Sorry, Sis," Kim said with a sigh. "I was gonna tell you earlier but, well, things came up," she said with a quick glance at the clone.

Kim turned and went to the console and pulled out a chair to sit on. She waited until Vinny had also taken a seat before speaking again.

"Sis, there's an amendment to the law which would allow Jason to marry you without divorcing me. He could be legally married to us both."

Kim watched her sister's face carefully. She saw the look of shock and disbelief slowly be replaced by acceptance of what Kim was telling her.

"Her," Vinny said, nodding at the clone, "he'll be able to accept, once he gets over the initial shock. But marry me? No way he'll do that, Kimmy. It will never happen."

Kim signed and shook her head. "Vinny, let me ask you something. Do you love him?"

Vinny lowered her eyes for a moment. "You already know the answer to that, Kimmy," she replied softly.

Kim nodded. "Ok, so let me ask you this. If you had the choice between spending your life as a Temple Virgin, even as a High Priestess, or being Jason's second wife, which would you opt for?"

"Kimmy, you know which one I'd chose, but it will never happen!" Vinny replied with a note of desperation in her voice.

"But if I can get him to do it, will you be his second wife? Vinny," she continued before here sister could answer, "There's no other woman in the world I would even consider doing this with, but I believe in my heart it will work for us.

"But before I go and try to convince him it's the right thing to do for all of us, I have to know that you'll go along with it and that it's what you want. If not, then I won't say a word to him about it."

Kim could see the torment in the eyes of her sister as Vinny stood and paced the room silently. Vinny finally returned to her chair and sat down. She glanced briefly at the clone before looking at Kim again. "If you can get Jason to go along with it, yes, I'll be his second wife."

"Good!" Vinny replied with a grin. She turned to the clone. "Now, let's get back to you and what to do with you." She laughed lightly. "By all the gods, Jason won't know if he's coming or going by the time we get through with him."

"You know," Vinny said to the clone, "you're going to have the men of Alazon going crazy. You'll have the same effect on them that Jason had on the women. Especially with that blonde hair and those blue eyes. Come on, let's go find you some clothes."

For the next couple of hours the three of them had fun going through the store rooms to find outfits for the clone. They laughed and giggled like school girls as they put together a collection of jump suits, dresses and other clothing suitable for Alazon. Kim and Vinny made the clone try on just about everything, giving her their opinions on what they liked and what they didn't. When they finally put together what they considered a complete wardrobe, they summed a servo droid to carry it all to a cabin she would use as her own for the time being. They decided it would be best for her to stay in a separate section of the ship for the time being so Jason wouldn't run into her.

"It feels strange to actually be able to experience the senses of touch and smell," the clone told them. "Everything is so new and different. So exciting. I can't wait to get down to the surface and see what it's like."

Kim smiled as she sat down on the bed and began absently folding the clothing and placing it in neat pies. "I wouldn't be in too much of a rush," she told the clone. "Right now there are other things for Jason to consider.

"If we hit him with too much at once, it will only confuse him, and we could end up blowing everything by doing that. Having you make an appearance right now would only cloud the issue of him marrying Vinny, and right now that's the most important issue we have to deal with."

"I agree," the clone replied.

"So, what will you do?" Vinny asked.

"Stay here for the time being," the clone replied. "Hide out until the time is right. Besides, I need time to get used to this body and see what all I can do with it. I'm still not a hundred percent comfortable with it yet."

"What if Jason comes up?" Kim asked.

"That's not a problem," the clone replied. "You see, even though I'm now in a human body, I'm still connected to the computer by way of a number of microchips I've implanted in the brain and body. In a sense I'm a physical manifestation of the computer itself. I know most of what the computer knows, and I'm also able to communicate with it at any time. It's sort of like two versions of the same entity."

"Like Vanda and Manda," Kim replied with a laugh.

The clone nodded. "Yes, to some degree, but more on a bio-mechanical level. The micro sensors implanted in my brain allows for communication between the physical body and the computer. It a way it's similar to the telepathy of the twins."

"So everything the computer knows, you know as well?" Vinny asked.

"More or less. Although I've limited myself somewhat to certain information and knowledge in the brain of this body so I can learn some things on my own. But I can also tap into the computer here on the ship any time I want as long as there's no more than five hundred miles between us. Anything over that and I have to use a communicator just like everyone else."

"That could be useful," Kim told her. "Hey, Vinny, can you imagine what Shon, Hass, Ster and Uncle Busker are gonna say when they see her?"

Vinny smiled and nodded her head. "They're gonna go crazy. But not just them. Every man above the age of puberty is going to have the hots for her."

"Do…do you really think I'm attractive?" the clone asked nervously as it looked down at its body.

"Try stunning," Kim told her. "That golden hair, those blue eyes, and that outrageous body is going to have the male hormones raging all over Alazon! Oh, hey, do you have the KLZ serum in you?"

"Of course. Once I finally got things right, I injected myself with it."

"You know, Vinny," Kim said with a mischievous twinkle in her eyes, "I think this is gonna be fun."

# THIRTY SEVEN

As sure as he knew his own name, Jason knew that Kim and Vinny were up to something. But he also knew they weren't about to tell him what it was until they were good and ready. That was a lesson he had learned the hard way after dealing with the two of them for over a year now. He thought of going to the twins to get them to try and find out what their older sisters were hiding from him, but the last time he did that, the twins had found out what he wanted to know, then laughed and refused to tell him.

When Kim and Vinny got home they went to the kitchen and began preparing supper. Jason took one look at them and decided to stay outside. He snatched Janella up and carried her over to the pool, where the two of them quickly stripped out of their clothes and dove in nude. As they played in the water he thought about taking Kim, Janella, Vinny and the twins on a short holiday to the planet of the dolphins. He was curious to see how the twins would react with Little One and the other dolphins. With the twin's own telepathic abilities, he knew they would probably love it, and the dolphins might even be able to teach the twins how to expand and better control their abilities.

Jason heard the shouts of the twins followed by dual splashes in the pool behind him and knew that Jarrell, Liet and the twins had arrived. As the nude bodies of the twins surfaced on either side of him they grinned at him mischievously, and he knew that they were aware of what Km and Vinny were up to. He also knew they weren't about to tell him.

Jason and the kids played tag in the water for a few minutes before he finally swam to the side and climbed out. He Dried of and slipped his jump suit back on. As he did, he saw the twins pull Janella off to one side and begin whispering in her ears. She looked up at him, her eyes going wide as she began to grin and nod her own little head. Within seconds he saw the same twinkle in her eyes as those of the twins, letting him know that Janella was now in on whatever it was going on with Kim and Vinny.

Jason walked over to join Jarrell and Liet at the table. It only took one look at their faces to realize that they were in on it as well. The last time this happened he had been crowned King of Preton on his wedding day, and more surprises like that he didn't want or need.

He sat down beside Jarrell, thinking of how this man had come to be like a father to him. He remembered all the nights the two of them had sat in the courtyard behind Jarrell's house just talking. Jason had done most of the talking while Jarrell had listened patiently, offering advice and consolation when the older man thought they were called for. More than once Jarrell had refused to make a decision for him, forcing Jason to make it himself. The older man had also forced Jason to accept the responsibility Jason sometimes tried to avoid in some manner or another. Much like Jason's own father, Jarrell never told Jason what was right or wrong, but forced Jason to look at it objectively. Like Mother, Jarrell would present all sides of an issue, then let Jason decide for himself which course of action to take.

The only thing they had ever really disagreed on was making Jason king. On that Jarrell had been adamant, even though Jason knew Jarrell was personally against having a king over the people of Preton again. But the older man had put aside his own personal feelings and beliefs, forcing both Jason and himself to accept it. But what had started out as a position of authority over one country soon became something he didn't think even Jarrell had expected; King of Alazon. But Jarrell had been there with him every step of the way to offer advice and a sympathetic ear.

"Would one of you like to tell me what's going on?" Jason asked as he looked from Jarrell to Liet.

"What makes you think something is going on?" Jarrell asked casually with a straight face.

"Your two oldest daughters have been giggling and carrying on every since I picked them up from the ship, and Mother was acting somewhat strange as well. The two of you show up for dinner in the middle of the week, and the twins are giving me that look which tells me that something is definitely going on."

Jarrell reached out to scratch Baby's head as the dog came over to the table looking for a little attention. She wanted a few friendly scratches before heading off to play with Janella and the twins, who were now chasing one another around the large yard in a game of tag, their nude bodies flashing golden and silver in the sunlight.

"Jason," Jarrell replied, trying to look dejected, "you hurt me with your accusations. Do you think I would hide something of importance from you?"

"In a heartbeat!" he replied with a short laugh.

Jarrell looked at him for a moment, the smile on the older man's face slowly being replaced by a look of seriousness that Jason was very familiar with. Jason knew then that whatever Kim and Vinny were up to, it was serous, and that worried him.

"You'll be told in time" Jarrell finally replied. "And by those whose interests are best served by it. It is not my place, nor that of my wife, to do so at this time."

Before Jason could respond to that, Kim came out to stand beside him. She called for the kids to wash off and get ready to eat. As she sat down beside him her face was now more solemn than it had been earlier, but there was still that impish twinkle in her eyes. He signed with resignation. "All right, I guess I'll just have to wait and see."

Liet grinned and nodded her head. "That's usually the best course where Kimmy's concerned," she told him.

"I'll be back in a minute," he told them.

He stood and went to the master bedroom, where he stripped off the jumpsuit and stepped into the shower to rinse off. He quickly dried and slipped on a pair of loose fitting shorts, tee shirt and sandals before returning to the table. The others hadn't bothered to wait on him and were already busy eating. He was quick to pick up on the quieter, more somber attitude of everyone than what was normal.

Jason ate without really tasting his food. Conversation at the table was occupied mostly by Janella and the twins, who talked about things they were involved with in school. It was as if everyone were deliberately avoiding the one subject he wanted to hear about, which, he knew from past experience, was exactly what they were doing. He put up with it, but wished the ingrained rules of protocol banning serious conversations at meal times weren't so adhered to.

Once dinner was over and he was holding a cup of coffee between his palms, rolling it slowly back and forth, he looked around the table at all of them. "Ok," he said, "I think it's about time someone told me what's going on."

His tone was no longer that of a husband, father and son-in-law, but that of the King of Alazon.

"You've all been hiding some big secret from me, but now it's time you let me know what's going on."

Liet cleared her throat and smiled at him. "Jason, before they tell you, I would just like to say that Jarrell and I have discussed it and are in complete favor of it.

"It makes sense, and it would make a lot of people happy, but I will understand if you don't feel the same way.

"Now, having said that, I think Jarrell, the twins and I should leave. This is something which must be discussed between you, Kim and Vinny, and even Janella, without us around. Our presence might possibly serve to influence your decision, and that would not be right. However, should you wish to discuss it with us later, don't hesitate to call or come over, regardless of the hour."

Liet stood up and motioned for the twins to do likewise. They were reluctant at first but finally complied. They came around the table to hug and kiss Jason, Kim and Vinny before joining their parents and leaving.

Once they were gone, Jason looked down at Janella, who had climbed onto his lap. She giggled and smiled up at him. He raised his eyes to Kim and Vinny. They no longer had the twinkle of amusement in their eyes. Now they both seemed somewhat pensive, as if unsure of themselves. Vinny lowered her eyes for a moment and then abruptly stood up, looking as if she were on the verge of tears.

"I can't, Kimmy!" she cried. "It isn't right. I know we talked about it and thought it would work, but it won't!"

Vinny fled into the house, but not before Jason saw the tears in her eyes as she cast him a pain filled glance. He looked at Kim, more confused than ever at this sudden turn of events. "Princess," he said softly to Janella, "do you know what this is all about?"

She nodded her head slowly. "Yes, Daddy, but I can't tell you. I promised."

Jason stood up and carried her in his arms as he moved around to sit one of the lounge chairs, following Kim's example. "That's all right, Princess. I understand. After all, a promise is a promise and shouldn't be broken."

"Daddy?"

"Yes, Sweetheart?"

"Then will you promise me that you won't be mad at Mommy or Vinny?"

"Well, I don't know what's going on but, okay, I promise not to get mad."

"Thanks, Daddy."

Janella turned her head to kiss his cheek before sliding from his lap. She went to Kim and kissed her as well before darting into the house.

Kim patted the chase lounge she was on. "This one's bigger," she told him.

Jason shook his head with a grin and moved to join her. As he sat down beside her, he wrapped his arms around her to hold her close. Neither of them spoke for a moment, and he knew she was thinking of the best way to tell him whatever it was she had on her mind. Kim finally turned her head to look deeply into his eyes.

"Jason" she said softly, "you have told me over and over that you would do anything in the world to make me happy, but I've never really asked you for anything, have I?"

"No, not really," he replied thoughtfully.

"Do you know what Vinny's plans are after the baby is born and I'm able to get around and do things on my own again without her help?"

Jason was somewhat confused about the switch of topics from herself to her sister and wondered what she had in mind.

"Not really. I haven't even thought about it. I take it that this big secret you've all been keeping from me has something to do with Vinny?"

Kim nodded slowly. "Yes. She...she's going to join the Temple of Lofa and go into training to become a High Priestess. She's also going to take the Sacred Vow of Chastity and Purity. Jason, that means she can never marry and must remain a virgin for the rest of her life."

Jason looked at Kim with a sense of confusion. What she was saying didn't make sense to him.

"Why would she do that?" he asked. "I mean, I'll grant you the temple would definitely benefit from her joining, and she would make a terrific High Priestess, but to remain a virgin and never marry? What about Naed?"

Kim shook her head sadly. "She won't marry Naed, Jason. She loves him, but not in the way he wants her to. Or the way she should if she were going to be his wife."

"That could change," he told her. "Naed's a good man and he loves Vinny a lot. In time I think she would come to love him the same way. Besides, I know he's patient and willing to wait for that to happen."

"It will never happen, Jason. I know it, Vinny knows it, and so does Naed. In fact, you should keep in mind that it was Naed who told me what it is I'm about to tell you."

Now Jason felt totally confused. He had no idea of what Kim was getting at, or what it was that Naed could have told her that would have such an effect on all of them.

"Jason," Kim said softly, "if you told Vinny you didn't want her to enter the temple, that you wanted her to try and see if things might work out for her and Naed, then that's what she'd do. She would marry Naed and do all she could to be the best wife possible to him, but she would do it because it's what you wanted, not because it's what she actually wanted."

Kim paused for a moment to give Jason time to reflect on that. As much as he hated to admit it, deep down in his heart he knew she was right.

"I don't like the idea of her going into the temple," he said after a moment, "but neither would I want her to marry a man she didn't really love. Even if that man were Naed. That would be wrong."

"Exactly," Kim replied. "So rather than do that, she'll go into the temple. But even there her heart wouldn't really be in it."

"Look, Kim, just because she may not marry Naed, that doesn't mean she has to shut herself off from the rest of the world by entering the temple. Why would she do that? It doesn't make any sense to me."

"She would do that, Jason, because the man she really loves won't marry her. Or so she believes."

Things were suddenly starting to make some sense to him. But it was a convoluted sort of sense, and Jason didn't particularly care for the direction of this conversation, even though he wasn't absolutely sure as to just where it was headed. He started to say so, but Kim held her fingers to his lips to silence him. "Hear me out," she said softly.

"All right," he said with a sigh.

"Remember when I tried to take my life because I thought I couldn't bear you a child?"

"All too well," he told her in a voice barely audible. He felt a shiver run through his body as he hugged her tightly for a moment.

"Well, I knew the law stated that if a woman was unable to conceive she had two options. The first being divorce, which I knew you would fight and never grant me, and the second being suicide. What I didn't know, until Naed told me last night before he left, is that the law was amended to make for another provision. To make sure of it, this morning I went and checked it out with Dad, who also checked with Mother to verify it. Naed was right."

Kim took a breath and let it out slowly before continuing.

"This amendment allows for a man to take a second wife, without divorcing the first, if the first is unable to conceive. But one of the stipulations is that the second wife has to be a sister. However, if she doesn't have a sister, or one of marriageable age and single, then it can be a cousin. I won't go into it all. If you want to know everything it says you can have Mother kick you out a copy."

Jason felt himself being boxed in. She had set her trap and he now found himself in it. He knew what she was leading up to and that

*Alazon*

frightened him. Although he loved Vinny dearly, he didn't know if he could do what he had a feeling Kim was about to ask him to do.

Jason also knew in his heart that if he looked at things realistically, if it had been Vinny he had met first instead of Kim, things might have been different for him now. He knew Vinny was in love with him. He had tried to tell himself that he was only imagining things for a long time, but finally came to accept just how deep her feelings really were for him. And, because of that, he had consciously made sure he didn't do anything to encourage it.

"Jason," Kim aid softly, interrupting his thoughts, "I want you to marry Vinny. I know it may go against the way you were brought up, but this isn't Earth. It isn't New Hope. It's Alazon, Jason, and things are different here."

"Kim...."

"Let me finish," she told him. "I don't want to see my sister lock herself away in a temple for the rest of her life. I don't care how much the temple and the people might benefit from it. If that's selfish of me then I'll just have to be guilty of it.

"Nor do I want to see her marry a man she doesn't truly love just to make you happy, which we both know she would do if she thought it was what you wanted.

"Jason, the law says you can take a second wife if the first is unable to conceive, which mans that it would have to be done before I have the replacement surgery. And," she added softly, "I won't have the surgery until you do."

It was finally out, but that didn't lessen the sense of confusion Jason felt at her request. Or the brief touch of anger at her emotional blackmail by stating she wouldn't have the surgery which would enable her to conceive on her own until he did this. Thinking he knew what she was going to say, and actually hearing her voice it were two different things.

Jason didn't know what to say. He felt a sudden urge to be alone, to get away from all of them to think this through. He wanted to talk to Mother. She would know what to do. Even if she were in on the secret, which he knew she was, she would still help him. Perhaps she could help him find a way out of this which would enable all of them to find an equitable solution.

"I've got to think about this," he told her as he stood up. "There's no way I can give you any kind of answer right now." He looked around nervously, as if expecting to see Vinny any second. "I'll be back."

He turned and hurried toward the small shuttle parked on the landing pad beside the house. He climbed in and started the engines, quickly lifting the craft into the night sky. However, instead of heading directly for the <u>Stargazer</u>, he flew around for a while, aimlessly following the path of the river which flowed past Lemac, heading south east. Two hundred miles later, where the river joined another, he finally lifted the nose of the shuttle and headed for the ship.

After shutting down the engines of the shuttle inside the bay, Jason noticed that Mother was strangely silent as he made his way to the bridge. He often liked to come to the bridge to sit and do his thinking. He could shut himself in with only the small, softly flashing lights of the computer and controls for company. He opened the shields over the view screens to take in the expanse of stars presented to him as he sat in the Captain's seat and propped his feet up on the console. "You're in on this, aren't you?" he asked after a few minutes.

"Let's just say that I know about it," Mother replied.

"I suppose you think I should do it?"

"Jason, what I personally think or feel has no bearing on this matter. The only thing I will do is point out the pros and cons of it, what options may or may not be open to you, and then let you make your own decision."

"All the rhetoric aside, Mother, I know you have a personal opinion on this."

"Of course I do!" the computer replied with a chuckle. "But whatever it is, it's mine, and it doesn't have any bearing on your decision. In a situation such as this, Jason, my job is to advise you of the various options."

"I know what the options are," he replied dryly.

"Yeah, I kinda figured you did."

"did you also know that Kim said she wouldn't have the replacement surgery unless and until I married Vinny?"

"That I didn't know," Mother replied softly.

Jason was silent. He thought of the love it took on Kim's part to ask him to marry her sister. Not just her love for him, but her love for Vinny as well. He knew this wasn't a decision Kim had reached lightly, but one she had given a lot of thought and consideration to before approaching anyone with it. He also knew she had carefully thought of all the possible consequences of it. The fact that she had gone to her father to check it out, and then have Mother verify it only proved that.

"Mother, contact Busker and Shon," he said after a few minutes. "Tell Shon to pick up Hass, and that I want to see all three of them as soon as they can get up here."

"Hold on and you can tell them yourself."

Jason started to argue, but then sighed in resignation. "All right," he replied weakly. He felt as if he were fighting an uphill battle against overwhelming odds.

"Go ahead," Mother told him a few seconds later.

"Busker, Shon, whatever you're doing, drop it and come up to the ship. Shon, pick up Hass and bring him as well."

"What's up?" Busker asked.

"I'll explain when you get here. Oh, and don't, I repeat, do not talk to any members of the family before you come. Is that clear?"

He heard their hesitation but it was Shon who finally answered. "We read you. We're on our way."

"Jason out."

He leaned back in his seat with a loud sigh. He was trapped. He knew that whichever decision he made it would affect the lives of a lot of people, especially Vinny and Naed. Naed loved Vinny. What would he think of Jason if he were to marry Vinny? Betrayal? Would their friendship suffer because of it? If Naed were to feel resentment over it, would it one day lead to the two of them having to face one another at the end of swords?

Then he remembered Kim saying that it was Naed who had told her about this provision in the law in the first place. Jason wondered why Naed would do that if he loved Vinny so much? Naed knew the possible consequences of what might happen once he told Kim. <u>Maybe because he loves Vinny so much</u>, he thought to himself. He let his mind dwell on the type of man Naed was, and the amount of self-sacrifice it had taken on Naed's part to reveal this amendment in the law to Kim, knowing exactly what she would do with it.

# THIRTY EIGHT

Jason was still thinking about Naed when the door of the bridge slid open softly behind him. Busker and the brothers came in and took seats. He wondered how they had managed to arrive at the same time, but decided not to ask. They looked at him expectantly while waiting for him to speak.

"Kim wants me to marry Vinny," he told them bluntly, nearly laughing at the looks of shock on the faces of Busker and Hass. But the slow smile on the face of Shon surprised him somewhat.

"Kim wants a divorce?" Hass asked.

"No," Jason replied with a shake of his head.

"Then…."

"The amendment," Shon said softly.

Jason looked at Shon through narrowed eyes. "You know about it?" He saw the confusion on the faces of Busker and Hass, who didn't have the faintest idea of what he and Shon were talking about.

Shon nodded slowly. "Naed came to see me last night after he had spoken to Kim. After he left I had a feeling this meeting would be taking place."

Hass looked back and forth from Jason to Shon. "In the name of all the gods, will someone please tell me what the two of you are talking about?" he finally asked in frustration.

Shon looked at his brother and grinned. "There's an amendment to the law which allowed Kim to attempt to take her life. It was made about a hundred and thirty years ago. It states that a man can take a second wife, without having to divorce the first one, or having her kill herself, if she's unable to bear children."

"Oh, I see," Hass replied. But the look on his face indicated otherwise.

Busker leaned forward slightly in his seat and places his forearms on his knees. "Let me get this straight. This amendment would allow you to marry Vinny, while still remaining married to Kim?"

"Right."

"Are you going to do it?" Busker asked.

Jason shrugged his shoulders and spread his hands. "If I don't, Vinny's going to enter the temple to become a High Priestess, and take the Vow of Chastity and Purity. While that would be a boon to the Temple of Lofa, I don't want to see Vinny shut herself away like that. It would be a waste of a beautiful woman who has a hell of a lot to offer a man.

"Her other option, or so she believes, is to marry Naed, even though she doesn't love him the way she feels she should. Or the way he deserves. NoR does she feel she could ever truly love him that way.

"In other words, it would be an arranged marriage, so to speak. But if she thinks that's what I want, then that's what she'll do. And she'd break her neck in trying to be the best wife she could to him.

"But I don't want her doing that either," he told them. "I wouldn't want her to marry a man, no matter who he was, that she didn't love in all the right ways, living a life which would be a lie. That would be even worse than having her enter the temple."

"May I ask you something?" said Shon.

Jason turned to him and nodded.

"Do you love Vinny?"

Jason hesitated a moment before answering. "Yes, but not the same way I love Kim. I mean, there's a difference that's hard to explain. Sometimes I think that if I had met Vinny first, things might have turned out differently."

"The difference you speak of may not be as big as you think," Shon told him softly.

"What do you mean?"

"Let's suppose for a moment that Kim's suicide attempt had been successful. What do you think would have eventually happened between you and Vinny? Stop and think about it before you answer."

Jason didn't need to think about it. He already had, and had a pretty good idea of what would have happened. "I probably would have eventually married Vinny," he said at last, his voice heavy with defeat.

"Exactly," Shon said with a nod of his head. "She loves you every bit as much as Kimmy does, she's just as beautiful, and just as smart, if not smarter in some things, and in time she would have gotten you to love and marry her. And she would have done it without destroying or replacing the love you had for Kim. Just as Kim did without affecting the love you had for Nadia."

Jason studied Shon's face. There was wisdom in Shon which surfaced from time to time like a gently flowing stream, surprising in its clarity.

"Okay, for the sake of argument, let's say I do this. What about Naed?"

"It was his suggestion in the first place, remember?" Shon replied. "He's the one who told Kim about the amendment, knowing exactly what she would do with the information."

"I know," Jason stated with a sense of exasperation. "And that's what I don't understand. Why would he do it?"

"Because he loves Vinny and wants her to be happy," Shon told him. "And if being your second wife would make her happy, and he knows it would, then that's what he wants for her."

"Damn it, aren't you people ever the least bit selfish?" Jason snapped. His voice was louder than he intended it to be, revealing the frustration he was feeling. "All of you go around looking out for the happiness of others, but never for yourselves.

"Your father puts aside his personal convictions and beliefs to make me king, Kim is willing to share me with her sister, and Naed is willing to give up the woman he loves for her happiness, instead of fighting tooth and nail to win her heart for himself.

"And Vinny is willing to shit herself away in a temple for the rest of her life, or marry a man she doesn't really love, just to keep from hurting anyone and to make me happy. And the three of you sit here and act like this is the most natural thing in the world. Once, just once, I'd like to see someone say 'This is mine, and to hell with you, buddy'."

There was a long moment of silence after his little tirade. "Jason," Shon said at last.

"What?" he snapped.

"Make it a small, private wedding."

"Oh, for crying out loud!" Jason moaned, throwing up his hands in frustration.

"I'm serious," Shon continued. "Don't make a big production out of it because Vinny wouldn't want that. She would never presume to take Kim's place in your life, or in the eyes of the people, and a big wedding would only be compared to your wedding to Kim. That would be unfair because it couldn't be matched or duplicated. This isn't a contest between them, Jason, but a commitment. Oh, and make Naed your Best Man," Shon added with a grin.

Jason looked at Shon as if the man had suddenly sprouted a third eye in the middle of his forehead. "You've got to be joking!" he gasped in surprise. "I seriously doubt if he would even show up!"

"He'll be there," Shon told him. "You can bet on that. And he would love to be your Best Man. Trust me on this."

"Do I have much choice?" he asked in resignation.

Shon grinned and shook his head. "No, not really."

Jason stood and walked to the front of the bridge. Placing his right hand against the view screen he felt as if he could reach out and grasp one of the stars. As he looked at one particular cluster he was reminded of the dream where Trish had told him that she and the others would always be with him. The two brightest stars in the cluster reminded him of the stars which had made up the eyes of his little sister in the dream. <u>"Trust them, Jay, and do what you know is right,"</u> a voice seemed to whisper softly in his mind.

He turned and looked at the others for a moment before heading for the door. "If I'm gonna do this, I guess I better go take care of something," he said over his shoulder as he left the bridge.

Busker and the brothers followed him from the bridge to the metallurgy lab. They stood silently as he opened various small compartments and selected the materials he wanted, then gathered around the work table and watched as he used a small laser torch to melt and fashion gold into an exact duplicate of the ring he had given to Kim, working entirely from memory. But when it came to the stone for it, he selected a pear shaped emerald instead of the emerald cut he had given to Kim. He mounted it into the ring and held it up for their inspection. "Think she'll like it," he asked them.

"Knowing Vinny," Hass replied, "she would settle for a simple gold band. Yeah, she'll like it. Hell, she'll love it!"

"When are you going to ask her?" asked Shon.

"I better do it tonight before I get cold feet and change my mind."

"Want us to go with you for moral support?" teased Hass.

"No. I don't want, or need, an audience for this."

Busker grinned and took the brothers by the elbows. "In that case, gentlemen," he told them, "I think the three of us should leave the man alone."

After the three men left, Jason sat on one of the padded stools to try and collect his thoughts. "Mother?" he called out after a few minutes.

"Yes?"

"Cut the crap and give me your personal opinion. Do you think that me marrying Vinny is the right thing to do?"

"Yes."

"I had a feeling you were gonna say that. Well, I hope you're right, Mother. I hope to God that all of you are right, because if you aren't, things could turn out very ugly."

"You worry too much, Jason. Look, if it were any other two women then I'd have some serious doubts about it, but not with these two. There's a special bond between them which can't be clearly defined, and I believe they can make it work. Providing you don't fight it and just go with it."

"It's times like this," he said softly, speaking as much to himself as to the computer, "that I wish my parents were here so I could talk to them. I still miss them, Mother."

"I know you do," the computer replied tenderly.

Jason left the lab and headed for the shuttle bay, his mind on what the future might be like for him now. He flew back to Lemac almost as if he were on automatic pilot. He remained in the shuttle for a few minutes after landing beside the house to try and get his thought straight. He finally left the shuttle and walked slowly toward the house. Entering through the front door, he nodded at the two guardsmen standing at the end of the walk. They weren't really needed since Jason had installed a complex electronic surveillance and alarm system that would stop anyone, but it was something they wanted to do so Jason allowed it.

Inside the house most of the lights were out. He found Kim sitting on the large sofa in the living room waiting for him. She was sipping a cup of hot chocolate, which was something she had developed a craving for during her pregnancy. He sat down beside her and slipped his arm around her shoulders, pulling her close. He tasted the chocolate on her lips as he leaned over to kiss her. "I love you," he said softly.

"I know," Kim replied with a warm smile. "If you didn't, then you wouldn't have all the doubts and reservations about this. It will work out for the best, Jason, I know it will."

"You seem to think I've already made my decision to do it."

"You have," she replied, "and it's the right one."

"I have a question."

"What?"

"Why are you doing this?"

"Because I love you, because I love my sister, and I want to see all of us happy. I couldn't do this if it were anyone else, but it's Vinny, and that makes all the difference in the world."

Jason kissed her forehead. "You know, Golden Girl, you really are something special."

"Yeah, I know," she teased.

He reached into his pocket and withdrew the ring. "What do you think?"

"Oh, Jason, it's beautiful," she replied as she smiled at him with tears of happiness in her eyes. "She'll love it, and she'll love you for thinking of it."

"Where is she?"

"Out on the patio."

"What's she doing out there?"

"She's been crying, although she doesn't think I know it. She expects you to come back and tell her you won't do it. Now, before you go out there and make her as happy as you've made me, I've got something to tell you."

"Please, not another surprise," he moaned, shaking his head.

Kim laughed lightly. "Well, sort of. Look, Alien, you and I haven't made love in over a month because it's been too uncomfortable for me, and I know it's been driving you up the wall."

"That's not important and you know it."

"Yes, it is," she replied. "Anyway, tonight is a special night for you and Vinny, and because of that I'm going to sleep in Vinny's room tonight, and I want Vinny to sleep with you."

Jason started to protest but Kim placed her fingers against his lips to stop him. "Hush, my love. I want it this way, Jason, I really do. Not just for you, but for Vinny as well. It would mean so much to her, and I think you'll find a lot more pleasure in it that you may be willing to admit, even to yourself."

Jason looked into her eyes and saw her love for him reflected in them. He wondered again what it was which made this family so selfless. He kissed her softly and held her close for a moment.

"You know you will always be first with me," he said softly.

"I better be," she replied as she playfully poked him in the ribs, "or you'll have one serious problem. Now help me up, and then go make my little sister the second happiest woman on Alazon."

Jason stood and helped her to her feet. He pulled her close and wrapped his arms around her to kiss her deeply. She clung to him for a moment after the kiss ended, then stepped back and walked away. She stopped in the hallway and turned to smile at him before disappearing into the darkness of the hallway.

Jason stood where he was for a moment, realizing he was almost as nervous now as he was before he had asked Kim to marry him. With a sigh and a shake of his head he headed for the patio.

Vinny was sitting on the large chase lounge he and Kim had occupied earlier. He sat down on the edge of it so that he was facing her. From the light of the small lamp burning on the table a few feet away he could see the redness of her eyes from her crying. "Hi," he said softly.

"I...I'll be leaving as soon as Kimmy is back on her feet," Vinny told him in a voice so low he could just barely hear her. As he looked at her she lowered her eyes, refusing to meet his. "And I'll try to stay out of your way until then."

"You've never been in the way, Vinny," he said softly. "In fact, I don't know how we could have gotten along without you here these past few months."

Vinny raised her head to look at him. He could see new tears forming in her eyes. "Look, Jason," she said in a voice just above a whisper, "Kimmy's idea sounded good at first, but I knew it was just a dream and would never really happen."

"Are you going to the temple?" he asked.

She nodded her head, unable to reply.

"Is that what you really want?"

"It...it's what's best for everyone."

"Well, if you do that, then what do I do with this?" he asked, holding the ring out so she could see it.

"You...you mean...?" she began, her body starting to tremble.

"Vinny, I'm probably just as nervous about this as you are," he told her. "A part of me is having trouble accepting the idea of two wives, even though it wasn't unheard of back on Earth, and a part of me says that if I do this I'll be hurting a friend I love like a brother."

He reached out and gently wiped a tear from her cheek. "But another part of me says it's the right thing to do. Sort of like your father setting aside his personal beliefs about having a king for the good of everyone.

"And, yes, I do love you, Vinny. It's not the same way I love Kim because you are two different women, but it is love. If it had been you out feeding the tollies that night instead of Kim, who can say what might have happened. I also believe that if Kim had been successful in her suicide attempt, that in time I probably would have married you.

"Now," he said with a rueful grin, "even though I've done this once before, it doesn't make it any easier the second time." He took a deep breath and let it out slowly. "What I'm trying to say, or ask you is, will you marry me and be my second wife?"

Vinny didn't reply at first. She could only stare at him in disbelief. "You really mean it?" she finally asked in a whisper.

"Yes. I do love you, Vinny, although, as I've said, it's not the say way I love Kim. I don't know if I'll ever love you the way I love her, if you know what I mean?"

"I do, and I understand."

"I'll admit that I still have some reservations about this, even though everyone else seems to think that it's not only the right thing to do, but the only sensible one as well. I guess I can't be the only one right, with everyone else being wrong.

"As Kim and Mother have pointed out to me, I doubt if this would work with any other two women. In fact, had it had been any woman other than you, I wouldn't even have listened to the idea in the first place.

"But it's not some other woman. It's you and Kim. I have come to love you in a very special way, and in some ways you mean as much to me as Kim. So, will you answer me, or are you going to make me get down on my knees and beg?" he asked with a grin.

Tears of happiness began to fill her eyes and stream down her face as her arms reached out to wrap themselves around his neck. "Yes," she whispered in his ear.

Jason pulled back from her somewhat and took her hand in his. Slowly he placed the ring on the middle finger of her left hand and then leaned forward to kiss her lightly. He stood and pulled her to her feet. "Come on," he told her softly.

She walked beside him into the house holding his hand. They went through the house until they reached the door of the master bedroom. Jason turned to look down into her eyes. "Kim said we should sleep here tonight. She's sleeping in your room."

Vinny looked up into his eyes as she placed her hands n his chest. "Jason, you don't have to do this. I'll understand if you don't want to."

Despite her words, Jason could see her desire for him in her eyes. He bent his head and kissed her. It started off softly and somewhat nervously hesitant, but quickly became more passionate as she pressed her body to his. Her arms wrapped around his neck and her lips parted eagerly to welcome his tongue. As Vinny kissed him, Jason knew then that he did want this, that he wanted her, and not just for the physical reasons.

When the kiss ended they were both breathing quicker and he could feel himself becoming aroused. The flushed look on her face let him know she was feeling the same way. As he opened the door of the bedroom, both of them gasped in surprise at what awaited them.

At the four corners of the bed were lit candles set into tall sconces. Beside the bed was a stand holding an ice bucket in which a bottle of wine and two fluted glasses were chilling. The bed was made up with blue and gold stain sheets, exactly the way the bed of his cabin aboard the Stargazer had been made the night he and Kim had been married. In fact, Jason realized, the entire scene was almost an exact recreation of his wedding night with Kim.

They stepped into the room and closed the door. To cover his own sense of nervousness, Jason poured each of them a glass of wine, handing one to Vinny with hands that shook slightly. Without a word they sipped the wine. Then, as if by mutual understanding, they set their glasses down and slowly began to undress.

Even though Jason had seen Vinny in a bikini or skimpy one piece bathing suit hundreds of times, he hadn't consciously paid attention to her figure. In fact, he had deliberately avoided doing so. But now, here in the candle light of the room as she stood before him with nothing on, he realized her figure was every bit as beautiful and sexy as Kim's. In fact, her breasts were a little larger and fuller than Kim's, making her already tiny waist appear even smaller.

As they lay beside one another on the bed he took her in his arms and began to kiss her. He felt her body shiver as his hands began a slow, gentle exploration of her. He wanted to take his time but Vinny had other ideas. She rolled onto her back and pulled him above her. Reaching between their bodies she grasped his penis and urgently guided him to her, almost demanding they be joined. As he began to slowly enter her, Vinny hooked her ankles behind his thighs and jerked him toward her, shoving her own hips upward at the same time. As he was forced all the way into her in a single plunge, Vinny buried her face in the hollow of his shoulder to muffle the cry that escaped her lips.

Jason didn't know if her cry was from her pleasure of them joining, or the pain of his entry into her virginal passage, as his own mind and body were now caught up in the heat of their passion. It had been over a month since he and Kim had made love and he knew it wouldn't take much before he climaxed, no matter how much he wanted to hold out and prolong it for Vinny.

Their movements became more passionate and demanding as they strove toward the ultimate release. As Jason felt his body explode in orgasm, Vinny arched up beneath him and cried out again. She wrapped her arms and legs around him tightly as they both rode out the storm of their passion.

"No!" Vinny whispered urgently, clinging to him as he started to pull himself from her a few moments later.

Jason looked down into her eyes. She pulled his head down and kissed him softly as she began to gently move her lower body to stimulate him again. Jason was surprised to find his body reacting so quickly to her actions. It didn't take long before he was fully aroused again.

This time their lovemaking was slower and more controlled. He was able to use his lips, tongue and hands to explore and stimulate her body. Much later she cried out again in joy when they both climaxed together once more.

This time, when he finally pulled from her, Vinny didn't object. She curled up beside him and placed her head on his chest and soon drifted off to sleep.

"Thank you, Kimmy," he whispered into the darkness of the room as the last of the candles flickered out.

# THIRTY NINE

The sun shone down brightly, but not too hotly on the wedding party, which consisted of just over fifty guests. All of them were gathered in the large backyard of Jason's house. They were mostly family members and close friends, with a small contingent of the Royal Guard in their dress uniforms, led by Captain Ster. At Vinny's request, Jason was wearing the traditional wedding robes of Alazon, as would she. She had made them for the two of them herself.

He understood her reasons behind the request, even though it was never voiced. Vinny wanted her wedding to him to be completely different from his wedding to Kim. She also wanted it to be a simple, traditional affair, without all the pomp and ceremony which had accompanied his first.

To Jason's surprise, over the past week Kim, Vinny and himself had seemed to become even closer than before. Kim had insisted he and Vinny spend two more nights together before she returned to his bed, sending Vinny back to her own room. She had also taken delight in teasing him about his nights with her sister. Jason was amazed by Kim's apparent lack of jealousy, as well as how much closer to one another she and Vinny seemed to have become. He had watched them, catching them whispering and giggling together when they thought he wasn't looking. The two of them would blush or laugh outright when he did happen to overhear their conversations about him.

When he stopped to think about it, it seemed to him that everyone was happier now, including Janella. His daughter had surprised him the most by immediately designating the two women as "Mommy Kimmy" and "Mommy Vinny". She went around telling everyone who would listen about how lucky she was to have two such wonderful, beautiful and loving mothers.

Jason had been relieved in his attitude in her, as it enabled him to quickly dismiss he own concerns about Janella's acceptance of this arrangement. To Janella, him having two wives was perfectly natural, especially since the two wives were Kim and Vinny.

The day prior to the wedding, Kim and Vinny told him that, due to Kim's condition, they had asked someone else to be Vinny's Maid of Honor. Jason had merely smiled and said "Fine'. He knew the sisters were going to do whatever they wanted, whether he agreed or not. Now, as he stood waiting for Vinny to come from the house to join him, he turned to look at Naed. "I'm nervous," he whispered.

"You're supposed to be," Naed replied with a grin. "That is all part of it. Besides, the fact that you are only goes to show that you're really not that much difference from the rest of us mortals after all."

The day after asking Vinny to marry him, Jason had flown to Bysee to see Naed. He hadn't been sure as to the type of reception he would receive, but Naed had been open and honest in his feelings. The two of them had spent the day talking and walking through one of the areas on the city's outskirts which had been damaged slightly by a small earthquake the week before. Naed had already inspected the area immediately after the quake, and was now directing the reconstruction of new homes for those who needed them. That evening, as the two of them sat on one of the open balconies of the palace, they had finally spoken abut the marriage, and the reasons behind why Naed had told Kim about the amendment. When Jason finally left, he had taken with him a new respect and sense of love for Naed.

Jarrell cleared his throat. Jason turned to look toward the house as Janella stepped through the wide double French doors. A big smile was on her face as she spread out a carpet of lower petals from the basket she carried. She was followed by the twins, who each carried a small silk cushion on which the rings he and Vinny would exchange rested. Jason had created a new ring for himself which would interlock with his original wedding ring to form a single band on his finger.

Following the twins was Vinny's Maid of Honor, whom Jason had yet to meet. Like Vinny, she wore the traditional robes, but she also wore a veil which covered her head and face. Jason thought that a bit unusual but merely shrugged it off. He noticed her hair was concealed in a tight roll on the back of her head, and for a brief second he could have sworn he saw tendrils of gold. But that thought was quickly banished as Vinny stepped from the house. Her robes of white silk were trimmed in gold and seemed to float around her like a cloud. She was escorted by Busker, who couldn't have looked more proud if Vinny has been his own daughter.

As Jason watched her approach he felt a sense of elation similar to what he had felt when watching Kim approach during his marriage to her. He looked down at Vinny as she stopped beside him and raised her head to smile at him. The sun glistened off the small tiara she wore, which was an exact duplicate of Kim's, and like Kim's, was a gift from Jarrell.

"Jason," Jarrell said to him, smiling brightly, "once again you stand before me to take a wife, and once again the woman you are marrying is a daughter of the House of Vehey.

"By your presence here today you are stating to all those gathered her, and to the gods of Alazon, that you also take this woman to share in your life in all things. That you will love her as you love your first wife, her sister Kimella, and that you will give to her the same respect and love you give to Kimella. Do you so avow these things?"

"I do so avow them," Jason replied as he turned to smile at Vinny.

"Vinette Vehey," said Jarrell, "you stand here now to link your life with this man for all time. Your presence here states to those gathered here, and to the gods of Alazon, that you will love him with all your heart. That you will be to him all that a wife, a woman, and a mother to his children should be.

"That you will strive to maintain the harmony of this house with his first wife, your sister, and that you will love them both for all your life as you do now. Do you so avow those things?"

"I do so avow them," she replied softly.

"Then as Mayor of Lemac, Senior Mayor of Preton, First Counselor to the King of Alazon, and extremely proud father of the bride," he added with a grin, "I hereby sanction this marriage under the laws of Alazon."

Jarrell stepped back and Seta took his place. She smiled warmly at the two of them. "The gods smile upon you," she told them, "for it is rare to find a love between three people such as the three of you have found with one another.

"As High Priestess of Lofa I find no reason this marriage should not be. Other than the fact that the Temple of Lofa shall have to look for a long time to find another woman of your qualities to become a High Priestess. But the loss of the temple is the gain of the king, so all is well.

"My Lord Jason," she said, turning t him, "you are taking on a responsibility few men could handle. There may be times when you feel as if this arrangement was the worst idea anyone ever had. It will be during those times that you will have to reach deep within yourself for the understanding and love which brought you to this point.

"My Lady Vinette," she said to Vinny, addressing her in the formal manner, "as Jason's second wife you must never attempt to supplant the position or love of his first wife, who is also your sister. You must remember that she will always be first in his life and heart. There may come a time when you wish it otherwise, but it can never be so. You must also remember that you are marrying not just a man, but a king. A man and a king whose responsibilities are greater than those ever known by any man or king of Alazon.

"There may come times when you have to put aside your own personal wants, desires and happiness to work with him, helping him do what is best for our world. And," she added with a warm smile of affection, "remember that my door is always open to you."

Seta took the gold, jewel laden goblet handed to her by another priestess. She sipped from it and then handed it to Jason. He took a sip of the wine and then handed it to Vinny, who also sipped from it before returning it to Seta. Seta then walked around the two of them to pour out the remaining wine on the ground to pay homage to Lofa. She handed the empty goblet to her assistant and then stepped back to allow Jarrell to stand before them again.

As Jarrell smiled and nodded, Jason turned to Vanda and took the ring from the cushion. As he did, his eyes locked with those of Naed for a second. He thought he saw a brief flash of pain in the eyes of his friend, but he also saw the love and approval for what was happening. Naed nodded slowly as Jason picked up the ring and turned back to Vinny.

"Vinette Vehey, on this day I take you for my wife," he said as he slipped the ring on her finger. "I will love and cherish you in all ways, and I will honor you and your love for all the days of my life. This I swear to you before all those gathered here and the gods of Alazon."

Vinny took the ring from the cushion Manda held and turned to Jason. She slipped the ring on his finger and looked up into his eyes.

"Jason Michael Stephens, King of Alazon, husband of my sister, I will do all within my power to be worthy of your love, and the honor you bestow upon me this day. I will stand beside you in all things and for all time. Together, with my sister, I will do all I can to make your life one of love and happiness for all the days of my life.

"I will honor and respect the love you have for my sister, never forgetting that she is, and always will be, first in your life and heart. This I vow to you with all the love within me before those gathered here today, and all the gods of Alazon."

Seta stepped up to stand next to Jarrell. She smiled at the two of them before addressing the guests.

"Let it be known from this day forward that the marriage of Jason Michael Stephens, King of Alazon, and Vinette Vehey, hereafter known as Queen Vinette Vehey Stephens, is hereby accepted and blessed by the Temple of Lofa, and that the gods smile upon this union and their love."

"It is done!" Jarrell shouted exuberantly.

Everyone cheered and crowded around them, surging forward to offer hugs, kisses and congratulations. Naed was the first to reach Vinny. "If anyone even thinks about kissing the bride before I do," he told the others as he placed his hands on Vinny's upper arms, "he better hope he's a better man with a sword than I am!"

Naed bent and kissed her cheek. As he started to step back, Vinny wrapped her arms around his neck and hugged him tightly. "I do love you, Naed," she whispered, looking into his eyes.

"I know," he replied softly, a smile of love on his own face. "But this is the way it should be. The best man won."

Vinny shook her head and smiled at him. "Don't ever think of yourself as second best, Naed. Not to any man, including Jason. You are a very special man, and one I could have loved in all the right ways had things only been a little different."

"Well, if this bum," Naed joked, jerking his thumb at Jason, "ever decides he can't handle the two of you, just let me know."

"You'll be the first," she told him as she kissed his cheek.

As the others came up to congratulate them, Jason noticed that the Maid of Honor wasn't among them. Curious, he looked around to find her standing by the doors of the house. When she saw him looking at her she lowered her head and backed into the house, glancing up at him briefly before disappearing. The woman's actions puzzled him. He wondered why he hadn't been introduced to her prior to the wedding and realized he didn't even know her name. As Jason glanced at Kim he saw her grinning at him with that all too familiar glint of mischievous amusement in her eyes.

"Oh, god, why do I have this sneaky suspicion that you and your sister are still up to something?" he asked with a shake of his head.

"Jason, why would you ever think something like that?" Kim asked with false innocence. "Especially on a day such as this?"

Jason didn't get the chance to answer as the other guests were coming up to them now to congratulate the three of them. For the next couple of hours Jason lost himself in the joy and happiness of the day, dancing, laughing and having a good time. He finally looked around and realized that the only ones left were the members of the Vehey family, along with Busker, Ster and Naed.

"Jason," Kim said as she took his right arm and Vinny took his left, "why don't we all go into the house."

Jason looked down at them and saw that damn twinkle in the eyes of both sisters. He shook his head in exasperation.

"You two are up to something," he told them. "I just know it. What now, a third wife? If so, you can forget it! The two of you are more than enough."

"Not a chance!" Vinny replied with a laugh. "It's just a little surprise for you."

Jason looked at Busker as they entered the house and went into the large living room. "Why do I have this uncontrollable fear that life being married to these two is going to be anything but dull?"

"Oh, hush," Kim told him. "You love it and you know it. Now, everyone please have a seat."

Jason sat on the sofa between Kim and Vinny and wondered what they were up to this time. As each of them took one of his hands in their own he could sense a slight nervousness in them.

Janella came to stand in front of him, her little face beaming brightly. She leaned forward to kiss his cheek and then ran out of the room and down the hall. He heard a door open and close and a few seconds later Janella returned holding the hand of the Maid of Honor. The woman was still wearing the veil over her face and hair. The woman stopped in the middle of the room as Janella went to sit beside Ster. She stood there for a moment and then slowly reached up to remove the covering from her head, allowing her hair to cascade down her back in waves of gold. Jason felt his breath catch in his throat and heard the surprised gasps of the others as well. No one on Alazon had blonde hair!

"Please don't be mad, Jay," the woman said softly as she continued removing the veil until her face was revealed.

Jason felt his stomach lurch and his heart leap into his throat as the woman's features were revealed to him at last. He stared at the blonde hair and blue eyes, his eyes, as he felt Kim and Vinny squeezing his hands tightly. The room seemed to spin around him as he finally recognized the facial features of the young woman stand before him.

"Trish!" he exclaimed weakly. But it couldn't be Trish his mind told him, because Trish was dead. His eyes had to be playing tricks on him.

"No, not quite Trish," the woman replied timidly. "The original genes were here's, but I altered them somewhat to conform to the height and skin coloration of this world."

"Mother?" he gasped.

The woman smiled somewhat hesitantly. "Again, not quite."

"No! This can't be!" Jason cried.

He jerked his hands from Kim and Vinny as he stood and walked across the room. He stopped in the archway to the dining room and braced his hands on the frame as if for support to keep from collapsing, keeping his back to the others in the room.

"Trish is dead," he said softly, his voice filled with anguish and pain. He whirled around to face her. "How could you do this to me?"

"Jason, please," the woman pleaded with him. "Yes, I used the genes from Trish to clone the body, but my mind and personality are those of Mother."

"Why?" he demanded in an emotion choked voice.

"Be...because I wanted to be human," she told him softly as she began to cry. "Because I wanted to know what it felt like to walk barefoot in grass, and to feel rain and sunshine on my face. I wanted to be able to hold a baby in my arms, and to know what it was like to be held in the arms of a man. Because I wanted to live, Jason, not just exist.

"As a computer," she continued before he could respond, "I can analyze just about anything, give advice or answers, even make decisions on my own, with or without human intervention, but I couldn't really _feel_.

"I could take apart a flower petal and break it down to its atoms. I could even reconstruct it a million times over if I wanted, but I couldn't feel the texture of it. I could analyze the odor, but I couldn't actually smell it! I knew what it was to love, but not to be loved!"

The woman burst into tears and slowly collapsed to her knees on the floor in the center of the room. Jason could only stand and stare at her. No one moved or spoke, all eyes darting back and forth from him to the kneeling, sobbing figure on the floor.

*Alazon*

As Jason listened to the sobs coming from her, something inside of him seemed to give way. Slowly he went to her and reached down to help her to her feet. "But why Trish?" he asked softly.

"Because I knew I couldn't come as Nadia," she replied weakly, glancing briefly at Kim and Vinny. "That would have been too cruel, to you and to them. But…but I thought that if I came as your sister than you might be able to accept me more easily. But maybe I was wrong. Maybe I should have selected the genes of someone who wasn't so close to you," she told him as she started to cry again.

Jason looked around at the others but saw no help coming from them. In fact, with the exception of Kim, Vinny, Janella and the twins, the rest of them seemed to be in as much of a state of shock as he was. He knew they were waiting for him to act.

"Damn!" he muttered as he left the room, going into the kitchen and picking up a small hand towel. Returning to the living room he eased her hands away from her face and gently wiped away her tears. After a moment she appeared to regain her composure, nodding her head and looking up at him. He handed her the towel and turned to face Kim and Vinny.

"How long have you known about this?" he asked them.

Kim smiled sweetly at him. "Vinny and I have known since the day you picked us up a little over a week ago. Janella and the twins found out the next day."

"And the rest of you?" he asked as he looked around the room at the others.

"They didn't know at all, Jason," Vinny told him. "We thought it best that way."

"You would," he mumbled.

He looked at the clone, who had now moved to sit between Kim and Vinny on the sofa. The three of them were holding hands, leaving him standing in the middle of the room. "What if I say I can't accept this?" he said to the clone.

The woman lowered her eyes for a moment before finally looking up to meet his. "Then I'll dispose of myself," she replied in a voice just barely above a whisper.

"You mean kill yourself? Just like that?"

She nodded and lowered her eyes again. Jason saw Kim and Vinny each place an arm around the woman's shoulders as they stared up at him, their eyes containing an open challenge to him. Busker started to speak but Jason silenced him with a wave of his hand.

"Jason," the clone said at last, "you are King of Alazon. You are also the last survivor of New Hope, and commander of the Stargazer. As such, I have an obligation to you to do as you wish. Therefore, if what you see before you is something you can't accept, then say so and I'll dispose of this body before the day is over and go back to being just Mother."

"You're manipulating me," he growled. "I don't like being manipulated."

"Then he sure married the wrong women," Hass quipped softly from the other side of the room, causing the others to smile and snicker.

Only the clone wasn't smiling. She was looking at Jason with steady eyes. She took a deep breath and let it out slowly.

"Jason, as I said, as King of Alazon, last survivor of New Hope, and Commander of the Stargazer, you have complete control and authority over me, both as a computer and as a human clone. And..."

"Oh, shut up!" he snapped. "I need to sort this out."

"Jason, if..." Busker began.

"Save it, Busker, and please stay out of this. There's a hell of a lot more involved here than you're aware of. Do you know whose genes she used to clone herself from?"

'No, but whoever it was, she was one beautiful woman," Busker replied, smiling bashfully at the clone.

"My little sister," Jason replied flatly.

The smile vanished instantly from Busker's face and Jason could see the understanding in the man's eyes now.

"Jason, may I say something?" the clone asked.

"Go ahead," he said with a sigh.

"As I stated earlier, I didn't select the genes of Nadia for the obvious reasons. It would have hurt you too much to see that face and body, knowing it wasn't really her. Nor would it have been fair to Kim and Vinny.

"But I know how much you loved Trish, and I thought that if I had a chance at acceptance with you that it would be as Trish. But with some minor alterations that would also allow me to conform to the standards of this world. If I had cloned Trish exactly, I would have been nearly as tall as you are and would have stood out too much. This way my only obvious differences are my hair and eyes."

"Oh, yeah, just a couple of minor things," he replied with a trace of sarcasm in his voice.

The clone smiled but other than that she ignored his comment. "I know," she continued, "that I could have selected from anyone in the gene pool from New Hope, or from various ones, mixing them any way I wanted, or I could have selected and mixed genes from any one of a million women of Alazon. But I chose those of your sister because of the love the two of you shared.

"I thought, I hoped, that by cloning myself as Trish, you might not be so quick to reject me. Maybe I was wrong to play on your heart and emotions in that manner, and if so, I'm sorry."

Jason stared at her. He really wasn't sure just what it was he felt. She was Trish, but a Trish he had never known, for his sister had died when she was only nine. This was no child, but a full grown, mature woman.

"Okay, let me get this straight," he said with a sigh. "You have the cloned body of Trish, matured, with some slight alterations, while your mind is that of Mother, correct?"

"More or less."

Jason shook his head in resignation. "Oh, god, what a combination," he muttered. "Okay, but if I tell you that this is just too much, that I can't accept it, you would…dispose of yourself and go back to being just plane old Mother, right?"

She nodded her head slowly.

"And yet," he continued, "everyone in this room knows damn good and well I could never order you to do that, don't you?"

His comment was answered by the nodding of heads and a few amused grins from the others.

"Why didn't you tell me you wanted to do something like this?" he asked softly. "I probably would have helped. Although, to be honest, I would not have selected the genes of my sister for you to clone."

"I didn't say anything because I didn't know if you would help or not," she replied, "and I was too afraid because I thought you would think I was being vain or silly and wouldn't let me do it."

He shook his head. "Mother, as the computer, haven't we always been able to talk? Don't I always come to you when I have a problem or situation I can't figure out on my own, or need advice with?"

"Yes."

"Then you should have done the same. And what's with the blonde hair and blue eyes?"

The clone allowed a small smile to come to her lips. "I decided there were enough beautiful, green eyed, silver haired women around already, so call it female vanity to want to be a little different."

Janella slid from the sofa and came to stand in front of Jason. She reached for his hands, tugging on them to get him to kneel down in front of her.

"Can she stay, Daddy?" Janella asked softly. "You won't make her go away and kill herself, will you? You're the king and your word is the law, but you're a good king and a good daddy, and you wouldn't do something that mean, would you?"

Jason gazed into Janella's loving, trusting eyes and knew that once again his mind had been made up for him by the women of Alazon. He smiled softly and picked her up. "No, Princess, I won't do anything like that," he told her.

Holding Janella in his arms he looked at Kim, Vinny and the clone. "Let me make something clear," he told them.

"I would have been a lot more receptive to the idea if I had been in on it from the beginning, but the deed is done. For me to tell you to dispose of yourself now would not only be like killing you myself, which you know I couldn't do, but it would also put me in the dog house with the rest of the family for a very long time. So, I guess you can stay."

Kim and Vinny yelled excitedly, wrapping their arms around the clone as the looked up at him with love and gratitude in their eyes.

"Hold it!" he told them. "I'm not done yet. First, we'll have to figure out how to explain you to the rest of Alazon. I'm open to suggestions on that one.

"Second, you will tell me everything, and I do mean every damn thing you are capable of. Knowing the Mother portion of you the way I do, I have a feeling you are a little more than human, and I want to know what to expect from you."

He glanced around at the others. "As for the rest of you, especially you two," he said looking at Kim and Vinny, "there are to be no more surprises of this nature ever again. Is that clear?"

"Yes, your Majesty," they replied in unison, grinning at him mischievously.

Jason stepped into the kitchen and returned with a chair. Setting in the middle of the room, he sat down facing the clone. He took a deep breath and let it out slowly.

"Okay, so how do we introduce her to the rest of Alazon? There are going to be a hell of a lot of questions raised by people, and we need to know how to answer them, especially since they've been told I'm the only survivor of Earth."

"Oh, don't worry, Jason, we'll figure something out," Kim told him confidently.

"Yeah, and that's what I'm afraid of," he replied as he looked at her and saw the amusement in her eyes. But he had no doubt that between Kim, Vinny and the clone they would come up with something to cover this. "All right, so what do we call you?" he finally asked.

"What about beautiful?" Busker asked softly, causing the others to grin.

"What about the name that comes with the body?" Vinny asked. "Unless that would be too difficult for you?"

"Trish? No, I don't think so," Jason replied with a shake of his head. "That would be pushing it too far."

"Not Trish," the clone said softly, "but what about Patricia, in honor of her. If that would be all right with you," she added, lowering her eyes briefly.

Jason glanced briefly at Kim and Vinny before returning his attention to the clone. "I guess I could go for Patricia, even Patty or Pat, but not Trish."

The clone stood up and crossed to where he sat. She knelt down in front of him, taking his face in her hands and kissing his cheek. "I've wanted to do that for a long time," she told him with a soft smile. "It's from me and Nadia."

Jason slowly shook his head from side to side before rolling his eyes at the ceiling. "I should have been a monk," he said with a sigh.

For the next two hours they all discussed how the presence of the clone would be taken by the rest of Alazon, and what role she might play in the overall scheme of things. He knew none of them would say anything about what had happened here until he said it was okay to do so. He looked at Busker, who seemed to have taken a somewhat protective manner towards her.

"I think Uncle Busker has the hots for her," Janella whispered in Jason's ear with an impish grin plastered to her face.

"Yeah, I think you might be right, Princess," he whispered back. "But you're too young to know abut such things." He nuzzled her neck to make her giggle and squirm around on his lap.

"I am not," she told him when she stopped laughing. "In fact, when I get older I'm gonna marry Captain Ster and we're going to have lots of babies."

"Oh, really? And does Captain Ster know about this?" Jason teased.

"Sure! Well, not the part about the babies yet," she added with a grin. "But I've already told him that I'm going to marry him when I get older. But sometimes I don't think he really takes me seriously."

"That could be a big mistake on his part. But don't you think that Beri is maybe just a little old for you?"

Janella's face became serious. "Not really, Daddy. He's only eleven years older than me, and besides, everyone knows that women mature faster than men. Not only that, but with the serum, once I'm old enough to marry him, it won't matter in the least about our age difference."

*Alazon*

Jason could see that his daughter had given this matter some serious consideration. "Well," he said after a moment, "don't you think you could do a little better for yourself than to marry a Guard Captain?"

"Daddy, by the time I'm old enough to marry Beri, he will probably be a colonel, or maybe even a general, so I wouldn't be marrying a captain. Besides," she added, "his rank isn't important to me. I'm gonna marry the man, not the uniform."

Jason smiled lovingly at her. He knew he shouldn't really be all that surprised at Janella's sense of maturity. She was an unusual little girl who had been through a lot in her young life, and it had served her to age beyond her years. And since her very first visit aboard his ship, she had taken every opportunity she could to learn from Mother, which placed her light years ahead of other young girls her age.

There were times when Jason looked into her eyes and saw not a child, but a woman in the body of a child looking back at him; a woman who was simply waiting for the outside to catch up with the inside.

"You now, Princess," he said softly, "I think Captain Ster is in for one very big surprise in a few years. I also think he's going to be one very lucky man."

"Of course he will," Janella replied with an impish grin as she snuggled closer to him. "After all, he'll be marrying me, the Princess of Alazon."

# FORTY

"What in the world are they doing out there?" Jason asked in amazement as he stepped back from the second story balcony of the temple. He turned his back on the crowd which had been growing steadily to surround the temple since before dawn as word of the impending birth had spread through the city like wildfire.

Jarrell smiled at him from his seat against the wall just inside the temple. The older man appeared relaxed and calm. "What they're doing, Jason, is awaiting the birth of the new Prince of Alazon. After all, it's been a while since the last royal birth here in Lemac."

Jason sad down heavily on a padded chair and gave his father-in-law a sneering look at the older man's teasing. "This is nuts," he said with a shake of his head as he got up and began pacing around the room once more.

"Jason," Shon said with a knowing grin from his own seat, "you may as well sit down. Pacing the floor won't make it happen any faster."

Jason turned and looked at Shon. "Hey, I'm about to be a father for the first time, so that gives me the right to be nervous. Besides, pacing for first time fathers is an honored tradition."

"True," Jarrell replied, "but Kimmy is in the best hands possible, so you should try to relax. Everything is going to be just fine."

Jason forced himself to sit down. He knew Jarrell was right. As Kim's delivery date had grown closer, Patricia had taken Vinny, Seta and two other women from the temple up to the ship and connected them to her computer self, giving them all the information she contained on birth and delivery. Then, when Kim had adamantly stated she was going to have her son born on the soil of Alazon and not on the ship, Jason and Patricia had brought down the equipment from the med lab to install a modern delivery room in the temple. He provided power for it by means of a small solar generator on the roof.

When Kim's water had broken two hours before dawn this morning, Jason had immediately flown her here to the temple. Within minutes word had spread throughout the city and people from all parts of the city and beyond had begun to make their way here, sitting silently as they awaited the news of the birth. Jason looked at the Royal Guard Sergeant who was sitting with a com-link, ready to send the news up to the ship, where it would then be broadcast to every city on Alazon via the communications satellites orbiting the planet.

As the door opened and one of the young acolytes stuck her head in, Jason leaped to his feet. "It's time," she told him with an amused grin.

Jason led the charge out of the room with Jarrell and the others on his heels. They rushed down the stairs to the observation room he had constructed next to the delivery room and pressed their faces up against the glass of the large window.

Inside the delivery room Kim was being gently lowered into a large vat of water via a birthing chair connected to a small electric winch. Liet and Vinny were already in the water tank, standing on either side of Kim. They were holding her hands and talking to her. Seta was also in the water and standing in front of Kim. The other women stood outside the large vat watching anxiously. Patricia was monitoring the computer connected to Kim via the leads attached to her stomach, heart and head. Jason couldn't hear what was being said and mentally kicked himself for not installing a communication system.

He saw Kim's breathing quicken. His heart leaped into his throat when she arched her back and clenched her teeth in pain. Fear and dread shot through him. I should be in there with her, he told himself. He had wanted to be, but for reasons known only to her,

Kim had been against his actual presence and participation in the birth of their son.

As Jason watched through the window he saw her in pain and began to worry. Kim was so small and the baby so large that he worried there might be problems. But Patricia had told him that giving Kim any kind of pain inhibitors should be held off unless absolutely necessary to prevent any harm to either Kim or the baby. At a nod from Patricia one of the women stepped forward and pressed an injector to Kim's arm. Kim immediately began to relax.

After that things seemed to speed up. Jason watched as Kim strained for a moment and then her body seemed to go limp. Seta stepped back, turning away from those at the window as she carried a small body to the side of the vat. She handed the baby to Patricia, who quickly gathered it to her and turned away.

<u>Oh, God, something's wrong!</u> Jason thought as fear and dread washed over him. He was about to go crashing through the door as they lifted Kim from the water and two women began to dry her off. The slipped a clean gown on her and helped her into bed as Patricia stepped forward and handed her a blanket wrapped bundle.

That was all Jason could take. He pushed passed the others and through the door to hurry to Kim's side. She looked up at him and smiled as she pulled back the edge of the blanket to let him see his son. He reached out and gently touched the soft, tiny face, which caused the baby's eyes to open.

"They're blue," he said softly.

"And his hair is brown," Kim replied as her fingers brushed the strands of dark brown hair covering the tiny head. She pulled the blanket back a little more and lifted a tiny hand with her fingers. "Five fingers, just like his daddy," she said with a grin.

"Maybe so, but he has your skin coloring," he told her.

As the others crowded around, Janella and the twins managed to climb up on the bed. Janella scooted up so that she was sitting right beside Kim, while the twins took up positions on either side of Kim near her waist. It was at that moment that Jason's son decided to test his lungs and let loose with a loud wait. Vanda and Manda reached out to take one tiny hand of the baby in their own, linking their free hands with Janella to complete the circuit. Almost immediately the baby stopped crying and a look of peaceful calm came over his features.

"He's hungry, and a little bit scared," Janella told Kim with a grin.

"Alright, everyone out," Patricia told them as he started to gently push bodies away from the bed and toward the door. "The baby needs feeding and the mother needs some rest."

"That means you, too," Kim told Jason as Vinny took him by the arm to steer him away from the bed.

"Hey, wait a minute! I'm the father!" he protested.

"Tough," Vinny told him. "No exceptions."

He bent and quickly kissed Kim. "I love you," he told her.

"You better, Alien, or you're in a lot of trouble."

"I supposed I'll get the same treatment when your time comes, too, huh?" he said as he patted Vinny's slightly swollen stomach.

"Maybe. But then again, if you ask nice maybe I'll let you stay when it's my turn," she teased.

Jason kissed her quickly before allowing her to push him out the door. As he joined the others at the window, Shon looked at him pensively. "What?" he asked the older brother.

"Today your first son is born," Shon said softly. "In a few months your second son will be born. They will be the first children of Earth and Alazon, and will growing up knowing of both worlds.

"You came here searching for a new world, Jason, and one day your son's will follow in your footsteps. They will lead the quest for us to find even more new worlds. This is only the beginning."

The End

Milton Keynes UK
Ingram Content Group UK Ltd.
UKHW022128160824
447080UK00010B/161/J

9 781438 993263